THE NEEDLE AND THE SWORD

Helen M. Stevens

THE SAXON TWINS

Published by New Generation Publishing in 2019

Copyright © Helen M. Stevens 2019

Author photo by Paul Bird

First Edition

ISBN
Paperback   978-1-78955-727-5
Hardback   978-1-78955-728-2

www.newgeneration-publishing.com

 New Generation Publishing

For Janice, with love.
… still crazy, after all these years …

'When you need a needle, you cannot use a sword'.
Brahmin proverb

Beneath the root of the great yew tree Irminsul, which rises into the Heavens and is known as the Pillar of the Universe, is the Spring of Destiny. Close by live the three Norns, the Daughters of the Night: Wyrd, Metod and Sculd.

Wyrd spins the thread of life and it is she who determines its quality, be it of the finest silk, or the coarsest wool. She is the Spinner.

Metod measures the thread of each life and decides upon its length, whether it be short or long. She is called the Measurer.

Sculd cuts the thread, and it is within her gift to give a clean cut and a good death, or a ragged and painful one. She is known as the Cutter.

Together they weave the fabric of all life. And all those who live must broider it with their actions. With love and hate, with good and evil, with bravery and treachery. The Web of Wyrd is infinity, and all is subject to her pattern.

FAMILY TREE

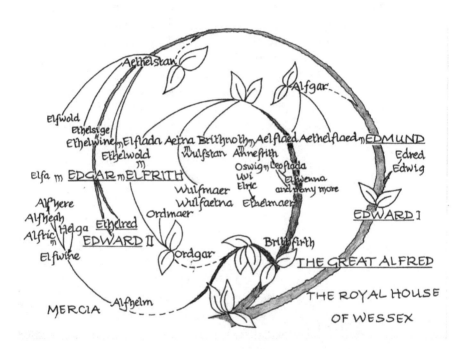

Aethelstan

Elfwold
Ethelsige
Ethelwine ᵐ Elflada Aetna Brithnoth ᵐ Aelflaed Aethelflaed ᵐ EDMUND
Ethelwold   Wulfstan Ahnefrith   Edred
                         Oswig Leoflada   Edwig
Elfa ᵐ EDGAR ᵐ ELFRITH   Uvi   Elfwenna
                  Elric   and many more
            Wulfmaer
            Wulfaetna Ethelmaer
Alfhere   Ordmaer
Alfheah   EDWARD I
Alfric Helga Ethelred
   ᵐ   EDWARD II
Elfwine   Ordgar   Brithfirth
                                                    THE GREAT ALFRED

MERCIA   Alfhelm   THE ROYAL HOUSE
                                            OF WESSEX

Alfgar

Cast of Characters (alphabetical, crowned Royals in **bold**)

Aelflaed	Wife to Ealdorman Brithnoth
Aelwarth	Ealdorman of Western Eastseaxe
Aethelflaed	Dowager Queen to King Edmund, sister to Aelflaed
Aetna	Deceased mother to Wulfmaer and Wulfaetna
Agnolo	Skop at Bathe
Alfhere	Chief Ealdorman and Ealdorman of Mercia
Alfreth	Novice at Bathe Abbey, later wife to **King Edward**
Anefrith	Deceased mother to Leoflada
Anselm and Sampson	
	Brothers at Bedeford Abbey
Aymore	Master builder at Caune
Bagshot	House priest at Corf
Bedricson	Landowner at Bedricsworth
Beleric	Edward's tutor at Wintancaestre
Beorndan	House priest at Tamweorthig and Wireceastre
Beornhelm	Brother to Beorndan, Bishop in Caledonia
Brandon	Dagmaer's eighth child
Brithnoth	Ealdorman of Eastseaxe
Cenfrith	Shire Reeve of Colencaestre
Cerdic	Member of Edgar's Court
Cillith	Kitchen thrall at Wintancaestre
Colley	Goodwife, Ethelred's nurse
Conferth	Ceorl at Caune
Dagmaeda	Eldest daughter to Dagmaer
Dagmaer	Wet nurse to the twins in infancy. Later servant/ companion at Radendunam
Dorwith	Parish priest at Caune
Dunstan	Archbishop of Cantuaria (from 963)
Eadwine	Son to Ethelwine
Earned	Monk at Cantuaria, Dunstan's emissary to Caune
EDGAR	King of Englaland, husband to Elfrith
EDWARD	King of Englaland, son to King Edgar
Elflada	Sister to Ealdorman Brithnoth
ELFRITH	Wife of Ealdorman Ethelwold, later Queen to **King Edgar**
Elfwenna	Eldest daughter to Leoflada
Elfwine	Nephew to Chief Ealdorman Alfhere, son to Alfheah
Elfwold	Brother to Ethelwold and Ethelwine
Elric	Brother to Oswig
Erdgor	Vermin catcher at the King's Worth
Ethel and Onwen	
	Serving women to **Aethelflaed**

Ethelmaer	Son to Elric, nephew to Oswig
ETHELRED	Son to Edgar and Elfrith
Ethelsige	Brother to Ethelwold and Ethelwine
Ethelwine	Brother to Ethelwold, later Ealdorman of East Anglia
Ethelwold	Ealdorman of East Anglia until succeeded by his brother
Father Aelmer	House priest at Radendunam
Flerrick	Reeve at Wenberie
Garreth	Man-at-arms to Edward, bodyguard to Alfreth in Sceo
Gorth	"The Eel-man" at Elig
Gorthson	Son to Gorth
Gorthwyrd	Mother to Gorth and guardian of St. Etheldreda's Shrine at Elig
Grindmaen	Tutor in swordsmanship to Edward
Gunnith	Youngest daughter to Leoflada
Guthric	Dagmaer's third son
Gyrrdd and Mennae	
	Serving thralls at the Sign of the Black Dog in Caune
Herrith	Nurse to Ethelred at Corf
Hilde	Baker-woman at Sceo
Irwin	Shire Reeve of Caestre
Kennyth	Head of the Clan Alpin, called the King of the Scots
Leoflada	Daughter to Ealdorman Brithnoth by his first wife
Leofwine (Leo)	Younger son to Wolstan
Lynet	Barmaid at the Sign of the Green Man in Bathe
Manfred	Companion-man to Ethelwold
Meggy	Whore at Caune
Meryasek	Tutor and companion to Ethelred
Morwen	Companion-woman/servant to Elfrith
Olferth	Nephew to Thoth
Ordgar	Sub-ealdorman of Dumnonia, father to Elfrith
Ordulf	Brother to Elfrith
Oscytel	Archbishop of Eoforwic
Oswig	Husband to Leoflada
Otter	Dagmaer's second son
Perry and Petrus	
	Twin sons to Leoflada
Petroc	Dagmaer's eldest son
Ranith and Carus	
	Landlord and landlady at the Sign of the Bull in Bedricsworth
Ratkin	Thrall and protegee of Ethelwold, later Companion-man to Wulf
Recene	Messenger at Uphude

Saewold	Senior apprentice to Thoth
Samuel	One of King Edgar's companion-men
Seward	Master Boatbuilder
Siferth	Representative of the Danelaw at Caestre
Sigar	Abbot of Glestingaberg
Sigewold	Elder son to Wolstan
Sinnyth	Daughter to Kennyth
Slean	Member of the Court at Wintancaestre, skilled huntsman
Thella	Dagmaer's youngest daughter
Thored	Ealdorman of Eoforwic
Thoth	Head of the kitchens at Radendunam
Thurstan	A Dane, petitioner at the Great Moot at Elig
Uvi	Younger brother to Elric and Oswig
Wolstan	Shire Reeve of Grantebrige
Wulfaetna (Aetna) and Wulfmaer (Wulf)	
	Twin niece and nephew of Ealdorman Brithnoth
Wulfstan	Father of the twins
Wulric	Archbishop Dunstan's brother

MAP

By God's grace in the second half of the tenth century since His Son's sojourn amongst us

October, 956

BEDRICSWORTH

"How shall I bear it? To leave them so soon, hardly to have known them and to be parted for so long? But bear it I must, for the thread is cut and the pattern which it wove to make my life is ended. Oh, I shall see them again, that I know, but whether in the strange cool, cloudy heavens Father Aelmer preaches, or on the far side of the Bridge of Rainbows in the ancient West, I am not so sure. Dagmaer seems sure it will be there, across the bridge, and it does sound a nice place to wait! But my pallet is made up here in the chapel, so that I may pray to Christ.

How long shall I have to wait before I greet them? Their threads are being spun, just meted out, beginning to unravel and reform even as the cords which attached them to my womb were severed. My magical, miracle babies! Only Dagmaer knows how magical – would Father Aelmer acknowledge them a miracle or denounce them as abominations? I did not think they could live when I first saw them, but Dagmaer saved them, and now even as I fail, they gain in strength. And I thank whatever powers spared me for the few days I have had to hold them, love them, and whisper to them in the night. To name them: Wulfaetna and Wulfmaer.

My girl and my boy. I thought I should tear apart as I tried to birth them. In the end Dagmaer took her knife to me and I hardly felt the pain of the cut, so great had been the agonies of my confinement. And then she brought them to me, wrapped so closely side by side in the blanket and snuggling together, for comfort, I thought, after so long embraced in my body. But then she drew back the covering and my heart stopped in my breast, for they were not only as like as one, they were one... joined together rib to rib, the little girl to her brother's left, as though leaving his sword arm free to defend her. And yet so perfect, and Dagmaer felt them all over, and said it was skin, just skin that held them together, and that she thought she could cut it as she had cut them from my body... but that it must be done now, now before anyone else saw them... before the priests said they were tainted...

And there was so much blood anyway, and I felt as though I was in a dream... I said yes, yes, do it, cut them! I heard them scream, two voices crying, I swear it, as if they could not bear to be parted, and then I heard and saw no more, everything was dark, dark as dried blood to begin with,

7

then black as the night sky without stars and then, gradually, stars began to appear, and then a dawn and... somehow, I was alive and so were they.

I tried to give them suck, but I soon had nothing to give. Dagmaer's breasts were still heavy from feeding her latest boy and she took them to her. She lay on the pallet with me, first to my right, then to my left so that the babes took turns resting between us as they fed, and when I asked to see their bodies, I was amazed to see such little scars... like tiny opposing crescent moons, with a few stars around each, the marks of the stitches that healed the wounds. In a few years, Dagmaer said, they would hardly be visible at all.

And now I must leave them. Strange, I thought that yesterday should be my last day on this earth, and this my last night, but now... surely the darkness cannot have passed so quickly! I can see the coming of a new morning: I can see a lightness. But wait, is that the East? No, no, the altar is at the other end of the chapel, that must be the West. Oh, the lights are lovely, such colours – all the colours of the... I will wait for you little ones, I long to hear what you will do, I will wait on the Bridge..."

Part I

THE SPINNNING

ONE

The last day of September, the Year of our Lord 961

WULFAETNA

Our wet nurse spoke with the old gods. Of course, these days a right-minded person would not readily admit to such a thing. Even fifty years ago, when I was approaching my fifth birthday and the world was a less bloody place – or so it seems to me now – such an admission was not to be encouraged, but Dagmaer spoke to them, and she did so easily and comfortably, just as she seemed to do everything else. The gods found a way into everything as far as she was concerned and so she spoke with them, not just to them. If she was particularly anxious that the milk should not curdle on a hot day, she might mention to Loki, the trickster among the gods, that she was keeping an eye on him. If her horse needed shoeing, she might call upon Wayland, the gods' smithy, to ensure that our own blacksmith had time to tend to her old nag, and often, or so it appeared, the gods replied. Sometimes, the gods began the conversation. Odin might send one of his ravens out upon some business and if Dagmaer spotted it she would likely make mention to him that she hoped its errand was not to her. And if, on a blustery, starlit summer night, the Lady Freya's wain was partially covered by scudding clouds, then Dagmaer knew that the Lady was warning that rain or high winds the next day might well keep both nurse and children indoors. And that there might be other ructions, too.

On such days, we stayed in the Great Hall, trying to keep out of the way of adults who were less sympathetic to our pastimes than Dagmaer, but as often as not getting under their feet anyway. On that particular autumn day, the rain was over by mid-morn and we were ejected into the wet, sweet smelling meadows behind the palisade. My brother's birthday was only two days away, like mine. Wulfaetna and Wulfmaer, two little troublesome puppies Dagmaer called us, and, like puppies we had rolled and run and cuddled and chivvied and generally exasperated our elders and our playmates alike. We were as like as it was possible for girl and boy to be, and although we would not be able much longer to pass twin for twin, we were making the most of the time we had left.

"Put a braid in that girl's hair, for the love of Heaven," my cousin Leoflada had said early that morning, "or I shall never tell which of them I have to teach and which I have to spank!"

Although it was said with a smile, I could hear something of the exasperation of the older, more grown up, woman-child in her voice. I knew, too, that we had been pushing our luck that day, for my blue tunic was longer than my brother's short one, and when we dressed before breakfast, my knees had been demurely covered. Now they could be seen to be as dirty as Wulfmaer's, and his were hidden by the longer dress. We were still able – only just – to swap identities. And fool everyone but Dagmaer.

The game was up when, scooped off his feet, and protesting loudly, my brother was close to the indignity of having his hair plaited. He insisted that it be left loose – it was for women to tie their hair back to keep it out of the way during domestic duties. A man would only plait his hair when preparing for battle, plaits which would then be wound around his head to cushion it from the hard metal of his helmet. Wulfmaer's shouts and my laughter were the final straw. A busy Hall with important preparations underway was not the place for us and so, reprieved, we tumbled outside with the other children.

The main gateway into the Hall's inner courtyard had not been held closed in anger for a generation. Once, when the Danes were rampaging, it was said that the ditch, the greensward on its innermost side and the palisade itself had held them at bay for over three days until aid arrived from Wessex. But now the ditch seemed little more than part of the scenery – an extension of our playground, to roll down and scramble up, and as for the main entrance, well, that remained open during the daytime unless, on special occasions, it should be closed just so that the great, heavy gates could be ceremoniously thrown apart to allow some important visiting party to make a grand entrance. Which is what would happen later that day.

But all we knew was that a watery sun was now shining and promising to get brighter as the day wore on. There were about a dozen of us altogether: children of the stead, surprised to have such freedom thrust upon us, when usually we were kept busy with whatever jobs were within our capabilities. It was clearly a boon.

"Plait my hair, indeed!" huffed my brother.

"But you make such a pretty little maid," chortled Guthric, one of Dagmaer's many sons. Just short of a year older than us, Guthric was heavier than Wulfmaer and had not yet been bested by him. Indeed, it was more often that Wulf had the bloody nose at the end of a battle. "My sister has some very fancy braids that would suit you just fine!"

Wulf put his head down and charged at his tormentor, butting him soundly in the chest. With a grunt, Guthric fell onto his backside, the air knocked out of him for a moment. Then he kicked out at Wulf's legs, a boot connecting solidly with one of my brother's ankles. I felt a tingle of discomfort in my own ankle.

"Ow!" Wulf was now hopping on his sound leg and Guthric aimed another kick at the uninjured ankle but missed. Wulf tripped over a bump in the damp turf and joined the other boy on the ground. I pounced on them both, pummelling with my fists, knowing that I would do no real harm to their already tough young bodies. Guthric rolled away – wrestling with a girl was beneath his maturing dignity. Finding my puny punches had little effect, I began tickling my remaining victim instead. I knew all his most vulnerable spots – but he also knew mine, and soon we were giggling helplessly, whilst neither wanted to be the first to give in. I grabbed a handful of grass, bright with daisies, and stuffed it down his neck. His ankle no longer pained him.

"Enough," he said laughing and trying to pull the grass out. "What shall we do now that we are out of there? I want to get well out of the way before they change their minds and find me any errands to run."

"We better change our clothes back before you get my dress any dirtier," I said, beginning to lug Wulf's tunic over my head. "I don't want your spanking any more than you want my plaits."

"Me, get *your* dress dirty?" Wulf loosened the woven ribbon braids which tied at the neck of my dress and slipped it off. "That's a good one!" Our bodies shone very white in the glinting sunlight, two strange little scars like crescent moons, even whiter. Our fair hair was still slightly damp from the wet grass and sticking to our shoulders. Quickly we slipped on our own garments.

"When you two have stopped playing at changelings, we'd better make a dash for it." Guthric gestured towards the door from which we had been expelled. Leoflada had just emerged bearing a bucket and was clearly looking for someone to commandeer as her assistant in whatever chore she was undertaking. Without waiting to find out what it was, we ran down the steep side of the ditch and up the other side, where we would be out of her sight in the scrubby bushes and trees which bounded the stead.

We could just hear Leoflada's sharp voice ordering one of the other children to be about some task, and the laughter of his companions cut abruptly short as they, too, were put to good use.

A stream ran through the trees, its banks eroded low in places where we had so often scrambled down into the water to paddle and search among the stones for bright pebbles and tiny shimmering fish. Wulf whispered in my ear, making a show of telling me something that our companion would not be able to hear.

"Let's hunt…"

"… for the treasure of the Rhine." I finished his sentence before the first words were out of his lips. He took my understanding for granted. He carried on as though the sentence had been all his. "You shall be Sigilind and I am Sigimund."

Guthric said pointedly "I *can* hear you, you know. Wulf, you have a whisper like the bellow of the Yuletide boar! But it'll be no game without a fearsome foe!"

Wulf turned to Guthric. "Do you want to be the dwarf Ragin or his brother, Fafnir, the dragon?"

"Both," said Guthric, rather shortly, "since whoever I am, I shall be killed."

Dagmaer had begun to tell us the saga of the Great Hoard of the River Rhine, a tale, she said, of long ago and far away across the sea which pounded upon the Eastern shores of our uncle's Ealdormanry, where our own people had once lived, before they crossed that same sea and made war upon the tribes which then held this land. The story was long and complicated, and the older children understood it better than we did – we could only remember the excitement of battles and strange gods, and the fact that two of the main characters were twins, boy and girl, like us.

For an hour or more we played, Wulf and I splashing in the rill, finding imaginary gold under every smooth stone, avoiding the water etins, who took part in our game conveniently taking the shape of sticklebacks, and tiny ogres immaculately disguised as frogs. Guthric did an admirable job, in turn, of being not only dwarf and dragon, but also assorted trolls, barrow wights, and a host of other unpleasant enemies with which Wulf and I resolutely dealt by means of magical swords, in the shape of stiff iris leaves, or hammers – for which it was harder to find convincing substitutes. Eventually, his memory of the tale little better than ours, he called out after one particularly gruesome death "Now I am reborn once more! Sigimund, meet your doom, for it is I, Loki, who challenges you to duel by fire!"

"No", I cried, "Not that, not Loki, not even in play…" I felt a cold prickle down the back of my neck.

"Father Aelmer would have you sent to bed with no meal if he heard you taking the name of one of the Old Ones so seriously," said Guthric descending from the stone on which he was perched ready to swoop down, impersonating the fire-wreathed god of trickery and deceit.

"And Dagmaer would bring me supper, together with a rune stave to keep under my head as I sleep and bring me sweet dreams!"

"One day my mother will go too far in antagonising that old man." Guthric laughed; he could see that I was unwilling to be cowed by his sneer. Loki was not to be impersonated, not if I was in the game. I had a nightmare horror of his cruel jokes.

"I would protect you even from the great prankster himself!" said Wulf, jogging over to us, half afraid that the make-believe was going to end in tears. He knew my nighttime fears all too well. But Guthric was never one to take a tease too far. Besides, he knew me well, too. My tantrums usually ended in me getting my own way, so why prolong the argument when the fun was over?

Dagmaer and Father Aelmer, our house priest, had a long and turbulent history of disagreement and mutual disapproval. One of the many things that Dagmaer did with ease was have babies. She was rarely without a babe on her hip, and another in her belly, which was the reason why, when our mother died giving us life, she took us to pap. Our father, Wulfstan, was grateful to his wife's brother, the Ealdorman Brithnoth, for taking us in. Brithnoth had no son – Leoflada was his daughter by his first wife, and his second Aelflaed, had shown no sign of becoming pregnant. There seemed little chance of more children and a sister-son would be a welcome addition to his Hall. A twin sister to that nephew was simply another small mouth to feed – and something of a curiosity. Ever since we could remember, Dagmaer had been a serving woman in the Hall, a free woman, not a thrall or a slave, but officially no more than a servant, though something in her confident stride and motherly manner made her more than just a mead-bearer. She was part of the family in a way which neither of us fully understood, nor questioned. At the age of around forty and with six children living what she didn't appear to have was a husband. Of course, Wulf and I knew that she must have a husband, somewhere… and one day he would turn up.

In the meantime, whilst we had an absent father and no mother, Dagmaer's brood had a mother but, it seemed, no father. It had to be said that if there was an acknowledged father, he would have been a remarkable man to look at, for her children shared the most disparate features it was possible to imagine in a single family. Guthric, with his wide blue eyes, freckled face and red mop was blessed with brothers and sisters with hair every colour imaginable from black to flaxen and eyes blue, green and brown. Petroc, the eldest son, was a tall young man with dark good looks and a short temper, whilst Thella, the youngest of the brood, barring the current babe in arms, was a fine boned, fair, curly-haired little flirt. At the age of two, she could charm my uncle's surliest thegn into picking blackberries for her or lifting her onto his shoulders to watch the jugglers in the Great Hall. Father Aelmer strongly disapproved. Dagmaer in turn found his sour-faced celibacy an affront against life itself. At church service, she stood doggedly still, eyes apparently focused on some distant object, hardly murmuring responses and clearly impatient to be about the day to day business of the Hall. And then, of course, there was the matter of her conversations with the old gods which she made no pretence to hide…

"I've had enough of this game anyway," said Wulf. "I claim the golden Hoard!" Guthric made no objection – he knew that in this game he was never destined to be the hero.

For a few minutes we all sat, the skin of our feet beginning to pucker and wrinkle in the running stream, enjoying the increasingly warm sunshine, our small disagreement forgotten.

"I wonder if Sigimund ever had to brush his hair and make ready for visitors," said Wulf, wistfully. "A warrior shouldn't have to concern himself with such things."

"And did Sigilind have to change her dress because her brother made it dirty?" I added.

"Back to that again, are we?" Guthric playfully tried to bump our heads together, and another scuffle ensued. I rolled off the bank and found myself sitting in the stream. "Now look, dirty *and* wet!" I shook myself like a puppy, and the boys hauled me upright.

Leoflada's voice was shrill in the distance. "Wulf, Aetna, where are you? Come in and change your clothes. Time to show yourselves. Now!"

"You notice she's not calling *me*," Guthric grinned. "I'm off to see if the others are back from the island. You'd better go home." He jogged off in the direction of the road which led to the coast. His elder brothers had gone fishing at daybreak.

"Come on then," Wulf said making his way downstream toward the palisade on the far side of the ditch.

I followed a few steps behind.

"Wulf?"

"Yes?"

"What you said about protecting me – even from you know…"

"Yes."

"Did you mean it?"

"'Course!"

"But I won't need protecting from him, will … I mean, neither of us will do anything …" I was not sure what I meant, nor quite what I wanted to hear.

"No, of course not! And in any case," Wulf turned around and waited for me to catch up the few paces I was behind, "he would have both of us to worry about, wouldn't he? Just like in the Saga!"

"But we don't know how that finishes yet."

"It'll be alright."

"Yes, but we won't if we don't get home soon. I know that tone in Flada's voice. We'll have to butter her up if we want to listen to the skop

14

in the Hall tonight, otherwise it will be early to bed for us and all the fun for the grown-ups."

"Race you, then!"

When we reached the small side door of the Hall, Leoflada was waiting for us, hands on hips, the little frown line which was already beginning to form between her brows creasing her otherwise smooth forehead. One of her mousey plaits was coming loose, beginning to escape the pins which held it in place and, where it touched her shoulder, becoming fuzzy with friction as it rubbed against the tabard which protected her gown.

"What in middle-earth do you two look like?" She was flustered otherwise she would never have used an expression which she had obviously picked up from Dagmaer. Father Aelmer would have tutted at the mention of an earth not wholly explained away by his biblical reading. Middle-earth smacked a little too much of a reality encompassing many more worlds that he acknowledged.

"We've been down..." Wulf began.

"... to the stream," I finished, our usual bipartite speech as natural as breathing. Something else that irritated Leoflada.

"But we did run ..."

"... all the way back!" I was still panting.

"I can see that!" Leoflada was standing on her dignity – determined to be counted among the adults today, and not with the children. "And rolling in the mud, to boot! Wulfaetna, when did you get that rip in your tunic? Well at least it's not your best one. And Wulf, where did you get that graze?" There was a bloody scab forming on my brother's knee where he had scraped it during his scuffle with Guthric. A wisp of hair from Leoflada's drooping plait tickling her cheek and she absentmindedly tucked it behind her ear. It made her look more like the young girl that she really was, despite her attempts at adulthood.

"It'll be me they blame if you two disgrace yourselves, as if I didn't have enough to do helping with all the..."

Wulf put his arms round her legs and hugged them – nearly making her topple over.

"Don't be cross, Flada! We've had such fun. I've been Sigimund and Aetna's been Sigi..."

"I've no time for that now," Leoflada was determined not to be placated. "Now go to your sleeping chamber, Dagmaer has laid out your fest-wear. Get yourselves properly dressed. And don't borrow my comb for those yellow tangles you call hair. I'll know if you have, last time it was full of grit when I came to use it. It's a miracle no teeth were broken!"

I remembered feeling rather guilty on that occasion – and, indeed, that we might have cracked one of the tines. Flada's comb was particularly beautiful and had belonged to her mother. Made of bone, it was set with tiny gems, and etched with a delicate scrolling pattern of interlaced beasts. Wulf had thoughtlessly picked it up and began to drag it through his hair when I saw the sparkle of its garnets through his fingers. Hurriedly I had snatched it from him and replaced it on our cousin's bedding – I knew she treasured it above any of her possessions.

"We won't, Flada, but can't we have something to eat first, it's hours since we broke our fast?" I had just realised that the hour of the midday meal was past, and there was no sign of the usual spread of food on the long trestle. In fact, now that I noticed, the whole hall looked different. The great trestle was moved to one end, beyond the larger of the two fire pits, turned so that it was across the width of the room, and a longer, but less robust table set lengthwise down the room in its usual place, between the fires.

"Everything is different today," Flada said, absently. Clearly her mind had already moved onto other matters. "Just go along, will you!"

"But…"

"No 'buts', go and get ready, there'll be plenty to fill your bellies soon enough! Please, you two, be good!" There was a little wheedling in her tone now. "I want everything to be perfect later on…"

"Can't we…"

"… just have some bread and cheese?"

"Oh, very well. Tell Thoth I said so, and come right out of the kitchens as soon as you've finished. And then for pity's sake get changed!"

The kitchens were to the side of the Great Hall, not too many steps away from the small side door where we stood with Leoflada, but out of sight of the main entrance. A door opened on the long side of the smaller building, opposite the side door in the Hall. Kitchens were habitually separated from other structures due to their propensity to catch fire. This was the domain of the kitchen thralls, but under the strict supervision of the Lady of the Hall – our Aunt Aelflaed. Ability to manage the day to day provisioning of the establishment, care of linens, hospitality and other wifely duties determined a Lady's status among her feminine peers as rigidly as the social and political rank of her husband. Such skills were already being passed on to me, just as elementary swordsmanship and an understanding of duty and fealty were beginning to feature in Wulf's education.

The building was low roofed, but for the area over the bread ovens, where it had been heightened to allow the intense heat to raise more safely toward the thatch and escape through a wide hole, and the door swung both inwards and outwards on leather hinges allowing for the constant stream of heaped platters and boards which left the kitchens full and returned empty during a meal – there were usually two dozen or more to feed at a normal sitting and many more on a special occasion. Sometimes the meat was cooked over the kitchen ranges and brought into the Great Hall, and sometimes, on high or holy days, it was skewered on huge spits and cooked over the fires in the Hall itself. This day was to be one of the latter.

Wulf made a dash for the door, just as it swung outward. With a howl he bounced backward, his hand over his nose, a trickle of blood oozing down over his upper lip. I felt a quick sympathetic twinge in my own nose and ran to pick him up. From the other side of the door came a word that Father Aelmer would certainly have not approved of our hearing (though we knew it already) and when it opened, Thoth, the head kitchen thrall stood, an empty wooden board dangling in hand, a broken pot at his feet, and a mess of crushed and partly crushed red berries, slippery with jelly, gently sliding down his chest and britches to pool in the cuffs of his boots.

"Did you not think, young wolf-cub, on a day such as this, that the kitchen might be busy?" Thoth was a man of good humour, rarely goaded to anger and with an ability to sail serenely through the most alarming culinary crises. "It's as well we have had a glut of fenberries this year, for this pot will not grace your uncle's table!" Any pretence at ill-will evaporated when he saw Wulf's bloody nose. He had a soft spot for children and Wulf was one of his favourites.

"Let's have a look at the damage," he swept Wulf up into his arms regardless of both jelly and blood and pulled away Wulf's hand. "Not too bad by the look of it, just another bruise to add to the others. You nose will still be just as pretty as your sister's."

"By dose isn'd preddy!" Wulf protested, as Thoth wiped the blood away with a kitchen cloth. "Ad I do't blait by hair!" he added rather irrelevantly. "I'b dot a girl!"

"Well, that's alright then." Thoth's mind was clearly beginning to get back to more important matters. "Now if you want some food – and I imagine that's why you're here – just take some cheese from one of the wheels that's already started. Don't spoil anything that's new. There's some misshaped loaves on the far trestle, and yesterday's milk in the grey jug – it's still fresh." He gave us both a smack on the backside. "And then get out of the way!" Thrall he might be, but he was master of his kitchen, under Aelflaed's authority.

We went to the far end of the room away from the ovens, where there was food laid out haphazardly for the sustenance of those at work. In my uncle's stead, it was hard to tell the thralls from the ceorls – the slave from the free servant – except that the thralls wore light metal collars around their necks, mere tokens of their enslaved status, and pale imitations of the heavy neck fetters worn in previous centuries. They were as well fed and clothed as the freemen. In a good master's hall, a thrall might arguably have the better life – his food and board were guaranteed, and he had several days in each year when he could offer his services in paid employment, enabling himself to gradually build up a small hoard of coin, sometimes enough to buy out the thraldom. Nor was it unusual to be given freedom upon the master's or mistress's death. A freeborn man, on the other hand, had full responsibility for his own and his family's life and well-being.

Wulf picked a gob of fast clotting blood from his upper lip, wiped the back of his hand across his face, and then the palms of his hands down the front of his tunic. For a moment, I reflected upon the fact that it was his tunic, not mine, and thanked the Powers (as Dagmaer would have put it) that we had swapped our clothes back.

"Good! That's what I want, food and bilk," only the odd word was now subject to his injury. He poured some into an earthenware tumbler. "And it doesn't matter if it is yesterday's bilk," he spluttered through a creamy moustache, a dribble of it added to the rest of the mess on his tunic. "It's Gillycrest's best! I can always tell when it's hers."

Gillycrest was our favourite milk cow, even-tempered and soft-eyed, she gave the impression that to be milked was a pleasure which she was graciously inclined to share with her keeper. She never kicked the maids, took the lead when, with her sisters, she came in for milking and tolerated our childish games. In the spring, we often made crowns of wild flowers and draped them over the softly curling horns, hence her name. She was, quite simply, one of our darlings.

We broke off great chunks of bread – special bread, topped with poppy seeds, a treat only on offer now as some of the loaves were misshapen – and, using the short knife left on the trestle for the purpose, cut wedges of cheese from the already well started wheel. Further down the table there were fragments of pastry, broken crusts from some great meaty creation still soaked with gravy and beyond that several heavy earthenware pitchers. Since we had not needed to tell Thoth what Flada had authorised – and he had not specified to what we were entitled – it seemed churlish to ignore them in favour of bread and cheese alone.

The pastry was heavy, yet crumbly and deliciously soaked with juices. Venison, pork? It was hard to tell, but there was also the richness of liquor, dark ale or maybe even wine. Our young palettes could not tell, but we knew it was food that we had not tasted before. Speechless with our own audacity, and not needing speech between us, we took several more morsels. Then Wulf's eyes lit on the smallest of the pitchers.

"That's small ale," he said.

"How can you tell?"

He had lifted it down from the board and sniffed at it. "I have smelt it often enough at meals, in the flagons and on Uncle Brithnoth's breath. And it's in the smallest jug!"

"Put it down, don't get into any more trouble." I knew we should be getting back to the Hall. "Flada will be getting her yarns in a tangle if we are much later."

"I shall be five in a few days, that's old enough to drink small ale," Wulf struggled to hold the heavy pitcher steady as he raised it shakily to his lips. More mess was added to the stains on his tunic. He snorted violently as the full flavour of the liquid hit his throat.

"It doesn't look the colour of ale to me," I said. It was almost as red as the berry jelly.

"It's quite nice though." He swallowed hard and took another hefty swig. "An' I've definitely smelt it before. Have some."

"I don't think so."

"Go on, you're five, too!" He wuffed noisily down his nose and then breathed in as if trying to clear his head. It seemed a little more than just another attempt to dislodge the now snotty blood from his earlier encounter. After a moment, he added "You're my twin shishter!" He hiccoughed.

I giggled. "Just one sip, then."

He held the crock for me and I took a mouthful. I echoed his first snort. "That's not small ale!"

"It wash in the schmallest jug."

"I don't think that's what it means."

He went to take another swig. "No, Wulf, don't! I mean it! If we get in trouble, we won't get to see anything tonight. And we won't go to the feast. It's not worth it." I grabbed at the pitcher, just as Wulf was about to drink. He lost hold of it, and with a crash it fell to the floor, smashing into pieces and splashing red liquid over our feet.

A dozen heads turned. We backed towards the door, I was trying for a look of surprised innocence and Wulf was sporting what I thought was a rather silly grin.

"Thoth said…"

"We only…"

"It just…"

For once our excuses did not seem to co-ordinate with their usual accuracy. We turned and bolted, more by good fortune than foresight, pushing through the swinging door without further mishap. I looked at Wulf. We giggled again and headed for the side door of the Hall. Now, if we could just make it to the sleeping chamber without running into Leoflada. But we were stopped in our tracks by the substantial figure of Dagmaer.

"How now, my pretty wolf cubs," she put a hand under each of our chins and turned our faces up to her. "What prey have you two been harrying, I wonder? Your young lordship looks a little worse for wear and my little lady rather shamefaced, too!"

"Oh, Dagmaer, we didn't…"

"It wasn't…

"We couldn't…" Our synchronised speech had failed us again and the idea of missing out on the day's events scrambled our joint explanation into a jumble of excuses.

"We're sorry!" This last in desperation – Wulf rarely found it necessary to apologise.

Behind us loomed a shadow of what must surely have been the Angel of Retribution, so favoured by Father Aelmer, swooping close to deprive us of our longed-for storytelling and entertainment. But it was only Thoth. He tried for an indignant voice, but there was a chuckle not far below the unconvincing growl.

"Dagmaer, your two noble charges have been creating chaos in my kitchen!"

"Have they, by the Powers? Well, it will be bone broth and a bed away from the fire for them in short shrift." Dagmaer's disapproval was a little – if not much – more convincing.

But just the thought of being ostracized on a day such as this was enough to bring the beginnings of tears to my eyes, and Wulf appeared to sober up remarkably quickly. Ever my champion, he confessed.

"Aetna had nothing to do with it – she tried to stop me," and in further excuse of himself, "It *was* only the small ale, in the smallest jug."

"Like you, young Aetheling, sometimes strong things come in small packages." Thoth could be strict no longer.

Dagmaer added, "I believe Father Aelmer would say 'Look not upon the wine when it is red'. You may have a headache later, young man. That will be punishment enough. I can see that Thoth feels there's no real harm done."

"Except for the breaking of my best small jug," but Thoth could hold back the laughter no longer, and truly Wulf was a laughable sight – stained from head to foot in various shades of brown and red. Although Thoth looked not much better – the remains of the fenberry jelly still smeared across his chest and streaking his britches.

"You look as though you have both been in the same battle," said Dagmaer, "and you needn't smirk, young girl-pup, your dress is almost as dirty and even wetter. Come now, both of you, off to your sleeping chamber – no, not to be banished," she saw Wulf's initial consternation. "But if we don't get you into some clean clothes soon Leoflada will have a moon-fit! Good day to you my Lord Thoth, I will no doubt see you at the story telling." Was that a flirtatious little wink?

"Till then, my lady Dagmaer." Was Thoth's tone also a little teasing? We looked from one to the other with the incomprehension of the very young.

"Away with you then!" There was the dimple of a smile on Dagmaer's cheek. She had no wrinkles, her skin still smooth, grey eyes bright and clear. Light brown hair was loosely plaited, wound in a single coil low at the nape of her neck. Childbearing had robbed her of the lissom figure of youth but replaced it with soft curves and a ripe aura of capable femininity.

Running ahead of her we went back into the Hall through the side door. The Hall was further transformed since earlier in the day. Already the two hearths were a-fire. Young flames rose from huge logs – they would later die back as the logs began their long, hot death. The wood would sacrifice itself to give us heat and comfort. "Never forget to thank the wood," Dagmaer had told us. "In dying, it gives you its life's hot, red blood." Blood which now spurted in orange flame from its once sap-filled arteries.

Between the two hearths the lower table was set already with wooden platters and bowls, earthenware tumblers grouped in sixes and sevens along its length. Long, low benches were drawn up on either side of the board. Straw was liberally strewn around and under the table, clean now and sweet smelling, mixed with woodruff and other herbs.

Beyond the second hearth (the one furthest from the main entrance) was the High Table. It ran widthways across the room, like the arms of Father Aelmer's Cross, though without the head part, making a shape not dissimilar, as Dagmaer had often pointed out, to Thor's Hammer, an amulet still occasionally – if surreptitiously – worn by those of the old faith. At its centre, facing down the room, was the Great Chair, usually pushed back against the wall, and beside it a smaller chair in the same style: high-backed with scrolling arm rests, and both now draped with red-dyed linen throws. The throws were magnificently decorated, embroidered with writhing, interlaced beasts, tails in their own mouths, legs embracing, wings enfolding wings. Green, blue, purple and black images all outlined in shimmering gold thread. Our Aunt Aelflaed's handiwork, these.

Other chairs were ranged the length of the table, all facing toward the twin hearths and the spaces on either side where the entertainment would take place. And on the table were things which we rarely saw, usually packed and well hidden away: silver platters and goblets, chased and engraved with more coiling creatures, tall horn flagons, banded with precious metals, and immediately in front of the Great Chair, where our uncle would sit, was the wonder of the Hall, a huge golden bowl, two full man hand-spans across and set around its belly with garnets and amber.

Despite our need to hurry, I was irresistibly drawn towards it. My head was only just above the level of the board, and I could see my reflection, hazily focussed and golden haloed in the buttery metal. My breath clouded its surface for an instant. It was the Great Hall's most valuable possession.

At the back of the Hall, beyond the High Table, a wattle screen disguised another door which led through to the private chambers: our uncle and aunts', ours – though Leoflada thought of it as hers, grudgingly shared – and a larger guest chamber which could be sub-divided by heavy hangings to give a degree of privacy to visitors. We scrambled into our chamber.

Two pallet beds, raised above the floor against drafts, and each with a palliasse, straw filling regularly renewed and freshened with herbs, stood on opposite sides of the chamber. One was Leoflada's, neatly patted into shape, the other ours, still shared, and usually a puppy-scrambled mess, but today uncharacteristically smooth. At its head lay Musbane, sunk in deep and luxurious sleep – comfortable as only a cat can appear to be. He opened one eye and chirruped a greeting.

"That cat has been the bane of no mouse this six-month," said Dagmaer, following us in.

"But he could if he wanted!" said Wulf, ever the champion of the persecuted. Musbane had been named rather in anticipation than in recognition of his skills. "He just doesn't want to!"

Only then did we realise what else was laid out on the bed: for me, a new dress, creamy buttermilk-coloured fine linen with – could I believe my eyes – a silk embroidered yoke and sleeves. And a kirtle of tablet woven braid, also in silk.

For Wulf... his eyes were as round as the garnets set around the great bowl in the Hall, as blue as the rain-washed sky, his mouth still smeared with various stains, open in amazement!

"Britches!"

Yes, fine, creamy linen britches together with a short tunic to match and plain brown tablet braids to cross garter his legs to the knee.

"You will be quite the little lordling and ladyship," said Dagmaer. "Don't let me down!"

Even the indignity of a thorough wash in very cold water – I know, because I needed one, too – could not dampen Wulf's spirit now, his short-lived contrition gone, embarrassment forgotten, and apparently with none of the retributive headache promised, he glowed with pride. I had to admit he looked splendid in his new clothes. We both did.

"I shall never be mistaken for my sister again," I felt a momentary pang and my heart seemed to contract for an instant. "But now I am truly Sigimund, and I shall be able to protect my Lindy from fire and foe, fetch and famine!"

My heart leapt back to its usual rhythm. I felt that I looked quite the part in my new dress.

"And should you fall in battle," at this point I jumped up onto Leoflada's pallet, scrumpling its cover into a mess, "I shall call you back, even from the Hall of Vallhal, to join me on my fire ringed mountain top..."

Dagmaer had finished dressing us, and with her own comb had teased out our tangled hair until it lay long and smooth against our new finery. She surveyed us with pride.

"My golden twins..."

Suddenly a dark shape shadowed the doorway.

"Woman, you see how your tales are corrupting these young souls." Father Aelmer's baleful eye was upon our admiring nurse.

"Stuff and dross, Priest! 'Tis but a game," she replied hotly, hardly bothering to look at him, though I noticed that the fingers of one hand were crossed in the sign of Odin's tree, to give the greater lie to her small untruth. "What games played you at your mother's knee, priest, always assuming your hallowed head ever passed the portals of a real woman's private parts? Perhaps like the great Julius you were snipped forth privily to avoid such contamination and never introduced to her?"

Aelmer bridled. "Woman, look to your charges, for there will be those present this night before whom no flippancy should be brooked – nor will be, if I have my way."

Dagmaer feigned bafflement, then, as if a thought had just struck her, said softly "Oh, you mean Dunstan, of course!"

"I mean," said Aelmer deliberately, "my Lord Dunstan, Archbishop of Cantuaria, as you very well know."

"My Lord...? Oh, yes, I forget, you have not known him as long as I... I remember a young man with a twinkling eye and a fine broad chest, who thought a kiss and a tickle in the kine-barn far more interesting that his studies. And not averse to the company of the kine-maid, for all his father's money. They were good times. The levels of Glestingaberg have kept many a sweet secret along with its other mysteries."

Aelmer's normally sallow face went an odd shade of purple. It was hard to judge his age: he had the look of an apple stored rather too long on the shelf – still edible, but not tempting. He was thin, not wiry but rather flabby, as though exercise was low among his priorities. You felt that his touch would be cold.

"Woman, I tell you..." but what he was to tell, we would never know, as a hubbub in the courtyard began to swell, heralding the arrival of visitors: jangling harnesses, clumping hoof beats, cries of welcome, barking dogs and the squawking of unwary chickens.

Turning on his heel, and without a backward glance, the priest strode away. Dagmaer looked us over as though judging her own handiwork. "You'll do," she said. "Now go and watch the guests arrive, stay clean and stop out of *his* way." She nodded in the direction of the retreating priest.

"Yes…"

"…Dagmaer."

"And where's Guthric? I haven't seen him since he was with you this fore-noon."

"He went to walk Petroc and the others back from fishing," said Wulf. "They should be home by now."

"If you see him, tell him he's wanted," said Dagmaer as we made to leave, eager to miss none of the excitement outside. "And Petroc, too!"

"Yes…"

"…Dagmaer."

I turned back to give Musbane a fare well ear-rub and caught an odd look in Dagmaer's eye. She was sitting on our pallet stroking him. Impulsively, I threw my arms around her neck and kissed her.

"Thank you, Dagmaer."

"For what? I'm just doing my job." But I knew better. "And what about you, Lord Puppy, too big for a kiss?"

Wulfmaer hesitated. Then he launched himself at her lap and smacked a wet kiss on her cheek. "Thank you, Dagmaer!"

We scampered outside through the door opposite the kitchen and along the back wall of the Hall, turning the corner abruptly at its end. Wulf skidded to a halt and I cannoned into him, both just keeping our balance. The usual workaday forecourt in front of the Hall was suddenly full of all the trappings of festival. Where carts normally unloaded their unremarkable contents: timber, sacks of grain or barrels of salted meat, patient mules awaiting their reward, there was now a melee of excited greetings, proud whinnying horses, servants unloading baggage and, amid it all, our uncle and aunt: he standing head and shoulders above everyone else, clasping right hands to the elbow with the other men, she seeming to be in all places at one time, kissing, embracing and teasing, and chiding the visitors for their long absence.

"We had not expected you to all arrive together, how so?" she cried. "So many friends all in one neat package! It is a joy indeed! Come into the Hall straight away and wash away the dust of the road with a welcome cup! Husband, pray make your official welcome brief for we need no ceremony upon these arrivals. Those who are not family are so long friends that they may pass as such!"

Our uncle raised his voice above the hubbub. "You are more than welcome, good friends. It is indeed my honour that this day of celebration brings you to my Hall … and now enough of formality! Come in, come in… Elflada, sister, you look radiant: Ethelwine, you are clearly treating her too well! And you have brought Oswig, I hoped you would! Aethelflaed, my dearest sister-in-law, were my wife not here I would pay you more compliment, but I must not risk sibling rivalry! Dunstan, old friend, you must have met with the others on the road?"

"No, indeed, I broke my journey at Aethelflaed's Hall, and we have had a pleasant few days of reminiscence this last week." The Archbishop shrugged a travel cloak from broad shoulders to reveal a plain monk's habit of good material, belted at the waist, cowl thrown back. Only a rich golden cross, studded with emeralds, on a thick chain suggested his high calling. His tonsure was immaculately shaved, and so small and neatly positioned that it could be mistaken for a natural bald spot. The rest of his hair was still a rich brown, with just touches of grey scattered through it. Dark eyes, full of good humour, but sharp and missing nothing. At fifty, he was still a handsome man.

Drawn by the fine horses and the air of welcome and general excitement, Wulf and I came up behind our aunt. I slipped my hand into hers, a little shy of so many fine guests. Wulf made to stroke the horses.

Elflada spotted me immediately. "Can it be… little Aetna, child, you are the image of your sweet mother, how she would have enjoyed today, so many good friends gathered together. It is hard to believe she has been gone these five years." She kissed my upturned face. "And where is that brother of yours?"

More interested in the horses, Wulf made some small resistance to being kissed, but was unequal to the task, for, once seen, we were both to be kissed by respective aunts: Elflada, our uncle's sister and Aethelflaed, his wife's. "They certainly take more after their mother than their father. Though now that I at look at them…" said Aethelflaed, smoothing back Wulf's hair. "Dunstan has word of Wulfstan…"

"Time for that later," the topic was changed hastily. "Take a cup now and your baggage will be carried to the guest chamber." Aelflaed swiftly re-assumed the role of hostess. "We are now awaiting only two more for our party to be complete. Have you news of how Ethelwold and Elfrith fare?"

"Wold is hardly his old self… and don't speak to me of that woman. Elfrith!" Elflada spat the word.

"Hush, let's not find ill even before she arrives," said Aethelflaed.

"Oh, Aethel, how can you say that? The woman is poison! When I think…" The women walked ahead of the men toward the Hall.

Brithnoth clapped Ethelwine on the shoulder. "You look well, Wine, how go the Marches of Grantabrycgscir? Still as flat as ever? And welcome to you, young Oswig. There's one here who will be more pleased to see you than I can say… your brothers are faring well, I hope?"

Ethelwine grinned widely. A head shorter than our uncle, and more slightly built, he pretended to be knocked sideways by Brithnoth's brotherly thump and stumbled into Oswig, who, playing along with the joke, caught him as he stumbled and stood him upright again.

"My Lord, I see you still don't know your own strength, sir! Thank you, yes my brothers send greetings." Despite the raillery, Oswig was careful to maintain a correct level of respect.

Ethelwine made a show of brushing himself down. "As do my brothers, Brit. Those who will not be joining us."

The conversation continued as the party made its way into the Hall. And now I begin to wonder how much I really remember of what was to happen in the coming hours. Of that day and the evening that followed I seem to remember everything. But how can I be sure that they are really my memories, when the tale has been re-told, discussed, argued over by others and I have heard those memories and those old arguments so often? Perhaps what I believe I recall of all that came after is really the memory of others, passed on to me for safekeeping. And of everything that Wulf came to know, experienced, survived? How strange is the manner of my sharing in his memories?

I can only tell what I believe to be the truth. If I explain it in the words of the woman that I am now, it will seem that the five-year-old I was, knew, and understood, more than her age would have allowed. Yet put it into such words I must. For without explaining how it all began, I cannot begin to make sense of how it has seemed to end.

TWO

By the time the westering sun had begun to silhouette the trees which enclosed my uncle's stead on its landward side, the remaining guests had arrived, not with the general celebratory air of the earlier arrivals, but with more ceremony. Outriders on horseback preceded and followed a large litter carried by eight thralls, whose generally exhausted and exasperated appearance made it evident that the journey had been neither quick, nor easy. Wulf and I had been watching the fires gradually burn hotter and hotter in the Great Hall – now we were once again drawn outside.

Shadows were already lengthening across the courtyard when the alarm had been called by the gatekeeper and my uncle and aunt went out to greet the newcomers. The rest of the company had retired to the guest chambers to refresh themselves and prepare for the evening's events. As the litter was lowered none too steadily to the ground (many hands, in this case, making for rather uncoordinated work) a woman's voice from within sounded querulous and irritable.

"God's breath, be careful you oafs! My Lord, *if* you could stir yourself, we seem to be here, for what it's worth!"   This latter in a tone both contemptuous and resigned.

A male voice replied, "My dear… softly, softly…"

One of the outriders, now dismounted, brought a small mat to the side of the litter, placed it carefully on the ground and drew back one of the heavy curtains which concealed the occupants. An elegant foot emerged, followed by an ankle enveloped by long drapery. The foot appeared to hesitate while its owner located the mat, at which point Uncle Brithnoth strode forward, holding out his hand, which was taken by a long, gloved, feminine counterpart. Finally, the lady herself came forth.

Her head reached to my uncle's shoulder – not an inconsiderable height for a woman – and her figure was slim, yet obviously strong, judging from the way she held herself: erect and taut. Her gown was soft brown, embroidered in silver, and fox furs swathed her upper body. Dark hair, deep brown with a hint of red was loosely plaited over one shoulder, the braid falling to her waist, its end captured in a piece of gold flecked fabric, which was tied into a rounded pouch by a ribbon. She had the look of a sleek wild animal, temporarily tamed.   I was fascinated. Inclining her head to Uncle Brithnoth she stood to one side.

"Lady Elfrith, you are welcome to our Hall… Wold, come on man, your lady is taking the lead!" My uncle released her hand and leaned into the litter.   I sensed a hesitation, and then he grasped the remaining occupant, hand to elbow, and hauled him out. "Ethelwold, Ealdorman of

All East Anglia!" a good natured, ironic emphasis on the title. "We are honoured this day to have so many dignitaries in our midst!"

Aunt Aelflaed came forward to greet her guests. She dropped a curtsey to the ealdorman, and as she rose, he wrapped his arms around her and lifted her off her feet, beginning to swing her around. "Come, little Flaed, none of that..." There was a pointed, though quiet, cough from his wife, and Aelflaed, restored to her feet, turned to her.

"Lady Elfrith, our Hall is graced by your arrival. The guest chamber is ready, you must feel in need of rest and refreshment."

Elfrith smiled. "I am grateful for whatever small comforts you are able to offer. The journey was indeed arduous. These idiots couldn't make a smooth journey if they were hauling a hot sledge over pack ice! I have been jolted to hell and back. Do you have a feather palliasse? No? Ah, well, my bruises can wait to fade until I am home again. They matter little to my husband, I am sure."

"My dear..." Ethelwold seemed about to remonstrate with her, but he was seized by a fit of coughing.

"Nor, indeed, do my headaches when I must put up with that infernal noise morning, noon and night," Elfrith turned away from him.

Brithnoth turned swiftly to the practicalities of the arrival. "Wold, your horses will be cared for in my stables, and your men are welcome to refreshment... the thralls may go to the kitchen, your ceorls will attend the feast later? Good!"

"Thank you, cousin. I see we are not the first to arrive?" Ethelwold had noticed the number of fine horses being rubbed down and given their evening rations. "Unless you have acquired a great many new beasts since my last visit."

"No, indeed, your brother is here, with Elflada. And Oswig with them. Aethelflaed has been entertaining Dunstan at Stoche this last week and they travelled together, so the family is gathered! Wulf, come here, pup, and welcome Ealdorman Ethelwold as his best friend's sister-son should!"

Whilst I had been gazing at Elfrith's gown and furs, Wulf had been studying the litter. He had not seen one before. He jogged over to Brithnoth's side and, remembering his manners, stood feet together and bowed his head sharply. "Welcome, my Lord. My uncle's Hall is..." Dagmaer's lesson in etiquette had been a day or so ago. I came to the rescue.

"... honoured by your footfall," I completed the sentence.

"I see you two are still speaking with the same voice!" Ethelwold ruffled Wulf's hair (I winced and thought of Dagmaer's careful combing) and then swung me onto his shoulder. "Ah, had I not already married the most beautiful woman in the realm I should have waited for you to grow up, Aetna!"

I remembered him saying something similar the last time I had seen him and being flattered by his attention – in fact for several weeks our games had included my new title "Lady of All East Anglia" until the new Saga had captured our imagination. He had been quite the hero of my immature heart – well built, tall, beard neatly trimmed on a full, firm jaw, blue eyes twinkling as he teased a willing victim. Now he looked different, though the game must surely have been less than a year ago. There was grey in his light brown hair, grizzled into his beard and moustache, his eyes seemed rheumy and his build less robust. As he put me back on my feet he coughed again, putting his hand to his mouth.

"You seem less than well, Wold." Brithnoth thumped him none too gently on the back. "Cough it out man!"

"It's nothing," Ethelwold glanced at his palm, and then rubbed it on his britches. "Nothing at all."

Aunt Aelflaed had already led Elfrith into the Hall, and as the men followed, Wulf and I on their heels, my brother whispered "That's everyone, I heard Flada say that once the Ealdorman of East Anglia and his lady were here things would really get interesting. I 'spose she meant that the jugglers would come in and the food start!"

"I don't know…"

"What do you mean?"

"I don't think that's quite the sort of interesting she meant."

Young though I was, I had been aware of an undercurrent of tension when the Lady Elfrith was mentioned by the other women.

"Hmph!" Wulf was unconvinced. "Well, I'm going to ask Thoth when the food will be ready."

"Remember what Dagmaer said about keeping out of the way. I'm staying in the Hall."

"I will. Call me if I'm missing anything."

He slipped across to the side door and out toward the kitchens. I hung back to watch the adults, Aunt Aelflaed leading Elfrith, who had declined immediate refreshment, through to the guest chambers, and Uncle Brithnoth who was plunging a hot poker from the lower hearth into a flagon of mead. It hissed and steamed, and, poker withdrawn, the flagon was passed to Ealdorman Ethelwold.

"Sit, sit, old friend, there will be plenty of time before the feast – the ladies will no doubt need another hour yet to be ready."

He pulled one of the rough benches from its place by the lower table and dragged it closer to the hearth. Both men sat down, Brithnoth stretched his long legs in front of him, and cradled his own flagon, warming his hands. The onset of evening had lowered the temperature outdoors. It was good to see the main doors closed against the chill.

"Five years, then," he said.

"Five years, indeed." Wold took a tentative pull at his mulled mead. "Hot!" He sucked the air over his lips and tongue, and then licked his lips appreciatively. A few drops of golden liquid clung to his moustache, unreached.

"We have much to celebrate this day." Brithnoth drained his flagon and looked into it as if wondering whether to refill it. "I shall save the toasts until this evening, but perhaps another of these is called for by way of a welcome cup." A tapped barrel was set to one side of the hearth, supported by a wooden frame which held it several hand spans above the floor, so that a large flagon could be slipped beneath its tap. Brithnoth stood his vessel in place and turned the screw until first a trickle and then a more substantial flow of mead splashed into it. The poker was already reheating in the fire.

The hanging at the back of the Hall was thrown back and Ethelwine appeared. He glanced at the thralls still preparing the High Table, snatched an apple from a carefully arranged pyramid (I waited for the pile to collapse, but nothing happened – did I imagine that he looked a little disappointed?) and strode across to the lower hearth. Taking a bite of the apple, he spoke with his mouth full.

"Well, brother and brother-in-law, I might have known that you were ahead of me… Brit, if that is not your first, you can make it mine, and take yours in turn. A fine host who allows his guests to languish with a thirst…"

"Peace, Wine, I know you like to live up to your name, there is plenty for all!" Brithnoth plunged the poker once again, handing the fizzing tankard to Ethelwine, who incautiously took a mouthful. The hot mead appeared to go down without touching the sides, as Dagmaer would have said.

"By the Saviour, that's good!" Despite the warmth in the room, his hot breath condensed. He looked like a happy dragon, a light smoke curling from smiling jaws, I thought. I giggled and the three men noticed me for the first time. "Laughing, little one? At me?" Wine opened his arms wide and made to run at me. I squealed and dodged behind my uncle for protection. But my erstwhile suitor, Ethelwold, proved by champion, and before I knew it, I was on his knee.

"Where's that brother of yours?" he asked.

"Wulf has gone to see when the food will be ready," I replied, happy to be the centre of attention.

"Another one whose belly is more important than his manners," Wold laughed.

"I hope you are not inferring…" Wine feigned insult.

"I infer nothing… you are my youngest brother, and I am used to your appetite. You always ate and drank twice…"

"Only twice?"

"Very well then, thrice, your allotment, when we were all four together." Ethelwold and Ethelwine were two of four brothers, eldest and youngest respectively. Between them, Elfwold and Ethelsige completed the foursome, though one favoured a monkish, and the other a bucolic, lifestyle.

"How do your brothers fare?" asked Brithnoth.

"Contentedly and well," said Wold. "I would like to see more of them, but Elfrith finds their company tiresome."

Brithnoth exchanged a glance with Ethelwine, who, with a covert grimace and gesture suggested that the feeling of exasperation with the lady in question was mutual.

"They visit us in Sawtrede often," he said. "Elfwold has been in contact with Dunstan recently, I know... something to do with his new plans for church reformation. I have not had time to keep up with them. And Ethelsige is as happy as his favourite sow in shit!"

Wold laughed. I was still on his knee and heard the rumble and rattle in his chest as the laughter turned to another cough.

Once again, the hanging at the back of the hall was thrown back. This time two new arrivals joined the party. Brithnoth stood up.

"Dunstan, good friend, come and take a tankard before the ladies arrive... you too, Oswig. If our plans fall out as we would wish you must learn to take the opportunity of enjoying male company when you can, a wife – especially a new one – can curtail such pleasures if she so chooses! And my Leoflada has a tongue on her when she feels the need. She takes after my first wife in that regard, may the Lord rest her!" My uncle produced two more steaming brews which were greeted with enthusiasm.

Oswig flushed slightly – though whether due to the brew or the allusion to his approaching marriage it was hard to tell. He was a slight young man, around seventeen years old, middling in height, clean shaven but for a small moustache, his brown hair falling to his shoulders, neatly cut and brushed back from his pleasant face. He and his brothers had estates bordering and enclosed by the Ealdormens' various holdings.

"To Leoflada, then," he murmured, talking a mouthful, though his toast was almost unheard as Dunstan's voice rang out in a churchman's full-throated tone.

"I give you all your very good health. Wold and Wine, to the continued ascendency of East Anglia; Brit, the same to Eastseaxe; Oswig, to your future. And to my... Church!" He quaffed back the tumbler's content in a single pull, and, having seated himself on the bench, slapped the empty vessel down on his knee.

Nestled as I had been on Wold's broad lap, he had not seen me until then.

"Little Aetna!" His handsome face beamed. "Why, here's a pretty chick to be sitting in so big a nest. Are you cultivating a taste for hot mead?"

I shook my head. The arrival of two, more unfamiliar, masculine faces made me a little shy, and for once I was mute.

"She's learning the knack of sitting pretty and listening – a fine accomplishment in a woman. The listening part, I mean!" quipped Wine. "And I'll warrant that the little lady now has an idea of at least one of the announcements to be made later." He winked at Oswig.

In truth, I had hardly half understood most of what they had said, but my feminine intuition had worked well enough for me to begin to understand why Leoflada had been so keen that the party should be perfect. I was glad that I had made sure that Wulf had done no harm to her precious comb.

There was a scuffling noise at the side door, as though someone was trying to open it whilst carrying some other burden. The company turned as one, hands instinctively reaching to their belts, where each carried a dagger. Though swords would not be worn in a friend's Hall, daggers or knives were always to hand, either for eating or, if necessary, defence. Even if danger was unlikely, the possibility could not be ignored. It was soon apparent that caution was not needed. Wulf struggled in, a drumstick – pullet or duck, I could not tell – held between his teeth, and two apples, smothered in honey and skewered on sticks, in his hands. A considerable amount of the honey was running up his arm as he attempted to keep the sticky mess away from his new clothes.

"Well, and here's the cock chick!" My uncle beamed at his sister-son and strode across the Hall to catch the door, which was threatening to swing back and repeat an element of this morning's kitchen disaster. Taking one of the honey-apples, he opened his mouth wide as if to swallow it whole. "This must be for me!"

Relieved of one of his burdens, Wulf removed the drumstick from his mouth, a smear of charcoaled grease appearing across his cheek as he did so. "Of course, Uncle, if you want it… but I really brought it for Aetna. I can run and get another – as long as Thoth is not looking!"

Brithnoth laughed. "No, little man, give the one you hold to your sister and I'll look after this one for you until you have finished your fowl! Though I may claim one mouthful as forfeit!"

For a moment, Wulf did not see me in my cosy place on Wold's knee. When he did, he looked a little jealous at my privileged position but then the Archbishop shuffled along the bench and patted it. "Come, Wulf, sit by me and tell me the tales of your day's adventures." Wulf handed me the deliciously sweet, honey coated apple and then settled beside Dunstan on the end of the bench.

"We have been playing at the Sagas," he said. "Dagmaer has been telling us the tale of the Rhine's treasure and we have been Sigimund and Sigilind." Wulf tore a chunk of meat off the bone and chewed it thoughtfully. "It's a very good game, but we need help to play it because there are so many monsters and foes to overcome!"

I wondered what the Archbishop would say, as Father Aelmer was so scandalized by our pagan play.

"It is, indeed, a wonderful game," said Dunstan. "I hope you will let me play it with you before I leave. I have a few days to spend here with your uncle and aunt and I can think of nothing I would like better." He could see Wulf's eyes were drawn to the beautiful gold cross on its thick linked chain. "Maybe we can even find some real treasure." He winked.

My voice returned. "We have turned over every stone in the stream but found nothing. Dagmaer says that the etins have taken all the old gold away." I hesitated for a moment. "And that people don't know how to look for it any longer."

"Does she indeed?" The Archbishop raised an eyebrow. "Well, we'll have to see about that!"

As if summoned by the use of her name, Dagmaer appeared silently through the hanging. "My lords," she said, "I am come to find the children, and to tell you that the ladies will be ready shortly." She was still in her workaday clothes, plain, but somehow so well suited to her that they might have been hours in the choosing. Her gunna, a long dress reaching to her ankles, was of a buttery yellow, a plaited belt of a deeper shade, tied at the waist, emphasised her figure. A kerchief, loosely catching back her hair, was white.

"Dagmaer!" The Archbishop rose from his seat.

"My Lord Archbishop." She dropped a half curtsey.

"You look well."

"Hard work is ever a source of well-being, my Lord – so long as it suits." She smiled at the company of men around her, a smile of simple pleasure, coupled with self-confidence. "Now, my wolf-cubs, come along with me, leave their Lordships to one last round before they collect their ladies."

Had I been older I might have wondered at an Archbishop standing at the arrival of a serving woman.

))))((((

By the time Wulf and I had been checked for any last-minute disasters – Wulf needed another pass of a damp cloth across his face and hands: thankfully the charcoal and honey had not extended to his fine new britches – the men had withdrawn, the fires fed to a new height, and the lower table filled by lesser guests. At the top of the table the High or Shire Reeves (the new name, recently coined for them by some, was Sheriffs) of the South Folk and Eastseaxe, together with their ladies, held court with their those of their minions lucky enough to have been included. In the middle ranks of the table, ceorls, freeman, their wives and reeves from the nearby villages were seated. Lower still were the performers who were later to entertain the company, together with others specially favoured by the ealdorman; Brithnoth's love of his hounds, horses and birds meant that the head dog warden, groomsman and falconer were also so honoured. The atmosphere was jovial, mead and ale were already flowing, and the noise of laughter and conversation came through the hanging and reached us in the withdrawing chamber.

Dagmaer took us, one by either hand, into the Hall, and we stood to one side to await the arrival of the occupants of the top table. Aelmer already stood waiting. He wore his usual priest's robe, though some effort had been made to brush it down and remove the worst of its accumulated stains. Vanity of dress was, he considered, a sin. Dagmaer had replaced her yellow gunna with one in a similar style, but of a russet red, and swapped the kerchief for a rectangular head-rail, draped over her hair and held in place by a tablet woven braid, stiffened to create a circular band.

At some pre-ordained signal which I did not notice, the lower table fell silent and the hanging at the back of the Hall was thrown back, a thrall holding it so that the doorway was fully exposed. Our uncle, Ealdorman Brithnoth entered, with the Lady Aelflaed on his arm, to a chorus of cheers and applause. Walking to the centre of the top table, where the two Great Chairs had been drawn back in readiness for them, they took their places, our aunt on our uncle's right, the golden bowl in front of them. Next to enter was Dunstan, accompanying the Lady Aethelflaed. They were the highest-ranking guests: Archbishop of Cantuaria and Dowager Queen, though it was always hard for us to think of our Aunt Aethelflaed as a queen: her husband, the late King Edmund had died ten years before our birth. They took their places, Dunstan beside Aelflaed, and Aethelflaed beside Brithnoth. Next in priority of position were the Ealdorman of East Anglia, my erstwhile champion Ethelwold, and his wife the Lady Elfrith. They went to their allotted places, lady alternating with lord, as the ealdorman's brother Ethelwine and his wife – our other aunt – Elflada, entered the Hall, and went to sit beside them. Finally, Oswig entered, and on his arm a blushing Leoflada. Somehow, she did not look like *our* Flada, usually so full of harassed business, the little girl, trying to look grown up. She *was* grown up! She wore no head-rail, as the married ladies did, and her hair was loose, softly falling to her waist – a circlet of stiffened braid, blue to match her gunnas, kept it from falling forward over her eyes. Like the other ladies, her undergunna was full length, and over it she wore a gunna, three quarter length and ungirdled, with bright embroidery bordering the neck, sleeves and hem. She and Oswig seemed reluctant to let each other go, but did as they must, Oswig moving to one end of the table to sit beside our Aunt Elflada and Leoflada to the other end, next to Ethelwine.

There were now just two places left at either extremity of the top table – one of each facing down the Hall, the others at right angles at the very edges. To the last of the "official" places Wulf and I solemnly walked, as we had previously, and with much repetition, been instructed. Dagmaer and Aelmer took up positions facing each other – separated, thankfully, by the entire length of the table. I found myself seated, therefore, between Oswig and (to my disgust) Aelmer, whilst Wulf (oh, he did seem a long way away!) between Flada and Dagmaer. I was not sure which of us was the more or less fortunate.

Whilst the rest of the company settled itself comfortably, Brithnoth remained on his feet. Thralls moved up and down the table, offering to fill the flagons with mead or ale. Since we had last seen the table earlier in the day more of the family's greatest treasures had been added. In front of each of the four central places green glasses had been set – precious Roman glass, rare and fragile. Only the host and his lady, and the two highest guests would use these if they wished to drink wine, the other guests – even at the top table, would use horn vessels, whatever brew they favoured.

A big spit had been fitted across the topmost hearth, and on it a skewered boar was turned by two small boys – they were around our age, red-faced and sweating from their proximity to the fire. Juices hissed and spat as they fell into the flames. The hog was already well cooked from the kitchen fire, brought into the Hall as the traditional symbol of festive hospitality, ready to be sliced and distributed later in the proceedings. First, great chunks of flatbread were being distributed amongst the guests, each a man's hand span across, and an inch or so deep. From the door, halfway along the long wall, closest to the kitchen across the way, a party of thralls entered, each bearing wooden trays and platters piled high with fowls and fish, roasted, baked and broiled, a delicious scent of herbs and wild garlic in their wake.

When the steaming food had been distributed along each of the tables – there was no distinction made between upper and lower – Brithnoth raised his voice. "My Lord Archbishop, I would crave your benediction on our festivities!"

Dunstan stood. "A pleasure, Ealdorman." He waited for a moment to allow silence to fall.

"We are grateful to God for his grace,
For fine food fairly given,
And the fealty of friends and family."

The hubbub from the lower table resumed and, as the Archbishop took his seat, Brithnoth pitched his voice so that only his personal guests could hear him. "Friends, let us enjoy a dish or two, and a tankard or three before the few formalities of the evening claim our attention." He sat down with a "Hurrumph!" of satisfaction.

I needed no second prompting and though I could hardly see him – there were eight adults seated between us – I felt sure that Wulf was equally keen, despite his earlier forays to the kitchen. The drumstick he had already enjoyed had looked so good that my first choice was to wrap my small fist around the leg of a fowl (again, I knew not what kind) almost the size of my forearm. Aelmer looked at me with distain, but said nothing, whilst Oswig grinned sheepishly.

"Well, Aetna, you and I will soon be cousins! How will that suit you?"

"Very well, I think." As an afterthought I added, rather irrelevantly, "I like your moustache." This seemed to please my companion and he smoothed it down with a single finger to either side.

"It is rather good, isn't it?" There was still much of the boy in this young man. "But I'll let you into a secret."

"Oh, I'm very good with secrets!"

"It's taken me six months to get it to look like this! And I don't think I'll bother with a beard for a while."

"No, I wouldn't!" This must have sounded rather rude, but I was disappointed that the secret had not been worthier to divulge to an imagined descendant of Sigilind. Oswig laughed. Nothing was going to spoil his evening, even if he had to sit next to a five-year-old, when he would rather have been with certain someone ten years older. He turned to his other companion.

"Lady Elflada, may I assist you to anything?"

"Thank you, Oswig, I have all I need for the present. Now, tell me how your brothers fare. Although they live so close on our marches, it seems I see little of them these days."

"Elric has still much to learn from our father, before he is ready to take over his two estates and there are plans for little Ethelmaer to enter the Church, though he is his father's son in temperament, and that may not work out! Uvi is beginning to make much of Coteham and Wivelingham."

My attention strayed. Apart from the food there was little, yet, to interest me in this gathering, except for the fine clothes of the ladies, and the best view of those had already been had on their entrance. The variety of their head-rails interested me, though. Both my Aunt Aelflaed and her

36

sister favoured the more traditional rail, a long oval or rectangular piece of fabric, with a hole cut in it to reveal the face, draped over the head and held in place with a circlet of metal. Despite her exalted social status, Aethelflaed's circlet was little different to our aunt's: a simple band of silver adorned with a few semi-precious stones. Elflada, our paternal aunt, a little younger, favoured the more modern innovation – a shorter, squarer cloth laid directly on the top of the head to fall gently to the shoulders, leaving more of the face and all the throat revealed. She, too, wore a circlet – hers a tablet woven braid stiffened with silver wire.

The Lady Elfrith, however, affected a very different style. She had changed from her earlier travelling garb into a undergunna and gunna both of bright red, embroidered with an interlaced design in black. Her hair was once more plaited, but now very loosely and in two braids, so that around her face, and to her shoulders, it fell almost as though loose – which would, of course, have been scandalous, as she was a married woman, not a virgin looking to find a husband. Once again, the bottom of each long plait was bound into a pouch of fabric – this time like that of her gunnas. On her head she wore a small, round rail, which just skimmed her shoulders and was surmounted by a deep circlet which glowed in the torchlight, unadorned with jewels but quite obviously made of etched gold. I had to lean a long way forward, or backwards, to get a good look and it was frustrating that I could not see all these pretty things more easily. To amuse myself, I next chose to eat a mackerel, which needed careful boning. I began to arrange the little bones around the side of the platter, ready to count then off the way we did with cherry stones and apple pips: "*Eena, meena, macca, racca...*"

Then Uncle Brithnoth was on his feet again. It seemed that the several reasons for the festivities were about to be made fully public. At Aelflaed's instigation, thralls hastened among the upper and lower companies making sure that flagons and tankards were all fully charged. The fashion for the lady of the Hall to serve her guests personally had fallen from grace, but it was still her responsibility to make sure that everyone was well catered for at all times.

"My Lord Archbishop, Queen Aethelflaed, Ealdorman, ladies, friends and companions. I welcome you all to my Hall at Radendunam and to my Ealdormanry of Eastseaxe. I rejoice to see so many familiar faces."

A burst of cheering and applause greeted him.

"You will know, I am sure, part of the reason for this happy gathering. It is five years since I took the oath of Ealdormanry and pledged my sword arm, my heart and my strength, for as long as it is mine to give, to the protection and administration of this land. They have been a good five years and I thank those of you who have laboured under me for your fealty. My task has been made the easier and the more pleasant by the proximity of my good friend Ethelwold in his position as Ealdorman of East Anglia, to which he ascended at the same time. Together, we have formed a strong bastion against those elements (and I will not name them here) who have threatened our way of life. Firstly, then, I give you a toast to Eastseaxe, to East Anglia and to our continued alliance."

He took a pull from his tankard, and the company did not need inviting twice to do likewise. Another cheer went up. Many flagons were emptied at a single draught, necessitating the thralls to scurry amongst the guests once again.

"Secondly, there is an announcement to be made which gives my wife, and me, much satisfaction. Our daughter, Leoflada – and she has become like a daughter to Aelflaed – is of an age to be betrothed, and we are happy to promise her, with her own consent, to Oswig of Dullingham. Oswig has fine estates, and a family of which we are proud to say we are friends. Welcome Oswig, to our Hall and our family. May God bless you both – now and in your future marriage."

Again, the tankards were raised and drinks taken, to the accompaniment of clapping, calls of congratulation and the odd ribald shout from the younger members of the lower table swiftly hushed by their elders.

"My next toast is joyful and yet tinged with a sadness that my wife, my sister and I have found hard to immerse in the happiness that has ultimately been its gift. My sister-son Wulfmaer, and his twin Wulfaetna, are soon to celebrate their fifth birthdays. And so, it is that we remember that their sweet mother, my younger sister Aetna, died that same five years ago. It has been my duty – a duty that I have come to believe is a blessing – to bring them up as my own. Wulfmaer is a fine, sturdy boy and his sister promises to be her mother reborn. I have decided, therefore, from this day, to take them both to be my own. Sister-son and sister-daughter, now my son and daughter. My inheritance, their inheritance, and so I shall swear. Raise your vessels."

I felt a rushing of blood in my ears, and a tingle over my skin. I knew Wulf would be feeling the same. This was a huge thing, and completely unexpected. Though we were too young to realise all the implications, we could hardly fail to be overwhelmed. There was a momentary silence in the Hall, and then a spontaneous burst of cheering. For a second, I thought our uncle – I could not yet think of him as 'father' – wanted us to do something, anything, to acknowledge the moment, and I did not know what! But then he went on with his address.

"Lastly, we are honoured to have with us a man who has been friend, companion and advisor to me and my kin for many years. He has been known to speak out of turn, to find fault with the great which has not been to his own good, to break rules only to rebuild them better and stronger than before. He has given up one fortune and found another, richer, more fulfilling and which he will distribute amongst all, rich and poor, high and low. He has been banished from these shores and is now recalled for the greatest of purposes. From exile to the Church's highest post in the land, under the King's hand, in just a few years. I give honour to my friend Dunstan, newly made Archbishop of Cantuaria!"

Brithnoth had been abstemious in the quaffs he had taken in the previous toast makings, but now he took up his flagon of ale and knocked what remained in it back in one gulp. Then, talking up the fine green glass, newly filled with red wine, he held it up toward his friend, separated from him only by his wife, raised it high and with a flourish downed the contents of that, too. Aelflaed also rose, embraced Dunstan fondly and kissed him full on the mouth.

"And now my lords and ladies," she cried, clapping her hands like a little girl, "I'll have no more speeches, just eat, drink and enjoy the entertainment!"

The guests, having obliged their host by drinking more of his liquor to seal the final toast, fell to with renewed enthusiasm.

The food continued to come. No platters were cleared away, as they rarely became completely empty, and so the tables almost groaned with variety and abundance. After the pre-toast courses, came cuts from the spitted hog, carved off the carcass in great lumps and bought to the tables to allow guests to slice off what they wanted – each with his or her own knife. Fingers became increasingly greasy as the meal progressed. Several of the ladies and a few of the men brought linen wipes to clean their hands, but many men, especially on the lower table, simply wiped them on their surcoats or britches. It seemed that Thoth had prepared an endless array of fine dishes which kept on coming: pigeons skewered together and broiled in wine, venison cut into strips and piled into layers with bacon and sweetbreads, pots of boiled root vegetables made aromatic with spices and always more warm bread, fresh and delicious. The bread platters became soaked with every juice imaginable, and on the lower table they were being eaten with gusto. The family guests left them in place.

Now, great wheels of cheese, both soft and hard appeared... I giggled to remember our escapade of earlier in the day, and then sweet dishes began to be set wherever the thralls could find space for them. The honey-apples already sampled made another appearance, resting stickily, fruit downmost in their honeyed sauce, their wooden sticks massed together, and looking like great hedgepigs. Pears were poached in cider, berries from the hedgerow mixed together. There were slices of honeycomb, still dripping their golden contents, and bowls full of cream, some smooth, some clotted in the way of the folk from Kernow.

At the same time as the sweet plates arrived, the entertainers began to ply their trade. They capered around the upper hearth, moving so that everyone could get a view. Jugglers tossed little sacs of sand and sawdust, sewn into balls, high in the air and caught them deftly, gradually increasing the number they had in the air at any one time. The oldest, and most skilled, then took short, pitched clubs, touched them to the fire so that they flamed, and began to juggle them, the flames whooshing and rushing at each upward thrust and flowing in a stream as they fell back towards his calloused hands. He never once allowed his fingers to get burned. Next, two slim boys and a pretty girl, all dressed alike came in. They bounced and tumbled about the Hall, flipping and cartwheeling, spinning in the air, until I could almost believe they were flying. Finally, the two boys stood facing each other with their hands linked and the girl leapt up so that she was standing on their outstretched arms, one foot on either side of their clasped hands. They bent their knees once, twice, three times and then threw her high in the air. She tucked herself into a tiny ball, spun over and over and then, stretching herself out again, landed once more on their forearms, regaining her balance by wheeling her own arms and then standing up tall to acknowledge the applause of the fascinated audience.

When the tumblers had left, a sharp whistle cut through the resumed babble of voices and clatter of vessels, as the company tried (largely in vain) to force down any more food. Then a tall old man, upright, wiry and with a shock of white hair, came into the Hall, apparently looking for something. For a moment the guests wondered who this interloper could be – he seemed to pay no attention to the gathering, whistling and clicking his tongue. Then it dawned on us that this must be another act, though what we could not imagine.

Abruptly, through each entrance, main door, hanging and side door scampered a dog, one black, one white and one brindled. The black dog jumped onto one of the old man's shoulders, the white onto his other, and the brindle ran around and round his ankles, the old man lifting first one foot and then the other so that the dog scampered in a figure of eight until it, too, jumped high and was caught in his arms. The company applauded appreciatively and the old man continued his antics, sometimes pretending to lose control of the dogs, sometimes to be exhausted by them, but always, subtly encouraging them to do more and more complex tricks. We laughed until our sides hurt, and then, at last, the three dogs jumping in somersaults quite as wonderful as those of the tumblers, the old man took his final bow and ushered his troop out by the side door.

Wulf had obviously asked Dagmaer sometime earlier if he might be excused his place and had come to join me. When Aelmer was not looking, I slipped from my seat, and together Wulf and I had scrambled under the table and out in front of it, sitting cross-legged side by side so that we had a better view of the entertainment. Only when the old man and his dogs had left was our disappearance noticed.

"Where are the twins?" Aunt Aelflaed's voice was raised above the general hubbub.

"Enjoying the show as if on the front row of Colencaestre's arena!" Brithnoth's height meant that he could just see the tops of our heads beyond the table top. The ancient burgh of Colencaestre still retained the ruined remains that bore witness to the Romans' love of bloodthirsty entertainment.

Our leaving the top table meant that two seats were now available facing down the Hall. Dagmaer moved to occupy one and even Aelmer was not sour enough to decline a better seat and view of the last performer. The skop, a story-teller, poet and singer of songs, came in with his harp.

He looked around at his audience, waiting for silence, and then, when he was sure that he had their full attention, he drew his fingers across the strings of this harp. Like the tinkling of a woodland stream, the notes seemed to conjure a picture even before he spoke, and then he raised his voice, clear and sharp, not loud but with a timbre that carried to the farthest corners of the room.

> "On a green grassy plain stands a bountiful bower,
> Dextrously decked by the Holy One's power,
> The wood a wonder of colours unchanging.
> A sweet scent fills the fields of that land
> And ever shall it echo joy until He who shaped it
> Shall make an end of his beginning,
> A beautiful bird, as wise as its wings are wide
> Lives its long life amid those leaves.
> Its name is the Phoenix and full fair falls any feather…"

The storyteller held us spellbound, his voice rising and falling, the strings of the harp vibrating in the air, cutting an invisible swathe through the smoky, still food-scented air. Finally, as the last of the strains of harp and voice died away, a moment's stillness followed. Then the applause and shouts of "More!" and "Another!" seemed to crash into the silence, like waves breaking on a rocky shore. But the skop was determined to leave his audience wanting more and resisted the cry for an encore. Brithnoth stood up and took a silver armband from his forearm, the traditional gift for a storyteller who had done well. Aelflaed, too, handed him something. He made a little play of hefting it in his hand and letting it clink next to his ear, so that we could all see that it was a small pocket of fine sackcloth, tied together at the neck.

"Thank you, my Lord, my Lady," the skop bowed to them in turn. "As ever, a pleasure to perform at Radendunam, and as ever a most generous recompense. May the Powers that be bless you both!"

At this Aelmer sat up abruptly, but Dunstan merely smiled. It was an acknowledged greeting and farewell, ambiguous in allusion only to the bigoted.

Brithnoth remained standing. "And now, friends, one last tradition to be maintained before we loosen our belts a little and take some more refreshment!"

He strode down the Hall toward the main door, which was thrown open, allowing in a gust of warm wind. The night had turned milder. Outside, some distance from the hall, but in line with the entrance and the main gateway into the compound blazed a fire. Turning in the doorway, silhouetted against the flames he called back to his guests.

"The bone-fire is lit! Bring you each a portion from your meal and give thanks for what we have shared!"

The top table went first, each carrying some small leftover, which they threw into the flames, Dunstan as jovial as the rest. Wulf and I took my bread platter with the fish bones neatly arranged, Wulf adding a chicken bone which he had tucked behind his ear earlier in the meal. When we got to the fire, we threw it into the crackling mass, our small contribution added to the rest. Even Elfrith, who had appeared vastly unmoved by the performers, comic and dramatic alike, appeared to take some pleasure in the ritual. Only Aelmer scowled.

Dunstan's great voice was raised again.

> *"Thank you, Lord, for love and laughter,*
> *Blessings received, brotherhood renewed.*
> *For meat and mead, song and story.*
> *Of your own do we give you!"*

It was not a huge fire, and soon began to burn low as it was not replenished. In the coming winter wood would be a valuable resource, so it was not to be used unnecessarily. The bone-fire had done it job, bringing an official end to the proceedings of the feast. Guests stood around it in two and threes as it collapsed inward upon itself, a stream of sparks flying up into the night sky. Gradually they drifted back into the Hall.

In our absence, the thralls had been at work frantically, rearranging the interior. The great tables had been pushed back toward the walls, leftovers still in situ, and the stools and benches which had surrounded the lower table arranged around the hearth. The top of the Hall had been partitioned off from the bottom, tall, woven hurdles ranged across its middle, allowing access via a narrow space opposite the kitchen door. This effectively separated the ceorls and lesser guests from the family, whilst allowing each to congregate around a hearth and extend the evening for as long as they wanted. The thralls still had access to both halves of the Hall, turning either right or left, to either side of the hurdles as they came through the serving door.

As we and the rest of the family, and their immediate guests, passed through into what was effectively now the 'Upper Hall', we saw that the thralls had arranged the seating around our own hearth. Wulf and I were flagging, the long day, excitement and food all making us sleepy. Dagmaer picked me up and as my head rested on her shoulder, I felt my eyelids begin to close. Brithnoth was already seated, and he lifted Wulf onto his knee. My brother leaned back against his uncle's chest, enveloped in his strong arms.

"Well, young Wulf, are you happy to be a man, in your own britches and in your adopted father's Hall?"

Wulf tried – manfully – to rise to the occasion. "Yes, Lord! I am proud and…" but the warmth of the fire, the many events of the day and the comforting, soft, solidity of the big man's body was proving too much for him. Like me, he was well on the way to sleep.

I heard Dagmaer's voice say, "I'll take the young lady to her chamber and return for my Lord's new young heir." And then the rumble of our uncle's.

"No, Dagmaer, I'll bring him. There may come a day when he will need to carry me, and I shall already have repaid the debt!"

THREE

Of the rest of that evening I remember nothing. Only later, much later, did Leoflada tell me of what happened. She and Oswig found themselves side by side – more by contrivance than chance, I am sure – and they had been speaking together softly, laughing quietly at small jokes, and beginning to know one another as a man and woman should before they come to the marriage table. Flada had been listening with half and ear to the conversation of her elders, employing the knack she had perfected of paying full attention to her partner, whilst still being able to catch her own name when spoken by others. By the time raised voices also commanded Oswig's attention the seeds had already been sown that would one day be reaped in such a bitter harvest.

It had all begun amicably enough. When Brithnoth returned, having deposited Wulf beside me in the sleeping chamber, there was a buzz of conversation and the occasional guffaw of hearty laughter from the Lower Hall, not raucous enough to make those in the upper speak more loudly than they wanted, and the party had disposed itself as it wished on the chairs ranged around the hearth. A low table had been placed to one side, within Aelflaed's reach, on which was wine and a few small sweet dishes, as well as cheese. She had waved away the attendant thrall and was making sure that the other ladies had what they wanted. In his host's absence, Ethelwine had assumed control of the mead and the ale and was ensuring that the several pokers provided for the purpose were heating to the correct temperature to mull it, if desired. He was clearly enjoying his self-appointed task and had sampled all the variations of wine, both spiced and plain, and brews, cool and hot.

He positively glowed with satisfaction as he beamed at Elflada. "My beautiful wife! And soon to be even more beautiful. Friends, would you not agree that there is nothing more alluring than a woman with your own child swelling her belly! A slim waist is lovely in a virgin, but give me a real, full bodied woman to my bed and board!"

His wife smiled indulgently at him. "Wine, you are again living up to your name. If you do so too often, it will not be very many times that you will see me so encumbered. Too much of the grape or the grain does little to keep small soldiers to attention." She blushed prettily realising that she was being perhaps a little too intimate in her joking. "I mean, we had to send Wulf straight to bed, didn't we?" She tried to extricate herself from her small embarrassment.

Elfrith sighed loudly and stifled a yawn none too effectively. "Oh, really…"

Wine crossed to his wife and kissed her. "Give me another boy like our young Eadwine, or a girl like little Aetna, and I'll be the happiest man in the Shire. And if it is a girl, I'll thank the good Lord that she is no blood kin to our sister-in-law here!" He glared at Elfrith.

Keen to change the subject, Aethelflaed sipped her own wine and took a taste of soft cheese. "Dunstan has been telling me of the fashion among the Franks," she said. "It seems they have strange tastes in many things, cheeses included! There are some they prize highly but which are quite green with mould before they eat them. Can you imagine? And gunnas are being worn tied quite tight to the waist, with a kirtle hanging only to the hip."

"Dunstan, you are a wonder!" Aelflaed laughed. "Firstly, exiled in a foreign land, studying the ways of the Cluniacs – which, Heaven knows, are less than easy to understand! Then learning that you are to come home to an archbishopric, no less, and yet still finding time to learn receipts and take note of ladies' fripperies! We have so missed you these last years."

"It is always better to keep busy than to dwell on misfortune," said Dunstan. "And I have to confess that my exile was entirely my own fault. It is simply not a good idea to berate a king on the day of his coronation, even if he has allowed his crown to roll under the table and left the Hall with not one, but two ladies of, shall we say, dubious integrity!"

"I shall never forget it," laughed Aethelflaed. "It is all in the past now, so we can afford to be amused, but at the time it was not so funny… although, oh, yes, it was!" And she broke into an irrepressible and infectious giggle, which her sister and Elflada found it impossible not to catch.

It was a familiar story to those in the know. The year had been 956 – the year of our birth. It was January, and King Eadred, brother to King Edmund (our Aunt Aethelflaed's late husband) had been dead some two months. Eadred had not married, and our aunt's title of Dowager Queen, therefore, still pertained. The new King, Eadwig, Edmund's son by his first wife, was enjoying his coronation feast. The great and the good of the land were gathered at Kingestun for the occasion. Most of those in the current party had been there (except for Elfrith, not yet embarked upon her married life), together with the rest of the Court. After the ceremonial and crowning at the hands of Archbishop Oda, the usual feast and festivities took place and the young King, at sixteen years of age, was determined to enjoy the event to the full. Having had a rather strict upbringing, first in his father's and then in his uncle's shadow, the trappings and privileges of power were new and as intoxicating as the wine. He was unmarried and had every intention of sampling the pleasures of his new position before taking a wife. At the height of the banquet, it became apparent that the King was nowhere to be seen. Worse still, the crown, so recently placed upon his royal head, was rolling around under the High Table, being kicked from one of his inebriated young friends to another. His stepmother Aethelflaed had her suspicions that he might have been indulging in unseemly behaviour and proposed going to find him. Dunstan, then Bishop of Glestingaberg, long-time friend of the royal family and tutor to the young princes, had volunteered to go in her place – fearing that there might be an unfortunate scene. He was right. When he found Eadwig, it was in the company of two ladies of the Court – widowed mother and unmarried daughter, all three in a state of undress and considerable insobriety.

Dunstan, forgetting that his one-time pupil was now his liege Lord and King, hauled the young man out of the non-connubial couch along the passageway and into a withdrawing chamber, cold and unfurnished, to sober up. Needless to say, Eadwig never forgave him. Once having regained his faculties, he immediately banished Dunstan, and the Bishop of Glestingaberg enjoyed the rest of his incumbency without setting foot anywhere near the famous Tor, or his abbey church, again. Only after Eadwig's death was he recalled by the present King, his brother and successor, Edgar. Since then the former bishop's rise had been meteoric.

The three sisters-in-law gradually supressed their giggles, trying not to catch each other's eyes and set themselves laughing again. Leoflada had heard the story before and was able to join in her elders' amusement. Elfrith raised her eyes to Heaven and sighed pointedly once again.

Ethelwold patted her on the knee. "You were just too young to have been there, my dear, otherwise you would appreciate it the more!" She twitched her gunna away from his hand. "For a while Court was certainly a lively place, with King Eadwig indulging any fancy that occurred to him. It made me feel quite the old man! Though I am used to that being the eldest of four brothers." He guffawed but the laughter once again turned into a racking, chesty cough.

Elfrith looked at her husband with distain.

"What news is there of Elgifu?" asked Elflada. Elgifu was the younger of the indiscreet ladies featured in the scandal. King Eadwig had, in fact, married her, only to be forced into having the alliance annulled two years later due to the revelation that her mother had been his father's mistress. It had even been suggested that they were half siblings.

"Well and happy and living in comfort in Lincylene, by all accounts," said Aethelflaed. "With her mother!" she added, the giggles threatening again.

"At least Eadwig appreciated a woman with some life about her," spat Elfrith. There had been rumours of late that the present Queen, Elfa, delicate before her confinement, was now, having given birth to a son, Edward, increasingly unwell. Edgar had apparently been attracted to her, so it was said because of her pale, wan, loveliness. His pet name for her – his little duckling – had led to her affectionate nickname the 'White Duck' at Court. Elfrith laughed, spitefully. "Elfa has now waddled from childbed to daybed, I hear!"

"Peace, my love, she cannot help her frailty," said Ethelwold.

"Any more than you can, I suppose," snapped Elfrith. "Old man!" she added, under her breath.

"God's breath, Elfrith, Edgar settled an unhappy wyrd upon my brother the day he sent him to meet you!" Ethelwine turned on his sister-in-law, unable to disguise his concern for Ethelwold's health. The drink he had taken was making his mood darker.

"Wine, be silent!" Ethelwold spoke low and harsh and gave his brother a warning look. But it was too late.

Elfrith's attention was already caught. She turned to her husband. "When the King sent you to meet me? What does he mean?"

"Nothing, my love, nothing, he's had too much to drink! What are you saying, Wine? It was good fortune that sent me to Elfrith's father's door, nothing more."

Wine took another pull at his tankard. "Pah!"

"If you have something to say, brother-in-law, say it!" Elfrith was now on her feet. The firelight glinted on her head circlet. She sensed that he wanted to speak. "Come, take another drink, it is a night for tales of the past."

"Well, there's nothing to be done to change it now," Ethelwine said.

"Wine, I tell you, keep your counsel!" his brother hissed.

"Be quiet, husband!" Elfrith said, steel in her voice.

"Why do you let her speak to you like that?" Ethelwine was indignant. "Very well, here it is. You will recall the day Wold and I came to your father's Hall? God forsaken corner of Dumnonia that it was! Did you really think that we would journey all the way from East Anglia to discuss cattle and sheep? King Edgar had heard that old Ordgar had a beautiful daughter – a daughter ill-suited to life in a far flung sub-ealdormanry, elegant enough to be a queen, educated above the norm. He wanted a wife, but he wanted to know something of her before he raised her hopes by inviting her to Court. Edgar is a considerate man. He asked Wold to look you over and report back... but Wold, Wold looked too long and too hard! On our journey back to Wintancaestre I heard nothing but how lovely you were, how clever, how virtuous! By the time we reached the Court he had convinced himself that he was in love with you! He begged me to keep quiet, and when the King asked, he said that reports of your beauty were much exaggerated. That you were, indeed, quite intelligent, but not blessed with charm! That you had not received the upbringing appropriate to a prospective Queen! The King, of course, dropped the

matter. In a few months' time Wold visited Ordgar again, and this time…
well you know the rest. And so here you are, Lady of East Anglia! And
speaking to your husband as though he were a thrall!"

Elfrith stood stock still. She looked around her, eyes resting on each
member of the family in turn. No-one spoke.

"How many of you knew this?" she asked.

Still there was silence. Leoflada slipped her hand into Oswig's.
Whoever else may have known, she certainly had not. The raised voices
from the lower Hall went on unabated, laughter, chatter, someone singing
a popular song. By the table, the serving thrall stood wide-eyed. This was
something to recount back in the kitchen!

Brithnoth cleared his throat. Aelflaed took a sip of her wine and
Dunstan kept his eyes on the fire.

"My love," Ethelwold, still seated, raised his hand toward his wife, as if
to take hers in his. Elfrith knocked it away.

"So," she spoke icily. "So, you raised me to the giddy heights of life in
East Anglia, when I might have been Queen! And you couldn't even
secure the place of Chief Ealdorman for yourself!" This cut deep, as
Ethelwold had been disappointed that the post had been conferred
elsewhere.

"Perhaps now we know why that was. Maybe the King had some
inkling of your deceit."

She flicked her long gunna back, smoothing its folds down over her
slim hips. Slowly she walked toward the hanging at the back of the Hall.
Turning, she said, "Don't even think of following me."

FOUR

If there were sore heads the following morning amongst those who had enjoyed to the full the revelries of the night before, Wulf and I were not aware of them. We were awake early, chattering and giggling under the great bearskin cover on our pallet. We could both only just recall having been deposited there, but we remembered everything else we had heard and seen the previous evening, from our uncle's announcements to the entertainment.

"But should we now call Uncle 'Father'?" wondered Wulf. "We do still have a father, after all. A real one, I mean."

"One that we never see," I replied, shortly.

"We saw him once!" Wulf was indignant. I could not remember this long-past event, and was not sure that Wulf could, if he was truthful. He had convinced himself, after telling the tale so often, that it was true. It might have been. I must have given a derisory little snort.

"Well, I did, anyway," he said. "He had a long moustache and was wearing a broad flat hat, and he picked me up and kissed me and..."

"I know, I know..."

"But you don't remember!"

"No, I don't, but I believe you. I do!"

"Well, I'm just not sure about calling Uncle 'Father', that's all!"

"We'll ask Dagmaer later; let's not worry about it now." I scrambled out from under the cover to discover that my long gunna of yesterday evening had been laid carefully out of harm's way across a beam too high for me to reach. I quickly found one of my older tunics and pulled it on over my undergunna. Wulf's new britches, however, were within reach, and he pulled them on, making quite a decent job of cross gartering them with strips of fabric which had been stuffed under our palliasse for safe keeping – it was where all such small items of attire were stowed. The splendid woven braid bindings of the night before were out of reach, like my new gunna.

Leoflada was nowhere to be seen and Dagmaer was about other duties, and so without comment on our choice of attire, we made our way into the Great Hall. The usual arrangement of tables, trestles, benches and stools had been resumed, the fire in the lower hearth was burning and a number of figures wrapped in their cloaks were still slumbering beside it. On the long table food had been laid out for those ready to break their fasts early. Much of what was there was reconstituted, with some slight variations, from last night's feast. That suited us well. Cold slices of roast pig could be slapped between two chunks of bread to make an easy, portable meal, together with a hunk of hard cheese each. There were several pitchers of milk, to which we helped ourselves before taking our food outside into the early morning sunshine. After yesterday's escapade, even Wulf steered clear of the jugs of small ale.

In the courtyard there was plenty of activity for us to watch while we ate. We may have been out and about early, but not early enough to witness the departure of Ethelwold, Elfrith and their entourage. We could hear the stable thralls grumbling about having to prepare the horses almost before light – and on a morning when they might have wished for an extra hour's sleep! I was disappointed that Ethelwold had left, secretly hoping that he would remember that it was my – our – birthday on the morrow, and perhaps have a gift for me. But gone they were, and there were still plenty of other visitors who would no doubt provide diversion from our usual routine.

We sat on a bench alongside the wall of the Hall, opposite the chapel. Wulf picked at a bit of pork stuck in his teeth. "What shall we do now?" he asked, examining the offending morsel, before popping it back in his mouth.

"If we see Flada, she's bound to find us something useful to do!" I said. "Let's see if we can find the boys and see what they're about."

By the boys, I meant Dagmaer's gaggle of sons. They were usually kept busy with some work or other but were good at escaping when they wanted to – especially our playmate Guthric.

Once the cheese had followed the bread and meat, we brushed the crumbs off our hands and laps and headed toward the stables – usually a good place to begin the search for Guthric and the others. The grumbling thralls had gone to eat in the kitchen, but we heard other voices coming from one of the stalls.

"He's a fine horse, m'lord, but he'll fill out a little yet, I'll be bound!" It was Petroc's voice, and as he spoke Oswig led a slim, black gelding out of the stall, the reins loose in his hand, the horse nuzzling his shoulder.

"Yes, my father gave him to me as soon as he was broken, and we've been together ever since. Learning from each other!"

"It's the best way, m'lord. When we lived in Dumnonia, I watched many a good beast spoiled by harsh treatment at the hands of those who did not understand how a young horse feels! He is a proud young soul, willing to learn and serve, but not to be treated as a slave."

"You were in Dumnonia?" Oswig, looked sharply at Petroc. "In whose Hall?"

"Old sub-ealdorman Ordgar. My mother was in the service of his wife for a while, after we left Kernow. One of many places until we settled here with the Ealdorman Brithnoth and his family."

Oswig said no more but patted his horse affectionately. "He's called Gran," he said. "How old are you, Petroc?"

"I'm not quite sure, m'lord! My mother is always a little vague on the subject…"

"It matters not. Are you determined to stay in the ealdorman's service, or willing to consider a change? I take it you are free?"

"I used to feel obliged to stay with my mother and the children to help support them, but these days their position at Radendunam seems settled. I am a free man; I can make my own choices. But I must have horses about me, always horses!"

Oswig swung onto Gran's back. "We'll talk more later, Petroc!" The horse picked its way delicately out of the stable, stepping around Wulf and myself as we stood by the door. Then he trotted across the courtyard and, as the small gate opened for him, cantered out of the enclosure.

Wulf ran across to Petroc and was picked up and, in one movement, hoisted onto the young man's broad shoulders. I pouted, a little jealous, and was easily lifted up to sit on the side of the stall.

"What are you two about?" asked Petroc.

"We're looking for the boys," I said.

"Guthric and Otter have taken their slingshots out to kill pigeons, and the others are getting ready to go fishing again," said Petroc. At this time of the year, the more fish that could be salted down, or smoked, ready for the winter, the better.

"What are you going to do, Petroc?" Wulf's voice came from on high.

"There's a mare in the village about to drop an autumn foal," replied Petroc. "I promised to go down and soothe her. If the foal comes today it should be strong of limb – it's the feast of Saint Mylor – so I shall encourage her to begin birthing if I can!"

We knew that Petroc was well known for his ability, seemingly, to 'talk' to horses. "I cannot take you with me. A lady in her condition likes her privacy!"

He swung Wulf back to earth and deposited me beside him. "Off with you! And if you see my mother tell her that I may not be back till nightfall!"

Frustrated in our attempts to find the others at a loose end, though we could have sought out the fishermen if we had had a mind, we wandered back toward the Hall. Leoflada came out. She was singing softly to herself – some silly song about a one-legged garlic seller – though it might as well have been a love song, for the dreamy expression on her face.

"Aha, I've been looking for you two!"

Our hearts – and, probably, faces – fell. "Oh, Flada, we were just going…"

"We have to…"

We desperately sought for a convincing excuse not to do whatever she had in mind. But for once she simply smiled at us. "Oh, you children!" Since when had she been so grown up? "Always with some little game to play! Don't look so worried, I won't disturb your make-believe!" Could this be the same Leoflada? "But I think you should know that the Archbishop has been asking after you... something about gold in the stream?" She laughed a little, light trill. "Ah, the sweet make-believe of childhood!"

This was too much! "Flada's a goose-girl, Flada's a goose-girl!" Wulf piped – a goose-girl was what we called a maid sweet on a young man.

"Indeed, I am not!" snapped Leoflada. That was more like the usual Flada. "I am a betrothed woman! And if you don't make yourselves scarce, I *shall* find you something more useful to do than be a nuisance to your elders and betters!"

We scampered away, and she called after us. "I told the Lord Archbishop where you usually splash about making yourselves look like a couple of thrall-urchins!" The last we heard was her muttering to herself, "What a man like Lord Dunstan wants with those two is beyond me..." and then she went back to her singing.

We followed the route we had taken the day before, through the palisade, across the ditch and down to the stream. At first, we saw no-one, and then strolling back towards us, from downstream, two figures came into view around the bend of the lane which ran along the riverside.

Dagmaer was once again in her buttery, cream coloured gunna, caught in at the waist today by a red tablet woven belt, her head uncovered, though her hair was drawn back and coiled high above the nape of her neck, as befitted a married woman. Dunstan, a head taller than his companion, wore a pain brown tunic over black britches, cross gartered also in black, so that the shape of his legs could be seen from mid-thigh to ankle. As the morning progressed, its early promise was fulfilled and it was unseasonably warm for the first day of October. The long slit at the front of his undershirt fell open, and some deep brown chest hair could be seen above it. He wore no cross today, and certainly from where we stood, his tonsure was invisible. Even at our age, it surprised us to see a priest, let alone an archbishop, look quite so informal. We could hardly imagine Father Aelmer ever appearing so – human.

Their conversation had been low – now, spotting us, they called out. "There you are!" As we reached them, Dunstan hunkered down next to us. "Well, who would have thought we two should be searching for gold ahead of the fabled twins! Sigimund and Sigilind, I do declare! Allow me to introduce myself: Dragon-slayer Dunstan at your command, and this the Lady Dagmaer, first among the swan-maidens!"

Wulf and I were delighted that the game should be afoot so quickly. "Lord Dunstan! Where have you searched so far, and what fell beasts have you slain?" Wulf was in character immediately.

"I have looked well in these reaches of the river, Warrior – and Shield-maiden," he was careful to include me in the game. "And have rid it of goblins and dwarfs. But downstream I fear there may be a troll or two, and where there are trolls... well you know how they like to guard things! It's the only pastime they enjoy – except for eating!"

"And farting!" shouted Wulf, already on their trail.

Wulf and I ran down the lane alongside the stream. Dunstan and Dagmaer, laughing, turned and followed us, retracing their earlier steps. In truth, the stream looked very little different to its usual self, but to us there was magic in the air. As we rounded the curve of the bank, we came to a place where the stream narrowed slightly. Decades before, a mighty oak had been felled in the nearby wood, stripped of its branches and the whole trunk split roughly in two lengthways, one half dropped across the stream, its cut surface now smooth and worn from the passage of a thousand feet. The other half of the huge tree had been left, again flat side uppermost, by the side of the rill. Over the years it had become a popular resting place, a convenient seat, even a lover's tryst. Many emblems of love had been carved into it.

"Beneath the bridge," panted Wulf. "That's where trolls hide!" and he scrambled down the side of the bank and splashed into the water. I was not far behind.

"Don't stir up all the mud," I admonished. "We will never find the treasure if you make the water all cloudy."

Although the stream was shallow at this point, the banks had been eroded over centuries of its passage, and the oak bridge was several feet above the level of the water. Wulf and I could get underneath easily, and with sticks and our fingers we began turning over all the pebbles and stones we could reach. We heard Dunstan and Dagmaer arrive above us.

"And so, you stayed away," she was saying, "until recalled by the new King."

"Until I was recalled," he agreed.

"And then..."

But their conversation was interrupted by a whoop from Wulf and a squeal from me. Beneath a large flat stone, we had found a coin. Both diving for it at the same time, we had succeeded in knocking each other over and now Wulf knelt, while I sat, in the bubbling stream, gazing at our discovery. Wulf reached in and carefully picked it up... despite Dunstan's encouragement neither of us had really expected to find treasure!

"What have you there?" Dunstan called down to us.

"A penny, a silver penny!" shouted Wulf.

"Keep looking, then, you may find more!" came the reply.

Dagmaer and Dunstan sat down on the fallen trunk. We crashed and splashed around in the water, with no real plan of action, but enjoying the moment. Wulf was in full character now.

"Sigilind, I must slay these trolls before we can continue our quest!"

"Very well, my noble brother, I shall help you!"

As we tired ourselves out in play-fight, occasionally taking the role of the trolls, as well as our own characters, to make the whole exercise more challenging (this was when we missed Guthric), Dunstan and Dagmaer resumed their conversation. Many years later she told me of what she had learnt that day – and what she had already known – of the man who was now head of the Church in King Edgar's Englaland.

Dunstan's boyhood and youth had been privileged. Eldest son of Heorstan, a Wessex nobleman, he was born in the village of Baltunesberge, close to Glestingaberg on the Sumersaete levels. He was his mother's darling and she later claimed that before his birth she had a vision foreshadowing that he would become a great man – but what mother doesn't have such ambitions for her son? He went to study with the monks from Iraland who, in the first half of the century, occupied the ruins of the ancient abbey, destroyed decades earlier by the Vikings and never rebuilt. He excelled at his studies, seemingly without having to try too hard, for he had time to enjoy the company of other young men, hunting, fishing and fighting and, also, the pleasures of female companionship. In short, he was an ideal candidate for admission to Court, and, together with his brother, Wulric, was soon numbered among the junior members of the retinue of the present King's uncle, King Athelstan.

It was toward the end of this time that he first knew Dagmaer. Her mother and her mother's mother had lived at the foot of the tor at Glestingaberg, by the White Spring. Only a child then, she remembered the young blades, back from Wintancaestre or some other great town, crashing through the low-lying waters surrounding the isle, disturbing the wildfowl and her elders together – the birds taking flight in great squawking skeins and her grandmother muttering that herbs could not be picked under such circumstances – they needed calm and tranquillity if their medicinal properties were to be maximised.

"His father was set on his marriage to a pert young piece from a well-off family, but he would have none of her," Dagmaer told me. "When she learned of his indifference, she made it her business to lay him low. Dunstan had ever been interested in the old ways, and though he teased my grandmother he sometimes came to our cottage to watch her prepare simples and to ask my mother about herbs used for dyes and preserving. The vicious little vixen accused him of trafficking with the Devil and

54

reciting poetry to invoke spirits. Such nonsense! But there were jealous factions at Court, and the King was persuaded to dismiss him. Not content with that, the bitch's brothers attacked him and beat him badly, finally throwing him into an open latrine. He managed to escape, but his wounds became foul after such a ducking and he was desperately ill for weeks.

"Eventually he came home to Glestingaberg, but his sores were so ghastly that it was rumoured that he had contracted leprosy! His mother despaired of his life, and despite the prayers of the monks, she thought she had lost him. In desperation, for she was afraid that the taint of witchcraft hung about the old woman, she sent for my grandmother. After many days of treatment, an improvement began.

"Poultices and herbal infusions, that was what saved him, not the prating of the priests, but Dunstan felt that both had played their part. He took Holy Orders and built himself a tiny cell against the old church of Saint Mary and there he stayed, playing his harp, working with dyes and inks, writing, silversmithing and meditating. His mother, not to mention his young friends, must have wondered what had got into him, along with the herbs!

"I was more than a child by then, and thought myself quite the pretty young thing... and using my grandmother's herbs and my mother's dyes for excuse, often visited the cell. He was a fine young man and though he now felt that the Church was his destiny, few monks and even fewer priests were truly celibate then – or now, that killjoy Aelmer excepted, and who would have him?

"In those days, nothing could persuade Dunstan out of the life he had created for himself. And I was pleased about that. What girl in her teens would not be happy to have such a man? And we were discreet, if not secretive. The village knew about our relationship and turned a blind eye. But then his father died and left him his fortune. He was beginning to be well known for his writing and other skills, and with money too, he became an asset to be courted once again by the highest in the land. King Edmund had come to the throne, and Dunstan was prevailed upon to return to Court. The last time I saw him he gave me the gift of a silver amulet – though he called it a Cross. I left Glestingaberg soon after, went to the West Country, first to Kernow and then to Dumnonia. I was in Petroc-stowe when my first son was born."

Dagmaer had heard something of Dunstan's history since then, but on that sunny autumn morning, many years after their last meeting, she heard the rest of the story first hand. On his return to Court, he found friendship with the new King, but his maverick beliefs, which had been compounded by his recovery, were hard for some of the more conservative churchmen to stomach. As well as friends, he made enemies and once again intrigue was afoot. The jealousy of others might have once more have been his downfall, but on a hunting expedition the King was almost killed when a stag he was chasing, and the hounds hot on its heels, had careered off a hidden precipice and his horse was within seconds of following. Dunstan was not present at the hunt, but the King swore that he heard his friend's voice warning him to rein in his horse – which he did just in time to avert disaster. Returning to his Hall, he immediately called Dunstan into his presence and appointed him Bishop of Glestingaberg, citing this miracle as evidence of Dunstan's sanctity. The two men rode side by side to the ruined abbey, Edmund prayed before the tumble-down high altar, thanking the Lord for the preservation of his life and swearing to give Dunstan every assistance in resurrecting the abbey to its former glory.

There followed several years of hard but gratifying work at Glestingaberg, interspersed with periods at Court, and as a member of the Witan – the King's governing and advisory council. During those years he first met our Aunt Aethelflaed, then King Edmund's Queen. In 946 Edmund was assassinated and his brother Eadred took the throne. Dunstan stood *in loco parentis* to the new King's nephews. On Eadred's death, when Eadwig became King, Dunstan's fall from grace was speedy and complete due to the unfortunate episode at the coronation, which had passed into family lore.

"I went first to Frankish lands, to the Court of Arnulf, who is a fine man and a good friend. He lodged me at the abbey in Mont Blandin. I visited Cluny and saw what a Benedictine monastery should be like. Disciplined, ordered and, above all, free. Free of the influence of the secular world, appointing its own ministers and not run by the family who endowed its land generations ago. And, sadly, my sweet, also free of women... other than the holy sisters, of course!"

"You've changed, Dunstan."

"I've finally grown up, Dagmaer. I'll not pretend that I do not still appreciate a pretty face or a trim ankle, but if the Church is to serve God it must live by rules, the Holy Offices must be held regularly – monks cannot tumble out of bed and into the abbey church and expect their prayers to be heard if they have just been tumbling..."

"Hush, hush, I understand! I asked nothing of you before and I want no explanations now! But it is good to see you again, and to talk, and walk and, maybe..." She laid a hand on his thigh.

Wulf and I interrupted them with our shouts.

"Another coin, another penny!"

"Well, that makes one each, then," said Dunstan. "And what shall you spend them on?"

"I shall keep mine safe and make it the heart of my own hoard," said Wulf. "One day I shall have a chest full of such stuff: arm bands and rings and..."

For once our intentions were not identical. "I shall ask Aunt Aelflaed if I may buy some silks of my own, so that when I embroider, I do not have to keep asking the other ladies if I may have some of theirs," I said.

"Two very fine decisions," said Dunstan seriously. "Young Lord, I hope I shall be permitted to ask for a donation to the Church from your hoard one day." Wulf looked rather uncertain about this... "And what pretty patterns are you stitching, young Lady?"

"I think it is the dragon, Fafnir," I replied. "Though when my aunt drew it, some of the lines came out rather wobbly."

"Perhaps you will allow me to draw you a pattern one day," said Dunstan. "And I will try not to wobble."

"Still the artist, then, Dunstan?" said Dagmaer.

Wulf and I looked back and forth between them, mystified by their strange intimacy.

"Yes, that foolish young man who drew pictures and wrote poetry for his sweetheart is still there, somewhere." Dunstan sighed.

"What young man?" I asked, hoping for a story.

"I'll maybe tell you another day, my pretty," said Dagmaer, with a soft smile.

The mention of a young man reminded me that we had a message for her. "Oh, Dagmaer, I forgot to tell you, Petroc says that he may not be back until it is dark. He is birthing a horse in the village."

"Petroc?" asked Dunstan.

"My eldest boy," said Dagmaer.

Wulf was getting restless again, and the morning was wearing on. "It's our birthday tomorrow," he said to no-one in particular, though he must have known that everyone present, except Dunstan, was well aware of the fact.

"Is it, indeed?" The Archbishop had a knack of appearing interested in whatever was said to him.

"Yes, and we shall be five. That's one third of the way to being a man, and I have britches."

"And shall you be getting presents tomorrow?"

"I hope so, sir."

Dunstan hunkered down between us, his twinkling eyes on a level with ours. "What did you like best at the feast last night?" The question seemed to be for both of us.

"The dogs," I said without hesitation.

"Yes, the dogs," echoed my brother, and he tried to dance a little jig, like the old man when the black dog had run in a figure of eight between his feet. "Woof, woof!"

"A dancer *and* a warrior, Wulf, you will be quite the courtier when you get to Court. No doubt Dagmaer recalls the steps… she was once quite…" but what she was, we were not destined to hear, not then.

"Come along, time to be getting back," said Dagmaer, briskly. "Work won't go away just because the sun is shining and there's treasure in the stream." Hustling us ahead of her she headed off toward the Hall, without a backward glance. Dunstan followed at a slower pace.

Our midday meal was little different to breakfast, except that much of the meat was now hot, reheated in great basting tins over the kitchen fire. Afterwards, Wulf went off with Guthric and Otter to continue their pigeon hunt (they had brought back a good morning's bag of game – five pigeons and two rooks, all of which would make good eating), Dunstan joined Brithnoth and Ethelwine on a hawking expedition and Dagmaer disappeared about her duties. Aelflaed, Aethelflaed and Elflada took advantage of the warm sunshine to sit outside the Great Hall, on the chapel side, and enjoy each other's company, at the same time working their embroidery. I went to fetch my own small piece of needlework and then joined them.

"Now, Wulfaetna, let's have a look and see how you are getting on." Aelflaed had been teaching me how to split my stitches to create great swathes of rainbow coloured designs, which, when I was older, I would work around the precious metal thread which was too valuable for me yet to use.

I showed her my efforts. The outline of a strange, imaginary beast was marked out on my fabric in a fine charcoal line – yes, in places a little wobbly. I had stitched over the outline in red and was now working around it in other bright colours: green, yellow, blue, all created by dyes carefully prepared by Dagmaer. My stitches were rather irregular, but generally placed as they should be.

"That's very good, my loveling," said Aelflaed. "Try not to work more with one colour than the others. It should not look as though any shade is more important than another. As in life, balance is everything. Your stitching is getting better all the time!"

I glowed with satisfaction. This was praise indeed. My aunt was famous for her skill with a needle.

"Thank you, aunt," I said, and told her about the pennies Wulf and I had found, and how I wanted to spend mine on silks.

"You are a good teacher, sister," said Aethelflaed. "And our little Aetna seems to have inherited some skill, too. Don't I recall that her mother was always happy with a needle in her hand?"

Elflada sighed. "Yes, my sister loved her stitching. It is hard to think of her gone from us these five years."

Mention of my mother made me bold enough to ask the question that Wulf and I had been going to put to Dagmaer. "Aunt?"

"Yes, little one?" Both Aelflaed and Elflada answered at the same time and then laughed.

"Don't leave me out," said Aethelflaed. "Child, you have an abundance of aunts!"

Sensing that I might be overawed by quite so many offers, Aelflaed, who knew me best, put down her work, placed her hand over mine, and said, "Ask away, little one."

"Last night Uncle Brithnoth said that we were now to be like his son and daughter. Wulf and I were wondering whether we had to call you mother and father now. But we did have a mother and a father... Wulf says that he can remember our father. I can't, but sometimes, just before I go to sleep, I think I hear a voice. A lady's voice, whispering. When I was little, I used to think maybe it was my mother..." I trailed off, not used to speaking so much, all at once, to grown-ups.

"Oh, Aetna, when you were little! You're hardly the size of a corn-doll now!"

"But should we, Aunt? Should we call you Mother now, and Uncle, father?"

"No, my love, no. Wulf is right, you do have a father, and your sweet mother should always be remembered. Your uncle simply wants to give you both all the privileges that our son and daughter would have been born with. I may never have a child, and Leoflada will soon be a woman grown, with a fine husband to care for her and a Hall of her own. That is all. Lord Brithnoth and I will always be your loving uncle and aunt. And I hope that you will love us back, as much as we love you," she added. "For you are, indeed, my little girl and Wulf is the son I might never bear!"

I looked deep into her grey eyes and saw some pain there. Dropping my work, I put my arms around her neck and hugged her. "I do love you, Aunt!"

"There," said Aethelflaed, "that's clear, then! But maybe it is time for you to hear a little about your father and mother. And the rest of the family. This seems like a good time for story-telling. Would you like that?"

It had always seemed that the subject of my parents had been avoided in our presence; Wulf and I discussed them sometimes, but always only between ourselves. For a moment I was dubious, but then I thought that I would like to be able to tell Wulf something he did not know.

"Yes, please."

"Sister, it's for you to tell the tale, I think," said Aethelflaed. Aunt Aelflaed picked up her embroidery again and stitched as she spoke. How much of the story I really understood at the time, I don't know, but I have since come to know it well.

"Your Uncle Brithnoth had two sisters. Their father was Brithfirth, a lord with lands in many places from the North, into the Danelaw, in Huntedunscir and here in Eastseaxe. Brithnoth was the eldest child. The family emblem, as you know – we've had to stitch it often enough – is the flaming star. It was seen in the night skies when his grandfather was alive, and again on the day of his birth. When he grew up, he was married to the Lady Anefrith, and she was Leoflada's mother. When Flada was a little girl, her mother gave birth to a baby brother, but he sickened and died, and she was never well again. When she died, it seemed as though the light went out of your uncle's life. Elflada had married the Lord Ethelwine, and that left Aetna, the youngest of the three siblings, still unmarried and living in Brithnoth's Hall. When I first met your uncle, she was the only one who could make him smile – but then she made everyone smile! She was so pretty! And she had as light a heart as you might never meet twice in a lifetime."

Aethelflaed added, "I recall when we first visited the Hall here at Radendunam, with our father... he was a straight-faced man without great humour, but she charmed him so that once I actually saw him laugh! I remember he called her his little Sunnebeam!"

Elflada chipped in, "When we were all children, she used to bring stray animals and injured birds into the Hall to care for them. No matter that the mangy dog might give us all more fleas, or the bird be otherwise destined for the table... they found sanctuary with Aetna!"

Aelflaed continued. "Your Uncle Brithnoth was in his twenty-first year and Aetna only her fifteenth, when King Eadred came to the throne. Of course, there were the usual celebrations, feasts and the like in everyone's Halls to celebrate. He was crowned in the August of 746 and the events went on all summer. And everyone was talking about a certain storyteller, a man everybody wanted to entertain at their banquets. Wulfstan, he was called: he could hold an audience in the palm of his hand, whether he was telling an old familiar tale or reciting a new poem. He wrote them, too. You only had to tell him whose deeds to immortalize and – poof! There was a new lay. The skops still sing his songs.

"When he came to Radendunam, Aetna was enthralled. And he was enchanted. It was as if the two of them were halves of the same whole. She would listen for hours to his stories, long into the night as his tales held her – and the rest of the audience – in a state of wide-eyed wonder. During the day time, he would sit and watch her sew, and they talked, talked, talked until it was impossible to believe that there were enough words in middle-earth for them to share.

"Of course, by the time Brithnoth realised what was happening – typical man – it was too late. They were in love. Tell her that it could never be, that it was a quite unsuitable match and she would simply smile. I never knew her to make a scene. When Brithnoth ordered him to move on, he did so, without argument, without rancour. Of course, it was all too simple. Within a week Aetna had disappeared, too. They had not gone far, only to Bedricsworth. They had found a priest and he had married them; it was as easily done as that! Where was the use in making threats, of being angry, of recriminations? They were a golden couple, sweet to look on, sweet of voice, sweet of nature and it was impossible not to fall under the spell of their happiness.

"Wulfstan gave up his life on the road and moved into Radendunam. With Aetna and Wulfstan in the Hall, the sadness left by Anefrith's death seemed to evaporate. Brithnoth became the open, friendly man he had once been, my father saw it and suggested that it was time he took a new wife: me. I was still young, but we were betrothed – my father's Hall was in Stoche among the South-folk of East Anglia. They were happy years, Aetna was about my age and we were like sisters – your aunt Aethelflaed, of course, was at Court.

"They had no children, which was their one small sadness, but they were like children themselves, even then. Oh, there was laughter and song, dancing and play acting, mumming and bone-fires almost every night! Then Wulfstan took it into his head that he would like to go travelling again, tell his stories once more, learn the new tales which only his fellow story-tellers could teach him. And nothing could stop Aetna going, too. They said it would not be for long, that they would leave in the spring and come back before winter. Who could stop them? Who would? They were like two beautiful young horses, eager for the open fields after months in the long-stable. When they left in March of the year 956 who could have known that Aetna was already with child – after waiting so long?

"We knew that their plan was to travel west, to Glestingaberg. They decided to go as far as they could before midsummer, and then head for home and be back during the autumn. They took a little money, but not much – they didn't want to risk being the target for wolfs'-heads and other ruffians. Story-tellers are usually safe as they travel – even outlaws enjoy a good tale around their campfires, and they rarely carry anything precious. Their reward is bed and board.

"At first all went well. Wulfstan was as spellbinding as ever, and Aetna enhanced his performances by singing whenever a tale called for it. They were feted wherever they chose to go. When they reached Glestingaberg, they were happy and relaxed, but already they had fallen behind the vague schedule they had set themselves. Then something bad happened, and I never really understood what…" Aelflaed had long seemed to have given up telling the tale as if to me and it was almost as if she was speaking to herself.

"Ladies, I can tell you. Perhaps I have been silent for too long." Dagmaer had come to see where I was. The others spun round swiftly, to see her standing by the wall, shading her eyes from the sunlight.

"What can you know of it, Dagmaer, when you only met my sister in time to help her in child-bed?" asked Elflada, sharply. I had always sensed that there was some tension between them.

"My lady, I knew your sweet mother-daughter before that, but she asked me to be still about what happened that summer. She ever hated there to be cause for ill-feeling and wanted no feud on her account."

I think that by now that they had all but forgotten about me, for there was no effort made to explain in a way that I would really understand – but that understanding would come with time.

"Sit then, Dagmaer, and tell us." Aelflaed made space on the bench. I sensed Elflada stiffen slightly.

Dagmaer took the offered seat. "When Aetna and Wulfstan arrived in Sumersaete, they went first to Glestingaberg. Wulfstan wanted to see the fabled Tor that featured in so many of the tales he told. They were given hospitality by the monks of Iraland and by the new brothers installed by Dunstan. Even monks enjoy the spinning of a good tale – and the lives of the Saints were some of Wulfstan's best yarns. It so happened that Dunstan's brother, Wulric, was at the abbey, and he asked them to visit Baltunesberge and stay at his father's Hall. They accepted and found quite a party of nobles in residence… Ordgar of Dumnonia was visiting, together with his young son, Ordulf, and Athelstan Rota – Athelstan the Red, they called him because of his wild red hair and beard – who was on the King's business, all of them eager for entertainment.

"On the day after their performance – Wulfstan had told the tale of the Walsings and Aetna sung the old songs that go with it – Ordgar approached them just as they were preparing to leave and head back toward home. He implored them to come back to Dumnonia with him, to entertain in his Hall for, apparently, his daughter – yes, now we know that was none other than Elfrith – was endlessly complaining of boredom, of having nothing to do and no civilized company on the edges of the dreary moorland beyond Escanceastre. He was quite desperate. Obviously, he doted on her, and she took full advantage – he was besotted with the idea of pleasing her. Wulfstan was not keen, but Aetna, always one to spread happiness insisted that they should go. What was a slight change of plans?

"They arrived in Tavestoch – it was much further than Escanceastre, and Ordgar had omitted to mention that they would have to cross Escanmor – after a long and tiring journey. That evening in May was the first time I met Aetna, she looked pale and exhausted. I had been living in Kernow for several years, and earned my bread making simples, ointments and philtres, helping to bring new life into the world, and easing the passage out of it, much as my mother and my mother's mothers had done. Then I had crossed the Tamar taken a position in Sub-ealdorman Ordgar's Hall. My children were with me. As soon as I saw her, I knew: she was with child and all was not well.

"Sweet girl, she came to me so quietly, not wanting to appear worried, not wanting to alarm Wulfstan. The last part of the journey had been too much for her. She said that she had suspected her condition a month earlier but felt well and strong. She had only begun to have pains this last few days, she said, such pains that she felt as though her back might break, but she had not spoken of them whilst crossing the Moors, for what could anyone have done?

"I felt her belly and laid a hazel twig on it, a sure way to tell if the baby is alive. Then I realised that she was carrying twins. And something more beside – she would not have an easy time. I told her she must rest, gave her preparations that I knew would help and stayed with her that night – while her husband performed in the Great Hall. Oh, he was a success as ever, and no-one would have dreamed that his heart was both bursting with happiness at the news of his coming fatherhood and shivering with fear that his wife's pains might mean that it would be over before it had begun.

"But she began to grow a little stronger. The pains still assailed her, in particular when she stood up, but they were growing less. She said that she wanted to return home in time for their birth... under normal circumstances there would have been plenty of time for the journey, but now? And how could they afford to travel by cart, or litter? Only by Wulfstan's working so hard that he hardly saw her. Aetna didn't want to send word home for money – she didn't want to worry anyone! She stayed at Ordgar's Hall, with that spoiled little cat Elfrith for company, while Wulf travelled around Dumnonia and Kernow, making enough to buy a wagon for them. At the time, I wondered why Ordgar did not simply give them the money, or loan them transport, but I later heard – my Petroc, even then, spent all his time in the long stable, and he had it from the ostlers – that Elfrith told her father that if he offered them horses so they could leave early she would lock herself in her chamber until Yule. She had taken a fancy to the story-teller and would not have mourned the loss of his wife. She whispered venom when she was alone with Aetna, suggesting that he had eyes for other women – that was why he spent so much time on the road. Of course, Aetna didn't believe it, but she was in no condition to fight back – even if she had it in her heart to do so.

"It took Wulf until mid-August to save enough, and then he bought them a covered wagon, two driving horses and a pack horse. When they were ready to leave, Aetna told me how scared she was of the childbed and begged me to come with them. She said there would be a place for all of us at Radendunam. I had never been further east than Glestingaberg, but she said that there was nothing to fear these days from the Vikings... that the Danelaw, the North and South folk of the Angles and the East Saxons were all as one now. In truth, I was tired of the West Country and was happy to go. There was room for my younger children in the wagon with Aetna, Petroc rode one of the driving horses and Wulf found me a nag of my own.

"We were a happy band when we set out. Aetna was getting huge – the twins were making themselves known – and was uncomfortable, but she never complained once, and the children loved her to distraction. I was almost jealous! She had a hundred little games to play with them as we jolted along, and Petroc whispered in the horses' ears to give her as smooth a carriage as they could. Had we known it, we must have almost passed Ethelwold and Ethelwine on the road, for it was only a matter of days after we left that they came to Ordgar's Hall – and we now know what events that visit set in train!

"Still, it was a hard journey and the weather was not kind to us. Summer ended early and there was heavy rain, turning the rutted track into a mire of mud and water. When we could, we followed the old Roman roads, but they are getting almost as bad as the greenways. We stopped at inns along the way – never longer than a night at a time, and Wulf would tell some tale to our fellow travellers. At Bedeford one of the cartwheels shattered and the wagon almost turned over, coming down with a terrible jarring crash. Aetna was as pale as a wight afterwards and that night she began to bleed. I was worried, gave her packs of herbs to try and stop the flow, and tinctures to drink, but it only held off the inevitable, by the time we reached Grantebrige, I could sense that I had a struggle ahead of me to save the babies – and her.

"Toward the end of September, we reached Bedricsworth – so close to home – and she could not travel any further. We took rooms at the sign of the Bull, where they had stayed on the night of their marriage and sent word to Radendunam. You know most of the rest..."

Dagmaer stopped speaking, put her face in her hands and sighed.

"It was Petroc who arrived here at dawn on Michael-mass Eve," said Aelflaed. "He had ridden all night, delivered his message and begged a fresh horse so that he could turn and ride straight back again, and Brithnoth rode with him."

"And he sent word to me as soon as he reached Bedricsworth," added Elflada.

Now they could all share the memories. But it was Dagmaer who completed the tale, speaking as if in a dream. "I tried all I could, but the babies were... too big. They wouldn't come as they should. She struggled for two days. Oh, I wished I had had my grandmother there! I tried to... but I had never seen... In the end, I had to cut her. Cut her and..." she stopped herself as if she had said too much. "I swear she didn't feel it. I had given her poppy draughts and more, and when she woke – I never really thought she would wake – she was able to hold the babes and even suckle them once. It was like a miracle, for a few brief hours I was vain enough to think I had saved them all. But then she began to fade.

"The monks from Saint Edmund's Shrine prayed for her and the priest who married her to Wulf came and gave her shrive. Brithnoth would not leave her side."

"And nor did I, once I arrived," said Elflada. "But she slipped away. Said she wanted to be alone to pray, in the chapel. When we went to her in the morning she was gone, but she lay with a smile on her sweet face."

"Thank the powers that I had only stopped feeding my youngest a month or so before – there are ways to start the breasts' flow again, and it was a comfort to be able to give those little ones suck. I swear I had loved her as if she were my own daughter," said Dagmaer.

"If how much a soul is loved in middle-carth counts when it reaches the higher realm," said Aethelflaed, "then Aetna is fortunate indeed. For she was very much loved. Which is why, of course, Wulfstan was never able to forgive himself – he felt to blame for her loss."

"He would not be comforted!"

"Never mind that she was as keen to take that trip as he."

Suddenly they seemed to remember that the story was, to begin with, being told to me. As if I might – or might not – have understood all that went before, Aelflaed now bent down, took my hands in hers and looked me straight in the face, her grey eyes solemn. "Your father was – is – a good man. After we lost your mother, he took a pilgrim's garb and an oath to travel to every shrine in Europe where sibling saints are honoured. He did that to thank God for you and your brother. And only once has he been home in these five years. That was two years ago, when he stayed with us but one night, and went in to see you and Wulf as you slept. Your brother stirred, and that must have been when he saw his father. You slept on!"

"So, I could never have heard my mother's voice?"

"Who can say that, child? She must have spoken to you as a babe, and it is well known that there are times when the fabric between this world and the next is stretched very thin. You have heard what you have heard." Dagmaer spoke softly but with confidence.

That was how I came to know, and have since come to understand better, how my brother and I came into this world. That night, when we cuddled up together beneath the big bearskin, I told him what I could remember of all that I had heard – especially about our father, for I knew that he would want to hear that above all things. But the following day, our birthday, we awoke carefree and careless as ever, and dwelt little upon the past, not knowing then how what has been always affects what is to come.

FIVE

Late summer, Anno Domini 962.

WULFMAER

Looking back on my childhood, certain scenes appear to me now to be stitched into the fabric of my life in higher relief than others. They are like my sister's embroidery: some remind me of fabulous, bold, bright designs, rich with precious gold, caught down lightly by strands of self-shaded silk. Others are a maelstrom of colours, a jigsaw of split, shattered stitches, swirling together to form: what? Those golden few days around our fifth birthday were certainly like the former. The following year, the first in a series of events seem to be emphasised as if outlined in blood red thread, the intertwining design set about with fractured motifs and reaching far into an unknown future.

Word had come to our Uncle Brithnoth that the Witan was to convene at Uphude, hosted by the Ealdorman of East Anglia – our Uncle Ethelwold – and that all members were to attend. There was also a pressing land dispute at Elig which required the King's attention, necessitating a Great Moot and convening of the Shire Court. As the two locations were relatively close, the Royal Progress to the Witan could divert to take in the latter. King Edgar had declared his wish to make a visit to his stepmother, Aethelflaed, along the way and also to worship at the fast-growing shrine to Saint Edmund at Bedricsworth. The King would leave Wintancaestre in mid-August, visit Londinium – where he wanted to check progress on a church being built close to Thornig Island – and then take the old Roman road up to Celmereford from where he, and the Progress, would make for Radendunam and the hospitality of our aunt and uncle's Hall. Brithnoth would join the party for the onward journey to Elig and Uphude, the Progress taking the old greenways across the Brecks, finally crossing the treacherous Fens to reach the Isle of Elig on which perched the ruined monastery dedicated to Saint Etheldreda. It was to be a family affair: Aelflaed, Leoflada, Aetna and I would accompany him.

Thought of travelling through the Brecks and the Fens put Aetna in me in an ecstasy of anticipation. We heard stories of the strange, wild, dry expanses of the Brecks where dust wights spiralled and skittered along the roadside. Tales of the watery bog-fested Fens were even more strange. There were whispers of the terrifying Will-o'-the-Wisp: his incandescent, shifting lights dancing in the dark to tempt unwary travellers off the few safe paths across the water. We could hardly imagine a more appealing trip. Through the last few weeks of high summer our games were all about following such shape shifters back to their lairs and relieving them of whatever ill-gotten fortunes they might have amassed from passing adventurers less well-prepared than we planned to be.

I know now that it had not been an easy year. Following a bitter winter, the spring had been late and wet and the crops had fared badly. There had been a poor harvest which, in one way, was almost a blessing as there would have been far too few field workers to bring in a full one. Following on the heels of the blighted spring, a vicious pestilence had killed many in the countryside and a rumour had spread that it had come from hogs lately imported from the country of the Franks. There was no way to know if this was true, but we were fortunate that our uncle had brought in none of this new stock, so our stead had escaped the worst of the plague and only fared ill because of the general lack of prosperity, meaning that the usual buying and selling of commodities for the winter was slow and wanting. Of course, we children knew and cared little of this, only mourning the fact that there was less to eat on our trenchers and if we wasted food, we were given a dressing-down from Dagmaer and, much worse, a lecture from Father Aelmer. Not that Aetna and I often overlooked anything on our, or anyone else's, trenchers. Any leftovers went straight into the mouths of our two new and best playmates. Before Archbishop Dunstan had left Uncle's Hall the previous year, we understood why he had asked what had been our favourite part of the celebratory performances. Perhaps, if we had said the jugglers, he would have given us a set of sand balls or hoops, but our quick reply that we liked the dogs best had prompted him to give us what Leoflada had said was more trouble than an elf-shot flitch. Flada had quite a turn of words when she wanted.

On the day after our expedition to the troll bridge, the morning of our fifth birthday, Dunstan had sought us out before his departure. We had, as so often during those few days, managed to escape Leoflada's delegated chores, and had made our way outside the palisade to play. This time we had not got far and we were taking turns rolling down the side of the great ditch. Aetna had not managed to get out of my way quite quickly enough and was trying to catch the breath which had been knocked out of her (and I was gasping, too) when we heard Dunstan's voice calling from the top of the rampart. Looking up, we could see him silhouetted against the blue sky the golden morning sun behind him. It was hard to see clearly, but he appeared to be struggling to hold onto something.

"Come on, you two! There are some introductions to be made!"

We looked at each other, hesitant, thinking that more visitors might mean that we would have to be back on our best behaviour.

We scrambled up the bank, blinking in the bright sunlight. From beneath his cloak Dunstan revealed the wriggling burdens he had been trying so hard to conceal: two small black puppies, curly coated, all squirming legs, wagging tails and wet tongues. We were speechless.

"One apiece," said Dunstan. "Both boys, I'm afraid no little bitches in the litter, but something tells me that's not going to be a problem..." He was already talking to himself, as our whole attention was given over to the puppies. Uncharacteristically, I remembered my manners first.

"Thank you, my Lord!"

"Oh, yes! Yes, thank you!" Aetna spluttered, the puppies licking her face. "What are their names?"

"Well, that's for you decide." Dunstan was clearly delighted at our pleasure. "They are your dogs, now. You must promise to look after them, though. I've spoken to Dagmaer and she knows all about them. Petroc brought them up from the inn early this morning – the old dog handler's been staying there and his bitch had pups ready for new homes. Their wyrd is in your hands. You must be sure to make it a good one." Looking back, I realise was a remarkable man Dunstan was. He was equally at home speaking to children or the High Witan, and could make both at their ease.

"Oh, we will, we will!" As so often, Aetna and I spoke in unison – as well as we were able for the puppies' attentions.

And so Bremel and Berrie came into our lives. It had not taken long for their names to be found. On the evening of their arrival, we proudly showed them to Guthric and he said their noses looked like the juicy, black berries that grew in the bramble bushes along the wayside. Bremelberries we had always called them. I had picked up the puppy which had seemed to have taken a special liking to me – he only differed from his brother by being slightly the larger of the two – and whispered in his ear "Bremel?" which resulted in another frenzied attack of licking.

"He knows his name already!" I announced.

The smaller puppy had been curled up on my sister's lap – both had eaten well and were ready to sleep in that instant, dead-to-the-world way that puppies have. Aetna made a kissing noise and called softly "Berrie?" A sigh of contentment and snuggling down of his nose seemed to indicate pup's approval and the die was cast. And according to Leoflada, from then onward, they made it their mission to trip her up, muddy her gunna and generally get in her way, "Even more than those demon-blessed twins!"

There was no question, however, that the following year Bremel and Berrie would come with us on our travels. They had quickly become part of the Hall's extended family of animals. Our uncle had two favourite hounds which accompanied him everywhere – one youngster, a bitch called Hunticge (Hunti for short), the other an older, retired dog, which he fondly called Waldi. Waldi only occasionally, now, took part in the chase and was more often to be found with his head on his master's knee in the peace of the evening. Our aunt Aelflaed had a little lapdog, Honig, white and golden like Biblical milk and honey (our aunt had said), bright-eyed and delicate, which pattered along after her as she went about her duties, and now Bremel and Berrie were added to the troop and treated with equal distain by Musbane, who, being the only indoor cat, enjoyed special privileges. It was a brave dog who thought to chase him... there were plenty of barn cats for those games! Nevertheless, the departure of the five dogs together with much of the household probably met with Musbane's approval, as peace descended in our wake. Aetna and I imagined him settling himself on our palliasse – or, possibly, on Leoflada's, as she was not there to evict him – with a contented sigh, Gilly's cream on his whiskers, and with a promise of kitchen scraps from Thoth to come.

The King's party had arrived two days previously, in the evening. Archbishop Dunstan was with them, as were a number of ealdorman and bishops, men who served on the Witan and advised the young King on various aspects of land and civil law, defence, tax and the general administration of the country. Up until this point, the King's Progress had been a business-like affair, but now it took on something of a holy-day aspect for Edgar had known Brithnoth and the family since boyhood and the planned stopover at our aunt Aethelflaed's Hall was one that we knew was anticipated with pleasure.

In the days since Edgar's arrival Aetna and I had reconsidered our concept of kingship. Until he arrived, our idea of a monarch – and Edgar was styled King of all Bryttania, and Chieftain of all Albion – was in the manner of Dagmaer's sagas: a king must be physically strong, visually imposing and wholly intimidating – but Edgar seemed to be none of these things. He was slight, at nineteen years old, a little over the height of Otter, Dagmaer's second son, just past his own thirteenth birth-fest. Edgar was softly-spoken but with a keen good humour. Light brown hair, swept back from his forehead, fell forward at his jawline softening still further the contours of his face; his chin, firm but not large, hazel eyes and something of the dimple in one cheek when he smiled, which he did often, combined to create an attractive whole. He was mindful of the well-being of his servants and, as we discovered later, not dismissive of children and their needs.

It was the last Thor's day before the feast of Saint Bartholomew (though Father Aelmer hated to hear the days of the week designated in what he called the pagan manner) and on the next we were to join the onward journey with the rest of the King's party. Shortly after breaking fast, the menfolk took their horses and hounds – Brithnoth's old dog, Waldi, joined the melee along with his younger companion – and cantered downstream along the lane towards the troll bridge where the previous year Aetna and I had found Dunstan's carefully concealed treasure. I had looked so wistfully after the mounted riders that my uncle had turned his horse back and swung me up to sit behind him.

"Hold me fast around the middle, young cub, or you will be bounced clean off and I will be riding too hard to miss you!" I grinned and locked my hands into my uncle's belt. Although I was able to ride alone (my riding master always chose me docile mounts) I had never joined a hunt and this was an unexpected double thrill: to be part of the party and ride on Fireflax, Uncle's magnificent red horse.

"You will not lose me, Uncle," I said. "I will hold tight."

Aetna watched me ride away with, I know, a twinge of misgiving, an echo of some small nervousness on my part. We had come to take such shared feelings for granted. I also felt a small pang of her jealousy as she was left behind working her embroidery. We were reaching the age when our respective pleasures and duties began to diverge. Aetna had been put in charge of little Thella – a responsibility not without its challenges.

The young King enjoyed the hunt, as did most men. Meat reared by village cottars, pork, beef and poultry were staples of the High Table, but game was the epitome of fine dining. Wild boar was considered vastly superior to domestic pig. During the autumn months, game would be hung, and perhaps smoked, for use over Yule. The Court's Progress would descend upon our aunt Aethelflaed's Hall in need of bed and board: the gift of a fine hind or hart, or perhaps a hog, would be small but welcome recompense for her hospitality.

The party rode west, and then turned north into dense woodland which stretched almost unbroken toward the ancient town of Celmereford, once a Roman citadel, now a small bustling market town set about by crumbling ruins, the relics of a time long forgotten and now mysterious. There were still some remnants of the Romans' buildings in the woodland, here a tumbledown temple, there a shattered statue, and it was by one of these, a female half torso, now so overgrown with ivy and creeper that it could hardly be recognised, that the party first halted waiting for the hounds to scent a quarry.

Old Waldi stayed close to Brithnoth's side, and allowed the younger hounds their head when a scent was finally caught and the chase was on. He loped after them in a nonchalant manner, seeming undaunted by the stampede of hooves pounding past him as the hunters piled in behind the baying pack. He was an old hand at this game. I clutched my uncle's belt and held tight, as I had promised, and was rewarded by being with the first of the men to reach the prey, held at bay by the hounds. Edgar had reached them first (though whether as the best rider, or because he was allowed to do so by his retainers, I wondered). Close behind him was Dunstan and then my uncle. Other Ealdormen came up behind us. Run to earth was a fine boar, not the largest of his kin – probably from one of the year's early litters – but agile, thick set and in the fullness of his youth and vigour. He had run a good race and now stood snorting down his long snout, the sunlight glinting golden brown on his bristly hide.

"Hold," called Edgar. "He's mine. A gift for my stepmother!" Edgar hefted his throwing axe in his right hand, finding its balance and judging the distance between himself and the boar.

Dunstan spoke low, so that only Edgar and my uncle could hear his comment. "Take care, Sire, this fellow's lively, throw askew and he'll charge us all." I was thrilled to be so close to the action, though my blood ran cold as the beady eyes of the young hog shifted from Edgar to Dunstan and back again. Brithnoth held his horse's reins with one hand and reached behind to give me a reassuring hug.

"I'll take him cleanly," breathed the King, drawing back his throwing arm and then whipping it forward. The axe few through the air, shaft over blade, once, twice and then buried itself in the boar's skull. The pig's front legs buckled beneath him. He was dead before his snout hit the leaf mould on which he had stood.

Behind the other mounted members of the hunt, the butchering party were catching up. This comprised several young men from the village, together with Guthric and Otter, and a lad called Olferth, Thoth's nephew, an apprentice from the kitchens with a good knowledge of how to gut and transport the kill. As Olferth approached from behind, one of the huntsmen's horses shied and its rider, losing his balance, allowed the tip of his spear to catch the lad a glancing blow to the right elbow, jagging up his arm to the shoulder, ripping through the fabric of his tunic and making a deep gash in his arm. Olferth clapped his left hand to the cut, bright red blood oozing through his fingers.

"Majesty," Olferth stuttered, more terrified that his misfortune had interrupted the King's moment of kill than of his own injury, and shock momentarily numbing the pain.

Edgar, though, was already off his horse, the boar forgotten in his concern for the injured boy. "Don't move, lad, you will lose too much blood. Dunstan, use your skills to help him."

Dunstan threw his leg over his horse's saddle and dismounted. Loosening a leading rein – a narrow strip of leather – he tied it around Olferth's upper arm, above the upper edge of the gash and tightened it, twisting a short stick into the knot to form a tourniquet. Immediately, the blood oozing between Olferth's fingers lessened, as the lad, white as a chalked fleece, sank towards the ground. Edgar turned to Guthric.

"Give me a knife, boy."

Guthric handed over his small side dagger, and Edgar made a nick in the fabric at the hem of his own tunic, tearing off a strip of linen.

"Bind the rest of the wound with that, Dunstan. It will hold until he gets home. And you, Cerdic," this to the unfortunate rider whose spear had caused the injury, "get off that horse. You clearly can't control it. The walk back to the Hall will do you good. Since we began this Progress your stomach has swelled as if you were with child. Our young butcher here has more need of a ride than you."

Olferth began to regain his wits, only to be struck dumb by the identity of his nurses. Wide-eyed, he looked from King to Archbishop. "My lords…"

"You'll live," said Edgar, and pushed his hair back from his face with a boy-like gesture. At that moment, he seemed little older than his patient. Then his attention returned to the boar, lifeless a few feet away. "Get that hog gutted and tied," he called to the other members of the butchering party. "And be sure to get all the bowels out – it will be a day and a half before my stepmother's kitchen thralls attend to it and I don't want to be riding with a stinking carcass in the train tomorrow!"

At that moment he spotted me, white-faced at the sight of Olferth's blood and still sitting behind my uncle, who had wisely not interfered in either the boy's treatment or the unfortunate Cerdic's chastisement. When both a king and an archbishop are taking action, it is a tactful ealdorman who stands back.

"Come, lad, it was just an accident, no real damage done. But let it be a lesson to you… a carelessly handled weapon can cause harm even at the most auspicious moments. It was Cerdic's carelessness that might have spoilt our day. Oh, but come, Cerdic, you will still be welcome at supper tonight – that stomach of yours will not go wanting! All's well!"

From that moment, I was the King's man. Here was a king full of humour, of compassion, quick to anger, but also quick to forgive. I desperately wanted to share all that had happened with Aetna, and was happy to take hold once again of my uncle's belt and be carried back towards the Hall. Waldi had appeared as if from nowhere, and trotted to our side.

The boar was gutted, efficiently, though perhaps without the finesse Olferth might have achieved, and its trotters tied together. Guthric and Otter cut a long, sturdy sapling, stripped it of branches and threaded the slender trunk through the animal's legs. They hefted it onto their shoulders and it swung between them, a little blood dripping onto the leaf mould. The guts were thrown to the pack, who noisily squabbled over the best bits.

"Sit tight, nephew," said Brithnoth as he swung out of the saddle. He snatched up what looked like the liver and threw it to Waldi, who wolfed it down, and then licked his jowls with what appeared to be a doggy grin.

"The old boy has been with me so long that he deserves his share, even if he hasn't had to work for it."

Edgar clapped him on the back. "What a sentimental pair we are, Ealdorman! I swear if the Vikings were to hack up this greenway now, we would be more worried for our dogs and our thralls than our gold and our silver!"

"Let us hope that we shall never be put to the test, then."

"Amen to that!" agreed Dunstan as he joined them, having seen Olferth onto Cerdic's horse, much to that chubby courtier's ill-disguised but silent disgust. "If we head back apace, we shall be in time to hear Father Aelmer ring the bell for evening service. And, I fear, his sermon."

)))))(((((

When we arrived back at the Hall, there was a flurry of consternation. The hounds and their whipper arrived first – which was unusual, as normally the mounted horsemen would have galloped ahead of the others to announce their success and accept the admiration of the ladies, before the arrival of the kill and the lesser members of the hunt. The riders approached at a sedate pace, and even from a distance it must have been obvious that there was a casualty among our ranks. In the general hubbub, the whipper's assurance that nobody of importance had been injured went unheard, and Aunt Aelflaed, Dagmaer and several of the serving women together with a couple of grooms ran out of the great gates to meet us.

Aetna had been sitting outside the Hall, working on her embroidery, on the same bench where, the previous year, she had heard the story of our mother's death. She was, she told me later, vainly trying to keep Thella from interfering in the work and business of everybody who passed them by.

I was tired and longing for the companionship of my sister, to tell her of the day's events and was relieved to see her in the usual sunny spot. She put her needlework to one side, and grabbed Thella, who was in danger of running under the horses' hooves in her excitement at her brothers' return, but Guthric and Otter were at the back of the party. Thella struggled to get free, and then saw me as I was lifted down from my uncle's horse by one of the thegns. Brithnoth absently ruffled my hair and handed the reins to his retainer, his mind on other things than his nephew.

As I walked toward them, Thella stopped pulling away from my sister, and stood stock still and rigid, staring at me. Her eyes were glazed, as though she was looking through me into a far distant place.

"*Ill fortune follows, when a wolf follows a boar!*" Thella's voice was a rasping whisper and not her usual high, childish babble. I felt sure that was what she said – though, truthfully, it was hard to be sure. "*Once, twice, then thrice, and the third the worst of all!*"

Aetna took her by the shoulders and spun her around. "What, what's that?" She thought she had heard my name and anything that concerned me concerned her, too. But Thella's eyes suddenly cleared and she looked from one to the other of us with her usual dazzling smile. "Where's my mammy? I'm hungry."

"With the others. Never mind that. What did you say, what about my brother and the hunt, the boar?"

"I don't know what you mean. Let me go!" Thella shook herself free of Aetna's grip and ran toward the door of the Hall, where Dagmaer could be seen disappearing, obviously taking charge of young Olferth.

Suddenly, the courtyard seemed very quiet. The hubbub of a few minutes earlier had subsided, the hounds were gone to their kennels and the horses were being rubbed down in their stalls, the grooms' voices low and subdued. I saw movement out of the corner of my eye and looked toward the chapel, its door just closing. I fancied that I caught a glimpse of Father Aelmer's dusty cassock being twitched inside before it was caught in the jamb. The sun went behind a cloud and a chill breeze swept dust in our eyes.

I shivered. "Well, if it comes to that, I'm hungry, too," I said. "Come on!"

"But..." Aetna still hesitated.

Taking her hand, I tugged her toward the kitchens. I had been tasked with the job of telling Thoth of his nephew's misfortune, which was a welcome excuse to fill my belly, since I had not attended to it since I broke my fast that morning – a lifetime ago! But Thoth had already heard the news and gone to make sure that it was no it worse than he had been told. The kitchen was a haven of calm before preparations began in earnest for the evening meal. A couple of thralls were sitting with their feet up on the irons by the side of the fire, one snoring gently, the other looking dreamily at the glowing logs, a tankard in one hand and a hunk of pork in the other. A dog lay at his feet, one eye on the meat, the other on the door. Should Thoth return, his footsteps would be enough to bring the dog – and so the resting thralls – to attention.

With a mouthful and of bread and cheese I recounted my adventures to Aetna: first the thrill of the chase, riding high on my uncle's saddle, then the kill and the King's skill with the throwing axe and finally the accident, Olferth's bloody predicament and the King and Dunstan's swift rescue. Aetna seemed underwhelmed by the details of the hunt, only really attentive to the story of the mishap with Cerdic's spear. When I finally stopped talking, she looked at me oddly.

"What do you think Thella meant? '*Ill fortune follows when Wulf follows the boar*'? She looked so strange."

"Hummph!" I was unimpressed. "She was just being cheeky. And anyway, she said '*a wolf*' not '*Wulf*'. You look very pale, did the sight of all those bloody bandages upset you? Have some food…"

"No, listen, Wulf, I mean it. There was something wrong with Thella, she wasn't herself. Her eyes were all…"

"Good thing, too, if she wasn't herself, the little piglet! Only last night I saw her taking the best of the bremelberries from under Thoth's nose and all he did was pat her on the backside, sit her on a trestle and wipe the juice off her hands for her! If it had been Guthric or Otter they would have had to make a run for it. It's like she casts a spell on people!"

Aetna gave up. "Oh, well, at least you have had an exciting day, I suppose," she said, rather petulantly. "More than me, I just sat with my needlework. Though Dagmaer and Aunt Aelflaed say that on my next piece I may use some real gold thread. That'll be the most excitement I get for a while, I dare say…"

"But you are looking forward to tomorrow, though?" I said, anxious that this petty jealousy should not spoil our anticipation of the trip. "Both of us together in the King's party, visiting Aunt Aethelflaed, and then the fens and everything?"

"Yes, of course, but just don't go off without me again for a while. It's not fair, just because I am a girl. I don't want to get left alone all the time and miss the adventures. I wish we could still swap our clothes sometimes."

"Well I don't!" I said with some feeling, and then realised that I had said the wrong thing as Aetna's lower lip began to tremble and her eyes moisten. Hurriedly, I tried to put things right. "But I know what you mean. Don't worry, we will do everything together, and none of the other children are coming so you won't get lumbered with *girl-childe* Thella again. It will be just you and me against the barrow-wights and the dust-demons and Willy Wisp, just as we planned. Unless, of course, the King commands me to…"

But what I thought the King might require of me was never voiced, as Aetna picked up a handful of sloppy curds and threw them at me. "Unless, of course, the King…" she mimicked, in a sing-song voice.

The curds had landed (most satisfactorily, to my sister's mind) with a splat right in my face, and now ran down my chin and onto my tunic. Mingled exhilaration at the success of her aim and the mess she had made, together with horror at her own audacity, crossed her face as I froze for a moment. Then I realised that we would both be in the hound-run if we were caught by Thoth treating his kitchen as our playground. The thought occurred to my sister at the same moment and we made a dash for the door, followed by the indignant cries of the kitchen thralls, left to clean up the mess, and the barking of the dog, who clearly thought that there was a game afoot.

We ran out into the courtyard and to the well. "Alright, we're even," I panted, sloshing water from the bucket over my head and scrubbing down my tunic as best I could. "And I can last out until supper now." Grinning, I dared to touch upon our earlier exchange. In a sing-song voice I said, "While I was with the King, my Lady, I expect you dined with the rest of the nobility at the High Table this noon." I took her hand and made a stiff bow.

"Indeed, I did, my Lord brother," Aetna essayed a little curtsey in reply, her voice also a strained falsetto.

My head was still full of the events of the hunt, and I confess that I paid little attention as Aetna prattled on about the ladies' noon-meal and the conversation which, it seemed to me, was wholly inconsequential: what they were to wear for the journey, and what for the banquets to come. Only when she mentioned the entertainments we were likely to enjoy at Uphude, was my interest engaged.

"Aunt Aelflaed said it was not likely that a dog act had been engaged, though," she said.

"Oh?"

"She said that a certain she-cat would not want her tail chased by such as they, only by greater hounds."

To my knowledge there had never been a house cat at Uphude. It seemed a strange remark.

It had been a long day and as the sun set, we were both ready to retire to our chamber. For once, Dagmaer did not have to chivvy us to bed after supper. As we snuggled down, Bremel and Berrie between us, it was with the promise of adventure to come, and we slept deep and sound, dreamless, until the early morning call of the cockerel and the bustle of the courtyard roused us.

SIX

Frig's day dawned bright and sunny. In common with the best planned departures, we were not on the road until a little later than had been anticipated. There were the usual delays as last-minute additions were made to the baggage train, things were misplaced and then found again, and a horse stood on its groom's foot and so a replacement thrall had to be found. To cap it all, Father Aelmer's sermon at morning service dragged on, or so it seemed, even longer than usual.

Finally, we were on our way, the sun only an hour or so into its own journey across the sky. Edgar's train, which was already seasoned to the trip, settled back into their usual routine easily enough, but it took a while for our little party to find our sea-legs. Brithnoth, as might be expected, rode ahead of us with the King and Archbishop Dunstan, the other ealdormen and members of the Witan a little behind, riding with friends and acquaintances, discussing politics or simply gossiping. Aunt Aelflaed had a litter in which to journey. The previous year she had so greatly admired Elfrith's litter that Brithnoth, keeping her ignorant of his plans, had commissioned it to be made in time for her natal-day the following June. Since then she had used it on short trips, but this was the first time it had been put to the test of a long expedition.

We could ride in it if we grew tired, but mostly, together with the dogs, we ran ahead of our immediate party – for progress was made at little more than a fast walking pace – rested until they caught up, and then rode for a mile or so, taking turns to clamber onto the tail boards of baggage carts and generally giving the adults a few small frights as we avoided horses' hooves and wagon wheels. Leoflada had appointed herself mistress of the wardrobe for the duration of the trip and was perched high beside one of the house carls designated to drive the cart containing the ladies' boxes of gunnas, shifts, rails and circlets. She insisted that it headed the baggage train. Our freemen, house carls and thralls kept pace behind it, watching that no baggage was jolted loose as, together with the other wagons, it bumped over stones and pot holes. Between the litter and the wardrobe wagon rode Dagmaer, close enough to hear if Aelflaed or Leoflada should call her – and to keep an eye on us. We never quite knew where she had acquired her riding skills (another of the small mysteries that she liked to keep) but she sat a horse well. A little post noon the whole train halted for some refreshment and when we set off again Dunstan fell back in the line and pulled his horse in beside Dagmaer's palfrey. The Archbishop was dressed as befitted his station, in a dark, sombre but rich tunic, gold embroidery at its neck and cuffs, with gartered leggings above black leather riding boots. A large, gold, bejewelled cross glinted on his chest. As he reined in beside her, Dagmaer raised an eyebrow.

"How now, my Lord. Come to ride with the hired hands?"

"His Majesty has gone ahead with some of the young thegns to give the horses a gallop before we halt for the night. It will give the Shire Reeve of Colencaestre palpitations when he arrives unannounced before the rest of us... I'll wager he has his scouts out watching for the party, tasked with reporting back so that he is ready with his civil welcome. He'll not recognise half a score of young bloods cantering through his gates, as if pursued by the hounds of Hel. There will be consternation and confusion afoot by the time we arrive!" Dunstan smiled his amusement.

Aelflaed pulled back the curtain of the litter. "Edgar is like his father in that respect," she said. "He likes to do the unexpected and see what effect it has on others. The late King always said that it was a good way to judge a man's character." She allowed the curtain to fall back and gave a little sigh of contentment as she settled comfortably into the cushioned interior. "Enjoy the rest of the ride: I am going to take a nap before we reach Colencaestre. I want to enjoy this evening's festivities." The litter-thralls grinned at each other. Aelflaed was not a heavy passenger and always rewarded them well after a journey. More than that, they loved and respected their Lady: they took pride in making her passage as smooth as possible. "Dagmaer, I shall have no need of you until we arrive. Ride where you wish."

Dagmaer and Dunstan pulled to one side of the road and allowed the litter and Leoflada's wagon to get a little ahead of them. Then they fell back into pace of the rest of the train. Between the wardrobe wagon and their horses, a baggage cart carrying extra food in case of delays or mishaps, rumbled along at an even pace, pulled by a single, broad-shouldered, amiable ox. Aetna and I were inside it, with Bremel and Berrie, all four of us tired after our long, scampering adventures. We lay in a companionable heap, my sister munching an apple and I, a pear, its juice dripping down my chin. The dogs were sharing a dried pig's ear between them. Above us a lightweight tarred linen protected the food and hid us from view. We could hear the adults' voices, but paid little attention until a name made us prick up our ears.

"Thella? Yes, she's my seventh child, after Guthric and before Brandon."

Dunstan's rich voice in reply, "She looks like you... I remember a fey little girl who turned into a beauty on the Glestingaberg levels. Who is her father?"

Dagmaer sounded suitably shocked. "Why, my husband, of course!" Dunstan let this pass and Dagmaer continued. "I never had quite the skills she is already mastering… she can charm the milk into cream and boys into milksops already."

"You had your moments! But, Dagmaer, be careful how you phrase your thoughts. I had that fool Aelmer talking some nonsense to me last night about Thella pretending to have visions and being able to see the future. He even suggested that she should be sent to a nunnery at the first opportunity to…"

"Over my dead body!" Dagmaer was indignant. "That man is an affront to your church, Dunstan. Why, even the White Christ would not have wanted such a sour old… to think of my Thella mired in with those dried up…"

"Peace, peace, Dagmaer, and keep your voice down. Thella will be what she will be, just as I hear that Petroc has some skills which are out of the ordinary – though an affinity with horses seems to be a more acceptable use of the Lord's stranger gifts than an ability to foretell events. Just keep her out of Aelmer's way. Does he know that she is your seventh babe?"

"I doubt it. I lost two close to birth and another in an accident three years ago. I wouldn't think he has been keeping score. He didn't even know me ten years ago. And he certainly doesn't know that I am my mother's seventh!"

"Good, keep it that way." Dunstan sounded in earnest. "I do not like Father Aelmer's ways, though I cannot fault him as a churchman, only as a man." For a moment or so they rode on in silence. "I have had enough of snide tale telling to last a lifetime. I shall tell him to attend to his church services and leave the bringing up of children to those who know what they are talking about."

Dagmaer's rich, throaty laugh rang out. "And that sounds like an angry young man I once knew at the foot of Glestingaberg Tor."

They fell to talking of other things and our attention waned.

"I told you that there was something odd about Thella yesterday," Aetna whispered. "You wouldn't listen then, but maybe now you will," she hissed and seemed about to try and draw me into her anxieties once again when we heard a sudden cry from the front of the train.

"Colencaestre's ahead!"

Evening was approaching. We had been travelling up the old Roman road which began at Londinium and went through Celmereford and on to Colencaestre. A mile or so back it had merged with Stane Street, leading from the west country. The road entered Colencaestre through the remnants of the old East Gate, which retained its place in the dilapidated Roman walls. Over the centuries, the walls had been alternately pulled down, in times of peace, to provide building materials, and shored up at times of war. They now presented a patchwork aspect of stone, lumps of

Roman concrete and wooden superstructure. Dagmaer had told us that in the time of the great King Alfred, people had been afraid to live among the Roman ruins for fear of the spirits of the Romans, but now, in Colencaestre and other cities such as Londinium and Eoforwic, the ancient buildings as well as the walls were gradually being put back to effective use.

Dunstan spurred his horse forward and rode up to the front of the entourage, where Brithnoth awaited him. As he had anticipated, there was confusion afoot. The train came to a halt and Aetna and I scrambled out of our baggage cart and trotted up to its head, the dogs at our heels. A corpulent figure in a dusky red robe, kirtled to what would have been his waist with a gold belt and sporting a shapeless three-cornered head-piece stood before our uncle and the Archbishop, seemingly at something of a loss. Behind him were several other worthies, together with a dozen or so men-at-arms, shuffling their feet and looking about them uncertainly.

The Shire Reeve, swept the oddly-shaped object from his head and essayed a bow – or as close a facsimile as he could manage, given his girth.

"Ealdorman," he boomed to Brithnoth, "we are honoured, as ever, to welcome you to Colencaestre, and our hearty good wishes and felicitations to the Lord Archbishop – it is he? I thought so! – but we had thought that His Majesty was with your party." He looked down the line of horses and carts, past Aelflaed's litter to the accompanying wagons, clearly disappointed to see no royal contingent.

"Be at ease, good Reeve Cenfrith," interrupted Brithnoth. "You shall have your royal guests, though my wife and the rest of my party will be grateful for your hospitality, too. But I fear that you have turned your back on your King!"

"What? What do you mean?" The Reeve was bewildered. Suddenly from within the town there was a clattering and clashing of hooves on the hard-packed earth and a party of young horsemen could be seen approaching from the other side of the Gate. The Shire Reeve spun on his heel, his paunchy stomach butting into his closest companion, who, at the sudden impact stumbled sideways into the man next to him, knocking him to the ground. The men-at-arms, not knowing which way to turn and half afraid that some sort of illogical ambush was taking place, tried to turn to face the newcomers and raise their spears, only to find that they had no room to do so, hampered by the closeness of the wall and the Gate. Several dropped their shields, one had his helmet knocked off and the rest gave up the unequal battle to appear at all soldierly and turned back and forth, looking first to the Reeve, then to Brithnoth and finally to the man at the head of the newly arrived party, who, it began to dawn upon all concerned, was the King.

Aetna and I were laughing as only six-year-olds can at the discomfort of their elders. The soldiers attempted to marshal their ranks, and the poor Shire Reeve looked as though he wished that the cracks in the ancient walls would swallow him up. Edgar's easy charm saved the day.

"Good Reeve, forgive my untimely arrival! My thegns and horses tired of the slow pace of our Progress, and we rode ahead. It is a long time since I visited Colencaestre. I remembered that there was something of the old Arena still standing and promised my men a race. We came in through the South Gate, rode through the town, around the Arena and now are come to disrupt your carefully planned welcome. Forgive a young man his thoughtlessness."

This seemed to throw the Shire Reeve into still greater flurries of consternation. "Sire, it is I who should apologise. My lookouts should have seen and recognised you at the South Gate…"

"Enough, enough. We are all here now and pleased to be so." Edgar threw a leg over the pommel of his horse's saddle and dismounted, his slight frame in striking contrast to his host. His men followed suit, their horses breathing hard from the ride. "And now, Reeve, we shall proceed at a more sedate pace to your Hall, for there are ladies in the party who wish to be rested and refreshed before what I am sure will be a splendid evening…" Much to Cenfrith's amazement his found himself walking arm in arm with his King at the head of the procession, while everyone else fell in behind them. The train wound its way through the Gate and into the city.

The streets were bustling, despite the lengthening of the shadows. Unlike many of the villages we knew, which were entirely built of wood, with an occasional stone walled church, there were remnants of stone and brick buildings scattered throughout, wooden structures enveloping them and joining one to the next. Goodwives and traders jostled between stalls and small enclosures where pigs and chickens ran, squealed and pecked and were occasionally hauled out into the general melee to be bought, sold or bartered. Despite our informal, pedestrian passage, it was clear that there had been some expectation of a more official entrance: the streets were not wide, but had been swept relatively clear of the accumulated filth that littered their edges. Animal droppings, waste from the market stalls and other rubbish had been rucked and kicked into small piles along the gutters, where stray dogs snuffled and rooted for scraps. Berrie looked askance at them and then looked up at Aetna. She lifted him into her arms as we passed, but Bremel, grown now into the more dominant of the two dogs, snarled when one of the vagrants raised its hackles at him. I slipped a braided lead around his neck and pulled him away, but was privately proud that he brooked no nonsense.

Banners and strips of fabric fluttered from poles wedged into crevices or tied to stalls, and the people fell back on either side of us as we passed, a ragged cheer going up when the crowd realised this unassuming young man was, in fact, their King.

We went straight on at two road crossings and then saw the old Roman castle ahead of us, its stone walls much eroded and fallen, shored up with roughly carved wood so that it presented an odd fusion of classical architecture and our own familiar style of Hall. The Reeve appeared to be explaining to Edgar how only the previous winter a large section of the wall had collapsed and had to be replaced by huge timbers. His previous discomfiture now forgotten, he was anxious to get the planned schedule back on track. This included making sure that the King was aware that he, the Reeve, was carrying out all his duties satisfactorily. The maintenance of the city's important buildings was part of his remit. He was responsible directly to Edgar for these, not to his ealdorman, our Uncle Brithnoth. As they reached the main entrance to the castle, Cenfrith paused and turned to the now congregated party. His confidence appeared to be quite restored.

"Your Majesty, my Lord Archbishop, Ealdorman Brithnoth and worthy guests, you are welcome to my Hall. Your footfall does me honour. This night I have the pleasure of entertaining you in this venerable place where once the Legions did battle against the ancient tribes of this land. It is my good fortune to be Shire Reeve at a time of peace, but I assure you that should the need arise, the Fyrd Commander of this shire would not find Colencaestre wanting." The men-at-arms, now regrouped, looked rather sheepishly at each other after the debacle at the East Gate.

"The guest chambers await you my Lords, my Ladies. Take your ease."

)))))))((((((

By all accounts the Frig's day evening feast went as well as the Shire Reeve could have wished. After the inauspicious beginning to the royal visit, it proved to be an enormous success and Cenfrith's choice of entertainment – a female minstrel accompanied by two musicians on harp and pipe – touched the young King's heart. As we heard later, his eyes were seen to be shining with tears as the *"Widow's Lament"* was sung, perhaps reminding him of his beloved Elfa left behind, and not in the best of health, at Wintancaestre.

Aetna and I did not attend the feast. We were not invited, being too young, and after the exertions and excitement of the day, we were asleep as soon as our heads touched the softly padded beres which had been provided for all members of the party in the guest chamber. We had eaten heartily soon after our arrival and had fully intended to wake up and remonstrate with our elders at our exclusion, but as it turned out we did not stir until the following dawn. By then, the promise of a new day eclipsed the old and we were happy to break our fast in the Great Hall, and listen to the gossip already circulating about the events of the previous evening and the expectations of the coming day.

Dagmaer, with whom we had shared a partitioned section of the guest chamber, was already up and about her duties when we came into the Hall. Having dressed ourselves in the same clothes that we had been wearing the previous day, we were possibly not looking at our best. It was early, and there were, as yet, few people looking for their morning meal, but the kitchen thralls were clearly leaving nothing to chance when entertaining a king, and the trestle was positively groaning under the weight of what remained of the last evening's offering, made over, as usual, as morning fodder. I was in my element. It was hard to choose what delicacy to try first.

There appeared to be only one young ceorl breaking his fast at this early hour, and with his back to us it was hard to see who it was. Judging by his leather jerkin, it could have been a page, or a messenger, stoking his inner fire before setting off on some mission. Aetna and I joined him at the long table, each taking a bread trencher. Aetna chose some fruit and a helping of curds whilst I piled mine high with cold meat, topped with a generous dollop of pickled apple. A jug of milk and some wooden tumblers were on the table just in front of the young man's plate. I leaned across to reach them. Only when he turned toward us did we realise who it was.

"S... Sire!" I was uncharacteristically lost for words.

"Why, it's the young Wulf-cub!" said Edgar. "And unless my eyes deceive me, his sweet sister!"

I bridled somewhat at the idea of Aetna being "sweet" – it was not a term either of us would have thought to use – but, rising to the occasion, and aware that I had already made much to her of my acquaintance with the King, presented her formally.

"Your Majesty, may I present my sister, Wulfaetna." I felt quite pleased with myself at finding the right words at such short notice.

"Bravely done, my man," said Edgar. He took her hand, kissed it solemnly and then winked at her. "Now, you cannot also be called 'Wulf' to your intimates, so I am guessing that you must be 'Aetna'. Am I right?"

My sister dropped a curtsey as she had been taught by our aunt. Dagmaer would have been proud of her. "Yes, Sire."

"So, here we have the two halves of my Lord Brithnoth's apple! No wonder he is a happy man. A sweet wife, a pleasant Hall and two pups to keep him entertained." He stepped back and made a show of looking us up and down. "You are as like as two grains from the same ear of corn. How I wish that my late brother and I had been so alike. There would have been less to make the thegns and Ealdormen take sides between us." He seemed to be musing on the past, lost in his own thoughts for a moment. Then, rather like a puppy himself, he almost physically shook off his reverie and was back in the present. "Come and sit by me and tell me what you think of the journey so far…"

We took our loaded trenchers and sat beside the King. Edgar's informality put us at our ease, and somehow it began to feel quite normal to sit beside him in this companionable way. He was, after all, just a young man, not much older than Oswig, who on his frequent visits to Leoflada, had become our friend over the last year. Aetna was even less in awe than me.

"You made me laugh yester-postnoon, sire, when you took the Reeve by surprise," she said her mouth full of fruit and honey. "The soldiers looked very silly, turning both ways at once and not knowing who was where!"

"I'll tell you a secret," Edgar was growing in our affections every moment: a secret from the King's own lips.

"Oh, yes, Sire!"

"I thought that Archbishop Dunstan was about to reprimand me, the way he once did my brother Eadwig!" the King grinned.

"Oh, but I saw the Archbishop laughing, too," I said. The conspiratorial tone was infectious.

"Indeed? And what might the Archbishop have been laughing about, may I ask?" We all three spun around and for a moment the King was just a lad making fun at the expense of his elders. Dunstan was leaning against the door jamb, his arms crossed, his eyebrows raised.

"Dunstan, you of all people should know that an eavesdropper never hears good of himself!" Edgar spluttered; his small beer had gone down the wrong way, as Dagmaer would have put it. Clearing his throat, he said, "Only that we were all amused by poor Cenfrith's confusion, yesterday! Especially my two breakfast companions, here."

The Archbishop chuckled. "Yes, it was funny, I'll admit."

"But he was quite recovered by the time of his splendid feast last evening, so no harm done," said Edgar.

"And we missed it!" I said rather petulantly, suddenly remembering that we had had every intention of demanding to be allowed to attend.

"So we did!" added Aetna, her memory returning at just the same moment. "What was it like? Did they have jugglers, or tumblers? A storyteller or a skop? Was there…"

"Peace, little lady, there was a fine minstrel and a sad song, which might have brought tears to your pretty eyes, but there were also some fine fiddlers who played merry tunes."

"Yes," added Dunstan, "Old King Coel himself would have been pleased to see his fiddlers playing such a lively jig."

"I've heard of him," I said. "Dagmaer used to sing of him to us when we were little."

"When you were little! And are you too much grown now to enjoy a story about him? He came from this very town."

"Oh, yes," said Aetna, always eager for a new tale. "I mean no, not too well grown, yes, please, a story!"

Dunstan took a bread trencher, piled it with meat and pastry and sat down opposite the King at the long table. Aetna had finished her fruit and propped her elbows on the table whilst I, on the other side of Edgar, was still manfully working my way through the cold pork crackling on my own trencher. Edgar put his arm around Aetna and she leaned into him, eyes wide, waiting for the Archbishop's story to begin.

"There was once a beautiful princess," this was guaranteed to have Aetna hooked from the outset. "She lived right here, in Colencaestre, though it was not called that in her times. Her name was Helena and her father was the King of these lands, King Coel. When the Roman Legions came to his city, their army was far stronger than his and he saved his people from hurt by paying much gold and silver to the Roman King – they called him Caesar, and he did not believe in Our Lord. He paid so much that he became quite poor, and the only valuable thing he had left was his beautiful daughter. Caesar heard of her beauty and said that if she would travel to Rome and marry him, that her father's debt would be paid and the people would be safe.

"Although she was very afraid, she left her home and her father and travelled hundreds of miles to Rome, where she met Caesar. Although he worshipped strange gods, he was a good man and she fell in love with him, so that when they married, they were happy until Helena began to have frightening dreams."

"I have bad dreams, sometimes," interrupted Aetna.

"Hush," I said, for I thought the story was about to get interesting.

"Well, these were very bad," continued Dunstan. "She dreamt that she had been buried alive, and that all she should do was dig downward, instead of upwards to get out. She woke up crying every night, and her husband prayed to his gods that they might explain the dreams, but no answer came. Then Helena prayed to Our Lord, and was answered. She was told to go to the Holy Land – we call it Outremer – and dig under a hill outside the great city of Jerusalem. There she would find the tree on which Our Lord was killed.

"Well, that's just what she did. The Tree was brought back to Rome, and a miracle happened: Helena had thought that she could not have babies, but she soon gave birth to a little boy. He grew up to be the first Caesar to worship Our Lord. When news got back to King Coel – who was by then a very old man – he called for his pipers, and his drummers

86

and his fiddlers to play music in honour of his daughter. And to this day, here in Colencaestre, on the Feast of Saint Helena – yes, they made her a saint – they play music all night, all day, and all through the night again!

"And did you not think it convenient, Sire," he addressed the King at last, "that Cenfrith still happened to have his musicians in attendance for our feast yester eve? He must have had them stay over for the week between Helena's festival and that of Saint Bartholomew. Cenfrith is, indeed, a most attentive host!"

"Aye, and a thrifty one, for I'll warrant that he did not pay them for their time in between the two!"

"Better that than a spendthrift."

The story appeared to be over, and the King and Archbishop's attention heading in other directions. Edgar released Aetna from his embrace and she slipped to the floor. "My Lord, I shall be Helena for the rest of the day, and Wulf may be Caesar." Her tone was imperious. "Come husband, I shall show you where to dig."

"I thought it was the princess who was supposed to do the digging," I grumbled.

"Ha! Wulf, have you not yet learned that when a woman says she will do something, whether she be your wife or your sister, she usually means that she will oversee YOU doing it?" said Dunstan.

"And that you have no say, whatsoever, in the matter?" added the King.

Their light-hearted talk turned to different things, our presence forgotten, and the last we heard, as we headed out of the Great Hall to find the dogs (we had not seen them since we had turned them out of the sleeping chamber earlier) they were happily deep in discussion as to whether old King Coel had actually lived at all, and if so, whether on the site of this very castle.

We ran out into the courtyard and found Bremel and Berrie squabbling with a couple of the resident hounds over some of last night's scraps. Dagmaer and Aunt Aelflaed came out of the guest chamber, carrying a large blanket between them, which they shook out and then folded neatly, standing opposite each other, halving and then quartering the fabric, until it could be tucked under Dagmaer's arm. She turned and saw us.

"There you are! Your aunt and I have been wondering if you were spirited away. You have been very quiet this morning."

"We have been breaking our fast with the King and the Archbishop," I said, aware of how grand this sounded.

"Have you, indeed? And where might this have been?"

"In the Great Hall." This was sounding better and better: I wished Leoflada had been there to hear it. As if to prove it, Edgar and Dunstan came out of the Hall at that moment. The women dropped curtseys.

"Come, ladies, if you do that every time you see me you will be suffering from the sickness of the sea before the next few days are over," said Edgar. "After all, we are family in all but blood," he added to Aelflaed.

"Sire," our aunt inclined her head gracefully.

By now, the early sun had burnt off any lingering mistiness in the sky and it promised to be another warm, dry day. Dagmaer excused herself, hurrying away to make sure that the blanket, together with all our other possessions was safely stowed away in readiness for the next leg of or journey. "Come, Aetna, your hair needs plaiting or it will be a rats' nest by the time we reach Stoche." My sister followed her reluctantly.

I was sorry to be leaving Colencaestre already. "I should like to have visited the Arena again," I said, remembering the time we had visited once before and I had seen a dancing bear.

"The Reeve tells me that some more of its wall has fallen down, so maybe not this time," said Edgar. "But I shall order that it is shored up – just for you – when I have the city walls reinforced, and then, when you serve in my army one day, and are stationed here, it will be ready and waiting for you."

"Shall I really be in your army one day?" I said. That time seemed such a long way off. "Who shall I fight for you?"

"My army, or perhaps my son's," replied the King. "And I shall hope that you do not have to fight, only to safeguard my people. For like old Coel, I would rather keep my country safe by other means than doing battle. But is easier to study the past than to predict the future."

With that, the King and Dunstan turned away, and though I saw much of them over the next few weeks, I never again had the chance to speak with them so informally.

SEVEN

WULFAETNA

Leaving Colencaestre, after the first and longest leg of our journey, we also left behind the old, straight Roman roads which had allowed us to make such quick progress. Taking the still more ancient greenways, which meandered through villages and around the boundaries of long-established steads, meant that our pace was slower and although Wulf was still content to trot alongside the wagons, seemingly never bored by the small problems and triumphs of the train's passage, avoiding potholes, manoeuvring around oncoming travellers and so on, I was grateful to accept my aunt's offer to ride with her in the litter.

For a while, every so often Wulf would pop his head through the curtain of the litter with some snippet of information or joke about places we were passing, but after a while he was offered the chance to ride with our Uncle Brithnoth at the head of the train. I knew that later I would be regaled with the story of his adventures there, in the company of the King and other nobility, and in truth I was pleased to have the opportunity to speak with my aunt alone, because there was something which was worrying me.

"Aunt?"

"Yes, my chick."

"Have you not had any babies because you do not want to die and leave Uncle Brithnoth?" I asked.

"Aetna, whatever makes you say such a thing?" My aunt was stunned. "No, of course not! The Lord has simply not seen fit to bless us with children, though it has been my dearest wish. To have a babe of my own would make my happiness in this life complete."

"It was something I heard the King say that made me wonder," I said. "He seemed so worried about..."

"Aetna, you should not be eavesdropping on other people's conversations," said my aunt, sharply.

"But he knew I was there. He was talking to Dagmaer while she was plaiting my hair before we left this morning; he came to sit by us on purpose." My eyes were filling with tears.

"Very well, then, that's different. But what is it that has upset you?"

"Well, the King asked Dagmaer if there was any more danger in having a baby very soon after a woman had already had one. He said that the day their little Edward was born was the sweetest of his life, and also the most frightening, because he feared he might lose Elfa. And now Elfa was expecting another baby, maybe too soon, he said. She was so frail already, he said, and he had put her in danger. He would never forgive himself, he said, but his love…" I was becoming more distressed and my words tripping over each other.

Aelflaed put her arm around me and drew me to her. "Ah, hush, little one, I understand now." She brushed my hair away from my forehead, where it had escaped Dagmaer's plait. "It is both a woman's joy and her burden that childbirth should be foremost in her mind once she is married. The joy is not given to all, and to some the joy is given, but only at the cost of their own lives. That was the case with your own sweet mother, as you know. But as to what befalls and to whom, it is only the Lord who decides. And it is not something that should be weighing on the mind of one as young as you!"

"I think Edgar – I mean the King – was about to ask Dagmaer if she could do anything to help Elfa, but just then the church bell sounded for morning service and he hurried off."

"Elfa has had one fine boy already, and there is no reason to think that she will not bear another – or perhaps a little girl, like you!" Aelflaed, cupped my chin in her fingers and kissed me on the tip of my nose.

"I think he would like to have a daughter," I said, remembering his story about the beautiful Princess Helena and the way he had allowed me to sit with him that morning. "I shall remember Elfa in my prayers – and her new baby. And I shall hope that it is a sister for little Edward."

"You are a good girl, Aetna," said my aunt. "And I am certain that your prayers will be heard. Now, what news shall we share with my sister, your Aunt Aethelflaed, when we reach her Hall tonight?"

Our talk turned to womanly subjects. I was keen to show aunt Aethelflaed the new embroidery stitches I had learned and Aelflaed was looking forward to her sister's advice on the latest fashions, for she still had many friends at Court and was always one of the first to know how head-rails were being worn, and whether a new shade of madder had been perfected in Wintancaestre's dye-makers' quarter.

After a while, the motion of the litter and the warmth of the sun through curtains made my head nod, and I dozed for an hour or so, until Wulf's grinning face appeared at my elbow, as he jogged along, keeping pace with the litter bearers.

"Shake yourself, Aetna," he said, "We are nearly there! I am so hungry I could eat a leg off Father Aelmer's old mule!"

"Wulf!" laughed our aunt. "Really!"

We had, indeed, missed the midday meal. The sky was becoming overcast with rain clouds and it had been decided to push on to Stoche, hopefully arriving before the storm broke and turned the dry track into a mire of mud. The next time the litter paused to negotiate some small obstacle, I climbed out and joined my brother.

The track wound its way up a gentle incline, at the top of which perched a small wooden church, and then followed the contour of the hill downward, until we came to Aethelflaed's Hall. The Dowager Queen had posted lookouts to send word of our approach, and she stood by the gates ready to welcome us. Wulf and I had worked our way up to the front of the party. Edgar dismounted is his usual leg over pommel style, and ran to his stepmother, embracing her warmly.

"Mutti!" he fell easily into the use of his childhood name for her; she was the only mother he could remember. "I swear you look younger each time I see you!"

"Tush, it was not at my knee that you learned to make use of such flattery," said Aethelflaed, though clearly pleased. She had to stand on her toes to reach her hands to his shoulders and he slipped his arms around her waist, lifting her easily, so that they were on eye level. "But it is good to hear," she laughed, "and to see you, too! Now put me down and let me greet my other guests!"

We stayed at Stoche for two days. On the first night, the King's gift of the boar, killed during his stay at Radendunam was the highlight of the evening feast and Wulf and I were allowed to stay up to enjoy the festivities. The next day passed quietly, the family catching up on news, and the ceorls making preparation for the onward journey. When we left the following morning, it was clear that the King was sorry to be parting from his stepmother so soon.

As the party mounted up ready to leave, he reached down from his horse and kissed her.

"And you will come to Court when my Elfa is nearing her confinement?"

"I have said so."

"Then I will rest a little easier in my mind," he said. "Fare you well until then."

We were on the road early, having broken our fast shortly after daybreak, and the morning mist still swirled up from the River Stur as the long train of horses, carts and wagons – and Aelflaed's litter – emerged from the gates of Aethelflaed's Hall and onto the track, heading north. From Stoche, the intention was to make our way to Bedricsworth by way of a number of small villages where Brithnoth and the family held estates and entailed woodland. I had looked so jealous when Wulf was invited to ride, once again, with our uncle, that Dunstan took pity on me.

"Aetna, would you do me the honour of riding with me for the day? I fear that I am missing the company of the ladies. It becomes very dull, with no conversation other than hunting and hawking!"

He reached down, took my hand and swung me up in front of him, just as the party was about to leave. Dagmaer, making her way back toward the baggage carts snorted, briefly.

"Incorrigible," I believe she said, though was not quite sure what it meant.

Throughout the day we passed through steads where the villagers came out to meet us. Polesteda, Caresia, Waldringa-felda, Stoche, Coche-felda, Rycebroc and several more: Brithnoth was recognised quickly and word went ahead of us that he was riding with the King and the Archbishop. We did not dismount, although the reeves of the villages invited us to do so, for the poor harvest and hardships of the past year meant that the people were already short of food and to accept their hospitality would have beggared them. Although they expressed their regret, the village elders must have been grateful that we paused only to water the horses and oxen. We saw no beggars, but when we passed a group of lepers, who quickly stepped off the road to allow us past, Edgar threw down some coin.

"Poor souls," he said, and crossed himself. "It is good, Dunstan, that the monasteries have mercy on such as these. I believe that the Lazar houses have been particularly full this year."

Dunstan nodded. "Yes, Sire. The infirmaries have been likewise overwhelmed, the hog-murrain has been a curse. But there are those who do not aid the Brothers in their ministry to the sick, but rather take the wealth of the abbeys for themselves."

"I am well aware of the schism, Archbishop, and when the time is right, I will give you my blessing in your crusade to rid the abbeys of the land-grabbers and coin-hoarders. But for now, I must allow the Witan to meet and discourse without the added distraction of the Monastic question."

"Sire."

Edgar sighed. "Dunstan, your silence is, itself, eloquent. But you know my position on this."

"I do, and I shall wait. But it pains me, nevertheless. Brithnoth, have you heard any news from your brothers-in-law on this matter?"

The three men were rising abreast, by necessity so close that their horses jostled for room on the narrow track. It meant that they could speak without having to raise their voices. The members of the Witan riding behind them would not have been able to make out their words above the clop of the horses' hooves.

"Ethelwold and Ethelwine have both had cause to reprove Abbots…"

Dunstan interrupted him. "Reprove!"

"Leave it, leave it alone for now," the King said, firmly. "I do not want this matter raising its head on this trip. I have said: when the time is right, I will act. Enough."

Wulf and I did not understand this talk, but the tension communicated itself to us. I wriggled in my seat in front of the Archbishop. "How far, now, until we rest?" I asked.

"Yes," said Wulf. "How long until we eat?" Once again, the party had ridden right through the usual hour of midday repast.

Wulf's customary preoccupation with his stomach eased the awkwardness of the moment and Brithnoth laughed. "As ever, young man, you have reminded us of the priorities! I think we are very nearly at Bedricsworth, so you will be able to fill your belly soon."

Indeed, the track we had been following from Rycebroc soon merged with the larger one from Suthbyrig and we were approaching the South gate of the town, an open wooden structure which arched over the road, supported on one side by a toll both, and on the other by a hut, which, as we came closer, revealed itself to be an anchorite's cell, its aged occupant sitting on a stool outside the door.

"You are well come to this place," the old man croaked, standing up shakily, and leaning on a rough crutch. "The blessed Saint Edmund's Shrine will be honoured by your footfall. You have made good time from Rycebroc, for the runner is only ahead of you by a few minutes or the Lord Bedricson would have been at the Gate to greet you himself."

Dunstan snorted at this. "Bedricson! First he will get his foot in the door of the shrine and then..."

The King spoke low but sharp to him: "Dunstan, I warn you, I want no politics at this holy place. The time is not yet for you to pursue your aims." Then, to the old man, he said, "Thank you, grandfather, we have no intention of standing upon ceremony, our visit is unofficial and in passing. Though we hope to spend the night in this fair town."

Gently kicking his horse forward, he led the way through the arch and toward the first straggling cottages, which gradually jostled closer together as we approached the town centre, a grid of streets to the West, the shrine and its grounds to the East, the main street running between the two. We were soon greeted by the party from the shrine, hurrying toward us.

"Your Majesty," Sub-ealdorman Bedricson – for it was surely he – essayed a low bow as did his companions, standing straight only when Edgar bade them do so. "I have had runners relaying your Progress since you left Coche-felda, I am mortified to miss your arrival at our Gate, but I hope I may have the honour of escorting you to my own poor Hall. We have room in the guest chamber for some of your party, and have instructed the inn to make the rest comfortable there, for we are still a small town, despite our fortune in have the blessed Saint Edmund at our heart."

Wulf and I had had enough of this conversation and were growing restless. We were helped down from the horses and ran back to our aunt's litter and to the baggage carts, finding the one in which Berrie and Bremel had been sleeping away the journey and roused them. As the procession moved off and through the town, we looked around curiously, for we both remembered the tale I had heard of how our parents had come here to marry, and later of our own birth and the loss of our mother. It had the air of a town enjoying its own expansion, with an expectation of even better times to come. New houses and shops were being built, stalls and barrows vied with one another for the best places to be set up, and street sellers hawked their wares from trays and handcarts. Everywhere visitors, the pious and the just plain curious, were heading to or from Saint Edmunds' Shrine, a wooden building fronting the main street with a stone chapel to one side.

"Pins, pins, Saint Edmund pins!" a man with a ribbon studded with small brooches, waved them under our noses. "Blessed by being left overnight beside the Saint's uncorrupted body..." but then, catching sight of the Archbishop – clearly a churchman of some importance, although I guessed he knew not who – the hawker made a hasty exit down an alleyway.

Several of the members of the Witan who had been riding at the head of the party dismounted to look at the stalls. One was haggling over the price of a splinter of arrow, said by its seller to be a fragment of one of the many that had killed the Saint. The corpulent figure of Cenfrith could be seen fingering the quality of a shawl, woven with emblems of Saint Edmunds's passion – arrows, a tree, and curiously, a hedgehog. Dagmaer was now walking alongside us.

I asked her about the design. "It is said that the saint was stuck so full of arrows that he looked like a hedge-pig," she explained.

The King's immediate party were already heading toward Bedricson's Hall, together with our aunt's litter, Leoflada's wardrobe wagon and a few of the senior Ealdormen. It had been decided that most of the baggage train would camp beside the river – the ceorls and other servants could enjoy what entertainment the town had to offer overnight, while the lesser nobles went to the inn. Apparently, Dagmaer had suggested that she, Wulf and I would be most comfortable in the latter group. She later told me that it would have been no fun for children to be mired up at the little Hall, but I believe that she, herself, was not overly keen to stay there. "I understand that the Lord Bedricson is partial to the company of churchmen. If I want to hear the endless prating of priests, I could have stayed behind with that fool Aelmer," I heard her say to one of the maids. I wondered what Dunstan would have made of such a comment.

We passed by the gates leading into the grounds of the shrine. At the crossroads in the centre of the town was a large inn, the sign of a bull, black-haired and red horned, over its door. Dagmaer ushered us through the porch and into the dark interior. As our eyes adjusted to the lack of day-light we found ourselves in a large flag-stoned room, trestle tables and benches set about and the floor strewn with rushes. A heavy woman in a brown smocked gunna approached Dagmaer with open arms. Her grey-streaked hair was drawn back from her face and tied with a plaited red band. A kirtle of the same braided rags was tied at her waist, holding a cloth in pace to protect the front of her skirt.

"Dear lady, how many years has it been? They have been kind to you. When news came that you were to stay here, I put aside the best cot in all the guest chamber – you are a sight for sore eyes. And these? These are surely the poor mites I last saw at your breast! Carus! Husband! Carus, come quickly, our guests are here!"

Dagmaer allowed the embrace, and another from Carus, a tall, thin man, who emerged from a side door. She propelled us forward. "This is the goodwife Ranith."

Wulf stepped up to the mark. "I am pleased to meet you, goodwife," his manners were well-rehearsed, I was proud of him. "I am Wulfmaer, son of Wulfstan, sister-son to Ealdorman Brithnoth and this is my sister, Wulfaetna."

Ranith looked back and forth from one of us to the other. "They are like as like!" she said. "And you have stayed with them Dagmaer. No more adventures for you, then?"

"I gave my word, and I have not regretted it," replied Dagmaer. "Now, I fear that if my young lordling is not fed soon he will swoon clean away, and his sister, too!" This might have been an exaggeration, but the thought of food was certainly welcome, and now the other guests were arriving, so Ranith hurried away to the kitchens.

)))))(((((

I did not sleep well that night. Despite the comforting presence of Dagmaer, and the familiarity of Wulfmaer in the cot beside me, the dogs occasionally snuffling in their sleep, and the distant snores of the other guests, I felt a chill of apprehension and loneliness as I lay in that place. The inn sign creaked outside our shuttered window and I saw, in my mind's eye, the great bull's head moving to and fro with each gust of wind. I imagined my mother and father, newly married and in love, not knowing what sadness lay in their future, and then, when that future had become their present, my mother's anguish as she came to realise that she would not see us grow up and my father's despair.

I tossed and turned and, though I tried not to wake him, eventually some of my fear and anxiety must have communicated itself to Wulf as he slept.

"Aetna, what's the matter? What's wrong?" he whispered.

"I don't know," I replied. "I'm sorry. I just have this horrible feeling, as though I am in a bad dream and I can't wake up, and everything is just *wrong*."

"Well, you are not, and it is not!" Wulf snuggled close to me. "I am here, and so are the dogs! We will keep you safe. Come, you are my sister Sigilind and tomorrow we battle sand demons together!"

"I do not like that great bull's head," I said.

"It's not real! Just a daub of paint, nothing more. And a squeaky hinge! In the morning you will see there was nothing to fear."

"I suppose!"

"Let's sleep now, or we shall wake Dagmaer. Or do you want to tell me how hard to pinch you, so that you will know you are not dreaming?"

I giggled at that and things began to feel normal again. For once I was pleased that Wulf did not share my fears of the unknown, of Thella's strange behaviour and of Loki's trickster ways. "No need," I said and when, eventually, I slept, it was without any dreams I could remember.

)))(((

We broke our fast the next morning in the kitchen with Ranith and Carus, the maids passing back and forth into the public room with leftover lamb, stewed overnight in watered wine, and pease porridge, steaming in earthenware bowls. The meat was tender and falling off the bone and Wulf and I ate it with fresh bread, hot from the ovens. Dagmaer had arisen before we were awake, and now came in from the courtyard, shaking the early morning dew from her skirts.

"A fine morning to be journeying," she said to us, and turning to Ranith, slipped a bunch of green herbs into her hand. "These are what you need. I picked them just as the sun came up. Crush them well and add the sap to water. If you drink it at midday it should ease your aches and pains without making you sleepy. Then heat the same mixture in the evening, take it with honey and wine and you will be sleep like a baby!" Carus looked doubtful. Dagmaer patted him reassuringly on the arm. "It is only mallow – cheese flowers to you – Ranith will be skipping like a young fawn before the next Moon's day."

"And now, you two, have you all your bits and pieces packed away? And where are those dogs of yours?"

In truth, we had little to pack away, we had slept in our under garments and only had to slip on our shoes, Wulf's tunic and my gunna to be ready for the day. At my waist hung a little pouch in which I carried my bone comb (a Yuletide gift from Leoflada, partly, I think, to stop me using hers) and spare hair ribbons. I also kept an extra set of leg bindings for Wulf.

From his braided belt was suspended his knife and mine, a catapult and two thin rope leashes for Berrie and Bremel. We were a single, compact unit.

"We are…"

"… all ready, Dagmaer."

"Good. Now thank our hosts for their bed and board." We did so, and as we headed outside, we could hear Dagmaer assuring her friends that payment would be made by the King's coin-bearer when the main party arrived from the Shire Reeve's Hall.

Above our heads swung the bull sign. In the bright sunlight of the morning it did not look so threatening, but I still did not like it and stayed close to Wulf, glancing at it apprehensively. Carus came out to wave us off as the Progress approached.

"Do you not admire our Bull, then, little one?" he asked me. I had to admit that I did not.

"He does not look like a very friendly bull," I said.

"Ah, I can explain that," said Carus. "You see, there has been an inn on this spot for as long as anyone can remember. My grandfather's grandfather was victualler here, and his grandsire before him, back to the time of the Legions. Back then, the Roman soldiers lodged here. And to allow new recruits to find it easily, they put a picture of their god – the god of soldiers, Mithras his name was – and his emblem, a bull, over the door. When Our Lord became known and the old gods were no more, they took Mithras off the sign, but left the bull behind. And he has never looked very happy from that day to this, however many times he is repainted!"

I laughed. Suddenly the bull did not look quite so threatening. In fact, I felt rather sorry for it.

"Poor bull," I said. "I expect he is lonely now that his god has left him."

"You are a kind-hearted girl," said Carus. "There will always be a welcome for you here at his sign."

As we stood beneath the bull's portrait, still creaking, but now, I felt, with a less threatening sound, the King's party approached from the centre of the town. Edgar, Dunstan and the nobles passed by us, Uncle Brithnoth smiling a good morning to Dagmaer and with a passing grin and raised eyebrow for us, followed by our aunt's litter, the wardrobe wagon, with Leoflada in her position of self-appointed authority and finally the several dozen carts and baggage carriers. A stable hand was leading Dagmaer's horse, and she mounted gracefully, giving him her thanks for his care. Wulf and I joined the procession, Bremel and Berrie at our heels.

Within an hour, we were rumbling through the sandy undulations of the Brecks. Leaving the town by the north gate we followed the valley of the Pryckewillowewayter, passing villages and steads where, again, the goodmen and wives came out to greet us. We crossed the Icenilde Way, which Dagmaer had told us was the oldest road in the land – ancient even when the Legions arrived – and took the route which led us West, through sandy grassland, sparsely grazed by shabby-looking sheep, and pocked marked in places by deep depressions, water filled and steep sided.

"Devil's dippers," said Leoflada, shivering. I was sitting beside her, Wulf trotting alongside, merrily swiping at wayside plants with a stout stick.

"Ha! Let the Devil's imps come forth, I shall slay them!" He picked up a stone and hefted it into the nearest of the pools. Just then a gust of wind blew up one of the long-anticipated dust-demons, which spiralled ahead of us to one side of the road. Even Wulf was a little taken aback at this abrupt reply to his challenge.

"I… I think I might ride…"

"…with us for a while." I reached down and helped him up alongside me.

"That's better!"

It had to be said that the landscape of the Brecks was not as exciting as we had anticipated. There was little traffic on the road, an occasional shepherd, as ragged and looking as poorly fed as his sheep, passed us, respectfully keeping his flock to one side. The villages grew smaller and more squalid and there was less interest in our passage the further we travelled, fewer curious faces peered up at us and those that did looked surly and, perhaps, even unaware of who was passing.

My poor night's sleep was catching up with me by midday, and after a short break to eat, water and rest the animals, when we set off again my head was nodding and finally, I slept, leaning against the comforting presence of Leoflada, who seemed happy to let me so do. For a while Wulf dozed too, but at some point, he slipped down from the wagon and made his way to the head of the train. It must have been approaching late postnoon when he came running back.

"Flada, Flada!"

Leoflada and I had both been sitting asleep for some while, companionably keeping each other just about upright despite the jogging of the cart, watched unobtrusively by the driver in case a sudden bump should dislodge us. He was not keen to take the blame for an accident involving the ealdorman's daughter and niece.

"Flada, wake up!" Wulf shouted. "Your love-sick goose-boy has come to meet you! He has ridden high and low, jumped ditches and skirted the fens, all take you in his arms…" He made several loud sucking and kissing noises.

Leoflada woke with a start, shrieked and disappeared into the back of the wagon. "Aetna, please, help me… I cannot meet Oswig like this! My hair is not braided! Oh, and I am in my work gunna… the dust! Where is my head-rail?" She stuck her head out of the awning "Wulf, you must keep him away! Take him to the victual cart for a drink of small ale, and tell him I shall be ready directly! Aetna, for the love of Heaven, where did we put my other day shoes: these are worn through!"

My cousin and I had reached something of an understanding over the last few days of the Progress. I was old enough to realise that a certain feminine solidarity in the face of predominantly male travelling companions was a definite advantage. The small comforts we could devise had to be shared. I was sympathetic to Flada's panic, she was not looking at her best, very untidy and rather travel weary. Better than search for hers, I took my own comb from my chatelaine pouch and straightened out the tangles in her hair, plaiting it for her while she laced up the front of a clean gunna – fortuitously on the top of the neatly packed contents of the closest chest. "Oh, sweet Saints, it is Aelflaed's... never mind, she will forgive me, this is an emergency!" she panted, pulling on slippers that were quite unequal to any heavy walking duties.

I found a bottle of rose water and poured a little onto a cloth. "Here, wipe your face, this will take away the dust. And put on this head-rail. Look, here is a ribbon to keep it in place. There, you look lovely!" And, somehow, she did; pink and breathless and bright-eyed with the unexpectedness of her lover's arrival. As she emerged from the covered wagon onto the buck board at the back, Oswig, refreshed by Wulf's offer of small ale, caught his breath for a moment at the sight of her, and even I was enchanted. Our Flada was becoming a beauty! How had that happened?

Oswig brought his horse alongside the back of the wagon, and putting his arm around her waist, lifted her easily up onto the saddle in front of him, where she sat side-saddle. Wulf and I were forgotten, and they rode up to Aelflaed's litter. Our aunt had been roused by the commotion, and looking out of her curtain, feigned shock.

"Flada, are you to be carried away from us already?"

"With your permission, Lady, just for a short distance and for a short while," said Oswig, reaching down and kissing Aelflaed's hand. "Alas, I know she is not mine yet!"

"Bear that in mind, and keep within sight," said Aelflaed, with mock severity. "But enjoy, sweetlings!" she added.

By early evening we had arrived at Saham, at the edge of the Fens, where Brithnoth had a large estate and a small but comfortable Hall. We were welcomed by his reeve, the King immediately shown to a private guest lodging, Dagmaer, Leoflada and ourselves to a family chamber within the Great Hall, adjoining another, larger chamber for Aelflaed and our uncle whilst the other Ealdormen, members of the Witan, ceorls and pack men were found accommodation appropriate to their various stations.

Though it was only planned that we should stay for one night, Brithnoth's retainers were well prepared. The kitchens were alive with activity, the fire in the Great Hall burning brightly, chambers aired and freshly strewn and in no time at all our travel-weariness seemed to fall away. Despite our protestations, however, we were fed and put to bed early, Dagmaer insisting that tomorrow's start would be at daybreak. I woke once in the night, when Leoflada came to her palliasse, humming and dreamily singing a love-lay to herself, but then I slept until dawn.

)))))(((((

Elig, when we finally reached it, seemed a poor place to be the destination for such a long journey. We had, indeed, started out very early that morning. The sun was barely showing above the horizon – and what a flat and distant horizon it was. We left the Hall at Saham in our usual formation, but travelled only a short distance before reaching the water's edge. The true fens lay ahead of us, chill and unmoving, dotted with tussocks of coarse grass and reeds, apparently stretching away to an infinity of the same.

A rough jetty jutted out where the track ended abruptly at the shoreline. Thick wooden supports disappeared into the water, blackened in places, and the boards of the walkway looked none too sound. Alongside, and on the edge of the fen, were moored several large flat-bottomed rafts and a number of high-sided, shallow keeled barges, each with a crew of two men, upright punting poles towering over their heads and disappearing into the water.

It took a long time for everything to be loaded. The animals were unhitched and led onto the barges, the high sides shielding the water from their nervous glances. Even so, the oxen were unwilling to board and their handlers had to bind rags around their eyes before they would be led along the jetty. The wagons and carts were unloaded and rolled onto the flat rafts, and our luggage and other possessions stowed beneath them. Everything was then lashed into place with stout ropes. As many people as possible were encouraged to find seats – of a sort – in the carts and the rest allocated standing space beside them, and told to hold tight and stand well away from the unprotected edges of the crafts.

Leoflada and I took up our usual places in what had been the costume wagon. The driver insisted on keeping his place, he said, "For 'tis the only wagon with paintwork and I don't want 'er ruined by them fens-folk."

Wulf squeezed in close to me on the outside, and the dogs settled uncertainly at our feet. Inside the wagon sat aunt Aelflaed, Honig in her arms (her litter had been dismantled and stowed), Dagmaer and two of the upper serving women. The King, Archbishop Dunstan, Brithnoth and

100

several of the Ealdormen took their places in another of the punts, standing tall and looking out over the waters, while the lesser members of the Court, the ceorls and other servants managed as best they could, perching on boxes, or taking their chances with the restless animals. The portly figure of Cerdic looked most uncomfortable.

At last, all seemed ready and, at an unseen signal from one of the puntsmen, poles were taken up and then plunged back into the water a little distance away, pushed and pulled, and the various craft began to move. Very soon an order was established, the King's boat in the van of the flotilla, the others following behind, like ducklings after their mother. The poles were withdrawn and plunged into the water rhythmically and with little apparent effort, the expert puntsmen propelling us through the water, which quickly became deeper. We could see that only a little way from the shore the poles began to disappear into the water and mud below by half their own length, but still the boats moved along smoothly avoiding the islets of grass and foliage, alder and reeds, heading toward some unseen goal.

There was no wind and hardly a ripple on the water.

"This must be the sort of place the water-wights hide," said Wulf as we passed a particularly lumpy mat of grass and alder. He leaned precariously over the side of the wagon to get a better view into the murky depths and suddenly jumped as a blue grey length of – what? – as thick as an archer's arm, flashed close to the surface of the water and disappeared into the tangled mass of vegetation.

"Urgh!"

"You may say 'urgh', young master," said one of the puntsmen, "but that were one of our famous great eels! 'E's come to greet yer, no more! Without the eels and the reeds that hide 'em, why, Elig would have nowt at all. They be our coin and our victuals, our leather and our luck. Don't you never mind 'em! You'll soon enough hear more about 'em from the eel-folk."

Wulf looked sheepish. "I knew what it was really," he muttered. All the same, he sat a little closer to me for the rest of the ride.

Eventually, what appeared to be no more than a slightly denser mass of watery skyline in the mist ahead resolved itself into a long shoreline. Low trees became visible and then another rough jetty, the twin of its counterpart at Saham, came into view. This, then, at last, was the Isle of Elig.

EIGHT

There was no sign of any building large enough to accommodate us. A short distance from the water's edge a few poor hovels clustered together around a central green – which was anything but green, the grass being trampled into a brown, muddy mess. Beside the jetty, ranged alongside the waterside, were some long, low sheds, open fronted toward the fen which seemed to be filled with elongated, funnel-shaped baskets, lengths of coiled rope and a few small, flat bottomed rafts, cluttered together with punting poles of various lengths, boat hooks and bundles of reeds.

The ceorls who, throughout the Progress, had always brought up the rear of the train, ill-tempered and bored-seeming, and suffering the dust of the rest of the party, with carts piled high with cumbersome spars, tarred linens and clothes, clanking pegs and ropes, for the first time appeared to relish their tasks. After a few short words with the King's retainers, they quickly unloaded the rafts which had carried their carts, taking the contents up onto slightly higher ground behind the village. With astonishing rapidity, they began to pace out distances, unfurl heavy tarps, erect poles, and hammer in stakes attached to long guy ropes. Before our eyes a tented Hall and courtyard began to take shape.

An elderly man, dressed in grey and brown rope-gartered trews, with a rough smocked tunic came forward deferentially from one of the huts.

Unsure which of the new arrivals was of the highest rank, he doffed his shapeless, felted skullcap, knuckled his brow and bowed shakily in the general direction of the noblemen.

"My lords?" he said hesitantly.

Brithnoth stepped forward. "Speak up, Goodman, and do not fear," he said. "What do they call you?"

"They call me Gorth, my Lord, though 'tis not my name," replied the man, sucking his teeth as he spoke. "That is, them that calls me anything. For hereabouts we all know each other without the need for fancy names."

Edgar came forward. "And how is that, man?"

"I am the Eel-man. My son, he is the next Eel-man, and his son will be... And my father, he were the last Eel-man, and his father... Rightly, my name is the Eel-man."

"And what do they call your wife?"

Gorth favoured the King with a toothy grin. "The Eel-wife," he said.

Edgar was enjoying himself. "They call me Edgar."

"Well come to you then, sir," said the Eel-man. "You have right many friends with you!" He looked uncertainly at the array of tents that were fast beginning to look like a small village of its own. "This land belongs to the King, you know, and there's them that are squabbling over it now. I don't know as how they will take to all this."

"Squabbling, are they?" said Edgar. "And who might they be?"

"Well, there's the Shire Reeve, 'im as comes up from Grantebrige once in a twelve-month of moon-days, with a big to-do every time, expecting me and mine to kiss his 'and for the right to be here. And then there's the North-man and he's slipperier than one of my eels! Always asking me how much I get for me catch, and where I sells it. I tell him I am here with the King's warrant, given me by his Reeve, but he still pesters us. Asks if we can recall when the old Danelaw first came to these lands. As if me and mine care for all that!" Gorth was warming to his subject now.

"Well, we are here to sort that out, once and for all," said Edgar. "But be assured, Gorth, or Eel-man, or whatever you prefer, your warrant will stand."

"It's good of you to say so, sir, but 'tis in the hands of them far above you, I'm sure."

"I think not," said Edgar, and made his way up to the tented village, leaving Gorth first to wonder and then to gape when he was told who the pleasant young man was.

Brithnoth, Dunstan and the other Ealdormen had watched the exchange with amusement and then followed the King up to the higher ground.

Dagmaer appeared at our side, as if from nowhere. "You two, keep out of the way, out of trouble and away from the water's edge," she said to us, hustling the other female servants before her, each carrying linens and crockery, pots and foodstuffs. "Don't upset the Eel-people, don't let the dogs chase those chickens and don't make me say any of that twice." We were free to explore.

Wulf's encounter with the great eel, and Dagmaer's instruction to keep clear of the water meant that it took us no time at all to decide upon the direction of our exploration. We struck off inland. Berrie and Bremel at our heels, we jogged up the incline toward the ever-growing encampment and then past it. The land became firmer and firmer the further we went, and eventually, we noticed what must have been the extent of the regular flood level, for the dark, silty mud gave way to sandy soil. In the time it took us to sing our way through *The Wife's Lament* (though, I confess, without remembering all the words) we saw ahead of us some low, ruined walls, piles of tumbled masonry and two small huts, one of stone, the other built of what looked like drift wood, but blackened, and like no wood that we had ever seen come from the sea.

We slowed our pace.

"The lair of Will-o'-the-Wisp?" whispered Wulf.

"So far from the water?" I said.

We crept forward. Wulf had, without me noticing, picked up a tent-peg as we passed through the encampment and now held it by its narrow end, like a short club. (There was probably an irate tent-man berating his underling at this moment!) He kept it raised.

"Who approaches the Holy Saint Etheldreda?" A cracked voice rang out shrilly.

Wulf jumped as though poked by a sharp stick. I swung around, trying to discover where the voice had come from. The dogs barked. There was a squawk from chickens somewhere unseen.

From the wooden hut, what looked like a bundle of rags emerged, bent almost double, but trying to lift its head to get a view of us.

"Children!" it said. "And none of those eel-scamps from the village! How came you here?"

The bundle resolved itself into an old woman. An ancient woman, rather, her face a mass of wrinkles and almost as black as the bog-oak of her cottage walls. She looked at us as though we were rare, strange creatures.

"Good day to you..." said Wulf.

"... Grandmother." I completed the greeting.

"We are here," continued Wulf, throwing out his chest with more bravado than conviction "with the King and the members of the Witan, to put to rights all that is ill in this isle." He sounded very grand. I was proud of my brother's rhetoric.

"Are you, indeed?" replied the old woman, obviously unimpressed. "And will that include restoring the honour of the Holy Saint Etheldreda?"

Wulf was clearly getting out of his depth. "I... I am sure..."

"... it will," I said, trying to sound confident.

A beatific smile spread across the face of the old woman. "Out of the mouths of babes..." she mused. "You are well come. Sit with me and tell me of the King, for it is a long time since I have heard any tales."

"I don't really know any tales," said Wulf. "But I do know about the King. He is a fine young man, is King Edgar, fair of face and deed." Wulf's mastery of the heroic style spoke volumes of Dagmaer's story telling.

"Would you like to visit the shrine of the Holy Saint Etheldreda?"

"Indeed, Grandmother."

Of course, we knew the story of Etheldreda. Three hundred years ago, the Princess Etheldreda was married to the Northumbrian King, despite having already taken a vow of chastity to the Lord. To begin with, her husband had tolerated the situation, mindful of his wife's high status as daughter of another King. But then he became frustrated by the sexless nature of his marriage and demanded she performed her wifely duties. Rather than break her vow, Etheldreda fled south to the lonely fens of East

Anglia, and, crossing the water by a hidden route revealed to her in a dream, found shelter in the Isle of Elig. There she founded a house of prayer for both women and men, though she only lived another six years before succumbing to the plague. There was more, but we could not remember it. Visitors to her burial place, first only locals, then pilgrims from further afield, claimed healings and miracles. Her shrine had flourished until the Viking attacks two hundred years later, when it was despoiled and almost forgotten as the Danelaw began to hold sway over the area.

"What are your names, little ones?"

"I am Wulfmaer, son of Wulfstan, and this is my sister, Wulfaetna. May we know your name?"

"I have been called Gorthwyffe," said the old woman, leading us toward the stone hut. "My son is the Eel-man and my husband was the Eel-man before him. Now my name is Mother Gorthwyrd, as was my mother's before me. It is my fate, as it was hers, to be the guardian of the shrine."

We entered the low, rough building. There was no light, other than from the small arch through which we had passed – there was no door – and a tiny rough hole in the stonework of the opposite wall, which, we could tell from the lowering sun at our backs, faced east. Almost covering the floor, with just a little standing room to either side and a low black wood table under the window, was a huge slab of stone. It was scuffed and chipped but still retained something of a sheen. It was of a stone that we had seen before in churches.

"This is all that remains of the shrine of the Blessed Saint Etheldreda," said Mother Gorthwyrd. On the slab lay a posy of tiny white flowers.

"Fen lilies," she explained, seeing my interest in them. "They grow hereabouts. There is nought else we can give her."

"They are lovely," I said.

There was a sense of peace in the place; both Wulf and I felt it. I kneeled beside the slab and laid my hand next to the flowers. Wulf shuffled awkwardly and then knelt, too. It seemed so sad, so desolate a place for a princess's remains. Mother Gorthwyrd put her hand on my head.

"Sweet children," she said. "There is no need for sorrow. The time will come when the Holy Lady will be honoured once again. Say your fare wells and come with me now, and have a drink of milk. I wager you will have not had the like before!"

We followed her out of the shrine. The low sun was still shining fitfully, and we made our way the short step across to Gorthwyrd's cell – for it was little more than a bare room with a stool and rough table, some pottery and a low, plank bed piled high with reeds and rushes. From the shady side of the doorway she picked up a pitcher and poured out a generous cupful of milk for each of us. It foamed as she poured it, rich and thick.

She gestured to a small, neat paddock behind the cell. Two golden brown, speckled does, each with a fawn at heel, grazed there, with a few scrawny chickens picking at whatever was in their droppings.

"Deer," I cried, utterly surprised. "This is doe's milk?"

"Indeed," said our hostess. "Once, when there was a famine in the land, and the Holy Saint's community was in great need, the Lord sent two does to give them milk. There have always been at least two does near the shrine ever since. I don't need to fence them in, really... it is more to keep other things out!"

She handed us the milk.

"Thank you," I said, tasting it. It was remarkable. "It is delicious."

"Almost as good as Gillycrest's," agreed Wulf through a milky moustache.

Gorthwyrd laughed. "And who is Gillycrest?" she said.

Wulf proceeded to tell her about our home, our favourites (the dogs had also been favoured with a taste of milk) and our family.

"So, the Lord Brithnoth is your uncle," Gorthwyrd mused.

"Yes, I am his sister-son," said Wulf. "And he has made me his own, adopted son," he added proudly.

"And you, my sweet?" she asked turning to me. "There cannot be a year between you and your brother. You are like as... two..."

"We are twins," I said.

"Like in the Sagas," Wulf added.

But Gorthwyrd's attention seemed to have wandered. "So, they are here at last," she said, apparently to herself. "And my Holy Lady's Shrine is to be raised high once again."

Wulf looked doubtful. "I don't know about that," he said. "From what I have heard, there are already people squabbling about what will happen to the island and asking the King for all sort of things. I heard nobody mention the Saint."

Gorthwyrd did not look at all perturbed by this. "I simply ask you both for one thing," she said.

"Of course," we both replied. The milk was all gone, but its taste lingered on our tongues, a deep, warm flavour of... what?

"Tell your uncle my story. Tell him before the Great Moot. Tell him of Gorthwyffe, the Eel-wife who became Gorthwyrd, the keeper of the shrine. That is all. Just tell him."

The sun was now beginning to get very low. "We had..." I began.

"... better get back," Wulf said.

"But we will tell our uncle all about you."

"And I will tell the King, too," added Wulf, sounding rather grand.

"May God and the Lady Etheldreda be with you, my children," said Gorthwyrd, and embraced us. She smelled terrible.

"And you," we said in unison, turning back the way we had come.

"And keep those dogs of yours away from my birds!" That sounded more like an Eel-wife than a nun. Why were Berrie and Bremel always being warned away from chickens?

)))))((((

Upon our return to the encampment, we could hardly believe the alterations which had taken place in our absence. A huge open sided awning dominated, presently empty but for a few eel-boys and girls, on their hands and knees, pounding the ground level with stones and strewing it with reeds and rushes. Beside it was a large, fully enclosed tent, where Dagmaer was currently supervising the tying back of two front panels to create a low doorway. Around these two main shelters there were many more tents of various sizes, between them braziers and camp fires, and one great cooking range, next to the main tent, with fire dogs on either side, supporting a cross piece on which was skewered the carcass of a sheep, dripping juices onto the spitting embers below. The lad turning the spit grinned at us, wiping his brow, and supposedly flicking the sweat away. The heat and light from the fires made the world outside their glow seem dark and chill, and we were pleased to be what felt like home.

"Ah, there you are," said Dagmaer, catching sight of us. "Go and make yourselves presentable. In here, quick, now! The family quarters are to the right, the King and my Lord Archbishop to the left. There's water in a bucket and I have laid out some fresh clothes for you both. Get a move on!"

She motioned us through the half-open tent-flap. A heavy hessian curtain hung down the centre of the structure. We could hear the familiar laughter of the King and Dunstan to one side and we stayed, as directed, on the right. The space was subdivided by another curtain. We peered behind it. A large pallet bed had been made up with a straw mattress and blanket. Aunt Aelflaed's costume trunk was beside it. In what we realised was our side of the hanging there were two bundles of rushes, neatly wrapped in blankets, with additional coverings folded at the head of each; one for us and one for Leoflada. We could tell which she already chosen: beside it was Flada's small travelling trunk, and on it her precious comb and some ribbons. Berrie eyed the make-shift palliasse.

"No, not there, we shall be skinned alive," I said. "This one, boys!" I indicated our sleeping arrangements. Both dogs immediately took

107

advantage of the offer and within minutes were fast asleep. "We can bring them some food later," I said to Wulf.

We washed and changed our clothes. I re-plaited my hair and lent my comb to Wulf. He left his loose, but slicked it back with water.

"I think we will do," I said, looking him up and down.

"I could do with a…" he said.

"Me, too…"

"I wonder where they have dug it."

"It won't be hard to find. All we have to do is follow our noses!"

We found the newly dug latrine on the leeward side of the camp, so that the prevailing wind would, to some extent, mask its presence, and then we made our way back to the centre of the tented vill.

Beneath the great awning, trestles had been set up, end to end, to create one long table, with benches to either side of them. We were beginning to understand why a Royal Progress was such a major undertaking. All the furniture, here and in the sleeping quarters, was assembled from flat planking, slotted and pegged together ingeniously to suit a variety of purposes.

An army of servants entered, carrying jugs, flagons and other drinking vessels, and placed them along the length of the table, making return trips bearing platters piled high with bread trenchers, bowls of fruit, slabs of cheese and other easily transported foodstuffs. One of the King's retainers came in to check progress.

"His Majesty has insisted upon informality, this evening," he said, as Dagmaer joined him.

"Agreed," she said. "But everything looks excellent. Are we ready?"

"I believe so," he said, nodding to a boy waiting patiently by his side. "Off you go, then!"

The lad perked up immediately and trotted outside, where he began to call "The King's table is set! The King's table is set!" He disappeared into the maze of tents and we could hear his voice fading as he circled through the camp. Almost straight away, those who knew that they were expected began to arrive. Despite the informality, those of a higher rank congregated at the upper end of the table, the rest happily jostling for position lower down.

Oswig and Leoflada came in side by side, so close together that they might have been holding hands moments earlier. Oswig waved. "Come, sit with us!" he called.

"Oh, really! Must they?" Flada seemed to have forgotten our recent empathy.

It didn't matter. Soon we were joined by our uncle and aunt, and several of the other Ealdormen, all familiar faces after our long journey together. Dunstan arrived and sat almost opposite us. Last of all came

Edgar. He looked as though, somehow, he had managed to bathe. He wore a blue tunic over soft, doeskin hose and a simple circlet of gold, with a single blue stone at its centre, on his forehead. His soft brown hair was brushed back beneath it and his eyes sparkled.

"Well, this looks like a fine party!" he said.

As soon as he had taken his seat at the head of the table – a chair had been placed there for him – the thralls began to bring in the meat, hot and steaming. As we ate, there was a hum of conversation from the adults, but for a while Wulf and I enjoyed our food in silence. Wulf, to his delight, found himself sitting next to Brithnoth, and, waiting for a moment when he would not be interrupting said, "Uncle, we met a strange old woman today."

"Did you?" said Brithnoth, picking a string of lamb from between his teeth. "And where was this?"

As we had promised, Wulf told our uncle everything that Gorthwyrd had said and, with a little help from me, described the ramshackle shrine, the poor anchorite's cell, the deer in the makeshift paddock and, finally, the milk.

"We told her that it was almost as good as Gilly's," I said, helpfully.

Suddenly, we realised that not only had our uncle been listening attentively, but so, too, had Dunstan and the King.

"And you say this old woman, this 'Mother' Gorthwyrd, and her family has been tending the shrine ever since it was destroyed by the Northmen?" asked Edgar.

"That's what she said."

"Were there any candles burning, any decorations around the shrine?" said Dunstan.

"Only a tiny bunch of flowers," I said.

"Archbishop," the King turned to Dunstan, "We will rise early tomorrow, before the Moot, and visit this place. It seems that there is more to be found on this isle than eels. These men who attend upon us tomorrow have not been wholly open in their petitions so far. There is more going on here than meets the eye."

The conversation turned to matters we did not understand and we lost interest. We slept soundly that night, and when we awoke, we found that Edgar, Dunstan and our uncle had already left for Etheldreda's Shrine.

)))))))(((((((

Of course, my brother and I were far too young fully to understand the complexities of the Great Moot. Only much later, as with so many other things, did we begin to appreciate that the decisions made that day would echo down through the decades and resonate in so many far-off times and places. We were keen, though, to attend the Moot, as it would be our first opportunity see Edgar in his majesty, as King of All Bryttania, wielding his influence and authority, not as the young man we had come to know and love as a friend. This was very different. In the past, we had often witnessed our uncle at the head of the Shire Court in Eastseaxe, sitting alongside the Bishop, and with the attendance of the Shire Reeve. It was a twice-yearly event and, to our eyes, always very grand, but this Moot was on an altogether different scale.

We broke our fast sitting on the ground outside our tent. The previous night's trenchers had been warmed over by the watch fires and were quite soft, and we had loaded them with scraps of left-over lamb and anything else that we could find in the communal kitchen tent. As we ate, we watched the new arrivals as they came into the encampment. The first to arrive, as we learned later, was the Shire Reeve of Grantabrycgscir. Oswig's nephew, Ethelmaer, had arrived in the early hours of the morning, with his father, Elric, and he now jogged over to join us. We had met him several times before when he came with the family to visit Radendunam. About a year older than us, he had proved to be a good playmate and had entered into our games with enthusiasm. We were both pleased to see him.

He pushed back his mop of fair hair, blue eyes sparking. "That's Wolstan," he said, pointing at the Shire Reeve. "He thinks quite a lot of himself." The Reeve was a heavy-set man, well dressed in a knee-length dark blue tunic, edged with embroidery, and a long dark cloak, thrown back on one side and held in place with large, round brooch. He was bareheaded, and his hair thinning, fair, through grizzled with silver.

"And who is that with him?" I asked.

"His younger son, Leofwine. He keeps him close to his side, I can tell you! Once, at the Hundred Court at Ditone, Leo and I sneaked off together to go fishing in the river. Along the way, we met up with my youngest uncle, Uvi. We spend a pleasant day on the river – caught enough loaches for a fine dinner that night – but when we came back, Lord, what a to-do! I was beaten, first of all, for suggesting the outing, and then Uvi was grilled as if there were no tomorrow – where had we been, what had we done? Then Leo was told never to go off with older men again – older men, poor Uncle Uvi had no more than sixteen years himself! and wrapped so fast in his father's arms that I thought he would suffocate. It was all very odd, I can tell you!" Leo looked to be about ten years of age, slight for his years and rather pale."

"Humph," said Wulf, his mouth full of lamb. "If that's the way fathers behave, I am glad that mine has been nowhere to be seen for so long." It was all bravado. I know that Wulf would have dearly loved to have a father so concerned.

"Well, I never got to spend time with him again, anyhow," said Ethelmaer.

The barges must have been making good coin again that day, and old Gorth exhausting his limited greeting speeches, as more and more newcomers began to arrive. I was delighted to see, at the head of the newly arrive party, Ealdorman Ethelwold, my ardent, though aged (or so it seemed to me), suitor from last year's gathering at Radendunam. He still cut a fine figure.

I jumped up and ran to him as he dismounted.

"Uncle Ethelwold, it is so good to see you. You do remember me, don't you?"

"Little Aetna," he beamed, and swung me up onto his shoulders. "And have you yet given your heart away to some other likely young man?"

"No, my Lord."

"That is well, then. For you are as yet far too young and too pretty to have been claimed!" He looked at Wulf. "And how do you fare, young man?"

"Well, my Lord, thank you." Wulf made a bow.

"And who is this fine fellow?" he asked, indicating Ethelmaer. Wulf made the introductions.

"I know your father well, lad," said the Ealdorman, and then squinting at me, through the sun, said, "Aetna, I do believe that you have been untrue to me. Surely this is your new swain."

I giggled. "No, indeed, my Lord, for Ethelmaer is already promised to the Church."

"Worse luck," said Ethelmaer.

From my point of view the conversation might have got even more interesting at that point, but Ethelwold began coughing. It was the same, deep, chesty cough that I remembered from last year, but worse. He put me down.

When he had got his breath back, he said, "Now, where you two are to be found, Dagmaer cannot be far away… I must find her and see if she has any of her throat tonic with her. I swear that I have not had a night's sleep since I ran out of the supply she gave me last year."

"She may be in our tent," I said. "But if not, she will not be far away."

"Thank you, my sweetling," he said.

He strode away. His two companion-men took his and their horses to the tented livery at the outer edge of the encampment, and we, having finished our breakfast, went to watch the preparations for the Moot.

Beneath the great awning, arrangements had been changed yet again. Now, a long, raised dais ran across the end of the open space. Placed centrally on it was a large, imposing chair, draped in a splendid red silk covering. Woven with a design of seated kings, the throw was edged with rich embroidery in multicoloured silk and gold thread, intertwining beasts and geometric patterns glittering where the sun caught the swirl of stitches. On either side of the throne (for such it certainly was) two slightly smaller chairs were adorned with less splendid, but still beautiful, covers. Five seats, but only one with the aura of true power.

The rough benches which had, the previous evening, ranged beside the long table, were now set across the space, facing the dais and behind them was standing space only for the rest of the spectators.

"We will never get a good view if we have to stand back there, and it is going to be a long postnoon," said Ethelmaer. "Come on, I know this isle better than most… and how to make us a comfortable place."

He led the way out of the assembly hall toward the water and the eel-peoples' huts.

"Gorthson, Gorthson," he called. Several faces, of various ages, appeared at barn doors and at the huts at the edge of the water. It seemed there was a Gorthson for every generation. Ethelmaer jogged over to the youngest.

Ethelmaer embraced him. "Gorthson, my good friend, can we borrow some bundles of reeds?"

"Aye, my Lord, that you can. Of reeds we have plenty! But why do you need them?"

"Must you work today, or can you come to watch the Moot with us?" asked Ethelmaer. "We have need of seats and back rests, for it promises to be a long day."

"As to whether I can come with you, I must ask," said Gorthson. Raising his voice, he called "Great grand-sire, may I go with the young Lord to the Moot?"

From the waterside, an old, cracked voice replied. "Aye, son, go along, for I ween that there will be little work to be done today other than to ferry folk back and forth and your wits are sharper than mine to tell what wyrd will befall after the Moot."

"Thank you, old father," called Gorthson.

Ethelmaer also called back. "I thank you, too, Gorth. I am, as ever, in your debt."

Between the four of us, we managed to pull, roll and carry eight bundles of reeds up to the tented Moot hall. We did not want to be too obvious in our intrusion, and so piled them against one of the weighty, load bearing poles a little way down, roughly opposite the second row of benches, two to sit on, and several behind us, so that we were effectively hidden from those outside the hall. Those with business at the Moot would occupy the front row – less important spectators the row behind, so we felt confident that we would not be ejected. Indeed, we were not the only people to be staking their claim to makeshift vantage points. Several of the lesser thegns and coerls, rather than occupy the standing room, had brought packing cases and trunks from the carts and wagons to allow them a certain ease in which to watch the proceedings.

"Now, we shall have a ringside view," said Ethelmaer.

"Almost as good as if we were in the arena at Colencaestre," added Wulf.

"What did you mean, about being in Gorth's debt?" I asked Ethelmaer.

"Oh, nothing, really. It is just that sometimes I like to come here to get away from Father and his plans for me. He would have me forever studying before my entry into the Church next year. My time before that is short, so I don't want to waste it mithering away at books and such. Sometimes I come here. To be alone. To watch the birds and follow the butterflies and, oh, I don't know, just to be free. Old Gorth is a good friend. He keeps his –and my – counsel."

"Do you have a boat, then?" I asked, intrigued.

"No."

"So, how do you get here?"

"One day, I may show you," he said, and winked.

Just then, a commotion erupted outside, behind our reed couch. It was past late morning – with the Moot due to begin at midday – and more people were already beginning to assemble. Leoflada, Oswig and his brother Elric, Ethelmaer's father, had taken their seats at the end of the bench nearest us – a mixed blessing, I thought, hoping that Leoflada would make no comment at our presence – and many of the lesser thegns were already taking their places at the back of the assembly.

The voice of Shire Reeve Wolstan could be heard; aggressive, shouting. "Stay away from him, Leo! I have told you before, your brother is dead to us!"

"But, Father," a young voice replied, in a low tone.

"Away, I said!"

Then another voice: unfamiliar, but clearly upset. "Sir, you are still my father, and, though you may be loathed to acknowledge me, I am proud to be your son."

There was no reply, only an angry stamping of feet as the owner of the deeper voice, departed, clearly dragging away the youngest of the group.

Another voice joined the furore. "Sigewold, leave it. There is time enough for this later." This last voice was deep and possessed of an accent which proclaimed it from the Danelaw, and so, probably, a Northman.

"It is so unfair, Thurstan," said the other. "Not to let me see my own brother."

"It is as it is," replied Thurstan. "You will never change how your father feels. His anger is too deep."

They walked around the outside of the Moot, and now entered under the awning at the far side from us, taking their places on the front bench, as participants in the proceedings to come. From our side, Wolstan and Leo came in and, leaving as much space as possible between the two parties, took their seats also on the front bench, Wolstan on the outside, quite close to us, and immediately in front of Oswig. The likeness between Leo and his brother, Sigewold, sitting at the farthest extremity of the bench, was quite striking. An older, more mature, version of the lad, he, too, was pale and shared their father's fair hair. But where Leo looked pallid and slightly unwell, Sigewold appeared smooth-skinned and pink-cheeked. His dress was quite the height of fashion, with bright red hose, cross gartered to the knee, slim fitting, black leather shoes, matching short tunic and cloak in green, edged with silver. Beside him, Thurstan sat very upright, dressed almost entirely in brown leather – jerkin, trews and boots. He was, as we had deduced from his voice, a much older man, maybe in his fourth decade, with dark hair and his moustache worn long in the rather old-fashioned style – to our eyes – of the Northmen.

There was, now, as we had anticipated, standing room only in the Moot, as all the benches were full. Ealdorman and members of the Witan from the King's Progress, lesser thegns and freeman – all part of the company that had made up our party on the long journey – had been joined by companion-men who had travelled with Ethelwold, Wolstan and the latest arrival, Alfhere, the Chief Ealdorman, who now strode in, and took his place in one of the chairs immediately beside the throne. He was closely followed by Archbishop Dunstan, who took the seat at the other side of the throne, but not before clasping Alfhere, forearm to forearm, in greeting.

"You are well come, Lord Alfhere," he said.

"I make apology for my lateness," replied Alfhere. "The journey from Mercia was tedious and beset by minor delays. I feared that I might miss this Moot altogether – though I was anxious to be at Uphude in time for the meeting of the Witan."

"No matter, you are here now."

Chief Ealdorman Alfhere of Mercia: we had heard his name often, but he had never visited us at Radendunam. It was only a few short generations ago that Mercia was another kingdom altogether, finally united with Eastseaxe and the other petty kingdoms by the Great King Alfred. There was still often tension between the shires and a jostling for position on the Witan by their Ealdormen, and although both Alfhere and Brithnoth could trace their fore-fathers back to the old royal house of Mercia there was now little love between the two. We had to admit that there was some family resemblance: Brithnoth and Alfhere shared the same Saxon colouring, the same athletic build and a certain squareness of the jaw, but the Mercian ealdorman lacked our uncle's height and easy, relaxed manner. A scar ran to one side of his right eye, long healed but angry looking, slightly puckering the corner of his eyelid, which made him look as though he were always searching intensely for someone or something. He did not look as though he smiled often.

Brithnoth and Ethelwold entered with Aelflaed between them, on her husband's arm. Our uncle escorted her to a seat between Leoflada and Ethelmaer's father, and then he and Ethelwold took their seats, on either side of Dunstan and Alfhere. Brief greetings were exchanged. The last of the seats were filled and the crowd at the back of the assembly was packed and jostling. A scribe came in, carrying a portable desk, which he set up at the far end of the long table, piling parchments upon it. A thrall brought him a stool and he sat. Everything seemed to be ready.

At some unseen signal, a horn sounded outside, one long blast, followed by three short and another long. Edgar entered the Moot. I caught my breath and Wulf clasped my hand. Could this really be the young man with whom we had shared stories and broken our fast so informally just a few short days ago? His companion-men had out stripped themselves in their transformation. Now we could see why his dress at the Saham feast was to be considered informal.

The King's tunic was of fine, smooth linen, cream coloured and shot through with a gold thread, which made the fabric ripple and shine in the sunlight flooding the end of the tent. His hose were of the same linen, but without the added gold, and his shoes of soft black leather, which extended to form long thongs cross gartering his legs to the knee. A purple cloak was thrown back over his shoulders and held in place at his throat by a jewelled clasp. Lined in black silk, the hems were embroidered with deep cuffs of coloured silk and more gold thread. A pearl and enamel brooch shone on his breast and was echoed by more of the same on the deep gold circlet which held his hair straight and brushed down over his ears.

Those standing bowed or curtsied. Those sitting, stood and did likewise. Edgar stepped up onto the dais and took the throne. The herald had followed him into the assembly, and with his horn now at his hip, raised his voice.

"Let all those with Petition to the King be forthcoming. You will be heard. The King's justice be done!"

Edgar smiled pleasantly. "Be at your ease, my good people," he said. He paused and looked around the assembly. As those with seats re-took them, his shrewd eyes rested upon the occupants of the front bench, appraising, summing them up in his mind. "Scribe, you have Petition in the matter of the land and appurtenances of this Island of Elig. Read it out."

The scribe made a great show of selecting the correct parchments from the collection on his desk – this was his moment – and then proceeded to declaim a lengthy description of the isle, detailing hideages and waterfront, the number of men of working age and their status. I thought briefly of the various Gorths, but my attention was waning as the diatribe went on and I was more intent on counting the pearls in the King's circlet. Eventually, the sonorous voice of the scribe paused, and he brought the Petition to its conclusion.

"All this land, the rights and appurtenances thereto and thereon, the service of the men both free and thrall, to be, upon Petition, ceded in tenancy, upon fair recompense to the King, to Thurstan, known as the Dane, of Lincylene and his heir Sigewold, lately of Grantabrycgscir."

With an air of satisfaction, the scribe took a deep breath, placed the document to one side and took up his pen in readiness to transcribe the outcome of the Petition.

Edgar spoke. "And Thurstan is present?"

Thurstan stood. "I am, sire."

"This is a correct record of your Petition? It covers the whole of your intention?"

"It does, sire though it does not speak in detail of our plans for the development of the isle's resources which I believe will make a good and profitable living for myself and my lad, and duly enrich the coffers of Your Majesty's tax revenue."

Sigewold shifted in is seat and tried to look across at his father, who deliberately looked away, although we could see that he was shaking with anger – what had been said that was so enraging? His fists were balled into the fabric of his cloak.

"I see," said Edgar. "And this Petition has been submitted several times, in the correct manner, to the Shire Court where it has, in my name, been repeatedly denied."

"Yes, sire," replied Thurstan. "Most unfairly."

"I did not ask for an opinion, sir, merely for the facts," said Edgar.

"Sire."

The King turned to Wolstan. "We have met before, Shire Reeve, and you have served me well. I have never had cause to question your judgement in the matter of my affairs. You have always spoken and acted wisely. Why has this Petition not been granted, or otherwise referred to a Higher Court?"

Wolstan rose to his feet, his fists still clenched. Making a visible effort to regain his composure, he said "Sire, I thank you for your confidence in my abilities." He seemed a little surer of his emotions, now that he was able to speak.

"The Petition has been rejected, sire, and unconsidered," he began, "because of the... the inaccuracies, the... illegalities, the misidentification, of the parties concerned. Inaccuracies which the Petitioner refuses to change. By implication these... inaccuracies... impugn the honour..." The Reeve reigned himself in and tried to resume the calm logic with which he had begun. "Sire, this Petition cannot be sanctioned with these irregularities – these unnatural irregularities – composite in its wording." His voice began to rise again. "Sire, you have a son..."

My attention was now refocussed on the Moot; I could not understand many of the words, or their implications, but I could feel the tension rising.

"What's it all about?" I asked, but the boys did not seem able to understand either.

"He's working himself up into the same state as when Leo and I bunked off with Uncle Uvi!" said Ethelmaer.

The scribe looked perplexed and, raising his hand deferentially, turned to the King. Edgar nodded. "If I may, sire, might I ask what inaccuracies exactly the Sherriff cites? The wording of the Petition is, as far as I can see, quite in order."

"Enlighten us, Wolstan," said Edgar. "This matter has taken up a great deal of time and administrative effort on the part of my scribes already. It cannot be allowed to drag on *ad infinitum* because of some technicality in the documentation! Come, man, there is more to it than this. Explain yourself."

Wolstan appeared to find it hard to continue. He seemed to cast about for the right words, and it was clear that he had hoped that his earlier explanation had been sufficient.

"Sire, I had hoped not to speak further. It is true that the feelings of a father cannot be salved by the application of the law, but his rights may be. This man," he gestured at Thurstan and almost spat out the word. "This *man*, has alienated my son, Sigewold, from me, from his family, styles himself my son's 'protector' (though from what, I have no idea) and calls him his 'heir' although there has been no legal deed of adoption or fostering. Nor is there likely to be. Sire, my boy is sixteen. Yes, perhaps that is entering manhood, but he is still so easily led, so under the thrall... it is impossible for me to see him, to speak with him..."

"That is not so!" Sigewold jumped to his feet, furious. "You refuse to see me, that is the truth of the matter!"

"I will not see you in the presence of that man!" Wolstan was now shouting, too. "And you seem unable to be parted from him for long enough to..."

"Long enough for what? To try to explain to you and Mother my plans, my hopes, my dreams? My feelings for... Without you raising your fist or her crying? Thurstan wants to create something for the two of us here, so you need not worry about leaving anything to me… leave it all to Leo, he will marry and produce heirs. Thurstan has money enough for the both of us, I want none of yours. Just leave me be to live my life…"

The King brought his fist down hard on the long table. "Enough!" he shouted. "Enough!"

I heard Leoflada whisper to Oswig, "I don't understand, what does he mean…"

"Has Father Aelmer taught you much of the Classics?" he whispered back.

"Some," she replied. "Why?"

"It seems that Thurstan and Sigewold's partnership owes something to the Greek style," said Oswig, quietly. Leoflada still looked mystified.

There was a general murmuring from the crowd.

Thurstan pulled Sigewold back and pushed him onto his seat, his hand remaining on the boy's shoulder. "Don't, Sigewold, don't!"

"Sire…" called Wolstan. "I…"

"Your Majesty…"

At a nod from Edgar, the herald blew several short, sharp blasts on the horn. The tumult died down and Edgar waited until complete silence had fallen before he spoke. Then he looked at the scribe. "Let me see that Petition." The scribe had long since given up the unequal task of trying to record the proceedings and was relieved to have something useful to do. He brought the parchment to Edgar and with a slight bow retreated to his desk.

The King scanned it briefly. "I was not entirely uninformed of this matter before these proceedings," he said, still looking at the Petition. "Tongues wag, gossip is not confined to washer-women and grooms-men. Sadly, the Courts abound with it." He glanced at Dunstan. "But we must look at the word of the Law. I can see no legal prohibition to styling one man another's 'heir', with or without the permission of his true father. However, I can understand any father's reluctance to sanction plans which remove and alienate a young son from his father's house, affections and duty. But, I fear, there is no recourse to law here. If the nature of the relationship between these two men is – unusual – that is as it is. The Great King Alfred made no law on the subject." He turned to Wolstan. "If there is remonstration to be made then it is a matter for the Church. Not for you."

"On those grounds, then, I therefore make judgement that the refusal of this Petition has been illegal." He sat back in his chair, allowing the implications of his decision to be understood by the parties.

Thurstan and Sigewold looked delighted. Wolstan was stunned.

"However," Edgar tossed the Petition onto the table, "I do not sanction this proposal. Thurstan of Lincylene, you are a Dane. Since the time of

King Alfred, the Danelaw has thrived alongside our own Kingdom. In later years, we have come together to form a great whole. The sum of our parts is Englaland. But I cannot forget that it was the Northmen who, some three hundred years ago, came to this place with hate in their hearts and blood on their swords and, on this very isle, killed godly men and women whose lives were dedicated to the service of a saint. Their bodies were crushed into this soil, their blood flowed in the fen waters, their homes were levelled and the shrine of the holy Saint Etheldreda desecrated. This very morning, I saw what remains of Etheldreda's Shrine, tended for generations by the women of one family – one family, whose rights would have been overturned in a single blow by this… Petition. They have maintained the shrine, living off only what Elig has given them, freely of its own will: eels and reeds. There was no mention of them in this document. It was not fully comprehensive. Therefore, I say again, it is not sanctioned.

"To cede this island to a Dane, whose fathers took so many lives, would be to compound the martyrdom – for such it was – of those monks and nuns who died here. There is much to be done to right this wrong."

He turned to Dunstan. "Archbishop, this land forms part of the See of Dorecaestre, does it not? Under Bishop Oscytel, lately made your fellow Archbishop – of Eoforwic?"

"It does, my King."

"I shall be having words with him… it seems his elevation has allowed his attention to waver from local matters. However, I decree that this land, with all its rights and appurtenances be made over to the Church. The shrine of the Holy Saint Etheldreda shall be rebuilt and rededicated. A new monastic house shall be raised up here at Elig." He looked over the heads of those seated toward the masses at the rear of the assembly. "And I do not forget those who have remained true to the Holy Saint. Is Mother Gorthwyrd present?"

There was a general craning of heads and looking backward among the crowd, for indeed, Gorthwyrd was present, but at the very back of the Moot, hardly even under the awning. Around her were many of the eel-people, Gorth included.

"Aye, sire," he called, "Mother is here!"

"Let her come forward."

Old Gorthwyrd looked as dishevelled as ever, and her son not a great deal better. With his hand under her elbow, he eased her through the crowd, until they reached the benches, and then down the side of the assembly. They walked right past us, on our makeshift seats. Gorth grinned his toothy grin, and his mother raised her hand, almost as if in blessing. She smiled at me. "Sweet girl," she said. "You see what happens if you have faith."

They came before the long table, and the King stood.

"Gorthwyrd, you and your people have preserved all you could of the sanctity of this place. All Christian folk are in your debt, for who knows when and where a Saint may choose to bestow her blessing. You will not be forgotten when this place becomes, once again, a place of pilgrimage and wealth. Yes, wealth, for where the Church comes, mammon is never far behind." He glanced at Dunstan, who declined to react. "You, Gorthwyrd, shall always have a place at the hostelry of the abbey, and so, too will every member of your family when they become infirm. And in their vigour, they shall have the right to fish and cut reeds throughout the isle, as they ever have, but with payment to no man. I have spoken."

"Your Majesty, we are your servants," said Gorth, head bowed. "May you live long in God's grace."

"A fine young man, fair of face and deed," said Gorthwyrd, seemingly to herself. Then she turned and looked at Wulf. "You were right," she said.

They crossed the floor to the far side of the tent, where, outside the assembly, a considerable number of Gorthsons had gathered, with wives and children, all chattering and patting each other on the back. Our companion bade us fare well and went to join his family.

"They will have a fine old time of it, tonight!" said Ethelmaer. "I am pleased for them." He looked at those still in their places on the front bench. "Though there are not many others here who are pleased with the day's proceedings!"

Edgar was once again seated, and the herald blew a single blast on the horn to call the Moot back to order. "If there any more Petitions or charges to be brought before the King, you are to declare them now." There were none. For a moment, Wolstan looked as though he was going to rise to his feet, but then he slumped back onto the bench.

Brithnoth spoke. "By your leave, sire, I would that the Sherriff remains behind after the Moot. There are some Shire matters to do with my estates that I need to discuss with him."

"So be it," said Edgar. There was a final fanfare from the herald and, the people rising to their feet in respect, the King left the tent, followed by Dunstan, Ethelwold and Alfhere.

People began to make their way out of the assembly, those at the back melting away in small groups, and those from the benches filing out singly. The far side of the tent was blocked by the still celebrating Gorths, and so the only way to exit the benches was on our side. We stayed seated as everyone passed, not wanting to get in the way. Wolstan was still in his place as Thurstan and Sigewold approached to file past him.

"*Nithing*. Sodomite," said Wolstan, quietly, but clearly.

Thurstan ignored him, but Sigewold, spun around. "You vile old man! Can you not leave us be? I have tried to build bridges between us, but you will have none of it. Well, now you will have none of me. If Lincylene is not far away enough to keep your influence at bay I shall go further, but rest assured you will not see me again!"

Wolstan came to his feet, and gripped Sigewold by the wrist. "Son, it is not you I want none of... it is... do not make me say it. Come home with me now..."

"Let go of me, Father, you are hurting me."

"You are just sixteen, boy, do not think that you are too old for me to lift my fist to you! Perhaps I should, and then drag you back to morality unconscious."

Thurstan stepped between them, and wrenched Wolstan's hand off Sigewold's wrist, pushing him to one side. "Do not touch him. He is right, you are a vile old man, and there is nothing you can do..."

Then everything became horribly confused. There was a flash of steel in Wolstan's right hand as he brought a blade out from under his cloak and stabbed it upward toward Thurstan. Sigewold grabbed his father's wrist and pulled it away, the blade's trajectory going wildly askew. For a moment they grappled, and then the dagger was somehow, appallingly, buried deeply in Sigewold's belly. His eyes widened in shock, his jaw clamped into a terrible rictus, a trickle of blood escaping its corner and his knees buckled. He sank to the ground, his hand still holding his father's wrist, his face buried in the older man's cloak and then, releasing his grip, rolled to one side.

Thurstan was on his knees beside him in seconds, calling his name, cradling his head, but it seemed clear that the boy was lifeless. Brithnoth leapt down from the dais.

Leo screamed and jumped up, running to the side of his brother, kneeling, blood soaking into his hose. Wolstan stood transfixed. The tumult had drawn others to the scene.

"What's happened?"

"Is he dead?"

"Who is it?"

The noise brought the King back. He strode in, his companion-men behind him.

"In the name of God, what is happening here? Brit, what is going on?"

"Sire, I fear there has been a terrible accident," said Brithnoth. Wolstan bent down to touch his elder son's face, stroking his cheek, as if the boy slept. Thurstan drew a knife and lunged at the Sherriff.

"Don't touch him! Murderer! You will pay for this!"

Edgar's companion-men flew at Thurstan, caught him, wrenched the blade free and pinioned his arms. He struggled briefly and then seemed to realise the futility of his action. He sagged against the men. "Murderer!" he said again.

The Sherriff seemed to regain something of his composure. "His body is mine," said Wolstan. "Sire, this was indeed an accident! How could I intend to take the life of my own son? This, this... man... had taken him from me. I was trying to defend what was rightfully mine..."

Leo was in tears, but looked at his father, and then at the King. "Sire, he didn't mean to do it. I know he didn't!"

"This is a poor day's work, indeed," said Edgar. "It was clearly unintended, but there will be a mighty weregild to pay. My scribe will advise you of the sum. This matter has been ill-omened from the start. Take your boy home and bury him with more dignity than he has had in death."

"Sire!" Thurstan was desperate. "He cannot be allowed to take him. He is the boy's murderer! It is I that Sigewold had chosen!"

"Thurstan, you are in no position to interfere," said Brithnoth. "You drew a blade in the King's presence. The penalty for that is death, if it is the King's wish."

"He had drawn, too," shouted the Northman, indicating Wolstan. "What about him?"

"He was not in the King's presence when he did so."

"There has been enough death today," said Edgar. "The law allows for an alternative, and so it shall be. Thurstan, you are banished from this realm. If you are found on these shores after two sunsets, your life will be forfeit. Go."

Thurstan shook himself free of the men holding him. He backed away, putting distance between himself and the others, ready to turn and run.

"I shall, and gladly, be away from this stinking, water-filled bog. But I tell you this, I shall not rest until I find a way to repay this day's doings. By the gods of the North I swear it. When the sun rose this morning, I had a life, a companion, hopes and plans. Now I have nothing. There will come a day, I know not how distant, when the name of Thurstan will be heard again on this Isle, and chaos will follow in its wake."

With one last look at Sigewold's poor, twisted body, he turned and ran toward the livery.

"Let him be," said Edgar. "I allow him his horse; he will be away from here all the faster."

Throughout this terrible time, I had been holding hard onto Wulf, and he, trying to shield me from the worst of it, had pushed me behind him. It had all happened so quickly, there had been no time to get out of the way. He was as pale and shocked as me. We had never seen blood spilt in anger and violence before. Ethelmaer was still on the other side of me.

"You should get your sister out of here," he said to Wulf. "And I must get back to my father. I will see you at Uphude." He ran off.

Wulf and I stumbled out of the assembly and ran back to our tent. Leoflada had just heard what had happened and was telling Aelflaed. They had both left before the tragedy occurred.

"Where have you two been?"

Something made us not want to admit to having seen what happened – we did not want to talk about it. Later, later, we would discuss it between ourselves and try to understand. Thurstan's threats were still ringing in our ears and we wanted to forget them.

"Nowhere…"

"…Aunt," was our reply.

The postnoon had turned sour and we were pleased to find the dogs curled up on our pallets, ready to wake up and play. We called them out and trotted off to find an out of the way spot.

"The evening meal will be ready, soon," called Leoflada. "Don't go too far."

But for once even Wulf did not have much of an appetite.

NINE

WULFMAER

Neither my sister nor I slept well, that second night at Elig. Memories of the day played around and around in our minds, the good fortune of the Gorths somehow confused with the death of Sigewold and Thurstan's threats.

When dawn came, we were pleased to be up and active early, watching the encampment dismantled and stowed away, as efficiently as it had been erected. The return trip across the water to the Saham side of the great fen was uneventful, and when the carts were all re-loaded, we were both pleased to take our places beside Leoflada in the wardrobe wagon and jog along in silence, each of us wrapped in our own thoughts.

We headed back toward Fordeham, through which we had travelled on our outward journey, and then turned west, skirting the edge of the fens, keeping to higher ground, but always with a view of the waters to our right. Aetna and I dozed for a couple of hours, and when we awoke, the sun was shining and a warm breeze from the seaward had blown away any traces of mist. The waters and tiny islets glinted blue and green, and the land to our left was well tended, crops looked as though they had not been a complete disaster, despite the year's poor weather, animals grazed and the trees were turning from their summer shades to autumn golds, brown and yellows. We had swung slightly inland, and there were also a few trees between us and the water.

Oswig cantered his horse up to our wagon and reined in.

"Look over there," he said indicating the landward side of the road. "The Devil's Ditch."

Crossing the landscape as far as we could see inland, and approaching the track along which we were travelling, a huge hump-backed bank cut a swathe through the countryside, falling away to a deep ditch alongside. Scrubby trees grew along its top in places and down its sides, which were also thick with brambles.

"What is it?" I said.

"Did the Devil really make it?" asked Aetna, dubiously.

"No, indeed he did not," said Oswig. It was quite funny to see Flada's rapped attention as he spoke, but we, too, were now curious about this strange earthwork. "It was built by our own people many centuries ago, before there was one king over the whole of Englaland, when East Anglia was at war with Mercia. But since then it has acted as a defence against those who would steal a single hide of Englaland. The King's grandfather,

Edward, held it against the Northmen and drove far into the Daneland with it at his back."

We were reminded, briefly, of Thurstan and his threats, but the thought passed.

"How shall we get past it?" I asked, for it looked as though it would cut off our path. We were now approaching the great ditch but as we got closer, we could see that it was not as deep as we had thought. Silt and soil had accumulated at the base of the rampart, and had begun to drift, like snow, up its side, making it less steep.

"Run up it and look ahead," said Oswig. The trees to our right had become more densely spaced, and we could no longer see the water of the fens. Aetna and I jumped down from the wagon, ran ahead and clambered up the incline. As we reached it, we realised that the track turned sharply to the right and began to run alongside the ditch, with the woods crowding in closely on the other side.

I was a little ahead of Aetna, and as I reached the summit, turned to help her up the last few steps. We continued to hold hands as we stood on the top of the bank, feeling like king and queen of a flat world, which seemed to stretched away in all directions.

"Ha!" I laughed. "This is more like it! The Sigi twins could have some real adventures here!" I broke a branch from one of the wind-blasted trees, and another for Aetna, so that we could have a sword fight.

"Be careful!" we heard Leoflada shout, and we realised that the convoy had turned north, following the track away from us. "Don't fall and don't get left too far behind!"

"She doesn't sound too worried, I must say," said Aetna. "Almost as though she is glad to be rid of us." From our vantage point, we could see Oswig pointing out various things along the way, leaning in toward her, and answering her questions.

We followed along the top of the bank, skirting the occasional tree, throwing stones down into the ditch, the dogs running at our side, delighted to be free of the confines of the journey. Ahead of us, and just to the far side of the bank, a small village nestled in its lee. The top of the bank gradually fell lower and lower, until it reached ground level. The carts had encountered some small hold-up, and we had now overtaken them. They rounded the end of the bank, following the track. Just as we reached its bottom, Oswig called out.

"Hey, you two! How many Vikings have you slain? Welcome to Reche – it is as far as the Devil's Ditch can reach! That's how it got its name, from here the waters of the fens protect us." Oswig had taken advantage of our absence from the wagon to climb up beside Flada, his horse loosely tied to the wagon, and trotting happily alongside. They were holding hands – again – and Flada's head was on his shoulder. The driver wore a resigned air.

"My Hall at Stecworthe is at the other end of the Ditch," Oswig said to Flada. "If you were to walk all along it the way the twins just came, you would arrive at what will be our home, my love, when you are my wife!"

We stopped at Reche to rest and water the animals and to eat our midday meal. It seemed like a prosperous little village. At its centre was a tavern which, Oswig informed anyone interested, served a good strong ale and fine small ale.

Brithnoth had dismounted and was helping our Aunt out of her litter. "Now that sounds like a good idea," he said. "Riding beside all this water for so long has given me a fine thirst for something a little more invigorating!"

Oswig went into the tavern to arrange for ale to be brought out. Dunstan and the King joined our group. Edgar was once again the young man who had entertained us with tales and good humour on the earlier leg of our journey. He sat on the ground, with his back against a tree. One of the thralls brought us all bread, cheese and apples. "A banquet," he said, "and to wash it down... ah, here it is!" The landlord came out bearing wooden trays of flagons brimming with ale, followed by two serving girls with more of the same. They moved among the men, flirting, giggling and pretending offence when slapped on the behind. A very small girl, no more than three years old came toward Edgar, urged on by her mother, with a posy of flowers.

"Your Majesty," she said with a slight lisp.

"When the Lord Oswig told us you were here, sire," said her mother, "my Elspeth said she must bring you these."

"Thank you, Elspeth," said Edgar, seriously. "You are most kind." He tucked the flowers into his tunic and then swung the little girl onto his knee. "And have you ever met a king before, my little princess?"

Elspeth was overcome with shyness and could not reply, merely smiling up at Edgar. "She is a sweet child," he said. "Perhaps this time next year I shall have a little princess, to be a playmate to my Edward and to bring me flowers every day." He lifted her up into the air and she laughed, and then he gently set her down. "It is for the sake of these little ones that we must keep the peace. I thank God that the Danelaw is become part of our kingdom and no longer the threat that made this great Ditch so necessary."

"Sire, you speak the truth," said Dunstan. "A kingdom at peace with others is a kingdom in the service of the Lord."

"A kingdom at peace with itself is even more to be desired," added Brithnoth. "Let us hope that the Witan can be in agreement when we meet."

We lost interest in the conversation, and having eaten our meal, washed down with watered small ale – for we were now quite grown, as I pointed out to Dagmaer when she offered us water alone – we amused ourselves throwing sticks for Berrie and Bremel until the call came to get underway again. Aetna and I graciously offered to ride in the body of the wagon, so that Flada and Oswig could continue their sightseeing.

Having navigated our way around the obstacle of the Devil's Ditch, the Progress turned away from the waterside, and took an easier route sweeping south west. Oswig and his brothers owned land and estates throughout this area and it would in time, as he had said, be Leoflada's home, so she was much interested in all that he had to tell her. He had a story about almost every village we passed, some prank he had played as a boy, or some tale he had heard about the people who lived there, making her laugh or gasp, depending on its nature. We enjoyed listening, too, but as the postnoon wore on, we dozed, lulled to sleep by the rocking of the cart and the voices of the adults, for Leoflada was quickly becoming the grown up she had pretended to be for so long.

We came to Wivelingham as the light began to fade and were pleased to be done travelling for the day. Aetna was tired and rather grumpy and it was all I could do to raise a smile from her. We were so alike, and had shared everything for so long I sometimes forgot that girls, even my sister, grew tired of eating and sleeping in different places for days on end.

"Cheer up," I said. "After tonight, when we get to Uphude, Dagmaer will be able to unpack and we can make ourselves at home for a while. Uncle Brithnoth said that after the Witan has met, we shall be staying on for a time with Uncle Ethelwold, and you know how much you like to be with him. You are his favourite!"

Aetna seemed to brighten a little at this, but still pouting and muttering about being tired of wearing her travelling clothes, she clambered out of the wagon with an ill grace. The Hall where we were to stay this night was much smaller than Radendunam, but looked welcoming. The evening was beginning to feel chill, and the warm lights glowing from within were inviting. There was a smell of roasting meat which made my mouth water. Dagmaer came up behind us, as usual bearing the essentials for our overnight stay, and ushered us forward. We followed behind the King and Dunstan, our aunt and uncle, Flada and Oswig. The rest of the party would make themselves as comfortable as possible where they could. They would be welcome, later, to food, and to sleep in the Great Hall by the fire, but the guest chambers were for family only – and kings and archbishops, of course.

Waiting to greet us was a young man who looked very like Oswig, a little younger and not quite as tall, but the family likeness was unmistakable.

"Sire, Archbishop, I am honoured by your footfall. Ealdorman Brithnoth and Lady Aelflaed, you and your family are most welcome in my Hall. I pray you all enter and take rest and food under my roof."

He bowed and Edgar raised him. "Uvi, it is good to see you again. A Hall of your own suits you, the boy has become the man. I am pleased to be here. By the saints, I am tired this day." It seemed that Edgar had not slept well the previous night either.

Edgar's easy manner, as ever, put everything on a relaxed footing. He clapped Uvi on the shoulder and strode past him into the Hall, followed by Dunstan, both making for the fire, where they stood warming their hands and then their backsides. Brithnoth and Aelflaed greeted Uvi warmly and Oswig embraced his brother enthusiastically, allowing him the liberty of kissing his wife-to-be. Flada blushed prettily. We brought up the rear with Dagmaer, as ever, keeping an eye on our manners.

"Leave those dogs outside," she said. We began to argue, but Uvi came to our rescue.

"Oh, let them come," he said, "There's room for all. The lady Aelflaed has her little pup, and my Lord Brithnoth's dogs are already making friends with mine. What are a few further wet paws, more or less?"

"Make your thanks," said Dagmaer.

"Thank..."

"... you," we said.

"We met with your nephew Ethelmaer yesterday," said Aetna. "He told us about you and him and Leo going fishing."

"Oh yes," smiled Uvi – he really was so like Oswig – "Those were the days! Before I had the burden of a Hall and an estate and... all this." He gestured around him, clearly very proud and happy to have such responsibilities, but, like his brother, always ready with a joke. I could see Aetna becoming more cheerful by the moment. This young man was winning her over already.

"Ethelmaer often comes to stay with me," said Uvi. "I shall miss him when he enters the Church. Now, why don't you let Dagmaer take you – yes, and your pups – through to the guest chamber. I must be about my duties as host, but we shall speak more later." He spoke to us as though we older than our years. I liked that and felt myself warming to him, too.

The guest chamber was set up along the usual lines – one pallet for Aetna and myself and another for Leoflada, with a curtain separating off a secluded area for our aunt and uncle. We took off our walking shoes, and put on lighter slippers, wiped a cloth over our hands and faces and were ready for whatever the evening would bring. In fact, it brought little for us, for after a welcome meal, the warmth of the fire and the good-humoured conversation and laughter of the family – Dunstan and Edgar now seemed part of that family – made our eyelids heavy, and despite our earlier naps, we were asleep and carried to our beds without the opportunity to bid the company a good night.

)))))))(((((((

The last leg of our journey to Uphude was uneventful. Uvi did not travel with us, he had no place on the Witan, and Oswig would bring back any news that mattered. It seemed that he was still enjoying the novelty of having his own Hall and estate and for the time being, had no wish to leave it. It was raining and Aetna and I were happy to travel once again in the wardrobe wagon.

"Did you hear what Oswig said to Uvi, just before we left?" I said.

"No." Aetna had been busy at the time chasing Aunt Aelflaed's little lap dog, Honig, which had been reluctant to spend another day in the litter, having enjoyed free run of the Hall for the night. "That little mongrel is a pest."

"He said that their father would have been proud of the way Uvi was running Wivelingham. I wonder if we shall ever meet our father again and if he will be proud of us."

"If you are serving Edgar and I am... well, doing whatever it is I am supposed to do, I am sure he would be proud of us." Then, she added under her voice, "Although I do not know that I shall be proud of him."

"He has his reasons for staying away, we know that now."

"Yes, well..."

The rain seemed set in for the morning, and we played nines (rather poorly, given the jolting of the wagon) and several games with a little travelling chess set that our uncle had given us for our birthday one year. I seemed to have a talent for it – Brithnoth had said it proved that I would be a good strategist, explaining what that meant. Aetna grew tired of it after a while and took to watching the scenery as it disappeared behind us. Somehow the order of the procession had altered slightly, and we were ahead of our aunt's litter. I went to sit beside Aetna, and we sat dangling our legs over the edge of the wagon, exchanging the odd word with the thralls carrying the litter. They seemed in good heart, nearing the completion of their task. When we reached Uphude, their duties would be light until the return trip.

We stopped only briefly to water the animals and take some small refreshment, as the general desire was to reach the end of our journey. The King and Dunstan were deep in discussion at the head of the Progress, and our uncle had come back to ride alongside Aelflaed's litter. She had thrown back the curtains to the side and front, and they were talking in low voices.

"What think you we shall find at Uphude?" said Aelflaed. "I thought Ethelwold seemed just a little stronger and in better health at the Moot. You saw him more than I. Am I right?"

"He has had a difficult year, as have many of us," replied Brithnoth. "The hog-fever took many of his men, and the worry has been draining him, I think. Uvi said that he had seen him at the summer sitting of the Shire Court and he had seemed distracted. He ate little at the Shire-fest, and returned to Uphude before nightfall. He left the Moot at Elig soon after it was closed – and thankfully missed that distressing debacle with Wolstan. I am pleased you did not witness it, my dear."

"Holding the Witan at Uphude is an honour, but a demanding one," said Aelflaed. "I hope it will not be too much for him. However," she added with resigned expression, "I am certain the Elfrith will not be found wanting when it comes to entertaining the King. I hear from Elflada that she has made great plans. I suspect Ethelwold rues the revelation that came about at Radendunam, she will not have given him a moment's reprieve, if I know her. She will have been like a she-terrier at a rat, worrying at that supposed slight. And all because her husband wanted her to wife so much! Most women would have found it a compliment. I wonder what Edgar will make of her – he cannot but know that Ethelwold was less than straight with him on the matter of his possible bride."

"Edgar is content – very content – with his own wife. It is a love match. The only good to come of the whole situation is that we do not have Elfrith as our Queen."

"May the Saints be praised on that score, at least!"

Up ahead a cry went up that Uphude had been sighted. Brithnoth reached into the litter and took Aelflaed's hand. He leant down from the saddle and kissed it.

"My love. I wish that all men might be as lucky as the King and I."

"Go on now," said Aelflaed but she looked pleased. Catching our eye, Brithnoth winked!

"Come on, you two! We are approaching your Uncle Ethelwold's Hall. I think there is room for you both on Fireflax." He swung Aetna off the wagon and onto the saddle before him, and waited for me to clamber off the tailboard and onto Fireflax's chestnut rump. I held him fast round the middle, and he settled Aetna between his arms as he held the reins.

"That is a precious cargo you have on board!" called our aunt. "Look after them!"

We cantered up to join the King at the head of the Progress. Two horsemen approached along the track ahead of us, Ealdorman Ethelwold on a fine, high-stepping grey and his companion-man slightly behind him on a more workmanlike beast.

Ethelwold rode forward to greet Edgar. Bowing in the saddle, he drew his sword with his left hand, and offered it, hilt first to the King.

"My shires and my Ealdormanry are yours, sire. As I am your man."

Edgar touched the sword and waved it back to him. "I thank you, Lord Ethelwold, and I return them to your keeping. There, that's the formalities over! We are weary and pleased to be at the end of our journey. No more ceremony this day, I pray you. I desire a warm tub, if you have one, to wash away the days of travel, a hot fire and pleasant company to set me back to rights. Lead on!" He nudged his horse into step and we trotted toward the slightly raised land ahead, where we could see a palisade, its gate wide open and the smoke from several fires rising into the late postnoon air.

Ethelwold turned to his companion-man. "Manfred, direct the Progress to its various quarters." Manfred trotted his horse to the first of the wagons, where he and our head steward set about organising the arrival and dispersion of the procession. "It is as well that I made good time on my return from the Moot," Ethelwold continued, turning back to us. "There has been much to prepare for the arrival of the Witan. Brit, I see you come with your matching pair of wolf cubs."

Brithnoth was about to reply when Edgar laughed. "They have been most entertaining companions ever since they joined the party," he said.

Aetna giggled – which rather annoyed me – and I said, in my most grown-up voice, "Thank you, sire."

"You will know, now, why I am so smitten with the lady Wulfaetna, sire." Ethelwold managed to keep a straight face as he spoke, though he clearly thought it a great joke.

"Indeed, it is well that we are both happily married," replied Edgar, with a slight edge to his voice. I thought I noticed Ethelwold wince as he realised that he had made an unfortunate *faux pas*.

Brithnoth came to the rescue. "Wulf has been practising his swordsmanship since we saw you last at Radendunam. I am hoping to visit the swordsmith in Rammesig to commission him a blade of his own. Maybe two, one for now and one for when he is grown. And a pretty dagger for Aetna."

"The smith there is, indeed, a fine craftsman," said Ethelwold. "We shall make a day of it and all go together. What do you say, children?"

I was overcome, but Aetna came to the rescue. "Thank you, Uncle," she said. "And thank you, Uncle Ethelwold, for your compliment." It was her turn to sound grown up.

The awkwardness of the moment seemed to pass, and we rode into Uphude's courtyard in high spirits.

Waiting beside the door of the Great Hall was Elfrith. The vanguard, with Ethelwold and the King at its head, followed by Dunstan and

Brithnoth, with us still holding on fast, trotted up to the Hall. Edgar dismounted in this usual fashion, throwing a leg forward over the pommel of his saddle and slipping gracefully to the ground. Ethelwold dismounted rather more stiffly.

"Sire," he said, "may I present my wife, the Lady Elfrith."

Edgar took her hand and briefly brushed it with his lips. "I am grateful, Lady, for your hospitality to me and to the Witan."

"Your Majesty," Elfrith curtseyed low. "Your footfall honours us. I have long wished to meet you, and I shall try to make your stay with us as pleasant as may be. Our Hall and all we have are at your disposal. My Lord Archbishop, Ealdorman Brithnoth." She inclined her head toward her other guests. We were ignored.

The litter approached. Brithnoth lowered Aetna and me to the ground, and dismounted. As the thralls set the litter down, he swept aside the curtain and, giving his hand to our aunt, helped her to step out.

"Lady Aelflaed," said Elfrith.

"Lady Elfrith," came the formal response.

Within the palisade, Uphude was very much like our home at Radendunam. They were arranged slightly differently, but all the buildings we recognised performed the same functions. Beside the Great Hall itself, the kitchen issued forth clatters and bangs, smoke came from its chimney – the new fashion for cooking in use here, too – and delicious smells began to drift across the courtyard. The chapel stood to one side of the enclosure, low stone walls surmounted by a wooden superstructure, and opposite it, the long range of buildings which made up the stables, various workshops and storage rooms. The well stood at the centre of the courtyard, and a steady procession of serving girls were busy transporting buckets of water into the Great Hall. The hot water for the King's bath was being prepared.

The rest of the Progress came to a halt in a great arc around the outside of the yard. Some of the carts were left outside the gate, to await unloading until the royal party and the family had dismounted and withdrawn inside. The wardrobe wagon, though, was brought up close to the entrance of the Hall. Dagmaer was already bustling around supervising the dispersal of its contents to the various guest chambers. The dogs had been sleeping in the wagon, and now woke, enthusiastically exploring their new surroundings. Little Honig joined them, yapping at Aelflaed's heels, and our uncle's hounds padded obediently behind him as we all made our way across the length of the Hall, to the chambers beyond, as at Radendunam, separated from the public area of the Hall by heavy curtaining. Elfrith walked beside the King as she showed him to the largest guest chamber. Edgar had complimented her on the quality of the wall hangings and she was dissembling, prettily. Her expression changed when she turned to see the dogs, scattering the carefully laid rushes across the floor as they scampered. Her lips tightened and she was about to say something when Edgar spoke.

"Now this truly feels like home. Dogs and children, what could be better?"

"Your Majesty," she inclined her head. Just behind her, her most senior waiting woman raised an eyebrow.

"Morwen," said Elfrith, "Make sure that the little ones have everything they need."

Both of Morwen's eyebrows were now raised in a look of surprise. "Of course, my Lady!"

The Hall, we could now see, was larger than at Radendunam, and we found that, for the first time, Leoflada had been accorded a portion of the chamber to herself, partitioned off, which meant that Aetna and I, in turn, had a small enclave of our own.

"And I want no mischief," said Dagmaer, when she discovered this fact. "This new idea of separating people up to sleep is a mixed blessing. I don't know…" Apparently, she, and our aunt's chief maid-servant were to be sharing a bunk in Morwen's space, just behind the withdrawing curtain.

"No Dagmaer…" said Aetna.

"Of course not!" I added.

The novelty of having a space of our own was heightened when we discovered that our chamber was close to one of the side doors which led out of the Hall into the alleyway between it and the kitchen. Having left our few belongings in our chamber, and with no instructions to the contrary, we slipped out and made our way back into the courtyard. Most of the horses were already stabled and being rubbed down, the carts and wagons positioned hard up against the inside of the palisade, to take up as little room as possible. A lad about our own age had been given the task of brushing down the wheels, clearing up the mud and carting it away. He wore the token neck ring of a thrall, but he looked well fed and contented with his lot. He grinned at us.

"The Lady Elfrith cannot abide mud in the courtyard," he said. "Or horse-shit, or chicken shit or dog…"

We said we got the idea and asked him what she could abide. It seemed like a good plan to keep on her right side. The expression on her face when she had first seen the dogs – and us – had made quite an impression, and her change of heart upon Edgar's comment seemed, to us at least, to have looked less than genuine.

The lad (he said his name was Ratkin) appeared to give a good deal of thought to the question. "She likes it when the peddlers come to the village, and when it is market day in Rammesig and the traders bring bolts of cloth and trays of ribbons to the Hall. She likes it when the Chief Ealdorman comes to see Lord Ethelwold and there is feasting, and all the company wear their finest clothes. She likes it when the tumblers come from across the water and speak of the fashions in the Frankish lands – then she and Morwen make over all their gunnas and rails to look different. She seems happiest of all when Lord Ethelwold must go away to oversee Shire Courts or sit on the Witan. Then we hear her singing and laughing with Morwen. Though they always stop talking stop when anyone comes too close. Oh, and she spends hours in the still-room with her wines and potions and herbs. I stay out her way as much as I can … but then, I doubt she would notice me, even if I didn't!"

Clearly, Ratkin had a fine knowledge of what kept his mistress in a fair mood. He was a pleasant looking boy, with a carrot top of red hair, blue eyes and a wide smile, which revealed the loss of a front tooth. We had nothing better to do, and it seemed ill-willed to watch him work while we idled, so I pitched in and scrubbed down the wheels of the wardrobe wagon. Aetna hitched herself up onto the backboard and offered her opinion on our work.

"You've missed a bit," she said, pointing to a large lump of chalky soil hanging from a rear wheel. I knocked it off and added it to the barrow load already collected by Ratkin.

"Is Ratkin your real name?" she asked.

"It's the only name I have," he replied.

"It's a funny name!"

"The Lord Ethelwold gave it to me himself," Ratkin sounded quite proud. "He says he found me and I looked like a little drowned rat!"

Later, we heard the full story. Four years earlier, when Ethelwold had been married to Elfrith for almost two winters, he was returning from Rammesig when he saw what looked like a bundle of rags on the side of the road. It was, indeed, a bundle of rags, but inside the bundle was a child, wet through, emaciated and filthy. The ealdorman had brought him to Uphude, put him in the charge of one of the grooms, whose wife had lost a child during the previous year, and Uphude was the only home Ratkin could remember. He worshipped Ethelwold, was fond of his adoptive parents and turned out to have enough wits about him to be a useful addition to the Hall. He was quite a favourite with Ethelwold and tolerated by Elfrith, who hardly noticed his existence, as he was careful to keep out of her way, which was, he said, the best course of action for children, dogs and anybody else that she had not expressly said she wished to see.

His chores finished, Ratkin dumped the last barrow-load of waste on the midden outside the palisade. The dogs had been nosing about in odd corners and now found an old boot on the midden pile, which they tugged between them, snarling playfully. Ratkin laughed.

"They look like two black bears, squabbling in the pit!" he said.

We were not sure that this was a compliment, but he assured us it was. "Last year, when the travelling performers came to Rammesig, they put two bears in together and threw a dog in, taking bets on which bear would kill it. They were splendid!"

"That's horrible!" said Aetna, her eyes filling with tears. She could never stand to see the cocks fight or even watch when Thoth wrung a chicken's neck.

Ratkin was not used to such sensibilities.

"I'm sorry," he said. "Don't cry! No really, don't! I didn't mean anything by it, it's just talk… I expect the dog was dead already!" He was not making things any better for himself. Aetna looked at him dubiously and sniffed. "Here, let me give you a ride in the barrow," he said and, intending only to manoeuvre the barrow behind her, accidently caught her behind the knees, making her sit down heavily in it. She struggled to her feet, the back of her tunic now filthy with mud. Furiously, she tried to rub it off, making it worse and smearing what was now on her hands onto the front of her dress as well. Trying to regain her dignity, she stamped, her foot sinking into more of the same. Ratkin's horrified expression reflected that he was not looking forward to explaining how he had come to reduce a visiting ealdorman's daughter to tears and then covered her in mud. My sister was lost for words – which was unusual, to say the least. It would not be easy to explain this to Dagmaer, either.

I couldn't help it – I burst out laughing. They both looked at me with something like resignation and then Aetna began to laugh, too. The grin returned to Ratkin's face and he, too, doubled up. We laughed helplessly for several minutes until, holding our sides, we sobered up a little.

"Oh dear," said Aetna, looking down at herself.

"We'll say you tripped and fell into the… the moat," I suggested.

"And you rescued her," added Ratkin.

"But I'm not dirty."

"That can be changed," said Aetna, and a large lump of chalky mud whistled past my ear, missing me by inches.

"Bad shot!" said Ratkin. "The least I can do is even things up a bit..." and he let fly with a handful which landed squarely on my chest.

"Why, you… little rat!" I retaliated with several handfuls of my own and soon all three of us were slinging mud and very possibly several other unpleasant substances back and forth and laughing again, joyful in our abandonment to dirt, whatever the consequences might be.

A little while later, having bid our new friend fare well, and promised to meet him again on the morrow when he had finished his duties, we tried to slip back into our chamber without being seen. We had knocked the worst clumps of mud off, and turned our tunics inside out so that the stains were not so evident, planning to hide them until later – much later – when we could claim that we had no idea how they had got so dirty. We had managed to cross the courtyard and slip between the kitchen and the Hall without being seen and were about to make a final dash for the blessed privacy of our chamber when, of all people, Archbishop Dunstan stood in our way.

"Well, now," he said, "What have we here?"

We were well aware that we were in no condition to be seen, despite our best attempts to conceal the worst of our dishevelment.

"Oh, um, well…" I began.

"I, I mean we, fell…" continued Aetna.

"Into the, well… well, not the well, the moat. Aetna tripped and I…"

"… and he…"

"He pelted you and with mud, and you threw it back, by the looks of it," said Dunstan, his eyes twinkling. "And what is Dagmaer going to make of this, I wonder."

"Well, we were rather hoping…"

"… we could…"

"Do you have water in your chamber?" asked Dunstan.

"I don't think so," I replied. "The thralls were too busy getting the King's bath ready to worry about us!"

"Quick, then, in you go, take of those things and hide them somewhere, while I get you some water to wash yourselves off…" and with a chuckle he trotted out of the side door toward the kitchens.

We might have felt more surprised had we not felt so relieved at finding such an unexpected ally in our subterfuge. We did as we were told, and stripped off our tunics, scrunching them up and stuffing them under our pallets. My hose were muddy at the bottom, and Aetna's under-shift was decidedly grubby, so we look those off too.

Dunstan returned bearing a bucket of water – warm water – which we told us the King could well spare, since he had finished his bath; he had seen the thralls emptying his tub.

"Come on, scrub up," he said, still grinning broadly. "I'll keep watch!" He stepped outside our dividing curtain, and we could hear him whistling softly to himself.

We had almost finished rubbing ourselves down, Aetna had washed her hair and I had made an attempt at doing the same, when we heard women's voices and then Dunstan's urgent whisper. "Keep quiet! Get dressed, I'll keep them at bay!"

Dagmaer's voice could be heard getting closer. "Oh, the children are quite used to eating at the High Table. Their manners are impeccable, I can assure you. They will be no trouble at all."

Morwen's clipped tone replied. "Well, the Lady Elfrith does not usually allow children to sit with the higher guests, but I suppose if it is..." she must have caught sight of Dunstan. "My Lord Archbishop, is there anything I can do for you? May I fetch you something?"

"No, no," Dunstan said nonchalantly. "I was just..." he cast about for some excuse to be loitering between the kitchen and the lesser guest chambers. "Just..."

"Yes?"

"Just... waiting to speak to Dagmaer."

We could imagine Morwen's active eyebrows raised once again in surprise and disapproval. "If there is aught you need, my Lord, it is I who should attend to it," she said. "I am head of the house staff."

"No, there is nothing, I thank you."

"Well!" We could hear her furious footsteps heading off toward her mistress's quarters.

"That will be recounted into Elfrith's ear within the minute," said Dagmaer. "What is going on here?"

"Going on? Nothing is going on, I was merely passing the time of day with the twins when..."

"But you said you were waiting so speak to me."

"Oh, did I? Yes, well..."

We had done as much as we could to make ourselves presentable and it seemed only fair, now, to come to our conspirator's rescue. We came out of the chamber, I, smoothing down my hair and tying it back with a leather thong, Aetna, ostentatiously, flicking some imagined dust from the shoulders of her gunna. Dagmaer looked at us suspiciously.

"You have changed your clothes," she said.

"We were getting ready for the evening meal," I said.

"And to sit at the High Table," Aetna added. "We heard what you said to Morwen."

"There is mud behind your ear, young man, and where are your shoes? And why has your sister washed her hair? And just look at the state of those dogs!" We realised that we had forgotten the tell-tale condition of Berrie and Bremel.

"Oh, come, Dagmaer, don't give them a hard time," said Dunstan. "They had a small accident, that's all, and wanted to save you the trouble of cleaning up after them."

"Save me the trouble...!" Dagmaer was speechless. She barged into the chamber. "Come along, where are your clothes? Oh, by the Saints, look at this muddy water, it is all over. And what have you dried yourselves on? Not the bed coverings! That bitch, Morwen, will have a field day!"

We trooped in after her, followed by the Archbishop. "It's not that bad, Dagmaer," he said. "We'll soon sort it out. They can have my bed covers and nobody need be any the wiser."

"And what am I supposed to do with these bed covers?" She was angry now. "And how am I to wash these clothes without... Oh, Dunstan, really, you can't just let children... if you had been there when your own..." She stopped abruptly.

"When my own what?"

"Nothing, nothing," said Dagmaer.

"My own what? You can't leave it like that. You have skirted around remarks like that before. Tell me!" Frustration was making Dunstan raise his voice, too.

Somehow it seemed that we, and our small maelstrom of chaos, were no longer at the centre of this confrontation. There was a sudden tension in the air. We didn't understand it, but it was there. Dagmaer sat down on our pallet.

"Petroc," she said.

"He's mine." It was a statement, not a question.

"Yes."

Dunstan sat beside her. For the moment, we were forgotten. He took her hand in his. "Why didn't you tell me?"

"When? When you began to climb through the ranks of the Church? When you were exiled? When you were made Archbishop? Our paths hardly crossed much, did they? Besides, there was no need. I met a good man. In Kernow. We were happy for a time, and then life just sort of..." her voice trailed off. She looked at us and smiled, her usual enigmatic, tolerant smile. "Well, sweetlings, it seems you have brought us all to a moment of truth!"

We must have looked dubious, for she said "There, don't fret, all is well. There's nothing here that a little more water cannot put to rights. And nothing in the world that love cannot put right, either! Life is what it is. So, Archbishop, you are forgiven, for this day's little adventure at least! Now, be off with you – yes, you and I will talk later – but now I have to get this place cleaned up, and these two got ready to do my Lord and Lady proud at the High Table! It will be a quiet day in Valhal before I let that Morwen think I am not capable of running THIS family's household affairs."

)))))))(((((((

That evening we were the epitome of decorum and, indeed, we looked the part. Like a whirlwind, Dagmaer had put our chamber to rights, finished our almost complete ablutions, dressed us in more suitable attire and presented us at the High Table, where we made every effort not to say a word, or put a foot, out of place. Morwen hovered behind her mistress and Ethelwold, and Dagmaer took her place behind our aunt and uncle, occasionally casting a look of undisguised hostility toward her counterpart, which was returned in kind. I overheard one of the thralls whispering to another that the King's taster (doing his job, as usual, in an inconspicuous spot to one side) might well be needed later when "those two" took their evening meal.

The presence of so many who had not been part of the companionship which had grown out of our long journey together made the meal rather stilted, although Edgar had insisted on informality. Chief Ealdorman Alfhere, who, like Ethelwold, had ridden ahead of our party, did not seem comfortable in such mixed company, and we had the impression that the King's lack of due regard for the hierarchy of the table was not to his taste. Though she hid it well, Elfrith also seemed uneasy with the arrangement.

The following day, the Witan convened. It was of no interest to us. We had already seen Edgar in his kingly role, and hours spent listening to the Chief Ealdorman and others debating matters far beyond our comprehension held no appeal. Ethelwold had set Ratkin free of his chores for the duration of our stay, so that we might have a playmate, and, now mindful of Dagmaer's repeated instruction not to get into any more trouble, we were happy to let him be our guide as we explored the village and surrounding countryside.

The Witan remained in session for three days. On the last, Oswig, who had not until then been in attendance was called and so, too, were his brothers, Elric and Uvi. There was some business to be done regarding their father's legacies of land to his three sons, and its allocation, although, far more important to us, was the fact that Ethelmaer was with his father, and therefore a further companion on our daily excursions with Ratkin. They both knew the surrounding area well, and there was some dispute as to where we should go that day. Ratkin had already taken us to the edge of the fen, where we had rowed a small coracle, woven from reeds and tarred to keep it water tight, over to some tiny islets where we could watch birds and dragonflies compete for small flying insects. On the second day, we had struck off inland to visit the village of Spaldevice where another of the family's estates boasted, said Ratkin, the finest pigs this side of the Danelaw. We should have realised, of course, that with the recent outbreaks of hog-fever, the farmer would not be prepared to let us visit them. In the end, the day was saved when his wife – another who had a very soft spot for Ratkin – said we could help her collect eggs from the scattered, hidden places where her unruly chickens had them hidden. As a reward, she made us griddle-cakes which we ate with honey dripping down our chins and a boiled egg each, the soft yolks the colour of early sunset.

The day Ethelmaer joined us was hot and sunny. He suggested that we follow the river along to the west a little way, where, he said, there was an excellent spot for swimming. The water held no fears for us, we had been swimming well for several years, and Ratkin said that he could certainly enjoy being a water-rat for the day. It was decided. We begged some food from the kitchen, and set off with cheese, bread, apples and cherry-plums wrapped in light linen and a reminder from Dagmaer to stay away from any rapids. The dogs trotted happily ahead of us, turning to make sure we were following and running for sticks.

We followed the river along for about a mile, as it meandered through meadows, cows grazing lazily and watching us with soft, curious eyes. As it entered a little wood, the trees closing above us in a green tunnel of dappled shade and reflected light, it opened out into a wider stream with broad, fern dotted banks sloping gently down to the water.

"Oh, this is lovely," said Aetna. "There must be fairies here!" It certainly looked magical.

"And etins," I suggested.

"And naiads," said Ethelmaer, whose lessons in preparation for a career in the Church had introduced him to classical mythology. Ratkin looked mystified. "I think they are sort of mermaids," Ethelmaer explained uncertainly.

"Then I'll be one of those!" declared Aetna, and stripping down to her shift, headed for the water. We boys had no such modesty, and quickly followed, trusting the water to hide our nakedness. We swam and dived, and splashed and laughed the morning away, and when we tired of chasing water demons and conjuring monsters from fallen trees, we returned to the bank to find that Aetna had set out the food, divided fairly for each of us, and had added bremelberries and some watercress, which she had found a little further downstream. We donned our hose behind the bushes and sat down.

"You will be a fine wife to a gallant lord," said Ethelmaer. Aetna smiled up at him.

"I thank you, kind sir!"

We pretended that the linen which had wrapped our food and which was now spread out for our picnic was the High Table, and we the nobility. As the noon of the day passed the angle of the sun changed and filtered through the trees which crowded behind us at the edge of the bank. We grew sleepy after our meal and lay back, allowing it to warm away any last chill from the water.

We must have dozed for some time as, when we woke, the sky had clouded over and it felt as though the postnoon was well advanced. There was nothing to pack away, but Aetna had neatly folded the linen and was putting her gunna back on when we heard voices from the other side of the trees.

"My Lady, I still advise patience. You are so close now, to hurry matters might be to put yourself in danger." It was the clipped tones of Morwen.

"I am tired of patience. I cannot believe that the old goat is still alive. He has taken enough in the last few months to kill a bull. But as his appetite fails, it is harder and harder to get the dose taken." We could hardly believe that the Lady Elfrith was out in the hedgerows, but so it seemed. And taking an interest in farm animals?

"You are right, though," she continued. "To increase the dose in food would be foolhardy. But a strong decoction, straight into the blood, would be... a merciful release from the current infirmity."

"Into the blood?"

"Who knows what little accident might befall in the preparation for the hunt? It would hardly be noticed, and the effect not evident until an hour or so later. Gather any plants with the seed pods still in place. The monk's-hood is well named. Poison hidden beneath a priest's cowl."

"We should, perhaps, have waited until after dark."

"No, the sun increases the plant's potency. We need to look a little closer to the water for the pennyroyal."

We froze. An encounter with the Lady Elfrith and Morwen was not the way we wanted our day to end.

"Quick," whispered Ethelmaer. "Behind the brambles – and keep the dogs quiet!"

As the two women approached the stream, we edged around the bremelberry bushes, keeping the dense tangle of prickly foliage between us. Berrie whined and squirmed in Aetna's arms.

"What was that?" Morwen stood still and peered into the undergrowth.

Elfrith paused and listened. "I hear nothing. It was likely just a bird." She found the plant she was looking for and broke of several tall spikes of purplish flowers. "Speaking of which, this should be plenty to deal with the ducklings!"

"Lady, have you ever gathered mandrake?"

"No, why do you ask?"

"There's to be a hanging in Rammesig, tomorrow. I have an... acquaintance... who has access to the gallows. If there is a mandrake at its foot, it could be bought – at a price."

"It would certainly be a useful addition to our collection. Come, we have enough of what we seek now, let us return before it gets any later.

The Witan will be disbanding this evening, there is much to do. Now, about this mandrake…"

Their voiced receded as they walked back in the direction of the Hall, along the path we had taken earlier, and we breathed easier.

"We'll let them get well ahead, before we head back," I said, not wanting to risk being noticed after our narrow escape. There was no reason why we should not have been at the river that day, but we felt that to have been known to witness Elfrith's activities would be dangerous. There had been a clandestine feel to her actions.

After a while, we allowed the dogs their freedom once again, and began to work our way back along the bank of the stream, stopping from time to time to skim stones.

"Did you understand what they were doing?" asked Aetna.

"Picking herbs," said Ethelmaer.

"Lady Elfrith is often in the still room, as I told you," said Ratkin. "But I have never heard her speak of ministering to the livestock before. And as far as I know we don't have any old goats… not billies, anyhow… they all get eaten before they get old! And… it is late in the year for ducklings."

"Aetna is beginning to learn the skills of the stillroom," I said.

"That's why I was curious," she said. "I have never heard either Aunt Aelflaed or Dagmaer speak of those herbs. I must try and remember to ask about them."

"Well, I wouldn't mention the gallows."

TEN

By the time we got back to the Hall, the Witan had broken up, some members had already departed and others were taking their ease, sitting in the courtyard, benches brought from the Hall, drinking ale and discussing the events of the previous three days. As we came in through the great gates, Ethelwold spotted us and waved us over. With him were Brithnoth and Oswig. Ethelwine, bearing four horns of ale, came out of the Hall, and passed the drinks around.

"So, here is the next generation," said Ethelwold. "Young Wulf, who will be an ealdorman one day, Ethelmaer, who will perhaps follow Dunstan into the hierarchy of the Church and little Aetna, who is sure to be a great Lady! And what of you, my Ratkin? What shall you do?"

"I shall serve, my Lord," grinned Ratkin.

"That you shall, my lad." Ethelwold was clearly very fond of his young foundling. "Brit, like me, you have no son, but you are fortunate to have your wolf cub; a sister-son to be your heir. I would that it were possible for me to adopt this lad, but Elfrith would never hear of it. Perhaps I will yet get her with child, though! If only my health will allow." A deep, rattling cough seized him once again.

I realise now, so many years after the events that were about to overtake us, just how ill he looked. His skin was sallow and his eyes sunken. Only a few years older than his brother Ethelwine, he could almost have passed for his father.

"You have heard that the shrine at Elig is being renewed," said Brithnoth. "Saint Etheldreda has worked miracles before now. Perhaps you should visit. Take Elfrith with you… who knows?"

"Ha!" Ethelwold laughed without humour. "I know, believe me, I know! Elfrith has little time for…" he fell silent and looked around as though he might have said something inappropriate. "But none of that! We have worked hard this last three days, now is the time to relax. We have much planned for this night."

We had been at Uphude for almost a week, and even Elfrith had ceased to notice our presence at the High Table, as the evenings went by. That night, as preparations for the post-Witan celebrations were completed, our attendance went unremarked. As we came into the Great Hall with Dagmaer, taking our usual seats, while she assumed her post at Aelflaed's shoulder, we were excited to see that this was to be no normal evening meal. The lower tables had been separated and pushed back to allow space in the centre of the Hall, and a group of musicians were tuning up their instruments to one side. This could only mean one thing – dancing. There were several new dances from the land of the Franks which had become quite the craze of late. Aetna had learned the basics of them from a group of travelling minstrels who had visited Radendunam, and she had shared them with me. I fancied we made quite the gallant couple and hoped that we would have the opportunity to show off. Mealtimes had become rather dull, now that we were permanently on our best behaviour.

The food was excellent, as usual; Elfrith knew how to maintain a very good table. The ale and mead flowed generously throughout, as did the wine at the top table. When the main courses had been finished and left overs removed by the kitchen thralls, the musicians, who had been playing quietly as we ate, struck up a lively tune, and Ethelwold stood.

"With Your Majesty's permission, may the dancing begin?" he asked of Edgar.

"Indeed, it may!" The King was already on his feet. Edgar's love of informality had conjured an atmosphere friendship and familiarity among the upper guests, which had begun early in our stay – outside of the Witan's formal proceedings – and now that the business of the Progress was entirely over, barring its return journey, he seemed younger than ever.

"And with your permission, Ealdorman," he said, smiling across at Ethelwold, "may I lead it, in company with your gracious lady, who has offered us such excellent hospitality this last week." He offered his hand to Elfrith. She slipped hers into his, and rose gracefully.

"Sire, you do me great honour," she said, without waiting for Ethelwold to reply.

They looked a golden couple as Edgar led her into the centre of the room. Elfrith's dark, fox-red hair was caught back in her usual favoured style – artfully allowing some of it boldly to flow loose, whilst the rest was secured by her plaits and headrail, as convention decreed. Her gunna fitted flawlessly and again she challenged convention by allowing her undergunna, richly embroidered with purple, usually a colour reserved for royalty, to show above her bodice. Beside her, Edgar's easy grace and slim frame was similarly engaging. A spontaneous burst of applause greeted them.

The musicians paused in their playing, waited until the couple faced each other and then began their tune again. Clearly, both Edgar and Elfrith were familiar with the steps, for they followed the prescribed patterns of the dance perfectly, completing one full set of figures before Edgar called for others to come and join them. More couples quickly obliged. The first were Brithnoth and our Aunt and soon the floor was filled with dancers – many with more enthusiasm than skill – Aetna and I among them, though keeping to one side of the floor and hoping that we would not be ordered to bed.

There was much laughter and chatter as the night and the dancing wore on. Voices became louder as inhibitions began to falter, and the strict measures of the dances began to give way to a more uncoordinated pattern of leaps, hops and twirls. At some point, dishes of honeycomb and clotted cream were brought in, with fruit and soft cakes and set out on the tables. Aetna and I had tired ourselves out on the dancefloor and were happy to find an empty space on one of the lower benches to enjoy them.

"Everyone is having a fine time," I said.

"Everyone except Uncle Ethelwold," replied Aetna.

We looked up toward the High Table. Ethelwold was seated alone, watching the antics of those enjoying themselves. As he moved, he winced and pressed his hand to his side.

"Shall we go and speak with him?"

"Yes, he looks rather lonely."

Weaving our way through the melee – Leoflada was prettily absorbed in a measure with Oswig, and was that Dagmar dancing with the Archbishop? – we made our way up to the High Table.

"Uncle Ethelwold, we have come…" I said

"… to keep you company," continued Aetna.

He laughed, though once again wincing. "You are kind," he said. "Did I look lacking in company?"

"You did…"

"… a little."

"Well, perhaps I was… a little!" He took Aetna onto his knee. "Now, what say you that on the morrow we go to Rammesig to get your brother measured for his sword, and you that pretty dagger we talked about?"

"Yes, please, uncle," I said, though the enquiry had not really been directed at me. "Can Ratkin and Ethelmaer come?"

"Ratkin is at your disposal, young man, but you had better ask his father if Ethelmaer may accompany us. Remember he is in training for the Church."

"I do not think that he is very keen on that," said Aetna.

"That is as maybe, but you must still ask his father, for he is determined to see him in orders. We shall leave early, so you had best seek them out before you go to bed and make your plans."

"Very well, uncle, and thank you, sir," I said, making my best little bow. Aetna kissed him on the cheek and he set her down. "We will see you in the morning."

"Off you go, then."

Suddenly, our beds seemed to beckon. We had had a long day, and the food and dancing – not to mention the lateness of the hour – meant that we did not wait for Dagmaer to chase us to our chamber, although judging by her enjoyment of the dance, that did not seem a likely scenario. We slipped through the hanging at the back of the hall and were skirting the curtained chambers before our own, when we heard a quiet chuckle. Edgar's familiar chuckle.

"You are right, Lady, it is indeed a very fine tapestry, but as to a likeness... I am not sure that I can claim similarity to Beowulf!"

"Come, sire, it is you to the life! See, the hair, the fine figure, the strong arm..." Elfrith's voice. We seemed to be hearing it everywhere today.

"Lady, you flatter me." Edgar sounded as though he might have taken a little too much fine wine.

"I swear to you, my Lord, when I first saw you, I thought it was my favourite poem come to life before my eyes! And now we have danced together as they danced in Hrothgar when the hero had killed the monster Grendel. Did you not think that we made a handsome pair?"

Laughter again. "Indeed, we did!" said the King.

There was a coquettish tone to Elfrith's voice which was unfamiliar. "And to think, if things had but turned out differently, we might have been a fine match in other ways. And danced many a step together," she said.

"Aye, Lady, that is so, but see how the Lord has sent us both a fine wyrd, nonetheless. For your husband is the Ealdorman of East Anglia and I have a sweet wife in Wintancaestre, and a fine son to boot!"

"That is true, sire, but..."

"And now we must get back to the hall," said Edgar. "For I must bid my goodnights and away to my bed."

"Sire, do you find me unattractive?"

"Lady?"

"You do not think me untutored, or ill-fitted for a life... say, at Court?"

"Of course not!"

"Then all is well. Come, sire, I can see that you are tired. We will call the revels to a close."

We had hardly dared breathe as we listened to this. There was nothing between us and the speakers save the curtain at which they were looking so closely. As we realised that it was about to be swept to one side, we dived for our own chamber, thankful that Elfrith's attention was more acutely focussed on Edgar than any slight movement beyond the partition.

We didn't know what to make of what we had heard. It seemed a little odd, but we thought nothing more of it, other than we were pleased not to have been discovered eavesdropping, albeit unintentionally, on our elders. Like a great many things that adults said and did, it made little sense to us. I went to find Elric and ask that Ethelmaer be free to accompany us on the morrow and Aetna began to get ready for bed. When I returned, she was already asleep, her arm around Berrie, with Bremel waiting patiently for me to join them.

)))))(((((

The following day, after almost a week of fair weather, the water level of the fen had fallen enough for us to make the trip to Rammesig on dry land. There was quite a holy-day feel about it; it was market day and the ladies had every expectation of finding trinkets and ribbons, fabrics and other necessities and the men were looking forward to visiting the swordsmith. Dagmaer insisted that Aetna and I wore our fest-day clothes – she said she would not have Morwen thinking we were on a bone-hunt – and Edgar insisted that he not be afforded any royal deference: he wanted to be an ordinary young man on a day out. To this end he had donned simple clothes: a dun-coloured tunic and trews and his favourite leather jerkin, which, though made of the finest calfskin, had seen better days. Ethelmaer joined us only just in time, as his father had insisted that he stay behind for extra prayers after morning service, which we had all attended in the Hall's chapel, and Ratkin made up our fourth. We were a jolly party as we set off on the two-mile walk – it had been decided that we would all travel on foot, as it was dry, sunny and warm. Even Elfrith made no objection.

Leoflada had her arm linked through Oswig's.

"It would seem our advantageous pairing has turned into a love match," said Aelflaed, as she and Brithnoth strolled along with Ethelwine and Elflada.

"As we hoped it would," he replied.

"It is fortunate that the next generation will have the same marriage ties with this Ealdormanry as we have enjoyed," continued Aelflaed. "The shires of Eastseaxe and East Anglia have always been close, both in miles and matters politic."

"And I am even more fortunate, because I have a wife who understands matters politic and matters of the heart!"

Ahead, Elfrith was walking with Edgar, deep in conversation, while Ethelwold contented himself with our chattering company. Ethelmaer and Ratkin were quite the comedic couple, playing pranks on each other, and laughing uproariously at their own jokes. Ethelmaer said that Ratkin should be jester when he grew up, but he said he would rather be a soldier. Then he fingered his thrall collar, and looked at Ethelwold.

"Though I may have to be a jester first, so that I may buy my freedom, my Lord!" He seemed to be not at all in awe of his master.

"All that is a long way off, my Ratkin. Time will tell!" He ruffled the lad's hair.

Behind us, Dunstan walked with Dagmaer for it seemed they had much to talk about and he had seen little of her whilst the Witan was in session.

We could imagine Morwen's disapproval at Dagmaer's inclusion in the outing.

"So, all is well with you? Truly? And you feel it better that the boy does not know?" Dunstan was saying.

"For the time being, at least. And yes, all is well, I would have it no different," Dagmaer replied.

Rammesig was a large, bustling village, and the market was in full swing when we arrived. People of all ranks jostled each other among the stalls, some well-dressed, others in tatters, merchants clearly buying in bulk, goodwives picking and choosing at the vegetable stalls, young girls and boys considering trinkets from the peddlers' trays. Food might have been a little scarce compared to recent years, but Rammesig was thriving. Around the village green, where the market sprawled, cottages and workshops overlooked the scene, some with their own stalls set up to catch the passing trade. Ducks and chickens fled from underfoot, dogs barked (we had left ours at Uphude) and donkeys brayed. Outside the tavern a scuffle was taking place, a young man being hauled off by an irate father and a girl and her mother shouting at them both.

"Just like my brother's coronation!" laughed Edgar, behind his hand.

"Your Maj..." began Dunstan.

"Shhhh! I am just Edgar today!"

"Well, ladies, let us see what the market has to offer," said Elflada. "My lords, we shall meet you outside the church when we are done." With that they all disappeared as one into the crowd, Aetna with them.

"We shall see no more of them this fore noon," said Ethelwold. "Brit, Wine, Your Maj... Edgar... let us to the swordsmith. It is an age since I last visited." He led the way to the far side of the market, skirted the stalls and turned down a well rutted lane. We passed a wheelwright's workshop, a huge wagon wheel propped against its wall, advertising its presence, then the blacksmith's open fronted barn, horseshoes tacked up along its eaves and finally came to a third building, also open fronted, but with a large sword hanging horizontally from two heavy chains above the archway leading to the interior. A furnace was burning low, the bellows folded by its side, but the room was still hot and the air dry.

"Master Smith!" called Ethelwold.

From a doorway at the rear the swordsmith emerged. He was well advanced in years, but strong and sinewy, the muscles on his forearms hard beneath skin pock-marked with scars and burns from his furnace.

"Lord Ethelwold," his face creased with pleasure, "And Ealdorman Brithnoth, as I speak to the Saints! It has been many years since we last met. Lord Ethelwine, too! Why I remember when you were all boys no bigger than..."

Brithnoth put his hand on my shoulder. "This is Wulfmaer, my sister-son, and my heir," he said.

"Son to that pretty sister of yours, may the Lord rest her. Yes, I can see the resemblance. My, but she loved market day here when your father visited old Lord Aethelstan."

"I wish to buy him a training sword, and for you to measure him for his fighting blade."

The old man smiled down at me. "So, your uncle still trusts my divining, does he?"

I was mystified. "Master Smith?" I said, looking back and forth between them.

"The Master swordsmith has a very special skill," said Brithnoth. "He can divine the stature of the man by looking at the boy. When I was eight," he continued, "Master Smith took one look at me and said, 'This lad will be a beanpole before he is eighteen!' He made me a sword so big that I could not lift it until I was twelve, or wield it until I was sixteen. And see, Master Smith, it is still here at my side! I grew into it and now it is as if it is a part of me. And the same will be true for you, Wulf."

The smith took a series of measurements: my forearms, my shoulders, my legs and finally straightening up, said to Brithnoth. "Not of your height, my Lord, but above average and with a strong arm in a fight. He favours his right leg a little, the left is just a fraction shorter. I will compensate when I make the blade. When shall you give it to the lad, Lord? How urgent is the order?"

"He will not be able to lift it for a year or so yet, Master Smith," said my uncle and I do not fare this way often, so add it to your worklist and send me word when it is ready. And for now, do you have a training sword which will suit him?"

"Aye, that I do, Lord, there are several to choose from…" and so saying he led the way to a rack of smaller swords; miniature replicas of the full-sized blades, but with edges not so highly whetted. "These are the finest training pieces you will find this side of the Danelaw. You cannot learn to fight with a wooden toy." He spat into the furnace and his spittle hissed away into nothingness. "A boy needs to wield iron!"

It took some time to find a piece which I was able to raise, but which would not become too small for me within a short time. Eventually we settled upon the right specimen.

"A good choice, Lord," said Master Smith. "When the lad has grown beyond it, send it back to me and I will be able to find its replacement amongst my stock. That way we will keep his sword arm busy until he can begin to use his own, special blade."

"As ever, Master Smith, you are ahead of me… my plan exactly," Brithnoth grinned. I was getting used to the feel of the hilt of my new weapon and barely listening. He ruffled my hair, affectionately. "And now, we must not forget your sister."

From a selection of knives and daggers, Brithnoth chose a pretty, narrow-bladed knife, with red stones on the hilt, for Aetna.

"Do you think this will suit her?"

"I think so, Uncle, though I fear she will use it to cut her embroidery threads rather than fight your enemies!"

"I hope that neither of you will ever have to fight in earnest with these blades, but this will serve both purposes, if it must."

When Aetna had stayed with the ladies, eager to visit the market and see what the traders and peddlers had on offer, Ethelmaer had remained with Dunstan (they had gone to visit the Church) and Ratkin had accompanied us. He looked wistfully at my training blade.

Ethelwold watched him, thoughtfully, for a few moments. Then, tuning to the sword-maker, he said "Master Smith, do you have another of those?"

"Indeed, my Lord."

"Then let us take it for my Ratkin, here! My lad, if you are to be soldier you had best learn how to fight, too,"

Ratkin, for once, was almost speechless. "My Lord!" he whispered.

Master Smith handed him a small, scaled down sword – not quite like mine, but very similar. "Every blade is unique," he said. "Respect it and keep it well cleaned."

"Oh, I shall!" he said and, turning to his benefactor. "Thank you, Lord Ethelwold!"

Ethelwold hugged him to the side of his leg roughly and smoothed the red mop of hair away from his forehead.

"You are a fine lad. It was a good day's work when I picked you out of a puddle!"

The exchange made me realise that, in my excitement, I had not shown proper appreciation for Brithnoth's generosity. "Oh, Uncle," I said. "Thank you. Thank you for both my swords. I shall be a true... I will always..." Words were beginning to fail me.

"Wulf," he replied, "You will be my strong right arm when I need it. That I know. It is enough. And it is a man's duty and pleasure to equip his son – or sister-son – and heir! We will say no more. Now let us back to find the ladies." Scabbards were chosen. Money changed hands and we made our farewells.

We returned to the market place where we had left my aunt and her companions engrossed with bolts of fabric, ribbons and sweetmeats, to find that they had moved on to the silversmith's cottage. We heard this from Dagmaer, who was haggling with a fishmonger over the price of dry-smoked eels, and beating the poor man down to a price she considered fair.

"For the price you are asking, my man, I should be able to buy smoked unicorn…" The unfortunate stall holder had a battle on is hands.

The silversmith's workshop stood on the edge of the green, where the main road through Rammesig crossed with a less well travelled road that headed away into the fens, in wet weather petering out altogether after a mile or so. Like the swordsmith's workshop it was open onto the road, the furnace smaller and less rugged, but still with a core glowing red. Unlike the sword maker, though, the silversmith had a separate room, behind the smithy, to show off his work. We could hear Elflada's and Aelflaed's voices.

"Certainly, two of those, and which are your very smallest needles? Ah, yes, they are very delicate. Master Smith, you are a great craftsman, I have never seen tinier eyes. They will surely take the finest silk." Our aunt sounded thrilled. She had often complained that there was not a skilled needle-maker anywhere near Radendunam. "Two of those, also, please."

"I will take the same," said Elflada. "Sister, have you seen these little shears? Are they not charming? Elfrith! Goodness, whatever to you need a needle that size for? Surely it is for leather-work, not embroidery!"

"Elflada, we are not all obsessed with gold threads and amber beads. Some of us have a thought to practical things," Elfrith replied sharply. "Come, let us make our payments and be gone, the day wears on." There was an impatience in her voice.

We had awaited the ladies in the smithy, in the company of a young apprentice, who, about the same age as Edgar, had unwittingly engaged the King in a discussion of how hard an apprentice's life could be.

"You are in training yourself, then, or a fosterling?" he asked Edgar. Fosterlings were sent by their parents to learn the skills of combat or other professions from men better placed than their own fathers. They were often worked harder than youngsters in training, for the latter paid money for their experience. Fosterlings did not.

"You might say that I am still in training," said Edgar. "I certainly still feel that I have much to learn!"

At that moment, the door to the inner chamber opened and Elfrith swept out, expecting to find only the apprentice present. She barged past him and into Edgar.

"Your Majesty, I am so sorry, I had no idea…"

"No harm done, Lady!"

"Your Majesty?" the apprentice was open-mouthed. But Edgar was in no mood to reassume his royalty so soon.

"Just a pet name," he said and propelling Elfrith before him made to leave, followed by the rest of us.

Like naughty children not wanting to be caught in a prank, we all hurried away, toward the church, where we could see Dunstan – also *incognito* – and Ethelmaer sitting on a low stone wall.

"A career in the Church can be a fine life, if you are suited to it," Dunstan was saying, as though Ethelmaer had been expressing his doubts, but their conversation was cut short by our arrival and that of Dagmaer, bearing a large basket of dried eels.

"Now, we have but to round up our love-birds," said Ethelwold, for Leoflada and Oswig were nowhere to be seen.

"We had better get the date set for that wedding," laughed Brithnoth, as the pair appeared, hand in hand, Flada carrying a bunch of wild flowers, and Oswig with a daisy chain on his head, which he had clearly forgotten was there.

"Nice head-gear," said Edgar.

Colouring, Oswig swept it off, but we noticed tucked it into his tunic.

"So, we are all gathered," said Ethelwold. Aetna was tired and Brithnoth lifted her onto his shoulders. Like any group of friends from a neighbouring village we made our way back to Uphude, and if anyone in Rammesig had recognised the Ealdorman of East Anglia, and guessed who his companion might be, they wisely said nothing.

))))(((((

The following day was set aside for a hunt. The party was due to break up on the morrow, but Edgar was keen to experience a hunt in the unfamiliar surroundings of the fenland borders and the plan was to ride across to Sawtrede, a mile or so to the west, where Ethelwine and Elflada had their Hall. Ethelwine assured the King that there was fine hunting to be had in his woods and refreshment could be taken afterwards, the host and hostess (for Elflada would accompany them) then remaining at their home, while the others returned to Uphude in readiness for their departure the next day. Dagmaer said that it would be a blessing to have the men out of the way while the preparations were being made.

I had asked that Ratkin and I might be allowed to go together on the hunt, though his station meant that he should be with the followers, rather than the hunters. Both Ethelwine and Brithnoth were happy for us to stay together, and we were found a docile old nag to ride tandem. As it seemed unlikely that it would be able to keep up with the horses in the front rank of the hunt, it was felt that we would be in little danger.

"Be careful," Aetna said, as I clambered up, stepping from the tallest mounting block to reach the horse's back. "Remember what Thella said."

"What's that?" asked Ratkin, as I hauled him up behind me.

"Nothing, just foolishness," I said.

"It is not foolishness," Aetna snapped. "She said that ill-fortune followed when Wulf followed the hunt."

"When a wolf followed... a wolf, not Wulf! And it was a boar, not the hunt," I said, testily, but then relented, as I could see that Aetna was genuinely worried. I could feel a little of her anxiety like a prickle under my skin.

"It seems that you remember what she said very well for someone who thinks it nonsense!"

"Don't worry, Aetna, I'll be fine. I have Ratkin at my back!"

The hunting party gathered in the courtyard. Aelflaed made her farewells to Ethelwine and Elflada, saying that, likely, their next meeting would be at Leoflada's wedding. Flada blushed, and allowed herself to be embraced tearfully by her aunt and robustly by her uncle.

Edgar was already mounted, his horse pawing the ground fretfully. "He is eager for the chase," he said.

"As are we all," Dunstan replied. "We only await Ethelwold, what's delaying him?"

The stable-hand had brought Ethelwold's horse into the courtyard and stood awaiting his master. He looked around abruptly, as did the rest of the party, when raised voices were heard from the Hall. Ethelwold strode out, scowling and rubbing his left wrist with his right hand. "Come, let's away!" he said to the waiting riders. Elfrith stood at the open doorway.

"I swear I shall never understand that woman," Ethelwold muttered to Brithnoth. "She never touches a needle if she can help it, and then when I am in a hurry to be away, she sees a frayed cuff to my tunic and insists on mending it there and then... and near flays me in the attempt!" A scratch ran across his lower arm and a little blood had soaked onto his cuff, staining the embroidery. Both men mounted and without looking back Ethelwold turned his horse and galloped out of the gates. Brithnoth raised an eyebrow to Aelflaed, blew her a kiss, and followed, the other riders in pursuit, raising a cloud of dust as the horses were given their heads.

"Hold on!" I shouted, and Ratkin did as he was told as our horse managed to raise a respectable canter and brought up the rear. I turned to wave to Aetna, and saw that she still watching, a look of concern on her face. She raised her hand, and I felt a pang of guilt, wondering how often I would be the one off on an adventure, leaving her behind. Soon, though, Ratkin and I were fully absorbed in our riding, and trying to keep our elderly horse motivated enough to catch up with the others.

The ride to Sawtrede was uneventful. There had still been no rain, and the trackway was dry and firm, so it was not hard to make good progress. Ahead we saw the rest of the hunting party taking things at a leisurely pace, Elflada's palfrey abreast of her husband's horse, Edgar and Dunstan in the lead, with Brithnoth and Ethelwold, apparently deep in conversation, bringing up the rear. We trotted up behind them.

"Uncle!" I called, and they both turned. "We are here!"

"So you are, and well ridden, young men," said Ethelwold. I noticed that he was still rubbing his wrist, and winced as he did so.

We chattered on and the Ealdormen, half listening to our prattling, and half continuing their own conversation indulged our excitement. This was, after all, the first time Ratkin had ever been on a hunt. I felt quite the experienced horseman, even managing to urge our mount to another desultory canter at one point.

When we arrived at Ethelwine's Hall at Sawtrede, Elflada bustled inside to arrange for small ale and mead to be brought out, a customary stirrup cup before the business of the hunt began.

Brithnoth said "Boys, you must be careful when the hunt starts, I shall not have time to watch you, and you understand it is a dangerous place to be once the chase begins. Stay at the rear of the party and should the prey double back, do not do anything foolish."

"We won't, Uncle," I said.

"I may hold back a little myself, Brit," said Ethelwold. "I am feeling as though I have something of an ague and I shall pace myself. I'll keep an eye on them."

At a signal from Edgar, the party left the courtyard at an easy trot, making for the nearby woodland. Ethelwold seemed a little less troubled by his wrist and rode off with them, Ratkin and I behind him. The lesser hunt followers who had journeyed from Uphude, were joined by a butchering team from Sawtrede and made ready to follow on foot, once the riders and hounds were a little ahead. We could hear their laughter and conversation as we rode off, but soon it fell behind us, as we all gathered pace behind the hounds quartering the ground and looking for a scent.

It did not take long for a quarry to be put up. The lead hound gave voice and followed by the others made a dash into a heavy thicket. A startled hind bounded out and into the clearing beyond, leaping over more tangled brambles and heading away along paths well known to her, leaving the dogs and riders to navigate the almost impenetrable undergrowth before they could follow. The chase was on.

For a while, impeded by the heavy late summer-foliaged woodland floor, the pace was slow enough for us to keep up, but gradually the older riders pulled ahead, and Ratkin and I were left in their wake, following the trampled pathway created by their passage, our horse content to co-operate, but reluctant to over-exert himself. We could hear the hunt crashing on ahead of us, and were happy to pretend to ourselves that we, as a rear-guard, would hold the hind at bay should she turn, despite my uncle's warning. We were weaving tales to each other of just this scenario when we entered a small clearing, where the going was easier, and came upon Ethelwold, his horse slowed to a walk. He was hunched forward over the pommel of his saddle, his right forearm pressing his stomach, his left hand dangling uselessly at his side. As we watched, he began to slip off his horse, trying to hold himself in place by leaning on his horse's neck, but loosing balance and hitting the ground with a sickening thud, his face to the earth.

Ratkin was off our saddle in seconds, running to him.

"My Lord, what ails you? Are you ill?"

I quickly dismounted, too. Ratkin had helped Ethelwold to turn onto his back, and was cradling his head in his arms.

"Uncle, Uncle, what can we do? What has happened?" I felt a terrible panic, as Ethelwold's eyes began to close. Ratkin gently tapped his cheek and they opened again, trying to focus.

"Ratkin, my boy, I don't know..." his voice was rasping and his breath shallow. Then a fit of coughing racked him. When he could speak again, he did so through gritted teeth. "Ah, my chest, my belly! And I cannot move my..."

"Quickly, ride on and catch up with the others. Tell them my Lord is ill. Tell them he is... just tell them," Ratkin whispered urgently to me. To Ethelwold he said, "I am here, my Lord, I am here. Lie still, Wulf will get help."

I clambered back up onto the horse, kicked him sharply and made off as fast as I could to catch the hunters. I could hear the hounds giving tongue and rode in the direction of their barking – now I prayed in earnest that the hind had turned and was heading back towards us, but it seemed that she was still leading the hunt away. I rode on, hoping at every turn to find them. The tone of the hound's barking changed: the deer was at bay, or down, and the whipper had called them off. All was quiet, someone was preparing to take a shot, to make the kill.

My horse barged noisily through a clump of young trees where the undergrowth was particularly thick and burst upon the scene. As I had guessed, the hind stood facing her tormentors, breathing heavily, her delicate nostrils flaring in fright and exhaustion. Both Dunstan and Edgar had her in the sights of their bows. My arrival destroyed the tableau. Everyone turned toward me, Edgar's arrow flew wildly askew, and Dunstan lowered his bow, swearing. The hind leaped high over the heads of the nearest dogs, and bolted away, while the hounds, their training deeply imprinted, continued to obey the whipper's last command and remained still.

"Wulf!" Uncle Brithnoth was furious. "What did I tell you? Get..." but I was already shouting, trying to make sense, though failing in my fear and urgency.

"It's Uncle Ethelwold! Come quickly! He's sick, he's fallen... I don't..."

Brithnoth's anger turned to concern. "Slowly, boy, slowly. What has happened?"

I tried to gulp down my panic. "It's Uncle Ethelwold, I told you! We found him in the woods. He is ill. Ratkin has stayed with him, but he looks so...!" My voice trailed off.

"Quickly, show me where!" My uncle rode up next to my horse, swung me off it and onto his saddle in front of him. He kicked Fireflax into action and we flew back the way I had come, again following the broken undergrowth, as I gasped out what had happened. Behind us, Dunstan, Edgar and Ethelwine followed.

The ride can only have taken a few minutes, but it seemed like an age. I did not realise that I had chased the hunt so far. When we came to the clearing, Ratkin was still on his knees beside Ethelwold, the ealdorman's head now in his lap. He had vomited, and Ratkin had done his best to clean his face and the front of his tunic, heedless of the mess on himself. Ethelwold was still breathing, but was gasping for air, and every breath seemed to be agony. Brithnoth was off the horse in seconds, and beside his old friend on the ground, leaving me high on Fireflax's saddle.

"Wold? What happened? Can you speak?"

"I... I felt a great pain in my gut, and could not grip the reins. I fell. The boys found me..."

"We will get you back to the Hall. All will be well. Rest, and we will..."

"No, no, there is no time, I can feel it. I am elf-shot to my heart. I cannot... Brit, witness me. Ethelwine, my brother, are you there?"

Ethelwine was, indeed, kneeling, too. Dunstan and Edgar stood to one side, horrified, shocked. Could this be happening?

"I am here, Wold, I am here." Ethelwine's voice was breaking as he spoke.

"Wine, witness me, too. My Will is made, it is in my great chest, and copies are with the Brothers at Petrideburg. Do not let Elfrith..." He coughed again and black spittle flew from his mouth. For a moment, he seemed unconscious. Then his eyes opened again.

"Ratkin, I give you your freedom, boy. I would that I had had a son like..." His eyes closed again, flickered once and then he was still. Ratkin wailed: a long drawn out cry of anguish and then his tears flowed silently. Silence, too, from those gathered around the ealdorman's body. Silence and shock.

The silence was broken as the hunt followers approached from the direction of the Hall. Chattering, laughter and good-hearted banter from beyond the nearest trees seemed as if it was coming from another world, another reality which had somehow separated from our own and was now quite unrelated to our existence. It stopped abruptly as the party took in what was before them.

Two of the King's retainers rushed to his side. "Sire, what has happened, are you unhurt?"

"I am quite well," said Edgar in a low voice, "but the Ealdorman Ethelwold is… gone. We do not know what has happened. Young Wulf and his companion found him grievous unwell and by the time we reached him…"

Dunstan had gently removed Ethelwold's head from Ratkin's knee and composed the body. With one arm around the boy, he was praying, the intercessions for the dead coming without thought, unbidden to his lips. He made the sign of the cross, and bowed his head in silence. Everyone fell to their knees, the King included.

I do not know how long we remained like that, but at some point, Edgar stood and took off his cloak. He laid it over Ethelwold, covering his face and turned to Ethelwine.

"Wine, I am truly sorry. Your loss is mine also, and that of his friends and thralls. He was a good man. Now we must take him home. How this harm came to him we do not know. He said he was elf-shot. That may be, for in the forests there are many dangers other than the beasts we can hunt with arrow and spear. It is true that he has not been in the finest of health for some time, and it may be that he was felled by an ill-stroke of that same malaise. This is a sad day."

I went to Ratkin. He was staring bleakly around him, as though he did not know where he was. "Come, Ratkin, let them carry him," I said. He looked at me without recognition, his mind elsewhere, but he allowed me to take him by the arm and follow the slow progress of the procession which headed back to the Hall at Sawtrede, Ethelwold laid on his horse's back.

PART II

THE WEAVING

ELEVEN

May, the Year of Our Lord 973

WULFAETNA

Ten years. Well, more than ten years. More than ten years since the day the hunting party returned to Uphude from Sawtrede: Edgar, ashen-faced, Dunstan, his eyes down, silently mouthing prayers under his breath and our uncle walking beside the hastily built litter, his hand resting upon his old friend's shoulder to steady him against the jolts of the road, as if Ethelwold's poor, cold body could still feel such discomfort. Ethelwine walked behind the litter, head low, leading his horse.

As the cortege approached the Hall, the lookouts on the palisade had called urgently that something was terribly wrong. The gates were thrown open and the household strained to see what was amiss. There was no sense of an expedition well ended, of a hunt successfully concluded. No butchered beast brought home amid congratulation and back-slapping to receive the attention of the kitchen thralls. Instead, just the silence of shock and disbelief. And the soon all-too-real evidence of our own eyes: Ethelwold, Ealdorman of East Anglia was dead.

Of all those at Uphude, I was probably the least shocked. I had known, known beyond all doubt, that something terrible had happened. Early in the day I had sensed Wulf's exhilaration at taking part in the hunt, I could almost feel the wind in his face as he cantered after the other riders, Ratkin behind him. Then his elation had turned to confusion and terror, desperation and an urgent, heart-wrenching need for help. And, finally, sorrow and an all-consuming compassion. I had been suffering a sick, dull ache in my belly which I recognised as fear for hours, and now I knew why.

As our Uncle Brithnoth walked beside the makeshift bier, Wulf and Ratkin rode upon Fireflax. Later, Wulf told me how Ratkin had begun the long trek home, like our uncle, walking beside the litter, refusing to be parted from Ethelwold, but as he became too tired to keep up, Brithnoth lifted him up on the great horse, and set Wulf behind him with instructions to hold him tight. Grief had exhausted him and, still mute, he seemed lost in a daze of disbelief and misery. Behind those at the head of the party, the other riders and the hunt followers rode and walked in silence.

Dagmaer and the Uphude serving women hurried forward. Brief explanations were made. The house-ceorls and thralls held back; this, the handling of the dead, would be women's work. A cry went up to send for Elfrith, where was she? Morwen appeared at the door of the Great Hall, and then retreated, presumably to find her mistress. After some minutes, Elfrith, leaning on Morwen's arm, and with our Aunt Aelflaed on her other side, was escorted across the courtyard and came to stand beside her husband's body. Edgar dismounted, handed his reins to a companion-man and hurried over to her.

"Lady... I cannot imagine what you must be feeling. This day is one of ill-fortune, indeed."

"Sire, you are kind." She took a kerchief proffered by Morwen and dabbed her eyes, prettily, though they did not appear to be wet. Aelflaed was openly weeping. She went to Brithnoth and buried her face in his chest. He at last took his hand from his friend's shoulder and wrapped his arms around her.

The King was all solicitude. "Every care has been taken," he assured Elfrith. "The Archbishop gave rites and prayers for the departed. Ethelwine and Lord Brithnoth witnessed the ealdorman at the last. He was truly a good man. His final thoughts were for others. He gave young Ratkin here his freedom."

"Indeed!" Elfrith seemed unimpressed, but then remembered herself. "Indeed? Well, that is much in keeping with his usual ways... Sire, if you will forgive me, I must attend to... there is much to..."

"Of course, Lady, of course. Do not think of myself or the Court, we shall not require your attention this sad night. You must be anxious to get to the chapel, and to see your Lord laid there ready for vigil. And... no, do not doubt it... I shall be part of that vigil myself. If I cannot give one long night to stay wakeful beside an old friend, then I am not worthy to be called such and, indeed, think of myself as friend, not just King, to my people."

"Your Majesty." Elfrith again put the kerchief to her face and allowed herself to be led back to the Hall, while the serving women took charge of the horse pulling the litter and escorted Ethelwold's body to the chapel. Ratkin made as if to follow, but Dagmaer held him back.

"No, lad, the laying out of the dead is not for you to witness. You may see your Master when he is made ready. Mayhap, then, you will be allowed to be part of the vigil, though you are young for such an observance. For now, go with Wulf and Aetna."

Ratkin made as if to object, but he had little strength left to do so. I put my arm around him and, with Wulf on his other side, took him to our chamber.

)))))))((((((

What can I say of the rest of our stay at Uphude? There was a pall cast over everything. Although the sun shone fair for the next several days, giving some comfort to those who travelled distances to attend the Ealdorman of East Anglia's funeral, it did not seem to warm us. Wulf had been deeply shocked by what he had witnessed and I was sadder than I had ever been before. True, Ethelwold had been only an occasional visitor to our Hall, but when he had been present, his long-standing pretence of being my aging swain had made me feel very special. In my childish way, I had loved him ardently. It seemed that a certain dimension of our fantastic games was lost for ever.

Far worse, though, was Ratkin's sense of bereavement. He was lost on an empty sea, rudderless and without hope of landfall on any familiar shore. His foster parents would have been happy to take him into their home permanently, and whilst he was careful to respect their feelings, and was grateful and affectionate toward them, it was Ethelwold to whom he had always given his deepest love and loyalty. It was Ethelwold who had saved him, given him the hope of a future, however vague, and who had now made him free of his thraldom. But to what end? He was too young to care for himself, earn a living, make a place for himself by virtue of his own talents and, now that he was free, no man had the responsibility of doing so for him. He was free indeed, but perhaps only to return to the muddy puddle from which the ealdorman had rescued him.

On the day following the funeral, which had seen Ethelwold laid beneath the flagstones of the chapel – Elfrith had insisted on a quick interment and would not hear of his body being preserved and taken to Petrideburg Abbey – Ratkin had sat with us beside the wardrobe cart, which was being packed, ready for our return trip to Radendunam.

"I have no place in this Hall any longer," he said. "I heard the companion-men talking; the King is to confirm Lord Ethelwine as the new Ealdorman of East Anglia before he leaves. And as for the Lady Elfrith's household, wherever it moves to, I shall not be welcome in it! Nor would I want to be…" Ratkin's dislike of his former mistress had deepened in the days since Ethelwold's death.

"What shall you do?" asked Wulf.

"I had thought, perhaps, to go to Rammesig and ask the swordsmith if he needed another apprentice, but though it would be a good place to pass a cold winter, I do not like the idea of being cooped up by a hot forge all summer long, too. And I would rather learn to wield a sword than make one."

"Then why not?" said Wulf.

"Why not what?"

"Learn to wield it. I shall be beginning my proper training soon – when we return to Radendunam I shall be six," said Wulf, proudly.

"So shall I," I added, sharply.

"And I am six already, I think!" said Ratkin, for the first time in days there was a sense of purpose in his manner. Hope for the future. "What do you think the Lord Brithnoth would say if I asked to become part of your household? Now that my Lord Ethelwold is gone, there is no-one I would rather serve. And you will need a companion-man of your own soon!"

I felt a little jealous. It was as though the boys were about to enter some great adventure of which I could never be a part. But their enthusiasm was infectious. I liked Ratkin and the thought of his being a permanent part of our lives was a good one. Whilst he could not yet muster one of his old, broad, gap-toothed grins, his eyes were shining with something other than tears, and he smiled.

"If I ask your uncle for such a place, would you stand up for me?"

"Indeed, I would," said Wulf, unable to hide his own grin.

"And I would, too," I said. Impulsively, I threw my arms around Ratkin's neck and kissed him full on the mouth.

"My Lady!" he feigned shock. I giggled, and the boys laughed, even Ratkin.

At that moment, our uncle strode out of the Great Hall, heading for the stables.

"Well, now, that is better! I cannot bear to see so many sad faces as we have had this last few days. Life goes on, does it not? And you, young Ratkin, how do you fare, as a free man?"

In that easy manner, and with little persuasion needed, Ratkin became a member of our inner circle. What did it matter that we knew nothing of his origins? Neither did he. Enough that he had been loved by one whom we had all loved so well. Our aunt, when she heard of it, was as pleased as our uncle. Dagmaer was, as ever, outwardly brusque, but comfortingly practical.

"Just what our Hall needs... another child! Do I not have enough to keep in order, I wonder? Well, little Ratty, if you are to be my young wolf-cub's companion we had better see about getting you better dressed - and rid of that collar! Has no-one thought to loose you of it yet? Must I do everything? Away to the workshop with you, for it will not take much to shear through that slight thing. In the name of the..." and she bustled away, taking her pretended indignation with her.

And so, in the decade that followed, we somehow left our childhood behind. The years between a sixth and a sixteenth birthday are momentous for any young person, and none of us felt any differently. Thella became my personal attendant and grew from a capricious little girl into a lively, intelligent companion-woman and between the four of us nothing passed unnoticed, either in the Great Hall or the servants' domain. We shared everything and no interesting snippet of information that circulated inside one or other of our spheres was missed. There were all the usual small sorrows and joys of growing up.

Poor Bremel fell prey to an accident with the horses in the stable yard, and his place was taken by a sturdy red and white hound – one of Waldi's descendants – who was, I confess, a better hunting companion for Wulf than the little black boy could have been, but Berrie was still part of my life, though he now preferred to potter about after me, or spend long hours by my side as I embroidered, rather than indulge in mad chases and games. Musbane appeared never to change, though he put on a little more weight and showed even less inclination to live up to his name, continuing to allow the outdoor cats to relieve him of the arduous duties of mousing. Gillycrest was no more, but one of her daughters still wore a floral crown at the Mayday celebrations – much to the disapproval of Father Aelmer, whose intolerance of such traditions grew more fanatical with each passing year.

There were greater joys and sorrows, too. The first large family gathering after the ill-fated trip to Uphude was a merry one, as Leoflada and Oswig married. Their happiness was so evident that it spread to all those present, and the cloud which had seemed to hang over the family since Ethelwold's death was dispersed in a three-day long celebration of love and in anticipation of the years to come. Flada had, of course, moved to her new home in Stecworthe after the wedding, but we saw her often, and she was now the mother of three daughters, Aelfwenna, Aelswith and Leofwaru, little imps, all of them, doted upon by their parents and spoiled by their uncles. Petroc, together with Dagmaer's elder daughter, Dagmaeda, had also moved to Stecworthe, he as head of the stables and companion-man, she as Leoflada's chief companion-woman, a position, I had to say, which I did not envy her.

But Wyrd had reserved the most tragic and extraordinary of her threads to be woven into Edgar's life. Upon his return to Wintancaestre after the events of 962 he was greeted by his beloved "white duck", well into her second pregnancy and his little son, Edward, now toddling. He found himself as he had ever wanted to be, at the heart of a happy family. Queen Elfa's confinement was approaching, and she seemed stronger than he could have dared wish, her only torment that of a debilitating waking sickness, which had not lessened throughout her time expecting. Before leaving Uphude, according to an admiring Edgar, Elfrith had, despite her own agonies of bereavement, thought to give him a philtre which, she said, was sovereign against such an ailment. Several drops in small ale when Elfa broke her fast, and the same again in wine at midday would soon restore her appetite and strengthen her for her coming labour.

Initially it seemed, indeed, to be an excellent tonic. Then, suddenly, in the seventh month of her pregnancy, Elfa was seized with appalling pains, and brought to her childbed early. Too early to save the child (which would have been the little princess that Edgar so long for), but too late to spare her the travails of a difficult birth. She became elf-shot and died three days later – to be buried with her tiny infant daughter.

Edgar was bereft. Inconsolable. Our aunt, the Dowager Queen Aethelflaed, went to him in Wintancaestre and, she told Aelflaed later, took him in her arms and rocked him as she had when he was a little boy. For weeks, months, he had done little more than fulfil his responsibilities as a king: attending courts, signing charters, hearing Petitions. He ate almost nothing, and his slim frame became emaciated to the point where his friends despaired of his life. But then, gradually, he began to regain himself.

Almost as if he was shy at being seen to do so, he began entering into a correspondence. He engaged a courier whose sole duties were to deliver and bring replies to his letters, the man almost permanently on the long roads between the Court (where ever it happened to be convened) and Dumnonia. Edgar, ever punctilious as to the niceties of etiquette, was conducting a very correct and restrained courtship. Anxious it should not appear that either of the widowed parties were hastily putting aside their mourning (which, in his case, was nothing but the truth) he had, he later said, received such moving and sympathetic words of comfort from the Lady Elfrith that he felt irresistibly drawn to her.

After Ethelwold's death, Elfrith had quickly returned to her father's Hall in Dumnonia, taking Morwen with her, but very little else to remind her of her time at Uphude. Within a year, Sub-Ealdorman Ordgar had been elevated to the position of full ealdorman with responsibilities throughout the long south-western peninsula of Englaland, the old Celtic kingdom of Dumnonia. Questions raised as to the capabilities of the elderly Ordgar were soon rendered immaterial as the reason became obvious: the Lady Elfrith, as daughter of this now important Witan member (and widow of another) was invited to Court. Chaperoned by her brother, Ordulf, and with the ever present Morwen by her side, apartments at Court were made over to her. It was only a matter of time before Edgar made her his new Queen, and they were married in 965. Three years later she presented him with a son, the Aetheling Ethelred. Elfrith was where she felt she should always have been – and unassailable.

In 973, Edgar was in his thirtieth year; for thirteen of those years he had been King, and was called "the peacemaker", for he had kept Englaland at peace with itself and the other nations with which it traded and shared the Eastern Sea, throughout his reign. There was talk, from time to time, of the Vikings and their ambitions, of their coveting the fertile swathes of Englaland, West of the Danelaw, but it was just talk, so everyone said. Even the weather and the way of the seasons had been fine in recent years. There had been no great storms, no floods or winters of extreme cold. Springs had been warm, autumns fruitful, harvests safely gathered in. It was time, so said a declaration from the Court, that Edgar should have the coronation which had been so long postponed after his brother's death, and, in a startling break with everything that had gone before, his Queen was to be crowned alongside him. Anointed and acknowledged as no woman had ever been in the history of Englaland. The ceremony was to take place at Bathe and it was to be followed by a Progress to Caestre, by land and sea, where a second, even more theatrical pageant was to be staged: every lesser "king" from around the islands of Bryttania was to swear their fealty to Edgar, consolidating the Long Peace which he had settled upon our lands.

Wulf and I, as part of Edgar's extended Royal Family – a distant part, admittedly – were, if not centre stage, then at least given roles to play in the wings of this great, unprecedented production. What could be more exciting for the two of us, six months shy of our seventeenth birthdays and just embarking upon our adult lives? It had been hard, especially for me, to become used to being apart from my twin, although our separation, we had both come to accept, was never entirely whole. Though we mentioned it to few, between the two of us we knew, without a trace of doubt, that our minds and spirits were linked in a way that could not be fully explained by rational argument. Just as we had once shared, as infants, the occasional physical hurt, the pain of a grazed knee, or a bee sting, or the gut-wrenching fear of each other's rare nightmares when we awoke, always at the same moment during the night, we found that we could now still sense the other's emotions, knew when the other was approaching, or when their plans had changed. Wulf was irritable when my monthly flowers were upon me, and when he had taken too much wine, I was laid low the following morning. Those were the less fortunate effects, but they were little in comparison to the overwhelming sensation of never being completely alone, even if we were parted by many miles.

Wulf had lately been in the service of the King, learning the ways of Edgar's Court and the skills of the battlefield – though, thankfully, never had he been called upon to fight in earnest. As promised, he had grown into the beautiful sword wrought by the Master Smith of Rammesig and now he was rarely abroad without it upon his hip. With many other young men of about his age, he travelled in the ranks of Edgar's royal processes, gradually advancing from running errands to more responsible duties: seeing that the King's ceremonial arms were always ready for use, checking, at first, that the ceorls were undertaking their own duties correctly and then, as he matured, that the lesser companion-men were correctly rostered, and on occasion joining the King on the hunt, or when he rode to falconry. His time of this apprenticeship was coming to its close, and decisions had to be made about how and where he would go into permanent service – at Court or back at Radendunam, to be groomed as a successor to our uncle, the Ealdorman Brithnoth. Ratkin had been at his side throughout: now companion-man to Wulf, as was my brother, in turn, one of several to the King.

Whilst his horizons had been broadening, I had stayed within the compass of the Great Hall at home. At first, I had been jealous of his opportunities, but I soon found that my increasing responsibilities were becoming also my great loves, opening the door to unexpected vistas. When Leoflada had left our Hall, Aunt Aelflaed turned to me to fill her place, and where Flada had found no interest in the comings and goings of those who ruled our land, meetings of the Witan and so on, preferring the day to day routines of the domestic Hall rather than the formalities of such entertaining, I found them both challenging and fulfilling. Where Flada's Hall was now a haven of informality and bucolic intimacy between her husband, her brothers-in-laws and their families, Radendunam, in contrast, was a place well run, well maintained and well known to many of the highest in the land. Whilst giving ease and relaxation to its Lord, it was famed for a fine still-room and kitchen, excellent entertainment, a Hall offering all the new comforts of separate rooms, integral hearths and, above all, with the facilities to welcome and play host to the Witan – and even the Royal Court – whenever needed. It was this latter that I found the most fascinating, for listening to the game of words, the play of politics and the management of affairs of State was becoming my true passion. I realise now that the time spent sitting on Ethelwold's knee or riding ahead of the King's Progress with my uncle had been more than just an opportunity to feel important. Although I could not, as a child, understand the implications of my elders' words, still I could sense their dynamics and loved to witness the cut and thrust of conversation, the ebb and flow of opinion and emotion. In becoming an integral part of the Great Hall, I was privy to much that remained beyond the ken of even some lesser members of the Court.

With the whole family now gathered at Bathe for Edgar's coronation, I could not have been happier. Anticipation of taking part in the celebrations, my brother's arrival and the knowledge that Aunt Aelflaed had the confidence in my skills to allow me much autonomy in the preparation of our hospitality to those who visited, gave me huge pleasure and with it a growing confidence in my own abilities. And the knowledge that whatever passed between those at the heart of the country's government, if it took place under our roof, would likely become known to me, added spice.

We had taken a moderately-sized Hall within the old city walls – like Colencaestre, the town was a jumble of Roman ruins incorporated into more recent buildings – and although we had only brought a skeleton staff of thralls and serving women, they were our best and most adept, so that under Dagmaer's immediate supervision it had been made comfortable and welcoming. It was the Feast of Saint Pachomius, two days before the appointed date for the great service of coronation on the eleventh day of May, and Archbishop Dunstan, who was being accommodated with the King and Elfrith, in what remained of the Roman castle, was to join the family for the evening. The ancients called the castle a villa – or so I had been told – and it stood close to the ruined bath houses where warm water still issued, like a miracle, from the regions of Hel below. It was only a short walk to our Hall and, typically, Dunstan had chosen to dress incognito allowing him to pass through the streets unrecognised.

He hammered on the heavy oaken door an hour or so before the light began to fade. It had been a warm, pleasant spring day. It was Dagmaer who opened the door to him, dropping a curtsey and, for the benefit of others present, greeting him formally.

"My Lord Archbishop. Ealdorman Brithnoth and the family await you."

"Mistress Dagmaer, it is a pleasure to see you once again."

"This way, Lord."

A small, curtained-off ante-chamber separated the hall from the door which opened directly onto the street outside. Dagmaer drew back the hanging to allow Dunstan's passage. I noticed that as he passed close by her, their eyes met and held for an instant. She followed him into the room. Her place in the household was still slightly ambiguous and now that she no longer had charge of me and my brother, her duties were more general. She had become more a companion-woman to my aunt – she had never entirely been a servant – but her social standing still prohibited her taking ease with the family.

There was a good deal of hugging and other greetings going on as Dunstan embraced Aelflaed and Aethelflaed and clasped arms with Brithnoth and Ethelwine, who had arrived with Elflada that postnoon.

By Aelflaed's leave, I was to play hostess that evening, and assumed the role. "Thank you, Dagmaer, you may be about your own pleasures now," I said. I added, keeping my voice low, "If he asks, where shall I say you are?"

166

"Lady?"

"Come, Dagmaer, don't be coy! Both you and I know that the Archbishop will not leave this Hall without passing some time with you!"

She smiled, pleased at the little tease.

"I shall likely be in the herb garden until sunset and then by the fireside in the still-room. If anyone should be interested," she added over her shoulder as she left the room.

Dunstan turned to me. "Wulfaetna! Why, you are a lovely young woman. Only two years ago you were but a long-legged filly, and now you... well, perhaps that was not the most flattering beginning! But you know my meaning. And if what I hear is true, you have inherited your aunt's skills and charm."

Aelflaed put her arm around my waist. "I will allow you the charm, for that is but a pretty compliment," she said. "But I fear that Aetna is already outstripping me in her husbandry skills. However, they say that the best a teacher can wish for is to be overtaken by their student, so I am content. She has many new ideas and I have said that for the weeks we are here in Bathe this is to be her Hall and that she may run as she wishes. It is quite delightful to take my ease and watch it all done for me!"

"Aunt, you know that I still have much to learn," I laughed. "But I thank you, Lord Archbishop, for your words. I can only hope that this evening's hospitality will not give them the lie, for this filly has been allowed her head tonight..." As we were away from home, informal and in something of a holy-day situation, Aelflaed had, indeed, given me permission to introduce some of the more neoteric – not to say controversial – fashions, recently arrived from the land of the Franks, into the evening's events.

"I am intrigued and enchanted," said Dunstan. "And may we expect the pleasure of your brother's company, too?"

"Wulf should be here directly," Brithnoth said. "He has been with us these two days, but it is hard to keep him out of the Waters. He was ever something of an otter, never mind a wolf, and he has been swimming dawn till dusk. He had something of a bruise, too, from sword practice, and he swears the Waters ease it."

"It has long been said that the baths here have a healing property," agreed Dunstan. "The ancients certainly believed it to be so. They left offerings to their gods in the pools so I am told."

"Well just don't mention them within the hearing of Father Aelmer," said Aelflaed. "Yesterday he and Dagmaer almost came to blows over the subject of the Waters! If I have to listen to another of his tirades against so-called paganisms at morning service I shall..."

What my aunt would feel impelled to do was lost, as hearty laughter was heard amid the clamour of the great door opening and the excited barking of a dog.

"Quiet, Rota! Ratkin, take him into the kitchens and find him some food. We left so early this morning that neither of us broke our fast. Feed yourself, too, for I will not need you again this day." There was some reply which I could not quite catch. "You will want your strength if you are to try your luck with that brown-haired, little she-kitten down at the sign of the Green Man. But she'll have none of you, I warrant!"

Still laughing, Wulf pushed the hanging aside and put his head and shoulders through the curtain. "Ladies, am I allowed to greet the newcomers as I am, or must I deck myself in finery first?"

Without waiting for a reply, knowing what it would be, he came into the Hall. Wulf. My brother, my twin, my other self. Golden hair tousled and still damp from the Waters, tall, over a *sixfot* in height, slim and strong, but without the heaviness of muscle that would come with greater maturity. Blue-eyed and with a smile that would light the black caverns beneath Irminsul.

There was no need for introductions. Dunstan knew Wulf as well as he knew me. The years had changed both of us, but not beyond the simple fact of our approaching adulthood.

"Young man, you look well. And wet!"

"Lord Archbishop, I acknowledge the first, and regret the second. I am indeed well, and hope to remain so, but the wetness can soon be rectified!" He essayed a short, ironic bow from the waist – it reminded me of the way he had often done so, studiously, as a child. "I am honoured to see you again, Lord."

Dunstan clapped him on the shoulder. I wondered if he was remembering the time he helped – or tried to help – in our little deception of Dagmaer close upon our arrival at Uphude so many years before. Wulf, and I, and been wet then, too.

"Sweet Aunt!" Wulf swung Elflada off her feet and whirled her around. "How are my nieces and nephews? Lord Ethelwine, you look... full of life and fair fortune." Ethelwine had gained a considerable amount of weight in recent years.

"We are all well," Elflada, allowed back to earth, smoothed down her gunna and took her husband's arm. "You see, my love? Even Wulf has noticed your..." she patted his belly, over which his britches were rather tightly strained. His over-mantle barely closed across it, and was held in place by a fine buckle, which looked in danger of tearing the fabric, so great was the tension under which it was put.

"Wife," he smiled at her fondly, "when my belly prohibits me from making yours swell, then I shall begin to worry. Until then..." He laid his hand over her slightly bulging waist and she slapped it away playfully.

"Again?" cried Wulf. "Aunt, I am sorry, I would not have been so rough!"

"All is well, my love," Elflada replied. "It would take a great deal more than a dance step or two with my handsome nephew to unseat this little one. With the blessing of the Lord, all my babes have found my belly too comfortable a bed to leave until the time was right."

Amid laughter and conversation, we made our way to the far end of the Hall. A heavy table stood to the left with benches on either side, a fire burning brightly in an open hearth ahead of us, while to our right several packing cases stood, partly emptied, with straw and hessian wrappings piled beside them.

"I fear we are a little short of room, Dunstan," Aelflaed explained. "The upper chambers have all been allocated for sleeping – Aetna now insists on the new ways in such matters – so the Hall has become something of a sorting room for all the paraphernalia of a household in transit!"

"Aunt, I was not to know that there would be no courtyard buildings in which to stow all our..." I was a little on the defensive, as, in embracing the fashion for private sleeping apartments, I had, indeed, overlooked the elementary need for storage. I still had much to learn, as I had acknowledged.

"It matters little, Aetna! We shall not be here long enough for it to become of importance."

Wulf and our uncle drew the benches away from the table and set them about the hearth. Brithnoth spread his arms wide, as though to embrace the whole company. "Come friends, sit, take your ease."

I excused myself and went through to the kitchens. Thoth had not travelled with us. Now in his sixtieth year, his health was beginning to fail him a little and at Radendunam he had become the grand-sire of the servants' halls, in a role which had lately been coined by some as a "bottler". One of his senior apprentices had travelled with us, a young man as keen as I to experiment with the new fashions in hospitality.

"Saewold, how have the short-eared hares cooked?" I asked. These strange little creatures, which made burrows and lived underground, had lately become quite the rage at some tables, I had heard. Saewold knew one of the kitchen staff in a household at Cyrnecaestre and had arranged for several brace to be sent up to us, though I later learned that they could often be found close to many old Roman towns, so we might have been able to catch some locally. I made a mental note to myself to tell Wulf –

maybe he and Ratkin could track some down; Rota had a fine nose for such things.

"They will shortly be done to a turn, Lady."

For the next hour I was immersed in my duties. It crossed my mind that it was a privilege to manage a meal – even an informal one such as this – with an Archbishop and the Dowager Queen of Englaland in attendance. Aethelflaed, like Dunstan, was accommodated at the castle with the rest of the Royal Family, but would dine with us this eve. The kitchen thralls efficiently set about the preparation of the table in the Great Hall, carrying the trenchers and cold dishes through while Thella, usually so light of foot, stamped around the kitchen banging down platters and flagons as through she would rather be bringing them down on someone's head. I pulled her up, sharply.

"For the love of the gods, Thella," I said, involuntarily glancing over my shoulder in case Father Aelmer should have heard me using one of her mother's favourite expressions. "Be careful with those. We cannot be sending back to Radendunam for replacements every half-moon."

"But I suppose it is alright for me to be here doing two people's work, when that block-headed Ratkin is away at his leisure down at the Green Man," she said.

"If my brother saw fit to let Ratkin have his evening free, that is his affair." In truth, Thella and Ratkin shared very few duties in common, but it clearly rankled that she was on call and he was not. Or perhaps there was another reason for her ill-humour. "In any case," I said, "you can hardly think yourself badly used: you spent the whole postnoon among the traders' stalls looking at ribbons for the coronation day!"

"Well, a girl must look her best on such a day," she said, somewhat chastened. She tossed her curls and for a moment reminded me of the little flirt she had been as a child. "You never know who you might meet."

"Well put that out of your mind for now and look to your work instead. I want you behind my chair when we dine, just as we practised."

When all was nearly ready, I slipped up to my sleeping chamber – shared only with Thella – to put on a clean over-gunna. I noticed a pile of ribbons on Thella's pallet. She would have one to match whatever she chose to wear for the next month! And no doubt some of them were meant for me. Where my needlework skills lay in embroidery, Thella's were more practical. She could turn a sleeve, alter a neckline and add a ribbon to any gunna and make it look quite the fashion overnight.

I returned and put my head into the kitchen. "Thella, with me! Saewold, say two *Fæder ures* and then bring in the hot food." In the time it took for the Lord's prayer to be recited twice, the company would have taken their seats.

Followed by Thella, I returned to the Hall. "My lords, ladies, pray come to the table," I said.

There was no seating plan, everyone took places alongside those with whom they were already in conversation. Brithnoth and Ethelwine had their heads together, Aunt Aelflaed and Elflada were laughing and joking with Dunstan and Aethelflaed, while Wulf came to sit by me. "Is my sister keeping you on your toes, Thella?" he said, as she took her place at my elbow.

"Do not tease, Wulf," I said. "This evening is important to me."

"I know," he said. "It will be fine."

Just as I had hoped, moments after the company was seated, the thralls began to bring in the dishes. Here was another innovation I had heard was becoming the norm in some places: a portion of meat was placed on each guest's trencher, rather than everyone simply helping themselves to heaped food set on platters in the middle of the table. Of course, they could still make free with the general dishes: fish, baked roots, coddled eggs and so forth, but the speciality dish – in the case, the short-eared hares – was served out with some ceremony. They had been braised in thickened meat juices and I had schooled the thralls in ladling them onto the bread trenchers without spillage. I was relieved when there were no mishaps. Dunstan gave us a short grace.

"Thella, see that everyone has their chosen drink," I said, but she was already circling the table, flagon and wine jar to hand, deputising, as tradition demanded, her mistress' once-obligatory role.

"Aetna, this is wonderful!" Aelflaed clapped her hands in the pretty little gesture that she had made her own over the years. "I have heard of these little creatures, but never tasked them. They do, indeed, owe something to hares, but the meat is less powerful."

"They do not need to be hung, Aunt," I replied, "so the flavour is sweeter."

"In the valleys of the Loire, they call them 'coonees' or some such," said Dunstan. "It loses something in the translation. The Romans thought them fine food. But then, they ate some very strange things – even dormice!" he laughed.

"Have you been across the water lately, Dunstan?" asked Elflada. "To see your Cluniac friends, perhaps? We do not see you as often as we used and I miss the stories of your travels."

"Alas, no, Lady. Disagreements on the Witan and the resulting uncertainties in the monasteries have kept me within these shores." He glanced at Brithnoth and Ethelwine. "Indeed, we have all been aware of the tension this last few years. I think it is one of the reasons that the King feels this is the time for his coronation. To demonstrate that despite internal wrangling, the Witan is still strong and loyal."

"You are right," said Brithnoth. "The King has been vexed by the arguments. It is hard to know where it will end, with the Chief Ealdorman stirring up dissatisfaction wherever reforms are mooted."

"Alfhere is, at least, mindful of his position and how his actions may be construed but the same cannot be said for his brother. Alfheah is becoming fanatical in his opposition to reform. And that brother-in-law of his, Alfric – now there is a man to be watched. I would not trust him as far as I could throw a hog!"

"And likely will remain so, when he benefits from the revenues his manors accrue from the abbeys on his lands," added Ethelwine.

"Alfhere may take care to distance himself from his brothers' activities in public," continued Dunstan, "but behind closed doors he makes no attempt to hide his opinions. He and the Queen are becoming increasingly vocal in support of the anti-reformation lobby and, of course, they both have the ear of the king."

Aethelflaed took a sip of wine. "But surely Edgar is not to be easily swayed," she said. "He has ever supported your aims to re-invigorate the Benedictine Rule in the abbeys."

"Edgar hates discord. He fears a fractured Witan. He opines for reformation but will not legislate against those such as Alfheah who breaks no laws but has no desire to see the abbeys concentrating upon their holy duties, which are prayer, the comforting of the sick, the care of the poor and the life Saint Benedict decreed. Instead he allows the monasteries to be coerced into electing Abbots whose families once owned the land on which the abbeys stand and the towns in which they must survive. Look at Bedricsworth. Or Byrgen Saint Edmund, as many are now calling it. The town thrives: that is good, the traders and market-men do fine business with all the pilgrims visiting the shrine. It is certain that there will be an abbey there before long. Who would be the foremost candidate for the Abbacy? Why Bedricson, of course. Scion of the family who has held all the surrounding land since before records were kept. Monies coming into the blessed shrine, once it is housed within the abbey, might as well go straight into the coffers of the local Hall. That it is in your Ealdormanry, Ethelwine, at least means that you would have some say in the matter. Fealty is owed to you and you see that the Church is not short-changed. But were Alfhere its ealdorman, as in Mercia, how much more would be syphoned off..." Dunstan took a long pull at his drink. "My apologies, ladies, I did not mean to raise my voice."

"It matters not, Dunstan," said Aelflaed. "You feel passionate about this matter. It is to be understood."

"I know that I am no saint," Dunstan caught my eye for a moment and again I was transported to the past – did he remember that Wulf and I were present when Dagmaer's revelation came out so abruptly? We had never mentioned it to a soul. "We are none of us worthy to be called servants of the Lord, but the manipulation of the abbeys is a sin not to be easily forgiven. Today, on the eve of the feast of the blessed Pachomius, he who first instigated the monastic life..." Dunstan fell silent.

"But why should Elfrith be so keen to take the Chief Ealdorman's cause to heart?" asked my Aunt Elflada, eager to change the subject slightly.

"Elfrith has an eye to the future," said Dunstan, and would be prevailed upon to say no more on the subject. "Speaking of the Queen, though, have you ladies been made privy to her planned wardrobe for the coronation?" He, too, sought to lift the mood of the conversation.

"We have been told what *not* to wear!" laughed Aethelflaed. "Red is to be the perquisite of the King and Queen alone."

"I fear that may be something of my fault," admitted Dunstan. "I confess that in the matter of planning the coronation ceremony Elfrith and I have laid aside our differences and have, I believe, created an event which I fervently hope will be the pattern for all the nation's coronations to come." This man was a welter of contradictions. Humble and prideful by turn.

We had, of course, heard much of the planned celebrations. My part in it – and I confess to being as heady about the upcoming day as Thella – was to be in the role of companion-woman to my Aunt Aethelflaed, who, as Dowager Queen had a place with the other members of the inner Royal Family. My ceremonial position was to see that her gunna and veil were perfectly arranged and to be at her bidding. The decree that red should be avoided had been with us early in the preparations, and we had duly commissioned gunnas in green, with undergunnas in soft buttery gold. The Dowager Queen's was, of course, to be finer than mine – but mine was still the most splendid that I had ever worn. Even now, it was carefully hung in my sleeping chamber, awaiting the final choice of ribbons to secure my head-rail.

The meal had progressed to the sweeter courses, platters of fruit, bottled the previous autumn and made delicious by the addition of honey and floral infusions, and curds with added spices. Reluctantly, I pulled my attention away from the conversation and to back to the evening's arrangements.

Thella had ensured that there was wine and ale set beside the fire, with pokers on hand to mull the brews for those who wished to do so. "I think we may retire to the hearth," I said, rising from the table. I had one more surprise in store. Wulf had told me of a skop he had met at the baths, one Agnolo, who had been entertaining those taking their ease in the Waters. He was young and newly arrived from Rome, so it seemed likely that he had tales and songs in his repertoire that we had not heard before. It was often hard to find such a one. He had been taking his meal in the kitchens, and I sent Thella through to fetch him. Judging by her flushed face when she returned, Agnolo had brought something of the heat of southern Europe with him to our cooler shores.

His entrance was dramatic, and he did not disappoint. A most enjoyable time followed as he held his audience spellbound, and I was delighted when Brithnoth favoured him with a broad arm-ring, after the time-honoured tradition. Wulf had explained to him that I did not have the wherewithal to pay him myself, but that if he pleased the Lord of the Hall then he was sure to be well recompensed.

"Aetna, you have done us very proud," Aelflaed once again clapped her hands lightly, like a little girl, and then slipped her slim arm around my waist. "I could not have wished for a more pleasant evening."

There was a general chorus in agreement and it was my turn to blush. As the party began to break up, my Aunt Aethelflaed took me to one side. "I must be with the Royal Family tomorrow, with the young princes," she said. "They need a little more schooling in their duties for the big day! But are you fully prepared, my love?"

"Yes, Aunt, Thella and I will be at the abbey at first light on Sunday. We will come to the Nuns' Door as arranged and will get everything ready before you arrive so that we may assist you dressing."

"Good, the Holy Mother will be awaiting you and promises that the Sisters will do all they can should you need anything, although as it will be Whitsun, I expect they will be holding even more offices than usual! Oh, dear, no, the life of a nunnery would not have been for me! Now, have a fair night, my lovely girl, and sweet dreams!"

Dunstan had said his farewells and I was about to offer to see the Archbishop to the door, when he said that he really must offer his congratulations to the kitchen, and was Dagmaer likely to be taking here ease there, since she had not been needed that evening? I mentioned that she was very fond of the herb garden, and that the still-room fire might have tempted her to a few quiet hours of solitude. Later that night, I could hear low voices rising and falling long after the rest of the Hall was asleep. As ever, he and Dagmaer had things to discuss.

TWELVE

The day of the coronation dawned fine and bright. A sharp shower overnight had left the sky rain-washed and a pale sparking blue, with just a hint of mist on the horizon, promising a sunny noon to come. Thella and I were on our way to the abbey as soon as it was fully light, as promised, together with Wulf and Ratkin, for two such attractive young ladies (my brother's words, not mine) should not be abroad unaccompanied even on such a holy day.

The streets were, indeed, already becoming busy. There was money to be made today: the hawkers and peddlers were eager to find good pitches from which they could sell their wares to the many spectators expected to line the streets for the coronation procession, some of whom were already staking claim to the best vantage points from which to watch. Goodwives and servants were hurrying to and fro, keen to have their chores done before the show began and there was a cheery, expectant feel to the morning.

It was Ratkin's turn to be a little jealous. He tweaked the tip of Thella's long, fair plait, which was secured with one of the many ribbons she had so carefully chosen. Her outfit was of a pale green to compliment mine, although, of course, she would not be seen at the ceremony.

"So much care taken, and not even to be part of the performance!" he teased.

"Ah, but which performance?" she said. "Never you fear, you shall be seeing me this eve before the celebrations are over!" I knew that tone in her voice; she was planning some… mischief?

"Thella…" I cautioned.

"Pah!" retorted Ratkin. "Talk is easy!"

We were approaching the Nuns' Gate, through which no man was allowed to pass, the Nuns' Door beyond it only to be entered by arrangement and after the ringing of a bell hung to one side.

Well," said Wulf, "you are safely delivered and this is as far as we can go. I am away to the Monks' Gate, and Ratkin, you are once again at liberty. I am beginning to think that of the four of us you have the best life. I warrant you will get a better view of the procession than we shall, even without you being in the abbey."

"Aye, Lord, you may be right!" grinned Ratkin. "I aim to find a spot by the West Door to watch proceedings, with a jug of ale to my right," he cast an eye at Thella, "and a pretty girl to my left, if I can spot one."

Thella snorted; not a pretty sound. I kissed Wulf briefly on the cheek –
having to stand on tip-toe to do so – and we passed through the Gate and
rang the bell.

A young novice opened the door. We were clearly expected and
quickly ushered through a small ante-chamber into the Nuns' section of the
abbey, which formed the western range of buildings to the south of the
abbey church. The monks' accommodation, toward which Wulf had
headed and where the King and his entourage were preparing for the
events of the day, formed the range of buildings to the south-east, a mirror
image of these.

"I am Sister Alfreth," said the girl. "The Reverend Mother has given
me permission to miss the usual offices today and do your bidding in all
things, so that when Her Majesty the Dowager Queen arrives, all will be as
it should." She seemed nervous of us, but none too disappointed to be
released from the Whit services, and I could see her eyeing our gunnas
with something like envy. As if shaking herself from some reverie, she
smoothed down the rough fabric of her habit and adjusted her off-white
veil. "May I offer you some early refreshment?"

"Thank you, no, Sister," I said, "not just yet, for we have broken our
fast already. But I would like to lay out these clothes as soon as possible
so that they will not crease." I had been carrying Aunt Aethelflaed's over-
gunna, carefully protected by cheese-cloth wrappings, over my arm and
was becoming aware of its weight. Alfreth indicated a low table set ready
for the purpose and with Thella's help I stripped away the cheese-cloth to
reveal the gunna beneath. Alfreth gasped. If she had been impressed by
our gunnas, this was beyond her wildest dreams.

Aunt Aethelflaed was a skilled needlewoman, but her sister, Aelflaed,
was mistress of the art and this was her handiwork. A deep, woodland
green velvet (no wonder its weight) formed the basis for the whole
garment. I was relieved to see that it had not been crushed as I had carried
it. Unlike less formal day wear, usually to the knee, allowing the
undergunna to be seen from calf to foot, it was full-length, with a long slit
at the centre, waist to ankle, artfully stitched open to reveal a cloth-of-gold
lining, itself intricately embroidered with a swirling interlace of green.
Around the neckline, cuffs and hem of the skirt, the embroidered pattern
was repeated, cloth-of-gold forming the ground of narrow borders applied
and held in place by stitches camouflaged under freshwater pearls.

"Oh!" the little Sister was speechless. Her eyes widened still further as
Thella similarly unwrapped her burden. A gossamer head-rail
embroidered with tiny sprigs of green silk, each bearing a seed pearl like
those on the gunna. There were a few creases in the light fabric. "I shall
fetch boiling water immediately," said Alfreth. "The steam will soon
soften those out." She almost ran to the door and off on her mission.

"It does not seem to me," I said, "that Sister Alfreth is entirely enamoured of life in a convent."

"Poor soul," agreed Thella.

It was not unusual for daughters to be handed over to the Church at an early age to become Brides of Christ – the blessed Saint Pachomius had indeed sent virgins to live with his own sister as early as the third century – often with little care as to their suitability to cloistered life. Whilst awaiting Alfreth's return, Thella and I agreed quietly with Aethelflaed's comment on Pachomius-eve: the life of a nun would not be to our taste, either.

Alfreth struggled back, a little while later, with a pail of water, steaming hot. She had laid an earthenware platter over the top of it, to retain the heat, and when she removed it, we carefully held the creased areas of the veil over the rising moisture and watched as the small corrugations in the light fabric disappeared.

"You have a knack for this," I said, and Alfreth beamed. The first real smile we had seen from her.

"I love beautiful things," she said a little wistfully. But then brightening, "The late Holy Mother said that I might soon begin my apprenticeship to the needle. One day, I should like to be allowed to work on the fine church hangings for the abbey, and maybe even be sent to the Daughter House at Wintancaestre to work on the royal robes." Her face fell. "But things have changed now, and I don't think any of that will happen."

"I am sure you will, if that is what you want," I smiled.

"What you want is not always what you get – not here, anyway," her shyness had ebbed away as we had worked together on Aethelflaed's costume. "But now, time is getting along, and you must surely like some refreshment before your duties begin."

The morning was wearing away and both Thella and I said that we would be pleased to have something to eat. Alfreth brought us honey-cakes, with dried fruit and some small ale. She was also careful to make sure that we had cloths to protect our gunnas, and clean, damp rags to wipe our hands before we touched Aethelflaed's finery again. Thella dressed my hair in readiness for the events to come – I had simply tied it back loosely before we had left the Hall to save time. Leaving the hair at the back loose she separated a layer above it, which she plaited into three fine braids, each incorporating a green ribbon of differing shades. Next, she plaited the three braids together to create a single rope of interwoven hair and ribbon, which lay atop the loose hair beneath. I had adopted the fashion of the shorter, square head-rail, simply held in place with a stiffened tablet woven silk braid, which allowed Thella's handiwork to be seen, as my long hair rippled down my back.

"Quite the beauty," she said, pleased with her efforts.

Alfreth had been sitting on a trunk, swinging her legs and watching my transformation. "When I take my final vows," she said, "I shall be allowed, just once, to wear silk."

"The Lord will love you just as well in silk or homespun," I said, trying to sound comforting, but, I felt, rather too like Father Aelmer to be so. Alfreth sighed.

The bell at the Nuns' Door rang once again. The Dowager Queen had arrived.

Aethelflaed swept in to the chamber, Alfreth once again responding to the summons of the bell to allow her entrance, swathed in a shawl and over-cloak against the morning air, for, as she said, there had been no point in donning a gunna only to take it off again and assume her coronation finery. She was accompanied by two goodwives, one bearing a small, heavy casket, carefully hidden within a hessian bag, and the other a basket containing various combs, ribbons and other small fripperies, which Aethelflaed bade her give to Thella.

"I see that you have worked your magic on my niece's hair, Thella. Aetna, you look lovely! I can hardly wait to see what those skilled fingers can achieve for me." The Dowager Queen, though she had been to many royal occasions, seemed as thrilled with the thought of the upcoming celebrations as we were. "Oh, and there is my gunna! My sister has truly excelled herself with those final touches, has she not? And the veil... beautiful."

"Sister Alfreth, here, has been most helpful," I said. "She worked wonders on removing the smallest of creases. She has a love of beautiful things, and a knack with them."

"Thank you, my dear," Aethelflaed smiled at Alfreth, who, at first overawed, began to relax in her presence. "Now, time for that gunna, I think!" Between us, we lifted the gunna so that it could be slipped over her head and smoothed the velvet down as it fell into place.

The chamber was becoming a little crowded with the goodwives in attendance, and Aethelflaed told them to take their ease in the ante-chamber until they were needed again. They took her outer cloak with them – probably, I thought wryly, to sit upon as the cold, hard stone seats in the outer reaches of the convent were in no way intended for comfort. Aethelflaed seated herself where I had been and Thella began work on her hair.

The Dowager was in her fourth decade now, but her beauty was little diminished: the looks which had brought her to the attention of the late King Edmund were still in evidence. Childless herself, her figure had retained its youthful lines, and the rigours of stepmotherhood had left her brow relatively un-creased. Yes, there were laugh lines around her eyes and at the corners of her mouth, but she had escaped any marks of plague or other illness and her hair was fair, so a few streaks of silver in the gold could be forgiven. As befitted a matron, she insisted that Thella should draw the bulk of her hair back but had given permission for one of the newer fashions from the Continent, and two long braids now fell down on either side of her face. Choosing two small, jewelled combs from the basket, Thella looped the braids up, and secured them on the top of the Queen's head, brushing any escaping tendrils into place, before putting the veil on, and anchoring it with a narrow coronet – taken from the small chest – which sparkled with emeralds.

Thella held up a disc of polished silver, also brought in the trinket basket, for Aethelflaed to see her reflection.

"Ah, if only my Edmund was still here," she said wistfully. "Thella, you are most clever, who would have thought you could do so much for an old woman!" My aunt was not above playfully fishing for compliments. She knew she looked lovely.

"You look glorious, Lady," I said. "Elfrith will be furious!"

"Oh, hush… as if I cared about that…" but there was a mischievous curl about her lips as she spoke. "I am sure Her Majesty will look…" she seemed to search for the right word, "… extremely striking. Had she chosen to come to the convent with us, we would be able to see for ourselves, but no, she has to break with tradition and stay with the King, ostensibly to keep an eye on the princes, though the last time she took any interest in them I cannot remember – poor Edward, anyway – and rely upon Morwen, as usual, for her female company."

"What did the Father Abbot think to her insistence upon entering the Monk's wing of the abbey?" I asked.

"The last I heard, he put up some token objection, but since both he and most of the brothers – not to mention the lay brothers – seem to have … amours … who regularly visit, he could hardly really argue the point. Dunstan, of course, disapproves, but in the spirit of reconciliation which he is currently trying to maintain with Elfrith, he has postponed his battles to another day."

"And Elfrith is really to be *crowned* Queen?"

"Yes, to be truthful, I cannot understand why Dunstan has agreed to it, but yes! It has never been done before, but Elfrith is to be crowned Queen alongside her husband. There has even been a new crown made, and after Edgar is anointed, so will she receive the holy oil and be enthroned. She wanted to wear purple, like the Sovereign, but that was one step too far and so she has had to settle for red…"

"And hence our prohibition!"

"Indeed."

As this conversation proceeded, Thella and I had arranged a gold kirtle around Aethelflaed's waist, from which hung her chatelaine, and chosen various jewels to further ornament her gunna. When all was done, we held up the silver mirror once more.

"Thank you, my dears, thank you. Now, how goes the hour, I wonder? Aetna, are you quite ready, or do you need a little more attention? You really do look quite charming, but I think…" she opened the casket "… this will set off your outfit to perfection." She drew out a blue green jewel, set in a filigree of gold and mounted on a delicate clasp.

Standing before me, she held it up as if wondering where on my gunna it would look best. Deciding upon a point just below and central to the embroidered edge of the neckline, she pinned it in place.

"It is for you to keep, my love," she said. "I have somewhat to discuss with you after this day, and I would have you think upon this: a girl of your age has many choices which are about to make themselves apparent. Your uncle – your adopted father – is a man who will allow you to make them for yourself. He will want you to be happy, but he will also want you to be fulfilled. It has never been the way of our family to push its women into any life they do not want. Leoflada has made her decision and she seems to be happy with it. I think you may want something more out of life. I watched you on Saint Pachomius Eve. Not just what you did, but who you are becoming. You listened… that is a rare accomplishment in one so young. When the Ealdormen spoke, discussed matters of State, you did not look away and count the sugar apples – though you were well aware of how the table fared – you wanted to understand. And in truth I think you are beginning to do so."

She put her hands upon my shoulders and looked into my eyes. "Now, enjoy the day, and we will speak more on the matter soon."

"Thank you, Aunt." I kissed her on the cheek. "For the jewel and…"

"No more now! Sister Alfreth, run out and see how close the time comes to our entrance. And ask Ethel and Onwen to come back in for a moment. But before you go … I think you must know this abbey well?"

"Yes, Lady, very well!"

"And you are at liberty from your offices today?"

"For as long as I am under Your Majesty's orders."

"Then I am instructing you – under my orders, mark you, if anyone, including the Reverend Mother, should ask – to take Thella and my two goodwives, and find them, and yourself, some high vantage point where you can see everything that goes on. There must be some spots amid the stairways and galleries above the church that will give you a good view. Take some honey cakes and ale up with you, mind, it will be a long day. I want to hear from my women that you stayed with them all the time – to care for their needs, of course – until the last pretty gown had disappeared from the building! Can you do that?"

"Oh, yes, Lady! And thank you. I..."

"Off you go, then."

Alfreth ran out of the chamber, holding up the skirt of her habit enabling her to do so the faster, and revealing spindly legs beneath.

"That child does not look as though she has eaten a square meal in a twelvemonth," said Aethelflaed. "Poor lamb."

Ethel and Onwen returned and exclaimed at their mistress's transformation: the fit of the gown, the delicacy of the veil, the excellent choice of jewels. Within moments, Alfreth, too, was back, with the news that the guests had all arrived and taken their places (they were to be seated, while the bulk of the congregation would stand, as usual) and that the Sovereign's party had left the monks' apartments and were making their way around to the West Door to make their entrance. It was time for us to take our places. The ceremony was about to begin.

))))))((((((

Ratkin later told us of the scene outside the great West Door of the abbey church. Throughout the morning, ealdormen and their ladies, members of the Witan, Reeves and Shire Reeves, Bishops and the wealthiest of the merchant classes – those who could bribe their way inside, even if to stand only at the very back of the great building – had been arriving to witness the event, welcomed by lay Brothers and escorted to their allocated positions, according to their status. When it seemed as though there could not be another square inch of room inside, there came a lull in activity, an expectant pause, while all heads craned toward the south-western corner of the abbey buildings, whence the King was expected at any moment, having left the Monks' Gate as the bell tolled for noon.

A fanfare of horns announced his approach. He walked easily, almost nonchalantly, toward the crowd, inclining his head here and there, smiling at the children, even pausing to pet a small dog held out to him by a little girl, all the time aware that Elfrith was to his left, her hand gently resting on his outheld wrist, and whispering the odd comment in her ear. Elfrith walked tall and straight, hardly seeming to acknowledge the crowd of lesser people ahead of her, or even the words of the King, so intent did she seem upon the pageantry of the day. Behind her, Morwen held up the train of her gunna to keep it free of the damp ground, and beside Morwen walked one of Edgar's favourite companion-men, bearing the King's long red cloak in similar fashion. In the King and Queens' wake followed the young princes, Edward, behind his father, and Ethelred following his mother. Just into his thirteenth year, Edward looked ready to enjoy the day, but his brother, only five years old looked sullen and ill at ease.

Behind the princes came a small group of nobles. But the crowd were not interested in them; it was the royal party they had come to see. General applause, which had continued since they had come into view, gradually reached a crescendo as they approached the West Door. Edgar beamed at the people, Elfrith even essayed a smile and they entered the abbey church.

From the moment they began the slow, stately progress down the aisle, I could see them. Aethelflaed and I were in our positions to the left of the Presbytery steps, where the long Nave narrowed into the most holy part of the church, surrounding the High Altar. We had been provided with seats but stood for the arrival of the King. When the royal party reached the top of the Nave, Elfrith would be on our side of the church. On the other side, awaiting the King were several more companion-men, including Wulf. He winked at me, but caught Aethelflaed's eye, too.

"That boy!" she whispered, but I could see a barely supressed smile.

Dunstan, resplendent in his Archbishop's robes, greeted Edgar and Elfrith at the Presbytery steps. The young princes went to seats opposite ours in front of the waiting companion-men. Edward smiled at Wulf and Wulf gave him a reassuring nod – during his time at Court they had begun to know each other well; with only three years between them, Edward felt comfortable in my brother's company, more so than with the older members of the Court.

Centrally placed, at the top of the steps and facing the congregation, were two huge chairs, one only slightly larger than the other, covered in cloth of gold throws, and cushioned in red velvet. Behind the two thrones, and positioned to face the High Altar was another, more modest chair. Dunstan turned and stood facing Edgar and Elfrith. The long service started.

Elfrith stepped to one side, Morwen carefully arranging her gunna and cloak to its best advantage. Dunstan took the King by the hand, turned him toward the assembled people and called for him to "Live long!" to which came the reply, "Long live the King!" The choir, which until now had been silent, sang words from the Bible – I recognised an anthem based on the First Book of Kings – and Edgar read a short oath, promising to rule justly and by the word of God. Then a Mass began.

I will confess that my attention wavered. I could not help but look at the gathered nobility, most of whom I had met, or at least seen, before and now facing us from the front of the huge congregation. Their clothes were splendid, but for once, I was more taken by their expressions. My Uncle Brithnoth and Aunt Aelflaed followed the course of the Eucharist with their accustomed sincerity, and Ethelwine and Elflada seemed their usual selves, but others? The Chief Ealdorman, Alfhere, seemed little interested in the service, but appeared rapt by the appearance of Elfrith: he hardly took his eyes from her. His wife was not present. By his left side was his sister, the Lady Helga, and further along, Alfric, her husband. Helga sat elegant and composed, but Alfric fidgeted, forever shifting in his seat, uncomfortable and ill at ease. Between them sat a young man, with the cool good looks of his mother, and little, it seemed of his father. In fact, he could be seen to glance at Alfric from time to time with something like dislike in his eyes. For a moment, he seemed to realise that I was scrutinising him, and looked back at me, but I quickly turned away, embarrassed to be caught so openly paying little attention to the service.

Old Ealdorman Ordgar, the Queen's father, had died two years previously, but her brother, Ordulf, stood in his stead. His eyes darted about the abbey, taking the measure of everything and everyone about him. Still comparatively new to his high status at Court, he seemed uncertain of himself in this elevated gathering. Archbishop Dunstan's brother, Wulfric, a long-time member of the Witan, seemed to be deep in thought, his chin on his chest. The dark, pretty girl by his side was so like him that she could be scarcely any other than his daughter, Dunna. I could see the family likeness in Dunstan, too, and was allowing my mind to wander along paths with no connection to the events going on around me when I was suddenly brought back to the present by words and actions which were not a normal part of the Eucharist.

I realised that Edgar had taken his place on the chair facing the altar – the coronation chair – and four of the companion-men were holding a canopy over him while Dunstan began the sacred ritual of anointing the Sovereign with oil. Edgar then stood, his red robe was removed and replaced by one in purple and cloth-of-gold. He resumed his seat, and was handed a rod, a staff and a great orb of gold. Finally, a magnificent crown was placed on his head. With another fanfare from the pages, their horns blaring in the echoing vastness of the abbey, Dunstan proclaimed him King. King of Englaland. Emperor of Bryttania.

Again, the congregation called out for the long life of the King and I saw that Edgar's eyes were wet with emotion. A tear rolled down one cheek, but with his hands encumbered by the emblems of power he held, he was unable to wipe it away. I looked at Aethelflaed and I believe that our thoughts were running along similar lines: in all of Dunstan's careful orchestration of this day, he had forgotten the human element. I wished that I could take my kerchief and dry the tear, but that would have been so far outside my remit that I dare not. I looked at Elfrith. Surely his wife would help, but no: Elfrith was anticipating her own great moment, just minutes away. She was looking inward, preparing for being the centre of attention and did not notice Edgar's discomfiture.

The great golden orb was removed and Edgar could breathe a little easier, the staff now in one hand and the rod on his lap, he was able to brush his free hand across his eyes. He stood and was led by Dunstan from the coronation chair to the front of the thrones, taking his seat in the larger of the two. Edward and Ethelred, went forward, kissed their fathers' hand and swore their fealty. Then Aethelflaed stood, took her place in front of the King and for a moment gazed into her step-son's eyes, with a shimmer of tears in her own. They smiled at each other – a sweet natural smile – and she sank to her knees and kissed his ring.

"Come, *Mutti*," said Edgar, softly. "This is no day for tears."

"I think it is too late to say that to either of us, my son," she replied, equally softly and then turned back to her place, where I checked, once again, that her gunna and veil were perfectly arranged.

Now, at last, it was Elfrith's turn. The moment she had been planning for so long. From her place to one side of the thrones, she stepped forward, Morwen at her shoulder, hovering in case of some slight disarrangement in her attire, and was led to the coronation chair. The anointing and crowning – she did not receive the symbols of power – proceeded as they had for Edgar and, finally, she was led forward to the thrones. She walked slowly, obviously relishing every second. The Queen's crown – newly created for her – fitted perfectly over her short head rail and her blood red gunna glowed with the many jewels which had been sewn into it. Her dark, fox-red hair, caught over one shoulder in a net of gold thread, shimmered and reflected the light of the candles set high around the thrones. As she sank into the cushioned velvet of the smaller throne, it seemed to embrace her body. She was where she wanted to be. The young princes, repeated their duties and Aethelflaed – I sensed her stiffen as she did so – hers. Dunstan called for the Queen to live long: the congregation's reply was respectfully given.

Now it was time for the nobles to swear fealty to the newly crowned King and Queen. Members of the Witan and the other ealdorman present, led by Alfhere, then Ethelwine and Uncle Brithnoth left their seats and swore their fealty to them both, Edgar first, kneeling, kissing his ring, and then Elfrith. When all had done so, the Mass continued. The coronation was over. All that remained was to celebrate.

)))))))((((((

How typical it was of Edgar that he should leave the planning of pomp and ceremony to others, whilst personally ensuring that his people should have the wherewithal to celebrate, whatever their station – and in doing so bind their hearts still closer to him. Word had gone out throughout the shires that work should be put aside and, after the customary Whitsun services, that the holy day should be theirs in which to make merry. The Reeves had been instructed to ensure that there was food provided, pigs roasted, mutton stewed and distributed, and at least one hostelry in every town and village was to be paid for a hogshead of ale to be made available to all for the asking. And nowhere was there likely to be greater observance of this royal decree than in Bathe itself.

The Court, nobility and those hangers-on able to make themselves indispensable to their betters – and who desired it – could expect a great feast at the castle, where Edgar and Elfrith would preside over elaborate festivities to befit the day, but Edgar had decreed that the whole town was to be invited to enjoy his generosity. As the spring evening began to lengthen, a great fire was lit in the yard between Saint Peters – the abbey church – and the baths, beside the main thoroughfare of the town, where the shoe makers plied their trade. The cobblers wisely shuttered their workshops and chained them fast, and those who did not want to join the revels would have done well to go elsewhere for the night, for there would be no rest to be had in the chambers above.

After the service had finished earlier in the day, Aethelflaed joined the rest of the royal party, Wulf and I dutifully accompanying her back to the castle, where, as I had expected, Aelflaed, Brithnoth, Elflada and Ethelwine were already enjoying the hospitality of the Court. I had not seen Thella since before the ceremony, and thought it unlikely that I would get any work out of her for the rest of the day, so I had made sure that the Dowager Queen's attire was suitably refreshed for the evening, looped up the train of my own gunna into my kirtle and was hoping that I might make my escape with Wulf to the bone-fire by the baths. There was general, good humoured conversation and laughter in the Great Hall of the castle, as the King's presence was awaited, and I slipped up behind Aelflaed.

"Mother?" I had taken to calling her that, on occasion, as it made her so happy.

"Yes, my love? Oh, you looked so wonderful in the abbey today, your Aunt Aethelflaed has told me, too, that you were in all ways the perfect companion-woman. I am so proud of you."

"Thella did much, too."

"I am sure she did, but you must take credit where it is due. The responsibility was yours."

"It was. And so, I am hoping, Mother, that I may be excused the Court this evening and that I may go with Wulf to the celebrations in the town."

She hesitated, and I knew what she was thinking. It was sure to get rowdy, there were a great many strangers in the town for the celebrations and even with my brother beside me it might not be the safest of evenings to be abroad. Wulf came over to us. He knew that I had been asking permission to go with him and could see from Aelflaed's expression that she had doubts as to the plan.

"Come, ladies, why the long discussion? Aetna and I must away if we are to see the arrival of the mummers."

"Wulf, I really don't know..." Aelflaed was saying when Edgar, Elfrith on his arm, entered the Hall. Behind them, the two princes, Edward and Ethelred followed. The assembly bowed and curtseyed as a single entity, and Elfrith looked around the room with an air of superiority, a slight smile playing at the corners of her mouth.

"My Lords and Ladies," said Edgar, "pray, be at your ease."

Heads inclined, and conversation resumed. Edgar scanned the faces before him, caught sight of Wulf and propelled Edward toward us.

"You ask, Father!" said the prince, hesitant to speak up for himself.

"Edward, you must be your own man," said his father.

"Cousin Wulf," Edward used the familiar term often employed at Court for distant members of the family, or, indeed simply good friends. "My father has said that I may be excused this evening's formal celebrations and see how the coronation is being enjoyed by the townspeople, but only if I go with you."

Wulf was a little taken aback. He knew that Edward had taken a great liking to him, and, of course, he had been Edgar's man since boyhood, but to take charge of the heir to the throne? Like Aelflaed, he now hesitated and wondered at the evening's safety.

"Come, Wulf," said Edgar, "you surely cannot mind taking the lad with you? I remember a time not that many years ago when I played the apprentice to your uncles and we had a day out unrecognised in Rammesig. What harm can there be? See, he has changed out of his abbey clothes and is simply a young man out for a good time with his elders."

Edward had, I noticed, exchanged his finery for a simple tunic and hose, and now looked little more than a young husbandman in training.

"Very well, sire, if it is your wish. My sister is accompanying me, too. We will be a very jolly party shall we not, Your High... sorry, Edward! Or shall it be Eddy for the night?" This rather deftly took any chance of opposition away from Aelflaed, who was still looking anxious.

"Did I hear mention of a party into town?" From behind us the fair-haired young man from the abbey – the Chief Ealdorman's nephew – joined us, though, suddenly realising that he was interrupting a conversation with the King, he went pale. "Your Majesty, my apologies for the intrusion, I wanted to speak to..." and he began to back away.

"No matter, Elfwine, of course you wished to speak with these young people, or perhaps it was more particularly this young lady!" He indicated me. "Or some other..." he cast about the room. "This is an evening for merry-making, not being mired about by the old folk." I thought it seemed as though he wished he were still our age. "Of course, you must join the party! And there is one more that I shall rescue from the boredom of their elders' company... Dunstan ..." he had spotted for whom he was looking, and called across the Hall to the Archbishop, lately arrived in the company of his brother. "Where is that lovely niece of yours? Come, do not make her endure an evening of your conversation... there is a much more interesting outing afoot!"

Dunna had been in the shadow of her father and listening rather half-heartedly to a long-winded explanation of Glestingaberg's monastic tradition which he was sharing with the local Abbot – who also looked as though he would rather be elsewhere. With a brief look at her uncle, who nodded his assent, she came over to us.

"Now, Edward, you are in fine company, indeed!" Edgar beamed. "Two young Ealdormen in the making, and two brave Shield-maidens. Away with you all... before I take off my own finery and am tempted to come along, too!"

"Right, lad, off we go!" Wulf ruffled Edward's hair – it was the same gesture that our Uncle Brithnoth so often used. For a moment, Edward bridled, unused to such informality, but then realised that it was part of the evening's ruse and grinned sheepishly.

"Yes... Sir!" he said.

As we left the Hall, we passed by Ethelred, close within his mother's circle, still in his abbey finery. He looked at Edward with something like a hint of jealousy and then turned back to Elfrith, leaning into her side and hiding his face in her gunna.

We were, as Edgar had anticipated, a merry group, as we made our way back toward the middle of town. Everywhere torches and braziers flared, hawkers were about selling hot patties and fruited breads, the tavern doors stood wide open, good humoured conversation and song spilling out onto the streets. Wulf took the lead, Edward at his side, with Dunna and me following along behind, giggling at Elfwine's antics. His cool demeaner in the abbey had belied his nature: he was a natural mimic, first walking like a fat, waddling merchant we passed, puffing and blowing and trying to keep up with his goodwife, then mincing along, in a perfect imitation of the lady herself, flouncing and pretending to consider purchases from the peddlers along the way. Then we passed a group of monks, making their way back to the abbey for the evening offices. Elfwine immediately assumed a beatific expression, clasped his hands before him and essayed the impression of holy superiority, walking upright and correct, until pretending to trip over a scrawny cat that crossed his path and using words which no man of the cloth ought to know. We were in fits of laughter as we reached the market yard where the bone-fire was burning high and bright.

Meat was being handed out on great chunky bread trenchers, and ale was flowing freely. Many people had brought pitchers and tankards with them, others paid a small coin to the brew-men to borrow a vessel, which they would return later for a refund.

Wulf turned to us, his arm around Edward's shoulder. "Watch young Eddy here, while I go and invest in some crocks," he said. "Ale for everyone?"

I half expected Dunna, who I did not yet know well, to demur at this suggestion. After all, her uncle was an archbishop, and she had spent much of her life surrounded by churchmen but she seemed as willing as the rest of us to enter into the spirit of the evening. Wulf pushed his way through the crowd to the trestle where the ale was served and Elfwine shouldered his way through the mass of people on our left to where we could find space to sit alongside the wall of the baths. Ancient masonry had tumbled down and obviously been used for centuries as makeshift seats.

"What a crowd!" I said. "Come, your High... Eddy, sit next to me." He hoisted himself up on to the stone, worn smooth by a million pairs of buttocks.

"Is it true," he asked, "that when you were a little girl you sat on my father's knee and he told you stories of princesses?"

"Why, yes!" I said. "It was in Colencaestre, a Roman town like this one! Fancy that he should even remember it... and tell you!"

"My father remembers many things from those last few years before my mother died," Edward replied. "He often speaks of that last Progress. It was very shortly before she and my sister passed. That is, he speaks of it when my stepmother, the Queen, is not within hearing." He looked a little wistful.

Wulf returned with a wooden plank bearing five rough earthenware mugs, somehow managing to keep them upright as he fought his way through the throng. "Grab them quickly!" he said. "My skills as a juggler are not up to this!"

Deftly, he made sure that Edward picked up the first mug to the right. He winked at me. "Drink up, lad! This will make a man of you!" Beaming, Edward downed a good half of his portion, and smacked his lips.

"Don't worry," Wulf whispered to me. "I made sure that one was well watered."

The rest of us supped our ale in silence for a moment, wondering when the mummers were to make their appearance, when we heard a cacophony of instruments tuning up, pipes and whistles, horns, flutes, the fluttering of stringed lyres, and tensioning of drumskins.

"Something's starting!" said Elfwine. "Let's find a better spot." Catching Dunna by the hand he hauled her off through the crowd toward to music. Wulf and I followed, Edward between us. Determined to be at the centre of things, we ruthlessly forged our way to the front of the gathering, where we could feel the heat of the great bone-fire on our faces. An area had been cleared for the musicians, with a space left for other performers, yet to take to their places.

"Lord!" a familiar voice came from just behind us. Wulf turned to see Ratkin, red-faced and beaming, his arm around a pretty brown-haired girl, her rounded figure pressed up against him as they jostled among the other spectators. The girl from the Green Man, I thought. It crossed my mind to wonder where Thella might be.

"Ratkin!" cried Wulf. "No need to ask if you have had an enjoyable day!"

"No, indeed, Lord, it has been most... entertaining!"

A chord in unison from the musicians announced that their instruments were fully tuned, and the performance about to begin. The music played for a few minutes and then, from one of the cobblers' workshops, clearly let out for the purpose to earn the owner a few shillings, came the mummers. Dressed in a variety of odd costumes, some looking like animals, others angels and demons, they cavorted about the fire, casting shadows across the square, which danced eerily on the walls of the abbey church and the Roman baths alike. It was difficult to be sure whether there was any plot to follow, but if there was it was incomprehensible to me, and, I suspected, to most of the rest of the crowd, but the lively antics, slapstick pranks and ribald exchanges with the audience made it immaterial. Finally, the players tumbled out of the arena, and back into the cobbler's shop, the last to leave executing a cartwheel as he did so. The crowd applauded enthusiastically.

For a few moments there was near silence as we wondered if the entertainment was at an end. Then the sound of strings, played in a rhythmic, yet strangely sultry, foreign style stilled the beginnings of any renewed conversation among those watching. A figure in motley – green, red and white – was silhouetted in the firelight. He played louder and louder, the strings of his lyre vibrating into crescendo, accompanied only by drumming, and then another figure appeared, swaying in time to the music, her slim form weaving its way through the mummers, who had returned watch. My first surprise had come when I recognised the musician – none other than Agnolo, the skop I had engaged for Saint Pachimous' eve, the second dawned on me slowly as I began to realise that I knew the dancer, too. Initially, it was the colour of her costume which gave her away. I knew that soft green: had I not seen it worked upon alongside my own gunna? But now the demur undergunna of earlier in the day was gone, replaced by a diaphanous red silk which billowed in her wake, the gunna itself left loose and flowing. Her long fair hair was mostly hidden beneath a black veil, shimmering with tiny round beads, giving it the look of a much darker shade, and her face, partly concealed by a strip of the same fabric secured across her nose with a ribbon tying it at the back of her head, also looked dark. Above it, her eyes were made huge and luminous with kohl. (Where had she got that?) Oh, Thella!

The music grew more rhythmic and hypnotic, and the crowd began to clap in time with it. Other musicians began to join in. Thella dipped and whirled, skipped and spun artfully (how long had it taken Agnolo to teach her all this – or did it just come naturally?) finally making a lap around the edge of the audience, just far enough away that the outstretched hands of some of the male spectators could not reach her, even if they had not been slapped away by wives and sweethearts.

As the performance came to an end, and Agnolo, came forward to stand with Thella and accept the applause of the crowd, she stripped off the veil and yashmak, to reveal her own fair features, only her eyes now strange and exotic. There was renewed applause, as Agnolo shouted something about a golden-haired Moor, his words lost in the general hubbub. Then the general dancing began. Wulf and I looked at each other, for a moment lost for words. Then the same thought occurred to us simultaneously.

"If Dagmaer hears…"

"… about this…"

"… there will be Hell to pay!" and we collapsed into laughter.

At some point Elfwine had refilled our crocks with ale and as we emptied them again, the thought of joining the dance seemed more and more appealing. Wulf whirled away with Dunna and as Elfwine took me by the hand, I turned to check on Edward. He seemed happy enough watching everyone. "Ratkin," I said, "will you keep an eye on this young man? Eddy, you will be alright? Just for a few minutes?"

"Of course," he said. I allowed myself to be pulled away into the dance. Then (as he told us later) a thought occurred to Ratkin. "Or maybe you would like to be able to say that you danced this night, too. Eh, lad? How does that sound?" and turning to the girl with the nut-brown hair, he said, "Lynet, will you not take young Eddy here for a turn?"

Lynet, who Ratkin had not seen fit to introduce until then, did not look entirely happy with the idea, but Edward blushed so endearingly that she relented. "You will wait here, Ratkin?" she asked. "And then we can…"

"Yes, yes, of course." Ratkin was not unhappy to see her off into the melee with her young escort.

I found myself hopping and skipping in Elfwine's arms, breathless and, I confess, feeling just a little tipsy. Wulf and Dunna spun past us in a blur of movement and laughter, and I thought I saw Thella being lifted off her

190

feet by Agnolo, skirts and hair flying wildly as he whirled her above him. Then I thought I saw… could that be Edward manfully trying to lead the brown-haired girl? The prince appeared and then disappeared in the throng. For several minutes the dance seemed to gather pace; faster and faster we flew around each other. Confusingly, I thought I could now see Thella in the crook of Ratkin's arm and then suddenly there seemed to be some sort of an uproar not orchestrated by the music.

The couple dancing ahead of us stopped abruptly and we cannoned into them, almost bowling them over. The dancers behind us collided as we came to a halt, and as I peered through the crowd to see what had happened, I could hear familiar voices raised in anger.

Agnolo: "Get your hands off her!"

Ratkin: "She is free to dance with whom she will!"

Lynet: "So, you send me off to play with a little bull-calf, while you seek out a cow!"

Thella: "Cow! Why, you brown-haired bitch!"

Lynet: "Very well, cat, then! And keep your cat's claws out of my Rat!"

Thella: "Ha! I don't need claws to keep a man near me! And everyone knows that a bitch is no good as a ratter!"

There was a resounding smack as Lynet punched Thella in the face.

"Cat fight!" called out some wag. Both Agnolo and Ratkin lunged to catch Thella as she fell backward, the Italian reaching her first.

"She was dancing with me!" said Ratkin, wrenching Agnolo's arm from around Thella's waist.

"And she said that you…" but what Thella had said of Ratkin we never heard, for Ratkin twisted his opponent's arm behind him and thrust him out of the way, with a yelp of pain. As Ratkin turned back to help Thella up, Agnolo regained his balance, spinning around to catch him a neat blow on the chin, sending him sprawling down beside her. He reached out to help her up. "Oh, get away from me!" she said. "Ratkin, my handsome… are you alright?"

"But…" the Italian seemed at a loss.

Lynet had turned on her heel, with a "Pah!" of exasperation and elbowed her way out of the gathering. Agnolo followed her lead, pausing only to collect his lyre from where he had left it with the other musicians. "You two deserve each other!" he said over his shoulder. "Come…?"

"Lynet," she said. "Lynet! And perhaps *you* will be able to recall my name in the morning!"

"*Ah, Tesoro…*" They disappeared into the crowd.

Tenderly, Thella touched her face, carefully feeling around the eye-socket, which was already reddening. She would have a fine bruise by the morning. Ratkin rubbed his chin which also sported the imprint of knuckles. Thella sniffed, and with the aid of Elfwine's outstretched hand, managed to regain her feet with a surprising degree of dignity. Smoothing down her skirts, she thanked him, unable to resist the temptation of a coy upward glance through lowered eyelashes. "What you must think..." she said.

"I think you are quite delightful," he played along. "You had every man in the crowd at your feet. You are a little witch!"

Suddenly, her playfulness was gone and she snatched her hand away from his. "Not a witch! Never say that of me!" she snapped.

Taken aback, he looked at me for some kind of explanation, but at that moment, a thought occurred to me. "Where's the pr... where's Edward... Eddy?" I looked about, scouring the faces around us.

Wulf realised what I was thinking and he, too, called out "Edward!" Then, to me, "Surely you didn't leave him alone?"

"No, of course not! I asked Ratkin to look after him!"

We both turned to Ratkin, now back on his feet and at a loss to know why we were so concerned. "I handed him over to Lynet for a dance," he said. "What's wrong with that? Why all the panic?"

"But..." Wulf and I were speaking over each other, and now Elfwine and Dunna had become aware of our fears and were beginning to look through the crowd for any sign of Edward.

"Ratkin, surely you realised who he was? You watched the coronation procession..." my voice fell to a whisper. "The Aetheling Edward..."

"I watched the King and that... Elfrith... but I was distracted when the rest of them passed." I imagined that Lynet could be quite a distraction when she wanted to be. "I thought he was just some lad you had taken under your wing!"

"Well he's not under it now, is he?"

"In the name of all that's holy, let's find him quickly," said Wulf.

We split up into pairs, Elfwine and Dunna heading toward the food stalls, Wulf and I working our way back toward the seats by the baths and Ratkin, with Thella, making a search through the teaming square, making sure that he was not hidden by any of the knots of laughing apprentices or still dancing couples. We met up back beside the bone-fire, which was now beginning to burn a little lower.

"Not a sign," said Elfwine.

"He's not in the square," said Ratkin.

"Then where..." but as usual, an idea occurred to Wulf and me at the same moment.

"Saint Peters!" I cried.

"The abbey!" said Wulf.

"Spabby!" was all the others must have heard as Wulf and I bolted toward the door of the great church, still illuminated by the flames of the dying fire making crazy shadows of the carvings decorating its lintels. It was hardly a decorous entry as the six of us burst into the holy building, but the peace within quickly stilled us. As our eyes grew accustomed to the low light from a few, sparsely placed candles, we spotted two figures on one of the low benches, lately at the front of the nave, but now pushed back against the South wall.

"There!" whispered Wulf, and we hurried toward them.

Edward sat, one leg curled up beneath him, like the young child he so recently was, with his head on the shoulder of... who on earth? He was asleep. As his companion turned to us, I recognised Sister Alfreth.

"Sister!" I said. "Thank the Lord, we have been so worried. How came he – and you – to be here like this? Is he alright?"

"Yes, of course," she spoke quietly, unwilling to wake him. "I couldn't bear to let the day end, it had been so wonderful. I should have gone back to the Sisters long ago – I shall probably be beaten for not returning immediately after my duties had been carried out – but I came back in here to remember everything I had seen. Oh, the gunnas, the flowers, the jewels, I shall never forget them! As I sat, a young man came in, looking a little lost and at odds with himself, and I offered him a seat. We talked. I do not think he realised that I knew who he was – but I remember everything of this day, every face, every word! He said he was tired – and I could smell that he had been enjoying the ale! After a while we found we were just sitting; sitting together and I felt his head nodding onto my shoulder. I wish that my future had been one that I might have had grand-children, for I should love to tell them that I had once been of service to..." Edward stirred and sat up, rubbing his neck.

"Oh, here you all are!" he said.

"Indeed – 'Eddy' – here we all are!" Wulf's concern gave way to irritation. "But where have you been? Why in the world did you wander off?"

"That Lynet tired of me! When she saw, oh! You!" He caught sight of Thella and then Ratkin. "With – you! Things began to get a little... well, I came in here and found a much more pleasant companion." He smiled at Alfreth. And then at Wulf. "Don't worry, I shall not mention any of this to my father. It has been a fine evening!"

THIRTEEN

Five days later

WULFMAER

Caestre Castle was worthy of its name. Like the Great Hall at
Colencaestre and many another, it was built upon Roman foundations, but
here much more of the ancient walls remained intact and in places there
were still even remnants of mosaic floors and painted walls. An upper
storey had recently been completed and Aetna's favourite new fashion for
separate sleeping chambers had been incorporated throughout – not
curtained-off areas, but fully partitioned rooms. When I arrived in Caestre,
she took pleasure in showing me to my allocated quarters, as though the
castle's status as a royal residence emphasised her own good judgement in
wanting to adopt the fashion wherever possible.

Despite a few sore heads following the coronation celebrations at
Bathe, the Court had been on the move the very next day. The second
element of Edgar's plan to demonstrate his authority over the whole of the
lands and islands that made up Bryttania was scheduled to take place just
one week later and it was essential that we reached Caestre ahead of the
other participants. While the ladies (much to Aetna's disgust) and less
active Court members travelled along the old Roman Fosse Way to
Cyrnecaestre, cutting across the greenways to Watling Street which would
lead them straight to Caestre, the King and the fitter members of his party
took the Ermine street to Glewcaestre. From there we followed the River
Saverna downstream toward the market town of Brycgstowe, a few miles
to our east, named after the bridge which spanned its river. Here, the
estuary was wide enough to harbour large boats. Many of the vessels,
moored on wharfs alongside the trackway, were seagoing and peopled with
despairing captives, for Brycgstowe was the centre of a flourishing slave
trade. Men, women and children captured during skirmishes in Walha,
those of our own land condemned by law to lose their freedom and other
unfortunates were held on board and then shipped to Duibhlinn where the
Viking rulers of Ireland would sell them on to destinations throughout the
world – or, indeed, back to Englaland to be collared as thralls. As we
passed by these ships, I tried to close my ears to the sounds of misery
issuing from them.

Beyond the slavers we came to three fine ships; these were the vessels
that were awaiting us, the plan to take passage around the coast of Walha,
along the Deva estuary and then up the broad river itself to Caestre. They

were magnificent. Edgar, riding at the head of the party, reigned in and called out as we drew level with the first.

"Ho! Ship-masters! When do we take to the water?"

Although he had exchanged his fine robes of state for more workaday clothes, the King still wore a circlet of gold on his brow and looked every inch the monarch that he had so recently been acclaimed with such pomp. Our arrival had been expected and the captains of all three ships quickly made their way onto shore and gave their obeisance. Edgar slipped off his horse (he still had that quirky way of throwing his leg over the beast's neck that he affected as a younger man) and raised them up.

"None of that, men," he said. "We are to be cheek by jowl for some days, and aboard your ships, you are the masters. But show me my new toy! And where is the boatbuilder?"

"My King, I am sorry to be tardy!" from behind us a man in dark, but expensive, clothes dismounted from a heavy horse. It needed to be a big animal for he was tall and broad; a strong man who had once, clearly, worked with his hands, but now oversaw the work of others. "I had hoped to be here when you arrived." He bowed and kissed the King's hand.

"No matter, Master Shipwright, you are here now… we have made good time on the roads. I only hope we shall make as sweet a journey over the waters!"

"I, too, Your Majesty."

"Master Seward, lead the way…"

The first two ships were empty, but for a small crew on each. There was seating for around twenty souls and low shelters constructed down their centres, wide enough to give some protection from the elements to a bare two or three souls. The third was larger and lay a little lower in the water, bearing, like a duckling riding upon its mother's back, another craft. This second vessel, with four rowlocks on each side, a tall prow bearing the head of a white horse and a stern built up in steps to support what could only be described as a throne, was a wonder of the shipwright's skill. The planks of the frame were smooth and polished a deep red and along each side, bosses formed in the shape of more animal and bird heads gazed outward: dogs, horses, eagles, swans, each expertly carved and painted. Where the mast should have been there was a tall cross, the figure of our Lord in glory facing the prow.

"My congratulations, Master, it is magnificent," Edgar was delighted. "Now, we have but to get it – and ourselves – to Caestre!"

I wish I could say that I had enjoyed the voyage. We did not have a great deal of baggage with us – most was with the other party, heading to Caestre overland – and it did not take long for what we had to be stowed and lashed. The ship bearing Edgar's "toy", as he persisted in calling it (for beautiful though it was, it was clearly not a practical craft) was to bear only the Master shipwright, Seward, along with its crew. The rest of us broke into two parties and boarded the other two ships, Brithnoth, Ethelwine, Chief Ealdorman Alfhere and several of the older members of the Witan on one, together with various of their attendants, and the King, some of the younger ealdorman and a number of companion-men on the other, including me, with Ratkin. Just before we cast off, the captain of our craft called out to his fellow masters.

"Wait, the Bore is coming!"

Ahead, I could see the water beginning to rise as though a huge, hump-backed monster was filling the channel and swimming inexorably toward us. I must have looked appalled as one of the boatmen slapped me on the back and said "Nay, lad, nothing to worry over. This is just a small'un! For a spring tide, anyway! You should see it upstream where the river narrows – now that's a sight!"

The wave reached our prow, and the ship rode it smoothly, rising and falling with the movement of the water. I looked at the other vessels; they, too, slipped through the wave easily. But that first lurch of movement was enough to make me realise that I was not cut out for a life at sea. My stomach turned over. As the Bore drove onward up the estuary of the Severn, we cast off, and with the King's vessel in the lead, the three ships made their way out, toward more open water.

The plan was to hug the coastline, far enough out to avoid shoals and rocky outcrops, but close enough to follow the shore. By all accounts, according to the crew, it was an unremarkable voyage, a little slower than on occasion, as the wind was against us some of the way, but with no really rough weather to concern us. My gut thought otherwise. Within minutes of being afloat, I was reduced to clinging onto the side of the boat, heaving my meagre midday meal, taken as the ships were loaded, down to the fish. Much of that postnoon, night and the next day passed in a blur of wretchedness, made little better by the fact that Ratkin seemed totally at home. Sometime during the second night aboard, I slept a little, and when I woke, to my relief, much of the nausea had gone.

My pathetic seamanship had secured for me the use of one of the shelters amidships, but the air inside had become stale and stuffy, so I crawled out, eager to feel a cool wind on my face, and even with the idea that a little hard-baked bread and small ale might be acceptable to my empty belly. We were cutting smoothly through the water, the gusts with us, filling the sail and tugging on the sheets. Crew and passengers alike were mostly asleep, wrapped in their cloaks and blankets, lying on the low deck, or propped up against the rails. Astern, a single man was at the tiller. I looked forward: another lone figure stood, steadying himself against the movement of the boat, hand on the curved prow, staring ahead at the sea-bounded night.

Avoiding the slumbering men around my feet, I went toward the bow.

"Sire?" I said, quietly.

"Wulf!" he seemed delighted to see me up and about. "I have missed you, lad! Are you now fully back in middle-earth? I have rarely seen one so elf-shot by the water! Have a little ale… see, there is some here. It will not be many hours until we break our fast, I think, though it is hard to judge the time, if you are not used to this life."

"Thank you, sire," I said, forbearing to comment on my seasickness, in case it should return.

"When you next see Edward, tell him how you have fared!" Edgar seemed in good spirits. "It may perhaps make him a little less disappointed that he did not accompany us. He was most put out to be staying with the women and old men – as he put it!"

"You did not think he might have benefitted from the experience?"

"Indeed, I did, but it was impressed upon me that to have the Sovereign and his likely heir both bobbing about off the Welsh coast was too much of a risk to be entertained. I am afraid the argument did not convince him, though. He was in a very ill humour when we parted. But look, ahead are the lights of Monez."

As the boat began to pull toward to *baecbord*, the lights gradually drifted to our right – they were sparse and dim, some, perhaps, lanterns hung to warn of the jagged coastline, some watchfires, for the Viking realm of Iraland was but a few short hours to the west, given a fair wind. Again, I marvelled at the skill of the man at the tiller – his steering oar gave the right side of the boat its name, the *steorbord*. In heavy weather he would have to use both hands to keep it steady, standing with his back to the left of the boat and giving that side its name: the *baecbord*.

"I believe the Vikings call it the Hooked Isle," I said. "Because of its jagged coastline, I suppose."

"Aye, and the Walha-folke, *Ynys Mons*. A place of many names and many strange tales. They say it was the last refuge of the Druids and some even claim the sorcerer Merlyn lies buried there." He seemed to withdraw into himself for a moment, and then murmured. "I think that sometimes I would be well served if I had such an advisor as old King Arturo had in Merlyn."

"A magician, sire? Surely not!" I spoke low: too many years living with the ever-listening ear of Father Aelmer, made me anxious that no such word be overheard. "Do you believe the stories of the old King, then, and his stately Court?" Dagmaer had told us these tales when we were children.

"I believe that there may have been a good, strong man who tried to rally his people after the Romans left. It is ironic, is it not? He was trying to protect these lands from invaders – from us! From our forefathers, at least. And now we think of this land as ours, to be protected, to be governed. And I wonder, does very much change? The intrigue at Caerleon, the need for defence against invaders... do I not face the same challenges?"

"Sire, the Witan is loyal to a man, and there have been no serious threats from the Vikings in many years. This is just the long night and the want of a meal talking," I said, for it suddenly felt as though an ill-omen was upon us, despite Edgar's earlier good humour. "The chroniclers are already calling you Edgar the Peaceable. There is nothing in this realm that threatens, surely?"

"There are many tensions on the Witan, Wulf. Singly, I would trust every one of my Ealdormen with my life; I have done so many times, sleeping unarmed in their Halls, eating their food without my taster – by the Heavens, don't tell anyone I said that! – hunting alongside them with their weapons unsheathed. But when men, even the best of men, are beset by disagreements concerning matters close to their hearts, their faiths and their coffers, factions begin to form. First, it is two against one, then three against four as sides are taken. Oh, it is all discussion and argument to begin with, but then – it happened in my father's time – passions boil over. A word is said that cannot be taken back. Before you know it, someone has stormed out of a Moot, a sword is drawn in anger. I come down on one side or the other and... well it is an old and tragic story, is it not? At the moment it is the Monasteries that are firing up the dissent: money is at the heart of it, of course, but Dunstan is determined to pull the Witan one way, and the Chief Ealdorman the other. What more explosive combination than God and mammon together?

"As for the Vikings, yes, they are quiet – for now. We are still holding the Danelaw to its oaths. But there are rumblings, always rumblings from across the German Sea. Tryggve Olafsson's boy – and he is still a boy, for he is younger than Edward – has already committed murder and claims he will do so again until he is a king himself, which day will come while his father, who styles himself "King of the Viken", still lives. If that is not a threat of war, I do not know what is! Kingdoms not inherited must be taken by force, it is the way of things in the lands of the North. And those who are dissatisfied with their lot in the Danelaw (there are always some) will plot and do treachery, and allow the door to be opened, just a crack, but that is all that will be needed to allow the whirlwind into the Hall!" He fell silent. I thought back, so many years, to Thurstan's threats at Elig.

"Wulf, I want you to be a friend, and more than a friend to my boy. Edward is yet young, and I sometimes fear that were I not alive... the Witan is full of powerful men: good men, but wilful and each thinking that his way is the... I can do nothing to change that, but if I know that he has someone to be himself with, someone without a personal ambition... it is a lot to ask. Could you be that man? Edward's companion-man?" He put his hand on my shoulder.

Without hesitation I dropped to one knee – rather clumsily, I fear, for the boat was lurching somewhat. "I can and I will, my King." Edgar laughed.

"A simple 'yes' would have sufficed; we have known each other too long for such antics! But I thank ye!"

The mood had lifted once again, and a pale dawn began to make itself felt at our backs. Men began to wake and stretch, the tiller-man was relieved by another and the morning routines began in earnest. Yawning, Ratkin appeared at my elbow, and Rota jumped up to greet me.

"He is as pleased to see you as I, my Lord," he said, slapping me on the back. "Do I take it that the sickness has passed? You certainly look better. Though it was a fetching shade of green you assumed, almost as fine as your sister's coronation gunna!"

"It is my devout prayer that it has passed," I replied. "I do not want to feel like that again for as long as I live. And now my belly is as empty as a hermit's bed!"

Ratkin found me some bread (double baked, so that it would not become stale during the voyage) and some hard cheese, and Edgar again proffered his crock of small ale. I was surprised by how little I could take before I felt full – my stomach had shrunk. As the morning wore on, though, and I found that I could repeat the experiment several times, I began to feel more myself. By midday I was beginning to exult in the sea-wind and the scudding clouds. I still found it hard to keep my balance, as the boat dipped and rolled, but at least my gut had become accustomed to the sensation.

Ratkin and I sat side by side, Rota between us, on one of the benches across the belly of the boat. Apparently, throughout my sickness the dog had lain beside the shelter, rousing himself only to eat – his appetite had not seemed affected – and to ease his bladder and bowels: the sailors had a trick of spotting when such an occurrence was about to take place, whereupon they held the unfortunate animal over the side.

"Aye, we've only ever lost a few!" said one, a swarthy mountain of a man, with a black beard, plaited and tucked into his britches. "Though the King's hound nearly made it into the company of those we have! He didn't take kindly to such handling from the likes of we... Nearly took my hand off, he did!"

Edgar barked a laugh. He was still near the prow, sitting now, with his arm around the hound in question. "Are we making good time, Master?" he called down the length of the vessel.

"Yes, sire," came the reply. "By tomorrow we shall be in the estuary of the Deva. The winds have been mostly kind, by the grace of God."

The rest of the day passed in conversation and tale telling. Edgar had a prodigious memory for verse, and he recited the long lay of the Seafarer. "*... I took my pleasure in the cry of the gannet and the sound of the curlew instead of the laughter of men...*" which was met with enthusiastic applause when he finished. Had he not been born to royalty, he might have made an excellent skop.

From time to time, favoured by a gust of wind which bypassed our sails, the ship behind us carrying the "old 'uns" as Ratkin put it, caught us up, and even ran alongside us. Generally, there was good-hearted banter and conversation to be heard, but late in the postnoon, there were voices raised in anger. I thought I could hear my Uncle Brithnoth shouting with a passion, and the clipped, furious tones of the Chief Ealdorman replying in kind.

"Come, men," Edgar raised his voice to reach the other boat. "What can be so contentious? Your ill-humour will be raising the spirit of Ran if you are not careful, and you will be taking your chances in her drowning-net!" Again, I almost winced at Edgar's easy reference to the old gods and their acolytes.

Ealdorman Ethelwine's voice blew across to us. "All is well, sire! Just a... vigorous discussion. We have been too long cramped together, that is all!"

"See that it is all!" Edgar was ill-pleased. He looked at me, and I knew he was recalling our conversation of early that morning.

The second ship dropped back behind us, and we could see the third vessel, bearing the King's rowing barge, not far behind it. Covered with tarred linen and lashed firmly amidships, the smaller boat nevertheless made an unwieldy cargo. I guessed that the Shipwright would be relieved to have his masterpiece safely delivered into the calmer waters of the upstream Deva.

I slept soundly that night, Rota snuggly wedged between me and Ratkin, forming an excellent hot-stone for us both. As the Master had promised, the following morning we began to navigate the mouth of the Deva, named, as Edgar informed us (really, Father Aelmer would be having a fit of the falling sickness!) by the old Britons as the "river holy to the Goddess". The wind had veered behind us and we kept the sails up, making a stately progress steadily inland, the sun in our eyes as dawn turned to mid-morn.

))))]((((

The sails took us almost to Caestre, but a mile or so before we reached the town, we struck them and the sailors took to the oars. It was easier, said the Master, to navigate the twists and turns of the river that way. While these preparations were made, Edgar changed from his workaday hose and tunic into something more befitting a king arriving for the second element of his coronation celebrations. We had seen a few people on the banks of the river along the way, though they did not seem to be aware of who was passing, but as we neared the old Roman walls, and could see what remained of the ancient bridge spanning the river, shored up and repaired – indeed, rebuilt – since the Legions left, a crowd began to gather.

Edgar had donned a rich, red tunic over soft leather britches, with a deep blue embroidered mantle, caught at his throat by a jewelled brooch. The circlet of gold with its single huge red ruby on his forehead, caught the sunlight. His light brown hair and neatly trimmed beard showed no sign of grey and he could have passed, I thought, still, for the young man we had accompanied to Colencaestre and on to the Fens, were it not for the worry lines forming on his pleasant, open face. He stood at the prow of the leading boat (we had maintained our order of progress), the wind billowing his cloak. Steadying himself with one hand on the carven horse's neck, he waved to the people with his other, accepting their cheers and good wishes, their cries of "Good King Edgar" and "Long life to the King", and on occasion, deftly catching a posy thrown by some young maid, or acknowledging a raised tankard as we passed by a waterside tavern.

The boats had rounded the last sharp meander of the river before the walls began to our left, on the north shore. Our Aunt Aethelflaed's namesake, the Lady of the Mercians, had re-founded Caestre as a burgh earlier in the century, when there was a real danger from the Vikings, and the Roman foundations had been capped and heightened into a formidable defence, as impressive as when the Legions had left. Along the top of them crowded several hundred people, waving pennants and kerchiefs, shouting and applauding, and as we came within reach of the jetty beside the nearest gate to the castle, we could see the welcoming party waiting for us; clearly, we had been spotted by the lookouts well before our arrival.

The Queen's Court, as I later heard it was beginning to be called (now, who should we suppose encouraged that?) had arrived in Caestre the day before, having made good time by land, and Elfrith, with the princes Edward and Ethelred, was standing by the mooring place, surrounded by the members of the Witan who had accompanied her. Among them Alfric, who had pleaded a dislike of the water, awaited Elfwine, his son, who had sailed with us and his father's brother-in-law, the Chief Ealdorman. The elderly Wulfric, so unlike his brother Archbishop Dunstan, was, as ever, talking though to whom was unclear, for Dunna, at his side, did not appear to be listening, her eyes on the arrival of our craft. To one side the Shire Reeve of Caestre stood beaming his welcome, lesser reeves and thanes around him, and a little further on other family members of those who had travelled with the King were waiting. As our boat came up to the jetty, the

King leapt ashore and embraced Elfrith, greeted his sons enthusiastically – Edward seemed a good deal more pleased to see him than his younger brother – and clasped hands with the Shire Reeve.

"Irwin, it is good to be in Caestre once again. Your townsfolk have given me a fine welcome. I think that the show we shall be putting on for them on the morrow's morrow will give them yet more cause to cheer!" Irwin, bowed and thanked him for his graciousness.

"No formality now, Irwin, I am tired and hungry for something more than hard baked bread. Hot food! And a bath... Elfrith how are our apartments? To your liking? Good!"

Without waiting for a reply, he strode up the bank toward the small gateway in the curtain wall. He turned back toward those of us still on the boat. "Come along, men, there is food waiting, and the ladies will be pleased of your company I have no doubt." The second boat had come alongside now and overtaken us to moor a little further along the jetty. The third, with its precious cargo was just catching up. "Master Shipwright," Edgar called, to Seward, "the Shire Reeve has arranged for a boat house to shelter the barge, the thralls will show your men where to take it. Be sure that it is safely harboured!" He seemed almost tempted to take one more look at it, but then remembered the hot food and bath he was looking forward to enjoying. "We will discuss its preparation for the ceremony tomorrow."

The immediate royal party followed the King into the castle yard, and we were free to greet those who had been awaiting us. Aetna ran up and embraced me, my aunts following.

"It is good to see you safe ashore, my love," said Aelflaed. Then, seeing Brithnoth approaching from the second craft she ran to him and was enveloped in his arms. Elflada greeted Ethelwine, as though they had been parted for a year, and he was all concern for her condition, patting her belly affectionately. "No, we are both quite well," she was saying. "It is just that I miss you so much when we are apart..." and so, chatting and laughing, we all made our way inside the city walls.

The Court's stay at Caestre was not expected to be as long as it had been in Bathe and, with the castle so large and well-appointed the whole Court could be accommodated within. Those who had not been allocated sleeping chambers of their own – or shared places – would take the more traditional course of making themselves comfortable in the Great Hall for the night, but as members of the Witan, the various Ealdormen and their families were each designated chambers. Aetna and I were, of course, too old to share a bed as we had as children, but she had been able to secure us two adjoining chambers, each large enough to accommodate us together with our companions – Thella and Ratkin – and, if necessary, other guests should the castle become too crowded. Fortunately, that did not appear to be the case, and we had some privacy. I had been dismissed from duty by Edgar, who wished to take his ease for the rest of the day and so, having found food laid out in the Great Hall, Aetna and I took trenchers up to our chambers.

She had reserved the slightly larger of two for herself ("ladies require more room for our gunnas and other essentials!") and so we took our meal and laid it out on one of her travelling trunks. Thella had disappeared who-knows-where and Ratkin appeared to have followed suit, so we were alone.

"It is good to see that you have your appetite back," said Aetna, as I tucked into a pastry. I raised my eyebrows. "Come now," she said, "you must know that I was fully aware of your water-sickness! I swear I was so nauseous myself that the other ladies were becoming quite convinced that I was with child!" She chuckled mischievously. "Thella told them that I must have eaten something which disagreed with me at the bone-fire but you know what chatter goes on…"

"I'm sorry you had to go through it," I said. "I swear I was beginning to believe that my guts had turned themselves inside out. My belly has never felt so empty and yet so little wanting food."

"It is a most unfortunate malady. I am glad that Edgar seems to have no weakness in that direction. It would be a tragedy were he not able to look his best at the water pageant."

Our conversation turned to forthcoming events, carefully planned by Edgar and Dunstan to confirm his over-lordship of the whole of Bryttania. It seemed that Aetna knew more of the plans than I: doubtless they had been the main topic of conversation on the road north. My enforced fast over the last few days had left me now with a ravenous appetite. I finished everything I had brought from the Great Hall for myself and cast a wistful look at Aetna's trencher. She was taking longer to eat than I was, as she prattled on about arrangements for the ceremony.

"Oh, go on then," she said, "finish mine. Just like old times."

I laughed; it was indeed like old times. And there were things I needed to share with her.

When I had finished eating, I supressed a belch as best I could and flopped back onto her palliasse arms outstretched, allowing my now full stomach room to begin its task of digestion.

"Aetna, the King has asked something of me. I have agreed, of course, but I need to talk to you about it. I fear it will dash our uncle's hopes for my return to Radendunam. I know that nothing had been decided, but I think he would have liked me to begin learning the skills of ealdormanship. He cares so much for our Shire and wants to know that it would be in safe hands if aught happened to him."

"I have something to discuss with you, also," she said. "Aunt Aethelflaed has asked something of me and I, too, must make a choice. But you go first."

I told her of Edgar's request that I become companion-man to Edward. I also explained somewhat of the King's fears for the future. I knew that her understanding of such matters was far beyond that of most girls of her age.

"Edgar truly fears that there may be difficult times ahead, then?" she said when I paused. "I felt something of the tensions myself when Dunstan was so emphatic about things at our Saint Pachomius-eve meal. I fear our uncle and the Chief Ealdorman will be at loggerheads."

"They already are. There was something of a heated dispute during our voyage. I suspect only the fact that they were in a small craft on a choppy sea prevented them coming to blows. Edgar believes that Edward needs someone closer to his own age than most of the rest of the Court as a strong right arm. Not a counsellor, or an adviser, but a true friend. He wants me to be a permanent part of the Court, and at Edward's back."

"And the prince certainly likes you," added Aetna. "He has never said a word about the incident at the bone-fire, except to me! And that was to say that he hoped he could go out on another adventure with you. He also said something cheeky to Thella which, I think, had he been any other than the King's son, might have earned him a clip around the ear!" She laughed.

"What is it that you have to decide?" I asked.

"I find myself in a place rather like yours," she said. "Twice before the coronation, Aunt Aethelflaed hinted that she wanted me to consider something, but only during our journey up here did she have the chance to speak to me at any length in private. We were sharing seats in the back of the wardrobe wagon. It has been my duty to look to its packing and care on this trip. Do you remember how jealously Flada used to guard that position? Well, it seems that our aunt also has her concerns about the unity of the Court, and, indeed, Edward. (She must have discussed it with the King, surely?) And Elfrith's growing influence worries her. She says that she has been impressed with my maturity this last sixmonth, and that she knows that I understand more than most of the discussions I have witnessed over meals and domestic visits. You know how often Uncle entertains members of the Witan at Radendunam – it is only natural that I have heard them discuss matters which worry them. But I keep my counsel. Anyway, she wants me to become her senior companion-woman. It would put a few noses out of joint; it will be said that I am too young. There are those in the Queen's Court who aspire to the post, but every word uttered in their presence would find its way straight back to Elfrith. Of course, I want to say yes, but I fear that Aunt Aelflaed will be disappointed... she says that she likes me taking more responsibility at home..."

"She cannot think that you would be at Radendunam for ever," I said. "Flada was married and away at barely your age. Though no-one would mistake Flada's character and ambitions for yours!"

She gave me a wry smile. "No."

"So, you must go. Or rather come! Yes, *come* to Court. We will both be there, how could we wish for more? It will be everything we dreamed of when we were children – together and with the people whose wyrd will shape history! It will be like living in one of the Sagas!" I was suddenly realising that the only thing which had been holding me back from wholly embracing the King's new trust in me was my separation from Aetna. However much we tried to ignore it, together we made a whole, whilst apart we were but two swathes of fabric, waiting to be stitched together.

She began to catch my enthusiasm. "It *would* be exciting!" she said.

"It *will* be exciting!"

"Let's..."

"... do it!"

"I have already sworn to the King," I said. "Will you speak to Aethelflaed again soon?"

"Yes, today. But I think we should ask that the positions remain unannounced until we return to Radendunam. We should think how to break it to Mother and Father: they think of themselves that way, you know."

"I know they do. And in truth they have been the best parents we could ever have hoped for. Our birth mother would have been happy to know that we grew up with so much love and support. And maybe, one day, we will be able to tell our birth father, too."

This last comment left Aetna unimpressed: she still harboured some resentment against our real father, although she knew the story of why he had left us. But nothing could now dampen our spirits. The future beckoned.

At some point during the postnoon Aetna had pulled off her head rail and tossed it aside. Her long hair was tousled where she had been lying back against the bolster; she had kicked off her shoes, too. I could not resist the temptation to tickle the sole of her foot – I knew she was ticklish. She shrieked and picked up the pitcher from amongst the remnants of our meal, tipping what little remained of the small ale over my head.

"Now look what you've done!" I said. "You've wet the bed!"

We collapsed into helpless giggles. It felt as though we were six once again.

FOURTEEN

The diplomatic manoeuvring and political embassies to and from the greater and lesser Royal Courts of the islands of Bryttania – some almost the equivalent of Edgar's Witan, others little more than a collection of ill-assorted brigands and bullies – had been extraordinary. These courts represented the eight "kingdoms" which made up the Cynewise, or Commonwealth, as some were now calling Edgar's empire. For the past six months, emissaries had travelled the length and breadth of the land, variously coercing, intimidating and bribing, with the result that on the Feast of Saint Brendan, the sixteenth day of May, as a watery sun arose glinting off the river Dee, eight men, who styled themselves Kings, were awaiting the arrival of their overlord, the man who, just five days earlier, had been crowned Emperor of Bryttania.

This day's events were to consolidate the sumptuous celebrations on Whit Sunday. The pageantry was to secure – and be seen to secure – the fealty of those who might otherwise be a threat to the stability of the realm. The men who had come to take part, some willingly, some less so, were to bend the knee take an oath which had been composed carefully and with much deliberation to formalise their duty to do Edgar's bidding and aid him in all things "by land and sea". Edgar was their monarch: that was already certain. All that remained was for them to acknowledge it formally.

But Edgar also knew that these men, these Kings, would not allow themselves to be seen as mere subservient vassals, but had to be recognized publicly as honourable and powerful in their own right. There needed to be a careful balance between the parties. The resulting performance was to be a brilliant piece of political theatre.

On the south bank of the river, a Hall had been erected some years earlier, when the threat from the north was perceived to be lessened sufficiently to begin building outside the city walls. It had been planned as a royal residence, and so commanded a fine view of the river and surrounding greensward as it dipped down to the water. Here, the eight kings had been accommodated, with as much honour as they, no doubt, felt was their due. They were to come forth, with their retinues, as independent lords, enter into Edgar's rowing barge – now awaiting them at the south jetty – and row out to the centre of the stream. From the north shore, Edgar would be rowed out to meet them, and then, alone, he would enter the barge and take his high seat at the stern. The kings would then each swear their fealty, and he would accept it. Whilst they gave him their service, he demonstrated his trust by being alone and undefended. Mutual respect and feudal hierarchy established in a single ceremony. The kings would then row their overlord upstream a little distance, before they all disembarked close to the minster church of Saint John, where a short service would be held to mark the occasion. Then there were to be revels in the old Roman amphitheatre.

From across the river, we could see that the kings appeared to be entering into the spirit of the occasion with some aplomb. Eight pennants fluttered, one above each of their respective parties, and each bearing the emblem of their house. There had been an upsurge in the use of so-called "coats" in recent years – the devices emblazoned on surcoats and shields to identify an individual and his followers in battle also used on banners and flags. It made a colourful and impressive show. Similarly, on our side of the river, a great standard had been raised, depicting gold coins and a lance – a play on Edgar's name, meaning "wealth and spear", the work of many hours of embroidery.

Aunt Aethelflaed had complained of a slight chill, caught during the journey from Bathe, and so had declined to attend the day's events, allowing Aetna her leisure. The pomp and ceremony of the coronation was to be replaced by a more sober and pragmatic approach to the day – festivities deferred until later – and so, whilst the chief members of the Witan were to follow the royal barge in a second vessel, the main body of the Court would make its way to Saint John's church through the town, the Queen going on ahead, ready to meet Edgar at the church. It was not a long walk, but Elfrith insisted upon travelling in her litter, Ethelred with her, leaving Edward free – as he put it – to enjoy himself.

The morning grew warmer as the sun rose higher, and as his boatmen rowed him out to the centre of the stream, where the royal barge bobbed at anchor, Edgar's slight frame seemed dwarfed by the men who awaited him.

"My father is not a big man," said Edward, as we watched from the north bank. "I wonder if I shall grow to be taller than him."

"The King has a great heart," said Aetna. "That is much more important than height or weight. And size does not denote strength. Your father is a great huntsman and a fine swordsman, too, though thankfully he has never had to wield his sword in anger."

The eight kings now aboard the barge looked formidable. It was difficult to make them all out at the distance we were from proceedings, but one, at least, was immediately recognizable: Kennyth, King of the *Scotti*, as the Legions had called Caledonia. As Edgar boarded the boat, Kennyth towered above him, as dark and broad as Edward was fair and lithe. A mass of black hair, bushy and merging into his beard, which jutted forward antagonistically, gave the impression that his head was larger than appeared normal. Whilst the other kings either bent the knee, or bowed, he merely inclined toward the King as Edgar greeted them. Beside him, a smaller, ill-favoured man in the costume favoured by the Northmen seemed unwilling to move far from his side.

The breeze was blowing away from us, and so it was not possible to hear the oaths taken, or Edgar's response. It mattered little; what was important was that the fealty was seen to be given. Each stood in turn and made his pledge and to each Edgar extended his hand in friendship. Then they took their seats at the oars and began to scull upstream. Edgar, at the stern, took the rudder and steered efficiently. I noticed, to our left, the master shipwright looking both anxious and gratified as his vessel responded to the King's lightest of touches.

"Come on," I said, "We had better make a move, the Queen will already be at Saint John's and we must be at the steps before His Majesty. Edward," I had been given leave to address the prince informally, "Do you have your words by heart?"

"I do," he replied. As the King's elder son, he had been given a role in the short ritual to follow. "I practised them all last evening. Ethelred was in a fit of jealousy!"

"Your brother is yet young," said Aetna. "He will soon enough have duties of his own and then I'll be bound he will not want them!"

"He never wants to do anything that he is asked," replied Edward. "Only what he thinks he would enjoy. Although," he added, "I suppose he is not allowed much of that, either."

My sister and I looked over the prince's head and exchanged a glance of sympathy. We had both witnessed Ethelred's tantrums and could not help but think they were partly due to his mother keeping him so close. From our vantage point beside the gateway opposite the bridge across the Deva, we returned inside the town walls, up Bridge Street and then turned right along a smaller street, heading toward Saint John's. There was a pleasant, relaxed feel to the procession as, without acknowledging the necessity to observe rank, Court and retainers walked companionably. Thella and Ratkin materialised beside us. I suspected they had been holding hands, though they now made an effort to appear nonchalantly indifferent to each other. Dunstan, of course, would be awaiting the King already, but his brother (not a significant enough member of the Witan to be awarded a place in the second boat, much, I thought likely, to his chagrin) huffed and puffed along, wanting to get a good place in the church. Dunna walked lightly by his side, and I noticed that Elfwine was making an effort to catch up with them, from his position further back. The houses and shops thinned out and as the road broadened into open ground, we saw ruined masonry jutting from the earth, relics of the Roman occupation of the town, and to our left the towering external walls of the amphitheatre. The minster church was just ahead.

It was a fine sight. Set on foundations of Roman stone, which were raised a little above ground level, the wooden structure of the building rose high above us, painted and even gilded, in places. To one side a long, low range of buildings opened onto the green in front of the church. These were the workshops of the stone masons, with tall, intricately carved stone crosses, some still in the process of being made, propped against plinths, lying on the ground or loaded onto carts to await delivery. The Shire Reeve, who had made his way to the front of the procession beamed at them. "Caestre's reputation for masonry…" he began to explain to his companions, but he was halted in mid-sentence by the imminent arrival of the King.

Edward had mounted the steps to the West door of the church and was standing to attention awaiting his father. Some of the party had entered to find advantageous posts from which to witness the ceremonies, but many others gathered around the foot of the steps, Edward's retainers keeping clear a passage for those about to arrive. Edward glanced over at us, a trace of nervousness betrayed as he slipped a finger under the collar of his tunic to loosen it a little. I gave him what I hoped was a reassuring grin and Aetna smiled and mouthed "You'll be fine!"

Heralded by a blast from the horns preceding him Edgar strode up to the steps and mounted to stand beside his son, the eight self-styled kings arranging themselves in a semi-circle below them. This was Edward's moment.

"My lords, Principals of the eight kingdoms, your presence in this royal city is welcome." The wording of this greeting had been carefully prepared to avoid calling anyone King with the exception of Edgar. "Kennyth of the *Scotti*, Massuc of the Southern Isles, Donald and Malcolm, Lords of Strathclyde, Jacob of Gwynedd, Morgan of Gwent and Glywysing and Siferth of the Danelaw, you have sworn your fealty to our sovereign King Edgar, and he, in turn, his fair and impartial protection of your lands. You are bid enter this holy place to make your thanks to God for these blessings."

Word perfect. Edgar beamed his pride, and with his hand on Edward's shoulder led the way into the interior of Saint John's.

)))))))(((((((

The service was not long. The rest of the Court and retainers – those who could find a place – piled into the church to witness Dunstan give thanks for this day when "peace among the peoples of these islands" was confirmed by "men of good will and God's wisdom". As ever, the alliteration of this prose made a powerful impact. Once again, the great crown designed for the ceremony at Bathe was placed upon Edgar's head –

we noticed that although Elfrith played no part in the proceedings, she was wearing her own crown already – and the kings made a final obeisance to their overlord. It was done.

With midday fast approaching, food, drink and entertainment were on offer in the amphitheatre, only a stone's throw away from the church. Tradition held that when the Legions occupied the town, Christians laid foundation stones of a shrine beside the eastern gate of the amphitheatre through which so many of their fellows had passed on their way to martyrdom. It was this shrine which grew into Saint John's Church. It seemed unlikely to me, from everything I had heard of the Romans, that they would have allowed such a thing, and voiced my thoughts to Aetna as we passed out of the church.

"They may have done so in such a way as not to be discovered," she said. "Perhaps just put a few stones together and marked it with a fish – their secret sign – hoping their masters would mistake it for... something else." Her attention wavered. "Just look at the great oaf," she said in a low voice, indicating ahead of us, where Kennyth and his companion – we could now see that the smaller man who had been beside him in the barge was Siferth, the representative from the Danelaw – were jostling and play-wrestling in an attempt to grab and pile as much food on each other's trenchers as possible, while quaffing down horn after horn of ale. Clearly, they had wasted no time in leaving the church and arriving at the well provided board. The other Lords stood somewhat to the side, whilst Edgar and the royal party had seated themselves a little way off.

"Ha, my Danish friend!" Kennyth was bellowing. "Pile up your meat. You will need your strength to defend the rights of our overlord. He may not be able to do the job for himself!"

"Indeed, Lord! For he is a small man to wear such a heavy crown!" The Dane threw an arrogant look in Edgar's direction. "Mayhap it will be too much for him one day! We must be ready to... assist!"

Kennyth strode over to Edgar, chewing on the leg of a fowl. He wiped his free hand across his mouth and beard, smearing fat still further across his face, and then unceremoniously slapped Edgar on the back with the same hand. "How now, Your Majesty, it does seem to me that it is a miracle so many provinces should be held by such a sorry little fellow as yourself." His grin was more grimace. Turning his back on the king he went to return to his acolyte. "Siferth, let us go and find some more... lively... company." He barged his way through the guests and past us.

"Not lively minded, for they would most surely eschew your company!" said Aetna in a loud voice.

He spun around and looked her up and down. "Where I come from, women do not speak unless spoken to," he said.

"Then I am glad that I have not been there." She turned away and began to walk toward Edgar.

"Perhaps it would do you good to be… taken… there, if you understand my meaning," he leered at her, Siferth laughing at his side.

"Aye, cousin, she looks as though she needs to be 'taken' somewhere!"

I whirled around at this, my hand on the hilt of my sword, but was suddenly stopped by another hand, clasping my own to my side.

Elfwine whispered urgently in my ear. "Wulf, do not forget yourself! You cannot draw your sword in the King's presence!"

"Brother, I appreciate your intentions," said Aetna, in her turn looking the Scot up and down. "I do not need defending from this 'little' king, when I am in the presence of a great one!"

Kennyth bristled but held himself in check. "One day, Lady, we may continue this," he said. "And you may not be so ready to scorn strength as beneath show. Today's performance is but words. Actions count for more in the real world."

"Have a care, my Lord," said Siferth, quietly, laying his hand on Kennyth's arm. "Time enough!"

"Yes, time enough, indeed. For now, let us enjoy the hospitality of the 'great' king." And he shovelled another piece of fowl into his mouth, following it by a huge swig of ale, much of which found its way into his beard.

With a disgusted look, Aetna swept her skirts out of the way and made to leave. Kennyth stepped to one side and blocked her, and as she stepped the other way, mirrored her actions, keeping her facing him. "So, you would dance, my Lady?"

My sister refrained from replying and managed to out manoeuvre him, stalking away toward Thella, who watched uneasily from a little distance. "Madam, that was not wise," she said.

"You can talk!" Aetna replied sharply. "Wisdom seemed to bypass you last time we enjoyed such festivities. Be about your duties, there must be something that needs doing."

I could not help but recall Edgar's sense of foreboding when we were on the ship together, and remembered that, for all the pomp of this last few days, he felt less secure in his kingdom than he wished to appear, with such as Kennyth and Siferth in its orbit. My appetite had suddenly abated, Aetna seemed in no mood to remain, and there was a chill mist rolling in from the Dee. Looking around, I could see that few appeared to have overheard the exchange, or if they had, were inclined to ignore it. Edgar seemed determined to do so, now standing with the Queen, his hand on Edward's shoulder, deep in conversation with Maccus of the Southern Isles. Edward cast me a worried look and then returned his attention to his father's words; he would not be needing me again that day.

"Come," I said to Aetna, "Let's slip away. I've had enough of this. And you look like thunder. Heaven know what you will say if anyone else crosses you!"

"Heaven knows, indeed," she said. "But you are right, let's leave. I should go and see how Aunt Aethelflaed fares. We will not be missed now that there is food and drink enough to keep everyone... amused." Her good humour was beginning to resurface.

Thella had made herself scarce, doubtless she had not found anything that needed doing as her mistress had bid, but had found the hand of Ratkin once again, for he was nowhere to be seen either.

We had entered the amphitheatre through the eastern gate. The boards of food and drink had been set up under awnings in the centre of the great open space at its core, the remains of seating and high walls still forming and almost complete oval, enclosing the arena where so many lives had once been lost to provide entertainment for the masses. I shuddered and for a moment sensed their fear. Was it, perhaps, not the most auspicious place in which to celebrate this conjoining of fiefdoms? I would be pleased to be gone.

Aetna took my hand and we slipped away, passing through the western gate, across the green and back through the town walls toward the castle.

"These walls look strong," said Aetna. "Do you remember the walls of Colencaestre?"

"I remember the King's prank played upon the unwitting Shire Reeve," I laughed. As we walked into the centre of the town it felt as though the fog, both real and imagined was beginning to lift. "When Aethelflaed, the Lady of the Mercians, defended these walls against the Vikings, she overcame them with hot beer and beehives thrown down upon enemy," I said, not sure if my sister had ever heard the story.

"So I believe," she said. "Now, there was a woman who did not wait to speak until she was spoken to! I should love to have met her."

"Well, don't you get any ideas about fighting," I said.

"Why not?"

"Because I do not want people saying that my sister is fiercer than I am! We could not now swap our clothes, but I sometimes think you would like to take a man's role on the Witan, would you not?"

"Perhaps, but I know that cannot happen. Though I shall be closer to it that most when I accompany Aunt Aethelflaed to Court – I wonder if she was named after the Lady of the Mercians. I must ask her."

We were almost at the castle, and the guard at the main gates opened up for us.

"My Lord, Lady. I am to request you to hurry to the Queen Dowager as soon as you are returned," he said.

"I hope she is not worse," Aetna said, hitching up her skirt and running toward the door to the Great Hall. "A chill can allow the elf-shot easy entrance if care is not taken!" I followed, the echo of my sister's fear roiling in my stomach.

The chamber our aunt had been allocated was in the overcroft of the Hall, and we ran up the stairway which had been built at an angle up and alongside the wall – wooden, like the wall itself – our outdoor boots clattering as we took two at a time, finally bursting into her apartment.

"Aunt! What is the matter? Are you unwell, what can I do?" Aetna panted. I must have looked equally concerned, for Aethelflaed rose quickly from her seat (she had been at work on her embroidery) and came to us.

"No, no, my loves, do not worry! Really, what in Heaven did that guard say? I only asked that you should pay me a visit on your return, not that I needed rescuing from some monstrous ill fortune." She laughed. "But I thank you, anyway. You are good children. Though I must stop thinking of you both that way, with Aetna coming to Court with me, and you Wulf, I hear, taking a full position with the Aetheling Edward. We shall all be at the heart of things. Come, sit by me."

There was a cheerful fire burning in the grate – another of the castle's modernisations: a flue taking much of the smoke from the room. Aethelflaed returned to her seat, indicating that we should make ourselves comfortable on the large, high-backed settle on the other side of the fire. Sheepskins softened the hardness of the wood and cushioned us somewhat.

"Aunt, we had not wanted to make our decisions public with regard to joining the Court until we had the chance to tell the rest of the family," said Aetna. "How did you know about Wulf's plans?"

"You will soon learn that it is hard to keep any information private at Court, Aetna. Your brother's appointment is still officially unknown, as is yours, but, believe me, you had better tell my sister and your uncle within the day, or the rumour mill will reach them before you do. It is somewhat to do with this that I wished to speak to you both. I had a notion that you would be returning before the others, and had you not done so I would have sent to the celebrations to fetch you – though given your reactions to my lesser summons, goodness knows the state you would have been in when you got here!"

Wulf and I exchanged a glance. "We will speak to our aunt and uncle this evening," I said. "We were worried they might be unhappy with our decisions. I think we were delaying for that reason. But we certainly do not want them to hear the news from anyone but us."

"I could not bear to see them upset," Aetna added, a little tearfully. The enormity of the upcoming change in her life seemed only now to begin feeling like a reality.

"Children... oh, there I go again! Aetna, Wulf, surely you know your adopted parents well enough to realise that they will only be pleased that you have both decided upon the direction of the future. That you do what makes you fulfilled will be all they ask. There are plenty willing to be part of their household: it is a happy one. Do not fret on their behalf."

Aetna sniffed. I cleared my throat. "There now," said Aethelflaed, "have a honey cake, both of you, and a mug of ale, and let us talk. We may not have much time."

She settled herself back in her chair, and picked up her sewing, for all the world like we were simply passing the time of day, but her expression was now serious.

"If I am truthful, I would tell you that if I had my choice, I would return to my Hall at Stoche, and take my ease with my stitching and my still-room. But I do not believe that I can make that choice. Life at Court has its compensations, of course, but in my heart, I feel that I have passed enough years following its progress from shire to shire, town to town – and when we settle for a few months in one place, I become tired of the endless coming and going of envoys and emissaries, the meetings of the Witan and the entertainments that accompany it all.

"But the late King, my beloved Edmund, entrusted me with the well-being of his sons when they were young, and though Eadwig was something of a disappointment, Edgar is as dear to me as any child I might have had of my own. Edward, too, is my very heart. I love that boy dearly. And I fear for him; I fear for them both. There, I have said it."

"Aunt?" Aetna and I spoke at the same instant.

"They are very like, Edgar and Edward. The same slightness of build, and, in many ways, the same all-too-trusting hearts. Oh, the King is no fool – he is like his father in that way – but when he loves he does so blindly and without limit. That was the way he was with his beloved Elfa – may the Lord rest her sweet soul – which was as it should have been, for she was as true and faithful a wife as any could be. When she died, as you know, he was totally bereft, I thought the melancholy would kill him. But, like many a man, he found he could love again. That it was Elfrith whom he loved did not alter his manner of loving, but..." she hesitated, and looked toward the door, "it might have been the better for him, for all of us, if it had."

Neither my sister nor I knew what to say, or even if we were expected to say anything. It seemed not, for Aethelflaed continued almost immediately.

"You both know the manner of her coming into our family. I must say that I rue the day Ethelwold perverted the course of events by engineering their marriage. Aetna, check that the stairs are empty and leave the door on the jar, so that we may hear if anyone ascends. Many walls have ears, but I believe this room to be private – and the Hall is still almost empty. You must both learn to watch where and when you speak when you assume your new duties." She laid aside her embroidery hoop.

"I believe that your Uncle Ethelwold lost his life as a result of his passion. Elfrith's demeaner toward him was not what a wife's should be from the first, but when she learned that he had diverted her on the path that would have led her to being Queen she... well, let us simply say that her husband's life became a burden she no longer cared to endure. I have heard something of the events on that fateful day at Uphude from my sister. I would that I had seen that scratch on your uncle's wrist, for it to give him such pain seems odd... and then his untimely collapse, there is much here that disturbed me then and worries me now."

Aetna and I looked at each other. Over the years we had at first discussed and then tried to put out of our minds, the ramifications of all we had seen and heard during our stay at Ethelwold's Hall all those years ago. We had never voiced our thoughts to anyone else. But now...

"Aunt," began Aetna, "there are things which we witnessed then that have always troubled us, too."

"There was a day," I took up the story, "when we went swimming with some of the other children. We saw Elfrith and Morwen picking herbs. We heard them speak of things that we did not understand at the time. And I am not sure that I do now..."

"But I begin to," continued Aetna. She had caught our aunt's feeling of insecurity as she spoke and continually glanced at the half-open door, although we could see there was nobody there. Nevertheless, she lowered her voice.

"They sought out monks'-hood, and spoke of giving it to an old goat... I remember Ratkin laughed that it was the first time Elfrith had ever taken an interest in the Hall's livestock. They also spoke of mandrake and... pennyroyal." Like all women, Aetna's education had included a knowledge of medicinal herbs. Mine had not.

"Sister, you told me of your concerns about the monks'-hood and mandrake, that they are both poisonous, but what of the other?" I said. I realised that we had not spoken of that day for many years.

"Wait," said Aethelflaed "let us be clear... you say monks'-hood? Mandrake is a vicious root, its actions would draw attention to a poisonous attack, but monks'-hood? That is a subtler weapon. A decoction smeared on a knife – or a needle... from a modest injury death would follow, but at a slow pace, slow enough to appear innocent to all but the most insightful."

"So, when Ethelwold became ill on the hunt..." My words seemed unnecessary, for the women had already reached a mutually agreed conclusion.

"I cannot say that I did not suspect something of the sort," Aethelflaed sighed. "But to have it confirmed... Did my sister not question the day's events?"

"We said nothing of overhearing Elfrith... we had too often been scolded for eavesdropping."

"Not that we ever did it on purpose." Aetna seemed to slip back into her childhood fear of being reprimanded for her natural curiosity.

"And Elfrith insisted on a swift burial: I recall hearing that," Aethelflaed mused. "Otherwise tell-tale signs on our poor cousin's body would become only too obvious."

"But, Aunt Aethelflaed, surely you cannot think that even Elfrith would use pennyroyal?" whispered Aetna. "Not to..."

I must have looked mystified. Aethelflaed assumed a more matter-of-fact tone.

"We must speak frankly now and then never voice the matter again," she said. "Let us have it said openly, between us, at least. You know that during that fateful Progress, Edgar was fearful for Elfa's well-being. When you visited my Hall at Stoche he made me promise that I would come to her in time for her confinement. But from all I had heard she was in good health, merely suffering from the morning-ills that beset many a pregnant woman. Edgar was ever a worrier. When he returned to her after the events at Uphude, he was even more concerned for her; he was anxious that the elf-shot which he believed had taken Ethelwold might somehow have attached itself to his person and been carried back to his loved ones. But all seemed well. Then – and it was still many weeks before the baby was due, so before I planned to visit – Elfrith sent him a philtre which she swore would ease the morning sickness. You know what happened – she appeared to improve, but then tragedy. Now you tell me that Elfrith and that bitch Morwen were harvesting pennyroyal. It is a herb used for little in the God-fearing stillroom. But whores use it to rid themselves of the ill-gotten consequences of their profession. It is as unholy a plant as any..."

"Oh, Heavens, Aunt, let it not be said," Aetna was as pale as snow, even though she had clearly made the connection before Aethelflaed put it into words for my benefit. I could not speak. This was women's lore, women's secrets. I realised what a gulf lay between our worlds.

"Now, to matters as they stand at present." Aethelflaed resumed her stitching to calm herself and then laid it aside again, unable to do her usual standard of work justice. "We need never speak out loud of these things again but be aware of this: I will ever strive not to allow that woman to harm Edgar or Edward, not while there is breath in my body. I, too, have knowledge and skills. But defence is a better way than outright aggression. Edgar adores her. Any word said against her will only strengthen her – she will twist it and use it to bind him still closer. She has risen higher than any woman not of royal blood since the house of Wessex took power. She is crowned Queen. I believe that will keep her content for the present at least. But as to the future? I do not like the way the Chief Ealdorman pays her court. I do not like the way she favours Ethelred over Edward, though it is only natural, given he is of her body. And I do not like the way she is beginning – slowly – to replace some of Edgar's closest retainers."

"Aunt?"

"Ah, you will not have heard yet... just last eve, the King's taster, Alwin, died. He has been at Edgar's elbow this ten years. Oh, there is no suggestion of foul play, how could there be? He has eaten the same food as the King every day of his service and yet it is strange that he should suddenly succumb to the falling sickness on the very day that it is announced Elfrith's own taster is to become wed to a man whose profession is the same as her own! Some might say providential. Others..."

We were beginning to realise that life at Court was not to be the joy-ride we might have anticipated.

"So, my loves – there, I no longer feel the urge to call you children – I am asking you to be a part of something which may take you a very long way from your comfortable home lives. You will be newcomers to the Court, you may get the chance to see and hear things that are kept from me as the Grande-dame of bygone days. Enjoy your new roles – Aetna, be sure that I will give you every opportunity to make friends with those who are both our allies and those who fall under our suspicion, and I am certain that being in young Edward's circle will afford you the same, Wulf. Be my eyes and ears. Elfrith thinks of me as a silly old woman, but she still keeps her own counsel in my presence. I think you have few secrets from Thella and Ratkin? I would trust them, too, but impress upon them the importance of this matter. They will be able to move amongst the lower retainers and there is much to be learnt from ceorls and even thralls. Go now, spend the evening with your parents; tell them of your new positions, but do not burden them with aught else. There may well come a time when everything is in the open, but for now, the fewer who know my fears the better. We can do nothing to change the past, and perhaps the future will hold no ill-omen. We must pray that it will be so."

FIFTEEN

November, the Year of Our Lord 974

AETNA

A full year has passed since we took up our positions at Court. The seasons have once again turned from spring, through summer and autumn and into an early winter before Wulf and I once again find ourselves with our whole family in a single Hall, but that last night at Caestre will remain with me always.

Wulf and I both felt that we had been on a wild ride of emotions, from heady, uninformed enthusiasm the day before, to an anxious mix of uncertainty and apprehension after our talk with Aunt Aethelflaed. That evening, as we had promised, we spoke to Brithnoth and Aelflaed. Their reaction was as Aethelflaed had assured us it would be: whilst there was some small regret that our childhood was over and our adult lives begun – that adulthood taking us, at least partly, out of the family circle – our aunt and uncle would support and approve our ambitions.

"Ah, Aetna," Aelflaed sighed, "I knew in my heart that you were too full of ideas and invention to remain with us always. The skills – and there are many – that you have learned at Radendunam will set you in fine form to attend at Court. Why, I have no doubt that you will have my sister's apartments rivalling those of the Queen for innovation before the year is out." And then with her accustomed little clap, "Will that not put the Lady Elfrith's nose out of joint?" I noticed that she still sometimes refrained, in private, from giving Elfrith her royal title.

"Sister-son, you know that you have been a son to me these ten years, and so you shall remain," said Brithnoth, as he and Wulf gripped each other wrist to elbow. "You are my heir, and I know that your duties to the King and the Aetheling Edward permitting, you will be my strong right arm, should we ever need, God forfending, to raise the Eastseaxe fyrd. I share your honour that the time you have already spent at Court has recommended you to the King for this, surely the most trusted of positions."

Wulf's eyes were bright. "You are my uncle, my father and my liege Lord," he said. "All that I am is of your making. Were I not sure that the King would release me if you ever needed me, I would not take this honour."

I was a little tearful, too. "Aunt and Mother," I said, "Like Wulf, I know that whatever the future holds for me, it is your love and training that has made me the person I am. You and Radendunam will always hold my heart."

"I am not sure of that, little one," Aelflaed laughed. "For I think there are likely to be many who will want to steal that particular jewel away!" She took my hands and held me at arms' length, looking me up and down. "Ah, yes, indeed!" She nodded her approval. "But come now, both of you – and you, Husband – there is dancing to be had in the Great Hall, and wine and food. We shall be home before the spring is over and there will be much to do to prepare these two for their adventures. Let us make merry while we can."

There was music and laughter in the Great Hall as we entered. Trestles had been pushed against the walls and loaded with food. The informality of the gathering allowed trenchers to be taken from great stacks at intervals along the tables and laden with whatever delicacies appealed. The "petty kings" had returned to their guest Hall across the river, ready to depart to their own demesnes on the morrow, leaving Edgar's Court free to celebrate the conclusion of the day's diplomacy. The younger members were dancing, or flirting in the corners, whilst their elders were chatting amicably. It seemed that for this evening, at least, all factions were united. Edgar – looking rather wistfully, I thought, at the dancers – and Elfrith were seated in large, straight backed, but cushioned and comfortable chairs, Edward and Ethelred beside them. Edward looked a little bored. His younger brother was playing with a cup and ball, the ball attached to the cup with a piece of string. He repeatedly tossed it up and tried to catch it again in the open mouth of the cup but was not expert enough to succeed very often. He appeared increasingly frustrated. When Edward caught sight of Wulf he immediately brightened and made to get up and come to us. The King gently put a hand on his shoulder and held him back. It was for a companion-man to come to his Lord, not the other way around. These lessons had to be learned young.

Wulf and I excused ourselves from Brithnoth and Aelflaed and made our way through the dancers toward the royal party, making our obeisance when we finally reached them through the crowd.

"I am so pleased to see you, Wulf," said Edward. "My father has told me that you are to be my companion-man. We shall have some fine times together, shall we not?" The twinkle in his eye reminded me of a young Edgar.

"Indeed, we shall, sire," said Wulf.

"And you, Aetna." My surprise must have been apparent as Elfrith spoke to me. Startled by this unusual attention, I almost forgot my curtsey as she continued. "I hear you are to be joining us at Court. As companion-lady to the Dowager Queen. You are yet young for such a position."

"Your Majesty." I could think of no ready reply to this comment.

"Do you think that your upbringing has equipped you well?"

"I do, Your Majesty." I could see little advantage in dissembling. "And the Dowager Queen has known me all my life. She is my aunt by marriage."

"Quite." There was a volume of implied criticism in that one word. She turned to Ethelred. "Will you stop that infernal clacking!" She wrested the toy from him. "Sit still and be quiet!" It seemed that her conversation with me was over.

"Sire," said Wulf looking to Edgar, "May I take the Aetheling Edward and find him a dancing partner?"

"Of course!"

"Come then, Your Highness," and they made off into the revellers. I curtseyed once more and followed them.

"I promise this time not to disappear on you!" he said.

The spring evening was still young. Through the windows of the Hall – another modern innovation: shuttered openings to allow air and light into the long building – we could see the light beginning to fade. A distant church bell intoned an invitation to evening offices. We could only hear it because the musicians had briefly stopped playing, to wet their throats with the fine ale which was flowing so freely. The town gate would be locked in an hour or so.

Suddenly, there was a commotion at the entrance to the Hall. The great double doors were closed against the encroaching night, but the small wicket gate, large enough only to admit one person at a time stood open in the body of the lower right-hand quadrant of its armoured height. The two sentries, who had been acting as little more than doormen on this convivial evening, were struggling to hold back a small, squirming figure, its determination to gain access apparently giving it more strength than its size would suggest.

"No, you don't, you little mud-*wyrm*!" the shorter of the two said, between gritted teeth as he grabbed hold of the scruff of the intruder's neck. "Get out and back to whatever dung-heap you came from."

A shriek of anguish came from the small form, which showed no sign of lessening its attempts to enter. "I must speak with…"

"You will speak with no-one here this night," The taller, heavier of the sentries tucked the struggling figure under his arm and began to manhandle it out of the door.

"The Queen, the Dowager Queen… please, you must let me. I have to…" But the wicket gate banged shut.

Aethelflaed had remained in her chamber, so it seemed that I must now assume my duties a little earlier than I had anticipated. With a glance at Wulf, I headed for the door.

"Let me out," I said to the remaining sentry.

"Lady…"

"I said to let me out," I repeated. "I am companion-lady to the Dowager. I wish to see what is amiss."

"It is just some creature who knows of Her Majesty's generosity and seeks alms in this ungodly way."

"Nevertheless."

Reluctantly, he opened the wicket and I passed through. His companion was walking back toward the door from the corner of the building, rubbing his hand.

"Bit me, the little bitch! Lady, do not go near, it is not safe!"

I bridled, wondering how much harm such an apparently small person could inflict upon me, let alone a man of his size. "It is a girl?" I asked.

"As far as I can tell, Lady."

"And what have you done with her?"

"Nothing, Lady. I have left her to crawl back to…"

I hurried around the corner. A pathetic form hunched against the wall of the Hall, rocking backward and forward, one hand holding up the torn shoulder of her… gunna? It seemed little more than a shift, a rag, really. There appeared to be some commotion going on by the River Gate. Some men were heading toward the castle, but seeing the sentries, looked to think better of it.

"Are you hurt?" I said, not getting too close, despite my concern, for the girl looked wildly about her and I thought that perhaps she was moon-struck.

"Lady?"

Something about that voice seemed familiar. I looked more closely at the sad little figure.

"Alfreth! What in middle-earth had happened? Why are you here? Who is with you? Why are you not in Bathe at the convent?" Too many questions, Alfreth was in no condition to answer them.

She appeared to rally the last of her strength and stood up. "Lady, I am cast out from the convent. I have nowhere to go. No-one to serve, few skills and nothing to offer for my bed and board but my body… and that I will never offer. I did not ask for the life of a nun, but it was all I had. The Queen Dowager was the only person ever to offer me kindness and a word that made me think there might be a different life for me. Except for you, of course, and…"

She faltered and tears came.

"Come, you are safe now," I said. "How long is it since you have eaten? And how came you here?"

"I have had no food in three days, Lady. I walked… but then…"

"No more now," I put my arm around her waist, though I am ashamed to say I wrinkled my nose against the smell of her. "We will get you cleaned and fed and then see what is to be done."

I had been so focussed on Alfreth that I had not heard footsteps come up behind me. When a hand fell on my shoulder, I gave a small scream and spun around.

"It's only me." Wulf looked concerned. "Great gods, what is going on here?"

Alfreth buried her face in my gunna. Again, I tried not to reel away from her filthy condition.

"Sister Alfreth has had a most unfortunate time," I said, but before I could say more, she spat, "Not Sister, never call me Sister again!"

"She cannot go into the Great Hall like this," I said. "I must take her up the side stairs to our chambers. Find Thella and tell her to bring water – warm if she can. It is yet early, Aunt Aethelflaed will not be abed, knock at her chamber and tell her what has happened, or as much as we know of it…"

Wulf turned on his heel only to cannon into another figure as it emerged from around the corner of the Great Hall.

"… can this poor girl have no privacy in her distress?" I said sharply, and then realising the identity of the newcomer, "Oh, I am sorry, your Highness, I did not see it was you!"

Edward recognised Alfreth immediately despite her sorry appearance.

"Little Sister!"

"Not now, Edward," Wulf slipped back into the familiarity we had enjoyed with the prince. Then more properly, "If you will, your Highness, help me to do what my sister says; we need to fetch the Dowager Queen. Women know how to deal with such things."

"Yes, yes, of course, anything I can do!"

They returned to the Hall, to run the errands I had given Wulf, and I helped Alfreth to the stair leading up to the private chambers.

She seemed to summon up some strength from an untapped reserve and with my steadying arm around her, managed the steps up to the sleeping quarters above. I took her into mine, and sat her down, wrapping a blanket around her shoulders.

"Lady, may I have a little water? I am fearful thirsty."

"Of course, and we shall soon have you clean and warm, too."

"I thank you, Lady. But now that I am here, I am afeared that I should not try to see the Dowager Queen… coming seemed the only thing to do, but I think in truth I never believed that I would be able to reach her. It was just a desperate dream! I shall surely be in even more trouble for being so forward…" Tears threatened again.

"No, Alfreth, I know that my aunt – you knew that she was my aunt? – will want to know of this. I am certain. She will be here soon."

At that moment, the door opened and Aethelflaed, followed by Thella, bearing a bowl of water and a cloth, entered.

"Aetna, what is happening? I had some garbled word of an emergency from the prince and met Thella who had had the same from Wulf. They said…" She saw Alfreth as I stepped aside. "Child! What has become of you? How did you come here?"

Alfreth was overcome, and I replied for her, telling Aethelflaed as much as I knew and as I did so, took the water from Thella, and began to clean Alfreth's face and hands with the warm, perfumed water.

"Well, she is clearly in no position to speak now," said my aunt. "Thella, go to my chambers and fetch Ethel and Onwen, this poor girl needs more than a passing wipe with a warm cloth and a sip of water: she needs a bath and a meal." Alfreth looked terrified. "Come child, we are all women here… you are safe now. But then we must hear your tale, for it seems a troubling one."

The goodwives were with us in moments, Thella behind them. With some clucking and tutting, they helped Alfreth out of the room, and I did not see her again that night. I returned to the Great Hall, where the evening appeared to be continuing to pass pleasantly, people eating, drinking, dancing and talking with all thoughts of the earlier slight disturbance forgotten. I looked around for Wulf and Edward and caught sight of my brother as he hurriedly took Dunna and Elfwine to one side and appeared to be explaining to them what was happening. Edward was still with him. I went to join them, and we found a slightly quieter corner where we could sit and talk without being overheard.

"I cannot help but think that this must have something to do with what happened that night after the coronation," Edward said.

"Perhaps I should tell the King the whole story," said Wulf. "If he is minded to retract his commission to be your companion-man – and I can see how he might, I lost you after all – it is better now than later."

"We were all part of it," Elfwine took a swig of ale.

"But the prince was in my care… Alfreth may have… I don't know, what *can* have happened?"

"We should do nothing until we have heard what she has to say," I said, decisively. "Elfwine and Dunna had no part in his care, no-one knows they were with us."

"The King does," said Dunna. "He was there when we all set out."

"But he does not know we stayed together. You should both just keep silent. There are those who feel Wulf is too young for such responsibility – and I for the position with the Dowager Queen. They will not treat kindly any who they feel might have spoken out but did not."

"What are you all whispering about?" A small, querulous voice intruded upon our conversation. Ethelred, elbowed past his brother and stood pouting in our midst.

"Nothing that need concern you!" said Edward. "Why are you not abed? It is too late for children to be abroad."

"My mother, the Lady Queen," he said, with a slight lisp, clearly rehearsed in calling her by that title, "says that it is important for me to be seen."

"But not heard!" responded his elder brother. "Be off!" He turned Ethelred around and gave him a none-too-gentle shove in the direction of his mother, who was now looking in our direction.

"Well, if this is to be our final evening before facing the music from the West, let us make the most of it," said Elfwine. "Come, Dunna, another dance! My friends, I am sure we shall meet again on the morrow, before we all depart. Or are dismissed!" They spun off into the melee.

There seemed nothing left to do that evening. Shortly afterwards, I bade Wulf and Edward a good night and headed, once again, toward my chamber. As I reached my door, I hesitated. I had to know what Alfreth had suffered, and why. It was getting late. Thella was awaiting me (she had, apparently, not been needed once Onwen and Ethel had taken charge of Alfreth) and was ready to help me prepare for the night. She heard me outside the door and opened it.

"Come," I said, and we went along the walkway to Aethelflaed's chamber. I knocked softly at her door and it was opened by Onwen.

"Come along in," said my aunt. "Onwen, you may go. Keep an eye on that poor girl this night. You and Ethel. She will sleep now that she has had that draught, but if she awakes may be confused. I would not that she is any more fearful, she has suffered enough this se'enight."

"Aye, my Lady. And bless your good soul for the taking of her in. I bid you all a good night. My Ladies. And you." This last to Thella.

"Aetna," said my aunt, "I now have Alfreth's story, and a sad one it is…"

It was an hour before Thella and I returned to our chamber. We were sharing a comfortable pallet, and soon she was snoring lightly, while I lay awake thinking through the day's events.

It seemed that I had hardly slept at all when there was a scratching at the door and a low whisper. "Sister, are you decent?"

"Decent enough for you!" I replied in a similar low tone. Thella grunted and pulled the blanket over her head.

"A little more than that, I hope," Wulf replied. "I have a visitor with me that I would not normally bring to a lady's chamber at this hour."

I had expected him to be accompanied by Ratkin – and so had Thella, for she sat up, shook out her long hair, and pulled the blanket up to her chin, pinching her cheeks to give then colour. I made sure that my night-shift was covered. "Very well," I said. "We are presentable."

The door opened as little as was necessary to allow two figures to pass in, Wulf carrying a candle which flickered uncertainly in the draft.

"Eddy, Edward... sorry, Your Highness! I had not realised..." I was nonplussed.

"Come, cousin, I have given your brother leave to call me by my given name – or something like it – and I extend the same to you. In private, of course. After all, we are family, be it ever so distant!"

"Very well, Edward." It still did not come easily to me, not when I was thinking about it. "I thank you for the honour. But what are you both doing here at this hour?"

"I could not sleep for wondering about Alfreth. I woke Wulf and he in turn Ratkin, who said that he had seen you entering my step-grandmother's chamber after you left the Great Hall. Do you know the story?"

At that moment, as though summoned by mention of his name, Ratkin scratched at the door, whispering my brother's name.

"Oh, come along in, Ratkin," I said. "Really, I have never had such a gathering in my bed chamber! I don't suppose you have the minstrels and a skop out there as well, do you? We might as well make an entertainment of it!"

Rather sheepishly, Ratkin joined us. Thella, tossed her hair to one side and smoothed it down over her shoulder. I glared at her. "This is not the time or place, Thella!"

"Blow that candle out, Wulf, I don't want anyone else seeing a light and coming to investigate. We will have enough to explain on the morrow – or is it now today?" I continued. "Yes, I do have the story. Well, you had better make yourselves at ease. There are cushions on the trunk. You stay where you are, Thella! Edward, there is a chair by the window, draw it up closer." And in a low voice, with a little moonlight coming through the cracks in the shutters, I told them all I had heard from Aethelflaed.

Alfreth, as she told my aunt and the goodwives, after they had given her bread and meat, and hot ale, was left at the doors of Bathe Abbey as an infant. She was in a basket, with a rough sack as covering, with nothing in the world to her name – and, indeed, no name. She was taken in, as foundlings often were, named and brought up by the Sisters, destined for a life among them. She was a happy child, easy to love, and became quite the pet of the Mother Superior, a good, kind woman. But that good fortune was not to last.

When she was six, the Mother of the house died. Her successor was of a different disposition altogether, impassioned with a desire to raise the convent in the ranks of its peers, eager to encourage the most important families to send their daughters within its walls, and to accept the dowries they brought with them as brides of Christ. Her own niece, a precocious seven-year-old named Elspeth, joined as a novice and Alfreth's life was soon to become a nightmare.

Elspeth favoured her aunt in temperament. She was spoiled and demanding, and, bringing with her both money and prestige (for the Abbess' family was of the local landed hierarchy) was excused many of the more laborious chores and duties customary for young novices. The added burden fell upon Alfreth, whose lack of pedigree, status and wealth placed her, in the eyes of both aunt and niece, as the lowest of the low. She was bullied by Elspeth and ignored by the other novices, all eager to please the new favourite.

Relegated to the most menial of tasks, and with no prospect of her lot improving, Alfreth made the best of it. With what little opportunity she had to follow her own inclinations, she learned to sew, though was never allowed more than to mend and patch, picked up a little learning and daydreamed of somehow escaping to the Mother House at Wintancaestre.

Years passed, and her childhood with it. News came of the King's coronation, to take place in their abbey church, and the convent joined forces with the monastery to prepare. The choirs practiced day and night and those who were not blessed with a voice had other duties to perform. It seemed that everyone had a part to play. Even Alfreth: she was to stay in the nuns' kitchen throughout the day, ensuring that there was constant hot water, hard and soft lye soap available, should anyone need it. Heaven forbid a habit became stained or hands dirty on such a day.

Elspeth, of course, was assigned an important role. She was to welcome and attend upon the Dowager Queen and her party in the hours leading up to the ceremony. The day before the coronation, however, Elspeth became unwell. Something trifling, really, just a bad cold in the head, but even the Mother Superior could see that despite her protegee's protestations, it would not be appropriate for her to attend upon the Dowager sneezing, coughing and soaking kerchief after kerchief as her nose grew redder and redder. There was no time to re-assign anyone else from their duties, all was planned down to the last door to be opened and page of music to be turned. The only person who did not have a public role was Alfreth. Elspeth was furious.

We knew of how Alfreth had conducted herself that day; that she had pleased Aethelflaed and helped Thella and me with the Dowager's costume, and how Aethelflaed had sent her to watch the events of the rest of the day with Thella, Onwen and Edith. We knew, too, that she had somewhat extended her leave of absence from the day's offices by staying late in the abbey church, and of her meeting with Edward. What happened next, we were only now to hear.

Elspeth, refusing, later in the day, to keep to her bed, went into the abbey church to see if aught remained of the finery and ceremony she had missed. There, keeping silent as she watched, she saw Alfreth sitting, talking, with a young man, sitting close by him, and his head nodding, falling onto her shoulder while she held him close. Her own head beginning to nod, until the two of them seemed to slumber...

When Alfreth returned to the nuns' dormitory, later than she should, but willing to take the consequences of her absence the next morning – she would doubtless be given some unpleasant task as penance – she found the Mother Superior awaiting her, with Elspeth bright-eyed and eager beside her. Several of the other nuns and, it seemed, all the novices were either sitting up on their hard wood pallets or crowded behind Elspeth.

"What have you to say for yourself?" The Reverend Mother's voice was as cold as the night air.

"Mother, I am sorry to be so late, I stayed behind to see if there was aught needed clearing away – and in case my Lady the Dowager had perhaps left anything behind." Alfreth realised that these appeared lame excuses, but at least, she thought, they could hardly be contradicted, and were within the remit of her brief earlier in the day.

"So, you have not been in the church?"

Alfreth did not want to deny that she had been in St. Peters. "I checked to see that all was well, Mother."

"You? *You* checked to see that all was well? And what might you have done if it was not? If, perhaps, there was some ne'er-do-well loitering about? Some young man? Might you perhaps have spent time with him as if he was known to you? Perhaps put your arms around him...?"

"She... she *slept* with him, Mother!"

"Elspeth, do you know what you are saying?" Even the Reverend Mother was shocked at this.

As she recounted the story, Aethelflaed suggested (rather generously, I felt) that Elspeth might not, at first, have realised the full implication of her words, but, seeing their impact and the furore they caused, she maintained her accusation.

"Yes, Mother, yes! I saw them!"

"Holy Mother, yes, we... *slept* together... but we did not, I mean, I would not... *he* would not..."

"So, you do know him, then? Tell me his name. He shall be held to account for this!"

"I cannot!"

"You can and you will. Otherwise it will be the worse for you!"

"But we did nothing wrong, Reverend Mother!"

"Then he may tell me so himself. Come now, I will know who he is!" The older woman slapped her hard across the face. As Alfreth stepped backward, appalled by the violence of the impact, she felt something catch her foot. Elspeth's dainty shoe (she was excused the rough sandals of the other novices) tripped her and she fell, her head glancing against the leg of the nearest pallet.

Alfreth felt the floor tilt beneath her. As her world went black for a moment, she said, "I will never tell you!" and when, just a few moments later, she came to her wits, she found herself being bundled out of the dormitory, down the stairs and toward the ante-chamber where just a few hours earlier she had been so happy.

"One last chance, you... immoral creature," said the Mother Superior. "I will have the boy's name or you will leave this holy place with what you brought in with you – nothing!"

"Mother, please!"

"Very well, nothing it is then! Elspeth, remove her habit – and her sandals. I suppose we must leave her with her shift for the sake of decency, though that bird has clearly flown!"

At this point in the tale, Edward gasped, "Then it *is* all my fault! I never dreamt... I must go and..."

"Eddy, be still, wait. There is naught to be done at this moment." Wulf put a comforting hand on the boy's shoulder.

I continued. It seems that by the time Alfreth had come fully to realise what was happening she was outside the Nuns' Door. She stumbled toward the light she could see coming from the bone-fire burning away to nothing as the dawn approached. There was nobody about. Despite her desperate situation, she felt a thrill of freedom, and then a rush of fear. What should she do? Her head was full of the events of the coronation day and she determined to follow the Court where, surely, she might find a job in the kitchens. But where to go? How to find them? And she could hardly be abroad in daylight wearing naught but a... her face burned red at the thought of it.

Keeping to the shadows, she made her way into the great open space where the revels of the previous night had left behind them the detritus always conferred by a great number of merry-makers with no inclination to clear up after themselves. Among the broken jars and flagons on the ground beneath an overturned trestle she found a long, dirty length of cloth – perhaps it had been laid atop the trestle bearing the ale – and wrapped it around herself as best she could. Scavenging though the other rubbish she found a single shoe, a kerchief and a length of string which she used to fasten her makeshift cloak. She collected odds and ends of bread, some scraps of fatty meat, and a hunk of cheese, fallen behind one of the empty ale casks, and wrapped them in the kerchief: it seemed more important to take the food than cover her head. Without any great hope of success, she turned the tap on the keg. It gurgled. Finding a broken crock, she filled it with the dregs of the ale, cloudy with sediment, but strong and warming as it flowed through her veins. She gnawed on the cheese, wincing at the bruise beginning to form on her cheek.

She needed a plan. She had not slept for a day and a night – if you did not count a momentary doze with the Aetheling Edward – she could hardly believe she was even thinking those words! Weariness suddenly hit her like a gust of autumn wind. She remembered that once, on one of the rare occasions she had been out of the Abbey confines, she had been sent to collect eggs from a cottar on the edge of the town. It had not been a long walk. The chicken keeper's coops were many and, she noticed at the time, not all in use. She recalled the laughter of the old man as he told her that his "girls" like to ring the changes. "And I lets 'em! Keep my girls happy, and they keeps me in coin," he had said. She was small enough to curl up in a chicken coop and get her strength back. Then she could find the Court. With a last, wistful turn of the ale tap to no avail, she shouldered her small bundle and made for the outskirts of Bathe.

As Alfreth had hoped, she found an empty chicken coop and managed to slip inside unnoticed, where she curled up in the straw and fell into an exhausted sleep. When she woke it was late postnoon, the sun beginning to fall toward the horizon, but still casting shadows across the farmyard. Again, the sense of freedom was a heady tonic, despite her desperate circumstances and as she ate her meagre store of scraps, she planned her next move. Back into Bathe and find the Court. She scrambled out of the coop, careful not to be seen, and made a hasty exit through the scrappy hedge surrounding the strip of land where the chickens scratched and clucked, unworried by her presence.

As she trudged back toward the town centre she kept her eyes open for anything else she could scavenge. A strip of sacking at the roadside proved useful as a makeshift shoe (she pulled the thong from the one she had found in the square and, wearing the shoe loose, used it to tie on the sacking. The kerchief, no longer needed to carry her food, became a head-rail. She knew she must look every inch the vagrant beggar she now was, and as she neared the market place her earlier confidence began to wane.

The previous evening's debris had been cleared away and the bustling market looked as it did usually on a busy Moon-day postnoon. She would have to put aside any shame she felt at her appearance and approach someone, if only to ask where she might find the Court.

She stood uncertainly at the edge of the market place, wagons and carts rumbling past as their drivers prepared to pack up and head home for the evening.

"You're looking lost, hen!" A woman called down to her, unaware how appropriate the term was, given Alfreth's most recent place of rest. She couldn't help but smile.

"Aye, mistress, that I am!"

"My man has got hisself dead drunk again at the tavern and left me to load the cart... lend me a hand and I'll give ye my broken pastry crusts – and help ye find where ye's a-goin'".

"Thank you, mistress. That I will, and gladly."

Alfreth followed the cart the short way to the woman's stall, where the remains of her day's wares were already piled ready to load, a small basket of broken pies and spoiled pastries alongside. "I usually give these to the leper house on my way home," said the goodwife, climbing down from the wagon. "Now, help me take down the awning and stack those poles – that's it, they go in the back, here."

Between the two of them, the task did not take long and Alfreth marvelled at how pleasant it was to work alongside somebody with good humour and without having to watch her every word and movement. When all was loaded, she looked longingly at the basket.

The baker-woman laughed. "Take what you want, hen, ye look as though ye need a good meal. Now, where are ye making for?"

"Do you know where the King has been staying?" asked Alfreth, her mouth full of pastry.

Her companion looked askance. "That I do. He's been at the castle, of course. Though this morn the Court packed up early and was gone. I saw them heading away as we came in through the town gate. The King and his men as proud as fighting cocks on their beasts, making for the coast, I think, and the rest of them toward the North. What business do the likes of ye have with them?"

Alfreth did not feel inclined to reveal her story, kind though this woman was. "I... I was looking for work in the kitchens."

The woman eyed her up and down. "Well, I don't like ye chances!" she said.

At that moment, a man reeled toward them. "How now, wife! Are ye gossiping again?"

She looked at him with a mixture of contempt and tolerance. "And doing the work of two, ye useless *wyrm*. With the help of this lass. Get in the cart! No, in the back, you can hardly sit upright, ye'll be a-falling out if ye sit up here." He managed to haul himself into the body of the cart and flopped down alongside the poles. Within a moment he was snoring loudly.

"Are ye staying in town, lass? Ye'd best make up your mind, for they will be closing the gate soon."

"I have nowhere to go."

The woman considered for a few seconds. "I don't usually trust beggars. But ye seem fair of heart. Ye can have a night's shelter in the warmth of my bakehouse and I'll see ye on thy way on the morrow."

Alfreth spent a cosy night among the flour sacks beside the pastry cook's oven. They had reached a village bakery, some miles outside Bathe after sunset, and before dawn she was roused by the goodwife's bustling activity as she began another day's labour.

"There's milk on the board, lass. Take a sup, and see, I have packed ye up some more of yester-eve's crusts. There's some stale stottie, too. Keep ye going on the road! Ye had best be away before my man wakes. If ye are set on following the Court's progress, though I think ye're moon-struck, take the straight way out of the village – not the winding lane, mind, but the Legion's road – and head North. After that ye'll have to ask the way." She paused, her hands, floury, flat on the board in front of her.

"I do not ken why, hen, but I like ye. I wish ye well. If I had aught in the way of work for ye, ye would have it here. My name is Hilde. If ye journey back this way, there is a place by the fire for ye. Just ask for Hilde, baker-woman at Sceo."

Alfreth's eyes filled with tears. Not since the death of the old Reverend Mother had she felt affection from – or for – anyone. "Thank you, Goody Hilde, you do not know what a blessing you have been! I feel that we will meet again one day."

"I hope so, lass. I hope so…"

At the well-spring in the middle of the village, Alfreth splashed a little water – oh, it was cold! – on her face, asked an ostler filling pails to point her toward the right road, tightened the rags on her unshod foot and set off. The weather was kind, a light breeze blew from the west, and bright sun warmed her back as she walked. Spring blossomed around her. She felt light-hearted. A vague notion of finding the Dowager Queen kept her going. She knew it was ludicrously optimistic to expect a happy outcome to her quest, but with nothing to return to in Bathe, the road North seemed as good an option as any.

At first, she kept her head down when passing strangers. There were so many different types of wayfarer on the road: waggoners, their carts loaded with all kind of wares, drovers with herds and flocks that took up the breadth of the way, making her take refuge against the prickly hedges at the roadside, pilgrims in their long cassocks and wide brimmed hats. And then the other travellers: the rich on horseback, the poor on foot, those of indeterminate status on donkeys or mules. Most ignored her. As her feet began to hurt, and her left foot, wrapped in sacking, to bleed, her pace slowed, and most of those travelling in the same direction as herself overtook her. She realised that she needed to ask further directions, though she was not sure to where. She began to smile, shyly, at those passing her in the opposite direction, and finally plucked up the courage to ask if they had seen the Court's progress at all. Most had not, but then a carter said he had passed a train of fine horse drawn conveyances and litters, with outriders and guards, on yester-morn. They were on the road to Cyrnecaestre. Yes, that was the road she was now on. About another fifteen miles.

According to the scattered milestones and their Latin inscriptions together with a few scratched wooden signposts (Alfreth had surreptitiously picked up enough learning at the convent to understand place names and numbers) she had walked about seven miles from Sceo and was approaching Froweholt. It was now almost midday and she had twice as far to go again if she was to reach Cyrnecaestre by nightfall. And the Court was a day ahead of her.... and she was not even sure if it was staying there. The unknown began to overwhelm her. But she had little choice, push ahead or sit by the roadside. She decided upon a brief rest, a bite of food from her supplies and then set off once again, trying to ignore her growing lameness and aching legs.

Somehow, she kept walking. The pain began to numb her feet, as though each step hurt so much that her brain could not process it. The sacking on her left foot became more of a hindrance than a protection and she cast the bloody thing aside, walking lopsided with only one shoe, which made her back ache, too. Finally, she threw away the shoe, and wherever possible walked in the long grass at the side of the road, the cool green a balm on her bare feet after the hard, bone-jerking road.

The Roman walls of Cyrnecaestre lay ahead. Of course, the Court was not there, it had moved on, and she spent the night huddled in the porch of the great parish church in the company of other beggars, one elderly man, two children and a woman a little older than herself. She was amazed by the camaraderie between those who had almost nothing – the woman offered to share her meagre blanket and the elderly man chased off, as best he could, a drunken boy who made lewd remarks to the girls. She unwrapped the last of Hilde's food and shared out the bread stottie, which, she discovered, had been filled with cold pease pudding. Her eyes filled with tears again at the baker-woman's generosity.

As they huddled together for warmth, she shared something of her story with her companions.

"Aye, you have missed the Court by a day," said the old man. "I was seeking alms by the Abbey gate when the Progress set out this morn – one of the ladies threw some small coin for us. I heard the gate-keepers say that they were headed for Caestre for some big how-de-do, so ye will have some travelling to do if you want to reach them."

"But if they are staying there for a while, then I may be able to catch them up," said Alfreth, as her head began to nod against the woman's shoulder.

She woke the following morning amazed by how well she had slept. She slipped out from under the light covering, tucked it around the still sleeping woman and made to set off once again.

"Here, lass," the old man whispered and slipped two tiny fragments of coin into her hand. "I can see you are not the sort to have been on the streets before... take this from a man who has. And this advice: get off them as soon as you can!" Two quarter-pennies – fourthings, as they were called – nestled in her palm, the smallest units of money in the kingdom.

She thanked him, calling him "sire" for his trouble, which made him smile, and was out through the town gates as they opened for the day. For the next few days she followed in the tracks of the Progress, asking passers-by where they had been seen, or where heading, sometimes getting a ride from carters along the way, always on the lookout for any cast-off or lost clothes she might add to her mismatched rags. She found quite a large square of cheesecloth, fallen, perhaps, from an otherwise empty wagon, and tied it around herself, under her breasts, to hold both the table covering and her shift in place. She blushed to see that it made her look like a grown woman, with a small cleavage. The clips of coin were long gone, spent on milk and stale bread.

On the morning of the fifth day – or so she calculated, for the was losing track of time – she felt too exhausted and hungry to walk. She sat by the wayside, staring vacantly at the passing travellers, automatically, now, holding her hand out for alms. A cart clattered by, the horse skittish in its harness, one driver trying to calm it and the other in the bed of the cart, trying to hold down its contents as they were bounced about. The horse shied, kicked out and stopped, snorting.

"These crocks will be a-broke before we are half way to Caestre," called the man in the rear.

"Could you not have hired a horse that knew how to step softly?" his partner replied.

"Well, could you not have packed these pots so they would not be a-knocking together with every jolt?" They glared at each other, fists clenched.

Alfreth snapped out of her torpor. "You're for Caestre?"

"Aye, though there will be little enough profit in it if this clod cannot drive a horse without..."

"I can help! Take me to Caestre and I will steady the horse, or the pots, or... whatever! Just, for the love of Heaven, let me ride with you!"

"You can horse-charm?"

"Yes," she lied, walking to the head of the animal, its nostrils still flaring, eyes rolling and showing their whites. How hard could it be? She had never had anything to do with horses, and up close it looked much bigger than it had when it passed, but she was desperate. Reaching out her hand, she allowed the horse to smell it, and then lightly touched its velvety muzzle, praying the while that it would not rear and kick her. It seemed to tolerate her attention, so she cupped its face in both her hands, and reaching upward breathed toward its nose and gazed into its eyes. For a moment the horse looked as though it would toss her hands off, but then its eyes softened, it bent its head low, and nuzzled into her shoulder. She hid her amazement by whispering sweet nothings, and then looked toward the men.

"See?"

The carters were impressed – and probably less surprised than she was – but the upshot was that she was offered a lift all the way to Caestre on the condition that she rode with the driver and jumped off to placate the horse whenever necessary. They covered the miles quickly and as evening approached, the city walls of Caestre were visible in the distance. The carters took her across the great bridge, through the city gates, and dropped her off, though she did not then know it, within sight of her objective. The castle walls loomed to her left.

Less shy of strangers than she had been, she asked where the Court was, and was directed to the castle when she suddenly became aware of what she must look like. Barefoot, in rags, with little in the way of a head covering, she would surely not be allowed within the walls of the castle, still less into the presence of the Dowager Queen. Her grand plan suddenly seemed untenable, and to cap her distress it began to rain heavily. The flimsy cheesecloth was soaked in seconds, as was her shift, clinging to her breasts and revealing the lack of any respectable under garments. A raucous band of men, laughing and shouting entered through the gates behind her and as she made for the cover of the gatehouse walls, she was caught roughly by her elbow.

"Why, here's a little bedraggled kitten in need of petting!" A big, black-haired and bearded man; twice her height, and reeking of ale. She pulled away, sharply, but his grip held fast. He rubbed his other huge hand over the top of her head and through the cropped hair, uncombed since leaving the convent, and now wet and spikey. "Your fur is very unkempt, Madam Kitten, surely you do not object to a little stroking. You might even return the favour. I could put a little cream in your bowl for you!"

Beside the black bearded man, his shorter, red-headed companion sniggered and took her chin between his fingers. She jerked her head away and spat at him. She could not reach her captor, but this little goblin... she instinctively raised her hand and raked her fingernails down his face. He yelped, clapped one hand to his cheek and reached for the knife at his belt with the other.

"Ha! The kitten has claws," roared the giant. "No, Siferth, you shall not skin this cat until I have had my pleasure." He twisted the knife out of the other's grip and held it to Alfreth's throat. "Then you can have your turn!"

Desperation made her impulsive. "Lord, a purring cat gives more pleasure than a spitting one... You need not be so rough." She stopped struggling and looked at him boldly, with what she hoped was an inviting smile. He lowered the knife and for an instant his hold of her elbow loosened slightly. It was all she needed. Twisting in his grip she ducked under his arm and flew away toward the castle gates, on the far side of the open square. Within a couple of strides, he had caught up to her and made a grab for her wet rag of a cloak. As it tore from her body, she tripped and sprawled to the ground, an agonising pain shooting through her knee. The smaller man made to step on her hand as she tried, on all fours, to regain her feet. As he put out his foot to do so he tripped his companion, the big man falling hard and swearing obscenely. The others in their party were laughing and urging on her tormentors, though some, she could hear, were placing bets on her chances of escape. With her last ounce of energy and courage she lurched away from the entangled limbs of her attackers as they tried to rise and headed for the castle door. Her unsuccessful attempt at entry was witnessed by all of us...

That was there I came into the story, and from there on we knew how it had ended.

"The Dowager Queen is appalled by what has happened to her and proposes to send a party to Bathe Abbey to see what the Reverend Mother has to say for herself. And it seems pretty clear who the two men in this city were..." I said.

"By the Rood," said Edward. "She has the spirit of a Shield Maiden!"

"That she does," Wulf agreed. "I doubt she will be minded to return to the cloister now."

"Aunt Aethelflaed intends to offer her a position in service. Under the protection of Onwen and Ethel... they have taken quite a fancy to her, too." I said.

"Did she tell my step-grandmother about what happened in Bathe Abbey church?" asked Edward. "Who the young man was? For if she did not, then I shall. No, Wulf, there will be no fault laid at your door, I shall see to that, but Alfreth's honour must be restored. She has done nothing wrong."

"My aunt did not mention it either way," I said. "But now, really, we must get at least a little sleep this night. We journey on the morrow and have to be abroad early." Really, even a prince must be told when it is time to leave a Lady's chamber!

"Of course," said Edward, rising.

Wulf kicked Ratkin, who was beginning to doze in his place on the floor. "Wake up, it's time to sleep!" Ratkin groggily rose to his feet. He had most certainly taken some ale that night.

As the prince left, he turned in the doorway. "You know, it seems that throughout Alfreth's story, the poor, the working people, offered her kindness on the whole, and it is those in positions of power who have abused her. When I am King, I shall remember this night."

SIXTEEN

We took the most direct route home to Radendunam, along the Via Devana, the old Roman road which ran between the Legions' two military strongholds at Caestre and Colencaestre. Aethelflaed remained with the Court, which was to make its way back to Wintancaestre. Wulf had sought, and was given, leave by Edgar to accompany the rest of the family, both in order to make his own arrangements for permanent secondment to the Court, and so that he could accompany me when my preparations were complete. The journey was uneventful, though rough at times, as in places the road was much broken, its paving removed and used in the creation of settlements which had sprung up along the way. I remarked that it seemed a foolish economy to save on building materials and then be unable to reach the very locations for which they had been pilfered because the roads were so poor. However, for the most part, we made good time and as we approached Eastseaxe, through the flat, wide open expanses of the Grantabrycgscir landscape the late spring sun was warm and young crops were swathing the ridges and furrows which for centuries had been farmed by local families. We made a slight detour to visit Oswig and Leoflada at Stecworthe.

As we approached their Hall, I reflected that the type of life which Flada had chosen might still be mine if I wished. There were sure to be many young men at Court with good estates and Halls in need of a Lady. I mentioned as much to Wulf, as he jogged along beside me – we had both opted to ride.

"Ha, sister," he laughed. "You would not last a candle-length! Tell me again how you feel after we have been in the company of all our little cousins for a fore-noon!"

I had to agree he was probably right. The family had grown. Flada bustled out to meet us, a babe on her hip, two youngsters tumbling in her wake (twins, like us, I thought, and almost envied them their play fighting) and an older girl – this must be Elfwenna, her eldest. She looked so like Flada as a maid that I could not help remembering her has she had been. But although her waist had thickened, and the frown line between her eyes had deepened, she was still our Flada – the cousin who had been half-sister, half nursery keeper and wholly exasperated by our antics.

Wulf was already off his horse and sweeping her up in his arms, she spluttering and slapping him down. "Wulf, you do not change, ever the scally! Where is that sister of yours? Why Aetna, you at least seem quite the grown up!"

I embraced and kissed her, Aelflaed stepping from her litter and our uncle dismounting, both greeting her in turn, our aunt then unable to resist the temptation of holding the cooing baby. "So, this is little Gunnith! What a sweetling. She has a look of you about her…"

"Yes, and the lungs of a fen-ogre!" Gunnith's doting father kissed Aelflaed as he joined the welcoming party. Oswig beamed at us. "Well, my two courtiers! Ah, you wonder how I hear such news so quickly here in my backwater? My nephew Ethelmaer had it from the Abbot of Elig and he from the Archbishop's envoy. Truly there is no faster way to spread news than to tell a cleric! You may think you are soon returned from Caestre, but I sometimes believe that the Church…"

"Come, Husband." Leoflada did not seem to feel it necessary to hear what he thought on this subject "Not now! Everyone, you will take refreshment? Of course! Come along in… Dagmaeda, fetch the wine, and there are fresh biscuits in the long kitchen, bring them, too! Perry, Petrus!" This to the young twins. "Get out from under everyone's feet. There must be something about twins… Elfwenna! Oh, you are such a treasure! Go find your sisters and tell them we have visitors. Dagmaeda, where is that girl? Oh, of course, gone to…"

The rest of our baggage train had rumbled into the Hall's courtyard. Dagmaer climbed down from the wardrobe wagon, and Thella and Ratkin appeared from one of the other carts. Dagmaer came up beside me. "Flada forgets that there is more than one family reunion to be had this day," she whispered in my ear. From the stables Petroc was bounding toward us.

"Mother! It is good to see you… and Thella! Why, surely still the prettiest little troublemaker this side of the Danelaw!" Thella tossed her head but did not deny it.

We stayed but a couple of hours at Stecworthe, and I confess that Wulf had been right: a Hall full of infants and young children, the warm odour of the nearby cattle-sheds competing with the more overwhelming aroma of the pigsties and the homely conversation about livestock and crops, neighbouring Halls and their petty squabbles and jealousies could not rival the idea of a life at Court. As we made our farewells, Leoflada took both my hands in hers.

"So, you are to be a Lady at the Court?"

"Yes, Flada. Though I think you do not envy me."

"No, you are right. I love my husband and my children – and my life here. But sometimes, I wonder… Aetna, will you do me a kindness? You were ever good at your letters, write to me sometimes. Tell me of your adventures. My reading skills have improved since our lessons with Father Aelmer. I now help with the farm accounts as well as those of the household and Hall." A look of the young Flada crossed her face; a little smug and self-satisfied. Then she was back to her present self. Tucking a wisp of hair behind her ear (she still had that habit, I noticed, and smiled) she continued, my hands still in hers. "It would be such a pleasure to be able to relate to my neighbours the doings of my 'sister at Court'. The other ladies will be as jealous as..." Yes, this was the Flada we knew, remembered and loved!

"Of course," I said, and kissed her cheek.

The men were mounting their horses, Aelflaed entering her litter and the baggage carts beginning to rumble into action. I swung up onto the saddle of my palfrey, urging her toward Wulf's place in the train, and waved to Oswig. In him, too, I could see his younger self. He smiled and waved back, so obviously happy with his lot that I could almost have wished... no, not really!

We returned to the Via Devana and made just one more overnight stop – at Grantebrige – before we reached Radendunam. We had been away a little over a month, but it seemed like a lifetime. Returning home brought the reality of my decision into sharp focus, already it felt as though this place, for so long the centre of my world, was no longer where I belonged.

There was a small sadness awaiting me, too. Poor Berrie had passed away and been laid to rest next to his brother in a quiet corner of the courtyard. Apparently, Thoth had come into the kitchen one morning to find him curled up in his final sleep beside the hearth. I took comfort in the knowledge that his passing had been peaceful but was still tearful as I stood beside his small grave, a few primroses set upon it by one of Thoth's little grand-daughters. Wulf came up beside me.

"Dagmaer would tell you that we will all meet again – and that Berrie and Bremel are waiting for us, on the other side of the Bridge."

"Father Aelmer says that animals do not have souls," I said, sniffing and blinking away a tear.

"Father Aelmer says a great many things, but we have not always heeded them."

"That is true."

"And if I remember my gospel correctly," put his arm around me, "Our Lord said that his Father remembered every tiny bird – so I am sure that he has a place for dogs in His kingdom."

"Berrie would have been too old to travel to Court with me," I said. "It is better this way. And you are right. There must be room for animals in Heaven." I smiled and Wulf tightened his arm around my waist in a brief hug.

"No more tears, then. Come, let us wash away the journey and begin our planning for the future. I fancy it will take us little more than a week to prepare, and then we shall be on the road again. To Wintancaestre!"

Wulf's idea of how long it would take to make ready for our departure was somewhat optimistic. Within a few days, he and Ratkin were fully prepared, but it was clear that my Aunt Aelflaed had no intention of letting me depart until my wardrobe was fully overhauled. Together with Dagmaer and the other women of the household, myself included, every one of my undergunnas and gunnas, head-rails and cloaks was inspected, cleaned if necessary, and then either embellished with new embroidery, lengthened or shortened at the hem or sleeve, collars turned or cuffs reworked.

"I shall not have you at a disadvantage next to the other ladies," said my aunt, as she smoothed down the soft nap of a velvet cape. "I kept my eyes open in Bathe and Caestre and noted the current fashions. You will look the part very well."

Indeed, I seemed to have a great many costumes for all occasions, which translated into a great many trunks and boxes to be loaded on the wagons loaned to us for the journey, when, after just over three weeks, we were ready to leave. Wulf's two chests virtually disappeared amid mine, to which were added our strongbox, containing my jewellery and extra coin for the journey. The casket, reinforced by metal bands, and held shut by a mortice lock, had the addition of a padlock, a rare device lately come from the continent. It had been stowed first, at the bottom of the first wagon, with planks hiding it from cursory inspection. Aelflaed offered me the use of her litter, but I elected to ride, much to Thella's disappointment: she would have loved to share the litter. As it was, she sat alongside one of the drivers – the older one, at Ratkin's insistence – grumbling that the dust from the road would play havoc with her skin. We intended to stop overnight at inns, or abbey guesthouses, but in case we found ourselves spending a night without such accommodation, we also had a stock of food and small ale. Our farewells were a little tearful on my part – and Aelflaed's – but my excitement overcame my sadness very quickly, and our new lives began.

Our first year at Court passed quickly, and I confess that I had never been happier. When we reached Wintancaestre, Wulf and I parted, he to the King's Court to take his position with the Aetheling Edward, and I to Aethelflaed's Hall. It almost seemed like another homecoming. My aunt, the Dowager Queen, welcomed me with open arms and enfolded me as though I were her prodigal daughter. Onwen and Edith greeted me warmly and Alfreth... I could hardly believe that it was barely a month since I had found her on the ground outside Caestre's Great Hall. That bedraggled, bleeding vagrant was transformed into a slim creature, light of foot and quick to smile, her hair already losing its unkempt, short spikiness, showing as a red-gold wave around a pretty face, blue eyes bright with curiosity and good will. Even Thella, not usually given to complimenting other women, had to admit that she was quite the beauty.

Aethelflaed's Hall was close to the Nunneminster, a little way from the East Gate into Wintancaestre, between the broad street leading to the centre of the town and the confines of the abbey Church and the monastery. The Benedictine Sisters tended their herb-gardens, which abutted our Hall, with great care, as much, I felt sure, for their beauty as their medicinal and culinary properties. A little to the West of the monastic complex was the King's Great Hall. Although the Romans had occupied Wintancaestre – they had called it Venta – there seemed to be little left of their making other than the foundations of the Walls. The Great King Alfred had made the town his capital city and rebuilt streets on a grid pattern, better to defend it should need arise. He also fortified the ramparts and barricades. Rather than live within the city walls, though, he had preferred to create a homestead – a *wyrth* – about two miles north of Wintancaestre. Edgar now used it as a hunting lodge and the "King's Worth" was a favourite spot to accommodate visitors.

The Queen's quarters were, of course, adjacent to King's apartments in the Great Hall, and the rest of the Court were housed in and around the complex. In the monastery, great drawing rooms full of light provided space for the creation of wonderful manuscripts and books, whilst in the convent similar provision was made for embroidery and tapestry work. Most evenings, in the long gallery of the Great Hall, a fine meal was provided for the whole Court, often with the King and Queen in attendance, sometimes simply as an excuse for everyone to gather and talk, debate politics, exchange views on the latest news from the Continent – France was only a relatively short journey away – and gossip. Minstrels played almost every night, and I developed a passion for dancing.

The King had been on just two Progresses since our arrival, and only took Edward, and therefore my brother, on one with him.

I saw Wulf almost every day. He and Edward took part in all the social activities of the Court; Edward was becoming a charming young man, his shyness and awkwardness lessening as he grew taller and more confident. Hunting parties sometimes stayed overnight at the "King's Worth" and it was rumoured that some of the town girls found their way out to the Lodge to entertain the men. I still felt a twinge of fear whenever I heard that Wulf was to go hunting, but as months passed and nothing ill befell, my anxieties lessened. The prince attended at the monastery every day for lessons in penmanship, theology and other kingly subjects, except when his "duties" (I came to understand these to be anything from feeling an urgent need to practise his swordsmanship to it being essential that he call upon his step-grandmother) proved more important. During the pleasant summer months, Wulf often spent that time with me, sitting in the Nuns' Garden or, in the winter, before my aunt's roaring hearth at the Nunneminster Hall.

On one such postnoon, in the spring of Our Lord's year 974, we strolled through the orchard alongside the herb garden.

"It is hard to believe that we have been at Court for almost a year," I said.

"Is it all you expected?" Wulf ducked under a blossom-heavy branch, careful to avoid the bees, busy in the pink-white flowers.

"Oh, yes, and more," I said. "What about you? Eddy is turning into such a fine young man, the King must be pleased with your companioning of him." In private we still sometimes called the prince by the name he adopted on our first, less than auspicious, outing together.

"I could not ask for a better position," said Wulf. "And, yes, the King seems well pleased with Edward's progress. In fact," he cast a look about to make sure that we were not overheard, "he is beginning to look for a likely bride for him."

"Not already, surely?"

"The prince turned fifteen at his last birthday, it is not too soon to begin…"

"Well, by the King's standard, then," I huffed rather sharply, "you and I must be well and truly left hanging on the tree: we shall be eighteen this year."

Wulf laughed. "Why so tart?" A fair question since it appeared I had likened myself to an apple! "You could have had many a young man to suit this last year. You said you did not want any of them!"

"Nor I did – nor do!" I replied, "but it is not pleasant to consider that some of the Court may think me getting… beyond the peak of my ripeness."

"Sister, that shall not be for many a long year yet! Why, look at me, I'm… Oh, Eddy's coming! He must have cut short his lessons – again! Do not mention what we were discussing – it is a sore point."

The prince vaulted over the low picket fence which divided the herb garden from the orchard and trotted over to us.

"Cousins! How now? This is a pleasant way to spend an hour or so, is it not? I shall join you. My, but the bees are a-busy, is there a swarm afoot?"

"I have not seen one, sire," I said. "Edward, why are you not at your lessons?"

"Need you ask? The sun is shining, the breeze is warm, and it is no day to be sitting in that chilly library. And I wanted to see… Aetna, is the Dowager Queen receiving visitors today?"

"She will always receive you, you know that! But this forenoon she went to the Nunneminster to discuss how the new altar frontal is progressing and is not yet returned. I expect her any time now, we can see the path she will walk from here. Let's sit a while."

The grass was dry and we settled comfortably, leaning against the gnarled trunks of the apple trees. Edward stripped off his over-tunic and rolled it into a cushion. "For you, Lady."

"Eddy, you should really not abuse your position by skipping out on your teachers at every whim," said Wulf, trying hard to sound responsible. "Old Beleric never tells the King that you have missed lessons, and if you fall behind it will reflect badly on him. It is not fair."

"Oh, I'll catch it up," said Edward, leaning back and tilting his face, eyes closed, toward the sun. "Never fear, I will not let the old boy down." He smiled serenely.

We were silent for a while, each wrapped in our own thoughts. Voices lilted across the gardens toward us, and Aethelflaed, accompanied by Alfreth, rounded the corner of the Nunneminster's low gatehouse wall. Edward was on his feet in a moment and ran toward them.

"Grandmother! I am rebuked by my companion-man for wanting to miss my lessons to see you. You will surely take pity on me and allow me to spend the postnoon in your company?"

"Edward, it is always a pleasure to see you, but what is so urgent that you need abandon your studies?"

"Urgent? Why, nothing, I simply felt the need for female companionship."

"And there was none at the King's Hall?"

"None to rival that which is here!"

I would have liked to think that Edward was enamoured of mine, and the Queen Dowager's, companionship, but some sixth sense told me that there was more to his eagerness to spend time in our company than he was admitting.

"Very well, but you will have to endure Aetna and myself discussing the embroidery of the altar frontal – and the new votive panels which I have promised to the convent church. Aetna, the Lady Abbess loves your designs. Alfreth has worked samplers of the stitches we shall use and we have just…"

I fell into step alongside my aunt, Alfreth behind us, Edward and Wulf bringing up the rear. I heard Wulf whisper "Eddy, you see? This is no place for us…"

"… given the novices the patterns for the borders. They are simple enough – even the youngest of them will be able to assist in the work," Aethelflaed continued. We were approaching the door of her Hall.

"Come, let us sit in the *peristylium* and enjoy this light. Alfreth, ask Edith to bring us some wine, and then set out your samples for Aetna to see."

Alfreth disappeared through the doorway, and we took seats in a small wooden chamber, with no front wall or roof, surrounded by a collonaded walkway, which had been built alongside the entrance. The chairs were free standing, like small "x"'s, with a pivot at their centre so that they would fold flat for ease movement and storage. We had a delightful view of the gardens but were sheltered from the breeze. A perfect spot. During our Progress the previous year Aethelflaed had taken a great liking to the various Halls built upon Roman foundations. Upon her return she had asked Beleric to scour his books for references as to how the Romans had lived. The idea of a *peristylium* appealed to her, and this "garden room", she was convinced, recreated at least some of its features.

"Edith will be with us directly," said Alfreth on her return, bearing a small table, which she set in front of my aunt. Really, this little outdoor room was delightful! She set out her stitched samples and we began to examine the various techniques which would bring Aethelflaed's embroidered panels to life. They were to be a gift to the Nunneminster in memory of the late King Edmund. Alfreth's work was exquisite.

"I still find it hard to believe that you have learnt all this since you came to us," I said.

"Alfreth has a rare and valuable gift. I feel sure that she was sent to me by divine providence," said my aunt. "Only by the grace of our Lord could she have learned that stitch so quickly – it is such a trying technique. To capture the sweep of a bird's plumage in stitches – no wonder it has been coined *opus plumarium*. Feather work, indeed!"

The creamy linen before us was rich with silk and gold motifs. Birds as lifelike as those in the trees of the orchard, butterflies, their wings vibrant and so closely imitating reality that they looked as if they could fly off the fabric, small animals, flowers, foliage, all caught to perfection. In and around them intricate swirls and interlace of gold and silver thread wove into abstract patterns. Alfreth explained the various designs and showed how little of the valuable threads has been "wasted" – unseen on the reverse of the fabric.

"Beautiful, and clever, too!" said Edward from over my shoulder.

I had quite forgotten that he was there. "Yes, they are," I said, turning to him. Perhaps he had been referring to the embroideries – but now he was looking at Alfreth, and she at him, though she quickly looked away, and kept her eyes upon the stitched work for the rest of the postnoon.

))))))(((((

The summer passed pleasantly and both Wulf and I had almost forgotten our conversation with Aethelflaed that night in Caestre when she had voiced her disquiet about Elfrith, and her worries over Edgar and Edward. We never discussed what she had said other than between the two of us, not even with our aunt herself, and it seemed as though her misgivings were, perhaps, unfounded. Certainly, life at Court appeared to be running smoothly. Business was transacted at meetings of the Witan, Ealdormen came and went with their reports and requests. In the North there were one or two minor skirmishes with the Danes – small numbers of longships testing the resistance of the local fyrds, which saw them off without great loss of life. Edgar commanded that he be kept fully informed of the situation, but there seemed to be little to concern us in the South of Englaland. There was news from North Dumnonia that ships had been sighted along the coast of Walha, but they proved to be slavers transporting unfortunates to the Danish ports in Iraland, and there were no landings along our coastlines.

When autumn arrived, and the apples were being harvested, about a week before our birthday, Aethelflaed called me into her *peristylium*, where she was taking advantage of the warmth still to be had from the late sun. As usual she had her embroidery to hand, and beside her, her workbox, open to show a vibrant collection of silks, catching the light and shimmering like the wings of the butterflies which they so often depicted.

"It is on postnoons such as this," she said, smiling as I entered, "that I miss my beloved Edmund more than ever. It is sad to think in this lovely autumn – of my life, as well as the year – that he will not share it with me. I know a king can never fully take his ease, but it does feel at present that all is well with the world."

"Madam, you are yet young – the autumn is but of another year!"

"Perhaps," she said wistfully. "But now, the reason I have called you is that I want you to find Wulf and bring him along to see me, too. No, no, there is nothing amiss, I have said. I have had a letter from your mother – your aunt, well, you know what I mean – and I would share it with you both at the same time. I believe, for once, that Edward is at his appointed lessons, I saw him a while ago heading toward the *scriptorium*, so your brother should be free of his duties at present. If he needs any added incentive, tell him that Ethel has just taken a batch of fresh honey and bremelberry cakes out of the oven!"

"I am sure that he will not need asking twice," I said and, throwing a light cloak around my shoulders, for there was a slight breeze away from the shelter of the *peristylium*, I made toward the Great Hall.

I loved the autumn. When the harvest had been good – as it had been this year – people had an air of satisfaction about them, of a job well done, and a sense that the Lord had been kind to them. They were quick to smile and laughed easily. The hardest work of the year was done, the winter was still a way off, and the bounty of the hedgerows offered sweet treats for but a little effort – such as the juicy bremelberries gathered just this morning and already cooked, added to Ethel's always delicious honey cakes.

The wicket gate in the tall door of the King's Great Hall stood open, sentries posted to either side, but I passed through without query or comment. I was now a well-known figure, and like many others of my station, could come and go without hindrance. I walked to the far side of the Hall, past the glowing tapestries and embroideries which caught the postnoon sunlight as it fell through the high windows, and the war shields, wood oiled and bosses painted, which hung between them. The floor had been freshly strewn with rushes and straw, herbs added to sweeten the air. Later that evening, as it so often was, the Hall would be full of music and laughter.

Stairs to the rear of the Hall led up the side of the wall to the private apartments. Another sentry was stationed beside them.

"I would to the Aetheling Edward's – and my brother's – chambers," I said.

"Very well, Lady."

The layout of the Hall was much as most modern residences – the fashion for private apartments was spreading swiftly – and I knew my way well. The King and Queen had chambers are the far end of the building (and a private stair), other chambers, divided by stout wooden walls, ranged around the inside of the outer wall, and many gave onto a walkway which overlooked the ground floor of the Hall below. Edward's apartment was the first on my right.

Despite my familiarity, I knocked at the door.

"Yo!" My brother's voice.

"It's only me!"

The door flew open. "Only? Only? Why, sister!"

I laughed, he affected such amazement and pulled such a foolish face. "How can you say that when half the prince's men are sick for the love of you?" he said.

"Hush, Wulf, they are only boys," I said. "Though many of them are fine dancing partners, I will aver. Elfwine is..."

"Don't say it! My ears are too finely tuned to hear..."

"Well, it is your ears that are wanted. Aunt Aethelflaed has had a letter from home and would read it to us both, rather than to me and then to you when you have a moment to spare from your heavy workload." I could tell from the scrunched blankets that he had been lying abed. "Why are you not out and about on a fine day such as this?"

"I was indeed out upon Edward's business all this forenoon," he said. "He had me up at dawn and down to the water meadows. We bagged a couple of braces of fine duck – he is becoming a rare shot with the bow – and then, would you believe, off he went knee deep in the stream to collect watercress! Apparently, he said, in the autumn the taste is more peppery than in the spring when most people collect it. Though where he acquired that piece of wisdom he would not say. We were back to deliver the duck to the kitchen before the bell began to ring for Terce, and then he said that he wanted me to oversee the austringer as he fitted the new goshawks for their jesses and hoods... he would have done it himself, he said, but he had to be elsewhere... So, I had to ride all the way out to the King's Worth. I have only been back an hour. I am assuming he has now gone to his lessons."

"Aunt Aethelflaed believes that is so. She says she saw him heading that way a while ago. So, now you are free? Good, there are bremmel-buns and small ale awaiting your pleasure!"

"Very well then, lead the way."

We retraced my steps through the Great Hall, and back to the grounds of the Nunneminster, to find the *peristylium* deserted, for our aunt and retreated into her Hall. As we entered, she was in conversation with Ethel.

"You have excelled yourself, my dear... ah, and look, here are more of your devotees come to sample your baking. Wulf, Aetna, see, the cakes are still warm!"

Ethel bustled away, well pleased with our compliments, for the buns were excellent. Wulf and I settled ourselves on a bench beside the long table and Aethelflaed on a high-backed chair, pulled up to its other side. From the soft goat skin pouch attached to her chatelaine she drew forth a much-folded parchment which she flattened out on the table before her. I recognised my Aunt Aelflaed's handwriting immediately. I had expected to see the flowery scrawl of Father Aelmer – for it was customary to dictate most letters to the house priest, allowing him the opportunity to earn his bread and board by doing a little more than officiating at the various offices of the day. But no, the letter was in our aunt's neat, precise hand, so familiar to me from the many notes, receipts and labels I had seen her create during our hours together in the still-room.

A second, smaller letter, its seal still unbroken, had been folded within the first, and Aethelflaed set this to one side.

"I shall read you my sister's letter to me first," she said. "Then you may read this, which is addressed to you both."

Wulf and I exchanged a glance of shared curiosity.

"Dearest Sister", our aunt began. **" Greetings from your family in Radendunam. We would that you were here with us this fine autumn, but rest assured from your last letter that you are well and in good spirit. We send you enwrapped with this message a letter for Wulf**

and Aetna, the content of which we are sure they will share with you. We ask the favour that if they prove reluctant to leave you and the Court for a brief visit to the Eastern Shires, that you will encourage them to do so. You may guess..."

"Ah, no the rest is but sisterly gossip!" she said, folding the parchment and returning it to her pouch. She slid the second letter across the table to us.

"Sister, you were ever the better at your lessons. I fear I have let my reading skills slip this last twelvemonth," said Wulf.

"Twelvemonth?" I raised an eyebrow. "Sadly, I fear a little longer than that, brother! But no matter." I broke the seal, quickly scanned the contents and then read out loud.

"My beloved children, I do not chastise you for your lack of writing, for I know that your lives must be full and the hours few for such pastimes, but I know from my sister that the King is well pleased with Wulf, and she with you, Aetna. My Lord husband, your uncle, and I are proud of your achievements, and much gratified by all that we have heard of you both.

In but a few short weeks you will reach your eighteenth natal day. I would that you were with us for that celebration, but have little doubt that there will be much ado made of the day. I console myself with the thought that you will surely like to come to us for a visit when it is past, and would ask that you seek leave to journey to Uphude in time to meet us there before the eight and twentieth day of November, at which time the new abbey Church at Rammesig will be consecrated. Your Aunt Elflada and Uncle Ethelwine offer us all their hospitality, and invite us to stay for the days of the Nativity of Our Lord in December.

Make haste to reply, my dears, and know that I shall be counting the days until I see you once more.

I send my love and prayers to you both. Your aunt and mother, Aelflaed."

"Wait, there is more," I said.

"Post scriptum." This was in our Uncle Brithnoth's strong, square hand. "Sister-Son and Daughter, greetings. All that I have heard of you this last year makes my heart light. I cannot command, for you are at the behest of the King and the Dowager, but I would most fervently ask that you seek the approval of those two Godly persons to your aunt's request. It is of import. I leave you in the love of our Lord, with my best thoughts and prayers. Brithnoth, Ealdorman + Eastseaxe."

"Aunt?" Wulf looked at Aethelflaed expectantly.

"Well, of course, my dears, I will release Aetna from her duties for a few weeks! It would be selfish in the extreme to deprive my sister and brother-in-law of the pleasure in her company that I now enjoy daily! And I feel sure that Edgar will feel the same – though Edward will miss you, Wulf."

"You know that is not what I meant," said Wulf. "What is it all about? It is surely more than just the idle whim of our foster parents to have us return for the celebration of Christ's Mass. That much is clear from the *post scriptum* if nought else!"

"Yes, Aunt, there is more in your letter that you have not shared with us," I added.

"If there is, then it is because I choose not to," replied Aethelflaed.

"But, Aunt…"

"You cannot think…"

"That is fair…"

As ever, when our emotions were heightened, our old habit of speaking with one voice emerged.

"I know not whether it be fair, but it is as it is. Now, I suggest, Wulf, that you be about Edward's companionship – he will be finished with his studies in but a while, and you, Aetna, need to attend to the taking of yester-eve's leftovers to the leper house cart. It will be departing the courtyard any time now. Curb your curiosity and learn patience. If your parents choose to tell you no more at this moment, you may rest assured that it is with good reason."

And, with that, we were dismissed. With a final, mutual glance, Wulf made for the *scriptorium* and I for our kitchens.

)))))))(((((((

Aunt Aethelflaed was quite correct in her opinion that the King's permission for Wulf to accompany me to Uphude would be forthcoming. Edward, when he heard, was as intrigued as we, and was even moved to ask his father's leave to come with us, but this Edgar did not approve.

I will confess that I was a little disappointed not to be celebrating Christ's Mass at Court. The previous year, the first in our new positions, was still vivid in my memory, and I felt sure that this season's masques, plays, feasting, dancing and merry-making would be just as enjoyable. Uphude could hardly be expected to rival it. However, our birthday revels at the beginning of October were all that I might have wished and when, some six weeks later, Wulf and I set off for Grantabrycgscir, the thought of seeing our loved ones again after almost eighteen months superseded any regrets. We travelled with Ratkin and Thella, and Edgar had assigned us two men-at-arms, in case of trouble on the road. We decided against taking a wagon, in order to make better time, and instead Wulf hired two sturdy pack-horses, which thankfully turned out to be well capable of keeping pace with our riding horses. I fancied that we cut quite a dash – all of us young (for the two men-at-arms had been trained but this last year) and, it had to be said, in my opinion, fair of countenance and well dressed. Ah, vanity, it is a sin hard to eschew in youth!

We were a merry party. Thella was looking forward to seeing her mother again – for Dagmaer would assuredly be accompanying our family – and perhaps some of her siblings. Wulf and I were in good heart and bearing gifts for everyone. Only Ratkin was a little apprehensive – the memories of his last visit to Uphude were not happy ones – but being with Thella ever lightened his mood, for though they still often quarrelled like sparring cocks, there was now always a subtle undercurrent of mutual attraction in their arguments, and in truth they were more often to be found holding hands than otherwise. It would surely only be a matter of time, I had long since suspected, before the two sought leave to become one. The days were short as the end of the year approached, but the weather held fine, and we spent every night at a different inn, and each day taking pleasure in the changing countryside and laughing as Ratkin mimicked the accents of the locals – out of their earshot, except for one occasion which earned him a bloody nose from a haystack of a farmhand.

Toward the end of the third week of November we approached the watery island landscape of the Fens. November – the Blood-month, it was called, for it was when the livestock not intended to be fed over winter was slaughtered, meat salted or smoked to feed hungry mouths during the coldest days of the year. But still the sun shone, and as evening fell on the final day of our journey, we rounded the last bend in the road with a blood-red sky behind us.

The welcome on our arrival was all that I had expected: warm and genuine, with a few happy tears from myself and my aunts, and much back slapping and hand shaking between the men. Ethelwine and Elflada had changed little since we last saw them, save that he was perhaps still a little stouter and Elflada now had a year-old babe in arms. They had called the child Edgar, an appropriate nicety, I thought, given that the infant, alone among his many siblings, had been present at the King's coronation and celebration of fealty, albeit within his mother's belly. Leoflada and Oswig had arrived a day earlier, and there was one more guest – whom both Wulf and I were delighted to greet – our old childhood friend Ethelmaer, now Brother Ethelmaer. As I had guessed, Dagmaer had accompanied Aelflaed and Brithnoth, and Thella was warmly embraced by her mother, and then immediately chastised for being "nothing but skin and bone". Was she not fed at Court? Thella smiled, dismissing her mother's comments and Dagmaer hugged Ratkin with affection, for he had been almost another son to her when newly come to Radendunam all those years before. Elflada showed us to our chambers and it took but little time to freshen ourselves after our journey, after which we made our way down to the Great Hall, where a fire was blazing and a table set for repast to come. Thella and Ratkin, together with our men-at-arms, had repaired to the kitchens where soon, doubtless, they would all be making as merry as us.

There were cushioned settles and the new style of "armed" chairs (Wulf and I had previously joked that it sounded as though they were about to fight off those who tried to sit on them) pulled up to the hearth, a large, knotted rag rug to protect the ladies' indoor-slippered feet from the prickly underlying straw and the delicious mingled smells of roasting meat from the kitchens and mulled ale, as it fizzed and sputtered against the red hot poker wielded by our uncle.

"We are all well met, my dears," said Elflada, raising her half-punt flagon. "Husband, give the *was heil* to our guests!"

"I will indeed, my love." Ethelwine rose to his feet, wincing slightly as his gout pained him, lifted his full-*punt* and, beaming, said "*Was heil*, my friends and family. I give you health and happiness and a hearty stay in my Hall!"

"*Drynke heil*!" we all replied, raising our vessels in turn and drinking.

The ale was good, strong and heady.

"Uncle, your gout seems still to afflict you somewhat," I said.

"Aye, it does, little one, but it is as naught compared to how I suffered before the miraculous intervention of Our Lord. There were times I thought never to walk again, but my fervent prayers and those of your Aunt Elflada, awoke the spectre of the blessed Saint Benedict himself from his slumbers. He appeared to me – well, you have heard the story – told me that Our Lord had heard our supplications and that I would be healed. The raising of the abbey at Rammesig is my oblation in gratitude."

I had, indeed, heard the story. Who, with a connection to our family, had not? Ethelwine's love of the grain and the grape made him a raconteur of considerable imagination, and the telling of this tale had improved, like his finest wines, with the years. But it was not for me to query its veracity. The truth was that his health was considerably better now than it had been. What more needed to be said?

"And the great abbey Church is completed in time for the Dedication," said Ethelmaer. He had grown tall in the last ten years, and, unlike many of his Brothers, who tended to have the pasty look of those who spent much of their time in the dim interior of a monastery, he had a ruddy glow of health and a hint of sunburn across his nose. "That is a miracle in itself! Like all projects of this kind it has had its problems, but with the grace of the Almighty, they are passed."

"Why? What happened?" asked Wulf.

"My Lord Ethelwine suggested – no, in truth, insisted," he grinned at my uncle, "that the abbey be built on the very spot where he saw the blessed Saint. The very spot. Unfortunately, the ground there is unstable. Too close to the edge of the fen, or so it appeared. The first two attempts at construction ended in the whole edifice sliding into the waters. It was only then that he remembered that he had been mistaken in his recollection of where the Saint had manifested himself. Happily, that turned out to be rather further within the shores of the Isle of Rammesig, and on much higher ground."

"How fortunate!"

"Indeed, it was," my uncle beamed. "The memory can play strange tricks when matters preternatural are involved."

That seemed to be an end to the matter.

"Tell the twins about the Sibling Saints," said Elflada.

"Ah, yes, the Sibling Saints," Ethelwine refilled his drinking vessel, and offered the flagon around.

Something piqued in my memory: where had I heard that phrase before? It was as though my ears caught a few notes of music and the tune was hovering in the back of my mind, without quite allowing itself to be played in full. Ethelwine warmed to his subject.

"Well, as soon as the abbey was nearing completion, I turned my attention to finding it's church some relics – you know how relics bring the people in – and after all, an abbey cannot live on bread alone, it needs a little cheese and meat! Not to mention wine. I asked my nephew here..." he slapped Ethelmaer on the shoulder; not quite his nephew but family enough, "... to look about for something. The abbey at Wakenig in Eastseaxe had a few pieces available, so he went down to take a look. The toenail of St. Nicholas... I ask you! Not even the whole toe, just the nail, and they were asking a ridiculous price for it. But I digress. They also had the bones of St. Ethelbert... the whole skeleton, mark you, for which they were willing to negotiate. Seems they needed the money and the Saint had of late been somewhat ignored by pilgrims in favour of the Holy Toenail. The price still seemed rather high, but then they offered to throw in the saint's bother, Ethelrede, at no extra cost... and he a saint, too! Well, two for the price of one was much too good a bargain to let pass. I have no doubt that we can weave the tale of the holy martyrs' deaths into a grand epic. Apparently, they were princes of Cent some three hundred years ago and murdered by their cousin when he ascended to the throne, though why I could not quite ascertain. Their relics, it is said, are famed for healing disorders of the feet – bound to be popular with pilgrims if we tell the story aright and gloss over the fact that their own uncle is reputed to have questioned the lads' sanctity. Families, eh? Impossible to please sometimes…"

"You did admirably!" said Wulf, still laughing at Ethelwine's words. "Are the Holy Saints now *in situ* at Rammesig?"

"Aye, they are. They were brought by Archbishop Oswald on the eighth of this month and will be honoured this coming Sunday. Oswald is staying with the Abbot. We are most fortunate to have the Archbishop of Eoforwic to officiate – thanks to the recommendation of Dunstan, who has also been kind enough to take interest in Rammesig. The Sibling Saints of the Fens. It as a splendid ring to it, does it not?"

Of a sudden, I recollected where I had heard the term before. I was about to blurt out something, when I looked at Wulf and realised that he, too, had been struck by an unexpected thought. We had decided between us that, although curious about the seeming imperative nature of our visit, we would not precipitate discussion of the matter. It was bound to be revealed in good time. But now, as I had an inkling of what it might concern, I felt a shock of apprehension. I think, perhaps, I went a little pale.

"Sister-Son – and Aetna," said Brithnoth, "we had not thought to bring this matter up on the first night of your stay, but I think, from your looks, you especially, Aetna, that the time has come." Aunt Aelflaed laid her hand on mine.

"What is it, uncle…" said Wulf.

"… Aunt?"

"When Ethelmaer was in Wakenig, he met someone. But I will let him tell the tale," Brithnoth allowed Ethelwine to refill his jar.

Ethelmaer took up the story. "Wakenig is but a small House," he said. "The monks have little in the way of luxuries – indeed Archbishop Dunstan would thoroughly approve of how they live by the Rule of Benedict, although I cannot help but feel that they would wish for a little better than they have, which is why they essay to make some money by redistributing their relics! I am not a man who demands comfort but sharing the dormitory with the entire brethren – they do not even appear to distinguish between lay and full brothers – was a little too… they were three a pallet!

"Anyway, I took a room at the tavern. It's a nice little place: warm and welcoming with a fine barrel on tap, a goodly cook and chambers as free of fleas and bedbugs as most, if not more so. And popular. The night I was there, the local Shire Reeve and his deputy with their ladies were making merry, there was a party of lads from the estuary fisheries celebrating one of their number's last night before he wed his sweetheart (and bemoaning the price of the *morgengifu* to be paid!) and a dozen or so pilgrims, freshly off the boat from the Continent, a good-humoured bunch, bound for the abbeys and shrines of the eastern shires.

"Everyone had eaten and drunk well when a cry went up for some storytelling. No sooner was this call made by the fishery boys, but the pilgrims piped up, saying that they had among them the best storyteller that ever drew breath. He needed but little persuasion, and setting aside his cloak, stepped up onto a settle where we all had a good view of him.

"The pilgrims had not exaggerated; the man was a genius. Despite his penitent wayfarer's garb, he told a tale from the old Saga of the Rhine. The part where Sigilind reaches her bother Sigimund through the fiery ring set about him by his enemies…"

I cried out involuntarily and Wulf caught his breath.

"Ah, I see you are ahead of me, but I will tell you how the evening unfurled," said Ethelmaer. "When the storyteller had finished, to a round of appreciative applause and more than a little coin in his pilgrim's hat, he resumed his seat, and shared out the coin with his companions. I went across to them and offered to stand him a mug of ale, which he accepted, and we sat together close by the hearth. I complimented him on his storytelling skills and he said that he had long been travelling and reciting the old tales, and that he had sometime been a gleeman, too, though that had been when his wife had been travelling with him. There was a terrible sadness in his eyes when he spoke of his wife, and I guessed that she was beyond the Bridge. I said that I was sorry for his loss, and he seemed not unhappy to speak of her. She had been, he said, the sweetest girl, with a lightness of heart and step and the voice of an angel. Then he paused and when he spoke again it was with a catch in his low, musical voice.

"'But had I not taken her with me she should not have died. There is not a day in my life that passes without my regretting my selfishness.' He seemed almost in a reverie. 'I did not know, you see… she was got with child before we took to the road, and we delayed returning home too long. She became weak, so weak that I never managed to get her back to her family for her lying in… and then, after the babies came – yes, they were twins – she could not regain her strength. She passed her last night in the Chapel of Saint Edmund, and in the morn she lay cold. But my children, my son and my daughter, they thrived. They were strong, but I was not. I could not bear to resume my life with her family, but without her. I knew the babies would be well cared for by their aunt and uncle and I took a pilgrim's attire. This eighteen years I have travelled the length of this land – and many others – to pray at the shrines of sibling saints. To thank our Lord for the gift of my children and beg forgiveness for my failure to be a father to them.'

"'Truly,' I said to him," Ethelmaer continued, "'The Almighty works in strange and wondrous ways.' I told him that I believed that I knew the family of which he spoke, that, indeed, I had played with those very children little more than five years after the loss of their mother, and that they were – and are – happy and healthy and much beloved. I think he knew not whether to laugh or cry. I told him, too, of my negotiations with the Abbot at Wakenig for the relics of the saints, and that I would be returning on the morrow to Uphude where his late wife's sister would, I had no doubt, welcome him.

"It took all my persuasive skills to get him to agree to accompany me. Whilst he was anxious for news of the twins, he felt that his reception would be less than warm. He felt that he had been a poor excuse for a father and in that…"

"In that he had been right!" I said, my cheeks now, I felt sure, flushed. From nowhere, I felt an anger that I had not known I possessed. "A poor excuse for a father, indeed!"

"Aetna!" Elflada's voice was full of rebuke. "He was grieving terribly when he left you. Hardly in his right mind. He was elf-shot with arrows of such misery he…"

"I knew it," said Wulf. "I knew it was my father. I remembered seeing all those years ago, with a broad pilgrim's hat and a voice as low and full as any I ever heard. He kissed us and then was gone. You slept through it, Aetna, but he did, he did remember us!"

"Once, and again now – so he says, though we have only his word that he returned for that reason – in eighteen years! Hardly a glowing testament to paternity!" I said. "Where is he now? Off on his travels again, I suppose."

"He is with the Brothers at Rammesig," said Aelflaed.

I could think of nothing to say. Wulf, too, was silent. "It is his dearest wish to see you, to know you, both," continued Elflada. "Your sweet mother was my and your Uncle Brithnoth's sister. If anyone has excuse for ill-will against Wulfstan then it is us. Grief takes its toll on all of us differently. He has devoted his life to pilgrimage, there is no shame in that. He has not begged, nor stolen, he has earned his bread by his own talent. And now he has returned – I know not what his plans may be, but I know that he loves you dearly. Though it is love without acquaintance and that is a sad thing!"

"I perceive," said Brithnoth, "that Wulf needs little encouragement to meet his father, but you, Aetna, I understand your reluctance. I will admit that when your mother first died, I, too, was angered at Wulfstan's desertion – yes, that was how I saw it – but I came to realise that he had given to Aelflaed and me the greatest gift we had ever received. We had the joy of watching you grow, mature, become the people you are now. He did not. In his misery, he denied himself that which might have brought him comfort. You have your mother's good heart, Aetna, surely you will not condemn a man for his own misfortune."

Wulf put his arm around me and I felt my eyes fill with tears. Not for my father, not him, I thought, but for those lost years. Although… those years were not lost to us, we had happy memories, whilst he had none. "Well, I suppose…" I began.

"We," continued Wulf "… must, of course, meet him."

I leant against him, his left arm cradling me, and felt the old, familiar comfort. "Yes, I suppose so…"

I slept little that night, despite my weariness after our journey. Wulf came into my chamber when I was abed and flopped down beside me. Thella had not yet returned from the kitchen and her reunion with Dagmaer – at least, I hoped that was where she was. Wulf mentioned that Ratkin was nowhere to be found either.

"Do not be vexed by me," he said. "I know I have ever been more anxious to meet our father than you, but you must be curious if naught else."

"Oh, I am not vexed with you. It is our father that vexes me. Eighteen years and now he wants to meet us!"

"No, not quite that long, remember he…"

"Wulf, will you never be still about that night? Very well, you saw our father, what do you want me to say?"

"Nothing, Sister, nothing. But do not condemn him, not until we have met him."

"I condemn no man, not before he has had a trial. We will meet him, I have agreed. Tomorrow. Let us have at it tomorrow, for neither of us will rest easy until…"

"…we have."

SEVENTEEN

December, *Anno Domini* 974

WULFMAER

To be back at Uphude after so long. Ratkin, I know, has had mixed emotions, for this is where his life changed so radically, from thrall to freeman, though he knew not where that would lead. It seems to be a place of catalyst, a place where the wyrd of life is rewoven in ways unforeseen and unexpected.

Who could have imagined that our summons – for such it was – to meet with our foster-parents and celebrate the foundation of Rammesig abbey would bring us to this, to the meeting I had so long imagined with our *byrth-faeder*? As we travelled from Wintancaestre, such thoughts were so far from my mind... it was still full of my position with the Aetheling Edward, of how Court life was so much more than I had ever expected, of my ambitions, of the future, not the past. And then...

Aetna was more shaken, even, than I. She tried hard to hide them, but I knew - I felt - her emotions. For so many years she had tried to supress the longing to see our one remaining parent. Not because our aunt and uncle had been in any way less than all we had needed, but as a link to our mother. And now, now, he was returned. Wulfstan, after whom we had both been named. On the morn after we had first learned from our cousin, Ethelmaer, of his arrival, we were to meet him – this on the insistence of my sister, who, having at first been reluctant, then wanted to take the hog by its tail and whirl it into whatever maelstrom was destined.

Thanks to the fair weather, the road to Rammesig from Uphude was dry and clear as we rode across the flat, open-skied landscape of the Fens. In ill weather some of the route we took would only have been passable by pole-jumping, a skill neither Aetna nor I had learned – why would we? But I felt sure that our companion for the day, cousin Ethelmaer, could have done so, if he had wished. He jogged alongside Aetna as we rode, our horses untroubled by the water on either side of us, regaling her with tales of the fen-folk, making her laugh despite her half-concealed dis-ease at our mission. I had never seen a churchman so at one with his wild surroundings. He seemed unlike any monastic brother I had ever encountered.

The planned celebrations at Rammesig and the veneration of the two boy-saints was due to take place in but one day's time, and already merchants and hucksters were making their way to the town to stake out the best sites for their wares. There was a holy-day atmosphere, and as we approached the newly built abbey, we could not but be impressed. Uncle Ethelwine must have been very grateful indeed for his recovery from the gout. The cost of such building would have been considerable. Two high towers rose from a two-storey church, twin beacons across the Fens, fairer, I had to admit, than the new abbey church at Elig, whose likeness had been shown to us at Wintancaestre – Aunt Aethelflaed being a patron. From each tower fluttered a pennant, a white heart on a ground of red.

As we entered the town, even Ethelmaer's banter could not distract Aetna's discomfort. She all but turned her horse back toward Uphude, but I caught up to her, jostling my cousin to one side and put my hand on her wrist as she tensed the reigns.

"Sister, we are here today at your behest. I would have given you more time to prepare, but…"

"But nothing, Brother! My hesitation was but a moment's weakness. I am resolved."

At that moment I loved her more than I could say… my sister, my twin, my other self. Golden hair tousled by the wind, chiselled jaw set, her pain ignored to allow my desire to be fulfilled, I knew. So be it.

Despite the moment, I realised that we were passing landmarks which brought back to me that day so long ago when we had last visited Rammesig – the Market Square where Dagmaer had haggled with the fishmonger, the turning to the swordsmith's workshop, the sign for the needle-maker… how long ago it seemed. The day when Ethelmaer had sat beside Dunstan and felt, perhaps for the first time, that a life within the church was still a life. But he was silent as we approached the abbey Gate.

It stood open. A lay brother came forward to greet us.

"My Lord, Lady… and Brother?"

"We are here in advance of the celebrations to…" said Ethelmaer.

"Aye, come you in then…" It seemed that there had been many visitors, on various errands. The precise purpose of our visit was not requested.

We passed beneath the gate. It, too, bore the insignia of Ethelwine's family, the pierced heart. I realised how similar it was to the pennants flying over the abbey. Our horses jogged toward the stone water trough just within the gates and we allowed them to slake their thirst. Ethelmaer dismounted.

"I will go and seek out your… father," he said.

I slid out of my saddle and assisted Aetna to do the same.

"So, this is it," she said.

"Yes."

"Our *byrth-faeder*."

"Yes."

"Do you feel at all disloyal to our uncle, our foster father, to Brithnoth?"

"I have sworn fealty to him. That can never be changed, nor would I wish it to. He is my Lord, my ealdorman. I love him with all my heart and my right hand and sword are his. That will never change."

"Aye, but I am a woman, I have taken no such oath."

"Aetna, your heart is as true as mine, you need no oath…"

Ethelmaer returned. "Your father… Wulfstan… awaits you in the vestry of the abbey church."

We tethered the horses beside the water trough and walked across the abbey courtyard, Aetna's hand in mine. I could feel it trembling slightly. Entering the abbey church, it seemed dark compared to the brightness of the day outside, and as we turned left and entered a small ante-chamber – the vestry – it was hard to make out the figure which awaited us as he stood, his back toward us. He turned and the light from a sconce which had thrown his form into silhouette fell across his face. It was suntanned and lightly wrinkled with a sadness about his eyes. His hair was sandy, tied back from his face with a thong, slightly greying at the temples, but full and with no sign of balding. His garb was long and dusty black, with a rope tie at the waist – he could almost have passed as one of the lay brothers were it not for a gold brooch pinned to his breast. It glinted with amber in the torchlight.

"Wulfmaer, Wulfaetna, I present your *byrth-faeder*, Wulfstan. I will leave you. I shall wait in the courtyard." Our cousin gave us – or was it intended for our father? – a reassuring nod and withdrew.

There was so much that needed to be said, but somehow no words came. From any of us. The silence seemed almost palpable as it hung between us. Then Wulfstan took a step forward. He held out both his hands, palms upward, as if in supplication.

"Thank you. Both of you." His voice was deep and clear, yet soft and with a hint of the lilt of many tongues, both accents from within our own shores, and strange languages. I realised that Aetna was still holding my right hand, clasping it tightly, in fact, so I raised my left hand and put it in his right. He squeezed it gently and smiled into my eyes. Then he looked to Aetna. He was tall, around my own height, and she had to look up to meet his gaze. It made her give that little, stubborn upward thrust of her chin that I knew so well.

"Aetna," he said, "You have your mother's spirit, I can see that. Do you also have her forgiving nature? Can you forgive my cowardice – for such it was. Fear of remembering her too well when I met you, and fear of the pain that would give me. But now I realise that any pain I feel is so far overshadowed by my joy at seeing you that I curse my foolishness at losing so many years of your acquaintance. Can you find it in your heart to take my hand?"

Aetna hesitated. Then, still trembling a little, she raised her right hand and put it in his left.

I do not know how long we stood thus, the three of us, hand in hand forming a small circle in the flickering light of the torch, a dim shaft of light coming from the high window. It was probably only a few short seconds, but it seemed to extend into eternity. And for a moment I had the feeling that there was another with us, that in the shaft of light the dust motes swirled together into the form of figure, slim, slight and with a soft smile on the indistinct features of her face. Then the spell was broken.

Wulfstan released our hands and brushed away a threatened tear before it could fully form. He laughed, a warm, rich laugh with a hint of embarrassment in it. "You must, indeed, think me a fool," he said.

"That, I think," I replied, "is something that neither of us have ever thought of you. For in truth we have known little about you, other than your profession, your later oath to become a pilgrim... and that you bore our mother a great love."

"What of you, little one?" he said to Aetna, for she had still not spoken a word.

"I... I know not what to say. It is often better to say naught than speak in haste. But I am glad to have taken your hand, and that is more than I believed I would say." She looked from Wulfstan to me and a slight smile touched her lips. "Aye, there is a family likeness of feature! But what lies in the heart is impossible to read so easily."

"You share the likeness," I said. "We are..."

"... twins, after all!" Her smile broadened as we spoke with our accustomed unison.

"Ha! That is a fine trick, two people, with but one voice between them," said Wulfstan with a chuckle. "Come, I think the Brothers will have some food on their board by this hour. Let us find young Ethelmaer and take some refreshment – together."

))))))((((((

The noon day hour and meal were well past before we headed back to Uphude late that postnoon. Wulfstan was clearly a welcome visitor at the abbey and we were accorded places at the Abbot's table in the Refectory, although the Abbot himself was not present, having, as we were informed by the young novice who showed us to our places, much to do in advance of the Dedication celebrations.

Breaking bread together proved a good way to become better acquainted. We were offered small ale, and wine, and whilst Wulfstan declined, explaining that he had forsworn such pleasures when he took the pilgrim's staff, I accepted some ale – and very good it was – and Aetna took wine. I asked him to tell us something of his travels.

"When I left Radendunam," he said, "I was still numb with loss. You may find it hard to understand, for I know," he looked at Aetna, "that you have felt me to be unkind in staying away so long, but the one blessing which I held in my heart was the thought of you – both. I have heard that some men, when they lose a wife, blame the child for her death, but I never felt thus. I blamed myself for that loss. I knew how she loved you in the short time she had with you, and that was all I needed to remember for my love to be greater than you may ever believe. But I could not stay with you. What did I have to offer? The life of travelling storyteller, or being burdened with a father who lived off the charity of his wife's family? Perhaps pride was my worst sin. Mayhap I should have put it to one side to stay with you, but I never had any talent for husbandry of a Great Hall – nor swordplay should the fyrd be called – so of what use could I be to your uncle, my brother-in-law? I was at best an embarrassment, at worst a useless mouth to feed.

"You seemed to me to be a miracle. How could two such perfect little beings appear on this earth in the wake of such sadness? It made me ponder the Lord's will. Then I began to read the lives of the Saints. Some of the stories I already knew – they were, after all, my stock in trade when I was on the road, and many were roistering good tales if told the right way! But I wander from the point..." His enthusiasm for his talent shone through his words.

"I found particular comfort in the accounts of those Holy Saints who, from birth, shared their faith and piety with their siblings; it seemed to me that in their filial bond Our Lord had given to this world a blessing that was more than the sum of its parts. I took an oath to visit and make my devotions at as many shrines to such saints as I could discover. When I left Radendunam, I returned, first, to Bedricsworth, to the Shrine of St. Edmund, where your mother lay. As I prayed beside her grave, an ancient Brother came to speak to me. Though I had told no-one of my quest, he lay his hand upon my shoulder and said, 'Go you first South to Wakenig.' I turned to speak to him, but he had already walked away – or so it seemed for there was nobody with me. With no other plan in mind, I headed toward the coast – for I had a hankering to see the sea – and followed the shore down past Dunwich, where ships came and went from and to the lands across the German Sea, back into Eastseaxe and finally to Wakenig. There I visited the shrine of the two saints whose relics this day lie in the new abbey church, here in Rammesig – how strange are the ways of Wyrd!

"At Wakenig I had my first taste of pilgrim life. I found likeminded folk, some treating their travels as if they were extended holy-days, some deeply spiritual and contemplative, and others, I fear, with an eye to the main chance of fleecing unwary travellers. The trade in false relics," here, Wulfstan glanced with a grin at Ethelmaer, "make those not as wise as your cousin easy targets. I fell in with a few pilgrims making for the Continent and together we took ship, landing in Frankish territory. From those more experienced than I in the way of pilgrimage, I learned of my first destination – in the region of Vermandois, where the twin Saints Medard and Gildard are venerated and from there I travelled to Soissons (Saint Crispin and his twin are entombed there), Paris, and the many shrines to Saint Benedict himself and his own twin sister, Saint Scholastica. This world of our has wonderful things to show, Wulf. Great skeins of strange birds whirling through the amber skies of the fjords; high mountain passes, crowned in snow and ice; flat plains that stretch as far as the eye can see. And Aetna! The beauty of the churches, they astound the mind. Some have towers taller than you can imagine, with glass in all colours of the rainbow, at Maaseik I saw embroideries that looked to have been made by the hands of angels – though they were, in fact, worked by sister Saints Harlindis and Relindis. As I quartered and criss-crossed the lands beyond the northern sea during the years of your early life, my agony began to lessen. No, perhaps not lessen of itself, but recede into a place where I felt it without such intensity. I felt the urge to go still further afield. But before I travelled South, toward the Holy See, I returned to Radendunam, for I had to see you both once again … and I did see you, but in that moment of joy, I felt my pain return with such a stab of violence that I knew I could not stay. Wulf, for a moment I felt you were aware of me, but Aetna, as I watched you breathing sweetly, calm in your sleep, I could not wake you. Dagmaer was a fierce guardian, and your aunt and uncle gave you the parenting I felt I could never offer. Without even breaking my fast the following morning, I left for Rome.

"Ah, Rome…" Our father seemed to be in a kind of reverie now as he recalled the years that were lost to us. Aetna glanced at me, and I took her hand, squeezing it gently. "Thank you," I mouthed silently. Ethelmaer's expression was rapt as Wulfstan recounted the glories of the Eternal City. He described the tombs of the twin Saints Mark and Marcellian, deep in the catacombs, where the breath of a thousand martyrs can still be inhaled; he told of Simplicitus and Faustus, beheaded by pagans, buried by their sister Saint Generosa, only to be martyred herself days later. And with each tale he drew us further into his experience, he shared emotions and described places and people in such a way that we felt we were witnessing events as they happened, riding the Apian Way, being born along the River Tiber through the ancients' ruined city and on to places still more distant. On, through Greece, across the lands of the Turks and Syria (where twin

Saints and doctors Cosmas and Damien are venerated) and on, on into the Holy Land, into Outremer, itself.

"And there, there... beside the blue Sea of Galilee, where the brothers Simon Peter and Andrew met out Lord, where sisters Mary and Martha sat at his feet, I began to feel whole again. I stayed in a monastery beside the Mount of Olives – they still grow there, just as they did when Our Lord must have picked and eaten them – where I met a group of pilgrims who, like me, had reached as far as it seemed possible to go, and were ready to return to their lives at home. We journeyed back together – and what travels they were, but you have heard me speak long enough – tell me of your lives, your loves, your hopes and, no, not fears, not today! For this is a day of joy!"

I began to tell him of our lives at Radendunam as children, of the family as it had been and as it was now, of how we had been at Edgar's coronation and our move to Court, and gradually Aetna started to join in, at first hesitantly adding short comments, then becoming more relaxed, and telling tales of her own. The Brothers had all returned to their duties and we realised were alone in the Refectory and the postnoon was beginning to wear away.

"So now," Aetna was saying, "we feel quite at home in Wintancaestre. It is a great city, not as great as Rome, of course, but still the finest in Englaland, I do believe!" She had become quite animated.

"You are both to be congratulated," said our father. "So young and yet so well placed. I am proud of you both, although I know, to my shame, that credit for none of your achievements can be accounted to me. But perhaps, from now on, I may be allowed to be a part of your lives? Aetna, will you let me try and make up for the time I have wasted?"

She hesitated, realising that her manner toward him had thawed in this past hour or so. Was it possible for her to return to her icy indifference? Or her anger? Did she want to? Her blue eyes swam with tears she was determined not to allow to fall.

"Time, indeed, will tell," she said. "Time lost can never be recovered, but time yet to come may prove a recompense. I am happy that this day dawned. Let us see what will befall..."

"And will you call me Father?"

Again, the hesitation. "I will," she said.

Silence. I broke it. "Shall you stay in Rammesig for the Nativity of Our Lord?"

"My plans had not been certain," said Wulfstan, "for I hardly dared hope... But, yes, I will. Now that I have met you both – and young Ethelmaer here – I can think of nothing I desire more than to celebrate the Christ's Mass with my family."

It was time to return to Uphude. The light would begin to fail soon, and the roads, although dry, would be none too easy for the horses if darkness fell. We took our leave of Wulfstan with mixed feelings. I think Aetna was emotionally exhausted and would be pleased to be away, despite the way the day had turned out. But I was sorry to go: there was so much more I wanted to ask. Ethelmaer declared that he would stay overnight at the abbey, and so one of the lay brothers, a burly fellow with a mop of wild foxy hair, accompanied us. I almost insisted that we did not need a companion but relented when Wulfmaer said that he would be happier to think that there were still four men in the party to protect my sister should anything ill befall. I did not want to argue with him over his newly acquired paternal anxieties. We met with the men-at-arms and headed for the town gate.

We got back to the Hall at Uphude just as the lamps were being lit and candles set about the long table. Aelflaed and Brithnoth had clearly been apprehensive as to how the day would pan out, and on seeing us in good spirits were obviously equally relieved. Our Aunt enfolded Aetna in her arms and hugged her tightly.

"Little one," she said, "I know this has been a difficult day for you. Are you pleased that you went?"

"I am," Aetna replied. "Yes, I am. At first..." Linking arms the two of them moved away, heads together, talking in low tones, and I knew that the day's events would soon be fully disclosed. I looked at my uncle.

"Well, sister-son, how feel you about meeting your *byrth-faeder*? Was he as you expected?"

"That is hard to say," I replied, "for in truth I do not know what I expected, but he seems to be a man I am not ashamed to call Father, even though you are still a parent to me, and always will be. Ethelmaer certainly seems taken with him."

"Yes, and thereby we may have some disquiet in the family this Yuletide, I fear. But that is for another day. Come, let us to the board. Though I wean you were fed well at the Abbot's table... if I know Ethelmaer he will have ensured that you were entertained to the best of the abbey's ability! He has a fine aptitude for such matters."

The evening meal was convivial and heart-warming. There was a general sense that the day had passed under a happy auspice, that a potentially ill-favoured event had turned out well, and the whole family was in celebratory mood.

Ethelwine raised a pot. "A toast to loved ones reunited," he said, and we drank. We all drank. For a brief moment I feared that Aetna faltered, but then she smiled and raised the horn to her lips.

"Yes," she said, simply.

The day set for the Dedication of Rammesig Abbey's fine new church dawned bright and fresh. Benches had been set out for Ethelwine's family and the most honoured guests, and Ethelwine himself sat in a fine chair, positioned importantly, on the left of the chancel, opposite the Bishop's own chair, placed to the right. Oswald, recently confirmed as Archbishop of Eoforwic, in the absence of Dunstan who was engaged upon duties at Wintancaestre, presided. Oswald and Ethelwine had collaborated on every aspect of the new abbey church and this day was the culmination of a project which had begun a full five years earlier. Aunt Elflada was serene in a blue gunna, edged with gold embroidery, and, surrounded by her children looked every inch the Madonna at she watcher her husband, love and pride shining in her eyes.

Cousin Ethelmaer's immediate family, his father Elric and Uncles Uvi and Oswig, had arrived just that morning, the latter with Leoflada, once more with child, and well along in her pregnancy. They had left their brood at home, with the exception of Elfwenna, whose presence, it seemed was indispensable to her mother, who she continued to resemble ever more closely. Ethelmaer, engaged today with his duties for the Abbot, was, so he had told us, not looking forward to the imminent family reunion, at which his future within the church was to be discussed.

Aetna and I were seated with Brithnoth and Aelflaed and were joined by our father. He would, I think, have liked to sit between me and my sister, but she closed her hand upon mine and did not make to move, so he sat beside me, adjacent to the aisle which had been left between the two ranks of benches at the front of the nave. Behind us the common folk of Rammesig – the Isle of Rams – crowded together to watch the spectacle. The deep, resonant chimes of a huge bell in the West tower boomed out.

To those who had not had the benefit of attending such occasions as Edgar's coronation, or the various magnificent celebrations we had been privileged to witness at Court, the service must have seemed very splendid, but I confess that Aetna and I, in our youthful arrogance, felt somewhat superior to the masses thus impressed. We could not help but compare the rather brash and self-important (as we considered it) ceremony to install the Sibling Saints' relics beneath the High Altar with the dignified and restrained, but nonetheless sumptuous, events in which we had participated at Wintancaestre. But Ethelwine was clearly enjoying every moment of his long-awaited opportunity to make good his promise made upon recovery from the gout. When the Saints were finally at rest in their new home and the last *te Deum laudamas* sung, a second bell, with an even deeper voice, boomed out, this time from the East tower. There was a loud crack and an alarming amount of dusty, fragmented plaster fluttered down from above the rafters. I remembered the profusion of dust motes in the vestry when we first met Wulfstan; like several others, judging by their expressions, I would not be sorry to be out of the church and in the crisp early winter air of the courtyard. Uncle Ethelwine, however, appeared to be undisturbed and brushed the white powder from his hair – he had been sitting directly below the worst of the shower. He smiled broadly at Oswald, who gave the final blessing and made his way, with, some may have thought, unnecessary haste, down the aisle and out of the West door.

When we gathered in the open space outside the church to congratulate the Abbot on his new church, and thank Oswald for his service, there was more than a little apprehension in the air. Uncle Brithnoth voiced the thoughts of many.

"Let us pray that your recollection, Ethelwine, of the location of your miraculous cure is this time sufficiently far away from unstable ground to allow your gratitude to be witnessed without danger to life or limb."

"The architect assures me that all will be well," replied his brother-in-law. "A little settling is to be expected." And that, it seemed, was the end of the matter.

Elflada left her husband's side and walked across to us, and to Wulfstan who stood uneasily on the periphery of the family party.

"Wulfstan, the twins may have told you that they, like my brother and his family, are invited to stay with us at Uphude until the Nativity and celebrate Yule. Christ's Mass is a time for families to come together. Will you not put aside your pilgrim's staff for one month and stay with us too?"

Wulfstan rubbed the stubble on his chin and looked at her with a world of gratitude in his eyes. Then he looked to Aetna and to me. I held my breath. Aetna broke the silence.

"Wul— Father," she said. "I cannot promise that in one month the losses of a lifetime can be recouped, but I would like to spend time with you. And I know Wulf would." She looked at me, and I could scarcely contain my relief. I would have stood by her, had she wanted no more of him than the meeting we had already had – but my heart would have been heavy.

"Then it is settled," said Elflada.

)))))))((((((

The weeks in Advent before the anniversary of Our Lord's birth passed quickly. As we spent time with our father, the sense of unfamiliarity between us lessened and even Aetna began to feel at ease with this man who, for so many years a stranger, seemed so quickly to be becoming a part of our lives. While the weather held fair, we spent time walking with him, often in the company of Ethelmaer, taking the winding, treacherous paths between the waters of the fens, while Wulfstan recounted more of his past life or, sometimes, tales from his repertoire of stories. Our cousin knew all the trackways and backwaters of this marshy world. It seemed that his enthusiasm for the natural world had lessened but little since his childhood. He could not hear enough of our father's travels.

"What provision is made for the well-being of the souls – and bodies – of the many pilgrims criss-crossing distant and not so distant lands?" he asked one morning, just a few days before we were due to celebrate the Christ's Mass. "If there are no chapels along the way, who performs the offices and services that they would attend in church? And where do they seek treatment for any ills they may suffer?"

"It depends," replied Wulfstan. "Along the well-trodden routes, such as into Rome, or between the most popular shrines in the land of the Franks, there are many hostelries where leech-men can be found to treat the road weary, and there are plenty of abbeys and churches too, with priests to officiate at the offices. But in out of the way places, and the further the pilgrim travels into the lands of Our Lord himself, then the more he – and sometimes she – have to rely upon themselves."

Ethelmaer appeared to be absorbed by this reply for the rest of our expedition that day. Even our unexpected discovery of a heronry, the great birds, disturbed from their peaceful feeding, wheeling in huge circles and landing inelegantly in the muddy waters, their indignant looks making Aetna laugh so much that she had to wipe the tears from her eyes, failed to rouse him from his reverie.

I caught Wulfstan's expression as he watched my sister. Love, yes, but also a sadness.

"Little one, you are so like your mother! I met her first when she was something younger than you, her laugh was just the same…"

Aetna took his hand. "Hush, Father, the time for sad memories is over," she said. "Cousin! What is keeping you so silent?" she called to Ethelmaer whose gaze was seemingly through, rather than on, the waters of the mere.

"I am thinking of the future," he said, and would be drawn no more.

We had walked toward the Isle of Elig and across the waters we could see a single tower rising heavenward, not as tall or impressive as Rammesig's twin belfries, but with a simple dignity that befitted the abbey lately risen upon the spot where so long ago, Aetna and I had happened upon the Eel-wife in her solitary watch over the shrine of St. Etheldreda. For the past many years it had been Ethelmaer's home, as he completed his training, took his final vows and, more recently, had been in the service of the Abbot.

"Think you not that your future lies at Elig, then?"

"I love and revere the Abbot there, he is a good and godly man, and does not think of nought but his coffers as some do," Ethelmaer replied. "But I have not changed so very much since we passed time in these fens as children – I still feel the urge to be out and about amid the wonders of Our Lord's creation, and to see lands far away, too. Before these Holy Days are past, I must speak to my father Abbot on the matter – and my natural father, too, though I fear that may be a difficult undertaking."

"Come," said Wulfstan, "we had best turn for home. The noon is far behind us, and even in your cousin's company I do not relish the idea of being abroad amid these waters when darkness falls."

"When we were last here," I said, "Aetna and I hoped to see the Will-o'-the-Wisp. We had heard so many of Dagmaer's stories that we were quite the adventurers ourselves! Sigimund and Sigilind!"

"We still have our moments!" added Aetna, her laughter ringing out again. "But you are right, we should away back to the Hall, I have matters to attend to before the Mass tomorrow. I promised to help Aunt Aelflaed wrap up gifts for Flada's little ones and to share with Dagmaer the secret of Ethel's bremelberry buns – though they may not be as sweet as when the fruit is fresh. We shall use the same dried fruit as in the suet pudding…" She prattled on happily, untroubled the fact that these mysteries of the kitchen were quite beyond our masculine ken. The sky had taken on a whitish hue, and flakes of snow began to fall, melting as soon as they came into contact with the water, but bringing with them, as though in hasty conspiracy, a fall in the temperature. Before we reached Uphude a light crusting of ice clung to the clumps of dead grass edging the track, and the snow began to cluster upon it. Soon, the landscape became a flat, white blanket hiding water and ice alike. It felt good to get inside.

We stamped the wet snow off our boots and made for the hearth. Aetna disappeared toward the kitchens, whence we could hear good-hearted chatter and laughter as the late postnoon darkened and torches lit around the Hall. A boy brought in warm bread and ale and we sat back to enjoy the refreshment – it would be some hours before the evening meal. We relaxed in companionable silence until it was broken by Ethelmaer.

"I do not know," he said, "whether it be better to speak to my father before the day of Christ's Mass and have it done with or wait until it be passed and so avoid perhaps – how shall I say it – lessening his equanimity before the celebration. My father has something of an ill temper when his wishes are not treated as orders to be obeyed. And Lord Ethelwine is of much the same mind."

"Ah," I said, non-committedly. I recalled how Ethelmaer's inclinations as a boy were ignored by his father and how he had been entered into the life of the Church without the chance of alternative. "What, exactly, do you want to tell him?"

Ethelmaer glanced from me to my father and back: it was hard to say what was going through his mind, although it seemed he was relieved to have the opportunity to discuss it with us before he went public.

"When I entered the Church," he said, "as you know, I had little joy in the prospect of a life mired up in cold abbeys and stuffy dorters. But as years passed and I grew to love the Abbot and the community at Elig, and to treasure my faith in Our Lord, I began to feel that I did, indeed, have a vocation. When the time came to take my final vows, I did so without regret. But I do not intend to remain behind the closed doors of a monastery, nor to spend my time as secretary to a Bishop – or even an Archbishop, for Lord Dunstan has expressed an interest in my literate talents and offered me a position in his service. No, I have spent much time reading the history of Our Lord's Church here in Britain, of the days before the great Synod of Witebi, when, as described by Bede - the venerable recorder of days – the traditions of the ministry of our Faith changed. The Rule of Saint Benedict insists that monks' lives are cloistered, that they should not travel, except upon specific and regulated pilgrimage, but our forefathers in the Celtic tradition saw things differently. They took their faith out onto the highways and rough lanes of the countryside. They preached to those uncertain in their souls of Our Lord's might, ministered to those in need in body and mind and even converted those to whom the good news of Christ's redeeming love had never been preached. They crossed seas, they scaled mountains and traversed the plains and deserts of distant lands. *Gyrovagi*, in the Latin tongue, those who circle middle-garth and wander the world. It is not a calling much in favour with the Sees of Cantuaria and Eoforwic but..."

"What is this nonsense?" We all started at the unexpected voice. Elric, Ethelmaer's father, stood beside the heavy curtain which divided the Great Hall from the smaller withdrawing chambers beyond. He was a heavily built man, with a double chin not entirely due to overweight – it looked more like the remnants of a muscled bull-neck that had, perhaps in his youth, been part of a sturdy build and bore witness to a belligerent temperament. His heavy brows were drawn together in a frown, and he was slightly flushed as though anger permanently simmered not far below the surface of his skin, ready, at any moment, to erupt in a physical manifestation of his emotion.

"You are already in disagreement with the Archbishop's See? You have not yet even taken up your position. Have a care that the Lord Dunstan does not withdraw his offer, there is many a young man just out of the *seminarium* who would gladly take your place, Ethelmaer."

"Father, I knew not that you were there. Do not fear, I have not been at odds with anyone." He looked into his drinking horn. "Yet," he added, quietly.

If Elric heard that last word, he chose to ignore it. "That is good," was all he said, and poured himself a drink from the large jug set beside the hearth. He took a long pull and sat down, extending his feet toward the fire. "It seems as though the snow may keep us from attending service at the abbey tomorrow, so it might chance that your first ministry will be to family!"

"That would be my privilege, Father."

"And then as soon as the weather clears you must send your acceptance to Cantuaria and make a date to begin your service with Dunstan."

"Father I have not yet decided to take the position…"

"What?" Elric's reply was in the guise of an eruption. He had just taken another draft of ale, which he sputtered down his jerkin, coughing explosively. When he regained his breath, he stared belligerently at his son. "Not… so, there is nonsense afoot. Of course, you will accept. Do you think I donated my hard-earned monies to the abbey at Elig for the pleasure of listening to its bells? Your education has cost me a fortune, boy, and now you would repay me by abandoning…"

"I am abandoning nothing, Father, but I feel that my vocation is not to be within the confines of any cloister, however exalted, even Cantuaria."

"Not this again, Ethelmaer, I thought you had outgrown the idea of preaching to the…"

"Father, please, do not become agitated."

"Ethelmaer…" Elric's voice was becoming louder and his colour higher. This was clearly a topic raised before, and not with a happy outcome.

"As I have told you before, I wish to minister to people directly, to be with them in their homes in their times of need, to learn the skills of the wise women so that I may help them in body as well as soul, even to learn the husbandry of the farm, and the ways of the wild beasts that I may succour all of the Lord's creatures. Lord Dunstan himself is known to have undertaken such studies in his youth – he told me as much many years ago."

"Yes, and we know where those early studies took him," shouted Elric. "Beaten and thrown into a latrine, sick unto death and then ignored by everyone who counted for a decade. But he had the sense to take the advice of St. Paul – he gave up childish things – and so should you. Good God, boy, you will be nothing more than… than… a *serabaite*!"

"Elric!" Elflada had entered the Great Hall from the kitchens, with Aetna and Thella and a number of serving women, to begin the preparation of the long table. "I will not have such language in my Hall! What is this all about? And on the eve of our Lord's Mass! Shame on you…" Aetna, too, looked shocked. This was a word not to be used in polite society. With its connotations of degeneracy, and indeed depravity, it was more commonly used to describe those *clerici* who had been expelled from the church for violent or unnatural crimes involving persons of their own sex, or even children and animals, and wandered the countryside, shunned by all but those like themselves.

"Lady, my apologies!"

"Well, I should think so… all this argument on such a joyous eve! Come, whatever is amiss it cannot be so bad as all that! Now, all of you, go and prepare yourselves for the evening meal. Perhaps there has been a little too much ale taken already." This last as she took the pot from Elric's hand, just as he was about to refill it. Elflada's long-practised manner of dealing with fractious parties – learned through the upbringing of her many children – seemed to work just as well on grown men and we all made, rather sheepishly, for our chambers. I noticed that Ethelmaer and Aetna exchanged a long glance as he passed her, and I sensed her sympathy for him; she knew more of this than any of us, I realised. On the long walk home that postnoon, she and Ethelmaer had been talking in low tones, heads together, almost the whole way, while Wulfstan and I were deep in our own conversation.

Little over an hour later, we were all back in the Great Hall, and had been joined by Leoflada and Oswig, with their brood of children, lately arrived from Stecworthe with their nurse. Most of them were happily, or in some cases less happily, playing together around the hearth with those of Elflada and Ethelwine who were not yet old enough to consider such rough and tumbles beneath them. Various dogs introduced themselves into the game, which became nosier and more boisterous as the hour of the evening meal approached. Brithnoth and Aelflaed looked on tolerantly – Brithnoth swung the youngest little boy up onto his shoulders and I felt a pang of nostalgic jealousy as I recalled when he did the same for me. Ethelmaer had been the last to arrive, together with Wulfstan, and they remained together when we took our seats at the long table, laden with meat, poultry, trenchers and pottage. Elflada kept her Hall in the old-fashioned manner (as I guessed Aetna was thinking) with few modern niceties, but her hospitality was none the less excellent for that: as the meal wore on and more wine and ale taken, the noise level from the older members of the family rivalled that of the younger. It seemed that the disagreements of earlier in the evening were, if not forgotten, at least put to one side. Fruit and honeyed tarts followed the removal of any trenchers left uneaten, and Elflada's head cook had made a pretty fair effort at recreating Ethel's fruit buns, though I had to confess they were not quite up to her standard. Thinking of Ethel, my mind ran onto Aunt Aethelflaed. As ever, it seemed Aetna's was working the same way.

"It is a shame the family is not quite complete," she said. "If only our other aunt could be with us, then we would be entirely whole."

"She has sent us all gifts and a letter to be delivered into my hand but addressed to us all," replied Elflada. "I thought it would be a fitting way to hold her close if we opened and read it together tomorrow, after the Mass."

"Wonderful," said Aelflaed, clapping her hands. "Though it is a good thing she did not entrust it to me, for I should never have had the patience to wait before opening it!"

"I confess it has been hard! Indeed, I gave it to my Lord to hold in case my curiosity got the better of me."

"Yes, and it has been safely in my keeping this se'enight!" laughed Ethelwine.

"Wulf, Aetna, you must think us quite the provincial rustics these days," said Aelflaed. "So excited to have a letter from Court. So eager for news such as you hear every day when you are there."

"Life at Court has its pleasures, Aunt," answered Aetna. "But so does time with those one loves."

"It has been a most agreeable month," I added. "More than that... it has brought someone back into our lives that neither of us thought we would ever meet." I grinned down the table at our father, who responded by lifting his flagon. "Yes, a toast," I said, but quickly looked at Aetna to check that I was not overstepping the mark. She had a much better sense of etiquette than I, but she seemed happy with my gesture.

"Aye, to our father," she said. "And the wholeness of family."

The general conversation recommenced as I resumed my seat, and Aetna leaned toward me.

"Though how long the sanguinity will last when Ethelmaer makes it clear to his father that he will not be swayed from his decision to take to the road is anyone's guess," she added quietly.

The children appeared to have worn themselves out and were dozing in a companionable heap with the dogs, enjoying the warmth of the fire when Brithnoth called for a story. We had, after all, he said, one of the best skops alive right in our midst. Amid general applause, Wulfstan stood and made his way toward the space between the hearth and the long table. Those with their backs to the fire, turned around and those already facing him settled themselves more comfortably. The children stirred into life with the promise of a story. Wulfstan passed behind Brithnoth as he made his way forward. Our uncle stood, held out his sword hand and clasped it to our father's arm, just below the elbow. Wulf responded by gripping his forearm in return. They stood, thus joined, for a moment, looking into each other's eyes, and then, with a firm shake of the arm, and a warm smile which reached his eyes as well as his mouth, Brithnoth propelled him into the forefront of the gathering. The breach, the estrangement, the pain of loss was healed. Time, separation and the memory of love had worked its magic. The two men who had both loved our mother so dearly, brother and husband, were fully reconciled.

Wulfstan dug deep into his treasure chest of tales and told us a story fit for the eve of Christ's Mass. It was a tale of heroes and monsters (Leoflada took her youngest daughter onto her knee), of maids and princes and talking animals and ghosts. We sat spellbound and when he was finished called for another, but he said that one such tale an evening was as much as he could remember these days. This with a little twinkle in his eye as he also said that it was time for him to find his pallet. That he was turning into an old man. No doubt he expected to be contradicted – and he was – but eighteen years on the road had taken their toll, and his sun darkened face did, indeed, look tired.

)))))))((((((((

Elric had been right. The snow continued throughout the night and the morning of the Christ's Mass dawned both bright with reflected light, glancing through gaps in the cloud, and with the threat of more snow waiting to fall from the strangely pink-hued greyish sky. Toward morning a brisk wind had blown up across the desolate fens and the snow had drifted against any building or other obstacle in its way. The road to Rammesig was impassable. By the ninth hour the entire family, together with thralls, and ceorls from the village were gathered in the Hall chapel, where Ethelmaer, together with Uphude's house priest blessed the sacrament and administered it to the faithful. I noticed that Dagmaer was absent, though Thella, with Ratkin at her side, was present.

Ethelmaer made a fine job of the commemoration of Our Lord's supper. His address for this joyous morn was brief, but meaningful and his voice soft but clear, somehow reaching to the very back of the chapel without apparently being raised. He had a talent and a love for this, there was no question. After the Mass, I noticed, he did not consume the last of the consecrated Host, as was usual, but put it to one side in a plain, but beautifully made, wooden box, which he covered with a white cloth. He glanced at Aetna and I saw her give him a brief nod of understanding.

The villagers dispersed to their cotts to make themselves warm as best they could and keep the holy-day as they chose and the family, together with the rest of the household, returned to the Great Hall. The day passed pleasantly, with much good food and entertainment. After the main meal Elflada called us all together to hear the news from Court in Aethelflaed's letter and – more importantly to the children's minds – open the gifts she had sent. We had already exchanged tokens of the day, several of the ladies were sporting new jewels and, in turn, their embroidered handiwork

273

was in evidence on their Lord's new cloaks, gauntlets and other garments. Smaller keepsakes had also been swapped between friends and cousins.

The Dowager Queen's gifts were distributed first and opened amid much delight and comparison of their contents. Then, with a gesture to call all our attention, Elflada produced the long-awaited letter and broke its seal.

"Come, it is time to hear our sister's news!" she said. "Aelflaed, she is your sister by birth, so you read it... besides, you are better at your letters than I! I always make such a hard task of reading."

Our aunt took the parchment, scanned it very briefly and then sat back on the armed settle and began to read out loud.

"My dearest family," it began "my love and greetings to you on this blessed season of our Lord's birth. May His grace be with you all, and the shining light of His star illumine all your ways.

"To my sister, Aelflaed and her Lord, Brithnoth, I send my fondest thoughts. And to my cousins and friends. It seems long since we were together. Here at Court my time passes pleasantly enough, but you are ever in my thoughts, as is my home in Stoche. I thank you for overseeing its running in my absence. There is a new breed of pig here, its meat all the rage at the Royal table, brought to these shores since the recent hog-murrain, which I would like to introduce to my Hall farm, and I will send the pig-herd across country with a good number, of which I desire that you take at least twelve for your own at Radendunam. I will brook no dissent, they are yours for the trouble you take on my behalf.

As I write, I realise how I miss my own Hall and farm. But enough. You will wish, Ladies, to hear of more delicate things. Preparations for the celebration of the Christ's Mass are well underway. There is a new fashion that began, I am told, in the land of Saxony to bring a tree into the Hall and dress it with mistletoe and holly berries and all manner of other gew-gaws, as well as candles, which, to my thinking, is a sure invitation to disaster. Of a course, The Queen, Lady Elfrith, has had to try it. It is pretty, but to my mind far too much trouble to become more than a season's fancy. She has lately also taken much interest in the Royal table, which has caused some surprise... indeed the new hog-meat is one of her less outlandish innovations. I confess that I am not sorry that my invitations to break bread in the Great Hall have been sparse. Apparently, these new dishes are all the rage in lands far away – some say even in the Outremer, or Filastin as the East-men call the land of Our Lord, but some of the flavours are quite beyond my palette. The King, of his very nature, will not hear a word

against her, but it is my belief that this strange food may lie behind his own ill-health. For he has not been wholly himself this winter, and, as is my habit, I worry over him. Edward is in fine health, and on good terms with his father, but for his stubborn refusal to even discuss the question of a betrothment, which adds to the King's dis-ease.

"Aetna, I do miss your company and assistance in my Hall, and I know that Edward will welcome Wulf's return. Sister, I long to see you again, and may perhaps hope that in the summer of this next year of our Lord CMLXXV it might come to pass.

"I leave you all in the care of Christ our Saviour and with the assurance of his mercy and blessing.

"I remain your sister, *Aethelflaed*". +

Aelflaed folded the parchment and laid it on her knee. There was a short pause, as its contents were digested. Despite the light-hearted tone, it seemed clear that there was some anxiety and disquiet behind the words. Elflada broke the slightly uncomfortable silence.

"Well, whatever next? A tree in the Great Hall!"

"Father Aelmer would be elf-shot, would he not?" Aelflaed essayed a laugh. "And with mistletoe? I fear he would we sprinkling the candles with holy water before the wicks had taken!"

Dagmaer and Thella, with Ratkin at her side, had taken places on the outer edge of the circle of chairs and settles which were gathered around the fire. Dagmaer snorted. "Aye, that he would," she said. "I never thought to hear of the Lady Elfrith being enamoured of the kitchens, either."

The conversation began to flow once more, but somehow the merriment of earlier in the day was muted.

EIGHTEEN

We had intended to stay at Upton until the year turned, but in the days following Christ's Mass we began to feel that the time had come to return to Wintancaestre. When we left Ethelwine's Hall, early in the morning of the Feast of the Holy Innocents – three days after our Saviour's own day, in that year of 974, we were pleased to have the company of others who might take our minds away from the nagging anxieties we felt as a result of the Dowager Queen's letter.

By some combination of argument and persuasion, Ethelmaer had convinced his father that it was likely that Archbishop Dunstan would still be at Wintancaestre, having no doubt celebrated the Nativity there, and that he must see the Prelate in person to discuss (or as Elric understood it, accept) the offer of a position in his service. We were also joined by Wulfstan. I could not have been more pleased: I was beginning to feel a deep respect for my natural father, as well as an affection which, though present as an abstract idea throughout my life, was now evolving into a real and genuine emotion. Aetna, too, seemed happy to have him with us. She was starting to become closer to the man who, for so long, she had strived to wish, if no ill, then no great good either. She became as fascinated as I with his tales, the places he had visited and the strange peoples he had encountered. Two more entertaining travelling companions it would be difficult to imagine: Ethelmaer with his deep love and knowledge of the countryside around us, and Wulfstan enjoying a seemingly never-ending supply of stories to while away the hours.

There had been a swift thaw on the Nativity's morrow, and by the time we were on the road, little of the snow remained, with the exception of slushy ice, churned by horses' hooves into a muddy mass at the edges of the way. Our men-at-arms were in good spirits, pleased to be on the road back to their sweet-hearts, and Thella and Ratkin their usual amiable if unpredictable selves. The first day of our journey passed swiftly. We took a midday meal at the newly built monastery dedicated to St. Neot, at Enylesberie, where the Prior was interested to hear the story of our uncle's acquisition of the Sibling Saints, as he himself was in negotiation with a small Cornish village for the relics of St. Neot. The haggling was not going well, and there was some ill-feeling between the parties, we were told. (Later I heard that a band of monks from Eynesbury removed the relics under the cover of darkness and before a final deal had been brokered. They were pursued back to East Anglia by an armed party of angry Cornishmen, but apparently the outcome was bloodless, and a compromise reached after much shouting and the exchange of more money than the Prior had bargained for. The vicissitudes of sainthood do not end with death.)

We spent that night at Bedeford. The abbey there was, like Eynesbury, only recently completed and still had the feel of newness about it. The stonework was sharp with the crispness of lately chiselled edges and the wooden superstructures were freshly stained and painted. The late Archbishop of Eoforwic, Oscytel, who died just three years earlier, was buried in the abbey church. His grave was very grand and when it was shown to us by the proprietorial and rather pompous Abbot, Thurcytel, we were informed that he, the Abbot, had every faith that Oscytel would, in due course, be canonized a saint.

"*Perveniens Reliquias apud pórtum,*" whispered Ethelmaer to Aetna, who giggled. "Relics in waiting." This was the same Oscytel who had allowed St. Etheldreda's Shrine at Elig to fall into such sad disrepair, so we doubted it, but kept the thought to ourselves.

The hospitality at Bedeford was excellent. A fine, well-cooked evening meal, accompanied by generous amounts of ale and wine were accorded to us, though I confess that the fact we were of Ealdorman Brithnoth's kin may well have been in our favour. The Abbot and more senior churchmen ate with us at the High Table, the lesser and lay brethren in the body of the refectory, where Thella, Ratkin and our men-at-arms were almost as royally fed as us. Wulfstan favoured the company with a stirring tale of saintly adventure, and when we repaired to our pallets it was with a sense of well-being and pleasurable drowsiness.

))))))((((((

I was awoken from a deep, seemingly dreamless sleep by a loud crack, which my befuddled mind thought, for a moment, was a crash of thunder. The slow creep of a winter dawn had begun to light the room through the small, high window. Then the ground beneath my pallet shifted violently and I realised that the sound was like nothing I had heard before. Ratkin and I, together with my father and Ethelmaer were housed in one of several guest chambers on the ground floor, adjacent to the refectory, Aetna and Thella in an adjoining room. We heard a scream from their direction and then another loud crack precipitated the fall of a huge beam, lurching down from the ceiling. Wulfstan and Ethelmaer were already on their feet, Ratkin scrambling from his bed and I, snatching a blanket against the cold, made a bolt for the door. The falling joist caught my father a glancing blow on the shoulder and he fell to the ground, which was still shuddering and emitting horrible grinding noises.

"I'll help the women," I shouted. "Get my father outside!"

277

"What's happening?" gasped Ratkin, as he rolled with the heaving ground.

"Don't know," I called back from the doorway, holding onto the wooden door frame to keep my feet.

Aetna and Thella emerged from their chamber, wild-eyed and clutching at each other in their fear. "Wulf, whatever..." Aetna found herself thrown against the wall by the violent pitching motion, Thella cannoning into her.

"Quick, outside!" I yelled and propelled them both before me toward the door to the courtyard. The others were already there. "Away from the walls," shouted my father. "Into the centre, fast as you can!" He was clutching his shoulder, where an ooze of blood was seeping through the fabric of his tunic.

There were cries and calls for help which we could only just make out through the unnatural noises made by the of the grinding of the ground beneath us. The Abbot appeared from his chambers, on the ground floor close to our own.

"Holy Lord! The end of times is upon us!" he shouted. "Repent your sins, my children, for the Almighty is surely about to judge us and find us wanting."

Our men-at-arms had been accorded the privilege of sleeping by the ovens in the kitchens, a comfort not allowed to the brothers and lay brothers who shared a large dormitory above the guest chambers. They appeared, crouching and retching, through the dust which blasted out of the kitchen doors, as timbers and masonry fell within.

"My lords? Ladies? Are you all safe?" called the more senior of the two.

"Yes, we are well, man!" I shouted back above the tumult.

The shouts from the second storey dorter, where the majority of the brothers were housed became louder and more frantic, as a huge crack appeared stretching the height of the wall. The window apertures were small and narrow. We could see arms reaching helplessly through them, hands snatching and grasping at nothingness and then with a terrible slowness one half of the building began to list away from the other and disintegrate as it collapsed to the ground. Amid the rubble, we could see the shape of men, stone, mortar, daub and wattle covering them, some moving with a strange jerking action, others still as death itself.

And still the earth shook.

The newly built abbey church had no tower, but a wooden superstructure above the nave roof housed a large bell. It clanged wildly with the motion of the building beneath it and its supporting timber splintered like a green-stick snapped in two. The bell plummeted down through the roof and into the church as the arch above the great west door

278

fractured and crashed down, turning the door itself into splinters hardly bigger than kindling wood.

"Dear God," moaned the Abbot. "Shall this never end?" Is seemed as though the maelstrom of destruction had been raging about us for eternity. "Sweet Jesus, who calmed the waters and stilled the storm, have mercy upon us!"

For a moment the ground was motionless. Then, as if to emphasise its shattering unpredictability, jolted us all off our feet. The roof of the cloister, protecting the monks' walkway alongside the southern wall of the abbey buildings, fell in with a mighty roar, more dust billowing into the air. The early morning light was thick with swirls of grey, gritty powder. From the kitchens a flicker of flame announced the coming of the next catastrophe: fire.

My father stood up first, shakily but strong and calm. "I have seen the like of this before," he said. "In the lands beyond the Middle Sea, and closer to these shores, where the sun is hot and brighter than you can imagine. Even in the icy wastes to the North. The earth quakes and buildings fall. It is death to stay too close to tall trees and heavy stone. Even when you believe it to be over, there can be sudden shocks and the ground moves again. Stay away from anything which may fall upon you."

"But the brothers…!" cried my sister. "Some of them are still alive, we cannot just leave them in their agony!"

"No, we cannot," Wulfstan patted her arm. "And we will not. But you – and Thella – are to stay here. We will bring them men to you, those that yet live, and you may tend them. But do not go near the buildings, and if the earth moves again lie flat."

The ground had been still for several minutes. The Abbot was on his knees, intoning prayer, and the kitchen well ablaze. "Now?" I said.

"Now," my father replied. "Check each man, if he is dead leave him, if he is wholly pinned and unable to move, leave him also, we will return to him. Move those who can be moved first."

"You are in pain, Father," said Aetna, noticing for the first time the unnatural slope of Wulfstan's shoulder, and the blood soaking his sleeve.

"It will keep, daughter. But, Wulf, I cannot lift. You and your cousin work as a team. You two!" He indicated the men-at-arms. "You are another team. Bring the wounded, lay them down and go back to fetch others. We cannot know how long we may have before the earth moves again and brings down the rest of the masonry. Pray God it may fall only upon those already with their maker!"

It was well that Bedeford was such a young community and made up of only a small brotherhood. Of the fifteen brothers in the dorter, nine were clearly dead, two alive but pinned beneath large clumps of stones, still held together by their mortar, and three less badly injured. These three Aetna and Thella tended as best they could, though under strict duress by our father not to return inside to gather necessities, their ministrations were restricted to bathing the men's wounds with water from the well at the centre of the courtyard – mercifully still intact, though the water level was falling slowly, seeping away through unseen fissures. Many of the lay brothers, and all the cleaning and other staff were still accommodated in the nearby village, from which we now began to hear wails of anguish and cries of pain.

Looking to the east, where the village lay, we could see the sun rising above the treeline on the horizon, huge and lurid red, the sky around it an unhealthy pinkish grey, blotched with iron coloured clouds which were spreading like angry bruises across its face. A low keening of pain came from one of the brothers still trapped amid the ruin of the dorter, the other, less badly injured man calling to him. "Have faith, Brother, the Lord has spared us thus far, he will surely not desert us now!" But the agonised moans continued unabated.

"Father, we cannot leave them," cried Aetna.

"Peace, daughter, we will help them soon," replied Wulfstan. There had been no shocks in the earth for several minutes. "Son, Ratkin, Ethelmaer, come with me." He headed toward the most severely hurt of the monks. "You two!" he called to the men-at-arms, "go help the other brother. But stay as clear of the walls as you can."

It seemed that the still fully conscious man was pinned beneath a large beam, in turn wedged under a jagged section of carved stone – part of an architrave from the fallen doorway. A mass of rubble and smaller debris needed to be cleared away before either could be moved to release the victim. Our men began to dispose of it, cautiously watching the larger debris in case it should shift and further injure its prisoner. The second brother was now silent, and as we began to lever away the block of masonry covering him, we could see that he was severely hurt. His body lay with his back turned at an unnatural angle and his right leg twisted away, crushed into an almost unrecognisable pulp. When we had moved the loose debris, it was clear that he was not trapped, but that the sheer volume of stone which had crashed down around him hand mangled his body and inflicted a deep injury to his head. He did not move. Ethelmaer knelt beside him and put his hand to the brother's chest, feeling for a breath, or heartbeat.

"He's still alive. Just."

With a grunt of pain, my father stripped off his long, wide pilgrim's cloak and spread it on the ground. "Carry him in that."

Gently we lifted the poor, broken body onto the cloak and carried him, Ratkin at his head, Ethelmaer and me at his feet, to the makeshift shelter by the well, which my sister and Thella had created by draping the blanket I had brought from my chamber.

"Dear God," said Aetna. "What can we do for him?"

"Little, I fear, Lady," replied Thella. "But we can try to ease his pain."

Moving the man had returned him to some level of consciousness, and once again he was moaning and trying, now, to speak. "My back. Oh, dear Heaven have mercy, my back!"

Thella lifted his right hand and took it between hers. Gently, with her thumb, she felt the joint between his thumb and forefinger, and the pressed hard on the fleshy area just above it. He gave a deep sigh, and appeared to relax under her touch, his eyelids fluttering.

"Ahhh, sweet Jesus, thank you!" Though whether he was expressing gratitude to Our Lord, or Thella, it was impossible to tell.

The other monk, now released, was assisted over to us, one of our men on either side, as he limped between them. He appeared, fortunately, to be able to put some weight on both legs, and his other hurts seemed relatively superficial.

"Anselm!" he cried, when he saw his brother. "Oh, Anselm!"

Brother Anselm now had a beatific smile on his lips. "It is well, Brother, I am in no pain, but I think I shall be with the Saviour sooner than any might have thought."

Thella released her pressure on his hand and then, more gently, reapplied it. "It will not be long now," she said.

The Abbot, who had been on his knees some little distance off, now approached, pushing his way through the other three brothers toward the dying man.

"Thank you, mistress," he said. "You may release his hand now. He is a celibate; it is not for you to minister in his last moments."

"Nor for you to return him to pain as he leaves this world," said Thella, sharply, retaining her hold on the brother's hand. "Say your prayers, Father, but I'll not be letting him suffer." She sounded like her mother at that moment.

The Abbot bridled, but as further argument would likely mean Brother Anselm would be dead before the quarrel was over, he knelt and performed the rites for the dying.

Suddenly, I was aware that my father was staggering. I caught him as he swayed and eased him to the ground. Without his cloak it was easier to see the extent of the damage to his shoulder. His right arm was hanging almost useless, and he supported it at the elbow with his left hand. A jagged tear in the fabric of his under-tunic revealed a long, bloody graze when the skin had been ripped away.

Aetna was quickly at his side. "We must find somewhere warmer than this," she said. A cold wind had picked up, and although it was now fully light, the heavy, grey sky made for a bleak aspect. Fire and smoke billowed from the ruins of the kitchen and was threatening to spread to the refectory and the remains of the dorter above. There was nothing we could do to save them. The only structure relatively undamaged was the abbey's single-storeyed chapter house. It stood some distance from the rest of the buildings (there had been plans to build a walkway and cloister between the two when funds permitted) and seemed, by comparison to any other option, a welcome refuge.

As the Abbot concluded his prayers Brother Anselm had slipped away. Thella released his hand and laid it across his chest, placing the other upon it. He looked peaceful, not like the agonized unfortunate who had been laid before us just minutes earlier.

"He is gone," she said. The Abbot gave her a long look but said nothing. Together with the other brother, who gave his name as Sampson, we moved him into the little shelter afforded by the canopy over the well, and put the cloak over him, anchoring it with stones. It was not safe to take him into the chapel. Brother Sampson knelt and said a last farewell. It seems they had been good friends. "He will be buried with the others when we are able, my son," said the Abbot, his tone softer that it had been earlier. "He was a fine young man. Come now, you need rest yourself."

Aetna and Thella helped my father into the chapter house. Built entirely of wood, it had fared better than the buildings with stone or mixed walling. The beams and planking had flexed together and moved with the shifting of the earth; all that appeared to be amiss was that one of the heavy curtain rails across the inside of the main door had split, and the curtain slipped off to lie in a heap upon the ground. This we took and spread on the floor near the grate, where the embers of the previous day were still, just barely, alight.

"Feed the fire," said Wulfstan. "I feel grievous cold." Ratkin went out to find small kindling and larger logs to build up a blaze, and Aetna helped ease my father onto the curtain. He lay back, finally allowing himself to rest.

Thella and Ethelmaer ran their hands over Wulfstan's body. "I have seen such injuries before," said Ethelmaer. "The pestle of his upper arm has come loose from the mortar of his shoulder. It must be put back or he will be permanently disabled. I have seen it done."

"What of the flesh wound?" asked Aetna. A long gash extended from just below his collar bone, toward his chest. A flap of skin had been peeled back by the force of the falling beam which had knocked his shoulder out of place. Blood had congealed on the exposed flesh.

"I think if we can get some balm into it, it will heal," said Thella. "I am more worried about the bones. They can be pulled back into place, as

Ethelmaer says, but it is a hard discipline and the pain is terrible – especially with the open wound so close to the other injury."

"Do what you must," said Wulfstan. He was beginning to shake, though whether from the cold or the pain or both I did not know. I worried that he might become elf-shot if we did not tend his injuries soon – elf-arrows can enter the body easily through a gash in the skin.

Ratkin had found a good supply of twigs and other wood and the fire was now blazing well, under his watchful eye. The Abbot, Brother Sampson and the three uninjured brothers were on their knees, intoning the prayers of the third office – Terce – for they estimated that the time was right, and our men-at-arms, at my instruction, had gone to the village to offer what assistance they could.

"Can you not allay his pain as you did for Brother Anselm?" I asked Thella.

"Brother Anselm's spirit was already part way to the Bridge," she replied. "To blunt his senses was but the work of a moment, but this is different. And your father's right arm will need to be worked back into place – I cannot nurse his hand as that is done."

"Is there nothing you can do?" said Ethelmaer.

Thella cast a look toward the Abbot, but he seemed engrossed in his prayers. "There is something…" She inclined her head so that we came closer to her and she lowered her voice. "I can send his spirit forth, away from the pain for the time it takes to right his body," she whispered. "But there are some who call it sorcery. Some who would rather witness pain than follow the paths of the old ways."

"I have heard of such things," said Ethelmaer. "It is done in distant lands quite openly. They do not consider it strange. They, too, work with the power of the body's threads as I believe you did for Anselm."

"Very well," said Thella. "But I would that you get the good Abbot and the Brothers away before we do this thing."

I called Ratkin from his vigil over the now hot fire. "There has been no quake of the earth for some while," I said. "I believe from what my father has said that it may be possible to approach the ruins now without fear of more shocks. Take the Abbot and the young brothers over to the remains of the dorter. Tell them I said that they are safe to pray for the dead… but do not allow them to try to move the bodies, there may yet be injury to be had without care is taken. We will ensure that the dead are found and buried in due course. Keep them out there until I call you back."

Ratkin looked at Thella, and she smiled reassuringly. "All will be well," she said.

The churchmen had finished their reciting of the Terce and were rising from their knees.

"Father Abbot, Brother Anselm," said Ratkin, gently. "Come, it is safe to pray for your fellows where they lie. Let their brothers give succour to their souls and speed them on their journey to the Lord." The Abbot acquiesced willingly, followed by the brothers.

Ethelmaer took charge. "Thella, what need you to do this thing?" he asked.

The ruin of Wulfstan's under tunic still hung on the left side of his body, and on it was pinned the amber jewel which Aetna had admired at Rammesig. "That will do well," said Thella, taking it off the tattered fabric. "Wulfstan, look at this stone…" Our father still lay on his back, with Ethelmaer now on his right side. "Look at the stone and listen to my voice. Only my voice. See the fire in the stone. Hear my words. You are walking, walking. There are steps before you, steps leading down into a beautiful valley. Walk down the steps, Wulfstan. Count them as you walk down…"

Wulfstan began to murmur numbers, almost silently, his eyes intent upon the amber jewel.

"You are at the bottom of the steps, Wulfstan. Where are you, Wulfstan? Hear only my voice and tell me where you are."

"I… I don't know," he whispered. "Ah, but it is beautiful, like the gardens of lost Eden…"

"You may begin," Thella breathed silently to Ethelmaer.

Our cousin turned to Aetna. "Lady, if you will put a damp cloth – do we yet have something clean? Good! – on your father's wound and hold it in place. I do not want to open the wound again if I can avoid it." There was a concave dip in the muscle where the skin was torn away, as if a hollow had been created where there should be none. "Do not be afeared to press it hard, it seems your father is feeling nothing." Miraculously this appeared to be the truth, for as Aetna pressed the cloth to his exposed flesh, he did not even flinch.

"Now, Wulf, go to your father's other side. Hold him across his waist and by his left arm and try not to let him move. I shall be pulling him toward me, so be prepared!" He sat on the floor opposite me and took my father's right arm, holding it at the wrist and elbow, and bracing himself against his body with his own left foot. Slowly, he began to pull. The tension across Wulfstan's body increased as Ethelmaer continued to ease the bone of the upper arm out of its unnatural position and I could feel the strain building. It took all my strength to prevent him slipping toward Ethelmaer: the pain should have been excruciating and yet Wulfstan showed no sign of being aware of it. Instead, there was a look of serenity on his face, and a slight smile played upon his lips.

Suddenly, there was a pop and Ethelmaer released his hold. The bone, it seemed, had snapped back into its accustomed socket. The odd contour of his inner shoulder was gone, and his arm was seated normally. Angry bruises were beginning to spread across his shoulder and down his arm, and the skinned area looked livid, but the ghastly dislocation was gone.

"It is done!" said Ethelmaer, and for a moment we were all silent with relief. "Bring him back, Thella. Please," he added.

"Wulfstan," said Thella. "Wulfstan, hear my voice. It is time to leave the garden. Come back up the steps. Can you see them? Good, that's it, count with me as you come up... count... three, two, one. Wulfmaer, you are with us now. You are back. How do you feel?"

Our father, seemed at a loss to know where he was. "Where...?"

"You have been asleep, Father," said Aetna gently, smoothing the hair away from his eyes. "Are you in pain?"

"Oh, was I dreaming? It seemed I had been away for a long time. In a wonderful... Yes, my shoulder aches like the very fury, and my head a little, too, but I am quite well." He made to sit up.

"No, no, lay..." I said.

"... still for a little longer," concluded Aetna, and, the tension broken, we laughed.

"We must find some unguent for that wound," said Thella. "I fear all my supplies are still in what remains of our chamber, Lady."

"Mayhap it is safe to see if we can get into the monk's dispensary," said Ethelmaer. "I will go."

He quit the chapter house and we could hear voices as he spoke in low tones to the Abbot, where the brothers knelt, praying for their lost brethren. A quiet chant of solemn song began, and our father stirred again. "Oh, by the Lord, I remember! Are you all unhurt? Where is Ethelmaer? How came we in here? I... I cannot seem to recall anything after that poor young monk died before us."

"It is well, Father," said Aetna. "We are safe, though I fear there is little left of the abbey, and few of the brothers left to repair it. No, no, do not fret, Ethelmaer is safe too. It is he who put your arm to rights, and Thella here who..."

"I simply soothed you while you slept," said Thella, quickly. "That is all."

))))))))(((((((

Thankfully, the earth kept still for the rest of the day and into the night. The dispensary had escaped the worst of the destruction – once again, it benefitted from being a wooden construction – and Ethelmaer had found some salve of marigold which, Thella agreed, would both help to heal Wulfmaer's open wound and reduce the swelling and bruising of his shoulder. There were bandages, too, and Aetna gently applied the ointment, binding it lightly, finally making a sling from her own undergunna's lining to support his arm.

At the Abbot's behest, though with reservations as to the safely of the decision, Ethelmaer, Ratkin and I helped the remaining brothers, to loosen the bodies of the dead from the debris and lay them beside Brother Anselm. Our men-at-arms returned from the village, and reported that there were three deaths, resulting from the toppling of the stone cross at the village crossroads. People had clustered to it, seeking the protection of the Lord when the ground began to grumble and shake, mostly the poorest villagers, as they had been sleeping in the open when the quaking began. Then, thinking likewise that it would be the safest place, the pompous and unpopular steward of the local Hall, known for his unfair, not to say illegal, interpretation of his duties and rights, arrived with his equally disliked wife and son and ordered the villagers away from the Cross, that his family might better attain its shelter. At that moment, the earth gave another vicious lurch and the Cross fell, crushing the unfortunate family and killing them instantly. Apparently, they were not mourned.

There being little, other than the market Cross, made of stone in the village, most of the inhabitants escaped with cuts and bruises and the odd broken bone. As it seemed fairly safe to access the dispensary, Thella and Aetna, with the help of Brother Sampson, who had some knowledge of medicine, made a search and found more medicines which they took into the village later in the morning, and returned with food, small ale, and the thanks of the villagers. We ventured also into the ground floor sleeping chambers and retrieved what we could of our possessions, together with blankets and some few comforts, as it was clear that we should have to spend the night in the chapter house.

We were grateful for the sustenance from the village, as there was little left of the abbey kitchens. The fire had burnt itself out and not spread to the fallen wooden superstructure of the dorter, as the wind had, thankfully, taken the sparks and embers in the opposite direction. We found that an early shudder in the ground must have found a weakness in the stable block, for the horses were not in their stalls, having bolted in terror before any harm could befall them. In the postnoon, Ratkin and I went looking for them, and found them, quivering with apprehension and cowering beside a windblown copse a mile or so distant. It was touching to see how relieved the beasts were to see us – and we were no less pleased to see that they were sound and well.

Wulfstan dozed on and off through the day, kept warm at Thella's insistence, close to the chapter house fire. Despite his protestations that he was fit to pitch in, his arm would not have allowed him to undertake anything strenuous and, in truth, once he accepted that she would not allow it, he seemed content to rest.

Late in the day a weary horseman clattered into the abbey yard. It was a messenger from Uphude. We were relieved to hear that all family and friends were well and uninjured by the quaking of the earth, both for their sakes and because we had been in a quandary: should we return to see how they fared or should be push on back to Wintancaestre, where we felt sure the King and Dowager Queen would be anxious for our return. Apparently, the upheavals had been less violent in Uphude and further to the North. There had been little damage to the Great Hall and adjacent buildings, but the splendid new Rammesig Abbey church had fared less well. Once again rebuilding would be necessary. The twin towers had been laid low and much of the structure of the nave and chancel damaged beyond repair. I was a little shocked at Ethelmaer's reaction to the news.

"Well, at least it will keep my father busy for the foreseeable future. And out of my business. He will doubtless be much involved with Lord Ethelwine in once more raising the abbey church."

"Ethelmaer!" reproved Aetna. "That is unkind."

"But true," he replied. "Although, I would not wish them less than good fortune in the task," he added, mindful that the messenger was one on his father's men, and loyalty would not allow him to demure if questioned about Ethelmaer's words.

"Lady," the tired man said, "My master and his guests will be relieved that you and your party are safe. I am under orders to return with news of how you fare as soon as I find you."

"But you cannot ride all the way back without rest," my sister replied. "Come, you must at least have food and ale – and a fresh horse, for that poor beast will be dead before you are half the way there, if you do not replace him."

Recene (was it, I wondered, because of his name, which meant "quick", that he became a fleet messenger, or did he enjoy that service because of his name?) accepted the hospitality gratefully. "I thank you, Lady, that would be welcome." Aetna hustled him into the chapter house and he sank down beside the fire, while Thella busied herself fetching broth and bread, thanks to the generosity of the village. By the time he was ready to ride again, having caught a short nap, the early winter dusk was already deepening into night.

"Shall you be safe?" said Aetna, as he mounted his new horse, a beast from the abbey's stable which he would return, collecting his own animal, at a later date.

"Aye, Lady, do not fear. I know these ways well. Though I am pleased I did not have to ride further to find you. The ladies at Upton were in a fever of apprehension to know that you were not hurt – or worse – and my swift return with good news will be the most welcome relief. I fare you all well. May the Christ be with you on the rest of your journey."

"And with you," I said.

"And pray give my father and Ealdorman Ethelwine my most earnest goodwill," added Ethelmaer.

"That I will, Brother. Lord, Lady, keep you safe!" He wheeled his mount and trotted out of the courtyard. In the still of the cold night we could hear him spur on to the gallop. There was moonlight to show him the way and we hoped he would have an uneventful ride home.

The next morning dawned fair and bright, although there was still a strange pinkish hue in the sky. Despite the basic comforts of the chapter house we had slept well – exhaustion is a great soporific – and Wulfstan announced that he was fit to travel. Thella loosened his bandage and applied more marigold salve to his wound, binding it once more and retying the sling which was still necessary to support his arm. The Abbot and Brother Sampson, together with the other remaining monks insisted that we took the lion's share of their supplies. More would be forthcoming from the village and their numbers were so sadly reduced that the future of the abbey itself would be in question.

We felt badly at leaving them alone to the unhappy task of burying their brothers.

"It is our duty and our honour to do so," said the Abbot. "They shall lie together. As they slept that fateful night in the same dorter, so they shall sleep for eternity in each other's company until they are awoken at the end of days."

"Father Abbot, we thank you for your hospitality upon our arrival at your door, and regret that the time we have spent with you was such a sad one," I said.

"That you were here was a blessing, my son," replied the Abbot. "We would have fared less well had you not been." He lifted his hand in benediction and made the sign of the Rood. "May the Cross of Christ protect you on your way," he said.

What shall I say of the rest of our journey back to Wintancaestre? As we travelled south and west, passing through the southern reaches of Mercia and on into north Wessex, the damage and loss of life appeared to become greater. Then, as we approached the middle of Alfred's old kingdom, and the ancient Roman milestones began to bear the name of Venta, Wintancaestre, the devastation lessened. Although we had not felt inclined to linger anywhere during our trek, we had made slower time than on out outward journey, as Wulfstan, though determined to keep pace, sorely felt the jolting of the road and needed rest from time to time. We stopped overnight mostly at taverns (and once spent the hours of darkness huddled over a campfire) as many of the stone-built abbey hospitals were in a sad state of disrepair. At last the city walls of Wintancaestre appeared in the distance.

We approached along the road which led to the Nunnegate. Darkness was beginning to fall, and the great gates already closed, but the small wicket stood open. From his station atop one of the lookout towers, a sentry called down to us.

"Lord Wulfmaer – and my Lady Aetna – you are a sight for sore eyes! Excuse my familiarity, Sire... Gatekeeper!" he shouted. "Gatekeeper, what? Are you already abed. See who is home safe!"

The Gatekeeper appeared at the door of the tower.

"May the Christ and all his Saints be praised! We have been a-waiting your return this five days. The King and the Queen Dowager have been sending to us every morn and eve and hour in between. As though word would not travel to the Court as soon as you were seen!" As if to illustrate the point a young lad sprang up from his seat at the foot of the wall and sprinted off into the city. "Their Majesties left orders that the moment there was news a runner was to come to them with it. And here you are!"

We dismounted to traverse more easily the narrow roads of the inner city. Our tired horses had their heads down, and we felt little better, though the warmth of our welcome cheered us, as did the news, by default, that the King and Dowager were safe and unharmed – and by association so was the rest of the Court, for it seemed that there had been little damage so far south. We heard later that the bells in King Alfred's New Minster sounded as the ground shivered and it was feared that the walls of the Old Minster would crack, but it seemed little else of note had taken place. It was not until news began to flood into Court from the rest of the country that the scale of the disaster was realised. Edgar had sent scouts out to assess the damage and to arrange for help to be given to the most badly affected areas. Services of thanksgiving for the safety of the Royal Family had been held in the New and Old Minsters, and the singing of the monks inside each became hopelessly intermingled as both took place at the same time.

We parted then, each going to their own journey's end: Aetna and Thella to our Aunt Aethelflaed's Hall and I, with Ratkin, Ethelmaer and Wulfstan toward the King's Court. As we approached the doors of the Great Hall, I suddenly realised that our appearance was not at all as I would wish, were we to see the King. Much of our attire – and we had travelled light – had been lost at Bedeford, and we had barely had a change of clothes or the chance to wash during the last several days on the road. If our horses looked ill-kempt and exhausted, then we looked little better, trudging by their sides. I thought we might be better served by making our way into the Hall by a side entrance and going straight to my apartments to make ourselves a little more presentable before reporting to Edgar.

But my plan was forestalled. News of our arrival had gone before us, and before I could lead my companions down a side road to approach the

Hall from a less populated quarter, I heard a familiar voice calling across the market square.

"Wulf, Wulf, you are returned! And with tales, no doubt, of the earth's quaking around you! Where are you going? Come, come, my father the King awaits!" Edward bounded up to me, his energy and vigour in sharp contrast to our weariness. "Thought you to slip in unnoticed? I fear that ship has long sailed!" He slapped me on the back, and all but embraced me, remembering at the last moment his father's admonition about too much familiarity in public.

"Your Highness," I said, "It is good to see you, too. And, yes, we have been in the thick of these strange events, though I am pleased to say both my sister and I – and our companions – are unharmed."

"That was my next question... the Lady Aetna is quite well? Good, my step-grandmother will be much relieved... as will Alfreth," he added. "And who have we here?" His youthful enthusiasm and curiosity was not to be gainsaid by my obvious desire to make a less immediate entrance into the King's presence.

I resigned myself to the situation. "Aetheling Edward, this is my father, Wulfstan, lately a pilgrim in distant lands. And this is Brother Ethelmaer, my... cousin, well, my cousin's husband's brother's... I will explain it later, but he and my father have travelled with us from Uphude."

Edward, seeing that Wulfstan was nursing some injury became solicitous. "Friend, you look less than hale. Come we will find you food and rest. And Brother Ethelmaer, you, too, are welcome." We entered the Great Hall through the main doors. Edward called to one of the serving women and ordered the guests to be found board. "Close to Wulf's," he said, "for it seems that they have shared much this se'enight."

"Indeed, we have, your Highness," said Ethelmaer.

Edward linked his arm through mine, unconcerned now for the show of informality, and propelled me toward the Royal chambers. "I know you are tired, Wulf, but I know, too, that my father will want to bid you welcome. It will be good to have you back – your counsel has been sorely missed. I need your advice as to how I may get myself back into the King's good graces. We are in disagreement on a certain matter..."

"Your Highness," I said, my fatigue beginning to overtake me, "I shall be happy to help, but first, when I have greeted your father, I must rest. I fear that any suggestions I might make at this moment would not be..."

As we entered the King's personal chamber, he and the Queen were apparently deep in some discussion, or perhaps argument. Elfrith turned and looked at Edward coldly.

"Do you think to enter the King's apartment without leave, Edward? And with a hireling at your heel?"

"Stepmother..." Edward began, but the King intervened.

"Wulf, my dear boy, you are a tonic to end the day! To see that you are safe and unharmed! And I hear that your sister is likewise returned to us. The Queen Dowager will be so relieved. But you look tired… Edward, you should have let Wulf rest before he came here."

The Queen snorted and swept from the room. "When you have finished consorting with the commons, Edgar, we shall continue our debate."

When she was gone, Edgar sighed. "It seems that my family are inclined to be ill-disposed to my opinions at present," he said. "But come, Wulf, before you go to your chamber, tell me briefly how your family fare. My stepmother has had no word and is worried, as am I. Did the earth's upheaval reach the Grantebrige levels? We have not heard from that quarter. Sit, sit, man. We will have no ceremony here in private, eh, Edward?" He looked somewhat drawn – and could that be a little grey hair amid the light brown? Surely not in barely a month.

In truth, I was relieved to sit. I told Edgar of our family's escape from the worst of the disaster, and of how badly some areas we had passed through had been affected, including the tragic consequences at Bedeford.

"I will send to them," said the King. "I have done so to a number of places that have fared ill, but, as I said, we have heard little from the East as yet, so I am grateful for your intelligence. Go and rest now, there will be time to hear details later. Edward, see that Wulf and his companions – I look forward to meeting them – have all they need. And give the man some peace until he is refreshed!"

)))))))(((((((

It seemed that Providence – some might still have called it Wyrd – was ill-disposed toward allowing Ethelmaer to compound the differences with his father with any unfortunate misunderstanding, or, indeed, downright untruth. Whilst he had convinced Elric, with what he said was logical argument, that Dunstan would undoubtedly still be at Court, both Aetna and I had grave misgivings as to its veracity. It seemed far more likely that the Archbishop would have returned to Cantuaria to see how his own abbey had fared, or even to Westmonaster. However, as we discovered later that evening, he was still at Court, and Ethelmaer's conscience bore no further stain.

Whilst I would happily have kept to my chamber for the next twelve hours, it was barely the eighth hour post noon when Edward knocked at my door, and entered without waiting to be bid. I had snatched a couple of hours of sleep and was still groggy with it when he flopped down onto my pallet.

"I know, I know, Wulf, and I truly beg your indulgence for I can see that you are spent, but you must come down to the Great Hall with me and take my father's mind away from his plans for me. Between him and Archbishop Dunstan, my goose is all but cooked – broiled and baked all at once – and for once it is not Elfrith basting the bird, it is my beloved step-grandmother. I hate to oppose her will, or my father's, but they have me pinned like a spatchcock."

"First a goose, then a spatchcock! There will be but few birds left to compare yourself with at this rate," I said. "What is it that they want you to do that is do far from your own will?"

"Why, you must know, Wulf! They want me to marry!"

"And why is this such a burden? It would be but a betrothal for now, a promise to wed the chosen bride when you and she are of age. It is the convention for such as yourself. Your father has a dread of the sibling rivalry he endured when his brother and he tussled over the throne. A betrothal signals a wedding in the making, and that, in turn, anticipates heirs to secure the succession. Their election is not automatic, but nowadays it is more than likely. Surely you can see why the King wishes you to go down this path?"

"My father is yet young. There is no urgency in binding me to some simpering girl I have never met."

"Nevertheless, if it is the King's wish…"

"Oh, Wulf, I thought I could reply upon you…" I had rarely seen him overwrought with such stubborn defiance. I could see it cost him dear, for he was not naturally disposed to be at odds with those he loved. His hands were balled into fists of frustration and his colour rose.

"Come, your Highness, Edward, this is not like you." I felt sure that it must only be uncertainly and fear of the unknown – and perhaps the implied mortality of his father – that was making him so intractable. "Do not worry, I will come down. My father and my cousin, too. You will like Brother Ethelmaer, he is but my age, so not that much older than you." I thought perhaps that emphasising his growing maturity might help him come to terms with the duties ahead. "And my father – well, he was once acknowledged the finest storyteller in all of your grandfather's realm, and he has not lost his touch, despite his pilgrim's weeds."

Edward seemed somewhat mollified by my promise and left me to wash and dress. I cast a wishful glance at my pallet as I left the chamber. Perhaps a horn of strong ale would set me up for a few hours, but I feared that it might have the opposite effect and I would be yearning still more ardently for my bed before the evening was spent.

It seemed that news of our safe return had spread throughout Wintancaestre and the Hall was already full of well-wishers and the plain curious, eager to hear what we had seen on our journey through the earth-ravaged shires at the centre of the kingdom. I collected Ethelmaer and my father from their chamber close to mine and we made our way down to the

Great Hall. Clearly there was to be no ceremony that evening, for the King was already seated, Elfrith absent from the chair to his left, and Edward sitting to his right. Edgar brightened when he saw us and waved us over.

"I would have you sit at the High Table this night," he said. "Wulf, go you beside my son, and this must be the famed Wulfstan, I have heard much of your skills, wordsmith, and I hope we may be favoured by a tale this night."

I introduced my father, and he replied that he would be delighted to render a story whenever the King wished. I turned to present Ethelmaer, but he was no longer beside me. Quickly, I scanned the Hall, for I wished him to meet Edward, knowing that his lively chatter would help to lessen the tension. He was a little way off and was in conversation with Archbishop Dunstan.

"Sire, Prince Edward, would you both excuse me for a trice, I would speak with my cousin," I said, fearing that this evening might yet descend into discord, if Dunstan was of the same mind as Ethelmaer's father, and took offence at the rejection of his offer to sponsor the lad's career. As I approached it seemed, however, that there was no friction between the two. Dunstan saw me and broke into a broad smile.

"Wulf, it is good to see you safe. And I hear Aetna is well, too. I am sorry to hear that your uncle's new abbey church is once more in need of rebuilding. Brother Ethelmaer here tells me that there has been much damage to the Lord's churches throughout the land due to this quaking of the earth. Bedeford all but decimated and many more beside. I fear that we must have displeased the Almighty in some ways more than the usual to have brought these things upon the Faithful. I will pray on it."

"Is all... well?" I said, hesitantly. "Between you and Brother Ethelmaer, I mean." I looked at my cousin. "There has been some little... disagreement... between him and his father in regard to your kind offer of..."

"Do not fear, Wulf, all is indeed well." The Archbishop smiled indulgently at Ethelmaer. "Ever since I first met this lad, I had the notion that a life in the traditional service of the Church might not be his lot. I made the offer of taking him into my service as a courtesy to your extended family, for as you know I consider myself almost one of you. But if his heart takes him in another direction that is well with me, though the life of a travelling mendicant brother is not one that recommends itself to many. And I can see why your father," he turned to Ethelmaer, "is not in favour of the plan."

"He seems to believe that I shall fall into the mires of depravity immediately I leave the discipline of the cloister behind me," said

Ethelmaer. "The Lord Ethelwine is of the same opinion, I think. The two have become very close since their shared patronage of Rammesig."

"I will make certain that they are disabused of any idea that you – or they – have lost my favour," replied Dunstan. "But should you change your mind at any time," he added, "my offer remains open. You remind me of myself at your age. I would not be gainsaid either. It would have been a welcome remembrance of my youth to have you in my employ. Do you have immediate plans?"

Ethelmaer glanced at me. "Brother Wulfstan – forgive me, but to call him brother seems natural, for his is so much the churchman, despite his lack of tonsure – is to take to the road once again when he is fully recovered from his injuries. I intend to travel with him."

I cannot say that I was surprised at this news. The two of them had struck up such a companionable relationship that I was almost jealous of my father's friendship, though I knew that his delight at being reacquainted with my sister and me was of an entirely different stripe, and that where ever and with whom he journeyed it would remain with him, a blessing once lost and now regained. He had something and someone to which he could return when the wanderlust abated.

"Alas, I shall not be dining with you this night, or I should have liked to hear more on it," said Dunstan. "I have matters pressing upon my time and must away to the New Minster to attend to them. We will speak again before our paths lead us each upon our way." He strode away, still the vigorous figure I remembered from my childhood.

"He is a great man," said Ethelmaer.

"That he is," I agreed. "But come now, meet the Aetheling Edward. I ween you will find him good company. He is a fine lad, as befits his father's son, but like yourself does not always appreciate his sire's plans for him. I would that you keep him entertained, for you seem to have more vigour than I this night! I declare I may well fall asleep in my broth if you do not keep your elbow in my ribs!"

And so the evening passed pleasantly enough, although I excused myself before my father began his storytelling and went to my pallet. Edward seemed happy in the company of my cousin and the King was enthralled by Wulfstan's tale – for he was still as enamoured of a good narrative as he had been in his youth. It seemed that new friendships were being forged and old ones comfortably renewed.

NINETEEN

WULFAETNA

Oh, Edward, Edward, who could have imagined that it would come to this? Was there a moment, an instant in which we could have had some intimation of the events which were to follow and perhaps tried to turn you away from what was to come? Should we have seen it in that first rumbling of a disquiet earth, and later that year in the red tail of the comet which hung for so long in the autumn sky? How were we to know?

When we parted late that January postnoon, Wulf, our father and the others toward the Royal Court, Thella and myself to Aunt Aethelflaed's Hall it seemed that we had weathered the storm well and come into a safe harbour. The lights in the windows of the refectory at the Nunneminster shone with a warm glow, and a little further on the familiar archway into the Dowager Queen's hall was lit with torches burning in their accustomed sconces. News of our arrival had gone ahead of us; a runner had departed for Aethelflaed's Hall at the same time as the King's boy had run to the Court. Our aunt emerged from the Hall, a blanket about her shoulders against the evening chill, which she allowed to fall unheeded to the ground as she opened her arms to embrace me.

"Child, it is so good to have you home!" she said, not releasing me from her hug, but rather holding me closer. "I was so worried. We all were. It seemed there was nothing but ill news from the direction in which you were coming – and none at all from further to the north east. Tell me quickly – no, you do not have to speak, I can tell from your lack of tears, all is well with my sister and the family... but there will be news to hear, I know. Though it can wait until you are warm and rested – and fed! Thella, it is good to see you, too. And no doubt that rascal, Ratkin, is with Wulf? Of course, he is! And I heard some garbled word that there were others in your party? Who..."

I had not had a chance to utter a word, Aethelflaed's questions – and her own responses to them – tumbling over each other as she ushered me into the Hall, Thella behind me. From the kitchens, Ethel bustled in, bearing warm ale, fresh baked bread and – could it be? – bremelberry buns, the rich aroma of the hot dried fruit swirling about her in an invisible cloud. And Alfreth, embroidery still in her hands, rising from her seat by the hearth, full of smiles and warm greetings.

"Aunt, Aunt!" I cried. "I am quite well, unharmed as you see, as is all the family. Calm your fears. Oh, though it is good to see you, too!" and I threw my arms about her once again. "I am as anxious to hear all the Court news as you are to hear of our travails! But let me first rid myself of this garb – I swear it have not had it from my back this five nights. The shaking of the earth has made for hard travelling and few comforts on the way!"

Thella and I ascended to our chamber, where we were delighted to find our pallets and clothes fully aired – we were to learn later that all had been in readiness for days, anticipating our return as if, in doing so, our safe arrival was in some way preordained. It occurred to me, perhaps for the first time, that this place felt, at last, like home.

Hunger hastened our ablutions and change of clothes, and within a quarter hour we were returned to the main chamber, sitting before the fire, warming our hands around horns of ale. It seemed that in my absence, Alfreth had become quite the lady's companion. Not a companion-woman, of course, for her lack of family and status made that title untenable, but certainly a source of good company for my aunt. She immediately vacated the settle by the fire when I approached, giving me precedence, and took a place further away, but Aethelflaed bade her come back and sit within the family circle.

"Alfreth has been a blessing during your sojourn. Without her, I fear I should have been quite the lonely old lady!" She laughed, clearly much exaggerating the situation for effect. "Although Edward has been solicitous in his attentions. Scarcely a day had gone by when he has not called upon me to tell of the goings-on at the King's table or regale me with some gossip he has heard on the hunt, or new direction in his studies with the Brothers, has he not, Alfreth?"

"In truth, Lady, the Aetheling Edward has been most attentive," Alfreth agreed.

"I am glad that you have not been alone, Aunt," I said.

"No, indeed. But tell me more of your trip. Not the sorry news of the shaking earth and its consequences, but of my family. And yours... I am agog to hear of your father. How do you like him...?"

The evening passed pleasantly. I found myself telling Aethelflaed of my feelings toward Wulfstan, and in doing so realised that they had changed much since my first learning of his return. He had acquitted himself bravely at Bedeford and was good company at all times. His obvious and genuine love for our mother and his heartfelt regret at not having been part of Wulf and my childhood had slowly but surely gained my respect and, yes, I will admit it, the beginnings of a real affection. Thella had long since gone to the kitchen and thence to her pallet before my aunt and I had brought each other up to date with our respective news. Alfreth, too, had excused herself. We were alone.

"Aunt, you intimated in your letter – which we read together on the day of Christ's Mass – that you were some little concerned for the King. Does his health still fare ill?"

"Sister-daughter, I fear so. He will not admit to it; indeed, he will not discuss it, but each time I see him it seems to me that he has lost a little more weight, and that he has a little less vigour. He professes to enjoy these new foods that Elfrith has had introduced to his table, but when I last attended a meal at Court (and that was on the eve of the Nativity) he eschewed them for the traditional dishes. Even Elfrith could not dissuade the kitchens from preparing the spitted hog and other tried and tested delights of the season, though I noticed that they had been obliged to make up some of her new fancy creations, too. I believe that much of what ails Edgar could be remedied by a thoughtful wife attending to his preferences rather than her own notions of how the Court should be victualled."

"Is there aught else that concerns you for the King?" I asked, mindful of our conversation so long ago at Caestre. Aethelflaed seemed suddenly in the same state of mind as on that occasion.

"I do not like the way the Chief Ealdorman acquits himself. In private he is constantly at loggerheads with Dunstan, even almost to the point of violence once – I heard this from Ethel, whose son serves at the High Table and had it from his cousin who attends the central hearth – and yet contrives to appear the epitome of fairness and reason in the King's presence. And he – Alfhere – seems far too confidante with the Queen upon matters of State. They are forever making suggestions a great deal too similar in nature to be mere coincidence. I fear there may be something inappropriate afoot. Oh, not an intimacy of *that* sort..." she saw my shocked expression. "But maybe something even more dangerous."

"Aunt!"

"Yes, well, I am pleased that Wulf is back at Court. He will keep his ear to the ground, no doubt. If only he could persuade Edward to be a little more tractable in the matter of an alliance it would be a weight off the King's mind. Although I cannot say that I am wholly unsympathetic to the boy's objections. Do you remember that frightful Kennyth, so called 'King of the Scots'? Apparently, he has a daughter... Edgar is concerned that his fealty is insecure. A marriage between Edward and the girl would do much to secure peace in the North. I can imagine what a harridan the spawn of those loins might prove to be. And that is just one of the possible marriages of convenience to be considered. Ethelred can count himself lucky that he is yet too young to be useful in such a way!"

"The responsibilities of royalty are many," I said. "And, indeed, of being a good son." I told Aethelflaed of Ethelmaer's contentious relationship with his father and of his self-imposed unconventional mission within the Church. "So, it seems that Edward is not the only one to be defying his sire," I concluded.

"Ah, well, perhaps a good night of sleep will put all into a fresh perspective, my love."

"It surely will, Aunt," I replied. "It is good to be back – to be... home."

"I am glad you think of it that way."

"I do," I said. And, at that moment, I truly believed that it would be so for many years to come.

"Sleep well, Aetna."

"You also, Aunt. Try not to worry. I am sure all will be well." It is unwise to feel too sure of anything.

))))))))(((((((

My life at Court resumed its earlier pleasant routine. The mornings I spent with Aunt Aethelflaed, in the stillroom or the herb garden or with any of a hundred small tasks, and in the postnoons at my embroidery, or with Wulf, and often Edward, too. As winter passed into spring, we took walks outside the city walls, and on occasion Ethelmaer would accompany us, his ever-surprising knowledge of birds, beasts and plants a constant delight. Alfreth, too, would be given leave to join us, and we were a merry band – Edward dressed in common garb, Ethelmaer in a habit which resembled none I had ever seen before – dyed a greenish brown with (he said) nettles, as befitted a "hedge priest" – Alfreth and I often with our gunnas kirtled high to avoid catching them in brambles and undergrowth. Wulf alone retained some semblance of duty: his sword at his side and with a sharp eye out for anything which might threaten Edward's safety. Really, as Aethelflaed had once remarked upon our return late one postnoon, we looked like a troupe of mummers come to entertain the Court, rather than a respectable group of Christians!

I might even have felt guilty about the number of evenings I spent in the King's Great Hall, dancing, eating at the High Table – for Edward always insisted upon us doing so – and enjoying whatever entertainment was to be had for the taking, if it not been with the explicit approbation of my aunt. Keeping my wits about me, and my eyes and ears open, I picked up many a titbit of Court gossip from my peers, and Alfreth, who was a frequent visitor to the lower tables, was likewise a fount of information gleaned from the kitchen, the laundry, and even the Queen's bedchamber, as Morwen – ever unpopular with the rest of the servants – was habitually the subject of their tittle-tattle. Alfreth and Thella had become quite the covert agents within the lower ranks of the royal household, while Ratkin, under Wulf's instruction kept a ware eye and ear on the stables, the kennels and the falconers' and hawkers' mews at the King's Worth.

On a postnoon in March, the sun bright and a sharp wind tugging at the heads of the yellow crocuses just opening in the grass, I sat with Wulf in our aunt's *peristylium* enjoying the warmth to be had when sheltered from the nagging breeze. Aethelflaed had complained of a slight headache and retired to her chamber to rest, Alfreth was about her duties somewhere and Edward at his studies.

"Ratkin is in Thella's bad books, again. She is not speaking to him," said Wulf.

"Oh?"

"He went over to the King's Worth yesterday, at my behest, for I wanted the austringer's lists – Edward seems to spend a great deal of time at his hawking, yet there is little to account for it in the ledgers – and, apparently, was becoming rather familiar with one of the kitchen girls in the Hall there. Thella got wind of it from one of the drabs in the laundry, and, well, you can imagine the rest!"

"I can!"

"He says he was only being friendly on account of the girl in question having been boxed around the ears by Morwen, who had been there on some errand of her own, for giving her lip. She had been badmouthing Morwen and Ratkin thought she might have something interesting to impart. But all he got for his trouble was a smack himself – from Thella!"

"I have told Thella that she should simply marry him and have done with it! She has had my permission for a sixmonth, and I know you would give Ratkin yours."

"Marry him?"

"Oh, come, brother, surely even you can see that it is sure to happen sooner or later – and sooner would be better for them both."

"But they are ever arguing, Aetna! Yes, of course, they flirt, but…" Wulf seemed aghast at my suggestion.

"Really, you men are hopeless! Of course, they fight. It is only because they do not make love! Thella is far too wise to risk a child which might be born… early. She will not give herself to him until they are wed, and she loves to keep him waiting. She was ever the minx! She is just waiting for him to ask her. Again." I tipped my head back and allowed the sun to warm my face. "She had better look to herself or this lass from the Worth may upset her plans."

"I must tell him," said Wulf, seriously. His expression of bewilderment made me laugh. "Speaking of plans," he continued, "what of Ethelmaer? You and he seem to spend much time in each other's company. When does he plan to begin his travelling? Our father tells me that they have had some thoughts of taking to the road together."

It was true that my cousin and I had been taking a great deal of pleasure in our friendship. As well as postnoons together with Wulf, Edward and Alfreth, we had taken to sharing our own special enjoyment of the stillroom, where Ethelmaer's knowledge of plants and herbs and mine of how to preserve and reduce them to oils and essences had prompted us to collaborate on a project to write down our experiments, with the conceit that we might create a manuscript useful to those who doctor to the injured and infirm. Ethelmaer had said that it would be a remarkable thing to be able to cure a man's soul and body from tinctures and simples that he could carry with him on the road. Unbeknownst to him I had begun to embroider a fine linen satchel for him to carry such remedies. Indeed, I was somewhat dreading the day he would leave and I would give him my gift, for I valued our time together.

"He has said that he wants to wait until Easter has passed," I replied.

"Hmph! He does not seem too anxious to leave on this sojourn of his that he was keen to undertake, despite his father's… misgivings. Easter is still a few weeks off. The fourth day of April, is it not, this year?"

I felt defensive. "Such a trip is not to be begun lightly," I said. "There is much to prepare. After all," and here I was voicing what I felt most keenly and would have preferred not to be the case, "he may be on the road for a very long time. Even years."

"Where is he this postnoon? Is this not one of the days you usually spend it in the stillroom together?"

"He was somewhat vague on the matter." I replied, shortly.

There was movement within the Hall, and our aunt came out into the *peristylium*.

"Still here, Wulf? Surely Edward should have finished his studies by now. Aetna, have you seen Alfreth? My headache is quite better now and I want her keen eyes to help me choose some silks before the daylight begins to fade. I can stitch by candle-light, but the colours change, as you know, and I must make my selection now."

"I am sorry, Aunt," I said. "I thought she was about some errand for you. I have not seen her since this forenoon."

"Come you, then, Aetna and we will choose the shades between us. It will be fun. Ah, this is what I missed while you were away… Wulf, you will excuse us?"

"Of course, Aunt. You are right, I had not realised how the time has ebbed away! I must go and find my errant charge. He is probably with Ethel, seeking refreshment after his labours in the *scriptorium*." He uncurled himself from his seat, tall, so much taller than me, now. As he lifted my hand to his lips, I realised how his Court manners had improved in the last years. "I shall see you this eve in the Great Hall, sister? There will be dancing. And shall you dine?"

"Of course," I said, though the thought of dancing was far more appetising than the anticipation of the food.

He embraced our aunt. "And you shall see me, too, young man," she said. "Do you not recall that His Majesty said that there was something of import to be announced this day. I would not miss it. Though I shall arrive after the food has been cleared away…"

"Indeed, then, Aunt," I added. "I will come with you and no earlier. I have a hankering for some of Ethel's recipes. I confess that eating at the High Table these days does not always agree with my constitution – like many another, I think! Let us hope that Edward has left some victuals in the kitchen, if that is where he is hiding himself."

Wulf left us and we went to sort silks and choose colours for Aethelflaed's most recent embroidery. It was an engrossing task. She had transferred the new design onto dense linen, pricking through the pattern with a fine, needle-like awl and scattering a minute line of powdered madder over the punch holes, allowing tiny pin-pricks of colour to fall through and outline the motifs on the fabric. Removing the parchment pattern, the line of dots was then merged together to create a fine meandering contour, which would ultimately be stitched in place – red silk overlaying the madder in split or stem stitches. Preparation was everything, she and Aunt Aelflaed had always taught me. We had a myriad of coloured silks from which to choose: yellows dyed from onion skins and weld, blues from woad, browns and pinks from tree bark, double-dyed silks twice treated, first with weld and then woad to create shades of green and a variety of reds, from madder and St. Johns-wort. We even had some highly prized purples made, so we had heard, from shellfish on the shores of the far-off Middle Ocean and shipped from Constantinople.

Aethelflaed allowed the lustrous fibres to flow through her fingers. "They are more than just threads," she said, dreamily. "It is like holding a glamour in your hands and using it to stitch together a fantasy! Just to think, if the Emperor Justinian had not sent his two monks to smuggle the poor little moths out of Cataya we would not be doing this today…"

"It is a romantic story, indeed," I agreed.

The time passed quickly as we noted down the chosen shades and gave each a symbol, which was then marked down upon the parchment pattern. By the time we had finished the light was fading, and Ethel was anxious for us to clear away the threads and fabrics from the table so that she could prepare it for the evening meal.

"Is Alfreth still not returned?" said Aethelflaed. "I am beginning to be concerned for her. It is not in her nature to wander off without leaving word of her plans."

"She is just this moment come in, Lady," replied Ethel. "And is gone to her chamber. Shall you wish her to dine with you?" In my absence at the turn of the year, my aunt had taken to having Alfreth eat with her for companionship. It had apparently been somewhat frowned upon by Ethel, who, though fond of Alfreth from their first acquaintance, still felt that her total lack of pedigree was an obstacle hard to ignore – especially when she was included, almost, into the family circle.

"No, she may eat with you this eve," said Aethelflaed. She was clearly a little put out by her protegee's thoughtlessness. "And you may tell her that I do not appreciate her coming and going without a word to anyone." Her tone softened. "I was getting worried."

We ate our meal with our minds still on the embroidery project. It was a narrative piece, telling the story of the late King Edmund's reign, from the death of his half-brother Athelstan, to his own sad death at the age of only twenty-five. Archbishop Dunstan had taken a hand in the preparation of the drawings. For Aethelflaed it was to be a labour of love.

"He was taken from me far too soon," she said. "So young and so handsome... ah, you must sigh to hear me reminisce so, I know, but it has been hard without him all these years. I loved him you know."

"Of course you did, Aunt."

"There is no 'of course' about it, Aetna. Marrying a king is not always a choice, but a duty. Though in our case the match became one of love early. It is my only regret that we had no issue... not that I would have any other than Edgar on the Throne!" She suddenly became aware of what she had been saying. "Mayhap if we had had a little girl... but I have you, my love, and you are like a daughter to me, as you know."

"And you a second – or third – mother to me!" We laughed at that and the conversation shifted toward what we would wear to the Court that evening.

When we arrived at the Great Hall some hour or so later, the tables had been cleared, but for the High Table, where the King still sat, with Elfrith and the two princes, some small sweetmeats and fruits to hand, along with wine. Dunstan had dined with the Royal Family and Wulf was beside Edward, talking to him earnestly and looking a little anxious. Ethelred was cramming his mouth with some sort of honeyed nuts, while Elfrith and Edgar appeared deep in conversation, the Queen's customary impatience carving deepening lines between her otherwise still smooth brows. When he saw us enter Edgar beckoned us over and bade us sit with them.

"Stepmother, Lady Aetna, will you both not take some wine, and a few dainties, if Ethelred has left you any!" He smiled indulgently at his younger son, who favoured him with a sticky grin.

"I will certainly take a little wine," replied Aethelflaed, "though I shall leave the dainties to the young people! Aetna, will you pour for us both – we may need our glasses charged for whatever His Majesty has to impart this evening."

"Ah, yes, indeed," Edgar cleared his throat, and glanced sidelong at his wife who avoided meeting his eye. "Yes, to be sure!" He seemed hesitant and on the point of putting the whole matter – whatever it was – to one side.

Without looking at him Elfrith said, in a low but clear voice, "Just do it!"

The King signalled to a retainer who stood to one side of the High Table. A rod was rapped loudly on the boards of the floor, disturbing the strewn rushes and making the dogs bark. "Silence for His Majesty!" Edgar stood and the Hall fell quiet.

"Friends – for so you are, we stand not on ceremony this eve – I have news to tell which will be of great import to our nation. It is now but some few short weeks until the celebration of the Resurrection of our Lord Christ. On that joyous Sunday my son, Edward, will become betrothed to Sinnyth, daughter of Kennyth of the Clan Alpin, sometime called the King of the Scots. The alliance will strengthen our over lordship of those lands and, with the blessing of Our Lord, unite our two houses in the persons of issue to come. I would that you make *was heil*!"

"*Drynke heil*!" came the resounding reply.

"Let us have music now, and dancing, and…" Edgar continued.

Edward flew to his feet, roughly shuffling off Wulf's hand which had been on his shoulder. The bench crashed to the floor behind him. He stood for a moment, fists clenched, staring at his father, as if about to speak, but then flung away from the table and ran from the Hall, disappearing behind the drapery which concealed the stairway to the private chambers. Elfrith's eyebrows raised and she shrugged as if resigned, though whether to the announcement, or to Edward's reaction, it was impossible to tell. There was a look of bemused curiosity on Ethelred's still sticky face. Edgar's expression was stony.

"Go after him, Wulf," was all he said. Wulf hurried out.

The assembly seemed uncertain how to react, but the musicians took up their instruments and began to play. The tune seemed inappropriately jolly, given what had just occurred, but it served to break the tension somewhat and one or two couples took to the floor, tactfully choosing to ignore the latter happenings in favour of the King's earlier instruction.

There was an uneasy silence at the High Table. Dunstan was the first to speak.

"These things are never easy. He is yet young. He will play his part in good faith; it is but a shock for him to hear it announced so. Knew he not that you would make it public this night?"

"It would not have mattered when it was announced," said Edgar. "He has set his mind against it. I swore that I would never force my children into actions against their will, but the threat from the North..."

"The boy is wilful," said Elfrith. "He always has been. He should have been sent for fostering after his mother died – hardened up to the real world, not coddled like some infant. Why do you not betroth Ethelred in his stead? He has as likely a destiny as Edward." Ethelred favoured us with another honey-smeared grin and forced one more nut into his mouth. His mother looked at him with something like exasperation. "Swallow!" she snapped.

Aunt Aethelflaed patted the King's hand. "Why do we not send Aetna after them? Perhaps a woman's perspective..."

"I am at my wit's end over it," he said. "She may have as fair a chance as any to make him see sense. It is not as if we ask him to marry the girl tomorrow, or even next year. Just to make the commitment. It is but a vow for the future."

Aethelflaed nodded to me and I rose. "Your Majesties, Your Highness, Archbishop." I made my curtsey and withdrew, leaving the hum of conversation and music behind me as the curtain fell back into place upon my leaving. Sounds from the Hall became muted as I ascended the wall-stair to the chambers above and I could hear the raised voices of my brother and the prince. I hurried along the walkway and tapped upon their door, but it swung open at my touch. Edward was red-faced, his hair wildly awry where he had dragged his fingers through it in anguish. He stood in the middle of the room. Wulf was sitting on the pallet bed, his head in his hands. Their friendship had long ago dispensed with the custom of waiting for an Aetheling to sit before his companion-man could do so.

When Edward saw me, he cried, "Aetna, cousin, surely you will not admonish me, too?"

I looked at Wulf and he at Edward. "Edward, I do not admonish you," he said. "I am trying to understand. You have ever known that a prince's duty is to his king first, indeed to his Kingdom. This is not such a great thing. The day of its fulfilment is yet far off... and a man needs a wife when all is said and done." I was not entirely sure that this last was a valid argument, but I let it lie.

304

"Edward, Eddy," I said. "Come, be calm, sit by me and tell me why this upsets you so. As Wulf says, it is no surprise to you that you are expected to take your place in the world."

I sat upon the palliasse, a little apart from Wulf, and gently pulled Edward down between us. I could see that he was near to tears, but angrily keeping them at bay. He was, after all, I thought, but a boy, and though not many years our junior, those few make the difference between childhood and maturity. And yet it seemed that there was little of childish temper in his demeaner. It was more a self-conceived righteous, and adult, anger. Tears of anger, yes.

"I am not a child," he said, as though reading my thoughts. "I know what my father expects of me... but..." Here, I felt sure, came the crux of the matter. "I love someone else."

Such a simple phrase. I suppose that deep down I knew this is what he would say. It was almost a relief. This, surely, could be dealt with.

"Oh, Edward," said Wulf and I, almost simultaneously. Wulf continued. "So, which of the lovely young things in your father's Court has taken your heart? Was she there this eve, dancing on the arm of some other man? Eddy, I fear there may be many such in the years before you are expected to make good the pledge to Kennyth's daughter. Though if you made your feelings known, I whist that some few will happily be your... companions! Is that not so, sister?"

This line of argument was not one with which I was entirely in accord, but I did not demur – at least not until I could see that it failed to be having the desired effect upon Edward. He looked at Wulf with an expression I could only describe as pitying.

"Wulf, my friend, that may be the truth in regard to the 'ladies' of your acquaintance," he spoke the word with an emphasis which belied my opinion of him as a child. "But she to whom I have given my... heart..." but then, again, perhaps I was wrong, "is much different. And she loves me." He put his hands between his knees and bowed his head to them.

Wulf and I looked at each other over his bent back. My brother raised his eyebrows as though in despair of knowing what to say next. I tried again.

"Come, now, Edward, this will not do," I said, trying for a matter-of-fact tone. "As the King has said, and as we have told you, these things do not come to pass in a se'enight! Even with the betrothal made, it will be years before a marriage takes place. Who knows how you will feel by then? You cannot have known this girl for long, when came she to Court? I can recall no new Ealdormen and their daughters arriving. She may, herself, have a change of heart! I do not seek to be unkind, but Eddy, remember I was a lass of your age but few years past, my feelings were as fickle as the wind." This was not strictly true, but it seemed a good ploy as I said it.

The prince sat up straight, and took a deep breath as though taking courage for what was to come. "Aetna, Wulf, I know you are trying to help. To change my mind and make me compliant to my father's wish. But I cannot." We began to remonstrate. "No, I mean it. Indeed, I cannot, even if I so wished – which I do not."

"Edward, you are not making any sense."

"I cannot because… because…" he took another deep breath. "We are already married!"

Not for the first time that evening, my brother and I were lost for words. Wulf regained his voice first. "What mean you?"

"It is not hard to understand, Wulf. We are wed. My love and I are one, in the sight of God."

For a moment I thought we had been misled. Wulf assumed the same.

"You mean you and this girl have taken vows, one to another. Alone in the moonlight, with the Lord in his Heaven above you. Told each other that your love will endure for eternity? Till the stars fall from the skies, that sort of thing?" he asked, hopefully.

"Yes," said Edward. A flood of relief washed over us. Only to be dashed away. "And in the presence of a priest, at the altar steps."

I closed my eyes for a moment to take this in. When I opened them, sadly, nothing had changed. Wulf leapt to his feet and strode to the centre of the room. He whirled around to face us.

"What? How has this happened? Who is this girl and how did you convince a priest to do such a thing? I do not know, but I think, I think this must be treason! We can, none of us, marry without the King's consent, but you! You, his own son! Oh, sweet Heaven, I shall be hung for this, for allowing it to… Great God, do you realise what you have done?"

"Keep your voice down, for pity's sake!" I said. "We shall have half the household in here if you do not. This, this is a…" I sought for the right word. "A surprise…" – something of an understatement – "but we can find a path through it all, I am sure." I did not feel one grain as confident as I pretended, but this needed a woman's calm head. "Wulf, sit down. Eddy, you must keep silent about this for the present. Go down now and make your peace with your father… no, I mean it. You need not lie. Say nothing other than you are sorry that you have pained him, and that you have thought further on the matter. He will be so pleased to see you in a changed mood that he will not press you on what your thoughts are; he will assume you have come to your senses. Dissemble, if you must, but you cannot speak of what you have told us outside this room. Smile, be your pleasant self. No, say no more now! Wulf and I will be down directly."

How I came to be able to order an Aetheling about in this manner, I have no idea, but my tone brooked no argument. Wulf looked at me open-mouthed, and Edward seemed quite content to comply.

"Very well," he said. "I shall make my apologies to my father, the King. But I shall not…"

"There is no need to worry about aught else for now," I said, I hoped reassuringly. "All will be well, but we must take time to think how to proceed."

Edward smiled, ruefully, turning to leave. Then, suddenly, there was something of the child back in his voice. "But you will come down soon?"

"*Pars minuta prima*," I smiled. We heard him walk down toward the stairway and hesitate before his footsteps began to descend.

Wulf turned to me. "What, in all the…?"

"Listen to me, brother," I said. "We do not know the full truth of this matter yet, but if we had kept Eddy up here any longer, someone – maybe even the King himself – would have come to investigate. He loves Edward dearly and cannot bear to have him unhappy. The need for this alliance with the Scots must have been pressing indeed for him to take this step. We must buy some time – for Edward, and this girl, whoever she is, for ourselves and for Edgar, too. And yes, even Englaland itself. For a secret marriage to be revealed just as a betrothal is about to take place would be enough to give that brute Kennyth an excuse to… well, I do not want to think about it."

"How did you become such a tactician, sister?"

"I listen, Wulf. I listen at the High Table. I listen to Aunt Aethelflaed as we embroider – she has been witness at the heart of this country's governing for decades. And I listen to my heart, also. There is more to this than a lad's passing fancy, mark my words. Now, compose yourself, for we find ourselves in the midst of an intrigue to rival those of Sigimund and Sigilind."

Wulf stood. I took his hands in mine and squeezed them. "You are right," he said. "We are not confounded yet!" He planted a kiss on my brow. "Come, Lady Sigilind, into the den of Fafnir!"

)))))))((((((

When we returned to the High Table, all seemed to be quite peaceable. True, Elfrith had her accustomed air of distaste and irritability and Ethelred was nowhere to be seen, probably sent to his pallet, or taken to be sick, judging by the lack of honeyed nuts remaining on the board, but there were no raised voices. The King looked quite serene, in fact, Edward speaking to him in a low, earnest voice and Aethelflaed in deep conversation with Dunstan. Wulf resumed his earlier seat and I slipped into a space beside him. Our aunt smiled her approval at me and mouthed, silently, "Well done, my love!" with a slight wink. The Archbishop, too, favoured me with a pleasant nod of the head before they resumed their discussion.

I confess that I found it quite unnerving to see how easily Edward dissembled before his father. I had thought it would be harder for him and, privately, I began to reassess his character somewhat. Wulf downed a large tumbler of ale, and I put my hand on his wrist, warning him not to become careless in his speech. I avoided making any further eye contact with my Aunt and was feeling very uneasy at the prospect of having to dissimulate before her upon our return to her Hall later that evening and during the early part of the next day before I could speak further with Edward and Wulf. In fact, I realized, I could not bring myself to do so.

I excused myself from the board, citing, rather unnecessarily, the need to make water and slipped away through the hangings. Leaving the Hall by a side door, I skirted around the outside of the building until I came to the kitchen entrance and went in. The kitchen thralls and ceorls were mostly taking their rest, the meal served and cleared away in the Great Hall, and availing themselves of the leftovers by way of their own repast. As one, their heads turned toward me, the steward and bottler rising to their feet.

"Be at your ease," I said scanning the room for a face I could use. I recognised a girl from whom I knew Thella had often garnered small titbits of intelligence and, lifting my chin to indicate that she should come to me, said, "Lucet, is it not?"

"Yes, Lady." She was a little thing, pert and pretty in a way. She wore the rough gunna of a kitchen drab but had somehow managed to tie it neatly to reveal a small waist and had a kerchief of unexpectedly bright red around her neck. A gift from a lover, I wondered?

"Very well. Lucet, I want you to go to the Queen Dowager's Hall and ask for Thella. Speak only to her. Tell her to come to me in the Great Hall – to come to the main doors, mind – and ask for me personally. She is not to say that I sent for her, rather that she must see me on a matter of great... well, tell her to say it is important that she sees me. Do you understand?"

"Yes, Lady."

"And do not mention this to anyone else. If I hear it whispered abroad, you will spend your time slopping out the pigs from now until Judgement Day."

"Yes, Lady. I mean, no, Lady, I will not!"

"Good girl." Ever the believer that the stick works best in conjunction with the carrot, I drew two fourthings from the little purse on my chatelaine and slipped them into her hand. "Be quick and quiet and there may be more where this came from," I added.

"Thank you, Lady!" Lucet hitched up her skirt and ran off in the direction of the Nunnegate.

I retraced my steps and returned to the warmth of the Great Hall. There were more dancers on the floor now, and it appeared that my father had been prevailed upon to give the company a story, for he was making his way toward the hearth – his favourite and accustomed spot to perform – shrugging his mantle from his shoulders in order that he might better gesture and emote the tale. I resumed my seat by Wulf.

"Where is Ratkin?" I whispered.

"I'm not sure," he replied. "I only hope, after your revelations this postnoon, that he is not back at the Worth with the little miss from the falconer's mews."

"It might be as well if he is," I said. Wulf looked puzzled, but then things began to happen quickly.

The musicians stopped playing and the dancers returned to their seats. Horns and cups were refilled, children not abed were hauled onto laps and there was a general air of settling down in expectation as a hush fell.

"I will give you first *The Seafarer*, a lay you all love," said Wulfstan. "Then I will tell you a tale of what happened next!" There was a murmur of approval at this. Both a favourite poem and a new story, what could be better?

> *"I can tell a true tale of myself,*
> *Tell of my travels,*
> *How in toilsome times I suffered terrible hardship*
> *And how I have borne bitter bile in my breast.*
> *Was made sad by sorrowful abodes on ships*
> *Amid the dread whiplash of the waves…"*

The wicket at the great door rattled. Voices could be heard without. I was suddenly reminded of Alfreth's dramatic arrival at the castle Hall in Caestre, perhaps that was why this ruse had occurred to me. This time, however, the small door opened and the man-at-arms ushered a figure in – followed by another. This was unexpected, surely Lucet would not have followed Thella? Then I recognised Alfreth, as though conjured by my recollection of that earlier event. No matter, I thought, she could easily be dismissed later. Thella flounced up the Hall, making a fine show of trying not to disturb my father's performance, whilst giving a splendid one of her own. She was made for this type of diversion.

"Just follow my lead," I whispered to Wulf.

Thella came up to me and bent to put her lips to my ear. "I am here, Lady, what is afoot?"

I essayed to look both shocked and censorious. "Thella!" I said, possibly louder than might have been entirely necessary. "I understand your distress, but it is not appropriate for you disturb the King's presence in this way! Be silent, I will have this matter explained. Come with me." Turning to Wulf, I said. "I am sorry, brother, but you must miss our father's performance this night. Your wretched man, Ratkin, must answer for his behaviour! Know you where he is hiding himself?" I hustled Thella toward the hangings, and Wulf rose, made his apologies and followed us. Alfreth, looking bewildered, trailed along behind us, casting a wistful look at... I thought... well, I was not quite sure.

When we were all out of earshot of the Hall, beyond the heavy hanging, I turned and faced the others. "Well played, Thella," I said. "Alfreth, I was not expecting you, but mayhap you can yet be useful in a little while. Wulf, I cannot return to the Nunneminster Hall with our Aunt this night, you and I must... discuss matters and I needed an excuse to be away from my own bed." I paused to consider for a moment. "Perhaps we should find Ratkin... it would make matters look more..."

"What about Ratkin?" asked Thella, suspiciously.

"Oh, he has nothing to do with this," I said. "I merely needed a ruse to get away."

"With what, though?" Her curiosity was thoroughly piqued now. "And in any case, someone ought to know where he is! If he is gone to that floosy at the Worth..."

"What floosy?" asked Alfreth.

"Oh, a little chit from..."

At that moment the man in question appeared through the side door, munching upon the leg of a fowl and with a horn of ale in his other hand. He made to ascend the steps to the upper level before he saw us, so intent was he upon his food, but then he stopped abruptly and returned our unified stare.

"My Lord, Lady Aetna, and... what do you all here? And with such looks?"

"Where have you been?" snapped Thella. The playacting was beginning to engender a life of its own. "If you've been..."

"I have been nowhere, my love!" His love? In public? This was something new. "Just about my duties. The falcons..."

"I knew it!" cried Thella.

"Enough!" I shouted, and then lowered my voice, glancing in the direction of the Hall. "Wulf, we need some privacy. Let's to your chamber."

I turned to the stair and went to ascend, my brother behind me. The others began to follow suit. "Not everyone!" I said, impatiently. "Does nobody understand the concept of privacy? Be about your..." This was not going at all as I had planned.

At our backs, the heavy curtain was pulled to one side and Edward ducked beneath it, Ethelmaer beside him. With an air of satisfaction, Edward said "I have told my father that I must retire to my chamber and pray. For forgiveness of my wayward behaviour and for the willingness to fulfil my duties." He looked at our cousin. "And Brother Ethelmaer is here to help me."

"Merciful..."

"... Heaven!" Wulf completed my outburst.

"Edward... Your Highness, we were just..." I was at a loss, now.

Edward took in the presence of the others – there were now seven of us gathered at the foot of the stair – and space was becoming short.

"Come," he said. "We will to my chamber. Aetna, I believe you are right: honesty is the best course now." I did not remember saying any such thing. "And I shall begin by telling you all." I was uncertain whether he meant that he would tell us everything, or whether he wanted us all to accompany him to his chamber, but the matter was taken out of my hands as, without further conversation, we all ascended the wall stair, crossed the walkway and entered his apartments.

"I must tell Aunt Aethelflaed not to expect me back this night," I said. "Alfreth, you may return to her now and make my apologies. Thella must stay as she is the one who has apparently instigated this... this... whatever it may be supposed to be."

"No," said Edward. "Alfreth must stay."

"What? Why?" In my irritation I forgot to whom I was speaking.

"Because it is my wish," said the Aetheling.

"Oh, very well! Thella, go down to the kitchen and tell Lucet to inform the Dowager Queen that I will stay in the Great Hall this night to set matters aright between you and Ratkin. Tell her to speak to my Aunt personally, upon my orders. She seems a likely girl, she will not be overwhelmed by the task. Say that I shall remember her for it. Then come you back here."

"She will manage aright," said Ratkin. "She is, indeed, a..."

"A what? And just how would know?" Thella snapped at him. "You seem to know a good deal about a great many girls..."

"I simply meant..." Ratkin stuttered.

"Just get on with it!" I said. Thella left the room with a bad grace.

Now that we had Edward back with us, Wulf clearly felt that his was his responsibility to take charge. He put a reassuring hand on Edward's arm – though the prince did not appear, now, to need such reassurance.

"Come, now, Your Highness. If there is more to tell, and if you wish for us all to know it then speak. It will not go beyond these walls." We could only hope, I thought. Those involved had already increased from two to eight, counting the invaluable, yet not wholly informed, Lucet. It was fast approaching a conspiracy.

Thella returned very quickly and, giving Ratkin a long, hard look, seated herself on the floor beside him. There was really very little other space left. Edward had seated himself upon the only chair in the room, with Wulf beside him on a long, low trunk, the other end of which was occupied by Ethelmaer. Alfreth and I sat upon the pallet bed.

"Your Highness?" I said.

"Yes, well…" He hesitated for a moment as if unsure where to begin. "My father has, as you all know decided that an alliance should me made with Kennyth of Scotland, in the shape of my betrothal to his daughter. I have nothing against her personally, indeed I know nothing of her. Whoever the King had chosen, my actions would have remained the same. I have wed the person I love in order that any such arrangement should be impossible."

"But who? Who is it that you think you love so irrevocably that…" Wulf interrupted.

Again, a silence. Edward looked, I thought, for a moment, at me. Then I realised he did not. Almost imperceptibly, Alfreth nodded her head.

"The Lady Alfreth," he said.

"Alfreth!" Wulf and I cried in unison.

Into another, this time stunned, silence, Edward spoke again. "I love her. With all my heart. She is good and kind and our lives have been drawn together by the threads of Wyrd, and now bound by the bonds of the Holy Church."

"And who found you to celebrate this marriage?" I asked, but as I said it, I knew. "Ethelmaer! You?"

My cousin now spoke for the first time. "I did not want to keep it from you, Aetna – nor you, Wulf. Nor, indeed, anyone. The plan was to tell the King this eve before he made the announcement, so that any – unfortunate – consequences of a retraction might be avoided. But then time became short, and, well, that did not happen. Then the King… well you know the rest."

"But when? When did this happen?" said Wulf, still as dumbfounded as I.

"This forenoon," said Edward. "As the bells sounded for the midday offices, we became as one." As he spoke, Alfreth rose from her seat beside me and went to stand beside him, laying a hand on his shoulder.

Wulf's expression suddenly changed to one of – what was it? Relief? Hope? "So lately?" he said. "Then this may surely yet be undone. If you have not consummated the marriage, it matters not how many times you have shared a bed before the nuptials – it can be annulled!"

For the second time that day, Edward looked as though he was going to strike my brother. But he held himself in check. "Wulfmaer," he said, "you have been my companion – and my friend before that – for some years now, and I love you like a member of my own kin. You will withdraw those words, or they will be the last I ever hear from your lips. Alfreth came to my bed this day as true and whole a maid as ever walked God's earth. She is above reproach, and this marriage is absolute."

"My Prince, Alfreth," Wulf went onto one knee. "I do, I mean, I will. I meant no disrespect. Truly I spoke without thought. But this has been, this is, a matter of such..."

Edward's forgiveness was immediate. "I know, I know... but come, not one of you has yet congratulated us. Surely a marriage day should be one of joy. Thus, it has been for me, but for that short interlude at the High Table. And for my love, too. Indeed, it was our shared joy which kept me from seeing my father earlier this eve... I fear our return from chapel at the Worth was somewhat delayed by it."

Alfreth blushed prettily and spoke for the first time. "I, too, regret the need for this deception, but my Lord was insistent. Aetna, pray, do not think too harshly of me. You know I have ever held you as my dearest sponsor. Were it not for you, I might surely have died – or worse – at the hands of those ruffians in Caestre."

Ruffians who, I thought, included Kennyth of Scotland, who must now be "insulted" by the King's withdrawal of his offer of Edward's hand. How strangely is the way this world is stitched? But I opened my arms to Alfreth and she ran into them. As we embraced, I felt her tremble. I felt most surely that she knew this love, though pure and holy, was a dangerous and ill-omened thing. "My sweet girl, Alfreth, and my Prince, Edward, I wish you both a lifetime of gladness together, of course I do. It is only my fears for you that temper my delight." I would have said more then – perhaps too much – but that the others now began to embrace Alfreth and take sword-hands with Edward. Ethelmaer spoke quietly in my ear.

"Aetna, will you forgive me?"

I was about to reply when there was a sound of footsteps along the walkway. Morwen's voice.

"I am sure they all came this way, Your Majesty."

I glanced at the door and saw that there was no lock that could be affixed from the inside, only a latch. There was nothing to prevent it being opened, and our gathering discovered. Only I noticed Thella make a quick gesture as though flicking something from her forefinger over her thumb and toward the door.

We all held our breath in mutual and instinctive silence.

The door rattled. And again. "I think there can be no-one within, Your Majesty," said Morwen. "These doors only lock from the outside – on your orders."

"Mayhap one of my less inspired decisions," said Elfrith. "The boy has likely made off with some of his low companions. No matter, what I have to say can wait till the morrow. It may yet be to our advantage. Ethelred is still..." Their footsteps echoed away along the walkway toward the Queen's apartments.

We allowed a few moments to elapse before we breathed once more. I saw Thella run her forefinger down her thumb and curl it into her palm. "By the Saints, that was fortunate," said Wulf. "Something must have jammed the catch." He walked across to the door, and it opened easily. "Odd."

I felt that we were in danger of allowing the whole night to pass in fruitless and idle discussion were someone not to call it to a halt with at least the essence of a plan of future action. "Your Highness," I said, "it is clear that you and Alfreth – Lady Alfreth," I hastily corrected myself, as Edward's brow creased. "That you and Lady Alfreth are, indeed, man and wife. But I counsel you that you must not allow this to be known for the present. Not until a way can be found to extricate your father from this announcement that is to be made binding at Easter. We will find a way," I added as Edward began to remonstrate, "but patience must, yes, my Prince, must be your watchword for the moment. Alfreth must return to the Queen Dowager's Hall as though nothing has happened and you must continue to dissimulate before the King." As the words left my mouth, I wondered if what I spoke was treason.

"But it is our wedding night!" Edward argued. "Surely, we may have this time together – and the dawn of the morrow, so that I may bestow Alfreth's *morgengifu*?"

I was tempted to point out that I believed there had been quite enough bestowing for one day, and that the idea of a wedding night was like unto a bird already flown. But the look on Edward's face – and on Alfreth's – was too ardent to be gainsaid, however much logic and prudence dictated that it should be. And there was still the matter of explaining the disappearance of myself, my brother, Ethelmaer and our companions in this extraordinarily – as most would see it – abrupt manner.

"May I speak?" Ratkin now stood by the door, Thella by his side, both intent that we should not be at risk of further intrusion.

"Yes, Ratkin, if you have aught in that head of yours that might help us find a way through this maze," said my brother. "Say on."

"My love," Ratkin turned to Thella, "this is not when and how I would have wished these words said, but will you marry me?"

"What?" It was Thella's turn to be speechless.

"Marry me. Listen, this night – I may say quite without justification…" He grinned roguishly, "… My honour has been somewhat impugned and it has been suggested that I have had – eyes – for some other. Nothing is further from the truth. I have known that we were meant to be together these past, I know not how many, years. Very well, I will play my part. Let us say that we have been betrothed some days, but that you heard I was straying and thus came in high dudgeon to find your Lady and ask her assistance in finding and, indeed, binding me. This night we *will* wed. That will explain my Lord's, and your Ladyship's, sudden disappearance from the High Table – and continued absence. Ethelmaer will wed us… we will go now to the chapel at the King's Worth. It will be but the cost of a few pints of ale to convince my friends there that I have been there all day – merely outside of their circle for the evening, perhaps with… but leave that for now. It will be thought that the twins are with us – but in fact they will remain here and ensure that the privacy of the prince's chamber is not violated. My lady Aetna can spend this night in her brother's room, beside the prince's, with no impropriety, it will be assumed that the Lady Alfreth has accompanied you as wedding maid, whilst in truth she will be with the Prince Edward, as his own true wife. We will return early tomorrow morning before the Hall is awake and return to our various stations with none the wiser. The fact that you and I shall be wed will be reason enough for most to ask no further questions… for, after all, it will simply be thought something of a radical solution to what appears to be a lover's fight! I will be considered rightly haltered… though in truth I shall be the happiest of men."

This was quite a speech, possibly the longest any of us had ever heard Ratkin utter. Thella stood speechless. Wulf and I gaped at each other, Ethelmaer stood motionless and Edward – Edward beamed. He put his arm around Alfreth's slim waist and pulled her to him. "Brilliant!" he said.

It was not the word I would have chosen. As a plan it lacked finesse and had several yawning holes, any one of which could spell disaster, but at least it had the advantage of tying up the loose ends left by my earlier ill-thought-through deception.

"Wulf?" I said.

"It could work," he replied.

"It will work," cried Edward. "My friends. My dear friends, I see that I have acted in a way that has put you into a difficult lot." He was not mistaken there. "But all will be well, I swear it. I will make it so. But now," he kissed Alfreth gently on the mouth, "now we will away for this one night, before I have to become my father's son for another day. Before I have to answer any questions, before…"

"We shall make it work. Come, my love," whispered Alfreth, softly. "Before this short night becomes an unwelcome dawn."

TWENTY

And, somehow, it did work. Neither Wulf nor I slept that night. We sat on the pallet with our backs to the wall, the palliasse giving us some small comfort and a blanket each as the cold of the night began to invade the room. Wulf put his arm around me and I rested my head on his shoulder. There was no sound from the prince's room beside us. Whatever love making took place was tender and quiet. When the morning came, as it always does, however much those in love might wish it not to, we waited for Edward and his Lady to come to us, unwilling to deprive them of any last moment before they must act as strangers, one to the other, before the rest of the world.

Ratkin and Thella returned from the Worth, Thella making some pretence of injury at having been cheated of her big day – for a wedding is a wedding, whether of the nobility or otherwise. Ethelmaer had, apparently, conducted a dignified, solemn, if quick, service (he must, I thought ironically, have been getting rather expert at it by now) and they were man and wife. Wulf and I promised that there would be a proper celebration, at our expense, before the se'enight was past. Alfreth returned with me to my aunt's Hall, where we explained away the previous day's events, with as few incontrovertible falsehoods as possible and with as much plausible vagueness as we could muster.

When Wulf arrived with Ratkin later in the day, Aethelflaed gave us all a very long, hard look. "I cannot but feel that there has been something taking place of which I am being kept in ignorance," she said. As we began to reply, she cut us off short. "No, do not speak! My years at Court have led me to believe that when those one trusts keep their counsel close, it if often better not to press for answers too vehemently. I pray you only to be careful, for your own sakes – and mine."

There seemed little more to be said. When Wulf spoke to Edward, the prince was still adamant that within a short while he would be able to find the right moment to convince his father that a betrothal to Kennyth's daughter would prove a hollow alliance and that point once settled, he could rely upon the King's affection to allow his marriage for love rather than politics. Both my brother and I were still dubious as to the likelihood of his hopes being met. In the meantime, some new domestic arrangements had to be put into effect.

Ratkin could continue as Wulf's companion-man, but Thella, now a married woman, was no longer a suitable personal attendant (or confidante – at least officially) for me. She must primarily be her husband's partner and help-mate. Ratkin had heard of a small cott, hard under the city wall,

316

by the Nunnegate, which had recently been vacated. With some little savings that he had accrued, a contribution from Wulf, and the bulk of the coin supplied by a grateful Edward, it was secured as the couple's new home. Whilst Thella's *morgengifu* could hardly be expected to rival Alfreth's (Edward had bestowed upon her a jewel of such glittering beauty that it must have been worth a king's ransom) it was, nevertheless, all she could have wished for. Ratkin had the ironsmith fashion a delicate chain from the old thrall's collar which he had never discarded since the day of his emancipation and Ethelwold's death. To it was attached a clasp and various rings to hold the household necessities which a goodwife held indispensable. A unique chatelaine, indeed, to which were added the keys of their new home. I had not credited him with such imagination.

It was one full week since the events which had so rocked our comfortable routines. Thella and Ratkin that day took up their new abode and, as Wulf had promised, were given the means to hold the celebration of their nuptials which had been impossible at the time of their solemnisation. The little house at the Nunnegate was full of well-wishers, the diversity of their social status remarkable even by the cosmopolitan standards of Wintancaestre. Even so, eyebrows must surely have been raised as the King's elder son arrived, bearing a barrel of fine ale and a garland of flowers – sent all the way from the warmer lands to the South - for groom and bride respectively. Thella vowed that she would dry the flowers and keep them always. The ale had no such chance of longevity.

Naturally, my Aunt Aethelflaed gave her attendance at the festivities – though not intending to stay long, for, she said, the young did not want the old spoiling their fun – and she was accompanied, upon her arrival, by Alfreth. A little while later she said to Alfreth "You stay, my dear. I shall have a couple of these fine young persons escort me back to my Hall, but you must remain and make merry." She said no more, but I had the feeling that she knew – or guessed – more than she was willing to admit.

In the few days she had available, Thella worked a miracle in the little house. When she first walked in, so she said, it had the smell of old men and even older cats about it. Now, swept and strewn, it smelled sweet and welcoming. Wood gleamed with wax polish, pots sparkled and curtains and hangings glowed, fresh washed in common mallow suds. The shutters were sound, and shut close when needed, but opened wide onto the street if desired – it could be converted into a shop quite easily, indeed, I thought that it had been so used in the past, though not recently. The sound of revelry floated through the open windows into the street beyond, and as more guests arrived – too many to be accommodated within – they, too, drifted out onto the hard-packed road, occasioning any travellers to take avoiding action, and carters to calm their shying horses as the noise level rose. Ratkin and Thella had become popular faces in Wintancaestre and both invited and uninvited well-wishers were welcomed with equal enthusiasm.

Wulf and I, with Ethelmaer and our father, found a spot alongside the off-road wall of the cott and watched the revelry.

"They deserve to be happy," I said. "They have both served us well – and will continue to so do in any way they can. I shall miss Thella's skill with the curling irons, but not her tantrums!" I added, laughing.

"Aye, and I am pleased that Ratkin shall continue at my side – for the time being, at least," said Wulf.

Our father swigged back what remained in his tankard and pushed himself away from the wall. "Well, I must away," he said. "The King is confined to his chamber this day, with the aches in his belly returned. It eases his discomfort to hear a tale or two and distracts his mind from the worries of State. I will bid you all a good day and a merry evening!"

He kissed me on the cheek and slapped Wulf on the back, affording Ethelmaer a companionable wink. The two were becoming good friends and I was only too aware of the approach of Easter, and their planned departure.

"And to you, Father," I replied. "And please give my… my love to the King. Wish him better ease from me, if you do not consider it too forward." I remembered that young man who had treated my brother and I as adults, or so we thought, when nobody else did; his smiles and laughter, which seemed all too rare these days.

"That I will, daughter, that I will. He will be pleased of it, I am sure."

Wulfstan eased his way through the throng and disappeared to bid his farewells.

I turned to Wulf. "How ill do you suppose the King really is?" I said. "There are so many rumours around the Court, people who seem to want to bend the truth to their own ends, it is hard to know."

"Even Edward is unsure," replied Wulf, looking around for somewhere to toss the chicken leg bone in his sticky hand. I had a flash of the little boy he once was – this seemed a day for reminiscence. In the end he settled for the back of a passing cart.

"Wulf!" I remonstrated.

"That fellow deserves it," Wulf snorted, indicating the carter. "I saw him try to run down a puppy in the road yester-eve. I gave him a kick on the arse for his trouble and took the puppy back to the Great Hall to see if someone would give it a home. It was a likely little thing!"

"Ah," I said, "so that is how Dunna got her new little companion. I saw her petting it this forenoon. Is it just the pup you gave her or did you hand over your heart, too?" I teased. Dunna was quite the belle these days. Many of the young men at Court had tried to impress her. I had even thought, fleetingly, that it had been she for whom Edward nursed a passion.

"I believe that Dunna's own heart is already given away," said Wulf. "Her father, though, would rather she entered the nunnery than give his blessing to..."

"Why is that such affairs so rarely seem to end happily?" interjected Ethelmaer. There was something of the petulant boy in his voice and – oh dear, my mind was full of memories that day – I recalled our times together as children. "I cannot say that I am unhappy in the life I lead; indeed, I have striven to make it my own to the consternation of my family. But..." He and I looked at each other and I wondered if he knew how I was dreading Easter and his departure.

"Enough of this," I said. "Wulf, you were speaking of the King's health."

"Keep your voice down – you know it can be counted treason to discuss such things..."

"But our father..."

"Should know better than to mention it."

I sighed, the conversation seemed to be going in circles. Wulf said, "I had better find Edward, we should away back to the Great Hall before nightfall. And you should return to our aunt's. Remember you have no companion with you now – how is your search for Thella's replacement?" But before I could reply, Thella herself rounded the corner to find us.

"Lady, Lord – and Brother," she smiled at Ethelmaer, "Prince Edward would speak with you. He is in the back chamber. Come."

We followed her around to the front of the house, through the open door, elbowing past those standing within and without, and went through to a small room at the rear, ducking beneath the stair which led to the chambers above. It might once, I thought, have been a storeroom, if the building had, indeed, been a shop, for there was a door, presently closed, which led outside and could be accessed down a narrow pathway, just wide enough for boxes and crates to be carried for delivery. Now, the room had been furnished with a small table and two stools, a large pallet bed, which seemed to take up more room than was sensible, and a few trunks set with candles and lamps, as yet unlit. One small window was in the same wall as the outside door, and we could see that the rear entrance was overshadowed by trees and quite private.

Edward and Alfreth were already there, waiting, it seemed, for us. The room was ludicrously too small to hold six persons and even when Thella withdrew, there was hardly enough space for us all to either sit or stand, even with the inner door closed.

Edward and Alfreth stood close, his arm about her slim waist, her head lightly inclined onto his breast. They were, in all truth, a sweet couple and was it not for their inequality of station, I would have agreed, a perfect match. "Aetna, Wulf, Ethelmaer," Edward's voice was low, though the noise from the other chambers hardly necessitated such a precaution. "You have heard, I think, that my father the King is unwell – again." We nodded. He continued.

"As you know, it has been my deepest desire to tell my father of my marriage, for I feel sure that he would, under normal circumstances, eventually be swayed to allow our happiness." He looked into Alfreth's eyes and a sweet smile played across her lips. "My love," she whispered.

"But this morn, a rider arrived from the North. From Scotland. It seems that there is much activity afoot. Harald Bluetooth has sent his son, Sweyn, for fostering to Kennyth – some say he is in exile – but, whatever the truth, my father is concerned that the Danes and the Scots seem on such friendly terms. The lad is yet young, but not so young that Kennyth might consider a match between him and his daughter preferable to... well, be that as it may, I would certainly dance at their wedding... but my father would not. He is now more adamant that ever that this betrothal should be made formal, to allay talk of such an alliance.

"I would still tell him of our marriage, but I cannot bear to think how such news would affect his health – how such an impediment to his hopes of peace would wear him down. Alfreth feels the same, and I would not take this decision otherwise. But I must, against my conscience, continue to dissemble. For the time being, this... this room... will be the only place where we will share our love, and our confidence, with just those few who already know of it. Ratkin and Thella will keep the door between the rest of the house and this locked and only Alfreth and I will have a key to the garden door. It will be our secret and our sanctuary, until such time as we are able to bring our love into the light of day."

We didn't know what to say. What could we say? It seemed as though events in far-away Scotland had made liars of us all. Liars and conspirators. I shuddered at the thought of it but could see no other way forward. It was impossible that Edward and Alfreth would forego seeing each other at all – they were young and in love – and this was as good a place to rendezvous as any, safer than most and involving no others in their trysts, saving those who were already complicit.

"Edward, are you sure that you can do this thing? Keep your own counsel and not reveal your true feeling to the King?" I said. It seemed impossible that he could be so duplicitous, even with the best of motives, and yet what other course was there?

"I take no pleasure in it, but yes, I can." He sounded older, now, than his years.

"*We* can," said Alfreth. "My Lord is not alone and never will be. If our marriage is never revealed to the world, still I hold it in my heart. That is all that matters. That and keeping what faith we can with His Majesty." Did Alfreth feel the weight of this lie bearing down upon her, also? I thought so.

"Very well," Wulf turned to practicalities. "Aetna and I will, also against our better natures, keep your confidence. But for Ratkin and Thella, this place shall be known to none but ourselves – and Ethelmaer, here – but I counsel you both to use it sparingly. If either of you take to disappearing for hours at a time with no good reason, questions will be raised and the more untruths told to answer them, the more likely it is that all will be discovered. I know, I know, you want to be together, but if you fail to act prudently then you will lose everything. Edward, my prince, you must know that Elfrith only needs an excuse to have Ethelred step into your shoes. If she gets wind of this then you will be exiled and Alfreth... very likely her life will be forfeit. Elfrith will conspire to make it look like treason of the most vile kind."

Alfreth went pale and Edward clamped his jaw tight as he held her against him a little more closely. They both knew this, of course, but to hear it spoken aloud... We all stood in silence for a moment. Then there was a crash from the front of the house, shouts, Thella's voice in high dudgeon and raucous laughter. The spell of dread was broken.

"Come, though," Edward said, spinning Alfreth around and kissing her lightly on the lips, "for now, let us rejoice with Thella and Ratkin – at least their happiness can be celebrated openly. This kiss," he planted another, harder, on Alfreth's mouth "will have to suffice until later, my love! You will now dance with my man, here." He slapped Wulf on the shoulder. "And I with the fair Aetna! They shall be our proxies, one to the other!" With a flourish he opened the door to the private greenspace beyond, and paired as he had decreed, with Ethelmaer behind us, we left the room and made our way around to the front of the cottage, re-joining the company as Thella was using a broom alternately to sweep up broken crocks and to whack the backside of the young blood who had broken them, cheered on by an appreciative audience led by her husband. A couple of musicians were tuning up their instruments and soon the roadway was full of twirling and stamping couples, most of them more enthusiastic than expert.

We all swapped dancing partners many times. At some point Edward and Alfreth disappeared, their departure unnoticed, I suspect, by any other than ourselves, and we did not see them again that eve. Ethelmaer and I found ourselves partnered a number of times – not entirely by accident, I must confess. For a priest and a Brother of St. Benedict he danced well, and his time under the tutelage of Archbishop Dunstan had clearly not been restricted to the *scriptorium*. Dunstan's many visits to our Halls had left me in no doubt of his acumen in the dance and as this thought passed through my mind, as if by miraculous intervention, the players struck up the "Dancing Day" carol.

> *"Jesus said baptized I was;*
> *The Holy Ghost on me did glance,*
> *My Father's voice heard from above,*
> *To call my true love to my dance."*

The rhythmic verses and chorus repeated many times and when, finally, the music came to a halt, I was breathless and flushed. I pulled Ethelmaer out of the crowd.

"I think that is my signal to return to the Nunneminster Hall," I said. Wulf had disappeared, probably, I thought, back to the Great Hall with one of the likely young girls who would need escorting.

"I will walk with you. It is time I made my way back to my rooms, too, and your aunt's Hall is by the way."

We bade our farewells to Thella and Ratkin and wished them a long and happy tenure of their new home. Thella was a little tearful at the thought of my night, the first of many to come, without her ministrations upon my retiring, but I fancy that was the effect of the ale on her heightened emotions. "I love you, my Lady," she said, and turned away quickly.

Despite the warmth of the spring day, the evening was chill. I wrapped my cloak about me as we walked, and Ethelmaer pulled the cowl of his habit up around his neck, although he forbore to cover his head. In the dim of the unlit streets he could have been any other young man in a long, loose tunic and over-mantle. He put his arm around me and our pace slowed.

"We have known each other some many years now, Aetna."

"We have."

"Do you recall our adventures on the blessed Isle of Elig?"

"Of course."

"It was there that I determined that if I must live a life dedicated to the Church that it would be one unlike my father envisaged. For I cannot be mired up in buildings of cold stone and dead wood. Life, life is what our Lord wants of us. The life of the wild birds and animals and the life of the living God – which he demonstrates for us every spring as the trees burst into leaf and the hedgerows into flower. Life and love, the two strongest words in all the languages of the world."

"Love?"

We stopped walking. We had reached the long, low wall surrounding the Nunneminster. Without the need of words, we both sat. Ethelmaer took my hand onto his lap and held it in both of his.

322

"From the time we have spent together, I know that you love these things, too," he said. "But you are clever, Aetna, perhaps cleverer than you know, and you understand much of what the Greeks called *politikos*. I have seen you listen at the High Table and at Court when such matters are discussed. The doors to your Wyrd are only just opening for you, and they open onto a scene in which I wish to take no part. The Church of Rome, the fate of the Great King Alfred's legacy in Englaland, the battles both diplomatic and death-filled to come – yes, I believe both will come – I do not want them in my Wyrd. Ah, but you, you I would have wanted! If only the passing of time could be reversed, if the Synod of Whitby could be made to fall out differently, I could ask you to be my wife. Why should a priest not have the benefit of a loving help-mate, a warm bed-mate? But no, the Benedictine Rule has the sway. We are to live as celibates. I took my vows and I must keep to them, that much I will hold to, I will not forswear myself, though in my father's eyes I will disgrace myself. I shall take to the road with your father. I shall minister to those who will hear me. I shall attempt to heal those who need me. I shall build what bridges I can between those of the old faiths – those who worshipped in the Groves, amid the animals and the birds – and a loving White Christ who died upon a tree for our souls. And I shall love you, Aetna, always and with a fire at the core of my heart that none shall recognise, but many shall feel as it warms them through my words and actions. I love you, Aetna. I may never say it again, but I say it now. I love you."

He lifted my hand to his lips and pressed them to it. Then I was in his arms, warm and strong, enveloped, held. Our mouths found each other and we kissed, long and deep. When we pulled apart, our faces kept close and we breathed each other's breath. I inhaled the essential masculinity of his being and felt him absorb the elemental spirit of my womanhood. We were one, as wholly and completely as any two people could be. The instant of the present stretched to an infinity of past and future and we knew that it would never end, just as it had never begun. It simply was. And we needed no more. Whether in greeting or parting, I know not, we lent our brows together for the briefest of moments and then stood.

"I love you, too." Mayhap I would never say it again, either.

I turned and walked toward my aunt's Hall without looking back.

)))))))(((((((

In later years, it has often occurred to me that I am amazed by the – occasional – capacity of the young to maintain discretion. Perhaps it is the irresistible attraction of the illicit, which would be lost if a secret came to light or perhaps the fear that, once exposed to the view of all, a situation once imbued with the romanticism of the forbidden, would become dull when openly acknowledged. Whatever the reason, Edward and Alfreth managed to maintain the concealment of their relationship, and of their trysting place, with admirable (or perhaps reprehensible) success.

They did not abuse their good fortune at having found a way to meet and to be together. It became their habit to do so just once each week on the same day that they had married and celebrated their first se'enight at Ratkin and Thella's cott. Each Frig's Day evening, Edward would leave the King's Hall, equipped with a waxed groundsheet and his bow, bound, he said, for a solitary night spent outdoors in order that he might practice his marksmanship at the first light of dawn without making a noisy arrival and scaring his prey before he could begin the hunt. Alfreth and I had secured special permission to study the manuscripts in the Nunneminster, in order that we might translate the illuminations into embroidery patterns. We would begin our work in the late postnoon, and later, when the *scriptorium* was empty but for ourselves, she would slip away, leaving me to do a little more work, before allowing myself the enjoyment of making free with the other books – the stories of the Saints' lives, early manuscripts dating back to the days of the Celtic church and even certain esoteric titles not usually available to lay persons. They afforded me many a pleasant evening's entertainment away from my usual duties. I would return to the Dowager Queen's Hall and leave the little wicket open in the side door close to my chamber, and Alfreth would let herself in quietly in the early morning. It was not ideal and it seemed to me that sooner rather than later they were sure to be discovered, but I tried to put the probable repercussions out of my mind.

The weeks passed. Easter came. The King's health continued to give cause for concern and so it was a muted ceremony which took place on Easter Sunday, when a proxy stood in the Princess Sinnyth's stead and the betrothal was made between Edward and his supposed bride-to-be, betokening continued peace between Edgar's Empire and the so-called Kingdom of the Scots. Kennyth had sent a delegation on the long journey from the Highlands, all tough, hardened men, without a woman amongst them, and it had been hard to keep a straight face as one of these bearded oafs stood, in representation of Sinnyth, and took the prince's hand, speaking the words of the oath. They were an outlandish crew, worse than I had remembered from Caestre. Even their clothes were strange. Later, Edward laughed that at least his "bride" was wearing a skirt – for apparently their traditional garb is called a *kjalta*, meaning a long *gunna* "kilted", or pleated, to the waist.

I was not much in the mood for laughing that day. Ethelmaer was due to leave on the morrow, with our father, and I would miss them – both. I had become close to Wulfstan. Of course, I had always loved and respected our uncle, Brithnoth, for so many years the only father I had known or wanted to know. But these last few months, first with Wulfstan recovering from his injury sustained at Bedeford and later as our acquaintance became closer, finally turning into a real affection, had been wonderful. He had spoken of our mother, of their short time together on the road before ill fortune struck, and of how he felt certain that she was, in some strange way, watching over us.

On the morning of their departure, Wulf and I met with them just within the Nunneminster Gate. It was bright but chill, the sky a pale blue. Rooks wheeled overhead cawing their raucous call into the wind. We were on foot, and walked slowly through the open gate, only stopping when we were outside the city walls. Wulfstan tuned to my brother, took his hand and pulled him forward into a bear hug.

"Son," he said, as though it were a statement. "We will meet again, and so this is indeed a time to wish you fare well, but also to begin looking forward. We have many more memories to make, one with another."

"God's speed to you, Father," said Wulf. I knew he was finding this hard. He had for so long nursed the wish to meet our father that to part now...

"And my little Aetna. I thank you, with all my heart that you have allowed me back into your life. I did not – I do not – deserve it, but God has granted you a kind soul. And me the greatest gift I could ever have wished for." He held me close and I embraced him in return. As he stepped away, he took my hand and pressed something into it. "Your mother's amber brooch. I should not have taken it when I did – it should ever have been yours – but now I have no need of it, for I have a greater jewel. Your love glowing in my heart is warmer than any amber, and more precious to me than any gold."

"Oh, Father, thank you." Tears filled my eyes. "I shall wear it for you both, you and Mother."

Wulf embraced Ethelmaer and they shook hand to elbow. "Travel safe, cousin – or brother – whatever!" he said. Ethelmaer laughed – that warm laugh that I loved. He turned to me.

The moment I had dreaded was upon me. Rather more brusquely than I had intended, I handed him the embroidered *saccellus* which I had made for him. "Something to…" I began.

"… remember you by? Coz!" He hugged me and his lips brushed my hair. He whispered so that only I could hear. "I need no reminder… I carry you in my heart." And then, stepping away, he examined the bag. "This is beautiful, Aetna, I shall treasure it. Thank you."

"Be careful… until we meet again," I said.

"Until we meet again!"

The weeks continued to pass and gradually the cool spring reluctantly began to give way to an indeterminate summer, fluctuating from chilly and bright to dull and muggy, but never quite managing to combine sunshine and warmth in a single day. Crops were slow to harden off, and it looked as though harvests would be slighter than usual. The King's health remained fragile, and the news from the North was unsettling enough for him to order the Navy – once considered a wholly unnecessary expense – to be bolstered and refitted.

Life at Court seemed to echo the disappointing weather. Dunna had returned to her father's house, as her mother was ailing, travelling some of the distance with her uncle the Archbishop, who had returned to Cantuaria. In her absence, Elfwine had felt the pleasures of being in the King's retinue were second to his desire to keep abreast of his father's activities, and petitioned Edgar for permission to go home, which the King granted, with the proviso that he, Edgar, be kept informed of any events in Mercia which might not reach him through official channels. The King, blind though he was to any failings of his wife, did not extend his tolerance to those whom she counted her favourites. Intelligence received from Ealdorman Alfhere of Mercia, whose marches extended almost to the borders of the disputed regions of the North, uncomfortably close to Kennyth's influence, was not always entirely reliable. The machinations of the Chief Ealdorman's brother-in-law, Alfric, Elfwine's father, whose interaction with the Northmen was becoming common knowledge, gave cause for concern. It was well known that ever since Edgar had favoured Dunstan's plans for church reformation, supported by the Ealdormen of the east, Ethelwine and Brithnoth at the forefront, Chief Ealdorman Alfhere had had an agenda of his own, an agenda which, whenever the occasion arose, the Queen was quick to advocate. There had not been a Court Progress, nor a meeting of the Witan for months. The rumour mill had it that the King was unwilling to gather all his ealdormen under a single roof, lest the simmering antagonism of the boat trip to Caestre should erupt into full-blown hostility.

Wulf and I still took our country walks, but without or our father and Ethelmaer, or Elfwine and Dunna, they seemed flat. Edward and Alfreth, naturally, tended to take the opportunity of being in each other's company and spent most of the time tête-à-tête and so we strolled along behind them, giving them enough space that they felt intimate.

On one such walk in June, when it was warm but threatening rain, Wulf and I had been silent for some while, when he said "How long do you think this can go on?"

"Brother," I replied, with some relief, "if I am truthful, I do not know." I had been wanting to express my thoughts for some time, but had hesitated, as it seemed that giving them voice would in no way help our situation. "Mostly I am just thankful to get another day over without the whole edifice of our untruths falling about our heads."

"And yet those two," he nodded in the direction of our companions, "seem oblivious."

"They are so young."

"Would we have been so foolish, just a few years ago?"

"No, perhaps not, but then neither of us fell in love!"

"For which may the Heavens be praised!"

"You may be right," I said ruefully, my heart heavier still at the thought of my own current emotions. "It seems – as I believe Edward once said – that love affairs rarely seem to be smooth sailing. I had a letter from Dunna, just this morning, bemoaning the fact that her father is not happy with the thought of Elfwine as her prospective suitor."

"Certainly, an alliance between Archbishop Dunstan's niece and Alfric's son would be one to keep the gossip mongers happy for many a day," said Wulf. "And Wulfric could hardly baulk at his family being joined to that of the Chief Ealdorman, surely?"

"Ealdormen – even Chief Ealdormen – can be replaced," I replied. "Alfhere can no longer count on the King's support, not since throwing his weight behind the non-monastic faction in the current disturbances. And I know that Edgar resents the Queen's favour toward him. Besides, I believe it is Alfric, rather than Alfhere that Wulfric so heartily mistrusts. And with good reason."

"Sister, you are quite the *politico* these days!"

"Ah, *'I am a wondrous creature...'* " I quoted the first line used in many of the popular riddles which were the staple of amusing wordplay around the fire of an evening. This seemed to lighten the mood and our conversation turned to other things.

Later that evening, I sat with Aunt Aethelflaed and Alfreth in the *peristylium*, allowing the last of the sun's rays to afford us daylight by which to embroider before we had to light the lamps. The Dowager was working on her narrative of the late King Edmund's life, while I was creating some small frippery which I intended to give to Thella as a late wedding present. Alfreth was pouring over some designs which I had taken the opportunity of tracing from the manuscripts in the *scriptorium* library during my late-night sojourn there the previous Friday.

"These scrolling acanthus would be a splendid motif for the borders, top and bottom, of your *broderie de memoire*, Your Majesty," she said.

Aethelflaed rose and went over to the table, looking over Alfreth's shoulder. "Oh, yes, they are charming. Aetna, it is so good of you to take so much time on this. I am afraid that my design skills are not equal to those I have with the needle. Without you and Alfreth – and Dunstan, he is such a talented man – I would be quite lost."

"They could be interspersed with motifs reflecting what occurs in the main panel. Perhaps a crown, during the coronation scene, swords and shields when Lindisfarne is attacked, holy symbols when the King visits the Shrine of St. Cuthbert and so on."

"Wonderful idea!" said my aunt, resuming her seat and taking up her work once again.

A quiet scratching at the door from the kitchen was followed by the entrance of Ethel.

"There is a young – person – at the pantry wicket, wishing to speak to the Lady Aetna," she announced.

"Who could it be at this time of day?" I said, for it was well progressed into the hour before it was customary to sit down to the evening repast.

"She would not give *me* her name," the emphasis and disapproving tone could not be missed. "But she said that it was a matter of which you would wish to hear."

Aethelflaed lifted an eyebrow, her curiosity piqued Alfreth studiously continued her perusal of the patterns. Like me, I suspected, she was anxious not to appear unduly disturbed.

"Very well," I said. "I will be there in just a moment. I will just finish this length of silk." Would that I had a fourthing for every time I had uttered those words! What embroideress likes to leave her work with the needle still threaded? I completed the motif I was stitching. Experience meant that at its conclusion the silk, too, was fully used up. Very little was ever wasted. Silk was far too expensive and precious a commodity for profligacy. Ethel retreated back to the kitchen.

Putting the work to one side, I stood up, smoothed down my gunna and tried to look as though my heart was not beating far more quickly than my show of serenity suggested. I felt sure that our intrigue was discovered. Who had uncovered it? And what did they want from me? Perhaps it was blackmail of some sort. At least the truth was not yet common knowledge; I would surely have heard if Wulf had been apprehended, or, indeed, Edward brought to book by his father... my mind was in a turmoil.

"I am sure I will not be long, Aunt," I said.

I entered the kitchen to find only Ethel busying herself at the range and the other kitchen thralls about their usual duties. I looked at Ethel, and she gestured toward the pantry door, closed, as usual, and I went in, shutting it behind me. The pantry had its own outside door – a small wicket, really – so that foodstuffs could be brought in and deposited without opening the door to the kitchen, thus not allowing its warmth, in the winter, to reach the supplies which needed to be kept cool. In summer it allowed for the air to circulate and so not overheat the contents, a screen of cheesecloth across the wicket to keep out the flies. It was not a part of the Hall which any other than the kitchen thralls usually had cause to visit. A shadow was cast onto the cheesecloth and I went out into the late evening sunlight, to find...

"Lucet! Whatever are you doing here? I am sure the King's bottler does not expect his thralls to be out from under his eye at this time of the day."

"No, Lady, but I made excuse. It is not hard to come and go if you are... resourceful."

"Indeed!" I said.

Lucet was as prettily turned out as ever. She had somehow managed to run a blue ribbon – really just a very thin strip of old fabric – through the neckline of her rough gunna, pulling it slightly so that it created a loose gathering effect, drawing the eye to her smooth, white throat. Another frayed ribbon held her hair off her face, though a few fair strands curled down, and lay along her neck. At her slim waist, a plaited straw belt (now, that was clever) cinched the material in to emphasise her figure. A mottled white and black pebble was enmeshed in string and stitched to her breast in imitation of a brooch. Out of nothing she had created much.

"Lady, there is something that I have heard that I think you should be aware of. It is well known that you love the King, and that he favours you – and your brother – above many in higher places than yours. I knew not what to do with this... this thing I have heard. Who to tell? I do not want to put you in danger, Lady, but I could not stand by and..."

It seemed, at the very least, that whatever had brought Lucet to the Nunneminster Hall, it was not with a view to causing me – us – harm. I breathed a little easier. I glanced involuntarily at the door toward the kitchen. It was unlikely that we could be overheard but I was not prepared to take any chances. I began to walk in the direction of the orchard and Lucet fell into step a fraction behind me. As we reached the low wall separating the orchard from the herb garden, I turned and faced her.

"Very well, Lucet, speak on."

Now that the moment had come, it seemed Lucet was not sure where or how to begin.

"Lady Aetna..."

"Come along, it cannot be that hard to say."

"Yester-eve, Lady, I was at the King's Worth. With... friends. I had cause to be there, Lady, for I had been sent by the second bottler during the postnoon hours to collect offal from the day's hunt, but I had not made haste to return. I have many... friends... there and they pressed me to stay longer. I did not think I would be missed in the kitchen, for the hour would be late by the time I returned even if I started back straight away, and I can always... well, be that as it may, I stayed on."

"Your extramural escapades are fascinating, Lucet, but get to the point."

"Well, we… made merry… longer than I realised and I did not want to walk back in the dead of night – there was no moon – so I took my ease beside the spit-grate where there was still some warmth from the embers. It may be near mid-summer, but there is still chill so late. I awoke with the dawn ready to make the walk home – home! Ha! – and had gone to the pantry to collect the offal from where I had left it the day before. I left the door ajar – I know, I should have shut it, but I was going to be hardly a moment and there was neither heat nor cold enough in the kitchen to affect the larder-wares. Also, I wanted to be away as quickly as possible, for even I would find it hard to explain why I was at the King's Worth at that time of the morning! I had shouldered my burden – and heavy it was, too – when I heard someone enter the kitchen and voices stopped in my tracks.

"A man's voice. I knew it quite well, it was Erdgor, the vermin catcher. He spends most of his time in and around the Worth, what with the rats in the mews and not being able to have cats there because they distress the birds. Hearing him was no surprise, but it was the second voice."

"Well?"

"It was Morwen, the Queen's… woman. I know her voice well enough, too, for there is hardly a day when she is not strutting into the Great Hall's kitchens with some complaint or other from her mistress, or some outlandish new demand for the High Table. But to hear her at the Worth, and with the sun barely chased up from the Underworld… my curiosity alone would have kept me listening, although I dared not try to leave for fear of being heard and discovered. She had no cause to suspect being overheard, but even so, she spoke low.

"'I care not, man, what excuse you make for needing to use the ovens – again – but the recipe must be made stronger. And the loaves must look as white as the rest of the bread on the High Table. It is well that the formula calls for wheaten flour or it would never pass unnoticed. If your usual *mus-brod* calls for one ounce, make it three. I imagine there is no lack of aconitum in your store – it was plentiful this year, was it not? It will be but the work of a few hours.'

"Erdgor sounded unhappy. 'Every time I do this, I am putting my life in danger, woman!' he said. And Morwen replied, 'Keep a civil tongue. If you do not do it your wife and your brats are in danger. Take your choice. I want it done by the morrow: bring it the usual way. There will someone waiting. And make sure that the madder-dyed cheesecloth has a strong enough colour. It must not get confused with the other loaves. Your normal formula is for a long-term solution – this will kill outright. It is meant for only one recipient.'

"Then it seemed as though Erdgor had a sudden surge of defiance. 'You are very sure that I will not seek out the King's men and betray you – and her. They would protect my family.' She laughed that croak of hers. 'Do you believe so? Try it. Your family will be dead before the next office. And you will disappear. Your death will not be so quick.'"

"His defiance collapsed, I could almost hear it deflate. 'So be it,' he said. The kitchen door opened and closed and they were gone. I went out by the pantry door and skirted the building, only stepping into the open when I saw Morwen's figure, on her palfrey, disappear into the trees on either side of the roadway. Erdgor was nowhere to be seen. I gave Morwen several minutes start, allowing her to get well ahead of me, and then started back to Wintancaestre. I was returned by the time the Court was breaking its fast. I could hardly bear to look at the bread. My mind has been in turmoil ever since."

I did not know what to say. Whatever I had expected to hear, it was certainly nothing like this. My own thoughts had been in such chaos since learning of Edward and Alfreth's relationship that my watching brief from Aethelflaed had been almost completely forgotten. I cursed myself for my negligence. Both Wulf and I had lost sight of our most sacred obligation – to the King.

To give myself time to think, I said "And you believe…?"

"Lady, I would not be here if I did not think that you would know what I believe."

"You are sure that there is no innocent explanation? Some old grandsire rat that is plaguing the kitchens of the Court? There are such cunning beasts, I hear…"

"I thought not to have to strive so hard to engage your attention, Lady Aetna! But no, there is no such creature. Nor likely to be for we have cats with the skill of Tibbert himself… I should know, for one of my duties is to tend to them: the regular offal collection is not meant for the dainties of the High Table, I can assure you. But Mistress Tabby and her cohorts thrive on it. We have no rat problem at the King's Court, nor no mouse problem, either. And no call for *mus-brod*."

Despite the urgency of the moment, my mind went back to old Musbane, lazing on our pallet at Radendunam all those years ago. Thoth had never allowed the baking of *mus-brod*, for he said it was a danger to more than the rodents. It looked (and apparently tasted) just like the finest white bread – made with wheat meal – dogs, chickens, ducks, even deer would eat it without hesitation. They almost always died. The lesser members of Musbane's fraternity, those who worked for their keep, kept the Hall and all the outbuildings free from vermin without recourse to poison. And so they did here, according to Lucet – but at the King's Worth there were no cats because of the falcons and hawks. *Mus-brod* would be the vermin catchers only recourse. My mind thoughts returned to the present.

"I had to be sure, Lucet."

"You may be, Lady. I shall speak plainly if it is what you need to hear. The King's ill health, his weakness, his lack of life-force: they all bear witness to some sort of corruption in his food. With these outlandish dishes the Queen has been introducing to the table, the whole attention of the Court is upon the taster's reactions to them – I do not believe he ever tastes the bread at all. And in any case, he is the Queen's creature, should he take a mouthful, he would know to vomit it up presently... at a low dose, a single bite would cause no more than a sore belly. But eaten every day it makes for great pain – and a heavy dose, such as three times more than in the normal receipt... I have seen ship's rats die of it. They puke out their entrails as a green slime at a fraction of the strength. It is a vile death."

Even without Lucet's colourful description of mortality, I did not need any further persuading. The horror of what had been happening before our eyes – while our attention had been so readily distracted by other considerations – hit me with the full force of delayed realisation.

"Oh, dear God, Lucet, I must go to the Dowager Queen at once with this intelligence. She will surely... and you must return before you are missed. You are a brave and good girl." Good? I was perhaps not sure that was quite the apposite word. "I have no coin about me at present, but keep your eyes and ears open, your mouth shut – yes, I know that you are well versed, already, in those skills – and you will be rewarded."

"Lady, I do not wish for money."

"Do you not?"

"It is common knowledge that you no longer have the services of a personal servant – a companion – I would that you might think of me for that role. You are about to say that we have no time to speak of it now, and you are right. I must be away, and you must... But, Lady, ponder on it. I will return, or send word, if there is aught further to tell. I will try to discover where this *mus-brod* is to be kept – I shall watch for loaves wrapped in madder cheesecloth, they will not be hard to spot. But who else would think anything other than some ill-dyed fabric is being put to a useful purpose? It is a resourceful plot."

Before I could speak again, she was gone. I really did not know what to make of her. Pert, with a manner above her station, but with a shield-maiden's way about her that made it of no matter. How came she to be wearing a thrall's collar? I had no time, though, to think on the matter. I had to speak with my aunt.

I retraced my steps, back through the pantry and kitchen to the *peristylium*, where I found Aethelflaed packing away her needlework in anticipation of the evening meal. "Oh, Aetna, I have not touched your work, for fear of misplacing the silk shades, but come, we must clear the table ready to dine... but, merciful Lord, what is wrong? You are as white as a winding sheet!"

"Where is Alfreth? This is for your ears only, Aunt." Alfreth had enough secrets of her own to keep at present.

"She will return shortly. She has taken the drawings to her own chambers. She wishes to peruse them further later."

"Then pray, Aunt, walk with me in the herb garden for a moment, we may claim a few minutes of fresh air before the night falls fully."

"Very well, I will fetch my shawl..."

"Here, take mine, no I do not need it, but come... quickly!"

"Aetna, you are beginning to frighten me. What on earth..." I took her by the hand and forgetting her station, and mine, in my anxiety pulled her to the main door and out into the evening twilight. I made sure that the door was close behind us and propelled my aunt toward the herb-beds.

"Aunt, the King is in danger!" I told her what Lucet had imparted, probably falling over my words and repeating myself in my haste to explain. Her eyes widened as my words tumbled out and she covered her mouth with her hands. Finally, I came to a halt. "What shall we do?" I said.

Even Aethelflaed seemed momentarily at a loss. Then she took a deep breath. "Praise be, we have this night, at least, before the danger becomes imminent, but we do not know at what meal on the morrow they plan to use this filthy poison. Oh, Edgar, my lovely boy! Yes, I know he is a man grown, and the King, but to me he is still that motherless child I came to love. I doubt that witch, Elfrith, and her minion will have entrusted their plan to many – save this traitor, Erdgor – but we must not assume that there are no spies in our own household. All must appear normal while we decide how to proceed, or they may anticipate us and move before we are ready to thwart them. We must return to the table. Send one of the thralls to Thella and have her commanded to come here immediately, with Ratkin. There is nothing untoward in that: it is quite usual that we might have need of either or both of them. Have them told to wait in the kitchen. We shall eat our meal and then see them at our apparent leisure. I shall send Alfreth over to the Nunneminster on some pretext – she is a loyal girl, but likely not able to dissemble well enough to be privy to these things. An incautious word could spell disaster."

I felt a pang of guilt at this last comment. Not able to dissemble? The girl was a mistress of the art, albeit for love rather than ill-will. "Very well, Aunt."

Dinner seemed interminable. I asked Ethel to dispatch one of the kitchen children to summon Thella and Ratkin and Aethelflaed told

Alfreth that she wished her to go to the Nuns' *scriptorium* and beg the favour of some very fine, thinly scraped, fresh vellum.

"I am sure we have plenty, Your Majesty, if you are thinking you need it for the transferring. I saw the stock this day, in the smaller chest."

"I desire the very finest, translucent skins for the tracings," replied my aunt. The designs are most complex. Or do you think that you already know better than I how these things should be done?" the Dowager said, sharply.

"No, madam, of course not. I am sorry, I did not mean..."

"It is well, Alfreth, I am sorry, too. I think mayhap I have stitched a little too long this day. I have given myself quite the headache and my temper is ill accordingly. Take your time and your ease. I believe that Sister Annyth has some new wine ready for tasting. Allow yourself the pleasure of giving her your opinion on it. Tell her that if you like it my household will have a dozen bottles to put down for the Christ's Mass this year."

When we had finally eaten our meal (I hardly knew what I was eating) and Alfreth was sent on her way to the Nunneminster, Aethelflaed bade Edith send Thella and Ratkin in to us. They had both enjoyed a cup of mead in the kitchen and were in good spirits. Their happy equilibrium was not destined to last long. Aethelflaed told them the gist of Lucet's intelligence, looking to me to make sure that she had it correctly.

"And Erdgor is to send this tainted bread, this *mus-brod*, to the Great Hall in the morning?" said Thella. "I remember him. A weak, *weosuling* of a man. Always whining about how ill the world treats him. No doubt he is taking coin from that bitch, as well as being threatened by her." I was not sure whether she was referring to Morwen or the Queen, but either was aptly described.

"We must intercept it, replace it with fair loaves and do so without anyone being the wiser," said Aethelflaed. "It is too soon to try and persuade the King of Elfrith's treachery, he will not believe it of her. She will deny all knowledge. Even if the bread is tested and found poisoned, she will simply allow others to take the blame. Then it will be harder to discover her at a later attempt. We must be sure that she does not know of our involvement."

"Then how...?" I asked.

"I have been thinking on this all the time we ate. I think we have no option but to further include Lucet."

Thella favoured us with one of her disparaging snorts. "That little..."

"She has been nought but true thus far!" I said. Thella sniffed but remained otherwise silent.

"Ratkin," continued my aunt, "I fear you must once again appear to compromise your wife's trust. None of us – you included – would seem to have any legitimate excuse to be in personal contact with one of the Great Hall's kitchen thralls. For any of us to do so would be out of the ordinary, and that we must avoid. You, however, might well indulge in a little dalliance with a pretty maid."

"Maid! Ha!" Thella's silence was short lived.

"But I am newly-wed," Ratkin objected.

"To my knowledge, that has never been an obstacle to a little flirting, if a man has a mind to," replied Aethelflaed. "Somehow, you must take her to one side and tell her what we want her to do."

"And what is that?"

"She must discover the whereabouts of these loaves of *mus-brod* and replace them with fair loaves. I will give you the bread from our own pantry – they are baked in the great ovens at the King's kitchen and look identical to those for the High Table. The tainted bread must be smuggled back here... it must be kept as evidence of what was planned. Ratkin, you must go to the Great Hall now, on some pretence or other, and seek out Lucet. Give her the bread. I will leave the details of the deception to you. Find some place to lay low overnight and watch for Erdgor at dawn, but do not challenge him. Lucet must keep her own watch, too, and see who else, if anyone, is involved. We can only pray that the *mus-brod* is left unattended at some point, so that the swap can be made."

"And I am then to carry the poisoned bread back here?" said Ratkin, dubiously. It seemed a fairly simple plan, if not immune to mishap.

"The only persons who will know that the treachery has failed (apart from us) will be those involved. It may well push them into showing their hand sooner rather than later. And we will then have proof of the plot – for at this stage all we have is the word of a thrall, against that of a queen – hardly of equal probity in the eyes of many."

"Does Alfreth know of this?" asked Thella.

"No, why?" My aunt looked at her sharply.

"Oh, no reason, Your Majesty, I simply wanted to know who was privy and who not. I would not speak out of turn."

"Nobody who does not need to know must be put in danger. Enough, now. Time is short. I will to the kitchen for the loaves. I shall tell Edith that it is for some poor soul in the town who is too ill to... something. She will be askance that I send the best white bread, but that is as may be..." She swept out of the room.

"My love," Ratkin took Thella's hand, "You know that you have naught to fear in this. I love you with all my heart and would never look at another..."

"I know, I know," Thella replied. "But I hate to be made to look the fool. It is not fair that I, and only I, have my..."

"What of my reputation?" re-joined Ratkin. "I am made to look the *lustling* in all this. Not married a month and already…"

"Oh, men can always rise above these things. You will simply be the scamp that is winked at by those who wished they were brash enough to do the same!"

"Oh, come, you two," I said, "remember it is all play-acting. We will be sure to rebuild Ratkin's honour – and yours, Thella – when all is done." Thella could hardly be said to be happy with this resolution, but there was no chance for further discussion. Aethelflaed returned with a cheesecloth bag – undyed cheesecloth – containing four loaves.

"I doubt you will find there are more than this," she said. "They would be too bulky to manhandle without comment, but if there are, simply leave these four and we shall have to hope that comment is not passed." Ratkin kissed Thella, which she accepted with somewhat bad grace, and made a short bow to me and my aunt. "Majesty, Lady, pray that I may do this thing without mishap – for all our sakes." And he was gone.

)))))))(((((((

We spent a sleepless night. Alfreth returned just before the bells sounded for the night office of Nocturn, and was told that Aethelflaed's headache had worsened, necessitating our sending for Thella, who would stay with her during the night. Alfreth offered to sit with her but was sent to her chamber on the pretence that it was thought that there might be some elf-shot loosed in the house. Better to be safely in her own bed for the night. By morning, doubtless the imps and their arrows would be gone. When the Hall was dark and quiet, I slipped from my chamber into my aunt's, where she and Thella sat in the semi light thrown by a shaded candle.

"We will not be heard if we speak low," said Thella. "Alfreth sleeps like she is awaiting the Second Coming." In the early days of Alfreth's arrival in the Dowager Queen's Hall, she and Thella shared a pallet on occasion.

We marked the passing of the hours by the bells of the Nunneminster, imagining the Sisters raised from their hard pallets to shuffle into prayer at the chapel, returning only to be raised again for the next office. It grew light early, as ever in June, and the morning song of the birds was raised in welcome to the new day. We wished that we were able to greet it so joyously. We imagined that, perhaps at that very moment, Ratkin was watching the covert arrival of Erdgor with the poisoned loaves, or Lucet was spying on some conspirator as they spirited them away to an ingenious hiding place. We had no way of knowing. It was not until later that day Ratkin told us what transpired and, later still, I learned from Lucet of the events in which she took part and witnessed.

As he made his way through the dark, almost deserted streets of Wintancaestre, Ratkin had pondered how to begin the enterprise. His first thought was to find Wulf, but he realised that to do so, and possibly rouse others at the same time, would simply pique the interest of the curious. He felt his best course was to go straight to the King's kitchens and, perhaps feigning a little drunkenness and citing a fictitious argument with Thella, seek out Lucet. He ducked down a side street – the same one which Wulf had attempted to navigate when he first returned to Court after the Christ's Mass – and made his approach from the rear, skirting the Hall itself and arriving at the side doors to the kitchen and pantry. He hesitated, wishing that he had had the foresight to take some little drink, both to steady him and lend some authenticity to his performance. A shadow detached itself from the doorpost of the pantry.

"Ratkin!" the voice was low, an urgent whisper.

"Yes? Lucet?"

"Come in here." The pantry door opened and she pulled him inside, shutting it behind them. It was almost pitch black, but for a dim line of light beneath the door leading into the kitchen proper, and an even dimmer line beneath the just-closed outside door, emanating from the few torches and glowing, candle-lit windows still in evidence as the townsfolk settled in for the night. "They have told you of what I heard?"

"They have. And the Dowager has a plan – of sorts – though I fear it seems to be up to you and me to carry it out. Or this night's part of it, in any event." Ratkin told her of Aethelflaed's wishes, still unsure of how they might be achieved.

"I think we can accommodate Her Majesty in that," said Lucet. "Listen. One of my duties is, on occasion, to take delivery of the bread supply at dawn. Several of us take it in turn. I have told Cillith – it was to be her task on the morrow – that I will do it. I had a notion that there might be games afoot! I made the excuse that I needed a reason to be out and about early as I would be returning from a tryst with a... friend. The lazy sow will not make it a swap of it, either, she will expect still to lie abed when it is my next turn, too. But that is of no matter. The bread arrives from the King's Worth, together with the hung game from the Lodge. There are two wagons, one for the loaves, the other the meat. They are unloaded into the pantry. Then whoever is on duty brings the bread for breaking the night's fast into the kitchen and places it ready for the bottler to inspect before it is taken to the tables in the Great Hall. The white bread for the High Table is set apart. Somehow, they have been swapping this filthy *mus-brod* for the loaves destined for the King only – I cannot fathom how they achieve that. We will remain watching after I have taken delivery, I know where we may hide. All being well, I will then replace the *mus-brod* with the Dowager's fair loaves and you will take the poisoned bread."

"I fear there are too many unknowns in this enterprise," said Ratkin. "But there is no other way, at least that I can see. Where can I lay low?"

"We have about four hours until it begins to get light," said Lucet. She glanced toward the kitchen. All was quiet, and the light showing beneath the door was extinguished. "We might as well take our comfort. And I will show you where you can hide." She put the bar across the outer door, and then cautiously opened the one into the kitchens. "It is as well to be careful," she whispered. In summer none officially sleep by the fire here, but there may be someone making free with the rules – like me!" She smiled, impishly. Fortunately, all was deserted, the fire burned down to glowing ashes, and they breathed a little freer.

"I think we deserve a little stiffener," Lucet opened a low chest and brought forth an earthenware jar, stoppered with a waxed cloth. She pulled out the wad and took a swig, handing the jar to Ratkin. "The bottler can spare a mouthful, I think." It was a strong, almost viscous, wine and Ratkin thought that more than a couple of mouthfuls would threaten their whole plan, such as it was, with disaster. Lucet took one more swallow, restored the cloth stopper and replaced the jar in the chest. "Now," she said, "this is where you will be while I take delivery... and where I will join you to await what happens next!"

A neat stack of wood was piled against the wall furthest from the fire – to lessen the obvious risk of conflagration. A little to one side of it an assortment of various cleaning implements was leaning against the same wall: brooms, long handled mops, and various other devices, the purposes of which Ratkin could not fathom. It had been many years since he had spent any appreciable time in a kitchen, certainly not on the business end of a brush. However, if he crouched low close between them and the wood-pile he could not be seen from either the pantry or main door and was shadowed from the long table. To complete his camouflage, Lucet threw a large square of sacking over him.

"There," she said, "Just stay still and quiet and you will not be noticed. People do not see what they are not looking for."

Ratkin was dubious. He levered himself into the space. "Cannot I just wait outside until the delivery is made and the swap effected?" he said.

"No, you cannot, *lufestre*!" Lucet laughed at his discomfort. "If something goes wrong, I want you right in here with me to come to my rescue, like the heroic champion you are!" She squeezed in beside him.

"See, there would even be room for me, too! Surely you are not afraid of us being... close." Teasingly, she lowered her chin and looked up at him from under her eyelashes, a slight pout on her pretty lips.

"Now, Lucet..."

"Pah! Do not fear, carrot-top, I jest… you are an old married man!"

"Not that old, I am but eighteen years – or thereabouts."

"Still too old for me!"

They emerged and sat on the bench alongside the huge, heavy table to await the dawn. Lucet's feet did not quite reach the floor and she swung her legs, suddenly like a little girl. Perhaps she was indeed too young for him – not that he was interested, he reminded himself; she was a strange one, Ratkin thought. Mention of his age, of which he was not altogether sure, led to conversation of sorts. Lucet seemed ill disposed toward telling much of her own history but was curious about his. Before long he realised that he had told her all he knew of his antecedence, of Ethelwold's kindness and of the ealdorman's death – of why he hated Elfrith and what he suspected she had done.

"I think I have said too much…"

"No, Ratkin, you speak from the heart. You loved and had that which you loved taken from you – of course you will hate the person who did that to you. I have no love for the Queen, either, but it is that bitch, Morwen that I really despise. She treats the thralls as though they were her own personal chattels. Bad enough to have to wear this thing," she fingered her collar, "in the service of anyone, even someone you respect, as did you, but a nobody like her…"

A sallow dawn was beginning to show at the edges of the shutters. "Time to make ready, I think," said Lucet. "Into your set, *beadlorbrocc*." She chivvied him into the space between the wood stack and the broom store and threw the sacking sheet over him. "Now you must be still."

"Wait," said Ratkin. "What if something is awry, should we not have a sign?"

Lucet thought for a moment. "If I say the word 'carrot', come to my rescue!" Ratkin was unsure whether she was serious or not but had no time to enquire. There was a muffled sound of horses' hooves and the clatter of wheels beyond the pantry. "The mumming begins!" whispered Lucet.

She opened the door into the pantry, just as a sharp knock sounded. Ratkin heard the bar being lifted and Lucet's voice. "Alright, alright, I come! Judas and all sinners, keep your patience, my head is banging already!"

A man's voice. "Oh, it is you, where is Cillith. Is it not her day to be awake?"

"She is still abed – and I am yet to get to mine, so be about your business. Bring that bread in, so I may get a nonce of shuteye before I am roused again. Hurry up!"

"Watch your mouth, you little slut – I'll warrant you have been in some bed this night, even if you got no sleep in it. Mind your manners with

God-fearing folk or I'll be speaking to the bottler. There's the rough bread, now, and I'll be fetching the white. Erdgor! Erdgor, get that game in here and let's be away."

There was the mumble of another male voice, and the thump of a heavy, soft object hitting the floor. "I had best hang this up, the meat will stay fairer that way," the second voice said. "Girl, get me a hook and chain." The baker made some comment about putting the wheaten bread by the other loaves and said he would be off now. Lucet came into the kitchen, rummaged about for a chain and took it back to the pantry without a word.

There was a cry of profanity. "What the…? Don't creep up like that, you little… give me that!" There was some clanking of links and a grunt as Erdgor hoisted the game – whatever it was – onto the appropriate hook.

"Right, that's me done!" And then a pause. The tone of his voice changed. "Unless you would like to earn a fourthing, of course…"

"Ha, I'd be wanting a good deal more than a fourthing to pleasure you, you weasel-faced maggot!"

"Whore!" The door slammed.

Silence until they were sure that both wagons had gone. Ratkin stretched painfully as he emerged from the restricted space. "Well, that was fun!" Lucet almost skipped into the kitchen. Then she led the way back into the pantry. The bread delivery was piled beside door, the rough brown bread in sacks, the wheaten in bundles of three, each in a cheesecloth covering.

"Here is the madder-dyed bundle," she said, indicating the packet. "That *cunte* must have swapped this for some of the other white bread while I was fetching the chain, that's why he jumped like a jack'nape when I walked back in on him. It is a clever ruse…" She opened the wrappings. The bread within looked perfectly normal: three white loaves, expertly kneaded and shaped, well baked and golden. They looked just as Ratkin remembered the loaves he had brought from the Nunneminster Hall.

It took several journeys to and from the pantry to ferry all the bread into the larger room. Lucet set it on the table, brown to the left, white to the right. The fair breads were still bundled in their trios, the rough loaves simply heaped up together. "Quickly, we may be taking too long," said Lucet, "someone could have been listening for the wagons and already be on their way. This is how it is left, and now that I think on it, there *is* often a differently coloured cloth – but I thought nothing of it, no doubt as all were intended not to!"

We must do the swap now."

But then… before she could retrieve the replacement loaves from beneath the table, there was a sound of footsteps from the Hall and Ratkin bolted for his hiding place. It was too late for Lucet to follow, as the door swung open before she could do so. She simply threw the sackcloth over him. Morwen entered.

"What are you doing here?"

"Mistress, the delivery was a little late, I have only this moment set out the breads. But see, all is as it should be now. Brown trenchers here… and the white loaves…"

"I have eyes in my head, girl, I see them. Be off with you now."

"Mistress, I…" There was a sharp smack as Morwen slapped Lucet around the head. "Do not speak back to me, girl. Go!"

Lucet had little option but to leave. The kitchen's main outer door to the yard was still barred, so she exited through the pantry, making a show of rattling the outside door closed behind her, that Morwen might feel at ease and alone. In his hiding place, Ratkin hardly breathed for fear of making some slight movement. He prayed that the dim light afforded by the encroaching dawn would not penetrate to his corner. He could not see what was happening, but he heard the unmistakeable scratchy squeak of a basket being filled, and the sound of the loaves being shuffled about on the table. Then footsteps toward the door into the Hall, a pause as if Morwen looked back to see all was in order, and the door opening and closing. Silence once again.

He waited several minutes before throwing off the sackcloth and standing up. On the table, the bread looked unaltered, save there was one pack less – the madder-dyed cheesecloth-wrapped loaves were gone. Another rattle announced the return of Lucet. There was a red welt across her cheek and temple. "So… it is as I thought!"

"Which is?" Ratkin was shaken by their narrow escape.

"Of late, the King has been breaking his fast in his chamber. The Queen has been taking it to him herself, and as we now know, direct from the hands of Morwen. That is how they have been feeding him – and only him – the poison. A little at a time. But if he takes any amount today… Ratkin, we must stop him!"

Now, Ratkin realised, was the time to involve Wulf. The dawn was well advanced and as his companion-man there would be nothing unusual in his attending upon his Lord at this hour. Wulf must then rouse Edward and tell him of the plot. Edward would need to think of a way to stop his father eating the tainted bread. They might yet forestall the whole plan without revealing their hand. He retrieved the untainted bread from under the table, breathing a prayer of thanks that Morwen had not noticed it.

"Lucet, you have done all you could, and that full well! But now stay here out of trouble and wait. Say nothing, whatever you hear. The Lady Aetna will make sure that you come to no ill through all this. I must go to her brother and he to the prince and… well, let us hope we are in time."

He could not resist giving her a quick hug. "Be careful." Before he knew it, she planted a swift kiss on his cheek.

"And you, *lufestre*!" Ratkin was about to remonstrate, but what was the point? He grinned, despite himself and she let him out into the main Hall, heading for the stairs to the upper chambers. Stepping as silently as he could, for fear Morwen might still be abroad, he ascended and made his way along the walkway to Wulf's chamber, beside the prince's. He scratched at the door and entered.

"Wulf, wake up. Wulf! Lord!" he whispered, shaking the sleeping form none too gently, and Wulf muttered drowsily.

"Great Gods, Ratkin, what is afoot? Why are you not at home with your wife? I thought we had done with the days when you stumbled into my chamber drunk or hungover!"

"Lord, I am neither, for pity's sake, wake up! As to what's afoot, it is treason and possibly murder if you do not!"

"What?"

"Here." Ratkin poured an earthenware tumbler full of small ale from a jug beside the pallet. "Drink this and I will tell you all." He swigged some himself straight from the jug, enough that even the weak brew gave him a much-needed steadying. Trying to keep the events straight, including those he had not witnessed personally, he told Wulf of everything that had happened since Lucet's visit to Aetna early the previous evening.

"So now it is your turn, Lord," he concluded. "Go to Prince Edward. Tell him as much or as little as you think fit, but he *must* stop the King from eating that bread. If he can find means to swap it, all the better, I still have the fair loaves here, but if not..."

Wulf was already on his feet and throwing on clothes. "Thank the Heavens that yester-eve was not a Friday, or Edward would not have been here... What can I say to him? I think, I think I must tell him all." He was speaking more to himself than to Ratkin. "But if I do... I know not how this will end!" He grabbed the bag of bread from the floor where Ratkin had dropped it and went to the internal door which led straight into Edward's chamber. He turned back to Ratkin and threw the bread back to him. "No, you keep this. Keep watching and listening. I cannot say how this will fall out, but if you get a chance, if the food is left unattended at any time, swap the bread over. Otherwise we will have to tell the King some version of the truth... Your Highness, Edward! Eddy, wake up!"

Ratkin watched from the doorway, keeping within Wulf's chamber.

Edward rolled over and grunted, then, sensing Wulf's urgency, sat up. "What's amiss? Is it Alfreth? Is she in danger?"

"No, my Prince, but your father is... but keep your voice low." Wulf gave an admirably succinct account of the situation.

"But we must tell him. Immediately!"

"No, think, your Highness. If we tell him all, then we must implicate the Queen. He will not want to believe it of her – and we have no proof of her complicity, only the implication overheard by a kitchen thrall. Elfrith will deny it and the King will believe her. She will sacrifice Morwen on the altar of her own survival, mark my words. She will say that the bread came to her from Morwen and she knew nothing of its poison; that Morwen acted out of some… well, that matters not. And say what you will of Morwen she would be loyal to the Queen, loyal unto the death."

"Then what are we to do?" Edward was on his feet, casting about for his clothes.

"At what hour does your father usually break his fast?"

"Around the time of the second bell after the Prime. These last few weeks, Elfrith has been taking his food to him in his chamber, and he eats abed. It is one of the reasons I know he is unwell – he would never allow himself such negligence if he was himself."

"We have some short time, then," said Wulf. "We must think of a way to get him – and Elfrith – out of the King's chamber long enough for Ratkin to slip in and replace the tainted loaves with fair ones."

"… which he just happens to have about his person?" said Edward, with a hint of impatience. Wulf had not mentioned this detail.

"As it turns out, yes… Ratkin! Get in here!"

"But what can I – can we – say to achieve it? I suppose I could feign illness; my father would come running, but Elfrith? No, I have it! Ratkin, say you that Lucet is still in the kitchens?"

"She was but a short while ago. I told her to stay put and…"

"Go and fetch her."

"Your Highness?" Ratkin looked aghast, and Wulf no less so.

"Edward, what are you thinking?"

"Just do it!"

Trying to be as silent as he had been in his ascent, Ratkin retraced his steps to the kitchens. Lucet was alone, curled up by the newly refuelled fire, which was beginning to warm the room a little, for the dawn chill till clung to it. "Lucet! Come with me!"

If she had been sleeping, she was fully awake in but an instant, her wits ready about her. "Why, Lord Rat, can you not stay away from me? Your wife will be sorry to hear it!"

"There's no time for all that now, just come along. The prince has some plan in his head and he sent me to fetch you… though what for I cannot think." He grabbed her by the hand, hauled her to her feet and toward the Hall door, just as it opened to admit the under-bottler and Cillith, her mouth wide with a mammoth yawn as she tucked her unruly, and seemingly unbrushed, hair beneath her kerchief. They almost barrelled into each other.

"Lucet!" cried Cillith. "What...? Oh, Master Ratkin, it did not take you long to revert to your old ways, did it? Now I wonder if Mistress Thella..."

"Hold your tongue," spat Ratkin, and pushed roughly past her, pulling Lucet behind him, "and mind your business. You, too, if you know what's good for you!" He glared at the under-bottler as he shouldered him out of the way. The door swung closed behind them. It took but moments to race up the stairs, though silence was sacrificed for speed. Wulf was keeping watch from the door to Edward's chamber.

"I am sorry, Lord, but the Hall is beginning to stir! We were seen," panted Ratkin.

"It matters not, all we need is a momentary diversion... by the time anyone can say anything all will be well, or else all lost! Quickly, to the Aetheling. Morwen has already taken the King's repast to Elfrith – she will be going to his chamber with it at any moment.

Lucet was gazing about her. Kitchen thralls were expressly forbidden the upper chambers of the Hall, let alone the royal apartments. Edward was back in bed. He threw back the blankets. "Lucet, will you trust me?" he whispered.

"Sire?"

"I need you to play-act. You will be rewarded, but now you may be in a little – trouble, shall we say? But do not fear, you will come to no harm, I shall see to that. So... will you trust me?"

Lucet's customary pert little grin surfaced. "That I will, sire! What do you want me to do?"

"Hop in, and just follow my lead. Feel free to improvise, if you like, we want to make as big a fuss as we can! I want the whole if the Court in here, if necessary! We are about to create a scandal!"

"Then, sire, if I may say so, you are overdressed!" Edward had thrown on his tunic and hose when he rose. "At the least you must bear your chest!" So saying, she stripped off her rough gunna, revealing a flimsy shift beneath, and dived under the blankets. Edward pulled his tunic off over his head, and pulled the pallet cover up above their waists.

"Now, quieter still! We need to time this just right. Listen for the Queen's footsteps along the walkway. Ratkin, stand ready with that bread – that's it, behind the door. Wulf, put on your best face of disapproval. Lucet, you do not look to me like a girl who would give away her charms for nothing, even to a prince!"

"That I am not, sire!"

"Then prepare to be full of righteous – or not-so-righteous – anger!"

The stillness that followed these imprecations dragged out, minute upon minute, until they began to wonder if their notion of the Queen's intentions was mistaken. At last, growing louder as they approached and softer as they passed, footsteps could be heard along the wooden floor of the walkway. A rap upon what must, surely, have been the King's door, was followed by indistinct voices. They paused for just a moment longer. Then...

Edward raised his voice, in a bellow of outrage. "Why you little... you will take what you are given and like it!"

Lucet rose to the proffered bait. "That I will not, sire! Why, I was a maid last eve, and now I am a... well, no honest man will offer me *morgengifu*! It is your obligation to... recompense me." She began a howling wail of distress. "I have no father to protect me! No mother to turn to! What if I am with child?" Surely, she should have been a player with the mummers!

Edward's voice now rose to an even higher pitch. "With child? With child? Well, that is small inconvenience for a night with your Prince!"

"Ooooohhh! Cruelty! Heartlessness! But you will pay. I may be but a thrall, but you will not ruin me without a thought! Why..."

At this moment – "At last!" thought Ratkin – there was a commotion without, not as loud as that within, but enough to justify him opening the door, to admit first Edgar, tousled from his bed, and behind him the Queen. When they were fully in the room, their attention upon the couple in the bed, Wulf standing awkwardly to one side, Ratkin went to slip out of the door, but as he took the first step, Morwen entered... and then several of the upper chamber thralls, wide-eyed and obviously enjoying the spectacle. Finally, a sleepy, querulous voice, as Ethelred pottered into the room. "Mama, I woke up!"

Seizing the moment, Ratkin left the room and sidled along the walkway and into the King's chamber. There, on a chest beside the pallet, was a wooden tray bearing small ale, honey, some diced fruit and – white bread, a loaf, thankfully not cut, but torn into four pieces. He swiftly took a loaf from the bag, divided it into four roughly similar quarters, and swapped them for the chunks on the platter, dropping the polluted fragments back into the bag. Making his escape, he returned to Wulf's chamber, from where he could hear the unfolding tumult next door.

"Edward, I know I instructed you that you were within your rights to lie with the thralls, but you should use some self-restraint. Virgins are always trouble! At the very least you should have taken her to the Worth... to have this uproar in the King's Hall is quite unsecmly!" Edgar was annoyed, but not without sympathy, though for whom it was hard to tell.

"Mama, why is that girl in my brother's bed?"

"Quiet, Ethelred, go back to your chamber – where is that nurse? Edward, get that slut out of the upper chambers at once! Not ready to wed, indeed? More than ready, I should say!" Elfrith's voice was icy.

"He took my maidenhead, Lady!" wailed Lucet. "I did not know what he was doing! I am but a... the bottler calls me a *bridd-braegen*!"

"Come, girl, Buffet, Stuffit, or whatever you name is," said Edward. You enjoyed it yester-night! Here, here is three fourthings! Enough for a..."

"Three fourthings! You monster! Ooooohhh, my belly pains me! You have, you have got me with child!"

Finally, Edgar's voice cut through the mayhem once again. "Edward, I think this little chit is, indeed, a simpleton. She must be, she seems to have no cognisance of... come, Wulf, there you are! How could you let this happen – take her back to the kitchens. Find some goodwife to care for her. We do not wish to be unkind but get her out of the way."

"Disgraceful!" Elfrith spat and spun on her heel to sweep back in the direction of the King's chamber. The thralls smirked behind their hands and went about their work. Ethelred was ushered away by his nurse and with a final long, hard look at his son, Edgar took his leave. Morwen was the last to exit. She said nothing but stared at each of them in turn, one black eyebrow arched. Slowly, her back ramrod straight, she turned and stalked from the room. Behind his back, Wulf made the sign to ward off the Evil Eye.

PART III

THE CUTTING

TWENTY-ONE

Wintancaestre. Anno Domini 975

WULFMAER

Edgar and Edward. Was there ever a father and son, either noble or base born, who loved more ardently and less wisely? In the weeks following the prince's supposed night of debauchery and the debacle of the following morning, an uneasy quietude seemed to descend upon the Royal Family. Whilst Edward still wished to tell his father of his secret marriage, the time never seemed right, either because of unsettling news from the North or some more local matter which vexed the King, making his son still more hesitant to add to his burdens. The Queen appeared all solicitude and encouragement when it came to matters of national import and even held her tongue on the subject of his son's behaviour, for which, in moment of quiet candour, he mentioned to me on a day when he had summoned me to enquire of Edward's new equanimity, he was extremely grateful.

Edward was, indeed, something of a new man. He had been deeply shocked by the treachery of his stepmother, and whilst he realized that with no proof of her complicity it was impossible to topple her from the King's affection, he began to be more attentive to the dynamics within his father's marriage, hoping to catch her out in some other duplicity. His love for Alfreth knew no lessening. Their weekly intimacies were the joy of his being, and opportunities to be in each other's company, even maintaining the secret of their love, were keenly sought by both. It was clear that their mutual love was mature beyond their years, and they deported themselves with a dignity and understanding of the situation's import and dangers that amazed both me and my sister.

But despite this outward calm, life at Court had undercurrents of increasing tension. Those of us close to the inner circle of the King could feel it building, like the strange prickling sensation of which one becomes aware before a great storm is loosed, sending bolts of fire and light across the Heavens.

The uncertain spring and early summer, wet chills giving way to wet days of oppressive warmth, had passed into a season of drought. The young crops, having forced their way through claggy mud now found themselves imprisoned by ground as hard as the Romans' man-made stone, baked into an unyielding crust by day after day with no hint of rain. Finally, the earth cracked and through the fissures more robust weeds emerged and strangled the few surviving shoots. Old grand-sires sat chewing leathery hawthorn leaves and spoke grimly of famine to come. Husbandmen and ceorls, unable to work the crops, contented themselves by moving their herds and flocks from one pasture to another in an effort to find fodder. Even the water meadows began to die back. Inevitably, there were incursions by one herdsman or another onto his neighbour's fields and ill-feelings stirred. These found their way up the chain to tenant farmers, landholders and finally ealdormen themselves. An occasional skirmish resulted in a few broken heads, but ill-feeling was the worst enemy. Petty discords at Court found an outlet in supposed violations of land rights and the bad blood between Ealdormen trickled down to those of lower station. Like an unhealthy miasma carried back and forth on the wind, Court and countryside breathed the same dis-ease.

Then, as midsummer passed, and July began its sweltering tenure, the great star that men of learning call "Comet" passed through the skies. In the dark of night, it was so bright that it seemed to dim the moon, red and livid in its passage, with a long, jagged tail that seemed to leave tiny offshoots of itself battling with our familiar stars. At dawn and dusk the strange fireball could still be seen, each day moving a little further across Heaven. Only during the full light of day did its unsettling presence disappear, and only then because the sun burnt down so brightly, forswearing any hint of rain, that eyes became tired of squinting and we retreated to the relative cool of Hall or cott.

The one blessing that we could count was that the King's health had taken a great surge for the better. Edgar forswore his earlier habit of breaking fast in the privacy of his bed-chamber and, after attending early Mass each day, he took his place at the High Table – though insisting upon informality – and ate a hearty meal. The Queen, likewise, made great show of joining him. Some of the younger wags even covertly commented that her great appetite for wheaten bread, which seemed to be affording her a somewhat thickened waist, was evidence that she was with child – though they made very certain that these suppositions never reached Her Majesty's ears. Edgar seemed to have returned to his old self, his energy renewed and his belly without the pains he had been suffering. It was a blessing for which we all gave most fervent thanks.

Despite the bickering at Court and the unnatural conditions of the season, the King seemed to be in better heart than for many months. He was, he said, convinced that the flaming star was a harbinger of good, rather than ill, fortune. He cited the great Star which hung over the stable at the time of our Lord's birth. Why should not this "Comet" also be the herald of peace and well-being? At times, of an evening, he seemed quite giddy with the pleasure allowed him by the Queen, who graciously stepped out into the dance with him. He was heard to comment that perhaps there might be another young prince – or mayhap a princess – soon to swell his family. Elfrith appeared to be all smiles at this, but Aetna later told me that she saw the Queen glance at Morwen, as ever a black crow at her shoulder, with a look of such exasperation as might wither morning glory on the vine.

During those weeks I spent more time in His Majesty's close company than I had since I was a child. Together with one of his own companion-men – from which he had many to choose – Edward and I would often ride out to the King's Worth and there join the whipper-in with the hounds on a mad chase through the woods or visit the mews where he would pick his favourite bird, in which case we would away to the heathland. Edward's skill with the hawks had increased over the last year and his father found great delight in teaching him further.

It was on just such a day, the sixth morning of July, the feast of St. Haddi, when Edgar and Edward, myself and the King's companion-man for the day, a pleasant fellow by the name of Samuel, were watching His Majesty's goshawk ride the high wind, circle and stoop in pursuit of pigeons, that Edgar, in a roundabout way, brought up a subject which Edward had both anticipated and dreaded. The morning had dawned bright and clear, with (we hoped without great conviction) a dampness on the browned-off grass that suggested there might have been light rain overnight, although it now seemed more likely that it had been just a heavy dew. Edward had, of late, taken to wearing his light dress sword throughout the day, slung low in a fashion that had come across the sea from the soldiers of *Germania*. His right hand rested on its hilt and he toyed with a gemstone set in the pommel.

"Your sword-master tells me that your swordsmanship his improving daily, my son. Though I wean that pretty plaything at your side would be of little effect against the Northmen."

"Indeed, Father, it would not! But, as I know you are aware, it is with the long sword that I practice with Master Grindmaen. And, yes, I believe that I would be able to give good account of myself."

The hawk snatched a collared dove from mid-air, its talons grasping the hapless victim in a vice-like grip. A pathetic flurry of grey feathers fluttered down, as the predator turned to return to the King's arm, bearing its prey. Edgar drew a dead chick from his pouch to offer as a reward.

"As you know, Edward," he said, "I have never had to wield my sword in anger, though at times I have felt the wish... but I fear in my heart that you may have to do so should you become King."

"What has brought this into your mind so suddenly, Father?"

"Let me reply with a question, my son. How feel you now in the matter of your betrothal to Sinneth? I know you gave your word in that travesty of a proxy oath-taking, but – and now speak to me truthfully – do you have it in your mind that you might break that pledge? No, do not think that I accuse you of planning to foreswear a sacred vow and damn your soul. There are precedents for such things. In affairs of state these... retractions, shall we say... are more commonplace than you might think. Indeed, from what I hear, we may not need to take this particular bull by its horns at all. It seems more than likely that Sinneth may make a match with Olaf Trygvasson, her father's fosterling. What I have to decide is whether to appear to take offence if Kennyth breaks the bond he made with us. Think you that you might like to take a war-party North and rattle sword against shield to make a show of righteous indignation?"

"Great Heavens, Father, has it come to that?" I had watched Edward's face as the King spoke, his expression turning from apprehension to relief and finally to dismay. "Surely we can simply send an embassy to express our disappointment and perhaps suggest some weregild by way of compensation." I could tell that he was longing to tell his father how relieved he would feel to be extricated from this abhorrent treaty.

"Perhaps," replied the King, a little dreamily, stroking his hawk's neck as he fastened the jess. He handed the dove to Samuel, who added it to the bag already caught – two fine pigeons and a few smaller birds. I made a mental note not to mention to Aetna that a skylark was amongst the haul. She had a great affection for the little song-makers. "Nothing is certain yet, but I would know that you are in full possession of the facts – and willing to make at least an exhibition of anger should the need arise."

"Father, I can assure you that I should be happier than you can imagine to set a lighted spill or two between the toes of that oaf, Kennyth." Edward was, of course, aware of Alfreth's close encounter with him at Caestre, and of his loathsome suggestions in the presence of my sister. "But... and you asked me to speak candidly... if he breaks with the agreement, I would not want to go to war in earnest with the aim of changing his mind back! I would, in truth, count it a blessing."

"That is as I thought, son. That is as I thought. And I have an inkling that there is more that you have yet to tell me, but let it lie for now. I am content. I do not believe that we shall need do more than bring the Scots to heel with a show of aggression. And Trygvasson is still a boy. He can wait, and for all he has sworn to carve himself a kingdom, he is little more than a heathen brigand. His father is well rid of him by sending him to Kennyth."

I could tell that Edward was longing to come clean and tell his father all. I saw him draw a breath as if to steady himself for the task, but then Edgar clapped him on the back with a hearty thump. "Aye, you are a good son. I am proud of you and my only regret is that your sweet mother has not seen you grow into the fine, honest young man you are become. My greatest wish for the future is to watch you – and Ethelred – find your places in this world. And mayhap to add to our family with another prince – or princess, eh? How would that sit with you?"

"What makes you happy makes me happy, sire."

"And now, come, we must away back to Court. Samuel, think you that there is enough in the bag that the cook might make an especial pastry for my beautiful Queen? I have it in mind that he should create a pie in the shape of... I don't know, let him conjure something... that may be set before her at the feast this eve. She has been so attentive of late I wish to make a show of my affection."

Samuel muttered some affirmative comment, but Edward and I were too rapt in our own thoughts to take much notice of it. I felt sure that our minds were both bending in the same breeze. We returned to the Worth, collected our horses and trotted back toward Wintancaestre. If only the season had been less uniformly dry and warm, we would had taken more pleasure, I think, in the day. The sky was an azure blue, with no more than a calligrapher's feather stroke of white cloud low on the horizon. There was a light wind which took the excessive heat from the midday hours, and the leaves tossed revealing their upper and lower surfaces, bright and pale green by turns in an ever-changing mosaic of shades. The blighted crops, alone, spoiled the glory of the summer's splendour.

We arrived back at the King's Great Hall about two hours post noon. There was already much ado, with thralls and kitchen men setting things aright for the night's celebrations, serving women scurrying back and forth with garlands and swathes of wild flowers and a band of mummers running through their performance and generally getting under the feet of everyone else. Samuel was despatched to find the cook and convey the King's wishes, and His Majesty bade us have a good postnoon, for he was away to his chamber. Edward had no lessons or duties and so we took our ease. With a couple of pots of not-so-small ale and a slab of wheaten bread liberally spread with a meaty paste each, we headed for the courtyard.

The Feast of St. Haddi was a particular celebration in and around the environs of Wintancaestre. The city itself, and surrounding villages, made much of the saint, who passed from this earthly life to that in the celestial realm in the year of our Lord 705. Next year, in the summer of 976,

Wintancaestre was already planning a great commemoration of the tercentenary of Haddi's consecration as Bishop. That formidable historian, Bede, tells of his wisdom and compassion for the suffering of both people and animals and it had become a custom not to clear away any dust which might collect upon his tomb, allowing those in pain to benefit from its properties, when mixed with water, as a cure-all. By all accounts he was a great and good man. His resting place in the Old Minster was, though dusty, much revered and the usual evening service of praise was, this night, to be one of thanks for his life and legacy. Much of Wintancaestre would try to crowd within its walls and those who came too late would gather outside. Even the New Minster, with barely a suggestion of jealousy, would participate by loaning their choir to raise its voice alongside that of the Old.

Edward and I found a shady spot in the shelter of an ancient tree beside the well at the centre of the courtyard and sat, our backs against its grainy trunk.

"I believe my father is becoming as broody as old Golden Comb himself," said Edward. Golden Comb was the cockerel of the Old Gods who sired all the chickens of middle-earth.

"Edward!" I spluttered into my ale, laughing.

"Well! At his age, to be talking thus!" How is it that the young always perceive their parents as old?

Our relationship was such that I could be candid. "I think we need not anticipate such a happy event any time soon," I said. "Elfrith does not strike me as willing to become a brood mare once again." I had not intended to exacerbate the farmyard analogy, but grinned, nevertheless, as the words left my mouth.

"It is good, though, to see him in such high spirits," continued Edward. "I was close to telling him all."

"I know."

"But then the moment passed."

"Indeed."

Edward hesitated. "The Queen," he said and paused again. "Think you that she truly wished my father dead? Could it not have been that she, perhaps, merely wished him not wholly himself in order that her favourites on the Witan could more easily have their sway? Could it be that Morwen took it upon herself alone to be the instigator of the greater ill? Thinking that she did her mistress some great service in this way?"

I had never told Edward the full story of our encounter with Elfrith at the time of Ethelwold's death, nor of our suspicions that she had a hand in the fatal confinement of his own mother. Neither Aetna nor I had wished to burden him with such information. But now... now he had to know of the dangers which might lie ahead. On that hot, sunny postnoon, as we sat beside the well, I told him all.

"Why did you not tell me this before?"

"Why think you?"

He sat silent. "And Aetna was a witness to all?"

"She was – she is. And the Dowager Queen, she, too, has been watching and waiting. She loves the King as if he were her own son. And you her true grandson. But this you know from the events of a few weeks past."

"Well, it seems now, at least, that Elfrith is brought to heel. I have never seen her more observant of my father's wishes. Nor more affectionate. It is actually quite unnerving!" He grinned despite himself. "But enough for now. I must wash and change before this evening's Mass. And though I may not speak to Alfreth this night, I hope that I shall see her at the Minster. I would not have her think I go to my devotions spattered with bird-shit!"

We returned to the King's Hall, each to our own chambers. The cooling breeze had dropped and the air was close and muggy. It felt as though there might be a storm, although still there was no hint of it in the sky.

)))))))(((((

Some little while before the sixth hour post noon, the congregation began to assemble at the Old Minster for the Mass in honour of St. Haddi. The usual office of Evening Prayer, Vespers, was replaced by this special service, and, as ever, the Royal family together with its intimates were afforded seating at the front of the nave, the lesser thegns and commoners standing to the rear. Those who arrived too late to gain a place within the church thronged the courtyard without, and it seemed that the whole of Wintancaestre had come together to celebrate the day. Great bunches of honeysuckle had been arranged to look as though they were climbing the columns which separated the narrow aisles to either side of the nave, their stems swathed in wet sacking, itself disguised by foliage to create a marvellously natural effect. (I heard later that this notion was borrowed from the Nunneminster which, in turn, had been told of it by Alfreth who remembered it from her time at Bathe.)

The cracks in the structure of the Old Minster which had occurred during the quaking of the earth earlier in the year had been inspected by the King's masons and proclaimed to be superficial, posing no risk to life or limb. Nevertheless, I noticed that the early arrivals found places well away from the fissures and it was only those whose tardiness afforded them little choice who stood directly below them. As the great bells sounded to call the last worshippers to their devotions, those situated closest to the fracture lines cast dubious looks at the walls and fervently made the sign of Our Lord's Rood.

The service progressed along its usual path. I am ashamed to say that my attention wavered. Of late, Edward had taken to attending early Mass with his father, with me in attendance, and the words had become so familiar that they washed over me, leaving in their wake only a sensation of well-being and comfort. My thoughts strayed back to the conversations earlier in the day and it was only when the Archbishop began his homage to the blessed Saint that I returned to the moment. Archbishop Dunstan was engaged at Cantuaria in preparation of that city's celebration of the Translation of St. Benedict, but by good chance, the Archbishop of Eoforwic, Oswald, had been in attendance upon the King for some days. The Old Minster's abbot had been delighted to entertain so eminent a speaker.

"... and when Haddi, of holy memory, brought the relics of Saint Birinus, within the walls of this place, he bestowed upon Wintancaestre, then but a small community, the mantle of greatness and set in chain the events which have made this city the foremost in His Majesty's kingdom. For Birinus brought together those who served Our Lord and those who had not yet heard his Gospel into alliance, then to draw those unenlightened souls into the company of Christians. When the great King Alfred..." Alas, my thoughts once again strayed.

To my left sat Edward, rapt by the oration, beside his father. Beyond Edgar sat Elfrith, her hand in her husband's lap, and beside her, Ethelred. A united and happy family. Why, then, was I, at this moment, so ill at ease?

The Mass, and the service, came to an end and we began to file out of the old abbey church, Edgar first, with his Queen, the two Aethelings following, Edward making much of his younger brother who, for once, seemed in good spirit. Ethelred had recently been appointed his own companion-man, a Cornish thegn from the Hall of his uncle, Ordmaer, by the outlandish name of Meryasek, whose company I kept for ceremonial purposes. He seemed a likely enough fellow and we were on good terms. We walked bestride.

"Look you forward to this evening's entertainment?" I asked.

"I do, Lord." He hesitated. "Will your esteemed sister be honouring us with her presence?"

"I believe so," I replied. "It is a rare entertainment which she does not enjoy."

Again, the hesitation. "Lord... I am uneasy to ask, does the Lady Aetna bestow her heart already?"

"Meryasek," I said, "My sister's affections are her own, I cannot..."

"Forget I spoke, Lord Wulfmaer. I am foolish. This eve I will… well we shall see."

Oh, Aetna, do you not know the power you wield? But we were about to enter the Great Hall, and all other thoughts took flight. The preparations which we had seen earlier in the day were but a foretaste of the decoration of the King's Great Hall which now revealed themselves. Celebration of the midsummer solstice had become too closely associated with the Old Gods, and so the rites and decorations once afforded a few se'enights earlier had, in Wintancaestre at least, been transferred to the feast of St. Haddi, just as in other places it had found outlet in the celebration of other conveniently timed Christian festivals. Greenery and other perquisites of the countryside had been brought into the Hall – ivy, that bugbear of the clerics – deftly intertwined with hops, bindweed scrolled around tall, purple thistles and everywhere honeysuckle, honeysuckle, the emblem and embodiment of fecundity. I wondered how these days were celebrated at Radendunam and how Father Aelmer interpreted the season.

Edgar escorted Elfrith to the High Table, Edward and myself to his right and Ethelred and Meryasek to the side of the Queen. The Dowager Queen, with Aetna beside her, seated herself further along the table, to my right. On occasions such as these the Court had become used to the King's insistence upon informality – in itself something of a dictate – and the usual arrangement of persons found an easy assemblage, Ealdormen and Shire Reeves toward the top of the long tables, lesser men and their ladies lower down. The hubbub was considerable. The King stood; silence fell.

"My people! To you, and to those who beyond these walls will come to know of my declarations…" Scribes were busy recording everything, to be decried in the days to come in towns and villages throughout Edgar's kingdom "… I declare my service and protection in the seasons to come. The Almighty has seen fit to test us with difficult times," here, a murmur of accord. "But He will, I feel assured, give us the serenity to weather these hardships and the courage to forestall the worst of their consequences. This night, as generations have before us in these days of short night and long light, let us make merry… and may the Devil, who has no part in these celebrations, take the hindmost part!"

A huge burst of applause rocked the Hall. Without further ado there was a general falling to of eating, drinking and – all in good nature – argument and discussion. It might perhaps only have been I, and possibly Edward (who was also scanning the assemblage for Alfreth) that noticed the arrival of the King's "fancy" for the delectation of his Queen. As the preliminary courses were removed, the cook's especial serving-thrall placed before her a pastry in the shape of a winged – what? Angel, bird, liberated soul: let later events decide.

"My sweetest of loves," I heard him murmur to Elfrith. "This day my hawk stilled many a heart's beat for you. As would I."

The Queen smiled sweetly, put her arms around his neck and drew him toward her. "Edgar…" was all I heard her say.

They kissed and Elfrith turned to Morwen, as ever behind her mistress's chair. "Ensure that only the finest wine is in my Lord's glass this night and that it remains charged," said the Queen. "See, he has had this pretty pastry created for me, and together we shall dine upon it and drink to our love!" How unlike the usual aloof Elfrith was this! She seemed almost skittish as she plied Edgar with more drink and insisted that he tasted the sweetest of morsels from her own *furca*, or fork. This odd contrivance boasted two prongs at the tip of a short shaft and was fashioned of bronze. Apparently, the Byzantine Empress Theophania had employed one at an Imperial banquet in Rome in 972, just a few years earlier, astonishing her Western hosts and it was rapidly becoming quite the thing to use, rather than relying solely upon knife and fingers. I saw Aethelflaed lean toward Aetna and heard her whisper "*That* thing will never become the norm… another fad from across the water!"

As appetites gradually became sated, the musicians tuned up their instruments and began to play, at first unremarkable traditional music, but soon the latest lively dance tunes which were all the rage at Court – it seemed every year there were new additions to the players' repertoire, and new dance steps to master. Aetna was already on her feet, skipping prettily to the rhythm of a catchy little melody, her fingers resting gently on the wrist of a likely young fellow whom I recognised as one of Edgar's new batch of companion-men, lately having completed their basic Court training. I cast a quick look at Meryasek and found his eyes following her every move. I excused myself from Edward's side, noticing that he, too, had found a subject worthy of his undivided attention, for Alfreth had entered the Hall and was chatting amicably with a lady of one of the lesser thegns. I walked a couple of places along the table until I stood behind the young Cornishman.

"Know you this caper?" I whispered over his shoulder. He jumped at my unexpected words.

"I… that is, I think… yes, I do!"

"Then at the next change of partners, I suggest you step up to my sister," I said.

"I would like to, Lord, but Prince Ethelred might need me. That is, I should stay by him, it is not seemly for him to be left unattended…" He looked wistfully at Aetna as she was about to cross to the other side of the floor, before returning to be caught up by a new escort as the figures of the dance demanded.

Ethelred seemed quite unperturbed. He was, once again, indulging his sweet tooth, on this occasion with a *sirop* infused with fruits. "Oh, take your leave, Merry," he said, quite pleasantly. "I am happy here. And for once Mama is not watching me! Go dance with Wulf's silly sister!" Ah, perhaps it was Elfrith's lack of supervision which made her son so light of heart this eve! I had wondered.

"Thank you, my Aetheling!" said Meryasek. Needing no further encouragement, he headed for the dance.

With little more than an instant's surprised hesitation at the arrival of a new and unexpected dance partner, Aetna's flawless execution of the figures continued seamlessly. Meryasek proved to be more than simply cognisant with the caper, but something of a master. His hesitance had clearly been due only to a shyness rather than confidence in his own ability. He pivoted and sidestepped, whirled my sister into each new step and by the time the musicians struck their final chord, had impressed not only Aetna but a small bevvy of other ladies, who hovered hopefully before retaking their seats, wishing that he might choose them to partner him in the next dance. Alas for them, his eyes were for Aetna alone, and it seemed that she, too, was content that he be her escort on the floor for the rest of the evening. Excellence recognises excellence. My job here was done!

I glanced at Edward and Ethelred. It seemed that there, too, the good will traditionally a part of the Festival of St. Haddi was working its magic. Ethelred appeared more mature than usual – his almost babyish petulance was missing and he was enjoying spending time with his brother. Edward was quite at his ease and fell back into a few of his more boyish ways, good-heartedly teasing and laughing with his younger sibling, pretending to make a grab for some sweetmeat or other, only to allow Ethelred to snatch it from under his hand – and then to pull a face of such desperate disappointment that the lad would relent and share it with him. The age gap between them seemed lessened and it was good to see them laughing and teasing each other thus.

I glanced down the table to the lower places where, seated below the lesser Ealdormen, reeves, freemen and companions were taking their ease. Alfreth caught my eye. She was with Thella and Ratkin and a few others I could not name but recognised from the Nunnegate quarter – presumably Thella and Ratkin's new neighbours. They were all having a fine time. I saw the softness in Alfreth's eyes as she watched Edward with his brother, and when she glanced back at me, I lifted my pot to her and took a drink. She, in turn, took a sip from hers, her lips slightly darkened by the wine as she smiled up the table at me. Oh, yes, I could see why Edward loved her.

Thralls were beginning to clear away the debris from the tables and I spotted little Lucet as she deftly balanced a pile of trenchers to be returned to the kitchen – there would be some good leftovers this eve! I could not but smile to myself as I remembered her atrocious over-acting on the morn following her supposed seduction by Edward. Aetna had told me that she was just waiting for the dust to settle and for all concerned to forget Lucet's face – though that might be a little harder for some than others – before she requested leave to buy her from the King's household. It was to appear a simple transfer of staff between Halls, but I knew my sister well enough to be certain that there was more to it than that. Lucet was a pretty, clever little kitten, I could not deny it.

My attention returned to the dancers. Could that really be Elfrith stepping with the King? And not with the usual ill-grace that attended upon her infrequent indulgence of his requests to dance; she appeared the very soul of light-hearted enjoyment. Edgar himself was most certainly having a delightful evening. He had eaten well, drunk somewhat incautiously and was in the arms of the woman he worshipped. His skills in execution of the figures might not be all they once had – a situation not aided by his continued drinking – but when a king dances, it is a foolish man who might point out such a thing. A cry went up that it was time to throw the last of the evening's offerings onto the bone-fire, and most of the assembly filed out into the courtyard. Edward and Ethelred were still together and I hesitated to break into the special familial time they were sharing, so hung back. I found myself close to Lucet.

"Do you not wish to join the celebrations around the bone-fire, Lucet? I am sure that the bottler does not grudge his staff a few minutes' respite on such an eve as this."

"I thank you, Lord, but I have seen enough fire and smelt enough burnt flesh to last me a lifetime. But it is good of you to ask." She dimpled prettily and smiled up at me, though there was a sadness behind her eyes which belied the coquettish look.

"You are yet young and with the Lord's good grace there will be a long lifetime ahead of you. Shall you never dance around the bone-fire then?"

"I think not, Lord. There are many places in which I find it much the more pleasant to dance. I have no lack of opportunities or offers of partners!"

"I can well believe it, Lucet."

"And now I must dance away to the kitchen, for although the bottler is in a good humour he would not, I think, approve of my loitering with the Aetheling Edward's companion." I stepped aside allowing her room to pass. As she sidestepped one of the dogs contentedly gnawing a bone rescued from its fiery fate outside, I thought that she exhibited a self-possession rare among those of her low rank. "A good night to you, Lucet."

"And to you, Lord."

))))))))((((((

I could not remember where my dream had taken me, nor what was happening in it at the moment when reality intruded upon the world of my sleeping self. Until I heard the cries of distress which awoke me, I had the feeling that I had been in a pleasant place, that light-hearted banter and laughter surrounded me – and perhaps that Lucet was somewhere close. But within seconds that was all gone. Foreboding crushed in upon me and I was up and off my pallet, through the door of my chamber and running along the walkway toward the frantic calls which became ever more desperate.

Oh, sweet Heaven, no! The King's chamber. The door stood ajar. As I entered, I found Samuel – lately honoured with the task of arousing His Majesty in time to break his fast – leaning over Edgar's pallet, his hands upon the King's shoulders, shaking his still form whilst continuing to shout for assistance.

"Samuel, Samuel, what is amiss? What has happened? You are making enough noise to wake the dead!"

"Would that it was so," Samuel's voice finally fell and became hardly audible. "I… I cannot say it! I believe… I believe His Majesty is… dead, indeed! Oh, Lord Jesus, that I should have to say such a thing. Wulf, Wulf, come, tell me I am wrong. Oh, please, tell me I am wrong…"

I went to the King's bedside. He lay strangely tidily for one who had enjoyed a fair evening's drinking followed by a hot, airless night. I know that I had thrown off all my coverings and slept with as much of my body as possible naked to what little breeze crept in through the shutters. Edgar was on his back, with just his face visible above a blanket, which was tucked in neatly on both sides of the pallet, a silk throw, smooth and undisturbed but for Samuel's shaking, covering all else. His face was tranquil, his head turned slightly so that his chin almost rested upon his left shoulder. There even seemed to be a slight smile playing upon his lips. Oh, but those lips were cold, so cold, and when I tried to lift one of his eyelids it would not move but remained tightly shut with an unnatural stiffness.

"Oh, God, Samuel, I believe you are right."

The space of time from my bemused entry into the chamber to this horrific revelation must only have been seconds, and yet the moment seemed to stretch into infinity. An instant of stillness passed and then the room became a maelstrom of voices and movement. Elfrith was the first to arrive, Morwen on her heels. Even in my state of shock, it went through my mind that she – and Morwen – seemed very well turned out for such an early hour, fully dressed and coifed. Edward burst in, like myself almost entirely unattired, in the process of tying a sham about his waist, but then letting it fall to the floor as the import of what he saw struck him. Ethelred trotted in, "… Mama?" His nurse and several of the upper chamber thralls crowded through the door. It was as if the whole *pantomimus* of a few weeks earlier was repeating itself – but as a tragedy rather than a comedy.

Elfrith approached the King's bed. "What is happening...? Edgar? Oh, Edgar, my love. What is wrong?" She knelt beside the pallet, placing her hands on either side of the King's face, as though he were a child about to be kissed better. But she did not kiss him. "Which of you was attendant upon His Majesty this morn? You, Samuel? Came you in and found him thus? Did nobody hear anything during the night?"

It seemed no-one had. Samuel was grief-stricken, but also terrified for his life. True, as companion-man his duties did not extend to being a bodyguard – there were men-at-arms stationed at the foot of the stairs up to the walkway and security was their remit – but the King's personal wellbeing was in his care. The Queen's capricious temper might well cost him his head if she chose to allocate blame in his direction. The men-at-arms now crowded around the doorway to the chamber, equally anxious that their attention to duty should not be seen as wanting.

Edward had been frozen by shock and horror. Now grief. Suddenly, it seemed, he was able to move again and elbowed his way past everyone and toward Edgar.

"Oh, no, no, no! Father! Father! How can this be? How?" Elfrith stood and twitched her gunna out of the way as Edward fell to his knees. Edward looked up at me, tears coursing down his face, a boy, a boy awakened perhaps, as I had been, from a dream and into a nightmare. "Wulf! How can this be? He was well last eve, so well. And happy. Happy, too!" He tried to take his father in his arms, but Elfrith stepped forward.

"Edward! Restrain yourself. Remember who you are. This is unseemly behaviour, even by your standards. It is not your place to touch the dead, that is women's work. Morwen and I will... and get some clothes on, for decency's sake."

"You will what?" Edward spat at her. "Well, I suppose there is little left for you to do to hurt him now, is there? You cannot now gnaw away further at his good heart and..." He took a deep breath, steadied himself and stood. "Wulf, hand me that sham!" I bent and retrieved it from where it lay by the door, passing it to him. He wrapped it around himself. He seemed taller than before he had knelt, the tearful boy morphing before my eyes into an angry young man.

"Very well," he said. "Very well. Be about your 'women's work'. But think not that you can speak to me thus any longer. The King is dead. The Witan will meet to elect the new King. Do not imagine that it will be any other than I. This day we mourn my father. But the business of state goes on, and the confirmation of my election is the first order of that business. Wulf, with me!" He strode from the chamber.

TWENTY-TWO

The Witan is a curious beast. For much of the time it roams the four corners of the kingdom obediently at the heel of the King, its master, if such an unpredictable animal can be said to have a master. When such attendance is not required it retreats to its lair, so well camouflaged that it is difficult to remember its character when last revealed. It is a chimera, composed of many disparate parts, any of which may change their appearance and allegiance when providential. And when its master is no more, as upon the death of a king, it awakes from its slumbers, if such they were, shakes itself and prepares for... battle?

The shock waves of Edgar's death took only hours to begin their journey, first through the former kingdoms of Wessex and Mercia, then into Eastseaxe and East Anglia, and finally reaching distant Northumbria. The common people mourned the King with genuine feeling. The "long peace" which Edgar had painstakingly preserved throughout his reign meant that a whole generation of young men had never known war; their mothers had never known the anguish of seeing their sons march away to it. On the whole, fathers and husbands had been able to provide for their families. Times had been good. Within the ranks of the nobility, mourning might, in some cases, be less genuine than others: *politicos* have their own agenda. Those within travelling distance of Wintancaestre immediately took to the road and headed to Alfred's old capital, keen to be part of the *"Witangemot"*, literally the "meeting of wise men". Whilst the succession of the King's eldest son was more often than not the outcome, it was not a totally foregone conclusion.

That day, 8th July, seemed to last a lifetime. It was Thor's day, and it seemed that the old God of Thunder himself was railing against the injustice of Edgar's loss. Toward evening a great storm broke, rain poured down onto hard-baked earth too parched to absorb it, and flash floods raced along roads deep in dust after so many weeks of drought. Huge torrents of filthy water rushed through the streets of Wintancaestre collecting and bearing with it the detritus of the city. The bells of the Old and New Minsters tolled in uneasy unison. As there had been no warning of the King's death, the Passing Bell had not been tolled, and the bell-ringers, without this usual *praeambulus*, had loosed the Death Knell immediately, furthering the day's sense of unreality. Its gloomy, doleful voice exacerbated the roar of the downpour, the blasts of thunder and, between them, the sounds of heartfelt grief in the Great Hall. Around mid-postnoon, the Death Knell stopped and the more familiar bell for Nones rang out from the tower of the New Minster calling the faithful to worship. It was a relief that the official mourning could begin.

There could hardly have been a soul in Wintancaestre who had not heard of Edgar's death, and few people who did not wish to assemble both to give and receive comfort among their fellows. The New Minster was larger than the Old, and so was the better venue for this first outpouring of regret, and those who could not find a space within crowded around its walls and spilled over into the precincts of the more ancient building, heedless of the pouring rain, for which under different circumstances they would have been so grateful. It was about the third hour post noon as I accompanied Edward down the central aisle toward the seating at the front of the church, whispers on either side of us.

"Look, here is His Majesty," and, slightly louder, "God bless you, sire!"

Edward acknowledged the murmurings with a nod of the head here, a slight raising of his hand there, but his eyes were focussed straight ahead, toward the High Altar, before which stood a bier surmounted by a great hollowed tree trunk, cut lengthways, its contents open to view. As we reached it, he gave an odd little gasp, as though holding himself tightly in check.

"Father!"

Edgar lay in a very similar pose to that which we had seen that morning. Indeed, one might have been forgiven for thinking even now that he slept. The wooden coffin had been padded first with fine woollen blankets, then with white linen. The King's head lay upon an embroidered pillow, still turned very slightly to his left. His face was serene. Like a bed covering, quilted silken sheeting lay over all of his body, tucked in on both sides with only his shoulders visible. He looked to have been closely bound, his arms to the sides of his body, the binding cloths disappearing beneath the bed-covers and giving the impression that he had been swaddled like a new born babe. Still, it seemed, there was the slightest of smiles upon his lips.

"Oh, Father!"

Edward took his seat at the very front of the assembly and indicated that I should sit beside him. To his right the Dowager Queen sat with my sister, who had taken her aunt's hand into her lap and held it there tightly. I had not seen Aetna all day, but I had been aware of her grief, suffering it with her, as she would have been feeling mine. Aethelflaed looked drawn and drained. Clearly, she had wept, but her eyes, though red, were now dry, her back straight and her chin held high. She looked straight at Elfrith, who had assumed a seat facing the congregation, in a chair placed to mirror the Bishop's throne, which had been positioned opposite, across the aisle, with Archbishop Oswald seated likewise, facing the people. Can

362

it really have been less than four and twenty hours since he officiated at St. Haddi's feast-day celebrations? The world felt very different this postnoon. Just behind the Queen's seat Morwen hovered, a malignant presence. Ethelred sat between his nurse and Meryasek. The boy had certainly been crying, and now he snuggled into the side of his nurse, seeking comfort and sniffling slightly, until Elfrith's cold eye caught his and he sat up straighter beneath her unforgiving gaze. Meryasek kept his eyes down. There had been no time for Ealdormen and others to arrive from more distant parts. This service, it seemed, was for but the immediate family – and the loyal people of Wintancaestre, who would never have gained such intimate access to their late King had the nobility begun yet to gather.

The office of Nones has ever been one of my favourites. Not a Mass, it is traditionally a time of quiet prayer in which to enjoy psalms and the beauty of the Bible's words, a tranquil, reflective service of meditation and thanksgiving, named for the ninth hour after dawn, the time of day when many begin to turn away from their labours, preparing to take their rest together with family and friends. And so this proved to be. Archbishop Oswald led us in an act of remembrance, recalling Edgar's life and integrating those psalms and prayers which he knew the King had loved. Time enough to prepare for the formalities of a funeral service when the Witan was gathered. Now, the loss was too immediate, the pain too raw. I might have wished that our old friend Archbishop Dunstan had been with us, to share memories and tell tales, but good Oswald gave us what we needed that sad day. Time to remember, to grieve quietly, to celebrate the small personal recollections of this man which many of us held so dear.

)))))))((((((

The people had returned to their homes. The wild weather had abated, water trickling away through cracks and fissures in the parched ground as soon as the violence of the floods lessened, and evening approached. Men-at-arms were stationed in the New Minster, by Edward's order, to watch over the body of the late King until the official vigil began later. Those chosen were aware of the honour afforded them. The Royal family and their close attendants were gathering in the Great Hall, food, largely untouched, prepared and set out, ale, mead and wine rather more in demand. It was the first moment I had had all day to speak to Aetna. As she entered with the Dowager Queen – that title, itself, now uncertain – she ran to me and I held her close.

"Sister!" There were tears yet unshed and they flowed now. "Aetna! Try to cry no more. This is a sad, sad day. But look at me, look... I saw the King this morn, second only to Samuel who found him. I would swear that he suffered not. He was at peace and left us with a smile upon his lips. He is now at the feet of Our Lord. Weep no more for him, weep if you will, for those of us who loved him and will see him no more until the Day of Judgement." I confess that there was a crack in my own voice.

Aethelflaed came and put her arms around us both. Sometimes I forgot that this fine, strong lady, this Queen, was our aunt and had known us since infancy. "Come, children, my loves. Tears will come... and they will go. Life will continue, joys will return. You know that I loved the King as though he was my very own son. And I believe that he felt the same affection for me. I ever tried to be his mother, for he could remember little of his own... that sadness he shared with you, both."

She began to straighten Aetna's rumpled gunna, as she might when Aetna was still a child. Turning to me, she reached to brush back the hair from my forehead, damp and windblown from the ferocity of the earlier storm. "Aunt!" I could hardly forebear to smile. "I am a man grown!"

"Aye, but we all need a little extra love on a day such as this has been. Come, now, we must take a little food, for making ourselves ill will be of no service to Edward, and it is he to whom we must now give our allegiance and our duty, as we did his father."

"Oh, I cannot eat, Aunt," said Aetna.

"I know you think you cannot, but you must," Aethelflaed replied. "I do not wish for anything either, but see, I shall a have a little of this..." She put some broiled fowl upon a trencher. "... and a tiny piece of this." A pastry stuffed with some minced fruits. "I shall take a bite, and then shall you, and before we know it – poof – all gone!" Truly, it was a shame she had no children of her own, for she was a natural mother! Even to those who thought that they needed one no longer. "You, too, Wulf!"

Despite the season – and the recent heat – the earlier downpour had made for a damp, chill atmosphere in the Hall, or perhaps it was just a symptom of the unhappiness of the day. The house thralls had kindled a fine fire in the central hearth. In the informality of that evening we gathered around it. Edward, who had slipped away for a time, returned and embraced his step-grandmother warmly.

"I should like to call you Mutti," he said. "I know it was my father's pet name for you... may I take it as my own to use, as I intend with all his other rights and duties?"

"My dear boy, Your Majesty, as I believe you will shortly be hailed, I can think of nothing that I would like better," replied Aethelflaed. He leant down to allow her to kiss him.

Ethelred was seated to one side of the firepit, swinging his legs, which were too short to reach the ground from the settle where he was perched. His nurse stood behind him, Meryasek, seated to his side. It seemed he had not needed a great deal of encouragement to recover his appetite. One of the stuffed pastries was already but a memory – a memory echoed by the many crumbs scattered upon his tunic – and a second, this one liberally spread with honey, was about to share the same fate.

"Mama says that I might be His Majesty..." flaky pastry sputtered forth with the words. "How think you 'King Ethelred' sounds? I heard Mama say it but this forenoon. I do not think that there has ever been a His Majesty King Ethelred before..."

Silence hung like a shroud. For an instant. Then...

Ethelred's nurse bustled around to the front of the settle. "Another pie, sweetling, that will keep you content, will it not? Now I wonder where your mama can be... perhaps we should go and..."

"Or perhaps I should take the Aetheling Ethelred to see the... er, the...? What was it your Highness was asking to do but yesterday?" Meryasek studiously avoided eye contact with anyone but his young master.

"No, no, I am quite happy here. And I will have a *saussiche*, Goody. Yes, fetch His Majesty King Ethelred a nice, fat *saussiche*! Ah, Mama, I was just..."

There must have been a sudden gust of air, perhaps due to the drop in temperature since the rain, for the curtain between the Hall and the stairs to the upper chambers suddenly billowed inward as if untouched by human hand and the Queen appeared with Morwen, as ever, a dark shadow in her wake. My mind, unbidden, had a moment's passing impression of Morwen shape-shifting from the woman we saw into the dark, black-beaked *Néofugol* of childhood nightmares, the bird which fed upon the bodies of the dead and rode upon the shoulders of witches. I mentally shook my head to disperse the image.

"Yes, I see and hear what you were doing, Ethelred. Nurse, is it not time that his... Highness... should be making ready for his bed? It has been a long day, has it not?"

"It has indeed, Your Majesty." Goodwife Colley dropped a curtsey. "Come, your... come Prince Ethelred, you may finish your *saussiche* in your chamber. Bid your mama and your brother a good night."

"Very well. Good night, Mama. Good night, Edward." Ethelred certainly seemed in a remarkably equitable mood. He looked about for the small toy sword which had, of late, been his favourite plaything. Meryasek spotted it beneath the settle, bent to pick it up, and then handed it to his young master. "Thank you, Merry. You may come and keep me company before I sleep." He favoured the company with a long, wide yawn and with a sticky smile left the Hall, his small retinue in attendance.

Elfrith watched him leave, an unaccustomed, tolerant smile playing about the corners of her mouth. "Sweet child!" she said. "And now, my dear... family... we have much to discuss."

We all, it seemed, glanced at each other with much the same element of uncertainty. In truth, other than her own son, there was none in the Great Hall that night with whom Elfrith shared any familial, or even foster, relationship. Edward was the first to rally.

"Yes, indeed, Step-mother, we do. Come, let us sit. But first – do you all have your vessels charged? – first, I wish to give the *was heil* in my father's memory." Vessels were, indeed, charged. "I give honour to Edgar, King of All Englaland, Emperor of the Kings and all peoples of Bryttania, Peace-broker, great-grandson of King Alfred and the fourth of his line to hold these lands and titles. And father of the next." His voice wavered, just slightly. "I give *was heil* to my father!"

"*Drynke heil!*"

In the short silence that followed, we looked into our glasses, our pots or drinking horns and each of us, I believe, remembered the happy times we had shared. Each of us? Who knew what was passing through Elfrith's mind at that moment? Her lips did not appear to be dampened by even the smallest sip, though her glass had been dutifully raised.

She gave sharp sniff. "Yes, well spoken, Step-son. Now, to the business of the next few days. Ethelred and I shall leave for Glestingaberg first thing on the morrow morning to arrange for the disposal... my pardon, I am mis-spoken... the disposition of the late King's body alongside that of his father in the abbey church. Edward, you may wish to accompany us, but I suspect that you would rather await arrival of members of the Witan, since you seem so eager to engage their goodwill. Step-mother-in-law, at your age – forgive me if I assume too much – you will probably feel it is too long a journey to be undertaken at such short notice: I quite understand! Perhaps, if Archbishop Dunstan sees fit to arrive in Wintancaestre betime, you may presume upon him to follow us and oversee the interment, otherwise I am sure that... well, I am certain there will be someone on hand in Glestingaberg to do it. By Sunday we shall be on our way back to Wintancaestre, and then the Witan may convene to... discuss matters further. And now, if there is nothing more, Morwen and I will attend to the sealing of the coffin. There will be no vigil." She stood and made to leave.

"Lady!" Edward was also on his feet. "There most certainly is more... You seem to have taken a great deal upon yourself without wider conference! How say you that my father will be interred at Glestingaberg, when his wish – I know it – was to lie here in the New Minster? And what necessitates this unseemly urgency? There must be vigil. And we must wait the usual nine days, arrange things with due dignity. The Witan will then be able to attend the committal..."

Still seated, the Dowager Queen's voice was low, but steely hard in its disapproval. "Elfrith, this cannot be... why, my step-son's corpse is not even properly prepared for burial! When I saw him in the Minster this eve... well, I thought that the hasty preparations were in order that we might be comforted by having him with us one last time. You surely cannot believe that he is sufficiently prepared. He is... he is... swaddled! There is no other word for it! I did not intervene today for I believed you would, at the least, call upon me to assist you in his laying out tomorrow, or even the next day. I thought, mayhap, that his poor body was suffering some unusually long stiffness of the death. And you cannot enclose the King in that wooden coffin... it is unadorned, it is..." Her voice had risen and she became lost for more words.

Elfrith froze half way to the curtain, and then turned to face us.

"You, all of you," she cast a look around the company, "forget yourselves. Need I remind you that I am now the only person in this court, indeed in the Kingdom, who is a crowned and anointed Monarch? And that the late King was my husband – therefore his body is mine to... well, be that as it may... I believe that he should lie beside his esteemed father. I cannot believe that you, Aethelflaed, of all people, should demur. And Edward, in this heat we cannot wait the customary nine days, would you that the corpse began to swell and smell like the tanners' quarter on a Moon-day's morn? The coffin must be sealed. And as for... well, I suppose I can understand an old woman's ignorance of the more current trends, but I can assure you, madam, that a more informal preparation for interment is quite customary these days upon the Continent. The Franks have long eschewed the outmoded manners of our court in this. I have said... I have no objection to any of you attending with us at Glestingaberg, but matters will progress as I have ordered, and that right soon."

Morwen held the curtain open for the Queen to pass, and Elfrith, without a glance backward was gone. There was the twitch of a smile at the corner of Morwen's mouth, however, as she cast a look behind her. Then she, too, disappeared behind the hanging.

Aethelflaed was the first to recover her voice. "I fear the... Queen... is right."

"What?"

"Aunt!"

Aethelflaed took a deep breath. "She is... correct. At this moment Elfrith is the most powerful person in the land, in name, if not entirely in law, and the law can be an uncertain palisade behind which to hide. Until the Witan meets, there is no king, but she, she is crowned and anointed. My poor Edgar's body is, indeed, his widow's property: she may make what arrangements she wishes. She can argue that the heat proscribes the usual nine day's mourning, and there is no valid reason why he should not lie at Glestingaberg. And mayhap I am outmoded in my..."

"No, no, Mutti!" cried Edward. "This cannot be! My father cannot simply be shuffled off to the abbey at Glestingaberg – I know, I know it is a fine church and he paid much toward its improvement these last years, even to the creation of the chapel that bears his name. And that my grandfather lies there. But he cannot be... dear Lord, he was not shriven, for nobody knew of his passing, but there must at the least be vigils and all the...." He became lost for words, too, as, for a moment were we all.

Once again, my aunt was the first to rally. "Aetna, look you behind that curtain, I would not that we were overheard. Wulf, check the wicket door."

My sister pulled the hanging aside and looked toward the stairs. "We are alone, Lady!"

I opened the wicket in the great doors. Only the usual men-at-arms stood without. "Admit no-one without announcing them first," I ordered. "No-one!"

That left only the door toward the kitchens. Aethelflaed herself opened it herself. The usual bustle was subdued and there were few comings and goings to other parts of the court but, at that moment, Lucet staggered past labouring beneath the weight of a heavy pail of water in each hand.

"Set those in the kitchen, girl, and return."

"Yes, Your Majesty."

Aethelflaed resumed her seat and it was but a moment before there was a quiet scratch at the door and Lucet entered.

"Stand just without, girl, and if anyone – anyone – approaches, make a loud show of entering with some message or other. You may leave the door ajar and hear what is to be said, but I do not, I am sure, need to tell you that what you learn this eve is more important than your life, and the lives of many here... if it reaches any ears other than those I prescribe, your end will be swift and painful."

"Aunt Aethelflaed!" Aetna had never heard our mother-sister speak so.

"Aetna, the time for dissimilitude is over." Here was the iron-clad Queen Aethelflaed of whom her namesake, the Lady of the Mercians, would have been proud. "Now, listen, all of you."

Lucet took up her position outside the door toward the kitchens, Aetna remained by the stairway curtain and I, certain of the men-at-arms without the great doors, returned to the hearth. I confess, I refreshed my drinking horn. Aethelflaed resumed.

"Matters are moving swiftly. Elfrith is determined that Edgar should be below ground within the next three dawns. For reasons which I cannot bear to put into words she is determined that none – save she and that wretch, Morwen – have a sight of his body. Even as we speak it is bound up like a suet ready for the pot in case any might try to gain such access. This nonsense about funerary fashions is but a smokescreen. We cannot

368

prevent her from taking him to Glestingaberg tomorrow, but it must not happen without witness. Aetna, you will go, too. I shall plead my age and distress – she has already given me the wherewithal to do so – and will stay here with Edward. I believe that my experience will stand me in good stead with the Witan and my support will be to his advantage.

"Yes, my love, I know, you wish to go with your father, but think… the members of the Witan will begin to arrive within a day or so. Elfrith has thought through all the permutations of her plan: if you go to Glestingaberg to honour your father, you will not be here to welcome them. I would place a good wager that Aelfgar will be among the first to arrive; he will begin a campaign to sway them toward Ethelred as King. Elfrith is relying upon your desire to see your father laid to rest. By suggesting to you that you stay to greet the Witan she challenges you to do so… and betakes the wager that you will not. By the Rood, she is cunning! Either way, she believes that she will have you on the back foot. Come to Glestingaberg and you will seem to have no care for the Witan; stay in Wintancaestre and you fail to honour your father! But at least the second case will go some way, hopefully, toward ensuring that Edgar's wishes are fulfilled. I and many others know that it was his desire that you be his heir."

"Elfrith and Ethelred will return from Glestingaberg in time for the *Witangemot*, there is no doubt of that. Bathed in the glow of righteous mourning. The Chief Ealdorman will have begun his campaign. There will be no evidence of ill doing on her part, and she, as anointed Queen will put herself forward as Regent during Ethelred's minority. You, Edward, will, I fear, be cast as the son of a queen uncrowned and therefore not the primary heir. Yes, the Witan will debate, but as to which way it will vote…" Her voice trailed off.

"But Mutti," Edward was still casting about for some way he could reconcile the two opposing courses of action. "Surely…"

"The Dowager Queen is correct," I said, putting my hand on his shoulder. "I know you wish to accompany the late King on his last journey, but it is more important to work toward his legacy. A legacy which would be upended if Elfrith and her cronies take power on the Witan. Ethelred is but a child, his mother will be ruler of this land if it is allowed that he be crowned. That cannot happen."

"I know, I know, but it is hard…"

"Edward, it is the first but not the last hard decision you will make in the years to come," said Aethelflaed. "Believe me, grandson, there will be many. Now, is it settled?"

"It is, Mutti," said Edward. "By the Heavens you are worth a dozen men on the Witan!"

"That remains to be seen. Now, Aetna, are you content to be my representative at the... well, I suppose we must call it a funeral?"

"Of course, Aunt. But must I travel alone? Thella is no longer available; her duties lie elsewhere."

Aethelflaed raised her voice slightly. "Lucet? Lucet, come, I know that you will have your ear set to the door... yes, I know I gave you leave! I did so because I feel there is more to you than meets the eye. Well, now I hear that my niece was to make an offer for your thraldom to the late King. But I know that in his Will he has made provision for the freedom of a number of slaves – and it is within my gift to choose the women so relieved of their collar. How think you to being the Lady Aetna's personal attendant? We will not call it companion-woman for the moment. You will have your letters of release but will be bound to my niece for a time. Does that sit well with you?"

"It does, Your Majesty, it sits very well!" Lucet pushed the thick, fair hair back off her forehead and looked down at her shabby, work-a-day threads. "But if we are to be ready to travel with the dawn, I must have something more suitable to... and I must see to my new Lady's things as well! And I know nothing of her preferences. Those are the last water pots I shall take to the kitchen... but I must make my farewell to the bottler, for in all conscience he has been good to me – and put up with much!" Lucet's usual aura of unruffled confidence was in danger of unravelling under the sudden weight of her new position.

Despite the gravity of the occasion none of us could fail to find at least a small smile for this ray of hope and happiness, as one person's life was made the better by the generosity of Edgar's will. And there would be more thralls freed in the days to come. It was a tradition long held to be of benefit to the departed's soul, and one which brought joy even at a time of sorrow.

"Peace, child, the Lady Aetna and I will make her preparations, you look to yourself. Here..." she handed Lucet a coin, "this will soon find you some clothes for the next few days and when you return... well, I dare say you will have time to discuss it on your trip."

Lucet looked at the *haelf-scilling* in her hand, a small smile of delight – which she manfully tried to hide – flickering across her lips. "Oh, Your Majesty!"

"Be off, then, and come to the Nunneminster Hall before dawn, that you may accompany the Lady Aetna to the City Gates. Oh, do you ride?"

"I do! Oh, yes, I do, Your Majesty!"

"That is just as well, then, for otherwise I fear you would have had a hard day's learning and a sore behind ahead of you!"

And somehow, in those few moments of preparation, of taking the situation, terrible as it was into our own hands and making our declaration of war against Elfrith – albeit, for now, only revealed among ourselves – the desolation of the day lifted and a small shaft of light pierced the darkness. The sadness was still there, and the loss. But the feeling that, despite our best efforts we had lost Edgar to… well, now, our task was to see that Edward was crowned King as his father's rightful successor.

))))))))(((((((

The funeral party, with the late King's body, left Wintancaestre at dawn on the following day as planned. It was only a small train, the family, such as it was, the Wintancaestre Great Hall's house priest, a small number of servants and a score of men-at-arms, for although there was no great show of wealth or ostentation, even a half-witted, half-blind wolf's-head would see that that there were persons of rank in the group – and that could mean ransoms to be had. But with ten armed riders before and ten after the family, and the bier not offering any kind of obvious riches we had little fear for their safety.

It had been a day of anti-climax and there was an air of unreality at court. Edward, on Aethelflaed's advice, told the kitchens to begin preparations for the arrival of members of the Witan. They were set to baking extra bread, churning butter, stewing fruits, anything to keep their hands busy and their minds on their work. Hunters were sent out to track down what game there was to be had – sparse now as the summer continued its parched course –and house thralls set to sweeping, re-strawing and strewing the halls and upper chambers. At around the ninth hour – once again the bell for Nones was chiming – Archbishop Dunstan arrived from Cantuaria, alone and with no ceremony, having only heard the news of Edgar's death late in the postnoon of the previous day. He had ridden hard, with two changes of horses along the way at abbey stables and was grim-faced and exhausted.

Edward and I were in the Great Hall, giving some instructions as to the arrangements for the visiting Ealdormen's thralls when he strode in, the wicket door slamming behind him.

"Edward, my son! I am cut to the heart to hear of your father's death. A rider arrived last eve with the news, but with no details. How? What happened? Was there some accident? I have told him a thousand times that trick of his, mounting and dismounting his horse like an acrobat, will kill him – though only in jest! Oh, Edward!"

Edward had known this man all his life; if there was anyone who stood in the position of a second father, it was Dunstan. The two hugged each other with a genuine affection.

"Dunstan, it is good, and more than good, to have you here," said Edward as they parted. "These last two days… but come, we must to a withdrawing chamber to speak… Wulf, send some food and drink through for the Archbishop, and then join us."

During the next short while, as Dunstan refreshed himself with meat and ale, Edward and I tried to make sense of all that had happened, not just in the last days but earlier and now more apparently relevant. By the time Edward had expressed his disgust at Elfrith's insistence upon the hurried funeral at Glestingaberg he was on his feet again, the tiredness black-ringed around his eyes and his hair still sweat-plastered to his brow.

"Then I must leave again, immediately," he said. "I must, no, I will not be swayed even if you tried, I must see him laid to rest. I can sympathise with your wish to have him lie here in Wintancaestre, but if it must be that he rests elsewhere, then Glestingaberg is a worthy place. A place of sanctity and power. She…" the tone of his voice left no doubt to whom he referred, "… she may come to rue the day she chose Glestingaberg to conceal her treachery."

I had sent word to the Nunneminster Hall to inform Aethelflaed of Dunstan's arrival when I ordered his food, and now my aunt entered, without ceremony or announcement.

"Oh, Dunstan, it is a joy to see your face, even in this time of sorrow! How we have needed your counsel in these last days. I knew you would come, but did not dare to expect you so soon. You must have ridden with the wind." They embraced.

"I did, Lady, I did. And now I must leave again, if I am to see our boy put to his last resting place. But I will return as soon as I see that all has been done aright."

The shared intimacy of those words, which brought back so many memories of Edgar as a child brought tears to my aunt's eyes. "Our boy… yes, he was, wasn't he? Oh, Dunstan I have had none with me here who remembered those days! I know you must go, I will not try to stop you – but will you not take some little rest? Just one hour or so that you may ride more safely? I could not bear that aught might happen to you!"

Dunstan hesitated. He knew that he was far behind Elfrith who would be travelling well into the light summer evening to make as good time as possible, but he also knew that to ride without rest would be dangerous.

"Very well," he said. "For you, my Lady and your peace of mind I rest two hours. Wulf, find me a pallet, and be sure to wake me, for if you let me sleep a nonce longer I will… well, the Holy Father in Rome would not approve of it!"

"Come to my chamber, Archbishop," I said. "You will have peace and privacy, and Ratkin will wake you at the very stroke of two hours! In the meantime, I will see to having the best and freshest horse saddled up for you, and food and small ale packed against the ride."

"Good man, Wulf. And, by the Heavens, it is a pleasure to see you – again, though, in sad times. And with your sister away in the enemy camp! I told her once she was becoming a *politico*, now I think, mayhap, she is an *espier* as the Franks would have it!"

"I would just that she keeps safe," I said, as we headed toward my chamber. Pausing only to pull off his boots, Dunstan fell onto the bed and safe in the assurance that he would be woken betime, fell quickly into a deep slumber.

)))))))(((((((

The Archbishop was on the road again, as he had intended, a little over two hours later. Upon being woken, he had taken little time in saying his farewells, assuring us that he would return with the rest of the court, and set off, his horse fresh and eager for the gallop, Dunstan only slightly less so. None of us had enjoyed much, if any, sleep in the last two days and so, as evening fell, Aethelflaed prepared to return to her Hall at the Nunneminster. Edward and I escorted her across the city. When we reached her Hall, Edith and Onwen bustled out to usher their mistress inside, with many tuts and sweet words, for they both knew how much she would be feeling the King's loss. It seemed that Alfreth had, despite recent events, gone to the archive at the Nunneminster to work upon the embroidery designs for the Dowager's *magnum opus*.

"I see," said Aethelflaed, a little coldly.

"Mutti, I will see you on the morrow," said Edward. "Wulf, will you walk with me?"

"And do you return to the Great Hall?" my aunt interjected before I could reply.

"I... er, yes... do we, your Highness?"

"Oh, well, I thought we might..."

"Come, come," Aethelflaed had finally lost patience. "Do you both take me for a silly old woman who cannot see the nose before her face? Think you that I have no inkling of what has been going on ... a quiet little conspiracy between all of you young folk? I know that my step-son has feelings for Alfreth, and that sweet girl has no face for mistruths, each time his name is mentioned she either turns away or finds a use for her kerchief. I just hope that you have not dragged her into some foolish course that will despoil her chances of as good a match as she can hope for. Each and every Frig's night you all disappear upon some errand or other... yes, I know Aetna is involved, too... and Thella and Ratkin, I'll be bound. The truth now, for there are harder matters afoot which must be dealt with in good faith, with no secrets between us."

"You are right, Step-mother, you are right," said Edward. "I have been foolish to try and keep things quiet for so long, but with my father wishing me to..."

"Come along within," Aethelflaed's tone softened as soon as she knew that the truth was about to be revealed. "Sit, take a glass of wine, tell me all. I was young once, too, you know!"

Onwen fetched some good Frankish wine, and we sat in the withdrawing chamber. As the light began to dim without, Edith brought candles, and set them upon the table. "Cakes, Your Majesty?" she asked. "I have some fresh bremelberry buns?"

"Oh, yes," smiled my aunt. "There is always a place for your cakes."

Edith returned with the buns, and then left, closing the door behind her. We were alone, the three of us. As the shadows lengthened in the orchard and the lights burned brighter within, Edward told all. Almost all.

"So," said Aethelflaed, "that evening, when the King was about to announce your betrothal to Sinnyth, and there was that ridiculous scene with Ratkin and Thella? What was that all about? Why their hasty marriage, what had it to do with this, this romantic entanglement of yours?"

"Theirs was not the only wedding that day, Mutti."

"Oh, by all that's great in Heaven, Edward, you didn't!"

And so, the rest of it came out. The marriage, Ethelmaer's involvement, the secret hideaway, everything. When Edward concluded Aethelflaed sat for a moment, speechless. What thoughts were passing behind those grey eyes? Anger? Disappointment? Perhaps even disgust, that an Aetheling should bind himself so, to a nameless, penniless...

Then, like a beam of sunlight, her smile appeared. That must have been the smile, I thought, that had made Kind Edmund fall in love with her, the sweet smile she shared with our own foster-mother. "So, now it all falls into place," she said. "Why, why did you not tell me? Think you I would have tried to stop it? Oh, well, in truth I suppose I might have, for you have certainly not made yourselves a comfortable pallet in which to lie, either alone or together. But now, what is done, is done. And I suppose that Alfreth is already awaiting you at Thella and Ratkin's cott? You have not been able to see her alone or to speak to her since your father's... oh, my sweet boy!"

With that, she summoned Edith. "Edith, we are going out once more. Stay up for me, I shall not return late, and Wulf here will escort me home. Pack up any more of those cakes as prettily as you may, for I wish to give them as a gift and add a pot of confiture from the pantry – oh, and one of the lavender-honey – and a flask of wine... quickly now!"

It took but a short while to walk to Thella and Ratkin's cott, beneath the city wall. Between us, Edward and I carried the food and other dainties

Aethelflaed had collected together. "Edward, you must realise that you have been supremely fortunate not to have been discovered in this matter," she said, as we rounded the last corner beside the little house.

"I do, Step-mother, of course, I do. But... we even have our own secret access!" He sounded almost like a small boy, proudly displaying his make-believe fort, as he ushered her into the secluded green space behind the cott. We opened the door into the back room. It was empty. Voices could be heard from the front of the house, and, opening the door cautiously, Edward put his head around it and then slipped into the room.

Alfreth gave a little cry of relief and flew into his arms. "Oh, my love, I have wanted to comfort you this two days past, it has been so cruel not to be able to do so. I... I am so very sorry about your father, I mean His Majesty... Oh, Edward, it is a cruel blow. You look so tired, come sit by me for a moment, Thella has some..."

The door opened more fully. Edward has his back turned, Alfreth's face buried upon his chest. It was only Thella and Ratkin who saw the entry of the Her Majesty, the Dowager Queen Aethelflaed. They both fell to their knees, Thella with her hand cupped to her mouth.

"Your Majesty!" Ratkin kept his head low. "I... I cannot... my wife knew nothing..." He stuttered on for a moment and then ground to a halt. I entered behind Aethelflaed. "Wulf, my Lord!"

The realisation that their secret was uncovered, almost brought Alfreth to her knees, too, but Edward held her firm. "My love, Ratkin and Thella, the Dowager knows all. She suspected much, but with all that has happened, it was time that she be told the truth..."

"And, children, whilst I cannot in all truth say that I am pleased, exactly, when love blossoms amongst those one loves, it is impossible not to be happy for it. Alfreth, I am sorry that you did not feel able to tell me of this, but I suspect that Edward had much to do with that..." She looked at him a little sharply. "Thella, Ratkin, I find no fault with you – you were but doing as your master and mistress bid. And, pray God, what your new king wished."

The "new king", those words were weighty. Yes, by all that was holy, Edward would soon be hailed the new King, it must be so. As if the magnitude of the thought had suddenly hit him, he sat, and pulled Alfreth onto his lap. "Mutti," he said, taking her by the hand, "thank you for your graciousness in this. I hated keeping you in the dark. And as for my father... for him to have died with this secret untold between us... it is almost the bitterest herb in the pot. I would that he could have seen what a sweet, kind, brave..." He held Alfreth to him afresh.

She sat up a little straighter on his knee. "Sweetheart, I, too, wish that your father, the King, could have known of our love and happiness," she said. "Although I never spoke to him, I know from all you have said that he was a good and full-hearted man..."

"He was," said Edward and there were tears shining, unshed, in his eyes.

"Know then," Alfreth continued, "that his bloodline continues. Edward, I am bearing your child, your father's grandchild!"

TWENTY-THREE

Wintancaestre, the Year of Our Lord 975

AETNA

I realise now, looking back, that it was as the last remnants of daylight passed and the fullness of night came upon us that I felt the first waves of emotion, hitting me like the buffeting of a sudden squall. Wulf. Something had happened. Initially, it was intense and not altogether pleasant surprise, melting into something like happiness, but with an overtone of anxiety and apprehension. What could have happened?

We had made excellent time on the journey from Wintancaestre, and now were resting for the night in a hunting lodge tucked away in a pleasant lea surrounded by woodland, just a mile or so outside the confines of Glestingaberg. Grudgingly, I had to admit the Elfrith was an excellent horsewoman. For the sake of speed, she had eschewed the use of her litter, and both she and Morwen had kept up a brisk pace. Young Ethelred, too. The horses pulling the bier bearing the late King were hard put to keep up, and it was well that a second pair had been brought along, which, having trotted along unburdened for half that day, were fresh enough to take over the task of pall-bearers at just after midday and complete the day's journey with the required momentum.

It had been an uneventful trip. Indeed, but for that presence of our men-at-arms, no-one would have given us a second glance, for we certainly did not look as though we had anything in the way of riches about us. It seemed a shameful way for King Edgar to make his last journey through the land he had so loved. The wooden coffin was set upon a workaday cart – so, the Queen said, that it might be tough enough for the rough trip over drought hardened tracks – with dun coloured cloths thrown over it and tied in place with hempen rope. Elfrith and Morwen were dressed not dissimilarly in dark gunnas, with light cloaks held in place with the basest brooches, and even the men-at-arms had been ordered to dress in such a way that they might draw as little attention as possible. It seemed that only I – and Lucet – had taken the time to ensure that our attire, at least, was in some way appropriate to the import of the day. I had worn a dark blue gunna, with an undergunna in a slightly lighter shade, kirtled and overlaid with a blue cloak of fine wool inconspicuously woven with a gold thread which added some richness. I wore my mother's amber brooch which made me feel close to both her and my father. Ah,

Wulfstan, I would that you had been there with me, for I confess that I was feeling lost and alone.

I was still a little unsure of Lucet – not her loyalty, that seemed unequivocal already – but what to make of her. She said little, but I felt that there was a great deal going on in that pretty, fair head. Her eyes were ever taking in everything and everyone. She had worked wonders with the coin given to her and outfitted herself in a fine-spun dark grey gunna (clearly a cast off made over, but how well!) with an undergunna of almost the same shade. A tablet woven kirtle cinched in her waist, and a dull red cloak was fasted with a brooch of some base metal, made attractive by the addition of what looked like a fine chip of flint-shaped and polished so that the striations of the stone flashed as it caught the light. Like me, she had opted for a plain, white head-rail held in place across the forehead with another braid, stiffened with arum. I had complimented her, that morning, on her efforts and she dimpled prettily. "Lady, if only you knew what a joy..." Then I noticed that she had not yet had time to get her thrall collar removed. Following my eyes, she had said, "It can wait, Lady, now that I know that it is not there for ever, it can wait!"

The hunting lodge was not large, and boasted only one good-sized main Hall, with a chamber off to one side. As occasional royal accommodation, when the King had been hunting in the area, it was permanently staffed with a cook, a few thralls and stable-hands. Needless to say, Elfrith commandeered the private chamber for herself and Ethelred, with Morwen in attendance, and ordered that the coffin be removed from the cart and laid in the main Hall. I can only imagine the consternation in the kitchens when we arrived! The cook, though, rose to the occasion manfully, and before long there was hot water for washing, hot food for sustenance and cold ale to slake our thirsts. Elfrith announced that she and Morwen would take the meal in their chamber and the rest of us could do as we pleased. At least she did not make any effort to stand on ceremony. Indeed, I had the distinct feeling that my presence was an irritation she could well do without. As Aethelflaed had guessed, she took no notice whatsoever of Lucet and any idea that this was the strumpet found a few weeks earlier in in step-son's bed clearly never entered her head.

As for so many nights, it was warm and sultry. I preferred to stay out under the stars. We had brought little with us but had thought to include blankets and Lucet surprised me – yet again – by knowing how and what to gather to create a comfortable bed of bracken and other dried herbage. We were sitting with our backs against a huge oak tree, when one of the kitchen thralls brought us bowls of broiled, spiced fowl in thick gravy, with root vegetables so long and slow cooked that they had taken on all the flavours of the meat. It was delicious. Warm bread in a woven straw basket enabled us to sop up every last drop. I had just emptied my drinking vessel and asked Lucet fetch us some more ale, when the shock hit me, and I knew that something had happened back at Wintancaestre. Something that involved Wulf. I put my hands to my temples.

"Lady, are you quite well?" Lucet saw that something was amiss.

"Yes… yes, Lucet, do not worry, it is just… I had a sudden dizziness, that is all. It has been a long day and none of us slept more than a short bell last night. Another sup of ale and a good night's sleep and I shall be ready for the morrow!"

"If you are sure, Mistress. Sit still, I will be back in just a moment." She trotted off toward the kitchen, the eyes of the men-at-arms, relaxing on the other side of the lea, following her. Those not stationed in the Hall, around the King's coffin were, like us, spending the night in the open.

I tried to imaging what could have happened for Wulf to have been so affected. Clearly, it was something of import, and yet not a tragedy – thanks be to the holy Saints, for we had had enough of that for a while – though it was something that gave my brother considerable pause and was fraught with consequence. I could glean nothing further from my intuition. I would have to put it to one side until we were home, but the feeling of unease remained.

Lucet returned. "Oh, Lady, you look better already. Pray the Lord it was, indeed, just a moment of tiredness. The cook – he is a scally! – has put a little extra dash of honey in the ale. He swears it will give us the sweetest sleep as his bees sup from the poppies hereabouts. Although…" she stifled a yawn, "like you, Mistress, I do not think that I will need any rocking this eve. See, I have plumped up your palliasse, such as it is, and if you keep a blanket below and above, you will feel no prickles and stay warm – my, though, it is a warm night once again!" This must have been the longest I had ever heard her speak, except for that night she came to warn me of the *mus-brod* plot. I warmed to her.

I drank about half the draught and put the rest to one side should I awake in the night. The camp fire lit by the men-at-arms had burnt down to embers, and their voices, low as they chatted amongst themselves with an occasional burst of laughter, was comforting. It reminded me of nights in the Great Hall at Radendunam when Wulf and I slipped in to sleep by the hearth and could hear the ceorls as they passed the pot around. I pulled the blanket up to my chin and snuggled into the nest of bracken. With Lucet beside me, and the connection I felt to Wulf, my misgivings of earlier in the evening began to subside. I felt myself beginning to drift off into sleep.

I do not think many minutes had passed, though it was hard to tell, for perhaps I had drifted off into that delightful half slumber before deep sleep summons the soul, when a tumult arose as though the Devil himself had come upon us, with the snorting of a horse hard ridden, a thunder of hoofbeats and a great swirling of cloaks. The men-at-arms closest to the trackway drew their weapons, those nearer the lodge roused, like myself, from slumber began shouting and scrambling for their swords and from within the Hall someone ran out with a flaring torch, flame and sooty smoke trailing behind him.

"Dear Lord in Heaven," cried Lucet.

"No, not quite, my dear, but his ambassador from Cantuaria," came a familiar voice. The Archbishop slid to the ground, staggering only slightly from his obvious fatigue.

"Dunstan!" I was on my feet and flying into his arms in seconds, quite forgetting any formalities due to his office. He hugged me close, and I could have wept for the sensation of safety and comfort his embrace gave me. "Oh, Dunstan! How come you here? When we left Wintancaestre this morning, we could only hope that you would be there with the others for the Witan upon our return. But no matter, it is so very good to have you with us!"

Dunstan threw the reins of his horse to one of the men-at-arms. "I received the sad news of our King's death yester-postnoon. One of my – friends – at the New Minster sent a message via several changes of horse the moment the tragedy was known. I lost not a moment in reaching Wintancaestre and then had but a long bell's rest and have caught up with you. Thank the Saints."

The men-at-arms had gathered around and, when they realised who our visitor was, had fallen to their knees. The only exception was the man holding the horse who stood on one leg dipping up and down, uncertain whether to kneel in the Archbishop's honour or retain his grip upon the beast's bridle. "Up, up, good fellows, none of that! But if there is a mug of ale and any food left after your supper, I would welcome it!" said Dunstan.

"Of, course, my Lord!"

"And my horse – the poor chap needs attention, too! Lad, your bobbing around will give him the sickness of the sea!"

"It will be done, Lord, pray take your ease." The men scattered on their various missions, and Dunstan turned again to me.

"So, Aetna, your brother tells me…"

"My Lord Archbishop," unseen and unheard the malevolent form of Morwen materialised beside us. "Her Majesty the Queen wishes me to inform you that she and the Aetheling Ethelred have retired for the night and after the vicissitudes of the day cannot be disturbed. She will speak with you in the morning."

"Ah," said Dunstan, as though considering this. "Yes, to be sure, the vicissitudes… she said nothing more?"

"Nothing, my Lord."

"Very well. Tell her I will attend upon her on the morrow."

"My Lord." Morwen turn and returned to the Hall as silently as she had approached.

When she was well out of earshot, the Archbishop looked at me long and hard. "Aetna, I fear that we are in the presence of a great evil, an unnatural and vicious deed has been done here, and I am at a loss to know what can be done."

I said nothing; I knew not what to say.

"Your brother – and your aunt – have told me everything of what happened two nights ago and since. There is something very wrong here. I am most disturbed by the unseemly haste of this so-called funeral. Is there no way that the body can be examined? No way without challenging the Queen openly?"

"The coffin is hard closed, Lord," I said. "Nailed and lead sealed. To insist upon opening it would be to make allegations that could never be retracted should they prove wrong. Believe me, the Dowager made every effort to see the late King's poor remains but was thwarted at every turn. Elfrith made sure to remind everyone that until a new king is crowned, she is the first and only law in the land."

"And wishes to remain so, should Ethelred become King."

"Indeed."

One of the kitchen thralls brought bread and ale, and the remains of the broiled fowl, hardly warm, but still with a delicious aroma. Dunstan sat beside us, his back against the great oak, and ate. When he had finished, he wiped his mouth on the back of his hand, successfully supressed a belch, and yawned.

"My apologies, Lady!" How strange it seemed to hear him call me that! I still felt like the little girl he had first known when I was with him. "Get you back to your beds. I will do likewise – yes, I shall be quite comfortable out here, there was a time I spent many a night out under far less benevolent stars than these – but first I must pray by the King's coffin. I loved that man like he was my son. When Aethelflaed became his stepmother, he was fortunate to have such a one in the stead of his own sweet mother, and when his father, King Edmund, died she and I often used to joke that we were of an age to be his true parents! In truth I almost came to believe that we might have been... in another life, perhaps... But fatigue is making me talk nonsense. I will pray, and then I will sleep, and in the morning... well, it will be another day."

)))))))(((((((

Birdsong and a clatter of pots and pans from the kitchens. Sunlight filtering down through the leaves and the crackle of bracken as I turned upon my makeshift palliasse. Opening my eyes, I found myself on a level with a huge bumble bee, busily foraging amid the tiny flowers of the woodland floor. It took me a few moments to remember where I was. From the activity around me it seemed that the whole of the camp was awake before me. I sat up rather stiffly, to find Lucet immediately by my side with a warm posset.

"This will take away any aches, Lady."

"Thank you, Lucet."

"There is bread and milk to break your fast, or would you prefer some cold fowl from yester-eve, and small ale?"

"The bread and milk will do nicely, with the posset. Quite the feast!"

"Yes, indeed, Lady. I will fetch you some."

She trotted off toward the kitchens and I wondered how I might make myself a little more presentable to face the day. I had not brought a change of gunna, but I did have a fresh cloak. My chatelain contained my bone comb, some spare hair pins and an extra ribbon or two, together with a fine silk head-rail, which was so light and rolled up so neatly that it could be carried with ease and still did not wrinkle too badly. I believe it cost a small fortune – a gift from Edward the Christ's Mass before last.

Lucet returned with a bowl of wonderfully fresh milk – I thought of sweet Gillycrest – and new-baked bread. Truly, the late King had had a treasure in this cook, hidden here in such an out of the way spot. I thought to mention him to Edward on my return, which brought my mind back to our immediate problem: ensuring that Edward was to be crowned the new King.

"Lady, I have brought you a damp cloth and some foaming mallow water that you may make your morning ablutions. It is just there behind the tree. Would you like me to dress your hair?"

"I think, Lucet, that I shall just comb it out loose this day and cover it with the light rail. I have ribbons to fix it. If you wish to look to yourself for a while, I shall be quite content."

"Thank you, Lady."

I leaned back against the oak and finished my posset, followed by the rest of the bread and milk. The sun was already warm. I shook out my hair and began to comb it, rather dreamily, reflecting upon what the day might bring. There was, as yet, no sign of Elfrith or Ethelred, but I could hear Dunstan's voice, as he addressed the men-at-arms.

"It is barely a mile or so to the abbey, and through open land most of the way, so I believe that we need not fear any wolf's-heads in that short distance. You men will have the honour of being the late King's escort to his final resting place, so smarten yourselves up the best you can, and when we leave, form a double line fore and aft of the bier. I have sent word ahead that we approach and the Abbot will be awaiting us at the abbey Gate. He, at least," he glanced toward the private chamber to the side of the Hall, where Elfrith had spent the night, "will ensure that the solemnity of the occasion is honoured."

I had passed the cloth over my face, arranged my head-rail and was standing smoothing down my gunna, when Dunstan approached.

"Lady, are you decent?" he called as he crossed the clearing toward where Lucet and I had slept.

"Yes, my Lord, and attempting to live up to your orders to the men!"

"My dear, you look charming, as always!" I was folding away my cloak of yesterday before donning my red one for the day when he said. "Aetna, it is shameful how little preparation has been made for this day… there is not even a respectable covering for Edgar's coffin. May I borrow your blue cloak to lay over it? I think it might almost be large enough. Edgar had many splendid attributes, but he was large of heart and not of body, the Lord bless him!"

"I would be honoured, Dunstan. Is there aught else I can do?" Lucet appeared at my elbow.

"Lady? My Lord Archbishop?"

"Speak, girl."

"Lord, I have made this. For the King. If you think it worthy, it might make his last journey a little less dour." From behind her, Lucet produced a wreath of woodland flowers, bound around and trailing down from a coronet skilfully twisted together from twigs and stiff grasses. Around its tines wound periwinkle and honeysuckle and at its heart moss was packed in a mound, smooth topped to create a look of green velvet. The floral crown rested upon a foliate cushion, from which a skirt of ivy, briony and clematis fell down in rivulets of colour. It was beautiful.

"Lucet!" Where and how on earth had she learned to create such a thing, I wondered.

"That is your name, girl, Lucet?" said Dunstan. "You have made something most lovely and fit for a king who loved his land and the simple people who dwelt upon it. He would have felt blessed to know that he went to his rest with such a crown upon his coffin. Blessed and honoured."

"Lord, it is I who am honoured." That pretty dimple showed once again. "I will place it in the cool of the shade until it is needed." Practical, too! No wonder I had the feeling that my brother was quite taken with her – though, please God, not another inappropriate liaison!

"You are a wonder, Lucet," I said.

"Lord Archbishop?" The hard-working cook, wiping his hands upon his tabard, approached, followed by the thralls and the stable hands. "We would ask a boon."

"Speak on, fellow."

"We would ask that we may follow the cortege into Glestingaberg, to honour the King. We would not wish to overstep the mark, but it seems there are few to walk him to his rest, and some of us here remember well his visits to our humble lodge. He was ever a man for the chase and the tall tales around the hearth afterwards. We loved him well."

"So you did and so you shall, and right welcome!" said Dunstan. "Well," he lowered his voice and spoke to me, "It seems that despite the wilful neglect of some, Edgar will, indeed be given..."

"My Lord." Once again Morwen had materialised by our side and claimed the attention of the Archbishop. "Her Majesty will receive you now. She is in the Hall." Dunstan raised an eyebrow at me and turned to Morwen.

"Very well, and I have somewhat to say to her." He followed Morwen toward the Hall and disappeared within. What passed between Archbishop and Queen I cannot say, but Ethelred came trotting out soon after Dunstan entered, as though dismissed and excused any unpleasantness which might follow, and whilst no words could be discerned there were most certainly raised voices to be heard.

Ethelred spotted me and Lucet packing away our few travelling accoutrements and strolled over. He was beginning to be quite a nice-looking little boy when in a good frame of mind and not assuming a petulant face. I smiled at him.

"Lady Aetna."

"Your Highness. This is a sad day, the burial of your dear father, but you must be brave," I said.

"Oh, I shall be. I wept the day he died, but Mama was displeased and told me that a king should never cry, especially on a day that was fortuitous."

"Fortuitous, your Highness? Surely that is not the word she used?"

"Yes, I am quite sure it was... Lady Aetna, that girl, your companion, is she not... was she not the... friend, you know, who spent the night with my brother a while ago. The morning my father got so angry?"

"Oh, ah... well, Ethelred, it is rather..." I looked at Lucet and silently prayed that she would come to my aid. She did.

"Why, yes, Prince Ethelred, how clever of you!" she said. "Yes, your brother and I were playing a rather silly game and we wondered if we could fool everyone... making me look different so that no-one would recognise me! But you did! Now can you keep it a secret for me?"

"It seems a funny sort of game... I shall ask Mama..."

"No, no, don't do that, she has much to do today... come away with me to the kitchens and I will find you something to take with you for the ride into Glestingaberg. We cannot have our Prince feeling peckish on his fine horse..."

Lucet gently hustled Ethelred away toward the kitchen and I could see her coquettish charms working their magic upon him. Soon, the "game", no doubt, would be one which made some sense to his childish mind – for what little boy does not enjoy a secret. I hoped so, anyway, for we had enough already to keep from Elfrith, without complicating things still further.

"Enough, neither of us should say more!" Dunstan's tone was clipped and he came out of the Hall. "You men," he shouted across the clearing, "Come now and bring the bier. Time to be about the business of this day." From behind the Hall emerged the cart that had bourn the King thus far. From somewhere the occupants of the little hunting lodge had found enough blankets and curtains to drape around its rough wooden sides and lay within. The bier was removed and taken into the Hall, to reappear a few minutes later with the King's coffin bourn aloft and then placed onto the bed of the wagon. I took my dark blue and gold cloak and laid it tenderly over the coffin. Lucet, back from the kitchen, then placed her wreath, surmounted by the cleverly constructed floral crown atop it. The wagon was drawn into the centre of the clearing, all four horses harnessed to it, and the men-at-arms formed up. Dunstan, at the head of the cortege, led the way, followed by five pairs of men. Then came the King's bier, immediately followed by Ethelred, sitting high on his brown mare. Behind him, the Queen, somewhat more appropriately dressed than on the yester, in a black gunna, white undergunna and head-rail. Morwen kept her palfrey close behind her mistress's horse. I followed, Lucet just slightly behind me and to my right. The second five pairs of men-at-arms came next, followed by the lodge's household. Thus began the funeral cortege of Edgar the Peaceable, King of all Englaland.

Dunstan's messenger, sent ahead to warn the Abbot of Glestingaberg of our arrival, had also spread the word of our coming along the way to the abbey. At every cott and farmstead, every forge and mill, there waited folk to see the late King pass, to throw flowers onto the coffin and to join the entourage. They filed into the road behind us, some bearing posies, some waving kerchiefs until we were followed by a great train of ordinary people, the people for whom Edgar had so cared, the people for whom he had maintained Englaland's peace. When we reached the abbey, the bells were tolling, the monks were signing and the people filed into the great church, those unable to find places waiting patiently without. Edgar's funeral was not the grim and disregarded event we had feared.

))))))))((((((((

We spent that night as guests of the Abbot. It was something of a sentimental journey for Dunstan, so many years the holder of that office, and the present abbot was at pains to make him and us as welcome as the short notice of our arrival had permitted. Abbot Sigar had held the position for five years and during that time stamped his presence on the place in a way of which the Archbishop fully approved. The Benedictine Rule was observed and respected. This adherence did not, however, preclude a fine table, especially when honoured guests were present, nor did it disallow expenditure upon the improvement and beautification of the abbey and in particular its church. During Dunstan's tenure, the church had been extended, both to the west and east, the latter chapel now the resting place of Edgar – beside his late father, King Edmund.

With Edgar safely below ground, Elfrith seemed more relaxed. The urgency of our mission was past and while she fully planned that the morrow's journey back to Wintancaestre should begin early and conclude only when we were safely home, she appeared more than willing to enjoy the evening's entertainment. Indeed, she seemed almost skittish, sitting between the Abbot and the Archbishop exercising her undeniable skill – when she wanted – at pleasant conversation and conviviality. Sigar had not stinted upon the wine, a fine red from his personal cellar, and Elfrith drank deep. I was not sure that I had ever seen her so conspicuously in her cups, but it seemed that some great weight had been lifted from her shoulders, or perhaps laid upon them, it was hard to tell, and the wine a necessary aid to her equilibrium. Morwen escorted her to her chamber while the evening was yet quite young.

Nevertheless, the following morning, the Queen was mounted upon her horse betimes and after thanking the Abbot and the brothers for all they had done, our party was on the road. The journey back to Wintancaestre was uneventful. Ethelred seemed to have taken quite a shine to Lucet – indeed, who did not? – and for a while, when his mother was deep in conversation with Morwen and not aware of her son's actions, rode behind her, his arms about her waist, leaving his horse to trot alongside. He chatted quite amicably to us both, and I began to wonder whether, without the constant carping of the Queen and the dour presence of Morwen, he might not turn into a likeable little fellow. He was, after all, his father's son, and I could see something of his brother in him, too. Perhaps young Meryasek would be a positive influence... my mind began to wander pleasantly back to that last evening before the King's death, the dancing and the... But then a sudden sharp summons from Elfrith called Ethelred back to her and, like a young hound inured to the jerk of its chain, he reluctantly obeyed.

We had the merest of rests at midday and pressed on into the evening. Now, it seemed, the Queen was anxious to be back in her own Great Hall. As we approached Wintancaestre, I began to feel apprehensive of what I would discover to be the origin of my intuitive knowledge that Wulf had experienced some shock or even – pray the Saints not – misfortune. We entered by the West Gate, Her Majesty and the rest of her party, together with the Archbishop, immediately heading toward the Great Hall, Lucet and myself through the city toward the Nunneminster. Wintancaestre was teaming. Ealdormen and churchmen were already arriving for the imminent convention of the Witan and all had with them men-at-arms, companions, thralls and various hangers-on. The merchants and shopkeepers were taking advantage of the sudden influx of potential customers, their shopfronts overflowing with goods, and as if by some alchemic attraction, hawkers and peddlers, cut-purses and street entertainers had flooded into the city, ready to take any opportunities which presented themselves. It was annoying to be so close to the comforts of our own Hall, only to have to shoulder our horses through the crowds and almost fight the way to our door.

I consider myself a fair horsewoman, but I confess that my backside was sore as I dismounted. Lucet, too, winced as we handed our reins to the stable men and headed into the Hall. I was just commenting that two solid days in the saddle with only a brief respite between would take a while to... when Aethelflaed, alerted to our arrival by Edith, came flying out to meet us.

"Oh, my dears, it is good to have you home! The city is become like a madhouse... it is ever thus at such a time... We were more afeared for you reaching home through the streets here than the rest of your journey. Edward sent Wulf and Ratkin to look for you at the West Gate, but they must have missed you in the crush. Edith, send one of the men to find Master Wulf and tell him his sister is safe home. The Witan is to be convened in two days' time... but come you in now, come in and rest and eat and... oh, you must be exhausted!"

We were, indeed, pleased to be home. Lucet had not yet spent a night at the Nunneminster Hall, so sudden had been her addition to the household before our departure, and she was now hustled away by Edith to find Onwen and be shown where our chambers were. Aethelflaed drew me into the *peristylium* and sat me down. Tumblers of cool small ale were to hand, and honey cakes. I drank thankfully but was almost too tired to eat. From what my aunt had already said, I was relieved to know that nothing untoward had happened to Wulf, but I was still curious as to what had happened on the evening of the day we left. My curiosity, though, would have to wait. Aethelflaed was anxious to hear about the funeral, and whether her "dear boy" had, finally, received at least some honour. I told her of all that had passed and she seemed a little comforted by the way things had fallen out.

"So, that cat, Elfrith, was not able to shuffle the late King away without the love of his people coming to the fore! It is as it should be, he ever loved the simple things…"

"And what of happenings here, Aunt?" I said. I had never mentioned to her the inexplicable harmony which, even at a distance, linked Wulf and my thoughts and emotions together. In fact, we had never told anyone – there were still too many, like Father Aelmer, to whom such mysteries smacked uncomfortably close to witchery.

"Ah, well, as you have seen, my love, the city is already being gripped with a frenzy in anticipation of the *Witangemot* and the confirmation of the new King. The Chief Ealdorman is already arrived, with his brother and brother-in-law, too. Young Elfwine is with them, you will be pleased to hear. We have had word that your Uncle Brithnoth and Lord Ethelwine will be arriving on the morrow. Archbishop Oswald is here already, of course, and Dunstan? Yes, I felt sure he would return with you. And, oh, there just seem to be more and more arriving all the time…"

"I really meant had there been any more… personal… occurrences, Aunt," I said.

She looked at me very straight and gave a little sigh.

"My dear, I have to tell you that your little – or not so little – deception concerning Alfreth and the Prince Edward is no longer unknown to me. No, no, do not look so distressed! I will admit that when I first learned what had been going on behind my back for so long, I was… disappointed and hurt, and, yes somewhat shocked. At the inappropriateness of the liaison, to say the least. But, well, these things happen. And more. Indeed, more has happened." She cast a look at the door. "Alfreth is with child! After I learned of the situation on the evening you left, we all met together at Thella and Ratkin's cott. She told us then."

So that was the shock which had coursed through Wulf like a bolt of lightning and shaken me at the same moment. "Aunt," I said, "I am truly sorry to have deceived you in this… I, we… knew not whether to… that is…"

"Peace, child, it is done now, and with this new revelation there are greater considerations than I believe Edward yet understands. I have forborne to speak with him, or rather them, upon the matter yet, but it must be done before the Witan meets."

"Where is Alfreth now?" I asked.

"This heat is making her feel a little unwell," said Aethelflaed. "She spends much time in her chamber. I fear that she is not as strong as she might be."

And, for the time being, that was where the matter was left. The time of the evening meal was upon us and Aethelflaed and I ate alone in the Hall, repairing to our beds shortly afterwards. As I drifted off to sleep, happy to be back in my own chamber, I wondered what the next few days might bring.

The following morning, despite some little sickness, Alfreth joined Aethelflaed and myself in breaking our fast at the long table. When she entered the Hall, I embraced her and, first making sure that we were not overheard, congratulated her upon her news. She smiled, a little embarrassed, and thanked me, but I could not help feeling that she was still anxious that my aunt had more, yet, to say on the matter and that in spite of her apparent acceptance of the situation it would not be anything that she, or Edward, wished to hear.

I was anxious to see Wulf, and as soon as I could politely excuse myself, called Lucet and informed her that we were bound for the King's Great Hall, for so I still thought of it, although, for just these few days, there was no king. Before we left, Aethelflaed beckoned Lucet to her.

"Child, the Lady Aetna has told me of the service you did my late step-son, the King."

"Your Majesty, it was but a token. But I am glad it was thought fair. He was a good, kind man."

"He was. Take this." She handed Lucet an unclipped penny. "Take it to the metal-smith and tell him to remove that thrall collar with all care. And that if he hurts you with those clippers of his, this will be the last of my money that he sees!" She smiled and cupped Lucet's face in her hands. "Edgar would be happy to know that that pretty neck of yours will no longer be encumbered."

"Lady, you are most generous. Thank you."

"Not I, Lucet, the late King. But I am happy to have you as part of our household."

Lucet dropped a neat curtsey and we were away into the hustle and chaos of the city, fighting our way through the traders and their animals, stepping over chicken coops and avoiding as best we could the accumulated filth and dust of the streets. When we reached the Great Hall, the men-at-arms immediately opened the doors for us, and, upon asking if they knew the whereabouts of my brother, I was informed that he was with Prince Edward in the withdrawing chamber. There were more guards at the curtain separating the Hall from the private chambers. Apparently, Edward had had enough of the visiting Ealdormen and had left orders that they should not be allowed access. We, on the other hand, were admitted immediately.

"Lady Aetna!" Edward was seated in a window embrasure, Wulf at his side. "It is good to see you. And the ever resourceful Lucet!"

We curtseyed and I kissed his hand. The dynamic was already changing. After all, if matters turned out as we wished, Edward would soon be our anointed King. Wulf and I embraced, and I searched his face.

He looked worried and tired. Edward, too, looked as though he had enjoyed little rest in the days we had been away.

"Your Highness," I said, "I have heard the joyful news of your impending fatherhood."

His expression lightened. "Yes, it is wonderful, is it not? How fared Alfreth this morn? I fear she is suffering somewhat from the sickness of the morn."

"She is well, sire."

"Praise God!"

"Lady," said Lucet, "if you have no need of me for the next hour, may I be allowed to run that errand that the Dowager Queen suggested?"

"Yes, of course, Lucet. Return here before the midday meal. Until then, your time is your own." With her customary pretty dimpling, Lucet bobbed a curtsey and left.

"Errand?" said Wulf, raising an eyebrow.

"She is to have her thrall collar removed," I said. "She has been a treasure this last three days..." I went on to tell Edward and my brother the details of Edgar's final journey and his laying to rest. As I had suspected, Elfrith's report had been less than comprehensive.

"Dunstan told us something of it," said Edward, "but last night he was too tired to talk much and this morning he has been ensconced with the Archbishop of Eoforwic since daybreak. They have been canvassing the Ealdormen who have already arrived and making plans to speak to those expected today. I am to have a meeting with him this postnoon. The Ealdormen keep pestering me for audience, but Dunstan says that it is better not to speak to any of them alone before the Witan gathers, that he will be my mouthpiece until then. It is hard to know... well, I suppose it can do no harm. But there are things that must be told..."

"Your Majesty," I said, glancing at Wulf as I spoke, "The Dowager Queen is anxious that she should be able to speak to you – and Alfreth – before the Witan." Before we left the Nunneminster Hall she had taken me to one side and impressed upon me the importance of such a conference. "She would that you come to Thella and Ratkin's house at sunset where she, Alfreth and I will be waiting. Wulf, you are to come, too. Sire, she said to tell you that your very future as king will depend upon it."

"Very well," replied Edward, without seeming to be at all intimidated by the implied imperative of the gathering. "I find nothing amiss at a chance to see my dear step- grandmother – and, of course, my beautiful wife."

Lucet returned promptly just before noon, and we were invited by Edward to join him for the midday repast in the Great Hall. It was busy with all manner of visitors, but the High Table was set apart and none allowed to approach without permission. We had barely finished our meal when, to my great joy, I saw my Uncle Brithnoth, together with Ethelwine and Oswig and a number of lesser thegns enter through the main doors, dusty and travel-stained, and in need of rest and food. Edward saw them, too.

"For your family, Wulf – and Aetna – I make exception, whatever the Archbishop may say… send down to them at once to come up here, never before have I been so pleased to see my father's old friends."

One of the thralls hurried down and bade the Ealdormen and Oswig to the High Table, while their companions found places lower down the Hall.

Ethelwine, as Ealdorman of All East Anglia, greeted Edward first. "Sire! For so it shall surely be within a day! My – our – greatest condolences on the loss of your royal father. This year's ill-fortune seems to know no bounds. My wife, too, sends you her love, if she may be permitted the intimacy."

"Good Ethelwine, it is always a pleasure to have you at court, and to receive the kind words of your lovely wife. Would, indeed, that my father was here to greet you one last time. And my Lord Ealdorman Brithnoth. You, too, are most welcome. And Oswig. Come, come, sit and eat, drink and take your ease. I fear we are a trifle over endowed with visitors, but I have made certain that a chamber has been saved for you in the King's Hall, here. Though I fear the three of you must bunk together."

Now it was Brithnoth's turn to speak. "Lord King," he kissed Edward's hand. "You are most generous. Aelflaed, too, was heartbroken to hear of the King's loss. She has sent you this small token of sympathy." From within his belt pouch my uncle withdrew a small package wrapped in parchment and handed it to Edward. He unwrapped it carefully to reveal a small silk kerchief, with the late King's cypher delicately embroidered upon it. "She had intended it as a gift for your father's next natal-day and hopes you will accept it with her dearest wishes."

"I shall, right gladly, it is a most thoughtful token. Please, when you return home, thank her most profusely. I shall hope to see her at *my* Court very soon! And now, my lords, you must excuse me, for I have a meeting with Archbishop Dunstan which I am to attend with all punctuality, or I fear that I shall spend this night doing some arch-episcopal penance!" He stood and withdrew into the private chambers.

Wulf and I remained for some time catching up on news from home. I introduced Lucet as my new companion. No need to mention her late status, for the thrall collar was gone without trace. I left to return to the Nunneminster Hall with Brithnoth's promise that he would call upon Aethelflaed as soon as time permitted.

As the shadows lengthened that evening, Aethelflaed, Alfreth and I left for the short walk to Thella and Ratkin's cott. As an afterthought, my aunt suggested that Lucet came too, for, as she pointed out, she was already so deep in our kin's convoluted involvement with the royal family that she might as well be hung for a sheep as a lamb! I expected Lucet to be somewhat disturbed by this, but she grinned impishly. "I should be honoured, Your Majesty!" was her only reply.

I suppose I should not have been surprised to find that Edward was already there, his eagerness to spend time with Alfreth undiminished. Wulf, too, was seated in the front chamber of the house, supping ale with Ratkin and they both rose to their feet in salute at our arrival, bowing to the Queen Dowager. Thella bustled about, offering wine or ale and small cakes. The room was not large and the eight of us had but little space, the evening hot and humid as had been the day.

Aethelflaed did not intend to waste any time. "Thella, I pray you, close the windows onto the street... Yes, I know it is airless, but there must be no chance we are overheard. The sooner some things are said, the sooner we shall be able to be away. I shall not mince my words. Edward, you know that I am ever only anxious to speak what I believe to be in your best interests. You will not like what you are about to hear, but I pray you, listen to me.

"Tomorrow, when the Witan meets, the future of this country will be settled for a generation to come. I believe that we, in this room, all have our suspicions about the late King's death. They cannot be spoken out loud, for we have not proof, but from all that has happened in these last few months it is clear that Elfrith is determined that Ethelred be King and that, in effect, it is she who will hold the reigns of this nation. This is not the time or place to conjecture upon all that would mean for the House of Wessex, nor for Englaland itself, but it cannot be allowed to happen. There are, thank the good Lord, many on the Witan who think as we. But there are good arguments which will be put forward in favour of Ethelred. First, he is the son of the anointed and crowned Queen. No, do not interrupt me, Edward, I beg your forgiveness, this must be spoken. No-one can suggest that your own sweet mother was not his lawful wife, nor that you are not an Aetheling, but she was not crowned a queen, and... well, you can see how the case could be made. Second, it is common knowledge that you and your father had not been on the best of terms recently. Ethelred is, of course, only a child, but he has never been at odds with his father... Elfrith will paint him as a loving and obedient son: the type of son his father would have named heir, had be not been taken from us so untimely. Yes, I know things between you and Edgar had improved of late, but your opposition to his wishes with regard to your betrothal have been the subject of much discussion.

"Now, listen, I take no pleasure in saying this, especially with Alfreth in her present condition, but fact of your marriage, and the expectation of your heir *must* be kept secret. For the time being at least. You simply cannot expect the Witan – even those members who are closest to you – to accept your alliance with (forgive me, Alfreth, it pains me to say this) a nameless girl, little above a thrall, plucked from the gutter by the church."

Edward, who I could see had been quietly fuming for some minutes, was on his feet, shaking with anger. "Step-grandmother, I cannot allow..."

"My child," Aethelflaed raised her hands in supplication, "I repeat, I wish with all my heart that I did not have to say these things, but you must harken to me. Apart from all that I have said there is also the question of the Scots. Yes, Sinnyth, has no wish to marry you, but her father will have every wish to fight you. This would be a perfect excuse. You will have slighted his daughter, not to wed some higher placed princess, but for a... well, I do not have to say it again. He is already, some say, conspiring with the Northmen, this would be the greatest gift you could bestow upon them. A legitimate reason to call our armies out. Even if, by some miracle, the Witan confirmed you King, do you wish your first action to have to be a march North to war? Next year there is sure to be famine, after this year's conditions, do you want to add terror and rapine to Englaland's troubles? Is that a fitting legacy in your father's wake?

"And one more thing. If you are not King, if Ethelred is crowned and you have a son. That child will not be safe. There are always those who will look for a likely challenger to any throne, you need only look at your own family's history. Elfrith would not allow such a potential threat to live. The child's life, and that of his mother, would be as nothing to her. As swiftly snuffed out as a candle. You might think you could protect them but... well, we have seen what she is capable of doing."

Edward had retaken his seat, apparently shivering slightly despite the heat. Alfreth was white as a sheet, her hand laid on her still flat belly. Thella, Ratkin and Lucet stared at the floor and Wulf and I locked eyes, each reading the other's thoughts. Aethelflaed was silent; she had said what she had to, there was no more. How long we remained thus I do not know.

Edward was the first to break the silence. "But, surely..."

"Surely what, my love?" Aethelflaed's voice softened.

"There must be some way?"

"Can you see it? Is there anything that I have said that, in your heart of hearts, you do not know is true? Edward, you have been living in a dream these three months. A lovely dream; a dream of love. But it cannot be. You will be... you are... a king. You have a destiny already chosen for you. But, you are yet young. You both are." She held a hand out to Alfreth. "Let your child be born away from here, in safety, my dear. Edward, take the throne, be a king worthy of your father. Make a reputation of your own and then, then, you may be able to bring your family together again. Once the Witan and the people have seen how you govern and have come to trust your judgement. Patience, that is the key. All may yet be as you wish. In time."

TWENTY-FOUR

The Great Hall was transformed. When we arrived the following morning to witness the preliminary arguments and deliberations of the Witan, we found the huge open space at its centre, usually encumbered only with the long and high tables, furnished with four great trestles, arranged to form an oblong, with armed chairs at the top and sides. At the centre of the arrangement a plinth was draped with cloth of gold, upon it the crown which had been placed upon Edgar's head at his coronation.

Around the walls, benches were ranged for those of a high enough status to merit them, with standing space only toward the end of the Hall. The bells for Terce had rung while we were making our way through the city, and, though it was yet early in the day it was already becoming hot and humid. The smell from the River Arle wafted across the streets and into the Hall. It had become a turgid, fetid stream, little eased by the flash flooding of the previous week. The alders along its length were looking sad and jaded. I pressed a kerchief containing mint and rosemary to my nose and wondered how long this meeting would last; I suspected longer than any of us wished. As Dowager Queen, Aethelflaed was accorded a place at the table of the Witan itself (though she would not have a vote, nor take place in the private deliberations) and I had a place reserved on one of the long benches. Upon Aethelflaed's insistence Alfreth remained at the Nunneminster Hall. Lucet remained with her. The revelations of the previous evening had hit Alfreth hard and we did not want Edward distracted by her unhappy presence.

The Ealdormen and Bishops took their seats toward the upper end of the central island, with lesser thegns and an occasional Abbot lower down. The places at the very top were, for the present, empty. Then the curtain at the back of the Hall was thrown open, and the Queen entered, followed by the two Aethelings and the Archbishops of Cantuaria and Eoforwic. Wulf, who came in behind Edward, made his way across to me, and squeezed onto the bench between myself and a portly woman – the wife of one of lesser, local Ealdormen. She was not pleased to have her space invaded thus and tutted pointedly.

"Your pardon, Lady," said Wulf, flashing his most engaging smile. "Were it not that my sister is unfittingly unescorted without me I should not essay to take a place beside such a beautiful woman without first being invited." The Lady in question simpered and was mollified.

"Do not drag me into your nonsense!" I whispered, though finding it hard to supress a giggle.

"Aunt Aethelflaed looks magnificent," he whispered back.

She did. Ethel and Onwen had done a fine job preparing her for this day. Her gunna and undergunna were both worked in cloth-of-silver and clung to her body revealing her still slim form to perfection. The traces of silver in her fair hair – the small amount showing beneath her head rail, which she continued to wear in the older fashion – seemed to be enhanced by her gown and added a glimmer to the gold. The stiffened braid holding the rail in place was woven with a pattern of diamond-shaped lozenges in red, almost as though she wore a coronet of rubies. She rose, as did the others at the table and rest of us who had seats, when the Royal party entered.

Elfrith took her place at the centre of the topmost trestle, Ethelred to her right and Edward to her left. It seemed that for this occasion she was in mourning. She wore black. A black gunna, with an undergunna in the same dramatic shade, though shot through with purple. It glinted like the iridescent feathers on a magpie's wing as she moved. Her head-rail, likewise, was black, but she still favoured the fashion once considered only appropriate for a young girl – the short, square kerchief allowing her abundant, deep, fox-red air to fall free.

Along the side trestles, to Edward's left sat Archbishops Dunstan and Oswald. Beside them, Ealdormen Ethelwold of East Anglia, Brithnoth of Eastseaxe and more Ealdormen and Bishops mostly from the shires of Wessex, South Mercia and the extreme West. To the right of Ethelred sat the Chief Ealdorman, Alfhere, his brother and brother-in-law, Alfheah and Alfric and next to them Thored of Eoforwic, before the lesser Ealdormen, largely from Northern shires. Thored's place, so high up the table, raised an eyebrow here and there – he was little known and must have come into someone's favour of late. There were a few churchmen among those lower down, but noticeably fewer than on Edward's side.

A horn sounded a fanfare at the rear of the Hall and a herald called the gathering to order.

"On this thirteenth day of July, in the year of our Lord nine hundred and seventy-five, this Witangemot is convened. May all those who have a place upon it speak fair and in the name of our Saviour, Jesus Christ. Let no weapon be drawn, nor any violence inflicted. Words alone are the means by which decisions shall be made in this place. Let the conference begin. Pray silence for Her Majesty Queen Elfrith, relict of His Late King Edgar."

Silence fell. Elfrith rose to her feet.

"Chief Ealdorman, Ealdormen of the Shires, Archbishops, Bishops and worthy thegns. Dowager." This last was a calculated snub. Our aunt did not choose to react. "I stand before you a widow, and speak as such, not as a queen, but as the widow of the great King that was my husband, Edgar. His untimely death has surely been that tragedy which was foreshadowed by the shaking of the earth at the beginning of this year and the fateful long-tailed star which hung in the heavens for so long in the spring. This summer the very heavens have rebelled against that which has come to pass in the harshness of drought. But God's will be done. My husband has been called to sit upon a more worthy throne and he is surely even now numbered among the fortunate few who are already upon the Lord's right hand. I pray," and here she put her palms together and looked, longingly, toward the heavens, or rather the smoke blackened rafters, "that he may speak now, through me.

"You meet together today to confirm the new King. My beloved husband was, indeed, fortunate to have two sons. The Aetheling Edward, son of poor Elfa whose frailty took her from him and my own son, Prince Ethelred. You may, perhaps, think that it is only my own, natural, maternal instincts which prompt me to speak as I shall, but," here she laid her hands upon her bosom, "it is in the interests of Englaland that I urge you to decide as I believe Edgar himself would have wished.

"The kingdom stands perilously close to the loss of that long peace which my husband worked so hard to maintain. An uncertain succession and all that brings would exacerbate the insecurity felt on our Northern boarders where the threat from the heathen Viking is at its greatest. Likewise, the hostility of the Scots – due in no small part to the Aetheling Edward's recent unwillingness to bow to his father's wishes – is undeniable." Where was this going, I wondered.

"It has been, in recent months, a heavy weight upon my heart that my husband's health has been so poor. He was ever a slight man – slight of stature and weak, some might say, in body – though stout of heart. Over the years, there have been many times when I have feared for his life, his stomach often pained him and I have used my own poor skills to relieve him. In the end... well, we know not what ill elf-shot took him from us. My fear now, yes, my honest fear, is that the Aetheling Edward, son of a delicate and short-lived mother and a father whose health was less than robust, might not be strong enough to shoulder the hard tasks which lie ahead. He has already proved ill-disposed toward the idea of marriage and the fathering of his own heir. Mayhap he is unsure of his own future health. Can such a future for Englaland be the best for which we may wish?"

Edward looked as though he might be about to make some outburst in protest, and I felt Wulf's will echo mine that he should remain silent. We watched him clench his jaw and take a deep breath to maintain control of his emotions.

Elfrith continued. "My son, the Prince Ethelred, is young, yes, but he is strong and has ever been willing to follow his father's behest. Already there is a possible marriage in train for him: Ealdorman Thored's daughter Aelfgifu is of his own age and such an alliance with a Northern shire would bolster the uncertain loyalties of the region." She paused for effect. "And do not forget, my lords, that Prince Ethelred is the son of a queen. The Lady Elfa, though my late husband's true wife – none dispute that – was not crowned. How can it be doubted that it was King Edgar's wish that his younger son, dutiful, devoted and the child of his father's only anointed Queen, blessed with the same holy oil that consecrated him upon the day of his own coronation, be similarly crowned? His youth should not stand against him: he has the benefit of his godfather, the Chief Ealdorman's, expert knowledge and guidance, and my own steady hand as Regent. Together, until the prince gains his majority, we shall hold the realm safe and secure."

She resumed her seat. Using the King's recent ill-health and the untimely loss of Edward's mother against him, painting the prince as physically weak and of uncertain manliness, this was a tactic that none of us had anticipated. And how cleverly she had slipped in Edward's antipathy toward his father's recent wishes. The Chief Ealdorman shuffled a couple of the parchments which he had in front of him and looked as though he was about to stand and speak, but he was pre-empted by Aunt Aethelflaed. She rose to her feet and looked around the assembly.

"Your *Majesty*, Highnesses and my lords, both secular and spiritual." There was just enough emphasis on the words to imply sarcasm whilst maintaining perfect correctness. "I, too, am the widow of a king. None have more experience than I, wife of King Edmund, grandson of the Great King Alfred, of the dangers of sibling rivalry. My husband was one of three brothers, all kings of this great land. Three kings, of different mothers, and yet each succeeded in turn to the throne without enmity or dissent, by due virtue of their age. This, surely, is the exemplar to which we should look. Prince Edward is his father's elder son. It is beyond logic to call his health into question: his mother, rest her soul, died as a result of a second and ill-fated childbirth – a sad, but not unusual occurrence. His late father, the King, was of perfectly robust health until…" She hesitated, careful in her choice of words. "Until most recently when, like many amongst us, he suffered some slight indispositions of the belly. Again, it is not an unusual occurrence when fashions in food change. He was, as a child, and he remained, like a son to me; his health was ever good, though his stature slight. Prince Edward, too, is of rude vigour.

"As to the suggestion that Prince Edward was unmindful of his father's wishes and that they were on ill terms… it is wholly without foundation. True, the prince was not in favour of the proposed alliance with the

398

Caledonian tribes but that was based on sound and considered beliefs, matters discussed with his father and ultimately agreed to be valid. Kennyth of the *Scotti* himself rendered a fiasco of the so-called betrothal, when he suggested an alternative alliance for his daughter. In all other matters King Edgar and his son were in perfect accord. And, unlike his younger son – I lay no blame, for the lad is yet young and had not the opportunity – he spent much time with his father. He has learned much of the late King's statesmanship, the skills which have kept this country at peace throughout Edgar's reign. He is become a young man of learning and letters, too, studying the history of this land. True, he is yet young, though not so young as to need a Regent! And should he be in need of advice, he has the whole of the Witan for that purpose." That was clever, to suggest that those present would play a part in the young King's growth toward full political maturity.

"And, should he be in need of more direct, personal counsel, he will have my experience and that of his extended family, the Ealdormen of the East, at his disposal and that of the Archbishops of…"

"Aye, there, there at last, we have it!" Alfhere banged his fist on the trestle and came to his feet. "Aetheling Edward is, and as King would be, in the thrall of the Church. All this talk of frailty or health, threats of war from the North or within, is as so much dross. The real choice is between a regimen cowed before the power and wealth of the Church and determined to facilitate its o'ertaking of this nation's lands or one which allows the honest estate holders and land owners to benefit from the profits of their own fields and fisheries. A king must, of course, be mindful of his bishops, but even Our Lord counselled to render unto Caesar…"

Now Dunstan was on his feet. "Chief Ealdorman, do not presume to quote the Holy Scriptures at me! Prince Edward is his own man. My brothers and I will serve and advise him in the best interests of Englaland – though if that course runs alongside scouring the abbeys of the impious, the secular lay-clerks posing as Abbots, their wives openly beside them and their whores in residence in the dorters… and the starving of the truly holy brothers and their missions to the poor and the infirm, then…"

"You have your argument well prepared, Archbishop," replied Alfhere. "Clearly this is, indeed, the aspect of the succession which has been exercising your…"

Within moments, Ealdorman Ethelwine, too, was standing glowering back at the Chief Ealdorman, beside whom his brother, Alfheah, now also stood, in his hand a sheaf of parchments which he waved toward the Archbishop.

"Ay, he does! These, these are the latest deeds making land over to the church in Bedricsworth – and the remains of the Holy Saint Edmund not even enshrined within an abbey yet! But in them he directly disenfranchises that good man Bedric and forbids him or his family from profiting... That land has been in the same family..."

Now Ethelwine waded into the fray. "Lord Alfheah, legal matters within my own Ealdormanry, whether relating to the church or otherwise, are of no concern to you. You should not even have indents and parchments in such regard! How did you..."

The assembly was disintegrating into chaos. There was a loud rapping upon the table-top. Elfrith, furious that the subject of the succession seemed about to be subsumed by a political free for all had taken hold of the nearest drinking vessel and was smashing it down repeatedly, continuing to do so until those standing and shouting – which now included a number of those lower down the Hall – resumed their places. Aethelflaed remained standing and stared the Queen down until silence once again reigned.

"I say only, now, to this 'meeting of wise men'. Look to your consciences," she said. "If the very mention of churchmen can prompt the dissent we have just witnessed, is it not evident that the counsel of the church is much needed? There are those upon this venerable board who would seek to influence the new King – whoever it might be – to break away from the rule of Our Lord. And those who seek to use it to maintain the peace and prosperity of Englaland. Let the natural law of succession come to pass. We do not need a Regent, nor the influence of a king-maker." Here she glared at the Chief Ealdorman. "We need the late King's elder son."

It was becoming increasingly hot and airless within the Great Hall. The smell of sweat and massed ill-breath made the room reek of humanity and once again I pressed my kerchief to my nose, wishing that I was able to escape the press of people, but they were hard-packed on the benches before and beside me. The arguments continued, and I was beginning to feel quite faint. When Wulf shook me gently by the shoulder, I realised that I had been almost insensible for a while.

"Aetna, wake up, are you unwell? By Heavens, it is hot in here, can you bear it a little longer? Look, the Aethelings are about to speak for themselves. Then the private deliberations will begin... we will be out of here then and you can take some refreshment. But you must hear this..."

Edward passed a kerchief across his face, wiping away the sweat, and stood. For the first time I realised how like his father he had grown of late. The same fine, light brown hair and straight nose. And his eyes, yes, they were like Edgar's, too.

"Your Majesties, Queen Elfrith, Dowager Queen Aethelflaed – stepmother and step-grandmother – Your Highness, my brother, Ethelred. Ealdormen, bishops and worthies, I greet you. I thank you for your solicitations and condolences on the loss of my father.

"You have heard many words from many great men – and women – who, I am prepared to agree, have more experience than I. More experience, yes, but not more love for this country, nor for its ways and its people. For the past three years, since my father's coronation, I have stood beside him as he deliberated the best course for Englaland: the best way to keep her safe, peaceful and prosperous. It is true that that there have been certain matters of a… a personal nature upon which I disagreed with him. But I am young. Not as young as my brother, but still young enough to think, on occasion that I know better than my elders." He favoured his audience with a wry grin and received a few sympathetic chuckles in return. "I am now in my seventeenth year. It is old enough to know my duty. And my duty, as the elder son of the King, is to govern our country as my father would have wished. The loss of a parent – a father in particular – does much to instil maturity into a son; it reminds him of his own mortality, of the need for a succession and I vow to you that I shall take that responsibility seriously. I do take it seriously." We held our breath for a moment, fearful that he might yet be tempted to reveal his alliance with Alfreth, but he continued in another vein.

"I am hale in heart and limb – my stepmother is over-zealous in her foster duties to think otherwise, though I thank her for her concern." Careful, Edward, the Witan is not fond of sarcasm. "And although my poor mother was not an anointed Queen, neither, for the greater part of his reign was my father himself an *anointed* King! Queen Elfa came from a noble family, long in service as Ealdormen to the Kings of this land, since the time of the Great Alfred himself." This was a well-made point, for Elfrith's lineage was unimpressive to say the least.

"Lastly, I say this to the *Witangemot*: much has been said of the role of the Church in the life of this nation. Of the influence of churchmen. The King of all Englaland leads his people under the laws of the Lord our God and his Son, our Saviour. If he does not, then he cannot expect the nation to prosper. Advice, counsel and direction from those appointed to the highest stations within the Holy Church are always to be sought. No King has ever been obliged to act on such advice, but not to hear it and think on it is to court disaster. Therefore, to have the good Archbishops Dunstan of Cantuaria and Oswald of Eoforwic and their successors on my right hand would, indeed, be my wish. However, regarding the Restoration of the Benedictine Rule, the conflict between the Lay Clerks and the Clergy, ownership and management of Church lands, these are matters for the abbeys and the Ealdormen of the shires in which they are situate to settle between themselves, each case upon its own merits. This," he looked straight at Chief Ealdorman Alfhere, "is not the time, nor the place to bring them to the table.

"My lords, I give you my word that as your king my reign would be based upon faith in our Lord Jesus Christ, fealty to this nation and to you in return for yours unto me. And fairness toward all, spiritual, temporal, noble or base-born."

There were murmurs of approval from many in response to this, and even a few hands pounding upon the table top. Wulf squeezed my hand and patted it. Edward had spoken well. But now it was Ethelred's turn. As he rose and took a short step forward, I could just make out that he had mounted upon a small wooden block, with the aim of making him appear a little taller than he was in reality – not too much, just enough to give him a slight boost in stature for his age. Elfrith had not missed a trick.

"My Lords of the *Witangemot*, and honoured guests." Clever – by this time everyone was getting tired of hearing the formalities repeated. "I am, as you are, saddened and bereaved at the loss of my father, the King. I will say but little, for those who understand these things better than I have already made my case. But I will pledge you my word, upon the honour of my father's crown, that under the guidance of the Chief Ealdorman, the rest of this noble Witan, the Holy Church and my mother, Her Majesty Queen Elfrith, who, by virtue of her coronation upon the same day as my father, stands in Regency for me, I will be a true King and guardian of this land, and upon my maturity take the reins of power unto myself."

He stepped down and retook his seat, turning to Elfrith. "There, Mama, was that not exactly as you taught me?" The Queen stiffened and her jaw tightened. Undoubtedly it had been, but the fact need not be emphasised. Poor Ethelred, he would not be receiving any praise from his mother after that last remark!

There was a general shuffling and scraping of seats as the Witan settled for its private musings. The herald signalled for the horn to sound once again and then called "Clear the Hall. The *Witangemot* is now in debate." The royal party, together with Aethelflaed, left through the curtains to the withdrawing chambers, everyone else filed out through the great doors, which closed behind us with a resounding thud. When they opened again the decision would have been made.

The square was already packed with those awaiting news, and a couple of enterprising local taverns had set up tables bearing tapped casks, doing a roaring trade in ale and mead. Wulf elbowed his way through the crowd, paid a premium for relatively clean looking drinking vessels and bought two large, foaming horns. We both swigged at them thirstily and then forced our way back toward the Hall, looking for a shady spot in which to wait. No-one, it seemed, had any intention of quitting the stifling, hot and smelly gathering until we knew the outcome of the Witan's deliberations. A familiar voice came from the crowd and Wulf received a hearty slap on the back.

"How now, you two, I see your positions both now warrant you a seat with the nobility! I had to find myself a place to stand with the *hoi polloi* at the back of the Hall!"

"Elfwine!" I cried. "How good to see your face. These have been difficult times!"

"Coz! Why did you not send word you were here?" said Wulf. "We could have found you a seat... though, no doubt, you were travelling with the Chief Ealdorman and his party, so I am surprised that..."

"Be surprised by nothing that comes out of Mercia," replied Elfwine, grimly. "I tell you," he glanced around to make sure that nobody was paying any attention to us, "Since the late King had me be his eyes and ears there, I have heard things..." He wrested Wulf's drinking horn from my brother's hand and took a long pull, handing it back half empty. "We will speak of them later in private, when, God willing we have a new King who... but no, I have said too much until we know which way the Witan leans!"

The press of the crowd had jostled us back in the direction of the great doors into the Hall, and from within we could hear loud voices raised in argument and although we could make out no words, it was clear that tempers were lost and emotions running high. I thought that I could distinguish the deep, melodic tones of our Uncle Brithnoth, but perhaps that was just my imagination. I envisaged him standing, so much taller than all his contemporaries, speaking out in favour of Edward, making the reasoned, reasonable points that were needed to get the result we so desired. I put up a short prayer.

"Have you word of Dunna?" I asked, really to ease my thoughts away from that which was so troubling them.

"We write," said Elfwine. "She says she is tired of her life with her father and longs for her own Hall. Would that I could offer her that, or even a settled life in the service of the court." He seemed very cast down. But then he brightened. "Who knows, though, perhaps after today things may change. 'Tis said that a new besom sweeps clean!"

Time dragged by a little longer. I was beginning to feel somewhat faint once again with the press of bodies and the smell from the river, which seemed to be getting worse as evening approached. Then there was a commotion from the other side of the great door, which swung open, sentries clearing the people from the front of the Hall, moving us all back into the body of the square. The herald emerged, followed by the royal party who formed up to one side. They would have been notified of the Witan's decision already, but it was impossible to tell from their faces what we were about to hear. Dustan and Oswald stood to the other side of the herald, and the other members of the Witan, appearing last, lined up behind him. Tempers looked frayed, but, again, it was impossible to guess who had gained the upper hand. A blast from the horn demanded silence and was obeyed.

"People of Wintancaestre and of all Englaland," cried the herald. "The honourable *Witangemot* has met and conferred. I pray you now give voice and call for the long life and happy reign of..."

We held our breath. Again.

"King Edward!"

)))))))((((((((

Five days later, at the King's Tun on the banks of the great River Temes, Edward was crowned King of the English and Chieftain of All Albion. By comparison to his father's magnificent coronation, it was something of a muted affair, but Dunstan contrived to incorporate the same features and elements, putting in train his desire that all future coronations should follow the example set at Bathe. I could see the sadness in the new King's eyes as the crown was placed upon his head and knew that he was thinking about Edgar. Aethelflaed stood beside him as he received the fealty of his Ealdormen and the good wishes of the people, but I could sense his feeling of isolation, with no blood relatives to share the moment and a wife whom he could not acknowledge.

Not surprisingly, Elfrith, now technically Dowager Queen, though eschewing the title, was conspicuous by her absence having, with Ethelred, sworn allegiance to Edward privily before the court left Wintancaestre. She pleaded exhaustion after the trauma of her husband's death and announced that by the time we returned from the King's Tun, she would have left to take up residence at Corf Gate, a pleasant, well defended manor on of the Isle of Purbecig, some fifty miles south-west of Wintancaestre. Wintancaestre, she said held too many sad memories. More likely, I thought, her hopes of assuming the title of Queen Mother and Regent in tatters, she required somewhere to lick her wounds. I commented to Wulf that Wintancaestre could only be a better place for her absence and for that of the sombre, brooding Morwen. I had it in my heart to feel for young Ethelred. Just as it seemed he was beginning to know and perhaps build a relationship with his brother he was removed from court into the stifling isolation of his mother's influence. At least the good Master Meryasek would be with him.

The revels following the coronation on 18th day of July were, like the service itself, unspectacular. There was a decent feast, food and drink was plentiful and music playing, but the court did not seem to be in the mood for such things, and the evening ended early. As I lay abed, I could hear that the poor people had no such compunction. As tradition demanded, free victuals and ale were provided and the coerls and thralls took full advantage of the largesse. Laughter and ribald jokes floated to the upper chambers of the Great Hall where we were lodged and the strains of music and song bore witness that the celebrations lasted long into the warm summer night.

We had contrived that Edward and Alfreth should, at the least, have this last night together. Some judicious swapping of pallets meant that they could share the King's chamber in privacy. Wulf, who would normally have a bunk alongside Edward's, spent the night with Ratkin and Thella shared a cot with Lucet in my chamber, much to the disgust of them both. Sleep was eluding me, but I pretended to slumber and it was some little amusement to listen to them, sighing and jostling each other.

"Will you be quiet! Snoring and tossing and turning, you will wake my Lady!"

"Hush, yourself, she was MY Lady long before she was yours! If you would just move over a little, perhaps I would be able to stay on the palliasse!"

"Some people could do with losing a little weight off their backsides. No wonder you are nearly on the floor. If I had an arse as big as yours…"

"Why you little…!"

I pretended to turn over in my sleep, with a little sigh.

"Shhh…"

"You shhhh!"

I must have slept eventually, for when I woke next morning both Thella and Lucet were up and about, apparently none the worse for their less than restful night. They seemed on quite good terms, all things considered.

"Come, Lady, the day is fine and it will be good to be back at Wintancaestre," said Lucet. "See I have found you honey cakes to break your fast, indeed, there are enough for all of us."

"I think I will just have a little bread and small ale, thank you all the same," said Thella. I wondered if she had taken Lucet's comments on the size of her backside to heart. "I must make haste, in any case, if Ratkin and I are to get Alfreth on the road before the court leaves."

Edward and Alfreth had done much soul searching in the light of Aethelflaed's admonitions before the meeting of the Witan. Alfreth had finally agreed that it would be safer for all concerned, especially her child, if they were to disappear for a time, but where? She had an understandable horror of returning to a nunnery, even as a guest, and her circle of acquaintance outside the Dowager Queen's Hall was all but non-existent. But then an idea struck her which, she believed, was inspiration from above. Remembering her long and perilous journey from Bathe to Caestre in pursuit of the court, and the many small kindnesses which she had been afforded, she recalled her overnight stay with the baker-woman at Sceo. She would tell the woman a story which was not too far from the truth –

with the omission of her husband's name and rank – that she had, indeed, found the court and gone into service. That she had met and married a man above her station, and that she was carrying his child. His parents had not approved of the match and until the time was right for him to acknowledge her, she needed a place of safety where she could await her confinement and, if necessary, stay with her child for as long as necessary. Money was not an object, though she did not intend to flaunt it. She would simply say that she had enough to pay for her board and keep, and that she was happy to help in the bakehouse in any way until the child came. She remembered the odd affection she had felt for Goody Hilde, after such a short acquaintance, and how it had been reciprocated. Yes, the bakery at Sceo would be her refuge.

It had been agreed that Thella and Ratkin would accompany her to Sceo, travelling much of the way along the "Devil's Highway" toward Bathe, before turning South to return to Wintancaestre, whilst Wulf and I would, naturally, accompany Edward, Aethelflaed and the rest of the court back home along Stane Street. There would be nothing untoward in a married couple attending Alfreth into her self-imposed exile, nothing to draw attention to her as anything other than what she claimed to be. As soon as I was dressed, I slipped along to the King's chambers – it still seemed strange to think of Edward as the King – to bid her God's speed. When I scratched upon the door and she bade me enter I found her alone. She and Edward had already made their farewells for they could not be seen to do so in public. She was tearful and full of apprehension once more.

"Oh, Aetna, will he forget me, once the business of running the Kingdom becomes a reality for him? Shall I ever see him again, think you?"

"Alfreth, Alfreth, of course you will." I hugged her and dried her tears with my kerchief. "He loves you dearly, you know that. And your child – his child – how can you doubt that he longs to know it? It may be hard for him to come to you for a while, but have no fear, he will write to you, and I wean there will be little gifts and keepsakes sent. And he will find a way to be with you when the child comes, I am sure."

"Oh, but that is so far off! And I do not care for gifts and keepsakes, as long as I know that he holds me is his heart."

"It is not that far off, Alfreth. And you will have a babe in your arms, and your husband by your side, if only for a short while. But you must take a care that you do not betray yourself in the meantime. There are those who would use it against him, as you know. Do not let your guard down. Remember your own safety and that of your little one. I believe that you will have at fine time at Sceo – better than sitting minding your manners at Wintancaestre while we are all getting used to our new positions! Although," I added with a grin, "it will have to be a better place without Elfrith and Morwen in residence!"

She managed a smile at that, and I hugged her again, saying that I would wave her off when she left, and that Wulf had said that he would be sure to do so as well.

"But not my husband!" she sniffed, tears threatening once again.

"No," I said, "not your husband. But be brave, Alfreth. You knew this would not be an easy road."

"I did, though mayhap I did not think it would be quite this hard. Pray God that travelling the 'Devil's Highway' is not a portent of evil to come."

"Nay, 'tis but an old name given it by those who forgot it's real origins. The Legions built it just as they did so many other roads. It is straight and true and will take you to where you will be safe. Have no fear!"

I returned to my chamber to find Thella already packed and away to meet Ratkin and their charge, and Lucet putting the last of our belongings into our saddlebags. Such a short trip had not necessitated our travelling trunks.

"Is Alfreth ready for the off?" asked Lucet.

"As ready as she ever will be," I replied. "I fear this is not a happy day for her. She is seeing ill-fortune and bad omens where ever she looks." I cast a final eye around the chamber. "It looks as though we have everything. Send one of the thralls to collect our bags before we leave, but let us go quickly now to see the others on their way."

We made our way down to the courtyard, where Ratkin was helping Thella and Alfreth onto their horses. Wulf was already there. "Well, brother," I said quietly as I stood beside him, "how think you this plan will work out?"

"They are neither of them happy," he replied. "But when Edward – I mean the King – came into my chamber this morning I had feared he might be more cast down than he was. He had said his farewells, promised to see Alfreth when the child comes and now... now he seems to have set his sights and his thoughts on the immediate future and our return to court. And all that comes along with it," he added.

"Aye, it is ever the woman who feels these things the deeper," I said, thinking of the day Ethelmaer left.

There was a single pack horse to accompany the little party bound for Sceo, tended by a rider alongside leading the animal on a long reign. Unless anyone cared to look closely it was impossible to see that the man was well armed with a longsword and knife and that concealed amongst the horse's other burdens was a sturdy bow with a good supply of arrows. This was one of Edward's most experienced and trusted men-at-arms, given the task of keeping Alfreth safe. When they reached Sceo he would make it his business to find unobtrusive work in the village and maintain a watch over her, keeping his own identity secret. With Ratkin in the lead, Thella and Alfreth behind him and Garreth, the body-guard, bringing up the rear, they trotted out of the courtyard, through the gates just opened by the sleepy gatekeeper.

Alfreth turned and looked over her shoulder, Wulf and I waved, but I could see that she was not looking at us, but rather to see if anyone else had come out to see them leave, or was perhaps looking from a doorway or window embrasure. But there was not. She turned back to the front and disappeared through the archway.

TWENTY-FIVE

Bathe, Anno Domini 976

WULFMAER

Companion-man to the King. For a whole year, companion-man to the King of All Englaland. There had been those who thought me too young, but then, the King himself was still younger and by the time he had reigned for a twelvemonth there were none who would gainsay his word. There were trusted advisors, yes, and those who might suggest, or even argue, alternative actions to those favoured by His Majesty, but none would oppose his final word on any given matter. If they did, they were subject to his not inconsiderable anger, for his temper could be short and his decisions were final.

And generally, his decisions had been good.

When we left the King's Tun, nestling alongside the Great River, on that summer morning in 975 there was still a suggestion of unhappiness at the loss of his father and regret at his enforced separation from Alfreth hovering behind Edward's eyes, but his mind was full of plans and ambitions and his heart of hope and faith in the future. Why not? He was youthful and fit, he had developed something of a taste for intrigue, he was in love and certain that it was reciprocated. He was returning to a court free of the one dark cloud which had hovered above it – his stepmother – and, above all, he was the undisputed King of a nation which had enjoyed decades of peace and prosperity. There was just enough hint of danger from the North to whet an adolescent appetite for adventure and nascent pride in his sovereignty was already beginning to suggest that there would be ways in which he could rival, or perhaps supersede his father's achievements, even if he knew not yet what they might be. He rode his high-stepping horse well and, word having gone ahead of our approach, graciously received the cheers of his people as they gathered along the roadside to greet their new king.

The crowds had gathered at Wintancaestre, too, to welcome us home. Colourful cloths hung from doorways and shutters as we made our way through the city, and fluttered from the market stalls and shop fronts. Some wag had even climbed the gallows and tied ribbons along its cross-bar, having first thoughtfully removed the tarred corpse which had hung there to remind other felons of their fate if caught. Edward laughed at the boldness of the jape and decreed that all prisoners held in the town goal should be released in celebration of his return to the capital. It was his first decree as King, and almost as popular as his second, which was to order kegs of ale set up on each street corner for the refreshment of revellers.

The Great Hall was merry and so it remained for the next few months as we all settled into our new roles. Without a wife and queen to grace the top table and take charge of the day to day running of the household, the Dowager Queen Aethelflaed stepped in to fill the void. Our aunt, I knew, had no real wish to assume the role, but she was content to be the titular head of the domestic establishment, while leaving a great deal of the day to day organisation to my sister. The kitchen seemed to run smoothly and the domiciliary thralls and ceorls, freed from the burden of Morwen's overbearing presence and constant interference on behalf of her mistress, were positively jovial in their work. Reluctantly, Aethelflaed gave up her residence at the Nunneminster Hall and moved into apartments close to the King. Aetna, with Lucet now firmly established as her right hand, did likewise. My own chamber adjoined Edward's who had taken over his late father's accommodation. Most nights there was music and dancing in the Great Hall, with storytellers, jongleurs and acrobats vying with one another to win the King's approval. Alas, they were not the only ones; many young ladies, both base and high born were also keen to gain his notice. Like any young man, he enjoyed the attention and was happy to take a turn on the dance floor with them all, but he favoured none more than any other and so, while there may have been some small disappointment among them, there was also undiminished hope.

Aetna received regular letters from Alfreth at Sceo, and always, folded neatly and hidden within the larger missive were little notes to be passed to Edward. Aetna, of course, knew not what they said, but guessed that they were full of love and devotion whilst, knowing Alfreth as we did, making no mention of her own longings and loneliness. Her letters to Aetna were outwardly cheerful, telling of the small adventures and comedic events inherent to village life, but there was an underlying current of wistfulness and a sad eagerness to hear everything of what was occurring in our own world, especially as it concerned the King. Aetna's replies were highly diverting – she had a way with words which I lacked, despite Father Aelmer's attempts at my education – and made every effort to keep her spirits up. Edward's replies were concealed folded in my sister's letters, though by no means of the same regularity as those from his wife to him. Often, he would ask Aetna simply to pass on his love and fidelity as a *postscriptum* to her own words.

The court made its Progresses and the Witan met without any particular incident, and for some time it seemed that the ill-feelings which had run so high during the brief interregnum were all but forgotten. True, the Chief Ealdorman whilst attending essential meetings, more often made his excuses with regard to more minor affairs and remained in Mercia, or, so we heard, spent his time at Corf Gate with the Queen, but there were no incidents which were cause for concern either from his quarter, or from that lady herself. Whilst Alfhere's brother and brother-in-law continued to pursue their avowed aim to support the clerics and lay clergy against the followers of the Benedictine Rule, there were no acts of violence, and from the North no problematical news from the Scots or from over the water.

Even the hardships brought about by the weather began to lessen. There was just enough grain to allow the hope that the fields would be sown in the spring and for the people to eke out survival through the winter. Though there was little left over to make merry by brewing ale for the usual harvest festivities, as autumn approached the hedgerows miraculously produced their customary largesse of berries and nuts, and pigs snuffled happily in the woods for acorns and mushrooms. It seemed that, after all, the Festival of Thanksgiving for the Harvest could be celebrated with some sincerity.

Our Lord's Nativity approached. There was still enough of the boy in the young man that the King was becoming for him to want the first Christ's Mass of his sovereignty to be one which would be remembered for years to come. With due deference to her domestic authority within the Great Hall, he approached the Dowager Queen first. Aethelflaed had reflected for only a moment before she replied.

"Oh, Edward, I thank you for your courtesy in consulting me, but it is not for those of my generation to be planning holy-day revels and the like, it is for the young. The Lady Aetna is far better suited to the task than I. I pray you make her your accomplice in this. I am sure that between you, you will conceive of a far more exciting season than I ever could!"

My sister was delighted. She had long wished to have a free rein to plan such an event, and she and Edward spent many happy hours, heads together, pouring over the festive arrangements, choosing entertainments, delegating lesser matters to trusted members of the household, seeking out new dances and games which had never before graced the Royal court.

"I think we should keep but one of the new ideas introduced by my stepmother," Edward had said, one evening when he and Aetna were, as so often, deep in discussion over some detail of the coming festivities. I confess I was not paying attention to their conversation for I was debating the best boar-hunting coverts in the nearby woodland with one of the other young men of the court. My sister recounted their words to me later.

"Which is that, sire?" she asked.

"The bringing into the Hall of the Christ-Mass tree," said Edward. "I know when 'twas first done it seemed strange, but it is like having some small part of the winter's stark beauty in the heart of the Hall with us. And I liked the notion of piling gifts about its foot."

"Well, I dare say that as long as the Bishops do not see us dancing around it like pagans, all will be well," Aetna laughed.

"Aye, all will be well," mused the King. "And only one thing would make it better." He spoke in a whisper that only my sister could hear. "If my Queen could be here to share it with me, or if I were with her. But I know that cannot be," he added. "These last months have made me come to understand much of the responsibilities which my father felt so heavy upon him. Neither he – nor I – could simply do as we please, for Kings are servants of their people as much as their people are vassals to them. Although we are at peace, I feel the weight of expectation upon me: the expectation that I should marry to create political alliance, that I should be available at a moment's notice should matters of state require my attention. And that I cannot, without good reason, simply disappear from court without explanation." Here, Aetna felt, he was coming to the rub.

"Lady, I swore to Alfreth that I would be with her for the birth of our child, but I now see that it may not be possible."

"Sire... Edward, if I may? This is a matter which has been upon my mind, also," she said. "I greatly fear that you may, indeed, have to be forsworn, for we cannot be sure exactly when the babe will come, and I can think of no legitimate reason for you suddenly to absent yourself from Wintancaestre and disappear who-knows-where – as the Court will see it – when a random messenger arrives. Gossip and rumour abound here as in any Great Hall. It would give ammunition to your enemies if you were seen to be thus capricious."

"Then am I to leave Alfreth uncomforted and without my presence throughout Christ's Nativity and her own confinement? It seems heartless..."

"As I said, sire, it has been upon my mind and I think I may have a way for you to spend mayhap several days with Alfreth before the coming of the Christchild's Day. On account of the terrible pain you have in your foot."

"What? What pain? There is nothing wrong with my foot! Have you lost your mind?"

"The pain, sire, on account of the mishap you will have tomorrow, which I am afraid will cause you to have a severe pain – bad enough to forestall your enjoyment of the coming festivities if you do not find a cure!"

"Aetna, will you stop talking nonsense! I am not a child any longer who needs tales of faerie and..."

Aetna raised her hands in surrender. "Enough, Edward, I am sorry, I do not mean to tease, but listen and I will explain..."

))))))))((((((((

The following morning – I believe it was the *ides*, the thirteenth day, of December – Edward came into the Great Hall to break his fast, with me in attendance, and Ratkin at my side. We were due to go to one of the outlying Halls close to the King's Worth and assess the value of a load of timber lately and illegally felled by a tenant – a task which would last all day and for which we needed a good, hot, morning meal to stave off the chill of early winter. The tenant farmer claimed that he had been led to believe the timber was his, as part of this legal entitlement. In fact, it belonged to the King – only the land itself could be sub-let by the local ealdorman. He claimed that he had made this clear to his tenant, but whichever way the Hundred Court – or possibly a higher legislature – chose to interpret the matter somebody was due to pay a heavy fine, possibly beggaring themselves in the process. Edward wanted to see the timber for himself.

The King wore a broad smile and called a cheery good-morn to the assembled thegns and others taking advantage of the always generous royal board. He strode up to the High Table, taking the steps up to the dais two at a time, and just as he reached the topmost, let out a stream of obscenities the like of which made me pleased that there were no ladies of breeding present.

"Sire?" I said. "Is aught the matter?"

"By the Lord's loaves and fishes, Wulf, something… God's breath, my foot! What have I done? It hurts like the very Devil! All I did was hop onto the top step there!"

I ran up the steps and supported Edward beneath his right shoulder. "Lean on me, sire, come sit at the table, it will be recovered in but a moment I am sure! Take some ale. Ratkin, look at that top step, see if there is aught which might have hurt His Majesty."

Ratkin dutifully examined the offending step, but there was naught to be seen.

"I fear you must have cracked some little bone, sire, it will surely swell up like a stuffed pig's stomach before the hour is out!" he said. "We should fetch the *medicus* from the infirmary."

"Aye, I think you are right, man!" said Edward, easing off his boot. There did not appear to be any injury, nor yet any swelling.

By midday, there was still no outward sign of impairment, no bruise or lividity, but the King asserted that he was in such pain that he could hardly put his foot to the ground. He hopped around on his sound left leg, just barely touching the toes of his right foot to the floor, swearing and blaspheming until we feared for his soul rather than his walking. The Brother from the infirmary applied a poultice, which Edward said made his skin itch as though he had fallen into a nettle bed. A large jar of strong red wine seemed to be the best solution to the day's ills and the King retired early to his chamber, the question of the unsanctioned timber's value left unresolved.

For the next two days His Majesty hopped and limped about the Great Hall, taking what little pleasure he could by the invention of increasingly explicit oaths. Strangely, there still appeared to be no apparent swelling or other symptom, and both the *medicus* and the wise-woman called in from the town were baffled. In the end, the latter declared that the King's foot had been impaled by a particularly sharp and vicious elven arrowhead. Elf-shot such as this was notoriously hard to either diagnose or cure. The Infirmary Brother looked dubious but, with no better explanation to be had, remained silent. We all stood around Edward as he reclined upon his palliasse in his sleeping chamber.

"Well," said Edward, "something must be done. I cannot be crippled by this pain for the rest of my life. How shall I be able to dance at the Christ's Mass celebrations?"

It had to be said that some might have thought the latter discomfiture was somewhat trivial when compared to the former, but both were fair points. The *medicus* and the wise woman remained silent, considering their options. This was Aetna's moment.

"Sire, I have heard lately that there is a Holy Well, a shrine recently dedicated, which has been found most efficacious in the relief of ailments of the foot. It is a freshwater spring dedicated to Saints Crispin and Crispinian, patrons of shoemakers, like that at Faversham in Cent – but much nearer, being just outside Bathe."

"Where just outside Bathe?" asked Edward, with an air of admirable ingenuousness.

"At Sceo, I believe, Your Majesty."

"Barely sixty miles!" he beamed. "Then that is the answer, I shall take a pilgrimage to the Holy Spring at Sceo! And I shall do it privily, with just a couple of companions. A humble penitent – *in cognito* – no-one shall suspect who I am. And I shall be cured directly, I feel sure!" Both the *medicus* and his rival looked relieved – they appeared to be released from their responsibility for the King's recovery. Edward clapped me on the back. "Well, Wulf, what say you, shall you and I and Ratkin take to the road this very morrow? Come let us find some pilgrims' garb and make our plans!"

Edward limped to the door to call for his body servant. The *medicus* began to speak. "Sire, are you not favouring the other foot? Truly this is an odd affliction..." His voice trailed off as the King scowled at him.

"Brother, you have been of no assistance whatsoever in this matter. You may return to your House. And you, woman!" Thus, dismissed, they hurriedly left.

We all collapsed into helpless laughter. When recovered, Edward said, "We must let it be known within the Court that I am taking this action in order for my affliction to be cured, and that I shall return before Our Lord's Nativity. None will question my absence for this purpose. Aetna, you are a genius!" He hugged her. "Will you not come with us?"

"I am pleased to be of service, sire!" she laughed. "But it will be a more convincing enterprise undertaken by the three of you alone. It is, indeed, most convenient that Alfreth mentioned in one of her letters that the spring at Sceo had recently become a popular stop on the pilgrim's route between larger shrines! And I hear that the excellent Garreth has invested some of Your Majesty's generous salary to him as covert bodyguard by opening a local tavern, which now provides accommodation for such travellers. I believe he has called it The Shoe! No doubt you will all be made most welcome. And, of course, there is a certain other at Sceo who will be more than delighted to see Your Majesty..."

And so it was that a bare week before the day of Our Lord's birth, what appeared to be a trio of pilgrims arrived at The Shoe, at Sceo, purporting to be an ealdorman's son, wed to the young matron who had be lodging with Goody Hilde at the bakery, and his two travelling companions. Alfreth's story of her ill-received marriage to a young nobleman had been accepted at face value in the village, and as she had become a popular character at the bakery and well-liked by the locals, their reunion was cause for muted celebration. Edward, or "Ned", as he was introduced, was afforded the best room that the tavern could offer (Garreth having once recovered from his initial shock of greeting his King, unannounced, at the door of his new inn) and he was joined by his wife for the duration of his stay. Ratkin and I slept well and deeply in an attic room, warmed by the good food and fine ale supplied, and not a little by the happiness which Aetna's plan had secured for the young King and his secret wife.

We arrived back at Wintancaestre on the postnoon of Saint Frithbert's day, which preceded the eve of Our Saviour's birth. The weather had turned and as our horses jogged through the city Gate, the first flurries of snow began to fall. Before the early mid-winter dusk descended there was a carpet of snow some inches thick and we congratulated ourselves on reaching home before travelling became too difficult. Ratkin left us and made straightway for his home and Thella's welcoming arms.

The Great Hall was ablaze with light and wonderfully warm after our cold journey. Edward strode into the Hall making much of the miraculous cure his elf-shot foot had enjoyed by virtue of the water at the Saints' Well and was greeted by Aetna and Aethelflaed, my sister flushed and slightly breathless as a result of her efforts to oversee preparations for the evening, and our aunt, as ever, elegant and flawless in her postnoon gunna. She, of course, had been let into the secret of our little deception, though she kept up the pretence of ignorance.

"Aetna, I am away to rest and change my dress before this night's entertainments. Be sure you come and tell me all your brother shares with you of the King's… sojourn… at Sceo. I am sure he was made most welcome!" She disappeared behind the hangings toward the private chambers.

"As ever, my stepmother is the epitome of discretion!" said Edward. "Oh, Aetna, your plan worked perfectly: Alfreth and I were able to be ourselves – and in company – for the first time… ever! I cannot say how wonderful it was to be able to sit beside one another and enjoy a simple meal with good, honest folk. And my love looked well, Aetna, her belly is great, but she is in good health. The babe kicks like a young mule, too!

"But now, I must be the King again, and just look at the celebrations you have prepared. Only we few will know that I am celebrating more than just, God forgive me, Christ's Mass!"

"Sire, I am so happy for you," said Aetna. "To have had time with you will have made all the difference to Alfreth's enjoyment of this season, too. But did you tell her that you would, likely, not be able to be back for her confinement?"

"Lady, I did not. For I did not want sadness to cloud her days or make her anxious. And who knows, mayhap I shall be able to visit very soon after…"

"Well we need not think on that now," my sister replied. "Come, you must both be tired after your ride, take a horn of ale and the time to catch your breath before we drink the *was heil* to Saint Frithbert this evening."

Aetna's transformation of the Great Hall was, indeed, to be admired. She had improved upon Elfrith's novel imported idea of the Christ's Mass tree, felled and propped in the corner of the Hall, by having the thralls dig up a whole young conifer, secure its roots within a huge barrel filled with soil and dragging the whole edifice into the centre of the room, where its topmost branches brushed against the cross-beams supporting the roof. Using long poles (or so I could only imagine) the house thralls had then swathed the tree in brightly dyed strips of fabric – and, where ever they could reach, hung painted pine cones and blown eggs, bright red holly berries and white mistletoe. Oh, Father Aelmer, if you could but see this…

The long table was already decorated with greenery, with piles of nuts and dried fruit at intervals along its length, with the High Table, in its place of honour, crosswise to the trestles, glittering with precious Roman glass and other colourful platters and vessels. Around the walls, supported by the shields and armaments which habitually adorned them, great swathes of greenery similar to that on the tables – holly, ivy, dried clematis, hops and briony – hung in graceful, looping garlands. In the firepit a great blaze of cracking logs sent dancing shadows over everything, despite the many candles. The smell of roasting meat wafted from the kitchens. I realized how hungry I was as my mouth watered in anticipation. Saint Frithbert's, for all his Saint's day was so close to our Lord's Nativity, was always an evening of peace and goodwill in its own right – his very name invoked peace, for *frith* meant freedom from molestation, protection, safety, security. And that was surely what we all craved, this and every night.

)))))))((((((

The winter which arrived in earnest on Saint Frithbert's day tightened its grip across the country in the following weeks. To begin with, snow fell steadily but unspectacularly, although, as the wind continued to veer and back, to and fro, from all points of the compass, drifts formed against every obstacle in its path. First one side of a lane would back up to the height of any wall or hedge by its side, and then as the direction of the icy blast changed, the opposite side would likewise be swamped. Soon every door and gate could only be reached by passage through a high white chasm. Then, briefly, the snow stopped and for a few days the temperature dropped so low that the fallen, drifted accumulations froze hard and icicles formed from the eaves of every dwelling. They grew steadily longer as heat from internal fires escaped from cracks and fissures, melting small amounts of snow, none of which remained unfrozen long enough to drip to the ground before it became part of one of the icy, sharpened arrow heads which lengthened with every drop until the icicles looked like witches' long-taloned fingers reaching down to snatch at the unwary.

Animals were brought inside, away from the worst of the weather. Where there were barns or sheds, they were packed together cheek by jowl, cows and donkeys, horses and mules, several families sharing the available space, for no-one wanted to see animals lost to the storm. If necessary, the beasts shared their owners' space – pigs and goats brought inside alongside children and dogs, chickens and ducks. Cats made their way up into the haylofts, to hunt rats and mice likewise trying to find shelter from nature's cruelty.

The fields had already disappeared under folds and mounds of snow. Bushes and shrubs were no more than mounds and hillocks of white and bare, black trees and woodland stood stark and strange like inky scrawls on pale parchment. The river froze solid, and first small children, then their older siblings and finally grown men and women walked from one side to the other rather than navigating the increasingly choked streets. Rubbish and ordure accumulated along its edges, frozen as solid as the river itself. All the filth of the city, which usually was born away by the water piled high and we could only anticipate the foul smells which would be released when the thaw finally came.

The snow began once again before the old year gave way to the new and 976 began, heralded by a storm of such ferocity that it was almost impossible to walk to either Minster to pray for good fortune in the twelve months to come. Somehow, though, we struggled to the service. The wind took our breath away and the ice underfoot was so slippery that we had to hold onto each other to stay upright, even then sometimes finding ourselves slipping backward against our will. Archbishop Dunstan had spent the Nativity at Court and preached at the New Year office. He had planned to be on his way back to Cantuaria before the turn of the year, but now we wondered for how long he would have to wait before returning to his own city.

On our return from the New Minster, we found the Great Hall ready, as ever, to offer entertainment and the long table laid with food, but the atmosphere was subdued and it seemed few were in the mood to make merry. Those whose own Halls were within walking distance preferred to get home before the storm grew worse still, and others, intending to take advantage of the Court's overnight hospitality, huddled around the fire pit, eating and drinking there, rather than at the trestles. Most of the ladies retired to their chambers. The musicians struck up a half-hearted tune, but no-one seemed inclined to dance.

"Come," said the King to those of us in his immediate circle, "let us repair to the withdrawing chamber." The storm was unabated and we could hear it howling around the Hall. "This is a night for quiet talk with good friends."

Aetna told Lucet that she would not need her again that evening, and she disappeared in the direction of the kitchens. Dunstan likewise dismissed the brother who had been attending upon him. Ratkin had already returned to his home, where Thella no doubt had a fine meal awaiting him. Edward instructed the thralls to bear wine and ale into the private chambers behind the Great Hall, and food later, and we passed through the hangings into the more intimate surroundings of the King's privy apartments. A fine fire burnt and wax candles threw a clean white light around the room. Aethelflaed sank thankfully onto a cushioned settle and stretched her hands toward the grate, as the rest of us founds seats.

"It is certainly not an evening to be out and about," she said.

Dunstan took a seat beside her. "If I may, my Lady…"

"Of course! You and I, Dunstan, have more need to warm our old bones than these young people."

"Lord Archbishop, Step-grandmother, I do not feel as young as I did this twelvemonth past," said Edward. "It has been a year of great changes." He cast a quick look at my sister and me. "I believe I understand, now, why my father often felt more weary than I then thought he should. I could not comprehend how a day sitting and talking could tire him so, but after experiencing a few meetings of the Witan myself..." He did not need to complete the sentence.

"Sire," I said, "you have learned much since the summer. And it has been noted. After the last meeting during our Progress to the West, I heard several of the Ealdormen commenting upon how quickly you were mastering the challenges of politics."

"But I must learn better to curb my temper," Edward replied. "When matters become complex and drag on, the Ealdormen arguing the same points over and over..." It was true, the young King was getting a reputation for being quick to anger and impatient when discussions became bogged down with legal niceties and entrenched viewpoints. "Often I feel that I wish I could just leave them to it and ride to hounds or be out with my birds."

Aetna had fetched her embroidery from her chamber and drew a candle forward, the better that she might see her stitching. "Archbishop," she began.

"Oh, Aetna, Dunstan please! You make me feel older still!"

"Dunstan, then," she continued, with a little throaty laugh. "I do not witness the meetings of the Witan, but often hear the Ealdormen continue their discussions during abatements, and even over the board at mealtimes. As you know, I like to try and understand the workings of the Council, but the complexities of these matters of reform in the Church and how they affect the Ealdormens' wealth and power elude me when I am privy to only piecemeal information. Would you mind explaining it so that I might understand?"

Edward groaned with an exaggerated shake of his head. "Oh, Aetna, now you will be sorry... I am sure the Archbishop would like nothing better! Where are those thralls? I have a sudden fierce desire for ale!"

Dunstan stared for a moment into the fire. "I will, Aetna, and I will try to give fair account of both sides of the argument, though, like His Majesty, I become vexed and impatient that it is often-times made to look more complex than it is. That, I fear, is the fault of... ah, but see, I am already sounding biased!

"The monasteries in Englaland are, as you know, mostly run under the Rule of Saint Benedict. Or so they should be, and so it is claimed they are. When Benedict established his Rule for the cloistered life, he decreed that each community be led by an Abbot who had authority over his brothers. The Abbot and the rest of the community were to live piously, chastely and holding their possessions in common. But there are many monasteries now which do not adhere to this Rule. Chief among the reasons is that powerful, rich men have founded some of monasteries, given the land they stand on, paid for the buildings, supported them in their first difficult years. I do not condemn them, they have done so to the glory of God, but it has been the case that in many, those men have thought it then their right to install members of their own families as Abbot. And these Abbots may have wives, children – even mistresses, forgive me ladies! If an abbot is less than chaste and lowly, how can we expect his underlings to be better than he?"

Aetna put her sewing to one side. She looked at Dunstan. "This bears upon Alfheah's comments at the *Witangemot* about Bedric and Saint Edmund's Shrine, does it not? He is afraid that if an abbey is founded Bedric will not be allowed as Abbot and revenues will be lost? Another precedent set which would undermine the power of the Ealdormen."

"Indeed, you remember correctly. The late King, with advice (I confess it, from me and my like-minded brethren) prepared the *Regularis Concordia*, an epitome, as it were, of the Benedictine Rule and those monasteries who have accepted it, have been swept clean of such practices and with them those Abbots who were not living according to the Rule. Power has been given to new men, and the influence of the families who founded the abbeys, and therefore the profit to be made from lands, fisheries and forests has been taken from them."

"Some Ealdormen have suffered – I use the word as they do – more than others in this regard. Alfhere, for example… in Mercia his forebears were called 'half-kings' and founded many monastic houses. Though he is Chief Ealdorman, he has no more right under the *Concordia* to profit from the monasteries than any other. Mostly he respects this – though grudgingly – but his brother and brother-in-law, Alfheah and Alfric, are less inclined to bow to the law. He turns a blind eye to their actions and even begins, now, covertly to join their rebellion."

"And this is why Elfwine was asked to report back to King Edgar regarding the goings-on in Mercia?" asked Aetna.

"Aetna, you are better informed of matters than many of the Witan!" replied Dunstan. "Yes, though his reports told us little that we did not already suspect. To add to the danger, the outer marches of Alfhere's Ealdormanry and his cohorts' lands, bound regions to the North where the Scots and the Norsemen would willingly come to their aid, or make pretence that was the reason for their aggression, if so asked. Money would change hands, even land, and once begun…" Dunstan allowed the thought to go unfinished.

Silence hung in the air uncomfortably. The repercussions of such treachery were all too obvious – and awful.

"So, it is money at the root of this dissent," said Aetna. "Money and the power it brings. Of course, what else? Elfrith is of a mind to support Alfhere, for the more money and power he has, the more likely – forgive me, Edward – he can yet influence the Witan that Ethelred might be the better King. And her own position elevated."

"Aye, they fight dirty," said Dunstan. "But I have some plans of my own that will…"

"Enough, enough!" cried Edward. "This eve is becoming like unto a moot-witan! I will not have it. Come, we shall drink and dance and chase away ill-thought!" He stood and strode toward the Great Hall. "If there are not enough high-born ladies unwilling to forego their beds this cold night, we shall call in the coerls and thralls… Aetna, summon Lucet and tell her to rouse the kitchen. You shall be my partner. Wulf, I doubt not that you will like to cut a figure with Lucet yourself… and do not think you are excused, my Lord Archbishop, my step-grandmother can still take a turn upon the floor, you will make an excellent couple!"

He disappeared through the hanging curtain and we could hear him call to the musicians.

"Come, minstrels, play up! Give us a merry tune, for this night is becoming more a wake than the wakening of a new year!"

As we followed him, I heard Aetna say to Dunstan, "Thank you, Lord, your words have made the matter of this reformation clearer to me. I can see why tempers often flare – and whilst I can understand the need for adherence to the Rule I cannot but feel sympathy for the clergy who must give up their wives… It is, indeed, a difficult subject upon which to feel wholly committed one way or the other!"

"Aye, it is as well that the King calls our discussion to a close, for I confess that my temper frays easily when such complications distract from the simple imperative, however hard that may seem. I fear that common sense and argument may not be enough – I may have to use unorthodox methods to convince my opponents of the Lord's will before long. But enough! Yes, sire, we are coming…!"

))))))))(((((((

It became a long winter. Spring came late and wet, and hopes that enough seed had been saved from the previous year's poor harvest were dashed when the chill earth refused to allow but one grain in ten to germinate. The common people were worried that famine was a real possibility – and the Court was concerned that the seething disagreements between secular and temporal sympathisers would soon boil over in the shape of actual aggression and violence.

In late February we received word that Alfreth had been delivered of a healthy baby girl. She named her Elfa after the King's late mother, though she soon came to be called "Effie" by all. Edward was thrilled and longed to return to Sceo, but the rumblings of discontent and ill-feeling between those supporting and opposing the *Concordia* made it impossible.

Dunstan prevailed upon the King to summon a Council as soon as the weather permitted ease of travel – it was neither wholly Witan nor Synod, but a convention of all the parties whose rights, possessions and manners of life were deeply affected by the sweeping changes to be affected by the *Concordia*. With his usual flair, he stage-managed the event in such a way – he hoped – that its outcome would brook no argument and that decisions made were final and definitive. He chose the Old Minster Hall as the venue, a fine, ancient hall both sacred to the Church (it boasted a greater than life size figure of Christ Crucified suspended from the roof beams) and often used for secular meetings, such as moots, the Hundred Court and even, on permitted occasions, celebrations of a personal nature, a substantial fee, in the guise of generous donation, being paid to the Minster itself.

The Council was scheduled to last but one whole day, though some delegates began arriving in Wintancaestre several days beforehand, determined to lobby support where they could, for the notion that this finally might be the event which determined matters once and for all was spreading. Chief Ealdorman Alfhere, with Alfheah and Alfric and their retainers arrived in considerable state – it was not easy to forget that he often referred to the fact that by birth he was a "Half-king". Our Uncle Brithnoth, together with Ealdorman Ethelwine and a number of other Ealdormen from the East arrived with only slightly less pomp. Clearly, both factions were keen to demonstrate their power and influence. Brithnoth seldom mentioned it, but his own forebears could be traced back to the same semi-royal branch of the family tree. Nobility rarely married far outside their own circle – so much so that Edgar had endorsed a law that no two persons sharing a grandmother might lawfully wed.

The Archbishop of Eoforwic, Oswald, arrived but one day in advance of the Council, and, as accommodation at the Great Hall was becoming scarce, was lodged at the Nunneminster. Only his closest and most trusted aides – those who were above any suspicion of lasciviousness – were allowed to share this privilege. In the current climate of accusation and counter-accusation all risk of a young novice's impulses toward a sister being acted upon had to be eliminated. The Reform party must be above reproach.

By contrast, the secular clergy who attended upon Alfhere and his companions were unabashed by any inference that their wives were not wholly legal – though the ecclesiastic aides referred to the wives, derogatively, as "concubines". The Chief Ealdorman's house priest, who had travelled with him, had brought not just his wife, but their two small children and a babe in arms, which the good lady nursed as she pleased. Uncle Brithnoth – frankly to my horror – had brought Father Aelmer. I had not seen him since my elevation to Edward's companion over five years earlier. He appeared little changed: somewhat more wrinkled, his tonsure less apparent as his hair thinned and his general air of righteous suspicion just as evident. However, he greeted me with a thin, slight smile.

"Lord Wulfstan, you look well. We have all heard much of the esteem in which you are held at Court. Perhaps you are now agreed that your lessons had some small merit, for all you wished to be about playing at the sagas with your sister?"

I should have known there would be some veiled rebuke behind the greeting. But I felt for the old man's inflexible, apparently joyless existence. "Indeed, Father Aelmer," I replied with what I hoped was a winning grin. "Your patience with me has paid dividends."

"We can only hope that those dividends will not be put to ill-gotten and ungodly ends," he said. That appeared to be the end of his interest in our reunion. My uncle had been watching with an amused smile barely concealed.

"You are at your liberty, Father," he said. "I believe there are some most holy and fascinating relics in both the Old and New Minsters. Pray, take some time for yourself to view them. I shall not be needing you again this day."

Aelmer withdrew. "He will spend a delightful postnoon, I am sure," said Brithnoth. "He has been agog at the thought of seeing Saint Swithun's tomb ever since we left Radendunam, and apparently there is a most thrilling heel-bone belonging to Saint... someone or other... which is said to hop up and down in the presence of anyone who... but come, enough of this nonsense! How are you, my boy? And where is your sister?"

My uncle and I had been taking our ease by the fire-pit in the Great Hall when Father Aelmer had joined us. The noon-day meal was past, and like many others, we were enjoying this day before the Council convened as an opportunity to meet old friends, make new acquaintances and exchange news. Ethelwine was taking the opportunity of spending time with the Dowager Queen, giving her an update on Elflada's health, which had been poor of late and, Brithnoth doubted not, trying to relieve her of some little donation toward the, now third, rebuilding of Rammesig abbey, in the aftermath of the earthquake. The King had given me leave to spend time with my uncle, whilst he and Dunstan had their heads together in preparation for the debates on the morrow. Strict orders were given that they should not be disturbed.

"Aetna has been most set about with preparations for the hospitality incumbent upon this occasion," I said, suddenly realising that I must sound rather pompous. "But she has made sure to be free this evening and bids me give you her love until then."

"Your aunt is most proud of the reports we have of her," he said. "And Father Aelmer spoke nothing but the truth when he said we had heard great things of you, too. Since Edward – His Majesty – became King, it seems you have been by his side at all times. You make me feel quite the provincial country ceorl!" He laughed; that great, easy laugh I remembered from my childhood. "Let us hope that this Council of his – yes, I know it is Dunstan who pressed for it – will allow us old rural yeomen to return to our farms in peace without worrying about whether the fate of the monasteries will heighten tensions. But tell me, you are privy to most intelligence at the Court, what, if anything, do you know of this *Scotti* Bishop, Beornhelm, I believe he is called. 'Tis said he is a fiery speaker and fierce in his support of the wedded clergy and the rights of the Ealdormen to profit from family associations within the Monasteries. And he is Danish by descent."

"Aye, you have heard aright, on all counts," I replied. "He travelled south with the Chief Ealdorman's party, for Alfhere's house priest is none other than his brother! The family name attests to it, too, Father Beorndan makes no secret of his Danish antecedents. His wife (I use the term loosely) though, would appear to be English. There is quite the enclave of Anglo-Danish at Alfhere's Great Hall it appears, for Thored of Eorforwic spends much time there and his name, too, betrays his northern his origins."

"That cannot be popular with the good people of Wireceastre – or Tamweorthig," said Brithnoth. "When a town has been sacked and laid as low as theirs – and not just once but many times – it is hard to forgive the descendants of the aggressors, even when several generations have passed."

"And yet it seems they must," I said. "By all accounts, Alfhere had this Bishop Beornhelm preach in Saint Edith's Church and it has only been rebuilt this last decade since the Danes destroyed it less than fifty years ago. That is scarcely two generations since!"

"What think you Alfhere seeks to gain by this dalliance with the men from the North? If they play true to form, he has no cause to trust that they will honour any compact he might make with them. If it is but the land and monies of the abbeys he seeks for himself and his brothers, he would be better – if that is the right word – simply to argue the doctrinal and legal points on the Witan."

"I know not, and he holds his markers close – even Elfwine, who has a finely tuned ear for conspiracy since Edgar sent him to Tamweorthig is uncertain. Elfwine has been pleased to have leave to return to Court since Edward was crowned. I believe he intends to approach Dunstan to intercede for him in the matter of a marriage to Dunna for he carried out his listening brief well, despite the lack of any real evidence that Alfhere is unreliable."

Our conversation drifted off into discussion of friends and family. There would be time enough for matters of state on the morrow.

The following morning, as the sun rose red above the grey city, the delegates to the Council of the *Concordia*, as some were calling it, began to make their way to the Old Minster Hall. Unlike the Witan which had met to elect the King, this assembly boasted no great attendant gathering of eager populace, no street hawkers or market traders bent upon making a profit from the day's proceedings, no eagerly shouted greetings or cat-calls as the various parties made their way to the Hall. It was as though this meeting, important though it was to the ruling class, was of no interest whatsoever to those whose main concern was to find enough food to keep themselves from the sparse charity of their fellow men. What the ealdormen and bishops were about was of no account, they felt, to their daily lives. Likewise, there were few spectators in the Hall. I was present, as companion-man to the King; similarly, some of the ealdormen had their own companions and house priests with them. I noticed Father Aelmer beside my uncle. The archbishops and bishops had their aides, scribes were there to record the proceedings and the King had ensured that there were clerks a plenty with copies of legal and church documents dating back to before his father's time in case precedents were needed. The clerks had brought runners, too. Young men swift of foot who could run back to the libraries and record halls to fetch more parchments, endless parchments, to corroborate those already to hand. I noticed Edward sigh heartily as the rolls of finely scraped calfskin were spread ready to receive more words, more legalese which he would have to spend time ratifying in the days to come.

Without ceremony, he took his seat at the head of the long table which stretched the length of the Hall, Archbishops Dunstan to his right, Oswald on his left. The committed attendees split themselves along partisan lines and were seated on either side of the table. Those without allegiance clustered toward the bottom of the board, opposite the King. Small ale was provided in pitchers along its length, drinking vessels clustered around each jug. The huge Crucifix hung above our heads, the sad-eyed Christ gazing mutely the length of the Hall, in the direction of the undecided. We heard the Minster bells ring, summoning the brothers to Terce and Edward called the meeting to order. Dunstan intoned a prayer and the Council was underway.

I had heard the arguments a dozen times. Would there be something new? Something which might, at last, put an end to the ill-feeling? Alfhere outlined the financial implications of the *Concordia* to ealdormen who had, for many years, considered themselves entitled to revenues from the abbeys on their lands. He pointed out that these revenues were taxed: the King's coffers, as well as theirs, would be the poorer without such income. He extolled the virtues of the married clergy; their long family service to the abbeys, the fact that the local populace, knowing that they were of the same water as themselves did not resent paying their tithes (this, I could not help feeling, was something of a moot point: did anyone, ever, not resent taxes?) and pulled at any heartstrings still unstretched by bemoaning the fate of wives and children cast from the only homes they had ever known.

Ethelwine, the respected Ealdorman of East Anglia, responded in kind. True, he said, the monies from the abbeys would be lost, both to ealdormen and the King's coffers, but the purpose of the abbeys was to garner spiritual riches, not temporal wealth. The prayers of righteous monks, unfettered by the unchaste responsibilities of family were worth more to Englaland than coin. If those who sympathized with the unfortunate state of the homeless concubines and their offspring were truly seized with the desire to assist them, let them give alms themselves. As to the common folk, a self-sufficient abbey with a hospital and accommodation for the weary traveller was of far more use to them, and their tithes put to better use than by supporting married clergy in their domestic bliss.

Those ealdormen and others who had not been whipped into supporting either faction appeared swayed by Ealdorman Ethelwine's words. Mostly, they were lesser nobles, men who understood the value of hard-won coin and kind, and took little swaying to be convinced that married clergy were an extravagance the church and state could do without – and that those of rank with the Chief Ealdorman were quite rich enough already. Besides, Ethelwine was popular. His stout, cheerful presence had been a welcome counterbalance to the haughty stance of Alfhere throughout Queen Elfrith's partisan patronage, and Ethelwine's brothers, the late Ethelwold included, were respected and trusted members of the Witan, unlike Alfheah and Alfric, who were known malcontents, ever on the lookout for means to make profit rather than offer philanthropy. There were mutters of approval, giving way to cries of "Yes, he's right!" and "*Concordia* not concubines!" Someone called out "Aye, East Anglia not Mercia".

Ethelwine beamed down the table to those who sat crossways at its far end. His words had seemed to win them over and with their approbation came a legitimate pretext for the King to overrule the Chief Ealdorman. Alfhere looked sour. As Ethelwine resumed his seat, Dunstan rose.

"Your Majesty, my lords," he said. "Ealdorman Ethelwine has spoken the very words that I might have said, but he, a man of the secular world has been able to do so in a way that I, as a poor servant of the Church, unskilled in politics, could hardly have mustered." (Oh, Dunstan, beware false modesty!) "I think it well that I add nothing. Your own voices have been raised in agreement. The *Concordia Regularis* must stand!" There were more calls of "Aye!" and "God bless you, Archbishop!"

Now Edward spoke. "We thank you, Archbishop. And good Ealdormen Alfhere and Ethelwine. You have both spoken well – and long. But your words, Ethelwine, which have so engaged those who are undecided among us, have moved me to my decision, and I would have it recorded..." Here the scribes bolted upright on their stools, all attention that they might transcribe the exact dictate as it came from the King's mouth "... that I find..."

Of a sudden, there was a commotion on the Chief Ealdorman's side of the board. Edward looked up swiftly, his eyes darting down the line of faces, some turned to him, some to the man who now rose to his feet. Beornhelm, the Bishop of Caledonian sees unknown to us, had risen and, hands clasped before him, as though in fervent supplication, spoke.

"Your Majesty," he began. "Pray you that a visitor to your Council, at the invitation of your Chief Ealdorman, be allowed to make some comment to this illustrious assembly before it is dismissed."

The King looked annoyed. He took a draught from the small ale, though there was but little left, and we heard the bell call out for Terce – midday approached. "The matter is decided, my Lord Bishop," he said. "The time for discussion is passed."

"Sire," Dunstan leaned toward the King. "If Bishop Beornhelm has seen fit, at Chief Ealdorman Alfhere's behest, to travel this distance to give us the benefit of his... eloquence... mayhap we should hear him? What harm can it do?"

Edward looked surprised. He had been about to close the meeting, with the outcome solidly in Dunstan's favour... though, he had to admit, there had been little said that had not been expressed before. He doubted if this would really be an end to the matter. Why would the Archbishop wish to allow the old arguments to be rehashed again – and so soon, before even this meeting was finished?

"Oh, very well. Bishop Beornhelm, say on, but I pray you be brief for the hour of the midday repast is close upon us."

Beornhelm was an imposing fellow, it had to be said. Tall, fair-haired with a tonsure expertly cut, the small pate neatly shaved. His costume was of more the priestly robe than the plain habit, and a costly jewel in the shape of a Celtic cross glinted on his breast. Father Aelmer, who was seated almost opposite him, looked up at him with dour disapproval.

My mind had been wandering somewhat and, feet on the stretcher of the table, head back, I had been looking idly at the crucifix above our heads and trying to gauge its weight. It was suspended from a crossbeam by two heavy chains, one attached to either arm, and anchored further by a stout hempen cable which stretched from the foot of the cross and disappeared through a small arch situated about half way up the wall at the back of the hall – which apparently let some light into a hollow space. Probably, I thought, there was a spiral or other staircase within the wall, leading up to the roof area. As my eyes followed the line of the cable through the aperture, I thought I glimpsed some movement within. A figure? A hat? My hand went instinctively to where my sword should hang, but it was not there – of course, we were among friends – but, nevertheless, it closed around the hilt of my knife. If the King was in danger… It seemed as though something stirred at the back of my consciousness, a childhood dream? Or perhaps familiar from a more recent memory?

I returned my attention to the men around me, surely there could be no plot afoot? Bishop Beornhelm was beginning a diatribe in favour of the married clergy. He voice was deep and full throated, lyrical in his lowland Scots accent, and his words, though I was paying little heed to their meaning, flowed pleasantly. He was an orator of some skill.

Suddenly, there was a grinding noise from above our heads, totally unexpected and alien. We all looked upward. Christ, on His Cross, was beginning to sway, initially with an almost imperceptible shuddering and then, gathering momentum, slowly swinging, first toward the East wall, and then outward to the West, until it reached the extremity of the retaining cable, which served to brake its movement and send it backward once again. Upon the third such swing, a voice echoed through the Hall. As a man, we all flinched, some covering their ears against the strangeness of it.

"Let this not happen… let this not happen! Ye men, ye have decided aright this day! It will not be well to change."

The words boomed around the chamber. As if from nowhere – and everywhere! As if from the lips of our Saviour on His Rood of pain. There was a shocked hush. Beornhelm was still on his feet, but he, like the rest of use was gazing upward and all around, dumbfounded. In an instant, Dunstan was also standing.

"Brethren, my brethren! Your Majesty, lords! What more proof could you want? You have heard the matter decided from the very mouth of the Divine!"

For an instant all was still quiet. Then, as though a dam burst around us, the calls came from ealdorman and companion alike, from priest and monk and cleric. "Aye, aye!", "So we have!", "The Lord has spoken, we have heard His voice with our own ears!", "It is surely a miracle!"

Edward, standing, shouted them down. "It is well, men, it is well. Scribes, I say what I was about to say. Record it thus: I find the *Concordia Regularis* upheld!"

)))))))((((((

Later that evening, alone in my chambers with Aetna, I recounted the events of the day. She had heard garbled and exaggerated accounts of what had happened. Already word was spreading that a great miracle had taken place, that the Holy Statue had spoken to the assembly at length, threatening all manner of dire repercussions if the *Concordia* was not immediately written into the Laws and the married clergy and their wives expelled from God's institutions. Apparently, as well as speaking, the figure of the Cross had also managed to extricate one hand from its impaling nails and blessed Archbishop Dunstan and the King. A huge and potent wonder had taken place amongst us.

"Aye, a tiny seed of such potency will grow to huge proportions in a very short time," my sister said. "But you mentioned that you thought you had seen something or somebody in the embrasure of the staircase... think you not that a strange coincidence? And why did no-one else see it, whatever it was?"

"I believe they were all too engrossed by what Beornhelm was about to say and the King's annoyance. It felt as though there might have been a tumult break out at any moment. Tensions were running high. The movement only caught my eye because I had been looking at the Cross and the archway directly beforehand."

"Well, whatever the truth of the matter, it seems to have had an affect most advantageous to Dunstan. The talk throughout the Court and already spreading through the city and beyond is that the Divine, in the words of Dunstan, has made His wishes clear. Surely there can be no further argument!"

At that moment, there was a quiet scratching at the door. Thinking that Lucet had returned and, hands full, needed assistance in gaining entry, Aetna, still looking over her shoulder at me, absent-mindedly walked to the door and opened it. The look on my face when I saw who stood without made her turn abruptly to the newcomer.

"Father!" she cried.

TWENTY-SIX

Aetna's shock upon seeing Wulfstan lasted but a few moments. Then she was in his arms, enfolded, as he kissed the top of her head, and asking, all at once how he had come there, and when did he arrive, why had he not told us of his plans...

"Peace, daughter, peace, time enough to tell all, but let me greet also my son!"

He strode into the room and we clasped arms, hand to elbow. A brief hug and he slapped me on the back. "Well, you are looking well. Responsibility suits you, Companion-man to the King!" And then it all came back to me; there he stood, in his pilgrim's garb, the round flat hat that marked him out as a traveller in our Lord's name. The hat that I had glimpsed as a child, half asleep and barely five years old. And the hat I had barely glimpsed, disappearing into the shadows of the stairwell in the Old Minster Hall. And the voice, the voice I had heard him use a dozen times as he intoned the accent of the Almighty in some great saga of story-telling, though never with such volume and impact.

"You! It was you! Father, what have you done..."

As I stood baffled and speechless, Aetna, too, was dealing with a surprise of her own, one still more pleasant. As she went to close the door after our father, another visitor appeared from dim interior light of the upper chambers' walkway. Bare-headed and tall, and his arms open to receive an embrace such as my father had enjoyed, though in that he was to be disappointed.

"Are you not pleased to see me also, Lady Aetna?"

"Ethelmaer!"

"Indeed!" he said. Aetna hesitated, glancing at me. I grinned despite my state of shock at my recent revelation.

"Of course... of course I am." She gave him a quick hug, an air of confusion, almost embarrassment, in her movements. "It is wonderful to see you, both of you." She turned back to my father, and only then seemed to become aware of the words which I had uttered in my amazement. "Father, what does Wulf mean? What *have* you done?"

Wulfmaer took off his hat and smoothed back his hair, looking around for somewhere to sit.

"Well, daughter – and my eagle-eyed boy... I suppose I should... but can it not wait until we have supped? Ethelmaer, I am sure, and I have a fierce thirst upon us for we have been about the Archbishop's work and he is a hard task master. Wulf, I cannot believe that you do not have a butt of something well rounded in your chamber! By the look of you, you could do with a draught yourself."

As it happened, I did, have a small cask of good wine which I kept on hand in case of visitors. Oft-times a young serving woman was in need of some sustenance when she came to my chambers by the way of her duties. Carrying chamber pots and linens can be thirsty work…

"Very well, Father," I said and tapped the cask, pouring wine into four round clay goblets. "Sit, sit, you too Ethelmaer – and it is good to see you, man! Aetna, take some wine." I pulled a chest against the door, for something told me that we did not wish to be disturbed for the next while. My wits were beginning to return and I was hoping against hope that whatever explanation was about to be forthcoming was not one which I might wish never to have heard. Aetna took a seat on my pallet, and Ethelmaer went to sit beside her, though, at the last moment seemed to realise the impropriety of such a move. My father had taken the only chair, so he sat on the chest, his back to the door. I sank down beside my sister and took her hand.

"I give you *was heil*, my children!" Wulfstan took down the wine in a single quaff and poured himself some more. "Ethelmaer, I assume you are happy for me to make plain your part in this little… matter?" Ethelmaer nodded, taking a sup of his wine. Aetna looked at him, her head a little on one side and a furrowed line of curiosity between her brows.

"Your part in this?" she said. "What…"

"All in good time," said Wulfstan. "You both know… of course you do, you are privy, between you, to all that goes on in this Court… of the difficulty this lack of settlement in the matter of the *Concordia* has been to the King. In his heart he would do what Dunstan wishes in a beat, but he has been unable to risk the discontent of the Mercians and their cohorts in the matter of lost revenue and, indeed, the self-conceived insults to their families should their scions be ousted from their monastic sinecures. Swords have been rattled; quietly, but they have been rattled!

"And so, despite the *Concordia Regularis* being sanctioned by the late King, Alfhere and his family and with them any who seek to line their pockets at the expense of the Church's rightful use of its resources, have continually thrown up barricades against those who would enact and enforce it."

"That is true," I said. "The King is constantly in a state of frustration, pulled this way and that whilst trying to content all parties."

"Just so," continued our Father. "It seemed to matter not what sensible provisions or assurances he made to the non-reformists, they were determined not to be swayed. Outright disobedience looms and that way could lead to armed dissent – even civil war, may God forbid!"

"But what…?" Aetna interrupted.

"Wait, Lady, wait," said Ethelmaer. "All will be made clear. May I, Wulfstan?"

"Go ahead, Brother."

"You will both recall that when I left Rammesig – to the disgust of my father – and told the Archbishop that I was unwilling to be in his service as a secretary, that Dunstan was unfazed by my decision, happily allowing me to take to the road as a travelling monk, virtually a mendicant, in the way in which my father felt so scandalous. What he asked me to keep secret – and I have his leave to tell you this now – is that he wished me to be his eyes and ears in places where respectable churchmen might not be welcome. As a hedge priest, not an eyebrow would be raised were I to drink in rough taverns, talk to those women who lie with both the high and the low alike, in short, those persons who know all, but often say little. The very souls who might be called upon to bear arms in the cause of – well, either side."

Wulfstan took up the story. "When Ethelmaer and I conjured the idea of travelling together, he put it to the Archbishop that between us we would have access not only to the baser but also to the nobler places on our way. For what Great Hall does not wish for a story-teller, and what kitchen has no place for a monk prepared to give absolution to the most common of sins?

"Since shortly after we left Wintancaestre, we have been sending reports back to the Archbishop of what passes in places where those who would be his enemies – and so, I do truly believe, the enemies of the King – gather and conspire. We heard that Alfhere planned to have this great orator, Bishop Beornhelm – whom he had met through his own house priest – attempt to split the Council to be held at Wintancaestre. As soon as winter was passed, we got word to go to Cantuaria. Dunstan was at his wits' end to find some way in which to settle the matter once and for all. And without troubling the King's conscience. His own ingenuity, my vocal skills and Ethelmaer's network of – shall we say underground contacts – which will spread the word far and wide, and quickly, have ensured there can be no further argument. The voice of the Almighty has proclaimed that the *Concordia* must be paramount. It is quite brilliant, though I make so bold as to say 'tis so myself!"

I was aghast. Aetna sat speechless.

"I have heard you 'throw' your voice before, Father, but never to such effect..." I said.

"Dunstan searched long and hard for a hall where the shape of the space would echo just as he wished and where there was a doorway or arrow-slit positioned just as we needed. That Our Lord on his Rood was also where it was, and that here in Wincancaestre... that was just good chance."

"Or, indeed, the hand of the Divine at work!" added Ethelmaer with a smile.

"But it was careless of me to allow myself to be seen," said Wulfstan. "When I saw you, Wulf, seated at such a high station, my pride in you took my attention. I came to my wits just as I was about to speak out, and thought that you had not seen me. We must have missed catching each other's eye by just a second. I pulled at the hawser to move the Cross and... well you know the rest."

"But how...?" Aetna could still hardly put her words together.

"How did we know it would all work?" said Ethelmaer. "We arrived in Wintancaestre two days ago. It has been hard to gain access to the Old Minster Hall in secret long enough to practise the performance, but between us and together with Dunstan, we ran through the exercise twice in almost complete darkness last night and the night before. If we could do it under those conditions... the only unknown factor was when Beornhelm would rise to speak. When the King almost disallowed him... well, Dunstan had to step in and ensure that he had his moment!"

"I wondered at the Archbishop being so equitable in encouraging His Majesty to permit it," I said. "And you have been lying low where?"

"In a tiny chamber off Dunstan's quarters. We could not risk being seen."

"And the King knows nothing of this?"

"He has not asked, therefore we need tell him no untruth," said Ethelmaer. "Those were the Archbishop's own words. As it is written in Proverbs, Chapter Twelve '*Qui loquitur veritatem ostendit iustitiae est qui autem mentitur testis est fraudulentus.*' 'He that speaks truth shows forth righteousness: but a false witness deceit.' We need bear no witness at all."

"And now, I fear," said Wulfstan, "we must impose on your hospitality for a few hours until it is dark and we can slip away. We took a risk coming to see you before nightfall, but I was worried that you might add two and two and go to the King with the total before we had time to acquaint you with our little... subterfuge."

"But surely you will not leave again straightway?" said Aetna, though I thought she looked more toward Ethelmaer than our father as she spoke. "It is so long since were... all of us... together!"

"Fear not, little one, no indeed! For tomorrow morning the good Brother and I will arrive at the Nunneminster Gate, travel-stained and weary and most disappointed to have missed the great miracle about which everyone is speaking." Father laughed his great, deep laugh and then remembering the need for secrecy pulled himself up short. "Oh, but you are both a sight for sore eyes, it does my heart good to see you!"

The following forenoon, just as our father had predicted, he and Ethelmaer passed though the city gate and made their way to the King's Great Hall. There they were greeted by Edward as the old friends they were, and if he had any suspicion of the ruse which had been perpetrated, he kept it to himself. The King was no man's fool, I thought, as he clasped Wulfstan's right arm and clapped Ethelmaer on the shoulder. He knew how keenly Dunstan had sought a way to settle this tormenting problem without putting his King in a compromising situation with the Chief Ealdorman and was grateful to whatever power, be it Divine or otherwise, which had made his life the easier. The Archbishop had set out at dawn to return to Cantuaria, well pleased.

"Wulf," said the King, turning to me, "send word to your sister of your father's arrival! And to the Dowager. Tonight, we shall celebrate together as a family, for, indeed, you are all the closest I have, now that I so rarely see my brother, Ethelred!"

We had withdrawn into the King's receiving chamber, where he had been about the business of signing documents. "Come men, sit, sit! Scribe, no more of this today, I pray you, my hand is as cramped as a whore's... I beg your pardon, Brother Ethelmaer!"

"Fear not, Your Majesty, I have heard much worse in my travels. The life of a mendicant monk does not allow for much delicacy, I can assure you!"

"I imagine not." A cheerful fire burnt in the fire-pit and Edward sat back on the settle and put his feet up on the fender. He turned to my father. "But tell me, Wulfstan, speaking of my brother, have your travels taken you to Corf Gate? Even my stepmother has need of entertainment, and a fine story-teller is turned from nobody's door on a long winter's night."

I thought of the unhappy history between my father and the King's stepmother, now so many years past but still, I knew, lying heavy on Wulfstan's heart. He would never forgive the delay which, he still believed, was in part the cause of our mother's death.

"In truth, Sire, we have avoided that ill-favoured place. The locals believe it is tainted in some way; there is even talk of witchery and other strange unholy doings behind the walls of the castle itself."

"'Tis true, Your Majesty," said Ethelmaer. "The barrows on its approach are said to house the spirits of the Durotriges, the tribe that dwelt there before the Romans came, and a whole legion is known to have simply disappeared as they passed through the gap in the Purbecig Hills which gives the place its name. They may still be heard at night, crying out in despair, unable to draw their swords and lost in endless fog. I would not wish to speak out of turn, but I almost fear for your young brother, being brought up in such a place."

"I had heard that the woods thereabouts were not a popular haunt for hunters and the like, but thought it only that they were, mayhap, mismanaged," mused Edward. "I am remiss, though, in not visiting Ethelred. He is a good lad. I would not that we two became less than friends. Wulf, remind me to make arrangements: soon, we will pay the Aetheling Ethelred the honour of receiving his brother, the King!"

The idea of a trip to visit Ethelred was not an unpleasant one, but the thought of his mother and Morwen... nevertheless, I made a mental note that as soon as the current furore over the Old Minster's miraculous cross had subsided, we would plan such an excursion. We might even be able to fashion some excuse to extend the trip toward Bathe, allowing the King an opportunity to meet his baby daughter. Yes, it was beginning to sound appealing. An opportunity to venture beyond the immediate confines of the city would be welcome, even if it came at the cost of spending some little time in the company of the Queen.

Aunt Aethelflaed arrived from her quarters and shortly afterwards Aetna joined us apologising for her tardiness – the upheaval throughout the Court since the events of the day before had thrown her housekeeping routines into chaos. Ceorls and thralls alike all wished to see the speaking Cross in the Old Minster Hall, though most had seen it a dozen times before without appreciable enthusiasm. The Minster brothers were in paroxysoms of joy over the episode – already their coffers, somewhat depleted since the New Minster had robbed them of many worshippers, were beginning to swell as those making haste to be among the first to follow the footsteps of the Council into the Hall donated alms. Soon, Aetna laughed, as she commented upon the mounting excitement in Court and city alike, the metal smiths would be fashioning pilgrim tokens in commemoration of the event.

"Which is as it should be," she added quickly, glancing at first at the King and then our father, "and befitting such a wondrous happening." She smiled brightly. "Such a shame you and Brother Ethelmaer missed the day," she said.

"Great-stepmother," said Edward, "we have just been speaking of visiting my brother at Corf Gate. I fear that I have been ignoring him. Would you like to join the party? What say you, Wulf, in about a fourteen-night? That should be time enough to prepare."

"I thank you, sire," replied Aethelflaed. "I think, though, that I shall not at this time. In truth I am just beginning to feel the benefits of the spring, but a long journey might be a little beyond me. But, Aetna, you must go. You have been working so hard all winter, a change of scene will do you good, and it will be of benefit to me to remind myself of all the duties you take from my shoulders if I see to the running of the household while you are away. It will not be too onerous – after all, His Majesty will not be here!"

"Ah, Ladies, it pains me that I am such a burden to you all!" cried Edward, blithely. "'Tis the curse of kingship!"

We spent a pleasant day. The Chief Ealdormen and his cohorts had left early that morning, Bishop Beornhelm, so it was said, having paid a visit before daybreak to the Old Minster Hall, apparently taking some time to look over the site of the miracle. I tried to put out of my head the idea that he may have nursed any suspicions as to the veracity of events. The other delegates drifted off, back to their sees or ealdormanries, carrying the story of the speaking crucifix with them. Soon only the Ealdorman of East Anglia and his companions remained. Ethelwine and Brithnoth came to join us in the King's chambers as the hour for the noon-day meal approached.

"Well," said Ethelwine, as he shook hands with Brother Ethelmaer, "it seems that not all your father's fears have come true! You do not look quite the hedge-priest for all your wanderings. And here you are taking your ease with the King! When I return home, I shall be sure to tell him that you are moving in high circles, and not, as he was so sure you would be, with the dross of the wayside."

"I should be grateful if you would, Lord. I thank you. Though I have not regretted one day of my life taking the word of our Heavenly Father on the road, my heart has been heavy that I caused him so much displeasure. But how goes the rebuilding of Rammesig?"

"Slowly, slowly, I am afraid. And meanwhile, at Elig, your uncle's patronage pays for the raising of a fine church where once old Mother Gorthson watched over Saint Etheldreda's Shrine. Aye, together we make the Fens a stronghold in defence of Christ's good people. And all without expecting a penny's revenue. Now, if that money-grabbing Chief Ealdor..."

"Enough, good Ethelwine," said Edward. "We have had enough of this subject for a while, and with God's grace the matter is now settled. I would hear no more of it now. Come, Brithnoth, tell us of how things fare in Eastseaxe. My late father was ever full of tales of how he spent time with you all there. He used to make my brother and me laugh at the story of his arrival in Colencaestre and how he caused the fat old shire reeve such confusion!"

Our uncle laughed. "Aye, that he did! Do you remember, Wulf? And Aetna?"

"I do, Uncle," said Aetna. "King Edgar stirred my young heart with tales of princesses in that city."

We spent the rest of the day enjoying the unusual pleasure of each other's company without either the weight of politics above our heads, or the presence of any with whom we felt the need to dissemble. If only, I knew Aetna was thinking, our Aunts Aelflaed and Elflada had been with us the family might have been almost complete. As the postnoon wore on, she excused herself, saying that she must attend to a matter in the herbarium. Ethelmaer asked if he might accompany her as his stocks of some medicinal herbs were low.

"Of course, Brother," she had said...

)))))))))((((((((

It was nearer three weeks than two before we were ready to leave for Corf. During that time the Court seemed to resume something of the atmosphere it had enjoyed in the immediate aftermath of Edward's coronation, before the tensions surrounding the *Concordia* had deepened. Wintancaestre bustled with unaccustomed travellers, all eager to visit the Old Minster Hall and the inns and shopkeepers were delighted with the unexpected increase in their business. It still seemed likely that there would be severe shortages of food as the year lengthened, but nobody was inclined to despoil the pleasures of the present with worries over the future. For now, at least, the sun was shining.

Our father and Ethelmaer decided to remain with us until we departed and, though still not willing to visit Corf Gate itself, planned to ride with us until we reached the Isle of Purbecig before heading off, once again, on their travels. Edward emphatically declared that this trip was not to be considered a Royal Progress, but nevertheless there was much to prepare. The King could hardly pay a visit to the heir to the throne and his mother without some formality and pomp. He purposed, upon leaving Corf, to swing North to Bathe where he would visit, upon the Dowager's suggestion, the convent and stay at the monastery. Aethelflaed had generously endowed the convent upon the appointment of a new Abbess, for it had grown considerably since the time of Alfreth's novitiate. At some point during his stay, Edward was determined to slip away to Sceo for at least one night to meet his baby daughter – and spend but a little time with his wife.

We had, of course, sent word ahead to Corf informing the Queen of our intentions and when we arrived, we were greeted cordially, our men and horses housed and fed well and we were made surprisingly welcome, in the light of Elfrith's disappointment at her son's lack of kingship. Young Ethelred seemed genuinely pleased to see his brother, and was keen to hear of what was passing at Court and the details of the Speaking Cross. Edward told him the tale of the miracle in great detail, rather exaggerating

437

the most dramatic elements and I contemplated how quickly and easily such stories became part of the great lore of the land. I wondered how long it might be before the anniversary of the miracle became a holy-day in Wintancaestre and perhaps even further afield. When Edward imitated the deep, resonate voice of "the Divine" Ethelred's eyes opened wide.

"Were you not terrified, brother?" he said, gazing at the King with something like awe.

"No, no, indeed, Ethelred," replied Edward. "My heart was lifted and my soul soared at being told that the course which I had, myself, favoured, was aright. I, and those others who were fortunate enough to hear the Voice, witnessed a great and wonderful thing. Our Lord betook Himself to speak to us in person. We were mightily blessed!"

I began to think that Edward had, in truth, begun to convince himself, if he had ever doubted it, that he had heard the Voice of the Almighty. He had made no comment since the event to either myself or, to my knowledge, any other that he was not completely certain of it. After several weeks in the company of my father, enjoying those splendid storytelling tones, he appeared, if anything, to be still more sure of it. Or perhaps it was just convenient so to believe.

We stayed a week at Corf. Aetna, in the moments we had in private together, confessed that she still found making conversation with Elfrith less than easy. The Queen, whilst scrupulously polite to my sister, who was clearly high in the King's regard, and representing her aunt, the Dowager Queen Aethelflaed, still managed to give the impression that she felt Aetna's youth and sex insurmountable obstacles to their intimacy. Apart from the ever present Morwen, Elfrith appeared to eschew female company. At the High Table she often recounted the visits of various Ealdormen – Alfhere chief amongst them – and her own political views, often shared by her guests, but rarely touched upon the womanly skills which (although perhaps I am foolish to think so) are such a joy to behold in one so beautiful, for she was still a bewitching woman to look upon. Often at these times, I found my eyes straying to Lucet, standing behind Aetna, as Morwen stood behind her mistress. I still could not quite make her out: so expert a servant, and yet there was something about her which made me feel that she was out of her natural place.

Corf was a small, enclosed household. Apart from a house priest who, on occasion, was invited to share our board, the only company for young Ethelred (other than his nurse) was that of his companion, Meryasek, who was almost always at the Aetheling's side. Meryasek's appearance suggested that he did not thrive in his new environment. His looks had become somewhat sallow, and the liveliness which had manifested itself at Wintancaestre seemed lessened. He hardly seemed to be the same young man as he who had been so eager to take the dance floor with my sister.

There was clearly a real affection between him and the prince, however, and he did his best to keep Ethelred entertained and in good humour when he had been in some way chastened by his mother, which was a common happening. Elfrith was almost obsessively exacting when it came to her son. If he spoke without her permission, or laughed excessively, or, so it seemed to me, acted in any way natural to a lad of his age he was reprimanded. And yet, if anyone other than herself spoke to him with less than what she considered to be his due deference her displeasure was shown swiftly and sharply. Poor Meryasek walked a permanent tightrope between treating Ethelred as an eight-year-old boy liked – with an element of cajolery and humour – and in a way which did not result in his own permanent dismissal. No wonder he was showing the strain.

On the final night of our stay, we were as usual taking the evening meal at the long board. There was no need for a separate High Table as there were so few diners, those household members of a lower station who would customarily take advantage of their right to eat in the Great Hall preferring the company in the kitchens. The house priest, Father Bagshot, was of the company, as was Meryasek. Edward was at the head of the table, with Ethelred to his right and Elfrith to his left. To his delight, Meryasek found himself seated beside Aetna, myself on the opposite side of the table, beside the Queen. We were quite the intimate little party, although as ever, Elfrith seemed out of sorts.

"Well, Your Majesty," she said to Edward, "how have you found your visit to our little Court? I hope that you have taken some pleasure from it. His Highness," (this was her habitual way of referring to Ethelred) "has most certainly enjoyed seeing so much of his... brother." She still managed to make the fact that Edward was a half-sibling sound as though it were some form of insult.

"Indeed, I have, Step-mother," replied Edward, "and I fully intend to make it a regular occurrence. We must see about getting the woods hereabout better stocked with game, too, for in the future I should like to hunt, and perhaps take the youngster here with me." He grinned across the table at Ethelred. "How would you like that, brother? It is high time you were not just sitting a horse but hunting, too."

"Oh, I should like that very much!" cried Ethelred. "Can Meryasek ride with us, too? He tells me tales, often, of how he rode to hounds with his father in Kernow. There was one time..."

"Ethelred, you should pay more attention to Father Bagshot and the learning of your letters than to your companion's idle tales," said Elfrith sharply. Then, her voice softening as she turned back to the King, she remarked, "It is hard to find reliable woodsmen hereabouts to care for the needs of the hunt, they speak some nonsense about wandering spirits and lost Legions. But we would be grateful for any improvements you would care to suggest, of course."

"Oh, but Mama, there *are* lost..."

"Enough, Ethelred."

There was a strained silence, Ethelred pouting. Then Meryasek broke it.

"Your Majesty?"

"Yes?" The reply came simultaneously from Edward and Elfrith.

Edward laughed easily. "My pardon, Lady, I forget that there are two crowned heads at this board! And one so much more handsome than mine!"

This was a pretty compliment, and the Queen smiled at it, but something had already put Elfrith back into a good humour. "No matter, sire! Speak up, Meryasek, what is it?"

"I... I happen to know that there is a piper taking his ease in the kitchen... he is the cook's brother, I believe. Yester-eve he was playing most jollily for the ceorls. Might he not be called to do the same for us? It is many moons since there was dancing in this Hall. On Your Majesty's guests' last evening, it might be pleasant to make merry. If Your Majesty approved, of course."

It was the longest speech we had ever heard him make to the Queen, and it was clearly done with the summoning of all his courage. His dark hair had flopped forward over his brow and he pushed it back nervously, managing a smile at Ethelred, who, without wishing to be reprimanded for speaking once again, was plainly keen for a reply in the affirmative.

"Oh! That is the way the wind blows, is it? Our Hall is to turn derry-down with the cook's brother leading the revels?" Both Meryasek and Ethelred looked so crestfallen that I almost laughed, but then Elfrith said, "Why not? I feel this last week has... but no matter! Morwen, off into the kitchen with you. Let us make the King's last memory of his visit one he wishes to repeat."

Morwen made small strangled noise, clearly not relishing her task, but did as she was bidden.

"We are short of ladies to dance, Mama," said Ethelred, tentatively. "May not Lucet join with us?" Ethelred had remembered Lucet from the sad ride to Glestingaberg with his late father's body. Aetna had told me that she had quite stolen his young heart. And, I confess, was beginning to steal mine, too. She stood so straight and strong at my sister's shoulder. And this eve she wore a most fetching gunna, pinkish red, over the top of a creamy under shift, which fell to the floor in soft, fluid folds. Her honey coloured hair was plaited and worn over her shoulder. It glowed gold in the candle-light, her light head rail a whisper of white above it. I held my breath, almost certain that Elfrith would veto the idea. But she seemed to be buoyed up by something outside our ken.

"Well," she said, "if we are all to embrace the spirit of the evening and dance the Haye, so be it! Ah, Morwen, good, you are returned. It seems we shall be in need of you on the dance floor, too. We shall be four to four and make the circle… Father Bagshot, you are excused from the dance, but pray find something to wield as a tambour, for I feel sure we shall require something to keep the beat!"

Could this be the same Elfrith that always stood so doughtily on her dignity and that of her son? What thoughts had passed through her mind to make her so willing to celebrate?

I didn't care, for as the cook's brother played on through the evening, 'Old Baggy', as I discovered the young prince called him, banging out the rhythm with a wooden spoon, first Ethelred danced with Lucet in the Haye and then he partnered my sister, his mother and the reluctant Morwen, leaving the delightful Lucet on my willing arm.

)))))))(((((((

We left Corf early the next morning and were on the old Legion Road of Portway by the time of our midday meal. Finding a pleasant inn, we stopped and allowed the horses to rest while we ate. The landlord was much flustered to find his premises hosting the King and his party, but rose to the occasion, finding us a passable ale and a very fine game pottage. I fear we must have eaten his kitchen clean, by the time our men were also fed. His regular customers would have to go hungry that eve, but Edward paid him well and gave him permission to hang a wooden crown outside his door to signify that royalty had patronised his tavern. I later heard that many claimed that the food at the "Sign of King Edward's Crown", was unequalled.

We would not reach Bathe that day, but purposed to cut across country and be at Ivelcaestre by nightfall, from there taking the Fosse Way up to Bathe. Runners had been sent ahead and we were expected at I'lcaestre, as the locals called it, accommodation having been arranged in the Hall of the local Reeve. No doubt the poor man was on tenterhooks, for I'lcaestre was not a large town, its position as a military garrison and financial hub under the Romans long since eroded by their departure.

Edward was in a fine mood. All morning he had been riding jauntily, humming one of the country tunes to which we had been dancing the previous evening and taking the salutations of those we passed. He downed his second tankard of ale and stood to stretch his legs before the postnoon's ride.

"What think you of my stepmother's sudden change of mood yester-eve?" he said. "One moment she was her usual stiff self and then... it seemed most strange!"

"Aye," I replied. "I think her humour lifted just after you suggested that your visits to see Ethelred might become a regular occurrence... and mentioned the hunt."

"I never recall Elfrith taking an interest in the hunt before," said my sister. "Except, of course that time at Uphude..." Her words tailed off, not wishing to dampen the high spirits of the day by recalling the tragedy of Ethelwold's death.

"Well, there may be hope for young Ethelred, yet," said the King. "He needs to come out from under his mother's wing. Perhaps I should suggest him being fostered."

"It would be a brave man, king or no, who suggested removing him for her nest just yet," I replied. "But perhaps a beginning can be made by the idea of the hunt..."

Lucet came through from the kitchens where she had been supervising the preparation of some small edibles that that we might eat on our way, and a few rag-stoppered flagons of small-ale to save our throats from the dust of the road.

"Lady," she said to Aetna, "I do not wish to hurry you, but I fear the weather is changing. We should try and reach I'lcaestre before it becomes too ill. I do not like the look of the sky to the west, there are clouds roiling on the horizon."

"Are there no limits to your talents, Lucet?" said Edward. "Actress," (he would never forget her willing compliance in the farce of his bed chamber) "Companion-woman and now weather prophet! You are indeed a rare find!"

"Sire, you do me too much honour." She dimpled in her usual pretty fashion.

I helped Aetna onto her horse, and then likewise gave the stirrup-hand to Lucet. "And yet we know nothing of your past, Lucet," I said.

She seemed to stiffen slightly. "I have told my Lady what is necessary," she replied, shortly.

"I... I'm sorry... I did not mean..." I stuttered. This was foolish. She was, after all, only a recently freed thrall. I had no need to apologise. But still, I felt that I had committed some indelicacy. She really was an enigma.

The men were already mounted and their horses, refreshed, were pawing the ground and eager to be on their way. We formed up and trotted out of the tavern's yard, the Landlord and his thralls standing at the door, exhausted but clearly happy.

"Fare well," cried Edward. "And the blessings of Our Lord upon you!"

"God save Your Majesty!" came the reply.

Edward and I rode abreast as we took the crest of the grassy greenway which would, we hoped, prove a shortcut between the high roads of the Romans. We would otherwise have had to travel all the way to Escanceastre to join the Fosse Way. The greenways were well travelled, but being unsurfaced were subject to waterlogging in poor conditions and often what started as a shortcut became a long, drawn out and exhausting marathon. The weather had been fine, but if Lucet was correct and a storm was on the way, we certainly did not want to get caught in it and become bogged down. But there seemed no immediate cause for concern, and we jogged along at a good pace, the miles disappearing behind us.

After a while, Edward kicked his horse forward. "I am going to ride for a while with the men in the vanguard," he said. "It is good to let them know that their King is one of them, that his backside sits a horse the same as theirs! Take your ease, Wulf, I shall not need you for now."

I reflected on how like his father he was becoming, and then just let my mind wander and my horse do the work. I was roused from my daydreaming by a light cough at my elbow. Lucet had ridden up behind me and was now trotted almost alongside my own horse, although as I had taken the centre of the road, she could not quite come quite level with me. I reined over to my right, allowing her to ride abreast.

"Lord Wulf," she said, "I am sorry if I was disrespectful when you spoke to me at the tavern. I forget my place sometimes."

I turned and looked over my shoulder at Aetna riding some short way behind. She smiled and nodded at me, and made a gesture as if to suggest that I should keep my attention with Lucet.

"Not at all," I replied, not sure how to proceed. Lucet had always troubled me, in a way. She had been a thrall, and was now a ceorl, but there was something about her that gave the lie to both those stations. Neither was she quite noble in her bearing. I found myself uncertain of how to act with her – I, I who never had a problem convincing a girl that she, and only she, had the arms in which I wished to lie.

I tried again. "Lucet, you are my sister's companion-woman. You are under no obligation to make yourself pleasant to me…" That did not sound the way I meant it to. "Oh, in the name of Heaven, I cannot put two words together today. Lucet, it is I who should be sorry. Your story is your own, it was not for me to tease you. I have spent too much time with a sister to whom I can say anything with no chance of mis-speaking. As you know, we are twins and when we are together, I become the inquisitive little boy I once was. Forgive me."

"I envy you that… a sister, a sibling who shares your memories. For my memories are mine alone and sometimes I would that I had someone to bear them with me."

"To bear them? That sounds as though they lie heavy upon you. Ah, but I am doing it again! It is well my name is not Tibbert, for I should surely be upon my ninth life by now!"

"I have ever had a fondness for cats," she smiled.

"I, too," I said and found myself telling her of old Musbane at Radendunam, and then of Bremel and Berrie, Gillycrest and all our other favourites.

Now Lucet was laughing. What a sweet sound! "Why, Lord Wulf, you have a soft heart indeed!" she said.

We heard a thud of hooves upon the springy ground beneath us and I turned to see Aetna cantering to catch us up. "It is good to see you both in such high spirits," she said, "but I fear Lucet may have been aright about the weather. Look yonder." She nodded toward the smooth, rounded hills which formed the horizon to the North – the direction in which we were headed. The sky had become a deep, angry grey, slashed with purple shafts where the lower clouds met the higher and caught the last of the sunlight. Already, beneath them there were diagonal striations reaching to the ground – rain was falling in the distance. A jagged flash of lightning split the sky. I counted slowly beneath my breath, approaching ten before the sound of the thunder reached us.

"It is still some way off," I said, "but we must find shelter, for we cannot reach I'lcaestre before the storm is upon us. Sire!" I called forward to where Edward still rode amicably with the men-at-arms. "Sire! Look to the sky ahead!"

The breeze was beginning to build and gusts buffeted us head on. The King stood in his saddle to get a better view of the surrounding countryside. There were no villages in sight. A bank of woodland to our right was tossing in the strengthening wind and looked to offer no refuge. Away to our left, some distance off the road was a low structure, little more than a rough hut, but there was a narrow track leading to it which looked as though it had been well used. "There!" he cried.

The vanguard of some six riders led the way off the greenway and onto the track, riding single file, for it seemed that little more than a handcart had ever been driven along it. Edward followed, with Aetna and Lucet, myself and the other men-at-arms bringing up the rear. The ground was claggy beneath the horses' hooves, and the light was becoming strange with that unearthly gloaming that precedes a tempest. There was a depression in the ground behind the hut which looked as though it might once have been another building but was now overgrown with saplings and young trees. The men began to arrange their waxed tarps among them to create a covering of sorts for themselves and the horses. Edward tried the door of the hut. It opened easily.

"Probably used now as a shepherd's hut," he said. "Though maybe once a home. Before the hog-murrain, perhaps, and the family died."

There were a few rough pieces of furniture within, together with some blankets, neatly folded and laid in a corner. The thatched roof looked waterproof and the single window still possessed a stout shutter. One of the men brought in the light trunks which were all that the King and my sister had brought with them by way of luggage. My own few possessions for the trip, and a clean pair of hose, I carried in my saddlebag. Lucet heaved off her shoulder the pack of provisions she had brought from the tavern, lately removed from her horse. Suddenly there was a white flash of light and almost immediately a crash of thunder. The wind whistled around the walls. At the same moment the rain arrived, beating furiously against the thatch and flung against the door and shutter by the ferocity of the wind. The storm had travelled faster than any of us had anticipated.

"Thank goodness we found this place," said Aetna. "The poor men, though! They have little cover – and the horses will be terrified."

"The men have weathered worse, and they will care for the horses, never fear," said Edward.

It was already well past mid postnoon, and was already becoming dark. The cloud cover was dense and with the shutter and door closed tight there was no light filtering in from outside. As our eyes became accustomed to the dimness, we fumbled about and found some tallow candles, set in rough clay dishes. Lucet fished out her tinderbox and after several attempts managed to get one of the rough wicks to light. From that she lit the others. They gave a poor, yellow light, very unlike the beeswax candles we were used to enjoying, and only when the lightning flashed could we really see much of our surroundings. Not that there was much to see.

"Well," said Edward, equitably, for nothing seemed fit to dampen his mood that day, "it seems as though we are to make the best of it for a while. What have you there, Lucet?"

"Sire, I have small ale, cheese and bread. And a hand of pork. And this…" From the depth of her pack she drew forth a stoppered flask.

"Beor!" cried Edward. "Lucet, you are a marvel. I thought not to see any this year, for the apple crop was so bad last!"

"In my homeland we call is *cisdre*," she replied. "When the landlord of the inn heard that you were giving him the honour of royal patronage, he bade me take it. It is from the year of your father's coronation."

We made ourselves as comfortable as we could. There was a low, rickety table, which Aetna brushed down, setting out the food. Of course, we each had our eating knives and the bread would serve as trenchers, but between us we could only muster two drinking vessels, small gold cup which the King always kept about him, and a tumbler my sister had in her trunk. Edward laughed.

"We shall let the ladies have the tableware," he chuckled. "Wulf, you and I shall swig straight from the flasks!"

"Sire, I cannot drink from a cup, while you…" Lucet was horrified.

"Come, Lucet, I think you have kept us in the dark too long. You are not the stuff of thralls or serving women, I knew that from the first time you put yourself forward to hinder those who would injure the late King, my father. You sit a horse like no slave I have ever seen, and I know that you have a little of letters and Latin. You knew how to be a companion-woman to the Lady Aetna with virtually no training and have an easy way with people of all stations."

Lucet had her back to us, fussing with the table as Edward spoke and I could see her stiffen. Then her shoulders relaxed slightly.

"Very well," she said. "Perhaps this is, indeed, the time for such a tale. For I do not think we shall be travelling any further this night." She turned to Aetna. "My Lady, here, these blankets are not too dirty to sit upon, and we have cloaks aplenty in the trunk for covers." She broke the seal on the flagon of beor and poured two generous helpings into the cups. Then she handed the bottle to Edward. He took a long swig and passed it to me. It was strong and sweet, and slipped down my throat easily.

"Come, let us sit where we may," he said.

For a time, the lightning continued to rip through the darkness and the thunder to crash, the wind whistling around the walls. Then, gradually, the worst of the maelstrom passed and gave way to a relentless pounding of rain, driven against the ground and hut in heavy, pulsating roar. We had eaten a little and taken several pulls at the beor before Lucet began to speak.

"You have heard of Richard of Normandy?" she said.

"Of course," said Edward. "They call him Richard the Fearless, do they not?"

"Some do. I call him Richard the Faithless, Richard the Coward. Richard, my father."

Edward was about to take another pull from the bottle, but stopped with it half way to his mouth. Aetna's eyes opened wide and I… well, we were all speechless.

"I am not exactly sure of the year of my birth. There are things from my childhood that I cannot remember, and others that I wish I could forget. But I believe it to have been about sixteen years past. I was my mother's third child born to Richard, after a sister and then a brother. They called me Luciette and there was a time when I was quite the favourite… but I get ahead of my tale.

"In the years just before my birth, Richard had reached the height of his power. Count of Rouen – the Norsemen called him 'Jarl' and were his allies. Many rivals had tried to take control of Normandy but he always pushed them back. He was Guardian to the son of Hugh the Great, King of the Franks, and betrothed to his daughter, Emma. Betrothed and then married. But she was not enough for him. He took his pleasures wherever he chose, and there were none to gainsay him.

"My mother was daughter to the head of the *Guilde des Tisserands de Tapisserie* - Guild of Tapestry Weavers. The family was not rich in the way of the nobility, but was wealthy and respected in Rouen. My grandfather did much work for the Church, although he was of a sect which did not willingly worship in the great buildings that he helped to beautify, being a member of the Manichaeus Brotherhood. They worshipped in private – in each other's houses. They were tolerated, but remained secretive and the accusation of heresy was never far away. *Maman* was beautiful and the Count saw her and wanted her as he had wanted and taken many women before and after. So, he took her, but unlike many men who will take a woman as mistress until he tires of her and then let her go back to her own life, perhaps to find a good man who would love her for what she was, he kept her. Richard had many wives – yes, wives. He married them *more danico*. Have you heard the term?"

"I understand the words," said Edward. "It is Latin for 'in the Danish manner', but I do not know how it relates to marriage."

"It means that a woman is taken to wife, as the Vikings take their women. She simply becomes her husband's property – not that that differs so much from the Norman way, though at least they limit their marriages to one at a time – but worse, he may put her aside as he chooses, with no honour, whether she wishes it or no. Any children are either legitimate or illegitimate subject to the humour of their father. That is how Richard took my mother. And for a while she was content enough. My father favoured me. I recall being dandled on his knee, told I was the prettiest among his children, even given my own pony once I was old enough. But time passed and his interest with it. My mother became just another of his wives... many called them concubines. But as she became less required in his bedchamber, so she became freer to visit her family and to live a life that was not unpleasant – for her or her children.

"Then one day there was a fire in the city. From the high windows of the castle we could see the flames fanning out across Rouen, moving south with the wind from the sea, heading toward the spinning and tapestry quarter. My mother ran toward her father's house to see if she could help them – perhaps even invite them to the castle to escape the fire. My brother insisted upon going with her, and they told my sister and me to remain behind. Of course, we didn't. We followed along, pushing through the throng of people making their way toward us and away from the fire, until we reached the square outside the Guildhall, next to my grandfather's house. My mother had just begun to climb the steps leading up to the great wooden door, when the wind suddenly changed. The inshore breeze which had been driving the fire south abruptly veered and my grandfather's house was saved. The fire swept through an adjoining house as though it was tinder, and in an instant a huge mass of burning timber fell, crushing many fleeing people beneath it.

"A cry went up 'Witchcraft'! The direction of the fire had changed so quickly it seemed unnatural. People pointed at my mother and accused her of whistling the wind. 'She is of the Brotherhood!' 'A heretic!' The cries came loud and fast. My grandfather came out of the house to help her, and then he was caught up in the accusations, too. The fire spiralled away to the east, and left death in its path. My grandfather, grandmother, *Maman* and my brother, sister and I were all arrested on charges of being heretic and turning the wind though sorcery.

"I will not speak of the time we spent in prison... only to say that Richard – the 'fearless' – was too afraid of his own people to intervene. He needed the unwavering loyalty of his citizens to keep his region safe from invaders: what was the fate of a few heretics, more or less? My grandfather was broken, not by torture, he withstood that, but by the threat of the same to his wife and daughter. He confessed to witchery hoping to save them. But we were all condemned. Even me, a girl not yet in her flowers.

"We spent three weeks in that pit of filth they called the city prison and were then led out to the stake. My mother had sent letters to Richard, first begging for justice, then for mercy. Then simply for him to save his own children, but she received not a word of reply. They burned my grandfather and grandmother first, and made her watch. Then they took her to the stake, and bound my brother and sister to the same pole, piling the wood around them. They were about to throw me on to the top of the pyre when a party of Viking rode into the square...

"'How much for the child?' called their leader, a great brute of a man with inked markings all over his arms. I had never seen such a thing before and was convinced he must be the very Devil. The executioner had me by the scruff of the neck and hesitated.

"'This scrawny little thing?' He named a price. 'We can buy a barrel of ale for that and drink to the death of all heretics!' The huge man agreed and I was tossed onto his horse. The last I saw of my mother, and the last I heard of my brother and sister, were the flames and their screams."

As Lucet stopped speaking the wind made a sudden shriek in the eaves and then all was silent.

"They took me to the slave ships. I survived." She seemed reluctant to say more. And we felt unable to speak at all. Finally, Aetna broke the silence. "Lucet…"

"My God…" I stood, my fists clenched. "I had no idea…"

"From then on I made it my business to stay alive. For them, for my family. Don't ask me, for I shall not speak, of what happened on those ships. Of the trade in human misery. Mothers and children separated. Men castrated. I passed through many hands. Eventually I was part of a cargo brought ashore at Brycgstowe. The old King's bottler saw me, and bought me. He was – he is – a good man. In the kitchens at Wintancaestre I began my life again. I am English now. I forswear Normandy and its ways and I tell you, Your Majesty, beware the Normans, for one day they will wreak as much havoc on these English lands as the Vikings. Beneath the skin they are of the same race and the same blood. And the same ways."

"Lucet," said Edward, "you have suffered much and until now spoken little. You are a remarkable girl and I am proud to count you one of my free subjects – an Englishwoman. May the shores of this island protect you – and us all – from such as they."

"Amen!" My sister and I spoke with a single voice.

))))))))((((((

The rain thundered down well into the night. Aetna insisted that we take some of the small ale out to the men, and I threw one of the blankets over my head and took out ale and bread. The men were grateful, but stoic: they had, as Edward had said, endured worse, and the horses seemed content in the shelter of the trees, now that the lightning had passed.

We four slept remarkably well that night, and when morning came it was with that rain-washed pale blue sky that so often follows a storm. We packed up and journeyed on to I'lcaestre, reaching it around mid-morning. The Reeve was relieved to see us unharmed. We decided to remain the day and night at his Hall to allow the men and horses to eat and get thoroughly dry and pressed on toward Bathe the following morning.

As we arrived, I recognized many of the places which had become familiar during our stay for the late King's coronation, and idly wondered whether I would get a chance to visit the Bathes. But foremost in my mind was the story we had heard on that stormy night, and the remarkable Lucet.

TWENTY-SEVEN

The Year of Our Lord 977

AETNA

Dear Heaven, why is it that fair weather always seems to be followed by foul – that a spell of sweet sunshine cannot give way to gentle spring rain instead of a cataclysmic downpour? Mayhap often it does, but it is the violent swings of fortune that remain in our memories. For two years, after our first visit to Corf, Wyrd threw her shuttle to and fro through the tapestry of Englaland, and our own lives, with an even, regular rhythm, the pattern growing with the addition of threads and colours, some a little darker than we might have wished, but on the whole bright and wholesome. Or so we thought. And now...

But on that late spring morning when we left Bathe to return to Wintancaestre, we were a merry crew. Even the men were cheerful beyond the norm. They had been given their leisure during the time of our stay, and many had taken full advantages of all that the city had to offer, including the waters of the Roman Baths and the many light scrupled ladies who plied their trade in their environs. Those who were faithful to their sweethearts at home were in high spirits at the thought of reunion. The King was elated. He had met his infant daughter and spent time with Alfreth. Wulf seemed in a perpetual state hovering between daydream and attentiveness to Edward, to me and – perhaps I was the only one to notice, for I knew him so well – in an inconspicuous way, to Lucet. She seemed to be more light-hearted than I had known her before. I sensed that reliving her ordeal by speaking of it had lifted some of the horror from her and the brittle quality to her humour had softened somewhat with the knowledge that she was truly among friends who now knew her story. Me? I had thoroughly enjoyed my status as representative of the Dowager Queen and I, too, had my private daydreams to enjoy.

We had stayed in Bathe for three nights, one day longer than we had planned, arriving late in the postnoon of the day we left I'lcaestre. The Brothers at the abbey, and their Sisters in the convent had arranged a fine banquet in the King's honour, and despite our arrival a day late, it took place as planned, for the ride had been easy along the old Fosse Way. We ate and drank well and retired to our chambers late that night. The following morning, Lucet by my side, I assumed my role as representative of the Dowager Queen Aethelflaed and was taken on a tour of the convent buildings to see how Her Majesty's endowments had been spent.

I would be able to report back to my aunt that she would be pleased. Her money had been used to beautify the Nuns' chapel – but not extravagantly – and to improve conditions in the refectory and hospital. A pleasing little stone had been engraved to the effect that this had been a gift from "Queen" Aethelflaed, with the date of its completion and set into the wall of the hospital, that all who saw it might be grateful. As I was taken through the rooms of the convent I had to supress a smile as I remembered what Alfreth had told us of her time there: the kitchens where she had been likely to spend the whole of the coronation day until she was ordered to see to our needs, the Church itself where she and Edward first met, the dorter where she was condemned by the former Mother Superior. The improvements had meant that the community had grown, and now justified the appointment of an Abbess. I spent most of the day in her company and was pleased to see that the community, whilst adhering to the Rule of Benedict in all things, appeared a happy one. During the postnoon hour of rest, quiet conversation and laughter could be heard and it seemed to be a very different place to that which Alfreth had endured.

Wulf had taken the King to the baths to enjoy the waters. Edward had been too young to visit them at the time of his father's coronation, and he found the experience most stimulating – though he forbore to take advantage of the other delights on offer. They returned to their chamber, adjacent to ours, just before the evening meal. We were still in the refectory when he complained of the return of a slight discomfort in his foot and declared that he would repair to bed early that night. (This mysterious ailment had proved to be quite a convenient excuse, on several occasions, when the King had wished to absent himself from some unwelcome duty.) When Wulf returned to the chamber it was empty – Edward had slipped away, taken the swiftest horse and made the short ride to Sceo, as he had said he would. We were not concerned. Dressed as a plain man, without possessions about him and armed with a good sword he was no target for robbery. He was not recognised at the city gate, where he gave the gatekeeper a generous bribe to allow him out – and back again before the dawn.

That morning we were due to leave. However, the King appeared blear-eyed to break his fast and announced that he had slept badly, due to the pain in his foot, and that he proposed to spend the day at the Holy Well in Sceo. Why, in fact, he suggested, did not Wulf and I go with him? The day was set to be fair and it was sweet countryside – it would please him to show me the Well and Wulf could spend a pleasant few hours at the Inn where they had stayed on their previous visit, he added. We would travel as commoners and did not need escort but for Lucet and one, particularly discreet, man-at-arms.

In truth, he could not forbear showing us his daughter. When we reached the Shoe Inn, Alfreth was delivering bread to the inn and helping Garreth set up the barrels for the day, little Effie cooing in a woven basket set on the trestle bar. Edward had fallen back easily into the role of Ned, Alfreth's high-born, though much absent, husband. She feigned a pretty surprise at seeing him (for, apparently, he had crept into her chamber the previous night without rousing Goody Hilde) and demurely greeted Wulf, whilst embracing me as her sometime estranged sister. This ruse Edward had added to the fast-growing imagined story of his and Alfreth's history. Really, I thought, he was taking a little too much enjoyment from this fabrication of events!

Effie was, indeed, a charming child. Only a few months old and already full of smiles and winning ways. Edward – Ned – was entranced by her. He could hardly stop coddling her for a moment, first dandling her on his knee, then kissing the top of her shiny curls – for she already had a mop of light hair, not unlike his own. I dutifully played the doting aunt and then, with Lucet and Wulf, went to see the Holy Well. The water was cool and sweet and we sat beneath a stand of trees enjoying the morning sun.

"Alfreth is making herself a fine life here," observed Lucet. "I wonder if she still has visions of being acknowledged the King's true wife."

"His Majesty loves her dearly," said Wulf. "Of that I am sure, but he makes no move at present to declare himself married. He is beginning to understand the value of his unwed status… the dangling carrot of a marriage alliance is more useful than wielding the stick of aggression when it comes to diplomacy. But fear not, Lucet, he is not made of the same stuff as your father. He would never forswear himself, nor put her aside."

"No. I did not think that of him. But did you notice the way Garreth watches her? There is more than the duty of protection and loyalty to the King in his eyes as they follow her."

"He is a good man," I said. "He has given up his old life to settle here. And it seems he prospers. The Shoe Inn fares well."

We spent a pleasant day. When evening approached, Edward could not bring himself to leave and, bidding the man-at-arms to tell the Brothers that he had decided to spend the night in contemplation of the miracles of Saints Crispin and Crispinian, sent him back to Bathe with the promise that we would re-join the party early the following morning in time to take to the road. And so it was, on another fair morn, that we found ourselves on the way back to Bathe and then on to Wintancaestre, in good temper and happy mood.

We could not fail to notice, though, as we passed through the countryside, that all was not well, and the commoners were far from sharing our high spirits in their day to day lives. Where crops had been planted, there were a few straggly patches of green, but much larger were the areas of ground where nothing by weeds were thriving, and others of bare earth. The beasts in the fields looked dejected and underweight.

"The hogs look scrawny," observed Edward as we passed through a village where the cottars had corralled all their pigs together in a single enclosure, the better to make the most of what meagre scraps could be saved for them. They had rutted the earth barren and obviously been moved from patch to patch where they had done to same. "Let us hope there will be no return of the murrain, for these animals have not the strength to resist it."

Some children ran out to greet us, for although we were not obviously a royal party, we looked well-to-do and might give alms. Edward threw them a few fourthings. "Where is your village elder?" he asked.

A lad who had already picked up several of the coins and, generously, allowed his younger companions to collect the rest, pointed along the narrow track between the cottages. "Yonder, the cott as the end," he said.

We jogged along to the outskirts of the tiny collection of buildings. An old man was sitting outside his half open door, stroking a scruffy dog and chewing a chip of bark.

"Three fourthings for a minute of your time, grandsire," said Edward.

"Aye?"

"How fare you in this village? Will you have enough to see you through the year if the harvest fails, for it looks like to do so."

"Lord, we struggle," said the old man, inspecting the coins which Edward had thrown him. "Last year's heat burned much cropping, and then the cold winter and the rains in the spring... it is like the Almighty lays us low. We try to pull together, but we receive no help from the Reeve. He is too busy ensuring that the Shire Reeve does not go without and blame him. And taxes still need to be paid." Suddenly it seemed a thought occurred to him. "We will pay, Lord, we will pay. But not yet, pray wait the time! Have patience!"

"We are not here for your taxes, man, fear not!" said the King. "In fact..." Edward mused. "I thank you for your words, you speak well and true." He flipped him another fourthing. "There, that makes a penny! Spend it on food, not taxes!"

"Thank you, Lord," the old man called after us, as we passed on. Glancing back, I saw him scratching his head and looking after us, surrounded by the children who had been watching the exchange. I wondered if he would ever realise who he had been talking to...

))))))))(((((((

Life continued not unpleasantly. At Court we were insulated from the worst of the food shortages which began to bite as the year wore on. Both in the cities and the countryside the rich, of course, are ever able to buy food and those who have plenty are often the ones to hoard more against a time when they can sell it and become even richer. Edward was much moved by the words of the old man in that nameless little hamlet and set to work to do what he could to alleviate the common people's want. He forbade the hoarding of grain by individuals and ordered Reeves to amass what remained of the previous year's crop and distribute it fairly. It was hard to regulate, but he sent emissaries out to check on the honesty of Reeves on a random basis and those who were not dealing justly were fined themselves. News of these measures spread and generally the system began to work well.

But still times became hard for the poor, and the unscrupulous used this ill-fortune to their own ends. There had been a lessening of unease between the secular and church parties in the matter of the *Concordia* since the intervention of the Almighty Himself in the shape of the miraculous speaking Cross, but then late in the year we began to hear reports, especially from Mercia, saying rumours were spreading that the abbeys were hoarding food for themselves and, as the secular bodies had no authority over them, there was no way by which this could be proved or disproved. In places the Reeves had demanded the abbeys open their grain stores, which had then been looted by the near starving townspeople whether they were full or, as in many cases, as near empty as their own. When Edward heard of this he had flown into a terrible rage and threatened to send men to hang the town Reeves on the spot. Instead, after taking – somewhat unwillingly – the advice of his permanent counsellors, he decreed that recompense be made personally by the Reeves to the abbeys which had been found to have little in their granaries, and that any abbeys that had been hoarding were to receive nothing by way of compensation. Since the Reeves were rarely popular with the common people, any more than were untrustworthy Abbots, this seemed to quell the worst of the unrest. Especially as those on either side who had been found at fault were also fined, the monies going to buy food for the people.

Wulf and I celebrated our twentieth birthday in October. As if to compensate for the previous few seasons' ill weather, conditions turned mild and pleasant. Day after day of warm autumn sunshine began to fill out the fruits which had promised to fall from the trees unripened, and soft overnight rain prevented the ground from hardening. Scrappy root vegetable plots began to yield unexpected crops and even the grass began to grow better, allowing for at least a small harvest of hay to lay up as winter forage for the beasts. A late and heartfelt service of thanksgiving for the bounty of the land was held at both the Old and New Minsters, and we began to look forward to the Christ's Mass of 976.

I will admit to one concern which was playing on my mind at this time and I know that Wulf, possibly with better cause than I, shared my disquiet. Edward was, I thought, not handling the stresses of his Kingship easily. His mood swings became quite acute at times. It was as though his persona as "Ned", during his infrequent visits to Alfreth exhausted all the goodwill and easy-going elements of his nature, leaving impatience and, it had to be said, depression foremost when he was at Court. There were times when a small mishap or possibly imagined slight threw him into quite the frenzy, and we dreaded the day when something major exploded into our world. And then, like a fork of lightning shattering a clear blue sky, it did. We received news from Mercia.

The Chief Ealdorman had personally led a party of his own troops and laid waste three abbeys, killing any of the brothers who resisted, plundering their treasuries and granaries and turning out the remaining monks to fend for themselves. His excuse? He did not see fit to give one. All three houses were in the heart of his own ealdormanry: Evesham, Persore and Derhest, each in the diocese of Wireceastre – Archbishop Oswald's original see, and still held by him in addition to his archbishopric of Eoforwic. Oswald had been an increasingly irritating thorn in Alfhere's side since the Council of Wintancaestre, hastening the reformation of the abbeys in the shire of Wireceastre and costing the Chief Ealdorman and his brothers considerable revenue. Clearly, he did not intend to allow matters to continue in similar vein throughout his ealdormanry. He was making a point and an example of these three houses.

Edward was incandescent with rage. The news had arrived with a rider from Cyrnecaestre on the Mercia-Wessex border, the Reeve sending word to the King as soon as disenfranchised brothers began to arrive at St. Mary's Minster in the town. He immediately despatched Aelwarth, the Ealdorman of Western Wessex, to Alfhere's Hall at Wireceastre with a summons that he should appear before the King forthwith to make explanation. Aelwarth returned a week later with word that the Chief Ealdorman regretted that he was too encumbered by matters of administration to be able to attend upon the Witan, as he chose, with deliberate insubordination, to interpret the summons. It so happened that the luckless Aelwarth arrived back in Wintancaestre late one evening, just as the evening meal was served. The King's temper had been simmering all day, he had been impatient for news. Aelwarth approached the High Table, unrefreshed from his long journey, and gave Alfhere's reply. The simmering pot of Edward's anger boiled over.

"Too encumbered... who does the Chief Ealdorman think he messages? It was not an invitation, man, it was a... command! His King's command,

and he is too... Why did you not enforce him?" Edward was on his feet and shouting into the face of the unhappy messenger.

"Your Majesty, I had but four men with me, and one of those a scribe. Your Majesty had insisted I left Wintancaestre with such speed. How could I enforce him? I had no order with *sub poena.* He had his entire... We, you, I, we all... thought he would come at your bidding!"

"Idiot!" Edward threw a chicken leg at him. "Get out of my sight!" He slumped back into his chair. "And the rest of you! Eat elsewhere this eve. Get out of my Hall! Wulf, whose *Tertium* is in arms this month? Fetch him... I swear I shall ride ahead of the Wessex Fyrd against that bastard! I have heard he is styling himself "Prince of the Mercians", like his damned Grandfather! Well, I am of the line of Alfred. He brought Mercia to heel once and so shall I! Aetna, where are you going? I meant for those fools lower down the table to leave, not you and Wulf. Where is the Dowager Queen this eve? And the Bishop... get me those I trust around me!"

I had already stood to leave the table as he spoke. Now I hesitated and resumed my seat. I knew, in this mood, Edward was unpredictable. Threatening to ride at the head of the Fyrd? This was tantamount to acknowledging civil war.

"Sire," I said, "I beg your pardon. I go but to seek out your step-grandmother. I believe she is in her chambers."

Edward ran his fingers through his hair. "Lady, forgive me, my temper flares. Of course, you stay! But send Lucet to go find the Dowager, and pray her attend me." He turned to Wulf. "Send a rider to Cantuaria, I would have Dustan here, too. Oh, God, my head hurts!"

As ever, Lucet stood at my shoulder. I nodded at her and she flew away, through the hanging curtains toward the steps to the upper chambers. Within minutes Aethelflaed appeared. "Edward, what has happened?"

The King had been sitting with his head in his hands and now raised his face. "Grand-Mutti," he said. "I thought we had settled this matter. The *Concordia.*" he said. "And now..."

How easy it was to forget that Edward was still so young. Confidence, self-confidence and then... confidence in those that surrounded him... only to have it betrayed. Of course, it was enough to unseat his lately acquired self-possession.

"Come," said Aethelflaed. "Let us withdraw. Let these good people have their victuals..." She indicated to the doormen to allow the lately ousted to return. "We shall to our private chambers. This is a matter for calm discussion..."

Our poor aunt... I knew that she had planned an evening in private working upon her embroidery. Her great *magnum opus*, the life of her beloved Edmund, was nearing completion and she had envisaged a late postnoon of stitching. Her hair was in dis-array, a light cloak thrown around herundergunna, she put an arm around Edward. "Come, my love, make no hasty decisions."

"But..."

"Time enough, time enough..." She drew him through the curtain, Wulf and the rest of us following.

))))))))))((((((

That evening Edward had been convinced to hold fast – not to rush to arms. But later events quelled any such fortitude. The Chief Ealdorman continued his persecution of the reformed abbeys and Edward could not be swayed. He would take up arms.

The *Tertium* of each sub-Ealdormanry of Wessex was called up. The Fyrd – the fighting body – was subject to raising one third of its men upon immediate command, and these the King corralled. They came to Wintancaestre in their tens, their fifties and their hundreds as they were summoned; poor men from the fields with their sickles, ceorls from the town with rusty swords and cleavers, thegns with old nags and battered lances and bows. They came at their King's command, for he had fed them when famine threatened; they were his. Word was sent to Mercia. No reply was received. On the first day of December the army assembled in the fields outside the North gate of the City.

And then... then, at the last moment, that for which many of us had prayed came to pass. The weather changed. The one factor over which the King had no control came to our rescue. Of course, we wished that the Chief Ealdorman had not acted as he had; of course, we wished that the King could find some other course to call him to heel; of course, we wished... but that was all swept away by the arrival of winter – winter, when there was no campaigning possible. No-one went to war in winter: it was suicide. Your opponent simply holed-up; they starved in their city, you starved in your field. Stalemate.

Snow fell. Snow fell. Not the freezing, bone-numbing ice falls of the previous year, but a soft, all-enveloping and incapacitating, ever deepening palliasse of soft, white, feathery down. Snow fell throughout the Christ's Mass, through the turn of the year as 977 made its cold presence felt. The eastern and western *Tertia* were sent home while they could still travel. January, February, March, still the snow fell... until we felt that spring would never arrive and yet, at the same time, dreaded the thaw, for then what would happen?

What happened was as near a miracle as we could have ever anticipated. As March lengthened, and daylight with it, winter finally relinquished its grip. Edward, by this time, was prepared to call up the full

457

Fyrd and take it on immediate campaign to Mercia, and we were certain that Alfhere's spies would have got word of his plans back to the Chief Ealdorman, meaning that the united Fyrd of Mercia would be standing ready. There was no question but that civil war would ensue. Easter Sunday was on 8th April, and Edward planned to leave with his army the following day. But on the very morning of our Lord's Resurrection a rider arrived from Wireceastre. Alfhere, in the most apparently abject terms made apology for his actions and proclaimed that he would do penance. He did not, the messenger reported, deny that his deeds had been hasty, and he should have notified the King of his intentions, but he maintained his belief that the abbeys which he had "purged" had illegally dismissed their rightful abbots and therefore their riches should be forfeit. By way of emphasising this he sent the King a sum of money equal to the goods looted from Persore – a humble, he said, recompense. He also suggested that there should be (yet another) meeting to discuss what he termed "these unfortunate matters" to be held at his own expense at Caune in Wiltshire. He even showed goodwill in suggesting this locale – it was over the border from his ealdormanry, within the safety of Edward's own Wessex.

Faced with this about-turn, and the very considerable cash consideration – over twelve hundred shillings, with more to come – Edward relented. He sent a terse acknowledgement back to Aelfhere, demanding to be told what penance the ealdorman intended and reminding him that it would be the work of but a few days to be at Mercia's borders with the Wessex Fyrd if he did not like the reply. From then on, as the snow melted, so the thaw in relations set in.

By our usual standards, I had seen little of Wulf while the crisis was in full swing. Although we often met at mealtimes, and managed to grab a little time together when the King, exhausted by his anger and military preparations, betook himself into his own chambers to rest alone, I felt that there was a great deal of which I was not fully aware with regard to how Edward was coping. Much of the time he seemed like a tautened bowstring, ready to snap at the slightest extra pressure. At other times he appeared almost impossibly optimistic, even eager to engage in warfare. Between times, he was dejected. When the tension was suddenly released, far from relief, he seemed ill at ease and restless.

The date of the meeting at Caune was set for the second week of May. One evening about a week after Easter, we had adjourned to the King's withdrawing chamber for the evening when Edward announced that he had made a decision.

"It is time," he said.

"Sire?" Wulf and I spoke simultaneously and then laughed. Edward looked at us sharply, not with his once usual good humour.

"It is time Alfreth took her place at my side. I shall use the assembly at Caune to announce our marriage. I am tired of this deception. I shall make use of this opportunity and proclaim her my Queen, in the full company of my Ealdormen and Bishops."

Had the year been sufficiently advanced for a fly to be clambering the wall of the chamber, it would have had a fine view of every person – Edward excepted – stopping stock still wrapped in their own shock and trepidation at this... well, it was not a suggestion, it was a statement. The King's statement and therefore... The Dowager Queen, hesitated in her stitching, needle poised midway between thread and fabric. Wulf, about to take a swig of ale, with his drinking horn just touching his lips. I, in the process of shuffling parchments, holding them before me just as I was about to tap them into tidiness upon the table. I was, perhaps, the first to regain my wits, and glance quickly around the room: thankfully there were no thralls present.

Wulf was the first to regain the power of speech. "Sire, do you not think that you should take advice on this matter... mayhap take Archbishop Dunstan, alone, into your confidence first and then..."

"No. No, I am determined on this matter." His voice began to rise to a shout. "Wulf, why must you ever gainsay me? I can find many another who will not question my words, you know! The Archbishop – both Archbishops – must be made aware at the same time as the rest of the Witan. It will be a matter of joy – a queen and a princess and, who knows, soon maybe an heir, a boy to follow me."

"My love," Aethelflaed set aside her embroidery and rose, walking over to where Edward stood, restlessly shifting from foot to foot. She put her hands on his shoulders and looked into his eyes. "Have you spoken to Alfreth herself on this matter? What is her thought? Could it be that she might not want to be thrown into the maelstrom of the Court at this time – there are dangers and uncertainties until this meeting with the Chief Ealdorman is fully concluded. For you, for her, mayhap for your child. We still cannot be sure that all will be resolved without bloodshed."

Edward's colour began to rise. He clenched his fists, and stepped back from Aethelflaed, disengaging from her hands and tossing them off, roughly. "You, too, Step-grandmother? You would argue with me? I am King. I say when... Alfreth is my wife and it is her duty to obey me." He looked around the chamber with a sudden wildness in his eyes. "It is the duty of you all to obey me!" Spittle was flying from his mouth.

"Sire, no-one intends..."

" ... to question your authority." Wulf and I spoke in tandem.

"You forget yourselves," he shouted. "All of you! I would be alone. Go!" He slammed his fist down on the table, making the candles jump and a spatter of wax fly onto his hand. "God's death, now look..." He rubbed off the wax, leaving and angry weald behind. "I mean it, get out! Out! Now!" He snatched up a tumbler of liquor and flung it against the wall. Turning abruptly, he kicked over the chair in which he had been seated, and then swept the other vessels from table. They crashed onto the floor.

We had seen Edward angry before, but this was new... surely there had been nothing in our words to prompt such sudden fury? As we hastened from the chamber, I looked back at him. He was rubbing his temples as if in pain. "Sire..." I began to return.

"No, Aetna, come," said Wulf.

"To my chambers," Aunt Aethelflaed led the way up the staircase to the private level. "We must talk."

When we entered Aethelflaed's withdrawing chamber Edith and Onwen were seated before the small fireplace working upon the Dowager's wardrobe, making slight alterations, tightening a seam here, adding a braid there and deep in the type of trivial conversation which makes such evening pastimes pleasurable as well as productive hours. As Aethelflaed swept in, my brother and I in her wake, they jumped to their feet.

"Your Majesty, we did not expect you back so soon. Pray, let us clear these things away. What can we fetch you? Wine?" Edith bustled to straighten the cushions upon which she and Edith had made themselves comfortable.

"Yes, Edith, thank you, I think we could all benefit from a draught of wine. No, no, do not fuss about tidying up... Lady Aetna and her brother have seen our closet before now! They are family, remember! And here, Onwen, take my embroidery and put it safe, I think I shall not be stitching again this evening." She handed Onwen her embroidery frame and a handful of silken skeins which had become tangled together in her haste to collect them and exit the King's presence. "I fear these will need your skills to separate them before I next thread my needle!"

She took one of the seats recently vacated by her ladies and motioned me to the other. Wulf pulled up a chair and sat close to us. His jaw was set tight.

"Now, Wulf," said Aethelflaed, "I know that the King has been out of sorts lately, but how often has his temper taken this extreme turn? Speak true, for you know I love him as a grandson of my own blood. This is not a natural fury, I think."

A nerve twitched by the side of Wulf's mouth. "Aunt – and sister – I hate to speak of it, for I feel I am doing him a disloyalty, but I will be frank. It is happening more often than I like to confess. Often, I can see his colour rising, and his fists clench and I manage to dismiss those present before his anger breaks, or dissipate it by changing the course of the discussion, or even engineering his leaving of the room. But it is becoming harder. And…" he shook his head "… I have heard that it has been the subject of comment."

"By whom?" asked Aethelflaed.

"Some of the lesser companions, visiting Ealdormen – even the ceorls and thralls. In the latter case I have disciplined them. But the Ealdormen will speak as they find if 'tis the truth. They are free men and have the right of free speech."

"Oh, Wulf," I said, "You should have told us! We love Edward and could have helped, surely."

"In the aftermath of such fits – for I believe that what they are – His Majesty is ever overcome with remorse. He hates himself for his loss of control and commands me not to mention it, though I have often told him that your counsel, in particular, Aunt, could only be beneficial. I believe he begins to fear himself. And then, often, when the storm of his anger is past – and also the doldrum of his despair – he becomes quite giddy with fair temper, carefree and in high, merry spirits. Every time the swing occurs, I am hopeful that his most recent outburst of foul mood will be the last. Aunt, is there anything we can do?"

"I think it is very much as I feared, Wulf. This winter of anxiety, of seemingly endless waiting for spring and with it the coming of civil war, his own doubts and fears have all taken their toll. He is yet young for such responsibility and many of those who should be helping to bear the burden – the Chief Ealdorman for one – have been the very people responsible for creating the crisis. For some reason, and I do not trust it, Alfhere has pulled back from the brink and offered an olive branch. It gives us time to help the King regain his right thinking and the first thing we must do is remove him from the Court for a while. He must be rested and himself again by the time of the Assembly. Did he not promise to make a return visit to Ethelred at Corf? Time spent there would raise no questions. I would not normally consider a visit to Elfrith a boon, but I believe on this occasion it might be our saving grace. But first, we must see the King settled back into his right mind. Now, Wulf, will His Majesty have calmed down sufficiently for you to go to back to him?"

Wulf looked at the hour-candle, burning down steadily on the table. "Perhaps, Aunt, it is hard to tell."

"Well, go and see. Stay with him, if he allows it. Be the good friend you are. Aetna, we must to the stillroom. Send Lucet to fetch Thella, for she is well skilled in these matters. Many heads may be needed. The good Lord has put many herbs on this earth which can be of service to the King, and we shall find out the best combination."

Wulf headed toward the door. "Shall I send for the *medicus*, too, Aunt?" he asked.

"No, Wulf, this is a matter better kept between ourselves, I think. It is women's work, we do not need the meddling of the *medicus*, however well intentioned."

)))))))(((((((

Aunt Aethelflaed and I, Lucet and Thella spent most of that night in the stillroom, Edith and Onwen keeping an unobtrusive watch upon its door, for we had no wish to be disturbed. We heard no more from Wulf, and so hoped that he had found the King in more peaceful mood and remained with him. By the time a chilly, misty dawn was breaking we were able to repair to our beds for some short sleep, Aethelflaed taking with her a stoppered flask containing a pretty yellow linctus which smelled like honey and tasted sweet on the tongue. Good medicine, she had said, did not have to taste good, but there was no harm in it doing so!

It was about the ninth hour of the morning when I tapped upon her door.

"Aunt? Did you manage a little sleep?" I asked as she bid me enter.

"Yes, sweetling, a little, but I wished still to be about early for the sooner we set about our mission the sooner shall we have our sweet boy back to us! See, Edith had brought me some bread and preserve, break your fast with me, then we shall see about..."

Another tap upon the door. I recognised Wulf's knock before we spoke. The Dowager bade him come in. "Did Edward rest?" she said.

"Yes, Aunt," he replied. "But he woke early and in a state of such remorse that I felt my heart was to break for him. He begs that he may come to you..."

"It is for us to go to him. He is the King."

"No, he wishes to come to you. He..."

"Oh, of course, I know, I know. Poor boy. Tell him to come now. My arms are open."

Wulf withdrew. My aunt and I looked at each other. There were tears shining in her eyes. "It is hard for him, so hard. My beloved Edmund felt the weight of the crown and so, I know, did Edgar, but they were older and both had their Queens by their side. And Ealdormen without their own hidden schemes. But we will have him aright soon."

When Edward slipped through the door, he looked terrible. If he had slept a little, as Wulf said, the repose had done him no service. His eyes were red rimmed and shot with blood, his skin pale and clammy looking. It appeared that he had rested in his clothes, though he was unshod, and his hair was tangled and askew as if he had spent many hours tossing and turning against his pillow.

"Step-grandmother..." he began. "I am so sorry..."

462

Aethelflaed took him in her arms and cradled his head against her shoulder. "Hush, hush, my love, there is nothing to be sorry for. You are the King, you have the weight of the nation upon your shoulders. But you are mayhap not well. I think you have not been resting as you should, and the troubles of these last months have filled your mind with dis-ease. But we will have you well soon. Aetna and I..."

He had been resting against her like a lost child, but now he raised his head. "Oh, Aetna, to you, also, I owe an apology. I bespoke myself so rudely and you have never been less than a sister to me. And Wulf – well, I have already bid him try to forget what I said. I would have none other as my companion."

"Sire, you have no need to speak thus," I said. "If we seemed..."

"Come, enough of this," said the Dowager. "Family needs no talk of apologies, nor of manners. But you must recover yourself, Edward, and the ladies and I have been taking advantage of the small hours of the night to make you a tonic which will set you aright. You will betake yourself to your private chambers for a few days. Then we are to Corf to visit your brother. You will rest, you will hunt, you will regain your spirits before the Assembly at Caune. We will stop at Bathe on the way to Caune and you may visit Alfreth. But first, you will imbibe this linctus, eat well, and sleep better. I shall accompany you all on this trip and by the time you return to Court you will be quite well." She looked him in the eye and he smiled ruefully.

"What have I done to deserve you, Mutti?" he said.

"You are your blessed Father's son, and his Father before him. You are the rightful King of Englaland. And I love you. Now, I would see you take a first draught of this tincture..." The mixture poured, gurgling like warm syrup, into a small cup and she handed it to him. "Poppy, to make you rest easily, chamomile to sweeten the rest and the herb of Saint John to lighten your spirits. And a few other things... it tastes sweet, does it not? Yes?"

"It does, Mutti, it does. But still, I..."

"No, I will hear no more. Betake you to your chamber. Wulf will make it known that you are not to be disturbed. You will be working upon matters of state. Thella will be in charge of your medicine. Several doses for the next few days and then... well, we shall see."

Ratkin and Thella were given chambers in the Great Hall, close to Edward's apartments. Between them, Wulf and Ratkin ensured that Edward was not left alone. Other companion-men were stood down with the excuse that the King wished them to take their ease after the tense months in anticipation of war. He, it was announced, once he had made all preparations necessary for his later meeting at Caune, would also be taking a break from his duties and visiting his brother. Runners were sent to Corf to inform Elfrith to expect the royal party within the week.

By the time we set off, the King seemed much improved. He looked well, natural healthy colour had returned to his cheeks and the haunted look in his eyes was gone, replaced by his familiar, open expression. The weather was fair and we made good time on our journey, following the same route as we had taken the previous year. We were a larger party. As well as Lucet, Ratkin and Thella attended Wulf and myself and Aethelflaed had brought Edith. We had a force of some twenty men-at-arms riding with us, together with foot soldiers, and a baggage train. Edward brought only two attendants, but they had been with the Court for many years and were experienced and discreet. I sensed that Wulf was protective and that he was keeping a close watch upon Edward. For a while we rode abreast of each other, keeping a little distance from the others, so that we could speak without being overheard.

"Brother, are you worried?" I asked.

"I am... cautious," he replied. "Our aunt's linctus seems to have worked wonders, and Edward has been sleeping and eating well."

"Then all is as it should be?"

"I hope so. Edward received a letter from Dunstan just before we left. The Archbishop will meet with us at Bathe before we go on to Caune. There was something in the tone of it that put me on my guard. He said that he would explain all, but not by letter. And I still feel uneasy at Alfhere's sudden volte-face. But the King seems calm enough now. He looks forward to seeing Ethelred, and Elfrith's recent letter was couched in the most affectionate terms. I hardly recognised it as hers!"

Edward had shown me Elfrith's letter. It was, indeed, something of a departure from her usual style. She declared herself "eager" to put Corf at the King's disposal, for as long as he wished. She wrote that Ethelred would be "overjoyed" to see his brother and hoped that the improvements which she had ordered made to the forests had ensured that the King would find pleasant sport in them. With only the slightest insinuation that her funds were not unlimited, she prayed that His Majesty – and his extended party – would all treat her home as their own.

"Think you that Elfrith has her own agenda in welcoming us?" I said.

"Hers or, mayhap, one of her allies. The Chief Ealdorman?"

Wulf and I looked at each other and said no more. He cantered ahead to accompany Edward, who seemed to be enjoying the ride, and I fell back to our aunt.

"You are concerned about something, my love?" she said.

"Just cautious," I said, echoing Wulf's words. "Just cautious."

The weather held fair and we arrived at Corf Gate on the postnoon of the twentieth day of April. Queen Elfrith's lookouts had spotted us pass through the gap in the hills which gave the Gate its name, and as we approached her Hall, we found her awaiting us, Ethelred at her side, Meryasek at his shoulder, and almost the entire household ranged up to greet us. A momentary flicker of annoyance appeared to cross her face as she noted the extent of the King's retinue – presumably she was mentally estimating the cost of their bed and board – but she quickly resumed her smile of welcome. It may have looked a little brittle, but it was a smile, nevertheless.

"Your Majesty!" She dropped an elegant curtsey as Edward dismounted, handing the horse's reins to Wulf. "It is a joy to have you with us again! And with so many… and *Your* Majesty, too!" This last was to Aethelflaed, as she and I rode up behind Edward and Wulf. "How very pleasant to have you join us. Ethelred… Ethelred, where have you gone?" She turned toward where her son had stood, about to urge him forward, but he had already flung his arms around his brother's waist and was hugging him. "Oh! Well, I see we are to have no pretence of ceremony!" Her laugh, like her smile, was brittle.

"Step-mother, your welcome is as gracious as your person." Edward had a pretty turn of speech when he wanted. "And brother! Ethelred, it is good to see you, lad. Why, you have grown since I last saw you – can it be a year since? You are quite the young man. You and I shall have some fine hunting together!" The young Aetheling beamed at this.

"Your Majesty, I have much to show and tell you," he said. "Mama says that I may stay up with you all in the Great Hall this night, and every night of your stay if…"

"Enough, Ethelred, remember yourself. You are a prince and heir to your brother's throne." Elfrith seemed no less sharp with the boy than usual, but he took it in good part and grinned at his brother with undiminished enthusiasm. Meryasek laid a hand on his shoulder, almost protectively. His eye caught mine and held it for a moment, then he turned away.

The horses were led to their stabling, and our men-at-arms to their quarters. Lucet and Edith saw to the delivery of our trunks to the apartments set aside the Dowager and myself, while Thella and Ratkin took charge of Wulf's together with the King's, overseeing their delivery to the same chambers they had occupied on our previous stay. It took but a short while for us to be settled and then we repaired to the withdrawing chamber where Elfrith awaited us. Edward and Wulf were already there.

"Ladies," said Edward, rising. "I was just commenting to my step-mama – I may call you that, may I not? – that we had noticed the woods looked in better fettle this year, despite the strangeness of the weather this last twelvemonth. I look forward to the hunt."

"I took note of Your Majesty's wishes," said Elfrith. "Whatever the Gate can offer Your Majesty by way of amusement is at your command. And now, before the evening meal, may I offer you some refreshment?" As she spoke the door opened and Morwen entered, bearing wine. Had she had her ear at the door, that she entered upon the split second of her mistress' word? As ever, her presence unnerved me somewhat. "Thank you, Morwen, and look to the comfort of our guest's companions, too, will you? Send one of the thralls to offer them ale before they join the other servants at the low table." One of Morwen's expressive eyebrows lifted, but she glided silently through the door upon her errand.

"I plan an informal meal this evening," Elfrith continued. "You will be tired after your journey and will not wish for aught else?"

"No, Lady," the King replied, "Let us begin our stay as we mean to continue – as family!"

TWENTY-EIGHT

The spring sunshine held fair. Edward's mood and humour likewise remained sunny. Whether the result of Aethelflaed's tonic, the welcome break from the routine of Court life and the stress of kingship or the companionship of his younger brother, who clearly hero worshipped him, the King was benefitting from this period of relaxation. He and Ethelred spent many hours together, practising swordsmanship – Edward was admirably patient, giving him tips on the wielding of his wooden sword, and promising that in but a very few years they would be sparring with the real thing! They rode to hounds in the woods, took Ethelred's falcon-gentle – a pretty female bird, sweet to watch in fight – onto the rolling hills surrounding the Gate and practised archery in the Great Hall when the weather was less amiable. Edward was determined to forge a relationship with Ethelred and told Wulf he could take his ease. Meryasek was likewise released from duty.

One postnoon when we had been in residence for several days, he approached me as I sat in what Elfrith called her "*solarium*". Ever one to embrace the latest fashions, she had heard that in Rome there was currently a passion for unearthing the remains of the ancients' houses and that these rooms, positioned to catch the sun were quite the craze amongst those who built new on the foundations of the old. Tradition held that Corf had been a Roman outpost, so she had a small south-facing room added and, at considerable expense, had the window glazed. The light was perfect for embroidery, and Aethelflaed and I had spent much time there. The Dowager was presently taking a nap in her chamber.

"Lady Aetna, may I speak with you?"

"Of course, Meryasek. You look well, but we have had little time for conversation thus far. Your charge seems to be faring most excellently. Ethelred is in good health and temper, I think."

I may have been a little flattering in complimenting Meryasek on his appearance of heath – as I had the previous year, I noticed that he looked a little tired and drawn, too drawn for a man of his youth, and the worry line between his eyes had deepened.

"The Aetheling is out with His Majesty again. Lady, you cannot imagine how good it is for him to be able to do so. He is quite the changed lad when the King is here."

"That is pleasing to hear. The company of the young prince is beneficial to His Majesty, also." I patted the bench beside me. "Come, Meryasek, we have known each other some years, sit alongside me.

Would I be right in thinking that perhaps something is weighing on your mind?"

He cast a look over his shoulder, ensured that the door to the *solarium* was fully closed and accepted my offer of a seat. "I am pleased to find you here, Lady."

"At Corf generally, or in this chamber with you?" I asked lightly – perhaps a little mild flirtation would do him good.

He seemed unduly flustered. "Both, Lady. But... well, in this chamber, and for a particular reason." His nerves appeared to be getting the better of him. "I... it... that is..." He ran his fingers through his hair, combing it back from his face. Now I could clearly see the anxiety there. I laid aside my stitching.

"Meryasek, if there is something you desire to tell me, I assure you that it will go no further than you wish. We both have Ethelred's and the King's best interests at heart. Of that I am sure. Whatever you have to say..."

He took a deep breath and seemed to put his uncertainties to one side. "Lady, you must first understand that I have had no desire to become involved in matters above my station. Nor to spy upon... but I must start from the beginning." Again, he looked at the door.

"We are quite alone," I said.

"Yes," he replied, "and that is one reason why I am pleased to find you... here. This is an old Hall. Older perhaps that you may realise. Many of the walls are still of the stones that the Romans raised when this was a garrison. They have been faced with wood, for they are crumbling, but between the stone and the panelling there are passageways which – well let us say that an inquisitive young boy, with few companions did not take long to discover many of their secrets. I do not think they were ever intended to be used as such, but they serve as a network of thoroughfares throughout the castle, and offer peepholes and suchlike in many places. But this is a new chamber – there are no passageways in these walls from which we might be overheard. I fear, you understand, that if Ethelred has found them, so, too, might others. Her Majesty likes to be aware of everything – everything – that goes on."

"And you fear that there has been something going on that may endanger...?"

"I do not know, Lady, for much of what I have heard, I have heard from the Aetheling, and he hears and understands only as a child. It was only once, of late, when I became disturbed by some of his prattling, that I betook me to... she would have me hung, if she knew... listening myself! And I wish I had not overheard what I did."

"Out with it, then!"

"It was two weeks since, Lady. We had visitors. They arrived one evening, quite late, and stayed but a night leaving the following morning. Though it was but a brief visit, the Queen made much of the Lord who led the party and the kitchens were ordered to prepare as fine a meal as they could at short notice. Neither Ethelred nor myself were to dine with them, their meal to be served in the private withdrawing chamber, whilst the rest of us ate as usual in the Great Hall. Meals are always rather jollier affairs when the Queen is absent, so we thought little of it, except to enjoy our liberty. The Lord's men-at-arms were churlish fellows at first, and had been ordered not to speak of their master but, as the ale flowed, they became more talkative and one let slip that the Queen's companion was none other than the Chief Ealdorman. He was soundly cuffed around the ear by his superior, and said little more.

"When the evening meal was over, Ethelred and I repaired to our chambers to play – he is becoming quite the little master at the chessboard – until it was time for him to retire. I had taken a little ale myself and was drowsy even as we played... I must have fallen asleep for the next I knew, I awoke with a crick in my neck, the fire burning low and my companion gone. I assumed his nurse – he still has a lady of the bed chamber – had taken him to his pallet and went to check that he slept – for then, I thought, I might take another draught of ale, but he was not there. I called down to the nurse, Herrith, but she was still keeping company in the kitchen and had not seen him. I spent a frantic time looking for him, searching the upper chambers – surely, I thought, he could have come to no harm, but the Queen is fanatical in her desire to know that he is kept close at all times – and I was about to admit that I could not find him and get assistance to search on the lower levels, when he suddenly reappeared.

"'Your Highness, where on earth? Look at you, you are covered in spider's webs and dust... what will Herrith say?' but in truth I was so relieved to see him that I could not be angry. And he had such a mischievous grin that my curiosity was piqued. 'Where have you been?' I asked.

"'Listening to Mama and the man,' he said. 'And I am to be King soon, so you shall have to call me Majesty and not Highness!' He skipped around the room. 'King, king, king! Will it not be fun when my brother visits – to have two kings?'

"'Highness, you have not been eavesdropping again! I have told you, the Queen would be so angry...'

"'A king is more important than a queen, Meryasek, like on the chessboard. Remember? You taught me that as we played. So soon it will not matter if she is angry, she will never again be able to... never...'

"'Well, your... Sire... be that as it may, you are for your bed and I shall call Herrith to see to it.' He went off happily enough with the nurse but my thoughts were in a turmoil. Of course, I knew where he had been and how he had got there. He had long ago shown me the entrance to the passageway that he had found in the corner of our private ante-chamber and despite my misgivings, we had not sealed it up, but rather neatened and camouflaged it so that we might better use it to play hide-and-go-seek and other games. I waited until I heard Herrith bid Ethelred a good night and then, shielding a taper which gave me only just enough light to see by, slipped behind the boards.

"The withdrawing chamber where the Queen was entertaining the Chief Ealdorman was below our apartments and a little toward the back of the Hall. I slithered down an incline of masonry – Ethelred insists on calling it 'our staircase' but in truth it is but where the stonework has crumbled in a series of short ledges – and arrived at the bottom making rather more noise than I wished. I stood still, but could hear nothing. I edged along the passageway, now becoming as be-webbed and dusty as the Aetheling, until I began to see a few slivers of candle-light through the thick planking. And now I could hear voices.

"'Elfrith...' it was the Chief Ealdorman speaking, and I was amazed at the intimacy; the Queen would never normally allow the use of her given name. 'Elfrith, you have ever been a woman of patience. Just a few more weeks and all will be settled. Surely you can see it is the better way?'

"'But I have been making my own plans this past year,' came the Queen's reply. 'Ever since the idea came to me last spring.'

"'This is safer. There can be no suggestion of blame. No connection to you. And I think it better that the boy is not involved, you know how he feels about his brother. He is too young to understand.'

"'Ethelred will do as he is bid...'

"'That's as maybe, but if this can be done far away from you both and with no hint of ...'

"Suddenly, the dusty, spiders' webbed air caught in my nose and I sneezed, though managing to supress the sound as best I could by hiding my face in my sleeve. But I must have made some muffled noise, for the two stopped their conversation dead in its tracks.

"'What was that?' The ealdorman had certainly heard something. I hardly allowed myself to breathe for fear of sneezing again, and I could sense them straining their ears for another sound.

"'Just the scuffling of a rat, perhaps,' said the Queen, though I could almost feel her eyes boring into the panelling, seeking out the slightest movement behind every join in the woodwork. Did she know of the passageways? I would not have been surprised.

"'Lady, we have said enough in any case. It is settled.'

"'Very well, but if it fails, we may need to be patient another whole year,' snapped the Queen.

"'Elfrith…' Lord Aelfhere's voice became a little lower. 'Come…'
She gave a sigh, and then a soft cry of, perhaps, pleasure, it was hard to
tell.

"I prayed that I might do so silently, and began to make my escape.
When I returned to our chamber, Ethelred was standing, waiting for me.
'Meryasek, I could not sleep. I came to find you …'

"'Indeed, sire, and you find me as dusty as you were but an hour past!
And never did I see such spiders!' I made light of things. 'Look, I have
some ale left here, let us drink it together like men, and soon you will sleep
with no difficulty, that I'll warrant.' He ever likes to be treated as an adult,
and in a very short time, Heaven forgive me, he had taken enough ale that I
was able to put him to his bed without him even realising it. He slept
soundly till morning, and seemed to have no reason to make anything of
the evening's antics. He never mentioned it again. But it has been much
on my mind, Lady."

"You fear they mean some harm to…"

"Lady, I do not know. I do not wish to speak it. The Aetheling may
have heard more than I, but I cannot ask him. If it is as I fear, then it is,
indeed, better that he remembers nothing of what he heard. Children have
died for less than being the innocent pawn in such a game. And so have
their companions."

"Will you trust me with this, Meryasek?" I said. "Trust me to tell only
those who I know will treat those who are innocent fairly? We have no
idea of what… how… harm may be engineered to befall the King…"
There, I had said it. The thought that had hovered unsaid since before
Meryasek's story began. "But they – and I – have had some experience in
thwarting such dangers."

"Lady Aetna, I had hoped that you would know what to do. I… I feel
so isolated, so cut off from any who might… I feel less of a man for not
being able to stand forth, but Ethelred has none other than me to prevent
him being used as a…"

"You are the prince's true friend and protector," I said. "One day, I am
sure, he will understand all that you have risked to keep him – and his
immortal soul – safe. He is King Edgar's son and an Aetheling of the
Blood, just as Edward is. He should not be mired away here with only…"

There was a sound at the door and Ethel bustled in. "Ah, Lady, here
you are. The Dowager would see you. My Lord? Can I fetch you
anything?"

"Thank you, no, I must return to my duties, Price Ethelred will return
from his ride shortly and his lessons await. Lady Aetna, it has been a
delight to spend time with you." He rose and made a pretty bow. Really,
he was a sweet young man, I thought, but then my mind raced back to
what he had told me.

"You also," I said. "We shall meet again at the High Table this evening, I have no doubt." He kissed my hand and departed.

Ethel gave me a little smile. "I believe that young fellow is smitten," she said.

"Perhaps…" I said. "But I must to my aunt. Thank you, Ethel." A thought occurred to me. "And Ethel, if you see my brother, ask him to attend upon us."

"Of course, Lady."

)))))))(((((((

By the time the household came together for the evening meal, I had told Aethelflaed and my brother everything that Meryasek had imparted to me. Wulf had tapped upon the Dowager's chamber door shortly after I had arrived from the *solarium*, Ethel having happened upon him as he returned to the Hall from a ride with Ratkin and Thella. They had visited the highest point of the Purbecig Hills, and were windblown and cheerful after a pleasant postnoon. I had repeated Meryasek's story as close to word for word as I could recall.

"So, all Elfrith's affability has, indeed, been a smoke screen," said Aethelflaed. "But to shield what? Mayhap we shall never now know, for it seems her paramour has made plans of his own."

"And we do not know what they are, either," added Wulf.

"We may not," I said, "but recall that the King mentioned Dunstan would meet us at Bathe before the conclave at Caune. Mayhap he has heard word which can throw light onto things and that is why he is so anxious to speak to Edward."

"Should we tell Edward what we now know?" asked Wulf, in a worried voice, tucking his wind-tangled hair behind his ears. The gesture reminded me of how he had looked as a child – my young hero. "I hate to burden him with more troubling thoughts. He has been so much more himself this last week. I fear such news might set him back… your tincture, Aunt, can only do so much in the face of the realisation of such treachery. And Ethelred, what of him? It seems he, too, is in a less than happy… what a mess!"

We remained wrapped in our thoughts for a few moments. The Dowager was the first to speak. "I believe that, for the present – and only for the present – we keep our own counsel," she said. "When we reach Bathe and Dunstan is with us, we tell him what we have discovered. In the meantime, we do not leave the King alone at any time. Wulf, you are our first line of defence, of course. It is more than natural for you to stay with him. Do so even when he is alone with the prince. Take Ratkin and Thella into your confidence, if you think it necessary. Aetna, I think we must also have Lucet in our party. Ethelred has a very soft spot for her and, if they spend a little time together – I am sure we can engineer something innocent – he may let slip some snippet he has heard but does not fully understand. I do not want to put the boy in danger of his mother's anger, but our first allegiance is to the King – though it makes my blood boil to see how Elfrith manipulates her own poor child!"

"I hate the thought that we are deceiving the King," I said. "I know it is for his own benefit, but if he comes later to think that we have been withholding things from him, his anger as we have seen it so far will be as nothing to what we may bring upon ourselves."

"We are not deceiving him," said Aethelflaed. "We are but awaiting the right time to tell him. He will understand that."

"I hope you are right."

For the remaining few days of our stay we maintained our vigilance over the King. Most of the time he remained in a good humour, aided by the presence of his brother, with whom he seemed to be enjoying a growing affinity. Lucet had managed to have some little conversation with Ethelred – she and Ethel made him sweetmeats – but had gleaned little more than we already knew. It seemed the boy was genuinely fond of his brother and certainly had no understanding that he might be a pawn in his mother's game. When the morning came for us to leave, I was relieved. Elfrith's apparent goodwill and hospitality had been increasingly hard to bear, knowing what had passed between her and the Chief Ealdorman, and at times it had been all that I could do to remain civil. I had on several occasions caught Wulf's eye and knew that he had been sharing my emotions. Before the formal farewells in the courtyard I sought out Meryasek in Ethelred's apartments. The boy was playing happily and I took his companion to one side.

"Meryasek, I want you to know that you have done us, the King and possibly the whole of Englaland a great service this week. My brother and I – and the Dowager Queen – are aware that it has been hard for you, but be assured that the Aetheling's well-being is also in the forefront of our minds. The King has great love for his brother and Ethelred is, when all is said and done, his heir. However these matters fall out, you need have no fear that harm will befall him, or you, from the King."

"I thank you, Lady," he replied. "And I assure you of my full allegiance to His Majesty, while my Prince Ethelred's safety is certain. I hope we shall have the pleasure of your presence with us again next year. Mayhap things will have turned out better than we fear. I pray our misgivings are misplaced."

"I sincerely wish that to be so," I said. I felt sorry for him, left to tread the difficult path between Ethelred's affection and the Queen's ambition. "I bid you fare well, Meryasek, and if you need to be in touch with me, or my brother, pray do so without hesitation." Impulsively, I embraced him. He seemed to need it. When, just a short while later, he stood in the courtyard with Ethelred and the rest of the household, his smile seemed more assured.

Before we mounted our horses, Ethelred hugged the King around the waist. "Come back soon, brother!" he said. Elfrith dropped an elegant curtsey and allowed her hand to be kissed.

"Step-mother, I am grateful for your hospitality and the warmth of your welcome," said Edward. I found my jaw clenched and noticed my aunt's all-but-silent sniff of disdain at Elfrith's duplicity, as the Queen smiled at her step-son with such seeming affection.

"Your Majesty, it has been our... honour," she said.

Other wishes to bide well made, we trotted out of the courtyard, our vanguard ahead, the King, Wulf and myself riding together, the Dowager attended by Edith and Lucet, with Thella and Ratkin, the pack animals and remaining men-at-arms bringing up the rear. As we had the previous year, we headed for I'lcaestre, intending to stay the night there, before pressing on to Bathe the following day. With no ill weather or other mishaps to delay us, we reached our destination in good time and spent a pleasant night. On the following evening we found ourselves approaching the old Roman town of *Aquae Sulis* – Bathe – in all her ancient splendour. Sunset was approaching as we arrived at the abbey and were welcomed by the Abbot.

"Your Majesty, it is a pleasure to welcome you once again to our House. And this time also to greet your esteemed grandmother." He brought forward the Abbess who had been standing a little to one side. "Welcome Your Majesty, the holy nuns in the sister House look forward to greeting you."

These niceties of etiquette established, there came a booming voice from behind the Abbot. It was typical of Dunstan to allow his lesser brethren and sisters their moment in the sun, but he could forbear his own greeting no longer. "Your Majesty! You look well!"

Edward beamed at the Archbishop. "Lord Dunstan, I *feel* well," he said, sliding off his horse in that same manner his father once assumed. "And all the better for seeing you! Have you been here long?"

"I arrived but yesterday, sire, being anxious to await your arrival... but come, let the good brothers show you all to your chambers, there will be time enough to catch up on news later." Turning to the Dowager he bowed and kissed her hand. "My Lady, Queen Aethelflaed, a pleasure, as always. Lady Aetna, Lord Wulf... quite the family gathering!" I fancied that I could sense a tension beneath his good spirits. But perhaps, I thought, recent events were colouring my perception. Or so I hoped.

Being a somewhat larger group than had stayed in the guest house the previous year, we had been allocated different quarters. Our men were billeted above the stables and given their liberty to enjoy the pleasures of the town, a small bodyguard excepted. Ratkin and Thella were offered a separate chamber as befitted their married status. The Dowager with Ethel, and I with Lucet, were given adjoining apartments and the King, together with Wulf, a splendid chamber which, said the Abbot proudly, had been added to the hostelry but this last year, for just such important guests. "Not that there could be others as important as Your Majesty," he added quickly, suddenly realising that he might be speaking out of turn.

Edward laughed – it was so good to hear him in such fine spirits, I prayed that we would have no cause to dampen them. "Father," he said, "within these holy halls, a king is no more important than the least of his subjects!"

It had been a long day and we were pleased to take our rest. We ate quietly, each in our own chambers, and I, for one, was happy to let whatever news Dunstan had for us wait until the following day.

It was hardly light when there was a scratch at our door. Lucet rose and wrapped a blanket around herself – the spring mornings were yet cold – opened the door a fraction and whispered through the crack "Who wakes my Lady at this hour?"

Wulf's voice, also in a whisper: "It's me… and I am not the first to be about this morn. Make yourself decent and let me in." Lucet pulled the blanket more tightly about her body and looked to me. Still under my own blankets I motioned to her to open the door.

"Wulf, you had better have good cause to be rattling around the halls at this…"

"Peace, sister, I do!"

Wulf's glance travelled over Lucet's trim figure, swathed as it was, and then he dutifully looked away. "Lucet," I said, "come back under the covers. You will catch your death!" Resisting the temptation to recline upon the palliasse as he would if we were alone, Wulf took a seat beside me, careful not to allow his eyes to stray toward Lucet. "What is so urgent that the proprieties are ignored?" I said.

"Where should I start?"

"At the…"

"Oh, hush, I know! Listen. I awoke about an hour since, and would have slept again, had I not seen that the King's bed was empty. He's gone to Alfreth, of course. I advised him against it when we retired last eve, and he said he would not, but clearly the temptation was too much for him and he crept out as I slept. I just hope he is being careful. And I don't like that he is not returned, for it is getting light and he may be seen… But if that was not enough, having resigned myself to an anxious wait, there was a

475

knock at the chamber door. I didn't want it known that the King was absent, so I went to answer it intending to send whoever it was away with a reprimand for trying to wake His Majesty so early... but it was the Archbishop! Dunstan himself, looking as though he had spent a restless night and could wait no longer before unburdening himself of whatever was troubling him. I began to bluster something about Edward being asleep, but he barged past me saying he had to speak with him... and he found ... no King!

"Have you ever tried pulling the wool over Dunstan's eyes? I tell you it cannot be done. I could think of no plausible explanation for the King's absence other than one that was not too far removed from the truth: that Edward had spent the night with a woman. Of course, that meant that the Archbishop wanted to know who... did I not know the dangers of allowing His Majesty to roam about the city at night? He is still but a lad in many ways! Well, in the end one untruth led to another and that got confused... I had to tell him the truth. I know, I know, Edward will... but at least our aunt will be able to assure Dunstan that Alfreth is a good, sweet child. In truth he was not as appalled as I feared he might be. And that, I have to tell you, is because he had greater worries besetting him."

All manner of scenarios had been passing through my mind as Wulf told us all this – not least of which was whether the Archbishop would hold us accountable for keeping such a huge secret from him. I was relieved, now, that Aethelflaed was a party to the deception. Dunstan could hardly accuse the Queen Dowager of acting without authority as he might us.

"I also told him something of our worries about the King's recent state of mind," Wulf went on. "Once I had admitted that the Queen Dowager was party to the King's marriage, it seemed pointless to hold anything else back. I said that he was presently much improved but that we – all – were concerned lest he fall back under the pall of his recent mood swings, especially with another round of these interminable talks on the question of the *Concordia* approaching. That seemed to remind him of why he had come to see Edward in the first place. He fell silent for a moment and then cast about the room for something. 'Is there no wine to be had?' he asked.

"'My Lord,' I said, 'the Brothers have not yet returned from Lauds, surely it is a little early... there is some small ale here...'

"'Early or no,' he replied, 'you may need a mouthful of something stronger yourself when you hear what... but now that you have told me of the King's recent... Wulf, you were ever Edward's best friend and protector; I think we must now do what must be done without allowing His Majesty to be burdened with it. The Northmen are on the borders of Northumbria sheltering under the protection of the Scots, the Normans – their brothers in all but religion – are to the South. The King needs a steady hand on the tiller and a clear head for these matters. Worrying over the loyalty of his own Ealdormen... and what you tell me of how these matters inflame his temper...'" Dunstan's words and apparently his thoughts had trailed off in a tangle of divergent threads. Wulf, too, as he continued, seemed to find it hard to bring all the strands together.

"Where is the Archbishop now?" I asked.

"He has ridden out toward Sceo," Wulf replied. "He hopes to meet Edward on the road as he returns in order that he might tell him that he knows of the marriage and..."

"Did he tell you what it was that was troubling him?"

"He did, though even he admits that he cannot quite put his finger upon what it is that makes him so uneasy about this proposed meeting at Caune."

"Well, what did he say?" I was becoming increasingly impatient. So far it seemed that Wulf had had no real reason for intruding upon our chamber at this hour other than his own – and now Dunstan's – unspecified apprehensions. Gradually, the story came out.

It seemed that a week or so before Edward and our party were able to leave Wintancaestre for Corf, and while Dunstan was still at Cantuaria he sent an emissary to Caune – one of the younger brothers from Cantuaria, a bright, friendly young man, not long having taken his final vows – with orders to become familiar with the town and take the measure of the local Reeve, such accommodation as they were to be offered and the suitability of the venue which the Chief Ealdorman had chosen for the meeting.

Brother Earned had arrived at the Caune town gates just before curfew, his mule tired from the long ride and the brother himself somewhat bedraggled and dirty, having stopped some few miles out of the town to help a man whose cart was mired by the roadside in deep mud – much of which had found its way onto Earned's habit, and, indeed, his hands and face during his energetic feat of assistance. He looked very much as though he had not seen the inside of a bath-house for a great many days and so, perhaps, it was understandable that the gate-keeper took him for one of the monks displaced by the implementation of the *Concordia*.

"Come you in, Brother, and sharpish unless you fancy another night under the stars – for it looks as though you have enjoyed some few of those, mayhap."

Brother Earned had, in fact, enjoyed the last several nights in the comfort of a number of well set-up taverns along the way, but he forbore to set the Gatekeeper aright, realizing suddenly how unkempt he must appear.

"I thank you, Keeper," he said. "I shall be pleased to set my feet before the fire of your nearest inn, if you will be so good as to direct me there."

477

"Aye, I dare say you would," replied the Gatekeeper, "but the nearest is at the sign of the Mason's Chisel and you will not find the Landlord there willing to take you in without his usual payment, which is too high for the likes of you, I'll be bound! Take the road to your right and bear around beyond the market place. Go to the sign of the Black Dog. They've sheltered many an expelled monk and even an Abbot or two, for a few fourthings. Don't expect much in the way of victuals, though, it'll be mostly what's left by the proper paying guests – but it's better than starving!"

"Oh, but I'm not..." began Earned, realizing the mistake the Keeper was making. But then he stopped himself. Perhaps it would be better to remain unknown, for the time at least. The Archbishop would surely be interested to learn in what regard those unfortunates – if they could be thus described – who had been removed from Mother Church by the *Concordia* were held.

"Not what, lad?" re-joined the Keeper. "Not yet starving? Give it time. You will find there are not many towns as friendly as ours to such vagabonds, even if they do affect to wear the tonsure!"

"Then I thank you, and God bless you," replied Earned, making the sign of the Cross. "I will do as you suggest. Come along, Nancy!" And with that, not wishing to get deeper into any falsehood, he jiggled his tired animal's harness – he was beginning to feel some affection for his bedraggled mule – and led her toward the market place as he has been advised.

"Nancy!" he heard the man laugh to his fellow Keeper. "I'll warrant he had a doxy of the same name to keep him warm in whatever abbey he came from... she probably disappeared to find a warmer, more profitable, bed and now he remembers her by riding his mule instead!" The two guffawed companionably as they drew the town gate closed for the night.

Brother Earned passed the lighted windows of the Mason's Chisel and looked longingly at the scene within, as a door opened to admit a well-dressed patron. An appetising aroma of stewed mutton and vegetables assailed him, but he resolutely pressed on to find the sign of the Black Dog, hoping that, if he offered to pay, he would receive more than leftovers. Beyond the town square the road became muddier and piles of ordure and other refuse were scattered along the gutters. There were no glass windows here, just shutters already closed against the falling dusk. A low creak caused him to look upward and there, swinging on what looked for all the world like a gibbet, hung the image of a Black Dog, its eyes painted a lurid red and its lolling tongue the same shade, protruding between sharply chiselled teeth. Hardly the advertisement of a welcoming hostelry, he thought, wryly.

There was no sign of a stable, so he tied Nancy to a hitching post, hoping that she would still be there when he returned, and opened the door. He was pleasantly surprised by the atmosphere which greeted him. Whilst clearly not rivalling the Mason's Chisel in the calibre of its custom, it was well patronized and there was a cauldron of meaty broth bubbling over the firepit. It took his eyes a few moments to become accustomed to the dim interior and then he approached the man he took to be the landlord, leaning on a bar of wood set across two huge barrels. Before he could speak, the man slapped the trestle hard with the palm of his hand.

"Ho, lads, here's another! Well, Brother, what are you? Novice, monk, abbot or priest? Kitchener or scribbler? The Archbishop cares not, I'll warrant. Ye're out of a home now, eh?"

"I, er... I... well, I... it's not as bad as all that!"

"I'm right glad to hear it!" He winked at several of his guests, who were taking an interest in the exchange. "So ye'll not be wanting free bed and board then '*in return for prayer and the gratitude of the Blessed*' as I have so often heard these last months?"

"Er, no, no. I can pay my way. I managed to put a little by in case of..."

"Hear that, lads? He '*put a little by*'! Had a hand in the Offertory, more like! Well, good for you, Brother. The Lord helps those who help themselves, that's what I say. Why should we expect those inside the monastery walls to be any different? There's none here will gainsay me. We have our own Brotherhood here! So, what can I do for you?" Earned reflected that under the circumstances he would rather be inside this fellow's brotherhood than outside it. The man was huge, fat around the belly but muscled, too. His forearms bulged within his tunic and his neck was as thick as a bull's. His *bonhomie* seemed a thin veil over an aura of supressed violence. He rubbed a rough hand, the size of a ham, over his black, unkempt beard.

"A bed for a few nights, a belly full of what's in that pot, a jar of strong ale – and a stall for my mule," said Earned, beginning to warm to his unaccustomed role. He jangled the coins in his purse and slapped a few pennies down on the bar-top. If he had to act the rascal in order to be the Archbishop's eyes and ears, surely the Lord would forgive him. "And a drink for these fine fellows." He indicated the Landlord's coterie who had gathered around during the exchange. He would rather have them as friends than enemies, too.

"Gyrrdd, go fetch the man's mule into the stable a-back!" the Landlord shouted at a skinny boy who had been hovering by the fire. "Mennae – where is that girl? – broth!" He turned the tap on a barrel and drew off a large cup of ale. "And by what name are ye going, man?"

"Br... No, just Earn... Earnest, now. Earnest. *Was heil*, Landlord!"

Earned spend a fairly comfortable night in the attic dormitory of the Black Dog. A row of sturdy pallets was ranged under the eaves, palliasses stuffed with horse hair and with an acceptable level of flea and bedbug infestation – he had stayed at worse in his travels. Although, upon taking his final vows, Earned had been afforded a private cell in his home community, he had slept long years as a novice in the common dorter and was used to the sound of his fellows' snoring, so the company of other guests troubled him not one whit. He awoke later than he had intended and by the time he came down the ladder into the room below, half a dozen or so were already tucking into a huge communal bowl of porridge, their wooden spoons clacking against each other in a jovial race to be the first to scrape the sides clean.

"Ho, lug-a-bed!" called the landlord from the kitchen. "I fear you will find little porridge left by the time these gannets have had their fill, but there's bread here, and cheese, or some fatty pork if you prefer."

Earned tried to recall what day it was: he had lost track of the date as he travelled. If it was a Friday, then certainly there seemed no imperative in this house to insist upon fish. To avoid meat, but appear unconcerned, he opted for the cheese. A jar of small ale was smacked down by his elbow.

"That'll set you up for the day! I'm told my small ale is not all that small, if you get my meaning!" The landlord took a long draught from his own jug and licked his lips appreciatively. "Now, if you'll pardon the inquisition, what are your plans? I ask because my brother – the builder – is looking for some strong backs to help him out for a couple of days. You say you have the wherewithal to pay your way," he looked Earned up and down discerningly, "but it never hurts to have a few extra pennies in your purse! You look none too flush to me."

Earned had done his best to remove the mud of yesterday, but he had noticed that in helping his fellow traveller he had torn the hem and sleeve of his habit in several places, and in common with others of his brotherhood, he travelled with little or no baggage or belongings. He might, indeed, be taken for someone on the downhill slide to vagrancy.

"Oh, ah, yes, well I have no experience in the building trade, but I can fetch and carry with the best of them," he said, wondering where this would lead him. "But first I must to the church, for though I am no longer a monk," he crossed his fingers beneath his cuff to fend off any misfortune his untruth might bring, "I would still make my prayers."

The landlord's bushy black brows rose an implausible way into the mop of curly hair falling into his eyes. "Well, you're a strange one and no mistake! Still, the colour of your money last eve was as fair as any, and your soul your own business. But if ye get your arse back here before the morgen hours end, I'll send you to my brother and he will pay you for half a day. Can't say fairer than that." He grinned at the others around the trestle with the clear intimation that if a man was fool enough to work nine hours and only be paid for six, simply to save his soul – well, what more could you do for him?

"I, er, yes, very well. I shall return before then."

Quaffing down the last of his ale, and with a hunk of cheese between two slabs of crusty bread, Earned left by the door through which he had entered the previous evening. He made a quick visit to Nancy, who looked content enough in an open stall behind the inn – the skinny Gyrrdd had fed her well – and then turned to make his way... where? He realised he had not asked directions to the church. Reluctant to re-enter the tavern, where he was obviously seen as a fool, though thankfully not a dangerous one, he headed in the direction of the market square he had skirted the night before. Someone there would point him the right way.

The town did not look any more prosperous in the light of morning than it had the previous day. It seemed that there was no night-soil carrier employed to remove the filth from the streets, and judging by the smell of fresh urine, no-one collected it and so it seemed likely that there were no tanners in the town. Some of the larger houses appear to be unoccupied and boarded up; the smaller all boasted heavy duty shutters to both doors and windows, as if householders distrusted their neighbours. A market was just opening up when Earned reached the square, stallholders shaking tarps and setting out their wares, stacking boxes of greens and sacks of root vegetables. Once away from the Black Dog, Earned had straightened and rearranged his habit as best he could, raised his hood and appeared, once more, the Benedictine he was. But he felt unfriendly eyes upon him as he passed, and one stall holder even spat on the ground at his feet.

He did not need to ask directions to the church, for as soon as he entered the square, he could see it, on the corner of a street leading off in the opposite direction to the one which he had taken previously. It boasted no vestige of a tower and, unlike many churches which were beginning to be stone built, looked more like the buildings of a couple of centuries earlier: a wooden construction, unwindowed and with the appearance rather of a shabby barn than the House of God. There was a small, lopsided Cross upon the apex of the roof. Hurrying through the market, he reached the church door, which was closed and upon pushing, opened with the grinding sound of ill-fitting hinges. The light within was almost non-existent and it look a while for his eyes to become accustomed to the gloom.

When he was able to make out his surroundings, they were shabby and none too clean. He made his way toward the East wall, where the altar, at least, appeared swept clean of cobwebs and the other detritus which lay about on the floor. A poor wooden crucifix hung above the rough table which bore two tall candles, unlit, and a shorter time-keeper whose wick sputtered and gave off a black, greasy smoke and a very small flame. Perhaps, Eadred mused, the taller candles remained unlit as a precaution against fire – this being a wooden building – in the priest's absence.

He knelt before the altar, trying to put the odd atmosphere in the town and the feeling of dereliction in the church out of his thoughts, and began to settle his mind into prayer, but he found it hard to concentrate. He could not help returning time and again to this being a strange place for the Chief Ealdorman to choose as the location for such an important conclave – especially as it was by way of an expiation for his sin in destroying three of the Lord's newly scoured and reorganised communities. However, he persevered and eventually began to enjoy the pleasant sense of tranquillity and remove that prayer always brought him, when he was suddenly jerked back to an awareness of his surroundings and once again in the here and now.

A hand descended upon his shoulder. He jumped violently at the surprise and was immediately afforded an apology.

"Sincere regrets, my son," a voice quavered. "I forget sometimes that my old feet do not make much noise, especially in these poor sandals! I frightened you. I am sorry!"

Earned's heart seemed to be beating in this throat, and his chest an empty, cold vessel, but he took a deep breath and turned toward the speaker, to find an old man, scrawny and poorly habited smiling down at him – for he was still on his knees.

"It is of no matter, Father," he said, trying to make light of his earlier fear. "You have every right to make free in your own church." He smiled up at the old priest, for surely this was the incumbent of the parish. He rose to his feet, thinking that the little prayer he had made would have to suffice until later in the day.

"Aye, that I do… and often there are few enough others about for me to need to have a care about it." He cast a doleful eye around his small, shabby tenure. "But you are a stranger – and a Brother, too, by the looks of it." For the first time he appeared to notice Earned's dress. "What business have you here?"

It seemed an odd question for a priest to ask a monk in a church! "Why, I make – or try to make – my morning prayer," Earned replied, and then regretted his quickness of tongue, as his companion looked so crestfallen and contrite at what he had obviously perceived to be a rebuke.

"Apologies again, my son, apologies. I am unused to visitors and my hospitality – never mind my wits – fail me. Please, will you not come into my room and take a sup with me? It is long since I conversed with a fellow Brother in Orders. Please." Earned looked at the time-keeper candle, it was slowly eroding downwards toward the line marking the end of the morgen-hours.

"I… I cannot stay long, but I would like to speak with you, Father," he said.

"And take a sup?" asked the old man, hopefully.

"Well, it is a little early, but…" The priest's hands were shaking. It looked as though he needed some fortification. It might loosen his tongue, thought Brother Earned, and by Heaven it felt as though there were things in this town that he needed to know. The old priest led the way through a curtain into a small, cluttered vestry – which clearly also served as his sleeping quarters, for there was a pallet topped by a few scrumpled blankets in one corner. A set of rough wooden shelves occupied the opposite corner, bearing several bottles – one clearly open – some black bread, a hunk of cheese and a few vegetables. He took down the open bottle, poured some of the red, viscous content into a wooden cup for himself and selected an earthenware cup for Earned. After blowing into it to remove accumulated dust he sloshed in a generous helping and handed it to the monk.

"Don't worry," he grinned, sheepishly, "it is not yet the blood of Christ. None of this little stock has yet been consecrated in the Eucharist! I may be a poor excuse for a priest, but I am not blasphemous! Sit, sit. But I forget my manners… my name is Dorwith."

"Father Dorwith, I thank you," said Earned, taking a sip of the thick wine and inclining the cup toward his host. He felt a little of his spirit returning with the warmth of the drink. Earned had taken the only chair, Dorwith perching himself upon his pallet. "Father, I hope you do not mind me saying, but your church seems a little… it appears as though… well, perhaps there is another church in the parish which benefits more from the tithe of the parishioners?"

"Another church? Oh, dear me, no. It is hard enough to scrape together the fourthings to keep this one standing and feed its poor incumbent – your brother and servant! You are not from these parts – well, clearly not, of course." The old man ran his hand over his ill shaven face, and across his rough tonsure. He looked furtively at the door which led into the church-yard, but it was securely locked, and then cast a glance at the curtain separating the vestry from the body of the church. He limped over to it, pulled it aside quickly, and seeing no-one without, allowed it to fall back and resumed his seat. "Foolish of me, really," he said, "there's few enough souls attending service these days and why I should imagine anyone was in the church now… that is why I was surprised to see you, my son."

"Father, I do not understand you."

"One hundred years next year, and still the town has not forgiven… neither the Church, nor…" he lowered his voice to a whisper, "the line of Wessex!"

"I am still not sure what you mean, Father. I see how poorly your church fares, and I confess that I was perplexed by the strange, contradictory reaction of the townspeople to me: some seemed to welcome me as a refugee from the Benedictine revivalists, some simply disliked me on sight for my habit. And so many of the houses, fallen into disrepair. What on earth happened here a hundred years ago – why, that was the year that the great King Alfred defeated the Danes, and forced their withdrawal from all these lands. Forced them into what became the Danelaw. The siege of Chepeham and then the Battle of Ethendon; all one hundred years ago, but how does that...?"

"Ah, the young, and even the not so young, know only what was written by the chroniclers. All you say is true, but what they did not record is... As King Alfred and his army remained besieged in Chepeham, congratulating themselves for their endurance, the Danes vented their wrath on us! They could not reach Alfred and his cronies, but us... the town was laid waste. Then, the King broke the siege, brought the Danes to battle at Ethendon, and again who paid the price? We did! Those men – they were more monsters than men – released from the confines of the siege laid waste to what little we had left. Any food the town had managed to hide from the Danes was taken, any virgin not despoiled was raped, any man not part of the 'Great' King's army was strung up as a coward. And what of the pious King? He did nothing. He was too busy making a treaty with the leader of the Danes, with Gudrun who became his godson when he 'converted'. Did the Church send aid? No, it was too busy patting itself on the back over the hundreds of new Danish 'Christians' it had acquired along with Gudrun. No, you will find few churchmen are welcome here – folk take pleasure in the abbeys' discomfiture as their patrons fight among themselves. And..." he lowered his voice still further "... the last collector of the King's taxes, dining at the house of the town Reeve, mysteriously choked upon a chicken bone. He is now in the churchyard through that door."

Time was slipping by. Earned suddenly felt that he must at all costs learn more of what was happening in this town if he was to make a full report to the Archbishop. He must return to the Black Dog and meet the landlord's brother. He, at least, appeared to have work to do and money to spend.

"Father, I will take you into my confidence. You are my brother in the Church and I must trust you. I am here at Archbishop Dunstan's direct order to ascertain..." he was reluctant to mention the King. "To ascertain how the town fares, for there is to be a conclave here in just a few weeks' time. You have perhaps heard?"

"Aye, the Reeve's Hall is being renovated as we speak. More money spent on useless politicking! Take care, Son, do not make yourself a

484

target. Our master builder, for one, has no love of King or Church – his family was decimated in the troubles."

"I am but a poor lay brother seeking a chance to make his way in a hard world," said Earned, his voice heavy with irony. "I shall hope to meet you again, Father, perhaps in more auspicious circumstances. And now I must leave you."

He looked back as he slipped through the curtain into the cold, cheerless church. The old man was shakily pouring himself another tumbler of wine.

Brother Earned retraced his steps to the Black Dog. A small group of men were gathering in front of the tavern door – clearly, he had not missed the end of the third morgen hour. He realized now why time was being kept in this archaic way – there were no church bells to announce the hours. The tavern keeper stepped from his door and hailed a giant of a man who was assessing these latecomers – his regular workforce would have been labouring for three hours already. The two big men were so alike that there was no mistaking that they were siblings.

"Aymore, this is Earnest, sometime ill-advised abbey-rat!" he said, indicating Earned. "Come by, lad, my brother will not be paying you even half a wage for holding up the line. Ye'll be happy to fetch and carry for the day, will ye not?"

"That I will."

The builder, Aymore, looked him up and down. "Spent more time scribbling and on your knees than in honest work, I'll be bound," he said. "Still, need all the help I can get if we are to have the Reeve's Hall ready for... by the Devil's balls, man," he shouted at one of the other workmen, who appeared to be playing a game of cat's cradle in an attempt to unravel a length of thin, hairy rope. "I told you to fetch good, thick rope not your wife's embroidery thread! Must I see to everything myself?" He wrestled the tangled skein away from the man and stomped off muttering to himself. The man grinned at Earned. "Master Aymore's temper is not improved by the Ealdorman's constant requests for updates on the progress of the work," he said. He was lean and sandy-haired with teeth that seemed a little too large for his mouth. "Conferth, ceorl of this fair town!" He held out his hand. After a slight hesitation Earned shook it. Apart from old Father Dorwith, Conferth's was the only apparently genuine offer of companionship, rather than surly tolerance, which he had received.

"The Ealdorman?"

"Not common knowledge, but my wife heard it from the fishmonger's... none other than the Chief Ealdorman himself, Alfhere of Mercia, is paying for the Reeve's Hall to be renovated, all on account of some great how-do-you-fare in a few weeks' time. Time, it seems, is of the essence, which is why our esteemed builder, Aymore, is taking on all hands. My wife – again – she heard about it and insisted I came and… well here I am, and I can tell you I would rather be popping my fishing pole into the Marden, downstream – or into her!" He winked as a well-endowed young woman, with an improbably low cut gunna, considering the hour and temperature, sashayed past, winking back at him and making eyes at the other men. Earned blushed.

Aymore returned with a coil of heavy rope beneath his arm. "Well, what in the name of all demons are you standing about here for? The Reeve's Hall isn't going to come to you is it? Thank the saints that I have some real workers already there, for if I was to rely upon you, poor excuses for…" The builder was, indeed, out of temper.

Following his companion, to whom he had introduced himself as Earnest, Earned joined the rest of the men as they made their way through the streets of the town toward the Reeve's Hall, which stood close to the river. It was, without doubt, the finest building in the town and, even allowing for the damage of generations past, which was now being repaired, an impressive one. The lowest sections of the walls looked, to Earned's eye, as though they were of Roman build, with later stonework added to shore them up where they had fallen. Above the ground floor, there was even what appeared to be a superstructure, an upper storey in its own right, not just an attic, once also made of stone but now almost entirely crumbled away and being rebuilt as a sturdy wooden construct. It was upon this stage of the renovations that the bulk of Aymore's workforce was concentrating. Great pulleys were hauling split tree trunks up onto the top of the stone walls and a floor of thick planks was being constructed within, currently held stable by props, but most of its weight borne by the rafters of the ceiling below.

"A fine Hall, indeed," said Earned. "And suitable, I am sure, for any great meeting the nobility desire to convene." He was careful not to let slip anything which might suggest that he knew more than he was admitting. He turned to where Conferth had been standing, about to ask what he hoped sounded innocent questions, but the ceorl was already climbing up the stone steps toward the partly built upper storey, at the top of which he straddled a great beam and threw a rope down to Earned. A leather strap at the end of the rope, complete with a sturdy buckle, was just the right length to girdle one of the smaller beams piled to the side of the steps. The rope went through a pulley to Conferth's side, and if he pulled on its other extremity the beam was quite easily raised up to him, to be unleashed, stacked on the part finished floor and its collar returned to the man below – in this case Earned.

"Come on man, strap 'en on, then!" called Conferth. Earned soon realised that he had the more taxing of the two-man operation. Each split log had to be manhandled into place, lifted to allow the strap to be put around it, buckled on firmly and positioned below the pulley. All his team-mate had to do was operate the pully, allow the log to swing of its own volition over the pile on the first floor, lower it and unbuckle – during which time Earned had to manoeuvre the next into place below. For some while he had neither the time, nor the breath, to ask any more questions. After what seemed like an eternity, Conferth called down that it was time for a break. The master builder was nowhere to be seen – from his vantage point above, Conferth had observed him hurry away on some errand and he saw no advantage in working when there was no-one around to chastise him for not doing so. The other odd-jobbers seemed inclined to do the same. Those above clambered down to ground level and pulled waxed packages of bread and cheese, onions and carrots from their belt pouches. Some even had small flasks of ale. With practised skill they found spots out of the wind to sit and rest.

Conferth groaned, arched and rubbed the small of his back. "My wife needn't think she is getting any pleasure from me this se'enight! Why, I can hardly move!" At that moment, the doxy from earlier in the morning passed by, again swinging her hips and smiling, knowingly, at the men. "Hey, Meggy, I shall have a full purse this eve, will you be at the Dog?"

"I... might!"

"I'll see you there!"

"We all will!" chipped in one of the other men, making a lewd gesture.

Meggy swayed off, smirking.

Conferth passed Earned his flask and the monk gratefully took a swig. He was expecting small ale, but found that he had swallowed a mouthful of burning liquor. "What ...?"

"Something to keep the cold out and the aches and pains away!" laughed his companion, retrieving the flask and taking several more draughts. Many of the other men seemed to be doing the same. To Earned, the thought of standing below as half tree trunks were unlashed above his head that postnoon was becoming increasingly unpleasant.

A number of the other, more skilled workmen had, by this time, also taken a break to eat something and gather themselves for the postnoon shift. They kept to themselves and appeared to be more interested in discussing the work than any passing whores. Earned wandered over, nearer to one of the small groups. They were munching hunks of bread and pastry and discussing some drawings etched out on rough parchment.

"But, I tell you, this makes no sense," one was saying, clearly repeating what he had said before, as his impatience was obvious.

"You don't have to shout at me," another grumbled. "I agree with you! I took the plans to Aymore yester-eve and told him that we were about to work on this today – and that it could not be right. I asked him what to do and he just said to do as we were told, follow the plans and get on with it!"

"Well, on his head be it, then," re-joined the first. "And it just might be, too!" They all laughed uproariously at that. "I shall have moved on to another job in another town, the consequences won't *fall* on me!" Again, the laughter.

Earned looked at his hands. They were red-raw. Aymore had been right – at least that he was not used to this type of physical work. He could not face another six hours of it. And yet he would like to learn more of… his train of thought was interrupted by a now familiar, angry shout.

"By Saint Edmund's liver and lights! Do you men never work? If I find any of you… if any of you drunken sots fall, the first man who tries to help them will wish he fell too! Get back to work, damn you all!"

"I need to piss," whispered Earned to Conferth. "I will be back in a nonce." He slipped around the corner of the building where the skilled journeymen had disappeared, followed by the master builder. He could hear raised voices.

"Not this again," Aymore was saying. "I told you last night, just follow the plans. Is that too hard for you? You are supposed to be professionals. The ealdorman has had these drawn up by some scribbler in the city and he wants it done as he…"

"But someone could be… I mean, if this is really what he wants it could be… surely someone should check again. Perhaps…" but there was a resounding smack and the speaker fell backward, only prevented from hitting the ground by colliding with the wall.

Earned could just see the top of his head from behind the woodpile where he had been relieving himself.

"Enough!" shouted Aymore. "Just get on with it."

Earned had just made himself decent and was emerging from the makeshift latrine as the builder barged past him. "Get out of my way, you idiot! And look at your hands. If you try working with those your likely to drop something and put one of my real workers out of action. Get off my site. And don't think you are getting paid!"

Perhaps, Earned thought, he should protest, but in truth he was relieved at his dismissal. Conferth appeared to have already found another partner and no-one was paying him any attention: he left the building site with the air of a man crushed, but secretly satisfied. He would have more than enough to report to the Archbishop. Returning to the Black Dog only to collect his mule, and pleased to avoid the inn keeper, he left Caune by the west gate and by that evening was enjoying the hospitality of a pleasant tavern in Avebury, surrounded by the ancient monoliths of the pagans, with a full belly and some marigold salve on his fast healing hands.

)))))))(((((((

By the time Wulf had finished recounting this tale as it had been told to him by the Archbishop, Lucet and I were both sitting up upon our pallet, in rapt attention, and completely careless of the impropriety of our positions and apparel. It was clear to all three of us that something was terribly wrong with the Chief Ealdorman's plan for the proposed conclave. But what was his intention?

Wulf had heard the story when he was barely awake and hurried to tell us straightway. In the retelling he was able fully to absorb the implications.

"And did you tell Dunstan of what we learned at Corf?" I asked. "For surely the Chief Ealdorman's words to Elfrith concerned whatever he is planning at Caune. Why can none of them ever speak plain? It is as though they fear the very walls might be listening, ready to pass on their intentions."

"Which is very much what they were doing at Corf," said Wulf. "Meryasek made a fine little fly – inside the wall!"

"Joking gets us no further along the path of understanding what they are plotting."

"Does Aelfhere plan to kidnap the King, perhaps?" Wulf mused. "Does he intend to take him by treachery – and so the upper chamber is being made easy to defend, so that he might hold Edward captive until he is able to carry him away into Mercia?"

"But why, then, were the journeymen builders so unhappy with the plans? If anything, that would make the building better, not make them so anxious," said Lucet.

"Whatever his plans are, Archbishop Dunstan is adamant that the King must not attend the meeting."

I shooed Wulf out of the way and got to my feet. "If he refuses, the Chief Ealdorman will say that Edward does not wish to make rational argument, and is not willing to accept his apology and appeasement. It will make Edward look weak and put the Reformists and supporters of the *Concordia* on the back foot."

"Once again, we have no proof that there is any treachery afoot," said Wulf, his pun unintentional. "Brother Earned's report is subject to interpretation, to say the least. But taken together with what we think we learned at Corf... the Chief Ealdorman's actions look pretty damning. But what it looks like and proving it are two different things. And Edward is desperate to believe that he can finally bring all sides together with this apparently miraculous about-face by Aelfhere – he *wants* to believe the ealdorman is sincere."

"Believing because you *want* to believe is a dangerous form of self-deception," I said. "I am just relieved that we have been able to hand it over to Dunstan."

TWENTY-NINE

WULFMAER

I left my sister and Lucet to ready themselves for the day and returned to my chamber to await the King's return. My mind was in turmoil. Would the fact that I had told Archbishop Dunstan Edward's secrets make him angry? Would Dunstan have told the King of his anxieties regarding the conclave at Caune – or perhaps the revelations of the King's marriage would be the first matter that he would raise. In any of these cases, I thought, I must prepare myself for Edward's displeasure, whether it be directed at me, the Archbishop or – most likely, in tandem with either or both of the first two – Chief Ealdorman Alfhere. I waited until I heard the abbey church bell toll for Terce, and then descended to the Great Hall, reflecting that it would arouse more curiosity in the King's absence for me to miss breaking my fast altogether than to make a late appearance, remarking that the King – and, therefore, I – had enjoyed troubled sleep and he had gone out early to clear his head, while I managed some late rest. We could, no doubt, cover the King's tracks on his return.

I was just completing my meal when Edward strode into the Hall, Dunstan at his side, his arm around the younger man's shoulder. They both seemed in fine humour. One of the house thralls immediately approached with a warm towel to wipe his hands and face, another offering a cup of steaming ale to dispel any chill after his morning ride. Edward passed the towel to Dunstan, who, after a cursory wipe of his hands, took a seat at the long table, opposite my own. Edward seated himself in his accustomed spot – his, by default, in any Hall – at the head of the table. There was meat and fowl on offer, cold from the night before, together with breads and cheeses of various types. Edward inspected the table.

"I have eaten already, at the Shoe Tavern out at Sceo," he said. Several of the other late-comers, still enjoying their meal, turned to him, eager to hear whatever their King was about to impart. "The landlord opens his board early for pilgrims, such as myself, who choose to make morning prayers at the shrine." He shared a knowing little grin with me. "And upon my taking the road home, who should I come upon but our Archbishop of Cantuaria!"

"I have to say, Majesty," Dunstan replied, "I think it inadvisable to roam around the countryside, albeit *incognito*, however compelling your desire to visit the Holy Well." He, too, essayed a slightly mischievous smile in my direction. Clearly, he and Edward had now shared the fact that the Archbishop was privy to the King's secret. He had decided there was little advantage in offering any negative opinion on a matter already accomplished – and the King seemed genuinely pleased to have another friend in on the intrigue. Dunstan had obviously made no mention of the state of affairs in Caune, nor of his suspicions with regard to the Chief Ealdorman. If he had, I felt sure, Edward's mood would have been considerably less sunny. The King drank down the tankard of warm ale in a single draught, and rose to his feet once again. Dunstan slapped a wedge of pork between two chunky lumps of bread, took a bite washed down with milk, and still holding the bread and meat, rose to follow him. My fast fully broken, I followed suit. The others at the table began to rise out of respect, but Edward waved them down.

"No, men, finish your meals. This is too fair a day to stand upon such ceremony!"

We left the Hall and headed toward Edward's withdrawing room – part of the suite of chambers of which the Abbot was so proud. I guessed that Aetna had broken her fast with our aunt, and acquainted her with Brother Earned's intelligence regarding the odd goings-on in Caune, and, indeed, as we approached the door to Edward's accommodation, she and Lucet, together with our aunt, made their way down the walkway toward us.

"Edward?" Aethelflaed's relief at seeing him safely back was palpable.

"There is nothing to fear, Step-grandmother, 'tis little over an hour's ride to Sceo!" he smiled. "In fact, I have to tell you that the Archbishop here is now fully aware of my... happy circumstances, for I met him this morn and have told him all. So, come you now – all of you – and we will make plans for the next few days." I caught Aethelflaed's glance of enquiry toward Dunstan, as if wishing to know whether he had yet broached the subject of Caune, and his slight head-shake, indicating that he had not. I think we all wished that we might have a few moments in which to discuss the best course of action, for the King appeared to be at the point of highest good humour in the seemingly unstoppable swing of his current emotions – and on occasion that was as dangerous as his lowest. However, it felt as though there was a tacit agreement amongst us that we should follow Dunstan's lead. His experience of intrigue and, sadly, treachery was greater than any of ours.

There was a bright fire burning in the withdrawing chamber. The morning was yet chill, though spring was well advanced – someone had arranged a bundle of furry catkins in an earthenware pot and stood it on a table. I could not resist the temptation of stroking the soft, fluffy buds. My mind went back to childhood caresses of the recumbent Musbane's velvety ears – how long ago those simple days at Radendunam seemed. Dunstan's voice brought me back to the present.

"Majesty, there are matters which need your careful consideration. I was reluctant to speak to you of them earlier, but now... now that I know that you are a husband and father, as well as King to your people, I can hesitate no longer, for I know you are sensitive to your responsibilities to both. I know, too, that you are also mindful of how your subjects – and your enemies, for I fear, sire, that you may have some closer than we feared – perceive your actions. But you have gainsaid those who doubted you because of your youth, and now, now you must add the virtues of prudence and patience to those of justice and generosity which you have already demonstrated." Had Dunstan had time to rehearse these words, or did they just flow naturally upon his demand? I thought I could see where he was taking his argument.

"Sire," he continued, "I have learned things from my sources that suggest that there may – I say 'may' not 'will' – be an attempt to disrupt the conclave or, still worst, to threaten your own freedom, perhaps even life, upon the occasion of this moot at Caune."

Edward frowned. "How so? And what sources are these of which you speak?"

"Sire, I sent a young monk to Caune, to check that all was as it should be in the matter of your Majesty's comfort and security... we thought it was strange, you will recall, that the Chief Ealdorman should choose a place for this conciliatory meeting so far from the borders of Mercia. It seems that strangeness is not confined to the ealdorman's decision, the place itself appears to be a hotbed of possible dissent and opposition to your father's line of kingship."

This is clever, I thought. Dunstan is not suggesting outright that Alfhere is plotting against him, merely that he could be ill-judged in his choice of location. And by suggesting disloyalty to Edward's father...

"Why have I not heard of this place before? What causes it to be ill favoured toward Alfred's kinship?" Edward asked, his brows furrowed.

Dunstan recounted the story of the town's ill fortune during the conflict with the Danes and subsequent abandonment, as the townsfolk saw it, to Alfred's victorious dogs of war. He even told how the Church's decision to take unto itself the surviving Danes after a cursory and politic "conversion" to the faith of Christ – spending church monies on elaborate ceremony rather than giving alms to the poor and dispossessed – had poisoned the town against the house of Wessex.

"In a way," Dunstan concluded, "It is a minor miracle that the town has not been more of a thorn in Your Majesty's side. I believe that the Reeve may have approached the Chief Ealdorman offering his fine new Hall for the purposes of this meeting, but with some ulterior motive about which Alfhere knows nothing." It must have stuck in the Archbishop's throat to portray his arch-opponent in the light of innocent dupe, but if it meant that the King would abandon this meeting without feeling that he appeared to be backing down from a head-to-head with those opposing the *Concordia*, then the Chief Ealdorman could wait – he would overstep the mark soon enough, if our suspicions gleaned at Corf were valid.

Edward took a seat alongside the board bearing parchments and other, rougher, documents which required his attention later that day – the day-to-day duties of kingship followed him where ever he happened to be. He put his chin in his hand and rested his elbow on the board. "It is an unhappy state of affairs, either way," he said. "I feel for this town."

"It is unhappy, sire," agreed Dunstan. "I feel for them too, but we cannot take risks with your safety, however much we would that circumstances were different. I suggest that we return immediately to Wintancaestre and send to Alfhere saying that we thank him for his offer of hosting the conclave, but circumstances impel our change of plans. Set a new date for the meeting – at Court – and summon him to attend. Knowing Your Majesty's sense of justice, I have no doubt that you are already planning succour for Caune: the town will rebuild its fortunes, given a little help. My researchers tell me that it was once quite a centre of commerce, when the Legions were still here..."

I began to hope that Dunstan's calm, measured manner, together with his decision to keep Edward in the dark, for the present, regarding Alfhere's possible treachery might yet offer us all an escape route from this precipice. This trip was ever intended as only semi-official and we certainly did not have enough men-at-arms with us to ensure Edward's safety if they were to be tested against a substantial force under the command of Alfhere – even though we could probably outfight the supposed threat from the towns-people of Caune. Better not to put them to the test.

"I don't know..." mused the King. "I am anxious that this matter of the *Concordia* be settled once and for all. I had truly thought the miracle of the speaking Cross had ensured it, but it seems..." He pursed his lips and then brought his fist down on the table top. "No, by the Saints, we will see it through. Now. And once the conclave is over, I will speak to the people of Caune. I will promise them..." Suddenly his face brightened. "But, in the name of Saint Cydd, I have forgotten to tell you the most splendid news of all! I wanted to wait until we were all together, but then all this talk from Dunstan about towns and torment... my dearest friends: my beloved Alfreth is with child once again!"

This sudden change of subject took us all by surprise. My mind had already been racing with the logistics of keeping His Majesty safe with our limited garrison, and I felt sure that as the King spoke Dunstan was weighing the advantages or otherwise of giving him cause to mistrust Alfhere – and perhaps even his stepmother. With so little proof, would he be inclined to belief or anger at the suggestion? And there was still the possibility that he might announce his base marriage, now, presumably, even more likely. How would that impact upon the loyalty of this other Ealdormen?

Aethelflaed rose to the moment. "Darling boy," she said, crossing the room to embrace him. "Your Majesty, that is wonderful news. How fares Alfreth, is she well? Her last pregnancy was a little hard upon her, was it not?"

The rest of us were still silent, still assimilating the news and trying to imagine how it would impact more pressing matters. "Grand-Mutti! You, at least, seem to share my joy!" He glared at Dunstan, whose expression was blank. He looked at me and I essayed to arrange my features into a smile – as sincere as I could manage. "She is, at present, quite well, I thank you. She is anxious, of course…"

"Why, yes, she must be. And this new intelligence will be of great concern to her … although, mayhap she already knows something of Caune, for it is quite local to Sceo, is it not?"

"Now that you mention it, Great-stepmother, she did seem out-of-sorts at the thought of me staying there, but she said nothing – you know how she is, never one to put herself forward when it comes to affairs which are none of her…"

"Come, come." Aetna was the first of us to realise what subtleties the Dowager Queen was working. "No more of that, now! Edward, you are the most fortunate of men, another lovely child with your beloved. We must celebrate! Oh, you men, do not look so dour, congratulate your King!" She kissed him lightly on the cheek. Lucet dropped a pretty curtsey, and Aethelflaed began to prattle on about baby-names – in a manner quite unlike her usual self. After a few minutes, she said, "Well, now we know why you were so determined to be away to Sceo yester-eve, do we not? Of course, you could not wait until today, Alfreth had told you in a letter, had she not? Ah, love between the young, so sweet!" She cast a guarded look at Dunstan. "And now, my sweetling, my King, we will away and leave you to your papers. The sooner you have them read and signed, the sooner you can once again to your love!" Like a mother hen she shooed us all, the Archbishop included, out of the chamber. "I will send your clerk in to you. We will see you at the noon meal, my dear!" and the door closed behind us.

"What… we cannot leave things like this," said Dunstan. "He has made no decision about the conclave, and I fear he was about to make the very one that we so little desired: that it should go ahead as planned, regardless of the still unknown risk factors."

"Can you not see," said Aethelflaed in a low voice, as she ushered us down the walkway toward the door which cut through the body of the building toward her chambers in the Nuns' House. "If we try to change his mind now, he will only become more stubborn. He is not yet twenty summers old. There is still enough of the boy in the man to make him contrary. There is only one who can make him alter his outlook. That one is Alfreth. *She* must convince him that he must not go to the meeting…"

Within a short space of time Aetna had sent to Thella, who was pleased once again to be within the inner circle of my sister's confidence – though her marriage with Ratkin was happy, he had mentioned to me that she had been missing such involvement – and, together with Lucet, the three were on their way to Sceo on fast horses, under the protection of six mounted men-at-arms. Later that evening, as my sister and I sat companionably by the fireside in her chamber, she told me of how they had fared. It had been a long day for both of us with revelations coming thick and fast.

All three women were excellent riders and made good time along the rutted roads to Sceo. The Legions' presence in this part of the country was still much in evidence, not only in their die straight, if now crumbling, roads, but in the shape of stony, outcropped ruins scattering the hinterlands on either side. Aetna had wondered how many of our own dwellings and other buildings might still bear witness to our passing some millennium in the future. The ride took something over an hour – as the men-at-arms insisted, for reasons of security, on bypassing some of the larger villages along the way. The Dowager Queen had advised the party make their progress as inconspicuous as possible. They crossed the Duncombe Brook and trotted the last half mile or so into Sceo at a pace which allowed conversation.

"Remember," said Aetna, "we do not want to distress Alfreth unduly, but we must impress upon her that we believe Edward may be in real danger if he attends the meeting. She is no fool and deep as her love for the King is, she knows that he can be unpredictable – and stubborn, too. But if we convince her, then I think she will be our best ally."

At the crossroads, by the one-time simple village well and pump, now the focus of much pilgrimage, they turned right toward to Inn. Several fine horses were tied up outside its doors. The time of the midday meal was approaching and there was conversation and laughter to be heard within. Two of the men-at-arms accompanied the women into the bar-room in case they might attract unwelcome attention, but there was none. Instead, Garreth, behind the bar and beaming with recognition, welcomed them warmly.

"Lady Aetna… and your lovely companions! What a pleasure! I had thought that perhaps we might expect a visit from you when… Ned… appeared so unexpectedly last eve. You seek Alfreth, I expect? She is at the bakery today. But will you not take a sup and a bite here before you go to her?" The smell of rich stew mingled with ale was overwhelmingly tempting, but Aetna declined.

"I thank you, Garreth, but mayhap later, before our return to Bathe – no, we shall not be spending the night," for she could tell that he was about to offer the hospitality of the house. "We shall to the bakehouse now. But our men may take their ease with you."

The bakery was but a few short steps from the inn. The arrival of our party could hardly be unnoticed in such a small community and already Hilde, wiping flour from her hands upon an apron, was making her way out through the doorway, a smile of welcome on her face.

"Why, it is… Alfreth, my love, come quickly! It is your friends. My, but we are having an abundance of visitors! Ned last eve and the ladies today! Come ye in, come in!"

From the living quarters at the rear of the bakehouse we heard voices, a soft cooing and the lilt of a quiet song, and Alfreth appeared, little Effie in her arms. "Lady! How wonderful to see you, Edw— Ned… said that you were all together, but I hardly hoped to see you so soon! Why, he can hardly have been back in Bathe but an hour or so before you left, for I fear he was quite the slug-a-bed this morning. My Effie has a fine pair of lungs and once she is awake, I fear there are none in the house than can sleep." She gave the little girl a playful toss and cuddled her to her breast. "Can they, my sweetling?" Effie gurgled as though in agreement and smiled showing a row of tiny, perfect, milk white teeth. She truly was an enchanting child. "Hilde, my dear, I know we are busy, but could you possibly find some food and drink for our friends – and come sit with us, too?"

"Food and drink I can bring, and that fair soon," said the older woman. "But sit I cannot, for I have a big order to complete. But take ye your ease, hen, for you looked right pale this morn, and I know the sickness has been upon you. If you can keep an eye on Mistress Effie there, then I shall about my baking as soon as I have brought the victuals."

The bakery's living chamber was cosy and well appointed. Whilst modest and unassuming, it was clear that everything was of the best. It could be assumed, by those not privy to the household's circumstances, that the bakehouse was simply doing fine and prosperous business, but even so, there was a well-to-do ambience which seemed a little less than likely in such apparently mundane surroundings. Alfreth could see that Aetna and the others were admiring some of the furnishings. "My… husband… is most generous, as you can see," she said. "Pray, sit, ladies." In this egalitarian home, there was no distinction between Lady and servant.

"Alfreth, you look well," said my sister. "And I hear that congratulations are once more due to you and… Ned." It seemed that Alfreth tried to maintain the use of the King's soubriquet even in the home, in case otherwise his real identity slipped out. Aetna followed suit.

"He is as thrilled as last time! He could not forebear to tell us all this morning almost as soon as he returned to the abbey."

"Aye, when I gave him the news last eve he was as giddy as a goat!" laughed Alfreth, and Effie joined in, sensing the happiness.

Hilde brought in some warm bread, straight from the ovens, slightly steaming in the basket. She set it down with golden butter, honey and cheese in which dark berries glistened.

"Chopped damsons," said Alfreth, as Aetna eyed the cheese. "They make the cheese sweeter and that seems to be my craving this time round. Alas for my figure." She did not seem to be showing and was yet as lissom as she had looked at Court. There was small ale in an earthenware jug and Alfreth poured some for each of them. Aetna drank thirstily for it had been a hard ride. She racked her brain for small-talk but it was elusive. Finally, she decided that the reason for their urgent visit had to be broached without further delay.

"Alfreth," she said, "it is, of course, a joy to see you and little Effie," she smiled at the child. "But I am afraid that we have another motive for seeking you out… and… the Ki – Ned – does not know that we are here. I know that your conscience will pain you for this small deception, but I pray that you will keep our confidence in this. I promise you that it is for his own protection."

Alfreth looked worried and set Effie down upon the floor to play upon her blankets. Unconcerned, the little girl picked up a silver rattle and sucked upon it. "What is the matter?" asked her mother. "Is Edward in some danger? He said nothing." The use of the King's given name was evidence of her concern.

My sister and I had had but little time to discuss how much we should tell Alfreth, but had come to the decision that if we were to rely upon her influence in this matter then we had to take her fully into our confidence. Quickly, and without trying to alarm her too much – though, Heaven knows, when taken together the circumstantial evidence against Queen Elfrith and the Chief Ealdorman seemed damning – she explained our fears, both those which had arisen at Corf and later. She outlined the strange events taking place at Caune, the inexplicable expense, in a town crippled by ill-fortune, of rebuilding an elaborate meeting-house and Alfhere's unexpected volte-face since his attack on the monasteries. Finally, Aetna mentioned my own idea: that mayhap it was the Chief Ealdorman's plan to kidnap the King and possibly hold him prisoner until he revised or even nullified the terms of the *Concordia*.

Alfreth's eyes grew wide as Aetna spoke. "And does the Archbishop know of this?" she asked.

"He does."

Then Thella laid her hand upon Alfreth's. "My dear, he knows, too, of your marriage. And he has made no objection. I believe that he is content – if maybe not yet happy – that His Majesty has found a true and loving soul to be his wife." Aetna cursed herself silently for forgetting to say something of the sort herself. But then the thought crossed her mind that perhaps only a married woman would think to reassure another on such an issue.

"Is it all true?" asked Alfreth, her eyes full of tears.

"Yes, Alfreth, it is." My sister looked deep into those tearful eyes and saw a quiet but desperate hope for a happy future suddenly seem to be in deep jeopardy. "And that is why we have come to you. You can help the King now, more than any of us, I believe."

"How so?"

"We have told the King of the possible dangers but he is determined to face Alfhere down at Caune. He fears that if he does not attend the conclave then he will be seen as weak and afraid to stand against him. We have not shared with him the concerns which arise from the rumours at Corf, for we do not know how he would react – his moods are unstable at present, and the comfort he has gained from growing closeness to Ethelred might be jeopardized. Family is becoming so important to him. That is why we want you to bring your influence to bear. If necessary, beg him to remain with you and let Dunstan go to the meeting in his place. He will stay away if he thinks it is important to you."

"Thinks? By St. Mary, it *is* important to me! But I do not believe you know him as well as you think. He will not allow himself to seem weak simply to allay my whims of fear."

Aetna took Alfreth's hands in hers. "Alfreth, you *must* convince him. He means to come to you again on the morrow – and the day after is that of the conclave. Time is too short to summon enough men-at-arms to do battle, for this was ever meant as an informal meeting and we did not bring enough from Wintancaestre. Who knows what plan the Chief Ealdorman has devised – and Edward is determined to walk straight into it?"

"Very well, I will do my best," Alfreth said unhappily. "But I fear we are dabbling in deceit and it will come to no good."

"There is one more thing, my dear," Aetna said. This, she knew, would cut deep. "Edward has a notion to announce your marriage, and the existence of the princess – and mayhap a new Prince." Alfreth smiled at that, and raised Effie onto her lap.

"Yes, he mentioned as much," she said. "It will be good to be able to be open about that, at least."

"Alfreth, you cannot let him!"

"What? Why not? He is the king; he has a right to marry where he wishes. He cannot be considered the child he once was, surely, he has proven that in these last two years. No, he has promised himself – and me – that he would confirm me his true wife and Queen. And our children his rightful heirs!" Her voice was becoming shrill and Aetna was afraid that the baker-wife would come to see what was amiss.

"Peace, girl! Calm yourself!"

"Do not address me thus! You forget who I now am! The King shall hear of this!" My sister could feel the situation slipping out of control. Alfreth had never before wielded her position, albeit secret, before anyone by way of asserting her standing. Little Effie sensed the tension and began to cry. Aetna was desperate.

"My apologies, Lady … Your Majesty … I am sorry. You are right, you are the King's true wife and have every right to receive the honour due to your status. The time is surely not far off when you will be hailed as Queen, but Edward must first weather this storm raging around the *Concordia* and how it is being used to undermine him. Everything is tangled up with it – his authority, the threat from the Chief Ealdorman, Elfrith's plotting – for she wants Ethelred on the throne and will stop at nothing to bring his brother down! I am sorry to say this, Alfreth, but if news of his marriage to you were to become common knowledge now… it might be enough to end his Kingship. It would label him the impulsive youth his father at one time believed him to be. Opinion would swing toward Ethelred."

Alfreth rose to her feet, still holding Effie. She walked into the middle of the chamber, her chin resting on the child's head. Finally, she gave a little sigh of resignation. She turned and faced the three women.

"Very well," she said at last. "You may tell the Archbishop that I will do my best to keep the King away from the conclave. But I will not lie to him. And I will tell him that I would rather he continue to keep our marriage a secret until after the new baby is born. That will be sometime near the Christ's Mass. I think he will agree to that. Have him bring Wulf with him when he comes to me on the morrow. I will arrange matters from then on. I cannot say that I am sure we are doing the right thing, but I will trust you. And you must trust me… Edward and Wulf alone. The rest of you stay at Bathe and prepare for the conclave as if all is to proceed as planned."

There was a hard edge to her voice which Aetna did not recognise. By being drawn into this intrigue Alfreth was beginning to lose her old self.

)))))))((((((

When they returned to Bathe, Aetna immediately sought me out. Edward and I had been to the ancient Roman Bathes and he was in a fine humour. He had completed his paperwork by the time of the midday meal (or, at least, put his signature to that which needed it, leaving the rest to his clerk) and we had spent the postnoon taking our ease in the warm spring waters. Now he was in the company of his step-grandmother and the Abbess being shown the fine stonework and wooden carvings which Aethelflaed had commissioned to enhance the Nunnery church. Lucet and Thella went about their business – they needed no reminder to keep silent about the day's events – and Aetna drew me into her chamber, where we would be unlikely to be disturbed.

"Wulf, I do not like this: Alfreth is unhappy with the idea of using her influence to keep Edward away from the conclave and she is becoming increasingly impatient with her situation as the 'secret' Queen. I almost forgot that she is younger, even, than the King, and her emotions still less mature than his. And now with this new pregnancy, they are ebbing and flowing with the whims of her body."

"Did she refuse to help, then?" I asked.

"No, I managed to convince her, I think. At the least she will tell Edward that she would prefer to keep news of their alliance quiet until after the new babe is born. And she will try – though I fear her heart is not in it, for she does not agree that it is necessary – to persuade him not to attend the conclave. I do not fully understand her thoughts, but she says that you, and you alone, are to accompany Edward to Sceo on the morrow, and that the Archbishop must continue with preparations for the conclave as though it were to go ahead."

"What? How can that work? If the conclave is to go ahead, Dunstan has plans for us all to leave on a Progress tomorrow, ride through Sceo at some time around midday where he will meet 'the young woman from the bakery' at the Shoe Tavern (apparently he says Edward is keen to show her off), they will then move on to Chepeham where the King is to be entertained by the Reeve, leaving for Caune the next morning and, pray God all being well, return to Chepeham that night. If the King cannot be prevented from attending, then at least his presence will be well advertised, and any treachery planned against him seen for what it is – treason."

"I don't know how it can be made to work," said Aetna. "But somehow it must, for it is the only hope we have of getting Alfreth to influence the King. She would have no opportunity to be intimate with him during a Progress. He would be lucky to snatch a private moment with her. That was the whole plan of returning to Chepeham after the conclave: he could once again slip away to his love during the night afterward. However, now, you must somehow convince him – it will surely not be hard – to go to her tonight. Tell him of my visit to her today and that she is anxious to see him. He will not take much persuading. Tell him that I will explain to Dunstan and..." I could see her mind working. "Yes, I have it!" she cried. "The King will complain of a return of the agonizing foot ailment which formerly afflicted him. He will appear to travel in a covered wagon, in such pain that he will not allow himself to be seen. He will privately visit the shrine at Sceo, in the hope of another miracle. But he will actually already be at the shrine. Then, if Alfreth has managed to convince him of the dangers, he can sadly, but resignedly, announce that the conclave must be postponed on account of his illness. And, God forbid, if she cannot convince him... he will be miraculously be cured, and continue on his journey to Caune. Either way, no-one will be any the wiser, or know that he spent the night before the Progress at Sceo."

"Sister," I said, "I am, as ever, amazed by your capacity to weave such intricate, duplicitous and yet believable masterpieces! No wonder your embroidery is the talk of the nunnery!"

"Is it?"

"I have no idea!"

"Oh, Wulf, this is serious. More than serious, it could be a matter of life and death – or kidnap and ransom at the very least."

"Well," I said, "I had better go and find 'Ned' and tell him that his wife will not be gainsaid and that he must attend upon her this evening. Should I use her condition, as leverage? Her expectant condition?"

"For Heaven's sake, Wulf, I know what condition you mean! Honestly! And no, do not tempt the fates by using that as an excuse. Women face enough danger in carrying and delivering their babes safely without... no, rather say that she told me how much it meant to her seeing him last eve and that she cannot bear to think of him so near and yet so far from her when she could be in his arms – you know the kind of thing, I am sure you have swayed enough young girls with such foolish, pretty words of love. You can even make out that part of the plan to smuggle him to her was hers and that Dunstan, the old romantic, is willing to play along. Then you and the King can leave tonight as soon as it becomes dark and be with her by the time we are sitting down to the evening meal here, which, incidentally he will appear to miss, confined to his pallet with his sore foot."

"I suppose it could work," I replied. "And we really have no other choice. Very well. With luck both the King and the Archbishop will be in the nunnery with the Abbess and our aunt. I will take Edward back to our chambers and tell him Alfreth wants him and you can take Aunt Aethelflaed and Dunstan into our confidence – they will need a little time to make arrangements for the covered waggon and to work out how to keep his absence unnoticed."

A plan, of sorts, was made.

)))))))(((((((

Leaving the rest of our small Court at Bathe, and hoping that we would successfully meet up with them again on the morrow, Edward and I stole quietly out of a back entrance to the Hall and around to the stable block, where Ratkin awaited us. The King's horse had been fed, watered and saddled ready for the ride, as had mine. On good, strong mounts, the journey should not take longer than something over an hour. I had been careful not to make Alfreth's request sound as though she was is distress, but rather, as Aetna had suggested, appeal to his love-lonely heart: he was rarely enough in the position to spend time with her that it seemed almost ungrateful not to make the most of every moment. As my sister had anticipated, he did not take much convincing.

We made good time. As we clattered the last furlong into Sceo, we could smell the aroma of hot food from the tavern, as well as from the cooking fires of pilgrims camped out along the road. The night was fair, warm for the time of year and the stars already bright. No-one paid much attention to two young men arriving at a popular destination, and making their way toward the bakery. If anyone had noticed us, they probably thought we were trying our hand at buying a stale loaf, so late in the day, at a knock-down price. We had not dressed as though we had any money to spare.

The door to the bakehouse was slightly ajar, Hilde, her arms covered with flour up to the elbow was kneading dough for the next morning's bake, dozens of loaves already proving on one side, close to the warmth of the fire. It was warm to the point of unpleasantness, but, so used was she to the conditions that she was quite happy and singing a cheerful ditty as she went about her work.

Edward knocked lightly at the door and walked in. Hilde cast a glance over her shoulder and then let out a little cry of delight.

"Why! Ned, I do declare. Twice in as many days. Alfreth will be so pleased. She is taking her ease at the back of the house, for she has been feeling a little queasy ever since your ladies left earlier. She does not complain, bless her, and would carry on helping me – and Garreth at the Shoe – if we let her, but we neither of us can bear to see the poor child looking so wan. Effie is already abed, but go ye through, go through!"

After all these months of pretence, "Ned" knew his way around the bakery well, and we passed through the steamily warm kitchens into the chamber at the rear as though it was his home from home, which, I reflected, it was in some ways.

Effie was fast asleep upon a child-sized pallet in a small cubby to one side, the curtain which would hide it from the main room when drawn, held back by a tasselled cord to allow Alfreth to watch the little girl sleep. Alongside it was a pallet, its palliasse neatly rolled and stowed at one end, allowing its use as a bench when not needed for its primary function.

Alfreth herself sat beside a small table bearing her sewing accessories, working, by the light of a fine candle, upon a tiny smock – too small, already, for Effie – clearly designed for the new babe. The intricate nature of its working bore witness to the fact that this was not a practical item of baby-wear, but rather a gown for an infant born to greater things than the need for hard-wearing hand-me-downs. She turned at our entrance and smiled over her shoulder.

"Neddy, my love, you came!"

"When Aetna told me how much it would mean to you, I… we…" he slapped me on the back, "came up with a plan which will fool everyone into believing that the interminable malady of my foot, which plagued me before, has caused me to travel privately tomorrow. Then, why, the Shrine will once again work its holy magic, my pain will leave me and I may journey on to Chepeham and Caune, healed and in excellent shape to kick the Chief Ealdorman's backside – and back to his senses. But let affairs of state not worry you, my love, let us enjoy this time we shall have together, as you so desired." He embraced her fondly and over his shoulder she cast a look at me… it was part rebuke that I should ask her to use his affection against him, even if in his own best interests, and party a supplication that I should keep him safe.

"Your Majesties," I said, "I shall away to the Shoe and leave you to your privacy!" Inwardly, I winced, hoping I had not spoken too loudly, but I could still hear Hilde singing and slapping the dough next-door, so reassured myself that she could have heard nothing amiss.

"Thank you, Wulf, I will not need you again this night." Edward sat down on the chair vacated by Alfreth and pulled her down upon his knee. "I bid you a good night."

"And you, sire. Your Majesty." This last I meant for Alfreth, who smiled sweetly. I gave a short bow and returned to the bake-room.

"Ah, Lord Wulf, will you not take a sup with me afore ye away to the joys of the tavern?" asked Hilde with a grin. "Do ye not recall that my mead is the finest in all Wessex, the Shoe's not excepted. That great lunk, Garreth," she said it with affection, "will one day wear out his tongue asking for my receipt! He may have the mead – and at a fair price, for he is a fine man – but not the makings. Not until I am in my grave at any rate!" She laughed a deep, earthy laugh, eyes sparkling. I thought, mayhap, she had already had a tumbler of her mead that night.

"I will that, Goody Hilde," I said, "and right happily."

Her hands were now clean of flour – for the dough had formed up clean and unbroken into a large rounded mound, set to one side with all the others to prove. Those which she had made earliest in the evening were already swelling beneath their muslin cloths, each a little larger than its neighbour, the newest still to begin the process.

Hilde bade me sit on a bench beside the table and slapped a tumbler on the table beside me. I took a long sup and licked my lips appreciatively. I look around the room.

"You have a fine business here, Goody," I said. "And if you ever gave up baking, you could give some brewers a run for their money. I'll grant you that."

She laughed again. "Aye, I am sorry to say it, but since my husband died, the business has come to life. It is hard to make a good living when someone drinks away all the profit. But there are times I miss him... not many, but some!"

Alfreth had told Aetna in one of her long letters of the old baker's demise. From what Alfreth had said of him – and the part he played in the story of her escape from the nunnery and flight to Aethelflaed – I recalled that he had seemed to be more hindrance than help to Hilde in her battle to make a success of the bakery. "I was sorry to hear of his death," I said.

The subject seemed closed. We sat in companionable silence for a while, sipping our mead and listening to the low singing of the water boiling in a pan on the fire. We could hear Alfreth and Edward's voices low in the next room – just the rise and fall of conversation, whatever the words, we could not hear them.

"That is what I miss," said Hilde. "Someone to chatter to about the day's events. In recent years the old fool was no company like that – too eager to be away to some tavern, or some doxy – but once upon a time... aye, we had some good days. Some happy days. I hope those two in there will be able to have some years together like that. Just simple days and nights passing as quickly as leaves blowing in a warm wind. We had whole years of days like that, if you asked me now to remember single events I couldn't, they were just days, contented, peaceful, ordinary days. But together they became something special. Yes, I hope they find their quiet times. Together."

I almost wondered if she was able to read my mind, for I had been pondering the unlikeliness of such a future for them. Then, almost like a charm, her words seemed to rise up against my gloomy thoughts and do battle with them. Would that her magic could overcome. It is sometimes said that those who work with yeast, that miraculous agent, can do such things.

The warmth of the kitchen, the long day and my lack of sleep the previous night, together with the pleasant effects of the mead made my head begin to nod. I shifted my boots on the flags of the floor and wished that I could take them off, but I still had to walk down to the Shoe to find my bed for the night. Eventually, my chin fell forward onto my chest, and I jerked my head upward violently in an effort to stay awake.

"Lad, it looks as though ye have had a long day," said Hilde. "Why do ye not bide here the night? Those two," she nodded toward the door, "will want for nothing more, I'll be bound, and I am away to my pallet. Stay here by the fire. Ye're welcome."

"I am grateful, Goody," I said, and pulled the boots off, stretching my feet before the oven.

"I will bid ye a good night, then," she said, slipping out of the front door. I heard her footfall for just a couple of steps, to the door of the cottage alongside the bakehouse and then the catch open and close. I pushed the bench up against the wall, that I had only one side from which I might tumble to the floor as I slept, pulled my cloak over by body and began to drift away into sleep. The last thought I remember before I fell into what seemed a dreamless slumber was that this was the very fire before which Alfreth had spent her first night as a girl free from the convent. So much had happened to her since. I began to say my night prayers, but before I could finish them, I slept.

)))))))(((((

I slept well and deep until just after dawn. As I awoke, I heard Alfreth's voice and, vaguely remembering my thoughts of the night before, believed that I was in some lingering dream, so rarely had I heard it raised in anger – though from what Aetna had said, Alfreth's temper was not as mild as it had once been. I had not heard the words which had prompted her reply, but they were not hard to guess.

"Demanding? How can you say that I am demanding? When have I ever asked anything of you for myself? Or even our child? I only ask that, now that you are here with us, you stay a little, and not leave again straightway for another meeting. Tell the Archbishop he may take the conclave himself. Have you not spent enough time on this matter?"

The King's voice was also loud and, in truth, belligerent. "Woman, have I not told you that if I do not attend this conclave, I will look weak before my Ealdormen? The Lord knows what moved Alfhere to make these amends and arrange this, but I must meet him half way. I cannot afford to insult him, he is too influential… and that is without mentioning that if I fail to arrive questions will be asked… and you have already made it clear that you do not wish our alliance to yet be made public – and in doing so thwarted my dearest wish: to openly declare you my Queen. Which, by all the Saints, I would have thought you wanted, too!"

It was clearly with some effort that Alfreth took a more conciliatory tone. "I do, my love, I do! But last eve you agreed how wonderful it would be to have a spring ceremony, with all the blessings of Easter-tide, to celebrate the announcement of our alliance. Mayhap even with a prince in your arms to consolidate your succession. Do you not remember?"

"Yes, yes, I do. And it would… it will. But do not ask me again to forego this day's events. I cannot. Let it lie."

"Of course, my love. I am sorry."

"And so am I." Edward sounded as if he was. But, clearly, he could not be swayed. I resigned myself to whatever this day might bring. Not wanting to surprise them with my presence in the next room, I purposely made a noise by rattling the fire irons, and throwing some wood into the grate. The main ovens, already fuelled by Hilde from her adjoining cottage, were throwing an ambient heat throughout the room.

I was shaking the creases out of my cloak and fastening the cross garters over my britches when Hilde tapped on the door and, without waiting for a response, entered. "The baking waits for no man – or woman," she said briskly. "How did ye sleep?"

"Well, thank you, Goody, very well," I said.

With a skill born of many year's practice, Hilde upturned the swollen, proved loaves of unbaked dough, placed them in the oven and pushed them back with a pole to allow more to be added and, repeating the process, filled the oven. "Nothing to do now, but wait on the cooking," she said. "And break our fasts."

We heard the latch lift on the door into the private room, and Alfreth, Effie on her hip, came in. "I bid you a good morn, Hilde," she said and then, seeing me, "Why, Wulf, you are about the morning early! I thought you might make a late night of it with Garreth at the Shoe."

"I confess, Lady," I said, "yester was a tiring day. My eyelids were drooping once Goody Hilde had favoured me with a mug of her mead, and then she took pity on me… I slept here before the fire."

Alfreth glanced uncertainly toward the back room, clearly a little concerned lest I had heard the earlier argument. "Oh, er, I hope…"

"And I hardly stirred until she came to fill the ovens," I added, crossing my fingers beneath my cloak to ward off ill luck attracted by my – however white – lie.

"Well, lass, how fare ye this morning," asked Hilde. "Is the rising sickness upon ye?"

"Not too badly, I thank you. I think I could manage a little porridge, with lots of honey."

"Ay, 'twill be a boy, mark my words. It is ever a boy when the mother develops a sweet tooth!" As she spoke, Edward entered, fastening his cloak with a great circular brooch of amber set in twists of silver. He fumbled with the pin which had to pass inside the circle, pick up two layers of the cloak, then re-emerge inside the opposite curve and stay firm against the silver, securing the cloak around his shoulders.

506

"And a fine boy, too," he said. "We shall call him Alfred after the great King of the last century and Edgar after my father, shall we not, my love?"

"As you say, dearest." Alfreth seemed a little subdued.

If Dunstan and the supposed Royal Progress had left Bathe on schedule, the plan was that they would arrive in Sceo at around midday. I slipped out to acquaint Garreth with our plan – he of all men could be trusted and would understand the clandestine rendezvous of the previous night. After all, he had been an integral part of this "secret" since the very beginning. As I entered the taproom of the Shoe, he greeted me warmly.

"Lord Wulf, a pleasure, as always, but am I amiss in my remembering? Was I expecting His... Ned this day?" He looked quizzically at the door, as if expecting him to enter.

"No, no, Garreth, you were not..." I quickly filled him in on how we hoped the events of the next few hours would pan out. "Garreth," I added, having thought long and hard about whether I should involve him in the under-plan, "there is another twist in this convoluted pattern." Trying not to sound as though I was disappointed at the King's decision, I explained how we had wanted Alfreth to remind Edward of his choices. "But," I concluded, "it seems as though His Majesty – whoops! Ned! – has his heart and mind set on facing up to whatever those who may be plotting against him may have planned."

"Well," said Garreth, "he has another strong right arm in me! It is a long time since I have hefted my sword, but I was ever skilled with it... that is why I was chosen as bodyguard to Ally – Lady Alfreth, I mean. I will not see her heart broken by the loss of the man she loves. When the Progress leaves for Chepeham – and Caune – I will be with it!" There was something in his eyes and in the way he spoke of Alfreth that made me think there was more to his protection of her than earning his wages, however generous the King had made them.

The morning was wearing away toward noon as I took the short walk back to the Bakery, passing the well, newly equipped with a simple pump, and the attendant shrine to Saints Crispin and Crispinian, a small wooden building, containing little more than a stone basin (always topped up from the spring) and an altar. I smiled at the pilgrims as they dipped their kerchiefs and rags into the holy water, binding them around their feet or toes. Some mumbled quiet prayers of supplication, some shouted of the Saints' mercy and to the glory of the Lord. Whatever makes them feel as though the miracle is more likely to happen, I thought, and sent up a brief prayer of thanksgiving for my own, and Aetna's, good health for we are all, ever, in the hands of the Lord.

The plan was for Edward to don a rough cloak and make his way unnoticed to the shrine, which would then be closed to the public for the arrival of the King. The covered wagon would back up to the entrance,

507

supposedly allowing its passenger to disembark and enter the chapel in privacy, there to pray for deliverance from his pain. "Ned" would then, after a suitable interval, climb into the waggon and it would leave, no doubt disappointing those who had got wind of what was purported to be happening and hoped for a sight of the King. We could not risk his alter-ego being recognised, but to mollify any bystanders who might be overly curious, a generous number of pennies and fourthings would be scattered by the royal hand.

It was nearing the time when we might expect the arrival of the Progress, so I went straight to the bakery to see that Edward was ready to slip over to the shrine. As I entered, he was wrapping the nondescript cloak over the better clothes he habitually wore as Ned. Within the waggon would be the royal robes he would need for the conclave. Effie was cooing in her basket on the bench, and Alfreth stood behind the King, as though about to help him as he struggled with the unfamiliar, rough fabric.

"... well if you *will* not stay with us," she was saying. There was a slightly wheedling tone to her voice.

"For the love of God, woman," Edward shouted. "How many times do I have to tell you..."

What happened next was over in seconds, but seemed to me to take on a dream-like quality which lasted an age. Edward spun around, clearly angry and ready to remonstrate with Alfreth, but still struggling with his cloak. She was standing closer to him than he had expected and his elbow caught her a glancing blow on the shoulder, making her take a step backward to try and avoid it. The back of her knee came up against the low stool where she habitually sat at her sewing and she fell, awkwardly and to one side, her head catching the edge of the table, which rocked violently enough to send a flagon of milk to the ground, where it smashed. Slightly stunned, Alfreth could not save herself from the rest of the fall and landed heavily on the floor at her husband's feet.

"Alfreth, oh, sweet Jesus, Alfreth! I am so sorry!" Edward cried.

She shook her head quickly as if to clear her sight. "It is nothing, my love, nothing. Not your fault..." She began to get to her feet and then sank down again. "Oh, oh, perhaps... Ah! Please, fetch Hilde. I think something..."

Before she could finish speaking, I was through the door and to the adjoining cottage. I opened the door without knocking and Hilde was already on her feet, throwing her shawl around her shoulders. "What is amiss? It sounds as though someone is breaking my pottery in there..." and then, seeing the consternation on my face, "... or it is something worse?"

"Alfreth... needs you," I managed to say as she pushed past me and ran the few steps which took her to the next door. I was but a moment behind her.

When we entered the stool had been righted and Alfreth sat upon it, bent over as though in pain, her hands clenched over her belly. She looked up, eyes wet with tears. There was a red weal over her brow, but it was the obvious agony in her body that filled me with dread.

Edward was on his knees at her side. "What can I do? What can I do?" He clasped at her hands where they were held tight over her still flat stomach. "Alfreth?"

Hilde jostled him to one side. "It looks as though ye have done quite enough!" she said, taking in his look of traumatized guilt, the broken pottery and spilt milk. "Away with ye! Both of ye! This is women's business." Little Effie, sensing her mother's pain and distress began to cry. "If ye want to be useful, go find a lass to look after the wee one," she added.

"I'll take her," said Edward, lifting the grizzling child from her blankets and holding her to him. "Come, sweetling, your Mama is not well... where?"

"Go ye into my cottage," said the goodwife. "I must get Alfreth to her pallet." Taking one of Alfreth's arms around her shoulder she helped her to her feet and toward the bed. Alfreth managed a weak smile toward her husband. "I will be alright," she said, though whether to comfort him, or herself, I could not tell.

Effie did not want to be parted from her mother and cried loudly as we left. Edward jiggled her in his arms and cuddled her to try and quiet her, but it did not seem to have any effect. He looked distracted. "Wulf," he said, "if anything happens... to the child... my own mother died losing a baby..."

"Sire, that was very different," I said, not really knowing if it was. As Hilde had said, this was women's business. "But we must find a girl to care for Effie... for the Progress will be here soon, and you must be ready..."

"But I cannot go now!" cried Edward. "How can I leave like this? No, no, I must stay with Alfreth. Oh, God, if only I had listened to her and decided not to go in the first place this would not have happened. I suppose you..." I had a terrible feeling I knew what he was going to say. "I suppose you are pleased this has happened. It plays out just as you wanted. You and Dunstan never wanted me to go, did you?"

"Your Majesty, that is a dreadful thing to say. I love Alfreth as a sister, I would never have wished..."

"No, no, of course not! Forgive me, it is my own guilt speaking. But, now, you must go to the Conclave. Be my eyes and ears. I know Dunstan will argue the case for the *Concordia* well – he ever has – but what the Chief Ealdorman has up his sleeve is anyone's guess. Go you now to the shrine and wait for them. Explain to Dunstan, tell him I will not – cannot – leave Alfreth, but tell him that I had wished to be there, and that you are charged with telling me all that is said and done. There are times when I am not even sure of the Archbishop – oh, I know he is loyal, but I think sometimes he thinks of me as yet a child to be led by the harness. I do not know that he tells me everything."

I felt a stab of guilt myself at that last remark, for I, too, fell within that category. But we had tried to make this work out well ... how could we have foreseen the tragedy which might be unfolding?

"Sire, I will do as you bid... God willing, all will be well here, but I will explain to Dunstan what has happened, and to the rest of the Conclave you will be suffering the agonies of the affliction which so assaulted you before. Do not be afeared, you will not appear to be absent of your own will, but by the will of..."

"Do not say it, Wulf. I fear that the will of God has nothing to do with what has fallen out this day. Oh, by all the Saints, do not let me lose her! She is my all, my only love!"

The King had pulled the remnants of his disguise from him and they lay in a heap upon the floor. Quickly, I assumed the persona of the nondescript pilgrim and made for the door.

"You are sure, sire? You will not come?"

"I am sure, Wulf, but tell me all the befalls. Every detail."

I slipped out of the door and, hugging the cottage walls, made toward the shrine.

I could only hope that I had managed to reach it without being seen. Somehow, as often befalls in a crowd, a communal awareness had arisen that something was about to happen. All eyes were upon the road from Bathe, and within moments the clatter of hooves, the rumble of heavy wheels upon rough flags and the measured footfall of men-at-arms could be heard. From beyond the bend in the road the vanguard appeared, followed by the standard bearers, and then the covered wagon which supposedly bore the King of all Englaland. Behind the wagon, Archbishop Dunstan rode, as ever upon a fine horse, his own accoutrements only slightly less splendid than might be expected for royalty, and behind him (did my eyes deceive me?) Aetna and Lucet. How, why, had they essayed to become part of this *pantomimus*?

The crowd being distracted, I had slipped into the shrine. I slumped against the wall. What could I do but await events? I heard the waggon being manoeuvred up to the door of the shrine. The leather suspension creaked and then, dressed in rich colours which were all that might be glimpsed and therefore attested from a distance, Ratkin strode into the holy space. Ratkin, of all unholy souls! We took one look at each other and – God forgive us – fell into a fit of inappropriate, uncontrollable laughter as stress gave way to relief and relief to hysteria.

"By all the Saints," I gasped, "you?"

"I could say the same!" came the reply. Gradually, sanity prevailed.

"Ratkin, this is not falling out as we would wish…"

"The King has not agreed to stay behind? Then where is he?"

"He is staying behind, but not of his own wish." I told him briefly of what had happened – what he feared, and that he would not, now, leave Alfreth's side. "But he has charged me, upon my honour, to bear witness to the conclave and report to him what transpires. He fears…"

I had been about to share something of Edward's forebodings with Ratkin, when the Archbishop strode in, allowing the curtain to fall back into place as he entered, and the door to bang shut behind it. Whatever he was about to discover, he did not want it shared with those waiting outside. There were already too many privy to this deception. "So, the King is not here, good…"

Once again, I had to recount the events of the morning. Dunstan, I could tell, was torn between relief that Edward was not still insisting on attending the meeting and regret at Alfreth's plight. Like me, he was not wholly blameless for the way things had transpired. "But," I said at last, "why is Aetna here?"

"She has been worried since yester-day that she had pushed Alfreth too far, in asking her to press the King to abandon his plans," replied Ratkin. "She will be devastated at what is happening – but it is well she is here. She…"

"Enough of this gossip," snapped Dunstan. "What are we, washer-wives? The plan is still intact. Come you, then, Wulf, if you must, into the waggon. We shall away to Chepeham and then on to… hurry, man! Ratkin get ready to throw more coins to the crowd, and make sure that neither of you are seen." He swept out and we heard him address those waiting outside.

"… Sons, daughters, I am honoured to tell you that the Saints have this day worked another miracle. The pain which has been assailing our King is greatly abated, but His Majesty is still weak from the affliction and cannot appear before you. He is, however, well enough to journey on and gives you his blessing – and coin!" The waggon rumbled out and Ratkin scattered a handful of coins in its wake. "In the name of the Holy Trinity and the Saints Crispin and Crispinian, go in faith this day, and serve the Lord." The Archbishop manoeuvred his horse into the Progress, behind the "King's" waggon and we trundled out of the village, I assumed without Aetna and Lucet, who had surely gone to find Alfreth – to be confronted by – what? It would be some time before I heard that news.

We spent the night at Chepeham in the relative comfort of the Reeve's Hall. Upon our arrival, Ratkin, still splendidly attired, had been ushered into the chambers prepared for the King, his head down, and supported by me and one of the men-of-arms – I only realised it was Garreth, as he bent low to take Ratkin under one shoulder – making great show of being in pain from his foot. I thought, wryly, that this whole masquerade would do the shrine at Sceo no favours: first apparently cured, only for the ailment to return, with a greater vengeance, before the postnoon was over. But that was the least of our worries.

To the great disappointment of the Reeve, it was given out that the King's affliction was too severe for him to see anyone, still less attend the banquet planned for his entertainment. Food was to be sent to his chamber, where he would be attended by myself and Garreth. Only the Archbishop would be admitted to his presence. The following morning it was announced that he would not be travelling on to Caune, and that the Archbishop would take his place. King Edward was to remain in his chambers, undisturbed. We hoped that by delaying the announcement until the morning of the conclave that news of his absence would not reach Caune ahead of us, and for that reason had made haste to get on the road early. Whatever plan the Chief Ealdorman had put in place, we wanted it to go ahead as intended – at least as long as was needed for us to ascertain what it was and, if possible, exactly who was involved.

We clattered into Caune about the middle of the morning, knowing that the conclave was due to begin at midday. Dunstan looked splendid. Riding astride his favourite grey, a huge beast bearing sparkling silver tack, he wore a garb which spoke of both his high ecclesiastic position and his secular place on the King's Witan. His accustomed black over-tunic reached only to mid-thigh over cross gartered leggings and riding boots, but was flowing in the manner of a longer, priestly robe, a nice mating of the two styles which emphasised his horsemanship.

Brother Earned's detailed information about the town and its environs had allowed us to make our way to the Reeve's Hall without recourse to asking directions, a preparation clearly not undertaken by any number of other attendees, who were looking increasingly surprised at the unusual location of such a gathering – the Hall tucked away as it was, close to the river and still, it seemed, only recently having been fully renovated. There were still building materials and other debris scattered about.

Despite what appeared to be a very recent completion of preparations, once we entered the Hall (having handed our horses to the stablemen on duty for that purpose) it was obvious that a great deal of time and money had been expended upon the venue. The most elevated of the participating Ealdormen had reached the town on the previous day – being accommodated at the sign of the Mason's Chisel – and were now standing about in knots of two or three discussing the debate to come and inspecting the renovations, impressed by the extravagance expended. The walls had been covered by embroidered and woven hangings, in the current fashion, and the windows were large, allowing considerable light into the rooms. A fine staircase ascended from the entrance hall into an upper storey, effecting an elegant curve – I had certainly never seen such a piece of architecture before. How strange that it should be here in this backwater and not in Westminster or Wintancaestre – or even in the Great Hall of the Chief Ealdorman himself, given that word was out that he had paid for this edifice. The floor was deeply strewn with rushes and fine herbs, which, together with the smell of still new wood, leant a most delightful aroma to the building. I wished Aetna could experience it. There was a large, well laden trestle to one side bearing foodstuffs of great variety. Many were already filling trenchers with meat and fish and quaffing from silver tankards. If it promised to be a long meeting, they did not propose to sit through it hungry.

There was no sign of Chief Ealdorman Alfhere, which obviated the immediate necessity to inform him of the King's absence. We had already agreed the ruse, if needed, of saying, that His Majesty was in some little pain from his foot and was reclining for as long as possible in the cushions of his covered wagon. The Devil knows, that wholly fictitious injury, contrived by my sister, had more usage than she could ever have imagined. I spotted my Uncle Brithnoth standing beside Ealdorman Ethelwine and upon receiving leave from the Archbishop went across to them.

"Wulf!" cried my uncle as soon as he saw me. "How are you lad? At the King's side, as ever?" He looked around the room, surprised that there had been no fanfare to announce Edward's presence. "Where is His Majesty?"

"It is good to see you, Uncle," I replied, unsure how much, how soon, to reveal of Dunstan's dis-ease. "Aetna will be jealous that I have had this reunion without her," I dissembled. "The King is, er…" I was relieved to see the Archbishop approaching.

"Lord Ethelwine and my friend and cousin, Brithnoth!" he called. "Well met!" Lowering his voice, he said to me, "Wulf, would you do me the courtesy of ascending this edifice and reporting back to me the arrangements up the stairs in the counsel-chamber? I would know the seating arrangements." So saying, he took the two Ealdormen to one side, his voice still low…

Knowing, now, that Dunstan had some idea, perhaps, of what lay behind this strange event, but still thinking that it was an odd request, I nevertheless climbed the wooden steps, up, up, to what seemed the implausibly high floor above. None of the other delegates had yet been invited to ascend and I half expected to be stopped but reached the upper level without being noticed. There was a landing and an arched doorway through into the assembly chamber. I heard voices and kept behind the door jamb, trying to make out what was being said. I recognised the voice of the Chief Ealdorman, but from where I stood could not see him – only a glimpse of several stewards or bottlers, well liveried and being briefed on the etiquette of the day.

"The King will be at the head of the board, of course," Alfhere was saying, and I caught the motion of his arm indicating a large, ornate chair placed at the far end of a long table. "The Archbishop will be at his right. On no account allow anyone to be seated immediately to the King's left – no-one, do you understand? Do not touch that seat. It is… reserved." There was a pause as he allowed these orders to be fully comprehended, and then some words from the other men indicating their somewhat bemused acceptance. "The Ealdormen from the East and South may arrange themselves as they choose towards the… towards His Majesty's end of the table. I shall be seated at the far end, together with my brothers and the Mercian Ealdormen." There was some query which I did not catch from one of the men. Alfhere's voice took on a scornful tone. "The other churchmen? Oh, they may dispose themselves as they wish. Is that all clear? When all that is done, you will withdraw." The stewards nodded vigorously. Alfhere added something in an even lower tone – I thought it sounded like: "If you know what's good for you." But I could have been mistaken.

The neatly liveried attendants came through the door onto the landing and I made as if I had just reached the top of the stairway and was about to enter the assembly room. Now I could see them clearly, I noticed there was a single, more officious individual, do doubt the bottler, and six stewards. The bottler was saying "I know it sounds odd, but if that's the way the Chief Ealdorman wants it… he's paying for the privilege." I tried for my most engaging, innocent smile and headed straight into the chamber. Alfhere whirled around as he heard my footfall.

"You!" he said, taken by surprise his face betrayed alarm, quickly masked, then superseded by – was it amusement? "But how fortunate! I had hoped that His Majesty might have his long-term companion by his side. I have a most excellent gift for the King, one which I would like presented to him at the commencement of this conclave… another token by which I would make amends for my ill-judged actions of last year."

"Lord?" I expanded my – I felt it must be – somewhat vacuous smile, hoping to look all eagerness to help. "If I can assist in any way?"

"Perhaps you would be good enough to attend upon my Lord Alfric when I have completed my words of welcome to those below – before we fully convene in this splendid chamber." He waved an arm, indicating the still freshly painted, plastered walls and carved beams. "He will give you the gift. Then I would prevail upon you to present it to His Majesty on my behalf. Bear it to him there, at the head of the board, where a seat is left vacant. You may take it, if you wish." He smiled. "A small contrivance of formality in this otherwise informal meeting."

"Indeed, Lord. It will be my pleasure. And I trust you will forgive a young man's curiosity in wanting to see this fine place before my betters. You have been most generous in your hospitality of today's event and to the good people of Caune."

"Ah, yes, generous, to be sure..." The Chief Ealdorman gave me a long and, I thought uneasily, perhaps wary, look. Maybe it had occurred to him that he had heard no clamour to announce the King's arrival – nor had he been informed. Did he fear that his plan, whatever it was, had been compromised? "Very well then, until after the noon meal," he said.

I returned to the lower hall. My uncle's party, with the Archbishop, were still in close conference. The rest of the assembly seemed to be getting restless, awaiting the presentation of the King, before which the conclave could not begin. Dunstan stepped slightly to one side to allow my entrance into their circle of conversation. I looked at him, and then at Brithnoth and Ethelwine. By their expressions I could see that they now shared our concern that all was not as it should be – and their relief that, whatever befell, the King was not here to be in danger.

"There is certainly something odd going on," I said in reply to the Archbishop's query as to what I had discovered. I recounted what I had overheard and my conversation with the Chief Ealdorman. "When are we to let it be known that the King is not here?"

"I'm not sure," replied Duncan. "Ideally, I should like to force Alfhere's hand into betraying himself, but that may not be possible if he knows his plan is thwarted before it begins. We will just have to play along with this charade as best we can until we..." but he said no more, as we saw Alfhere, together with his brother and brother-in-law, Alfheah and Alfric, descending the stairway into the lower hall, the latter bearing a bulky and apparently heavy strongbox. Taking the initiative, Dunstan crossed the floor and greeted him.

"Chief Ealdorman!"

"My Lord Archbishop. I thought that you were travelling with his Majesty, but mayhap I was mistaken." He looked around the hall to make sure that the King had not made an informal entrance.

"Our plan has, indeed, been to keep company," replied Dunstan, sidestepping a direct response, and taking Alfhere completely by surprise with a show of hearty comradeship, slapping him on the back, and continuing the conversation without allowing the Chief Ealdorman the opportunity to speak. "Well, Lord, this is a fine, a very fine, Hall. And you have funded its refurbishment yourself, I hear, for the purposes of this moot and for the benefit of the town. You are quite the philanthropist, are you not?" He put his arm through Alfhere's and with an unending, unbroken flow of words, complimenting the woodwork here and the woven hangings there, ushered him toward the stairway "... and this, this... contrivance – does the architecture have a name? – I cannot contain my curiosity to see the upper chamber." Turning to the other delegates he called over his shoulder. "Enough eating and drinking brothers, the time has come for words. Let the moot begin!"

I had never thought to see the Chief Ealdorman hustled, but had I ever considered such a thing, I suppose I would have imagined that the only person who might achieve such a feat would be Dunstan. Dunstan the master of dissembling – I remembered him as a younger man when Aetna and I were trying to evade Dagmaer's wrath and how easily he had spun a tissue of half-truths and contrivances to mislead her. But this was a more meaty challenge. Somehow, he had ushered Alfhere and the assembled Witan of Ealdormen and clerics up the stairway and into the upper room, where they found the stewards dutifully awaiting them. Only as the various parties began to take their seats did the Chief Ealdorman regain the initiative and shake loose – both metaphorically and in person.

"My Lords, my Lords, wait. I need to welcome you formally to this conclave and to greet the King... my Lord Archbishop, where IS the King?" His annoyance was beginning to show, however hard he tried to conceal it.

"The King? Oh, a thousand apologies my Lord, I assumed you had been informed. I regret that His Majesty cannot be present this day. He is incapacitated by the unfortunate..."

"Not here?"

"No. Indeed, as I was saying..."

"But the whole... How can we settle this matter of the *Concordia* without..."

"His Majesty has requested that I inform you that you are aware of his opinions in this matter. They will not change..." Dunstan's voice became hard for a moment, but then he reassumed his more conciliatory tone. "And you, my friend, as Chief Ealdorman, in his absence, must take the head of the table. You and your comrades from Mercia, no, no, I insist and I am certain his Majesty would agree. Sit in his place." His tone was still light as he propelled Alfhere toward the Great Chair set in readiness for Edward. Light, but brooking no argument. Alfhere was clearly uncomfortable, but seemed unable to find a good reason to demur.

Most of the attendees had by now ascended the stairway, crossed the landing and were entering the upper hall, milling around, unsure whether to be seated or not, as the strange behaviour of the Archbishop and Chief Ealdorman continued. "Come, my lords," said Dunstan, turning to the Mercian party, sit, sit. Here, in the company of your over-lord. I am sure the Lord Alfhere wishes to welcome you – us all – to this splendid assembly hall." Alfheah strode over to his brother's side and took the seat to his right, smiling affably. "Come, brother," he said "Do not look so concerned." He lowered his voice. "Mayhap the King's absence can be to our advantage. And, indeed, you look well in the Great Seat."

"Shut up, you fool!" snapped his brother. "You do not... where is Alfric?"

There was a great deal of noise as the other ealdormen and bishops, clerks and observers found seats – the former and foremost at the great table, the latter and lesser around the walls of the room, where they could lean, or, if the meeting dragged on, sit on the floor. I looked toward the doorway. Alfric stood, hesitating, still carrying the strongbox – which was clearly becoming a greater burden the longer he held it. It certainly looked exceeding heavy and I wondered how much coin it could contain. Having corralled the Mercian factor toward the head of the table, and successfully coerced Alfhere into the place of honour, Dunstan took his place opposite him, at the lower end of the table. "But of course!" He was laughing to a neighbour. "Humility is the watchword of the Benedictine order!"

Alfhere attempted to call the meeting to order, beating with his fist upon the long table to signal silence, for he was unprepared for this particular duty. Alfheah brought out a thick, sturdy, wooden cosh, which had hung on his belt. "This will bring them to attention, brother!" He smashed it down onto the table top, effecting a loud, resounding series of bangs, the heavy table vibrating at each strike. Alfhere grabbed his brother's wrist. "For the Lord's sake, stop it, you'll..."

But the desired effect had been achieved, the hubbub lessened and Alfhere stood. I thought for a moment he caught my eye, and, perhaps wanted me to take part in whatever was to happen next, as he had intimated earlier, though, without Edward's presence, my own seemed ill-met. Nevertheless, I quietly made my way over to Alfric where he stood by the door.

"I believe you are required to let me have that," I said.

"Not likely, boy! I liked not the idea of handing over this much coin to the King himself, and it was only on my brother-in-law's insistence that I have brought it here at all. If you think you are getting your paws on it... be off with you!"

The long table had no more seats to spare – and indeed without the King, my own status was hardly high enough to merit one, so I took my place among the other spectators, against the wall behind the Archbishop, from where I could see the whole assembly – and had a fine view of the Alfhere himself, now standing where, if the yester had not fallen out as it did, Edward would be awaiting the official welcome from his Chief Ealdorman and whatever gift of coin was in the strongbox.

"My lords, both spiritual and temporal," he began. "As you may have understood, it is my unhappy task to inform you that His Majesty, King Edward, will not be attending this conclave. His... infirmity... keeps him abed. It falls to me – to us – to discuss once more the position regarding the unjust treatment..." He began to warm to his task. His *ad libitum* words concerning the King's health echoed his original argument against Edward's accession. I was glad that Edward was not able to hear them and dreaded his reaction when they were reported to him.

The Chief Ealdorman continued. "Last year, my own discomfiture at the hostility toward, and callous ousting of, such innocent men as wedded clergy and those whose family connections bound them to certain monastic houses, moved me to unfortunate zeal. That I admit, and it had been my intention at this worthy gathering to offer to His Majesty, as an act of contrition, and as a *weregild* for the lives lost, a sum in excess of... No! What are you doing? Get back!" His voice rose from its usual persuasive tone to a shout of... what? Fear? Panic? For he realised that Alfric was fast approaching, bearing the strongbox and within moments would be at his elbow.

"My Lord," Alfric was saying, "surely these worthies should see the evidence of your generous *weregild* for themselves..."

There was a cracking sound as Alfric reached his brother-in-law's side and took the empty place at his left. At first nothing more seemed about to happen but then, as with a grunt of effort, he heaved the strongbox onto the table before the Chief Ealdorman, another deep creak seemed to come from... where? The floor beneath the far side of the great, heavy table shuddered and with a sound like the screeching of an unoiled anchor chain grinding against a ship's deck, several huge, thick-shafted nails emerged head first from the floorboards, as if propelled upward by some unseen force from below. The wide floorboards themselves began to bow and a depression appeared centred upon the area of the Great Chair. Other chairs began to slide toward it, some slipping alongside the table, others pinning their occupants against the table-top. Then, unbelievably, a huge crack appeared in the floor, more nails screeched their objection to this unnatural turn of events and shot, like crossbow bolts, into the air. One buried itself in the cheek of a Mercian lord, who fell to the floor screaming, blood pumping from his ruined face, just as an aperture began to appear, the floorboards separating to reveal the void below.

In the few moments it took for all this to happen, there was first an oddly frozen stillness amongst the delegates. Then, seconds later, the chamber erupted into a frenzy. The floor's disintegration accelerated and where there was, just an instant earlier, a crack and a small opening, there was suddenly an ever-widening gap. Several chairs disappeared and the huge table, no longer able to maintain its position by weight alone slid with a groan toward the figure of the Chief Ealdorman, still, somehow on his feet. It pinned him against the Great Chair and then chair, man and table all vanished through the ever-widening timber maw.

Those on their feet around the outside of the chamber rushed for the doorway onto the landing. With a sound like the crash of a huge tree felled in the forest and bringing downfall upon its fellows alike, a great beam broke in two, one half tilting upward and smashing through what remained of the floor, the other plummeting down to the ground below. Cross beams shattered with its demise. The last few chairs appeared almost sucked into the abyss, as if devoured and pulled underwater by a hungry whirlpool. Where the extremity of the floor was ripped away from the walls, jagged masonry jutted downward at a strange angle and the ends of beams looked like the stubs of rotten teeth. I found myself standing on just such a stump, clinging to a wall hanging, whose strength, thankfully, was far in excess of its appearance. Several others had saved themselves similarly and a fair number had escaped through the door, but by far the majority of the chamber's occupants were now moaning upon the floor below, where the boards once laden with food, wine and ale lay in splinters beneath them.

My precarious hold on the hanging made it hard for me to turn back into the room to witness the almost total destruction of the upper level, but I managed to shuffle around on the remains of my crossbeam and look down the length of the chamber. As though held aloft by the hand of some benevolent Higher Power, Dunstan alone remained. A single, solid beam spanned the width of the room. A few jagged – or were they? – floorboards remained attached to it and, surmounting this strange, miraculous raft, the chair in which the Archbishop was seated appeared to have its legs wedged between them. It was the chair in which the Chief Ealdorman would have been seated had Edward, and not he, now been at the bottom of that pile of carnage below us.

THIRTY

It had been a long day. Dunstan, Ratkin, our men and I returned to Sceo after nightfall. There was no light in the Tavern, but we rousted out the stable hands and got our horses cared for, the men bedding down beside them. Garreth settled the Archbishop in the best room in the house, gave him food and then insisted upon accompanying us to the bakery. Candles flickered in both the back room of the bakery and Hilde's adjoining cottage, but all was – we hardly dared think the word – deathly quiet.

We went to the cottage first. Aetna sat with little Effie upon her lap, Thella lay asleep before the fire. Old Hilde was rolled in a blanket upon her pallet. They all looked exhausted.

I embraced Aetna, and swept the soft hair back from little Effie's sleeping face. "Alfreth?" I said.

"On her pallet," my sister replied. "The King is with her."

"Is she…?"

Aetna sighed and gently laid the sleeping child aside. She put her finger to her lips and beckoned us toward the door once again. It was a mild night. We stepped outside and closed the door behind us. There was a bench beside the wall. Aetna and I sat upon it, Ratkin and Garreth on the ground. She spoke quietly. Such was the emotion in her speech that I can recall it almost word for word:

"At first, we thought that Alfreth would almost certainly lose the child. She was in pain and bleeding. Hilde cleared the room of everyone but myself and Thella. I felt to be of little use, but for fetching and refilling the water pot, bringing its contents to the boil, soaking cloths and folding them neatly to stem the flow of blood – then rinsing the interminable number of them returning steeped bright red. But gradually the number lessened. Still, thank Saint Mary, there was no evidence that the tiny soul had abandoned its hold on life. As her pain ebbed and Alfreth, pale as mist, lay back against her pillow beres, Hilde stroked the hair back from her forehead.

"'Aye, the wee mite has a powerful wish to live,' she said. 'Lie ye still, my love, and we may yet save ye both!'

"I lost track of time, and presently my services were no longer required. After some long discussions, Thella and Hilde decided upon the best brew to keep this particular child in the womb and as Alfreth sat swathed in blankets, sipping the medicine, I went to find Edward. He was not in here in the cott – though according to the girl watching an exhausted Effie, presently sleeping after crying for most of the day, he had been there throughout the long hours when Alfreth's pains caused her to cry and moan. Eventually he had been able to listen no longer and had made off toward the Shoe. I took the opportunity of changing into a fresh gunna – one of Alfreth's, for mine was stained, and washing my hands and face. Casting an eye upon the sleeping Effie, I smiled at the girl watching her. She returned my smile. 'It is ever the woman who suffers,' she said. 'My own mother died giving me life.'

"'As did mine,' I replied, suddenly struck by the fineness of the thread which bind us all to life. 'But I pray this day we have cheated Death of his prize.'

"'God willing,' she said, and I went to find the King. He has been with her ever since.'"

)))))))(((((((

In the first few months that followed the events at Sceo and Caune we never seemed able to regain that intimacy and trust with Edward which we had once enjoyed. Whilst, superficially, the King seemed to welcome my presence as he ever had, enjoying my company upon the hunt, at the High Table and in discussion of affairs of state, it always seemed that there was a slight inability upon his part fully to be at ease in my company, as though the depth of confidence was somehow lacking. He never said outright that he blamed any of us for the jeopardy in which Alfreth had been put, nor for the danger to the life of his unborn child, but he spoke of her less, as though she were a precious thing set apart from our world of intrigue and politics and that in sharing his thoughts of her with us, he might somehow, once again, risk losing her. He did not mention, either, his own loss of temper.

He spoke little, too, of the fact that our fears for his own safety had been proved to be all too well founded. The aftermath of the disaster at the Reeve's Hall in Caune had, to some extent, been downplayed by all parties. Dunstan had immediately set in train an investigation into the collapse of the hall, but there was no trace to be found of the architect who had designed it, nor of the Master Builder who had overseen the construction. Both appeared to have vanished into thin air. Even the local builders – including the brother of the landlord at the Black Dog – had either mysteriously received news of work elsewhere (although no-one seemed to know any details of it) or had, they said, never been in possession of any overall plans, and had merely worked piecemeal upon whatever aspect of their project was their own particular *metier*. Several of the attendees, including a number of lesser Ealdormen, had lost their lives and a great many more had been gravely injured, including the Chief Ealdorman, whose condition was, for several days, considered to be critical. His brother and brother-in-law were likewise incapacitated and unable to be of assistance in the matter of the investigation.

Alfhere gradually recovered and offered to pay *weregild* to the families of all those who had lost members – and compensation for other injuries sustained – being a goodwill gesture, he said, for the fact that they were attending the meeting at his behest. The majority of these monies were paid from the gold and silver which had, with the unfortunate delegates, fallen through the floor. The shortfall (for a certain amount of these riches had somehow become "lost", during the rescue operation) came out of the Chief Ealdorman's private pocket. A new architect was employed to redesign the Reeve's Hall. Our uncles, Brithnoth and Ethelwine, both came through the adventure unharmed as, of course, did Dunstan. News of the strange fact that he, alone of all those within the upper chamber, did not fall, but remained safely seated in his chair, wedged into the strong ceiling beam of lower chamber, looking down upon the unfolding chaos below, spread like wildfire. It was, said public opinion, final proof that the Benedictine faction and support for the *Concordia* was divinely inspired. How else could these events be interpreted? The fact that the King was not in attendance and that even before the disastrous accident the meeting was already disintegrating into mayhem played no part in the story. In private we could only conjecture upon Alfhere's exasperation at the outcome of his design. Another miracle.

Gradually, life returned to normal at Wintancaestre. The day to day events at Court settled back into their usual routine. During the summer months, the King went on official Progress twice. In July the whole Court packed up and travelled to Westminster, stopping off at a number of southern towns and villages along the way. Relations between Edward and Dunstan became a little less frosty as the Archbishop spent a good deal of time with the King, showing him around the little abbey which he had founded together with Edward's father in the early years of the decade. Tradition held that a young fisherman – Aldrich – had a vision of Saint Peter on the banks of the great River Temes, the Saint asking him for a meal of the salmon which the boy had caught that morning. Aldrich cooked and served the Saint the fish in question, and upon leaving, Peter gave him a blessing. The boy had rushed to tell his parish priest and the story spread. Now a thriving little Benedictine monastery stood beside the river at the centre of which was a Shrine to St. Peter, himself a fisherman. It was a pretty story and appealed to the King.

Dunstan later reported that Edward had said "At least the matter of the *Concordia* is at last settled. The holy monks at this place will live according to the Rule for many years to come. I wonder just how many?"

The Progress had swung North and passed through Eastseaxe, visiting our Uncle Brithnoth at Radendunam and then turning toward Grantebrige before beginning the long journey home to the South. We skirted the Mercian border and Edward made no mention of visiting Alfreth. We knew that they were corresponding, but still he seemed reluctant to allow any of us into their thoughts and plans.

Aunt Aethelflaed had remained at Wintancaestre during the progress, and Aetna, to her disappointment had remained with her. Lucet, too, of course. My sister was sorry to have missed the visit to Radendunam, and I had regretted that the opportunity had passed for my uncle and aunt to meet Lucet. Lucet was more and more in my thoughts. Back at Wintancaestre I found myself looking forward to seeing her and realised that while I was away, I had spent a good deal of time wishing that she was on the Progress with us. When August came and preparations began for the summer's second Progress, I was more pleased than I could say that Aetna and Lucet were to be in the party. Our departure for Mercia – for we were to make a visit to the Chief Ealdorman's shire, his recovery now complete – was to be a parting with other friends, though. The Dowager Queen Aethelflaed had decided that her time at Court was to come to an end. She intended to return to her estates in Eastseaxe and settle into the quiet retirement which she had planned but abandoned years earlier. And Ratkin and Thella were to return with her.

It had been a hot day in July when Ratkin came to me, his face serious and without a trace of his usual carefree air. Although still in my service I had seen less of him these last few months – indeed, years, since Alfreth's removal to Sceo. The little chamber at the back of his house had been turned into an apothecary's shop, where Thella brewed simples, worked ointments and made pills to ease common ailments. Their dearest wish had come true, too, for she was with child. I was in one of the upper chambers in the King's Hall, looking through some papers which Edward had found too boring for his own notice. Ratkin had scratched at the door and entered hesitantly.

"Come in, man," I said. "What's the matter, you look as though… there's naught amiss with Thella, is there?"

"No, Lord, thank the Saints, she is well and swelling!" At last, there was a grin and the Ratkin I knew so well.

"Then what ails you?" I asked, for he was clearly uneasy.

"Lord, we have been together now many years," he said. "I… I owe my whole life to you. Yes, the Lord Ethelwold saved me from starvation, and gave me my freedom, but if you had not persuaded me to ask Ealdorman Brithnoth to take me into his Hall, I know not what would have come of me."

"And you have ever been at my back," I said.

"But now… now I have a hard thing to tell and ask." He ran his hand through his still carrot-red hair. I noticed that, somewhere along the years, most of his freckles had disappeared.

"Spit it out!"

"My Lord, Thella has it in mind that she would like to return home – she thinks yet of Eastseaxe as her home – and to her mother for the birth of our child. And I, too… I would like to be away from the city, and back to country ways. Pray God, this will be but the first of our children, and I feel the pull as well. The Dowager Queen has offered us a place in her service – if we want it and you allow it. I confess that I find it hard to imagine a life not… but, well, things change, and…"

I felt a cold chill through my heart, for Ratkin was more than a companion-man, he had been a true friend for so many years. From boy to manhood. But, still, I could hardly forebear to laugh, for he looked so needlessly anxious.

"Ratkin! By all that's Holy, I thought you came with some dire news! Of course, you must make a life that is right for you and Thella. I shall miss your presence more than I can say, you fool, but I would be far more distressed to think that you gave up a chance such as this out of loyalty to me. Why, to be in the service of a queen, albeit the Dowager, is a step up from the companion-man to a companion-man – even one to the King! You are to be what? Her steward?"

"We had not discussed it so far, Lord, for I said that I could agree to nothing until I had spoken to you." His relief was palpable, though I could see that he was still torn.

"Well, go you now and tell Thella that she may begin making plans. I will tell Her Majesty that we have spoken and that all is well." But then a sudden thought occurred to me. I wondered that it had not come to me before, earlier that morning when the King had mentioned his step-grandmother's retirement. I had not yet had a chance to speak with her in private – nor with Aetna. Aetna! And Lucet! Were their plans also to remove themselves to Eastseaxe?

"Wulf?" In his relief, Ratkin reverted to the use of my given name. "Wulf, what's the matter? You have gone as white as milksops. Are you unwell?"

"No, no, it is just that I… I have remembered something that I must do. It need not worry you. Go you to Thella, all is well!" And saying no more, I jumped up, scattering the King's papers as I did so, and bolted for the door. Ratkin stared after me as I clattered along the walkway above and around the Great Hall below, to the other side of the building where the Dowager and my sister had their apartments. I hesitated outside Aethelflaed's but then went straight to Aetna's door and knocked.

There was some slight movement within and Lucet opened the door. "Lord Wulf?"

"Is, uh, is my sister at liberty?" I asked.

"What is it, Wulf?" I heard her voice from within. "Come you in, Lucet and I are just discussing preparations for the Progress. Such a to-do. Still, I missed all the excitement last time, so I suppose I cannot…"

"Aetna, may we speak… alone?" I said. She turned and faced me. Lucet had not yet completed plaiting my sister's hair and one side fell loose down her breast whilst the other was neatly braided.

"Why, yes, of course! Lucet has not even… may she not…? But no, I see whatever it is cannot wait. Lucet, you may as well go now and speak with the bottler. Ask him to ensure that all our trunks are set to one side for a good airing for they have not been used this twelvemonth. Thank you." Lucet gave me a somewhat surprised glance, but tripped past me and along the walkway. I closed the door behind her and sat down on the pallet.

"Sister, the King has told me about our aunt's plans. That she will leave with the Progress but then away to Eastseaxe. Will you…? Do you plan…? Will you take Lucet?"

Aetna laughed. "Oh, so at last we are admitting the way the wind is blowing, are we? Brother." Her tone became teasing. "I am flattered that you are clearly so distraught at the idea that we shall no longer be serving at Court together, but it seems you are more worried that…"

"Aetna, just stop it! Tell me!"

"Very well. No. I do not plan to return to Eastseaxe, and I shall not be parting with Lucet just yet either! Our aunt does not feel the need for a companion-woman in her retirement, other than Thella, who is to accompany Ratkin, who is to become…"

"Oh, I know all that! Ratkin, the fool, thought I might stand in his way and this morn sought my leave, as if I would hinder his plans! I am pleased for them both. But, er, I… well, you and I began this adventure at Court together, did we not? I would feel it a hard blow to lose all my childhood confidants in one fell swoop."

"And that I might have taken Lucet…?"

"Oh, well…"

"Come, Brother, I know you too well! You can dissemble no longer. I have seen the way you look at her."

I will not record the painful efforts Aetna made which finally succeeded in my admitting to her – and myself – that I would, indeed, have missed them both. That was as much as I was going to confess. But she knew, she knew.

)))))))((((((

Chief Ealdorman Alfhere had spent most of his convalescence at his foremost Hall, in Wireceastre, and was still in residence there. Edward had decided that we would strike North along one of the smaller old legionary roads and then continue on to Wenberie along Ermine Street, a route which would take us through some of the smaller towns that he had never visited. At Silcaestre, we bade fare well to Aunt Aethelflaed, Ratkin and Thella. As we watched them ride off, with a small company of men-at-arms, along the old Devil's Highway toward the East, Aetna was in tears, and I confess that I was hard put to it not to join her. It was difficult to remember a time when Ratkin was not with me, and Thella had been part of our lives since almost before we could remember. Aethelflaed, too, had become like a mother to us these last few years; a mother whose counsel in the turbulent life of Court would be much missed. I looked at the King. Like us, he found the parting difficult. Catching my glance, he gave me a smile, ran his fingers through his hair, in that old familiar gesture, and appeared to remove a dust mote from his eye.

As usual, we travelled only about fifteen or twenty miles each day, stopping off at various Halls and taverns along the way. Wenberie was at the foot of a tall escarpment, and traditionally was held to be the place where the Romans watered their horses before ascending the steep incline to the Merleberge Downs above. We, however, had just crossed the Downs and had descended into the pleasant little town, which was roughly half way upon our journey to Wireceastre. Edward decreed that we would spend several days in residence, which would allow time for news of his arrival to spread among the villages nearby, allowing people the opportunity of a sight of their King.

The Reeve's Hall was small but comfortable. The Reeve and his wife had, naturally, abandoned their chamber for the King's use, and he and I settled ourselves in on the first evening of the stay with something of the old air of comradery between us. Being on Progress suited him.

The Reeve did not boast a large household staff, nor a bottler, but we had been informed of the hour of the evening meal and had a little time to kill before we were to meet Aetna and the other companion-men in what passed for the Great Hall in this modest place. We would hear the church bells ring for the evening hour.

"Wulf, I would speak with you," said Edward, seated upon the low pallet.

"Sire?"

"Things have not been, well, comfortable between us this last few months. No, do not deny it, I have not behaved in the way a king should. I begin to feel now, now that time has passed, that you and Dunstan were in the right all along about the conclave at Caune. I have prayed on the matter. The Lord knows how I have prayed... at first that my beloved Alfreth should keep the babe in her belly, and when that seemed to be answered that I should never again lose my temper as I have in the past. And as I thought on that... and when we were at Westminster... well, much of my anger abated. Dunstan has ever been a good friend to me, as have you, the Saints know that!"

"Your Majesty, it has always been... Sire, I need not say it. If you will forgive my presumption, I have loved you not just as my King and friend but as a brother, ever since your father honoured me with the responsibility of your entertainment that evening in Bathe all those years ago! Mayhap I have made mistakes – as I did that night – but never have I had less than your wellbeing and security as my aim."

"I know, I know. And now, with this visit to Alfhere and my step-grandmother's departure, I begin to understand that in many ways I have been a trial to you! I wonder sometimes what my father would have made of it had he ever known about Alfreth... but I love her, Wulf, I love her and there is naught I can do about it. I know it makes the matter of alliances and the succession troublesome, but we shall, we must, find a way around it. It is but a few weeks now before my son may be born."

"Aye, sire, I pray it may be!"

Edward slapped his hands onto his thighs and jumped up. "And so, Wulf, I mean to be a king – and a man – worthy of the name. From now on. And I shall begin with this visit. Whatever Alfhere may say or do, I shall not lose my temper, but nor shall I leave him in any doubt that I am the King. I know he has thoughts of suggesting a marriage for me with one of the Northern Ealdorman's daughters, but I shall forestall that plan this week. No, do not worry, I will not speak of Alfreth – she does not wish it yet either, as you know – but I shall intimate that I have plans of my own, plans which he need not be privy to. That will also make it clear to him that I do not need his influence on the Witan to steer my course. Then, next spring..." His voice trailed off and I could see that he was already in that happy place, when he planned to announce his marriage, with a wife and a baby daughter at his side and an heir in his arms. "But, until then, it will be all statesmanship!" He put his arm around my shoulders. "What say you Wulf? Are you with me?"

"Always, sire!"

"You have not called me by my name for a long time..."

"Edward, then! Yes, Lord, I am with you!"

We heard the single bell in the roof of the wooden church count the hours. It was time to eat. I suddenly felt as hungry as a horse, a horse with a huge weight lifted from its back. Edward flung the door open just as Aetna approached. Lucet was with her.

"Sire," my sister said, "I would crave an indulgence. As we are in this little out of the way Hall, with only ourselves and our delightful host and his household to please, may Lucet join us at the table? I surely do not need to be served this eve, and I would not have her lower down with the ceorls."

"Lady, it will be my pleasure!" Edward beamed as Lucet came up behind my sister. "Though you have never again spoken of your antecedents – yes, and I know, do not wish to think of them – I know that there is noble blood in your veins. Mayhap, one day..." He looked, I know, at me, but I was pretending to collect together some of our belongings which had become scattered as we unpacked them earlier. "Never mind, of course, and you shall be introduced as Lucet de Normande, confidante to the Lady Aetna."

"Sire, you are most gracious," said Lucet. She hesitated.

"Say on, Lucet, there is something more?" asked the King.

"It is just... Normande, Normandy... It smacks too much of my father. May I be Lucet de Rouen? Rouen is but a town, and for all my bad memories, it holds some dear ones, too."

"Of course! I should have remembered – I spit on Richard of Normandy for his actions toward you and your family. 'The Lady Lucet de Rouen': it has a fine ring to it!"

That evening felt like the parting of the clouds after a long, dreary spell of weather. Our host, Flerrick, had left no stone unturned in his quest to entertain his royal guest and companions. A very passable minstrel sang, the Reeve's own young son recited a long, noble poem recounting the campaigns of the Great King Alfred – very well indeed, for an amateur, it had to be said – and then the whole company partook in a game of riddles, which lasted until well into the night. We had eaten and drunk well before we headed for our pallets.

I awoke early. Edward was still snoring – it is one of the more exasperating aspects of a companion-man's life that he cannot mention to his Lord such failings – but I did not mind as I knew that I would not have been able to sleep again. I had awoken from a dream of Lucet as she had appeared the night before. Aetna had lent her a gunna, in a pale red shade which suited her well and showed off the colour of her unbound hair to perfection. The practical, demure braided locks of a servant were replaced by a bouncing mass of deep gold which fell to her waist, with the merest of head-rails to cover her crown, held in place by one of Aetna's many woven, stiffened circlets. Her conversation had been lively but intelligent, her manners immaculate and her success at riddles superseded everyone's. It was hard to believe that she had not spent her entire life as part of the nobility – which, I supposed as I lay thinking, in some ways she had.

Edward woke suddenly and in moments was up and about. He had never been a lie-abed once morning had come.

"By Saint Cuthbert's ear, Wulf, I wish we had our hunting birds with us... That would be a fine way to start this day! But whatever is all that noise?"

Stirred from my reveries, I came to realise that there was a great deal of noise coming from without. Not raucous, but certainly excited, many voices blended into a low hubbub to which was added the clip-clop of horses' hooves, the shuffle of feet and the occasional call of street vendors offering pies, small ale, bread and milk. The King pulled back a shutter and looked out at the scene below, dodging back a little as the light streamed into the chamber.

"Look at this, Wulf!"

Where Ermine Street crossed the lesser road, the town square was packed with people, jostling, laughing, breaking their fast upon the wares of the hawkers, all from time to time glancing at the Reeve's Hall. News of the King's presence had spread already. Our appearance caused some slight stir, but clearly two tousled young men fresh from sleep, peering blearily from their embrasure did not convince the crowd that their monarch had yet emerged.

"A day for the fawn leather jerkin and trews - and the silken cloak, I think!" said Edward. "And... the second-best coronet? No, hang it, let's make it the best. I like this town!"

Hearing the conversation within our chamber, the young companion in training, who had been sleeping outside the door entered. "You are ready for your clothes, Majesty?"

And so the day began.

)))))))(((((((

Our stay at Wenberie continued as it had begun, and any lingering mists obliterating the sunshine of our friendships appeared to clear, as if by a warm breeze. Edward seemed quite his old self once again, the anxieties of the past months forgotten. Somehow, Lucet never reassumed her role of companion-woman as such and became more and more Aetna's confidante and friend. It was good to hear them laughing and chattering together as equals, for Lucet seemed older than her years – I supposed because of all that she had been through in her early life – and although Aetna had not seen as much of Thella in past months as he had previously. She must have felt her absence. When we pressed on to Wireceastre, stopping as before along the way to greet the people and, it had to be said, almost bankrupting some of the lesser Ealdormen with whom we stayed, it was with lighter hearts than we had enjoyed for many months. Edward felt no compunction in descending upon the Ealdormen as, he said, they could quickly recoup their expenditure by tightening their belts for a few months – Ealdormen lived well. When we spent time with lesser hosts – as with Flerrick at Wenberie – he insisted upon gifting them extra lands, or perhaps handing over some exquisite jewelled trifle which would reimburse them. Like his father, he had a great affection for the common man.

Our stay with the Chief Ealdorman was a less jolly affair. Although Alfhere was scrupulous in his attention to our every need, and at all times deferential to the King there was a chill in his Hall. The way the house ceorls scuttled about their duties set my nerves on edge. At the High Table there seemed to be little genuine good humour, even between the ealdorman and his family, whilst those who had been invited to share the board appeared strained and ill at ease. At the lower tables the usual raucous geniality was also missing. The subject of the unfortunate affair at Caune was studiously avoided, other than the ealdorman enquiring after the King's painful foot and Edward's reciprocal query regarding Alfhere's recovery from his injuries. It seemed that the matter of the *Concordia* was, at last, no longer up for discussion.

We were all pleased when our stay was over. We left Wireceastre, and headed South to Glewcaestre, re-joining Ermine Street and pressing on to Cyrnecaestre where we took the well-maintained Fosse Way to Bathe. Of course, it went without saying that Edward intended to visit Alfreth. We stayed at the abbey, as ever, and Edward affected his now well-rehearsed nocturnal trip to Sceo, returning, like a well-behaved school-boy, in good time to slip into our chamber and appear well rested and ready for our onward journey. I almost managed to pass the night without the overwhelming anxiety I had felt over his previous excursions.

And so home to Wintancaestre. The old city did feel like home. As our tired horses clopped through the streets, the familiar sounds of the Old and New Minster bells competing with each other as they rang out for service welcomed us. There were some not unexpected changes awaiting us at the King's Hall. With our Aunt Aethelflaed's departure, Edward had no family at Court, and the Dowager's chambers had been made over to Aetna, who now took charge of the more familial aspects of the household, with Lucet at her right hand and the bottler running the public Hall with his usual rod of iron. My position as head companion-man remained unaltered. But we were now a young and merry Court. The King's good humour continued and reached dizzying heights when news came to us, via a tired messenger, that Alfreth was safely delivered of her baby. The fact that it was another girl, not the much longer-for son was only a passing disappointment, for Edward was now determined that in the new year – during the spring, as Alfreth had desired – he would make his marriage public, bring his Queen and princesses to Court and, with the support of a loving God, he would have many more children, amongst which, no doubt, would be an Aetheling.

Summer had worn away into autumn and winter was upon its traces. Once again, the Christ's Nativity was celebrated and the year turned into that of our Lord's nine hundred and seventy-eighth. Edward was eighteen years of age, and entering the third twelvemonth of his reign. Why should we not rejoice in the hope of a happy future? We had had trials enough, or so it seemed in our youthful exuberance. The winter sun sparkled on a snowy landscape, the barns were once again full of grain and the blood-month had allowed the salting and smoking of many beasts. Rich and poor alike skated on the River Itchen and there was ale and pies for all. The ceorls and freeman danced in the taverns and we danced in the Great Hall. Lucet was in my arms and all was well with the world.

Easter would be early in that year of 978, and almost before the celebration of the new year was over, Edward had raised the question of when he should make his annual visit to his brother, Ethelred. We knew that they had been corresponding – Ethelred was now ten years old, and quite the penman, the King was a conscientious correspondent, always eager to ensure that his younger brother felt part of all that happened at Court, even if his mother did not allow him to visit. My sister and I often wondered whether she read all of his letters, or whether Meryasek managed to smuggle some of them away without her knowledge. In either case, there never seemed to be anything in them which was at all worrying; Edward showed them to us, proud of Ethelred's literacy. Mostly they were accounts of the boy's small adventures in the lonely Hall – companionless but for the faithful Meryasek – and his fierce desire to see his brother once again. In the King's mind, this put any reluctance on his part to attend upon Elfrith, despite her implication in the previous year's treachery, out of countenance. He could not disappoint Ethelred.

The feast of Our Lord's resurrection was an event which was too important for celebration elsewhere than at Wintancaestre. Traditionally, the first ambassadorial visits of the year tended to occur within a short time afterwards, and Edward did not want to postpone his visit until the late spring. Also, though he had made no specific mention of it, it was in our minds that he still held firm to the plan of announcing his marriage this spring. It was decided that we should begin our excursion to Corf on the tenth day of March, remain for two weeks and return with about seven days to spare before Easter Sunday. By the end of the first week of the month we were near ready. As the King's companion-man, I was, of course, in the party and Aetna, together with Lucet, were also to accompany him. As usual, we would take with us a small but efficient force of men-at-arms. But, essentially, this was a private expedition.

531

We were enjoying our evening repast at the High Table, a few days prior to our departure when Edward said "Wulf, I forgot to mention: do you recall young Slean? I have sent him on ahead to Corf. I value the experience he has gained on the hunt this last season or so and I am keen to see how my stepmother has succeeded in her plans to re-stock the forest with deer – so many were lost during the year of the famine and the cold winter that followed. I have told him to inspect the woodland and report to me as soon as I arrive. We shall have a fine time of it, I hope. My brother is of an age to join me on the hunt this year!"

"Excellent, Your Majesty, a good idea. In fact, now that I think of it, I was wondering earlier where Master Slean was hiding himself. He is not at the table today, now I know why!"

The King laughed. "Yes, he generally has a fine appetite! For many things, I believe. There are a number of young ladies present who may miss him while he is away! And," he lowered his voice, "a few other young women in the city who may be missing the fourthings he has to pay them to support his... indiscretions, shall we say? Pardon the inference Lady Aetna, Lucet!"

Aetna and Lucet laughed. "It is hardly a matter for levity, but we appreciate your concern for the niceties!" said Aetna. It had been a matter for Court gossip for some time that Slean, a dark, curly-haired fellow, whose father had sent him to Court around a year past, had fathered a number of children in the stews of the town. "We have both heard a great deal worse!"

"Indeed!" said Lucet.

"And witnessed much worse, too!" I thought, remembering her history. She was amazing. I had decided that during our stay at Corf I would declare my feelings to her. She must have guessed them. She was always my first choice upon the dancefloor and more often than I cared to think she had caught me looking at her with what must have been a moon-struck expression. If I waited any longer then someone else would snap her up, her lack of attested status not-withstanding.

Our journey to Corf was uneventful. By now, the way had become quite familiar to us and it was pleasant to notice small landmarks and scenes which we had commented upon before. The early spring was fair and the waysides and forest floors were carpeted with daffodils, swaying masses of yellow in the mild breeze.

"Affydowndills!" cried Aetna. "They are so pretty! Wulf, do you remember when we used to pick flowers and put them on..."

"... Gillycrest's horns! Of course I do!" I laughed. "She was so patient with us."

"They are called jonquilles in Normandy," said Lucet, in a quiet, faraway voice. "*Dames-a-bonnets*: ladies-in-bonnets." It seemed for, for once, she had a happy memory of her past. "The merchants' wives and daughters would wear wide straw hats for the Easter mass and tie them below their chins with ribbons. They looked for all the world like these flowers!" We hardly wanted to speak and break the spell, for it was so rare that Lucet spoke of her early life. But she said no more, just shook her head lightly, as if dispelling a distant dream and turned to Edward.

"Look, sire," she pointed to the gap in the ridge ahead of us. "There is Corf Gate, we have made splendid time."

The King sent two of our riders on ahead to warn the household of our arrival – though if I knew anything of Elfrith, she had her own men on watch and we would have been seen approaching long before we had reached the Gap. Aetna and Lucet dismounted briefly to tidy themselves before arrival, bone combs tucked away unruly stands of hair, and gunnas were smoothed of some of their travel creases. They both pinched their cheeks and bit their lips to add a little extra colour to their already healthy complexions. Suddenly, as they remounted and we began to climb the incline toward the Hall, Lucet looked anxious.

"Think you that Queen Elfrith will accept me as a member of the party and not a thrall – or ceorl?"

"You have been given your freedom – which should never have been taken from you – by my step-grandmother, and it is confirmed by me," said Edward. "What you may have been in the interim is of no matter. And I will make sure that it stays that way. And, if I recall correctly, my brother has always had a soft spot for you... he will be delighted to have you seated at the High Table, I'll be bound!"

"I would hazard a wager that Elfrith will not even recognize you," said my sister. "She ever had a blind spot where ceorls and thralls are concerned. They might as well wear sacks over their heads for all the notice she takes of their features!"

That brought a laugh to all our lips, and as we approached the tall gates set into the protective palisade, I believe it was only I that noticed a large black crow dip and swoop above the King's head, disappearing into the dappled shade of the encircling forest. Dagmaer would have had a brief word with the old gods.

The gates were thrown open from within and we entered the courtyard. Queen Elfrith awaited us upon the steps of her Hall, the Aetheling Ethelred at her side. He had grown considerably in the past year, and was now almost to her shoulder, but he was still slim and for the first time I believed that I could see something of his father in him. His hair was now styled as Edgar's had been, smooth on either side of his cheeks, and it was of the same shade as the old King's. He smiled, at first shyly, but then, as his brother dismounted and approached without ceremony, openly and with a touching enthusiasm.

Edward bounded up the steps. "My Lady, Queen Elfrith, Step-mother!" he cried, and kissed her full on the lips. "It is good to see you... and you, Ethelred. Why, you had me fooled, I thought there was some other handsome young man standing there. How have you become so tall? But, I suppose, at ten years of age, you are quite the gallant now!" Ethelred beamed at him and then appeared to remember his duty of hospitality.

"Welcome, Your Majesty, to our Hall," he said. "We are honoured by your footfall. Allow me to offer you the cup of welcome." A young page came up behind him with a splendid gold cup, shining with jewels, and handed it to the Aetheling. In turn, Ethelred offered it to Edward, who took a long sup, stepping backward and passing it to me.

"There," said Edward, "now we are done with the formalities. Step-mother, brother, you know my companion, Lord Wulfmaer, his sister the Lady Wulfaetna. You will not have been introduced to the Lady Lucet de Rouen. She is just recently invited to be a member of Court." This was true enough, I thought.

Elfrith spoke for the first time. "Your Majesty, it is as ever a privilege to have you at Corf. Of course, I recall your companions... and... the Lady... Lucet? You seem familiar, Lady, though I think the King is correct that we have not been introduced."

Lucet dropped a deep and elegant curtsey. "I am honoured, Your Majesty."

Once we had all tasted the welcome cup, the men-at-arms were dismissed to find their billets, the stable hands took possession of our horses and the house thralls busied themselves taking our trunks, unslung from the trusty mules which had been transporting them, to our various chambers. The King and I were in the same accommodation as we had previously enjoyed, whilst Aetna and Lucet were in chambers nearby. It was late postnoon and the evenings were not yet sufficiently lengthened to permit enough light indoors without tapers, candles and lanterns in the chambers.

"Morwen," said Elfrith, and we saw for the first time the shadow of her serving woman, as ever, at her shoulder. "Ensure that there is enough light for our honoured guests. Pray," she turned to us, "take your ease and rest. The evening bell will ring in advance of our meal. Ladies, I see that you are travelling without body servants. How... unusual! Do you wish for the use of one of my girls?" It had not taken long for some form of implied disapproval to become apparent.

"Thank you, no," replied Aetna. "Your hospitality here at Corf has always been... intimate. We do not expect the necessity of high formality. We shall do very well for ourselves."

"As you wish."

As we ascended to the chambers located above the gallery of the Great Hall, the stairs hugging the wall of the building in the customary manner, I reflected that Chief Ealdorman Alfhere, upon his visits to this place, had clearly not suggested any revolutionary architectural innovations in the Queen's Hall. I wondered how much of the panelling concealed passages and hollow spaces such as Ethelred and Meryasek had explored. The place had an aura of age about it which had ever made me slightly uncomfortable. Nevertheless, the King's chambers were well appointed, as before, and though I missed the cheerful presence of Ratkin, for so long my companion upon such jaunts, there was no reason not to look forward to the coming days with anything more than our customary dis-ease at being in the presence of Elfrith. Certainly, it seemed as though we were afforded a very genuine welcome by the young Prince.

"Wulf," said Edward, laying back on his bunk and kicking off his boots. "Before you take your ease, oblige me by discovering where Slean is keeping himself and how he has got on with his assessment of the forests. I have it in mind to hunt with Ethelred on the morrow, and I would like to speak with Slean this evening. Tell him that he may join us at the High Table."

"Very well, Sire."

I retraced my steps to the Hall below, which was now empty but for the thralls setting up the table and trestles for the evening meal, and asked one of them where I might find the King's man, Slean. I thought I noticed them exchange a furtive look or two, but felt sure I must have imagined it, and was told that he had been given a billet in one of the buildings in the courtyard, backing onto the palisade. These were the apartments generally put on one side for respectable travellers who might, if there was an abbey in the vicinity stay there, but, in the absence of a monastic house, might crave the hospitality of a safe haven such as a Hall. Wolf's-heads and other vagrants made it dangerous to be on the roads at night without protection and such beneficence was the norm at most establishments. I wondered how often Elfrith, though, welcomed such uninvited guests.

There was smoke curling from the hole in the roof of only one of the little cotts when I crossed the courtyard toward them, and I guessed this was where Slean had been accommodated. The door was closed and I banged upon it with my fist. There was a clatter within and the door opened. "Master Slean! The King has arrived and is anxious to know your opinion of the hunt. You look to be comfortably housed here."

He did, indeed, look at home. A long pallet was covered in a number of blankets, a bolster at its head, he had obviously been resting with his feet up when I knocked. A pitcher of ale had been at his elbow, with a tankard by its side, and judging by the presence of a collection of weapons and that of a number of rags, he was occupying himself by polishing his blades: a short, sharp dagger, a longer knife, designed to be worn on the hip and the type of sword which could be strapped to the thigh. There were also a couple of cross-bows on the low table. Clearly, all aspects of the hunt were his passion.

"Lord Wulf, welcome!" he said, after a brief hesitation, during which he glanced around his room. "I had not thought to see you this day – His Majesty must be keen indeed, to be so eager in his enquiry."

"So keen that he invites you to join us at the High Table to report your findings," I said. "I trust that you have apparel for the honour."

"I will endeavour not to embarrass myself!" he said, with a slight air of impertinence. He was, after all, only a very minor member of the Court, I reflected. The thought went through my mind that Elfrith might not be at all happy with him being seated so high.

"Yes... well... good. And have you accomplished what the King asked? You have made a survey of the forest and the game; the state of the deer herds and other beasts?"

"I have, Lord."

"Excellent. Then we will see you at the evening bell."

I left him leaning on the jamb of his door, one leg crossed over the other. A couple of serving girls were making their way across the courtyard and, seeing him, they giggled and ran off together casting looks over their shoulders. I could not deny that he was a fine-looking fellow – and the type that women fell for, in my experience. Dark, a little brooding, but with a smile to charm the milk into butter and the... well, that sort of thing. I returned to our chambers.

Looking in on Edward, I found that he was taking a nap, so I made my way along the walkway to the apartments where Aetna and Lucet had been housed. Scratching on my sister's door, there was at first no reply, but then I heard an inner door open, and Lucet greeted me.

"Lady Aetna has gone below to find Master Meryasek," she said.

"And the King is resting, so it seems we are thrown upon each other's company," I replied. "Unless, of course, you prefer to be alone," I added, fearing to assume too much.

"Not at all," she smiled.

"Shall we... I believe the herb garden is pleasantly sheltered from the wind. It is becoming a little more chill now that evening approaches," I suggested. She turned back into the chamber and picked up a light cloak. I held the door open for her. As she passed me, I smelt a sweet fragrance of roses. She still enjoyed working in the stillroom, but now could take the time to press flowers for their perfumed oils. It was also one of Aetna's favourite pastimes.

We descended the stairs once again. This time I led the way not toward the main door, but toward a side entrance which led out into an enclosed area neatly separated into small areas of planting. Herbs and other early plants were bordered by low, clipped hedges and pickets. There was a bench on the far side of the enclosure and we strolled toward it. The late postnoon sunlight slanted over the walls, barely reaching us. Most of the garden was already in shade. We were overlooked only by the solar-chamber where Aetna had spoken with Meryasek the year before. Now it was empty.

"Shall we sit?"

"By all means," she said.

Both she and I spoke at the same moment: "Lord Wulf"; "Lucet". We laughed.

"That is a trick you usually share with your sister," she said. "Mayhap I am spending too much time with you both!"

"Aetna and I complete each other's sentences," I said, still laughing. "It has been like that for as long as I can remember. But if I speak over her... as you know, she likes to be heard... and you have certainly not been spending too much time with us!"

"She has been a wonderful friend to me."

"I hope that you feel I have, too."

"Of course! You and Lady Aetna – Thella and Ratkin – and I hardly like to sound so presumptuous, but the King, too. It is a very long time since I felt I had family. But I do. Now."

I swallowed hard. "Lucet, you must know that I think of you... as more than... well, yes, family, but..." I was making a boar's arse of this.

We were sitting close together, for the bench was not large, and she turned to me. Her eyes were a little misty with... were they tears? Her hand trembled as she laid it on my arm. Her lips parted. Should I...? "Wulf," she said. "You know of my history. I... I am not... things happened to me when I was with the Vikings. I thought you understood."

"I understand that you were treated... as no woman should be treated, and that you were little more than a child. I understand that you were brave, and resourceful and that you did what you had to in order to survive. I understand that when you came to Aetna in Wintancaestre fearing for the safety of the old King that you were risking much..."

"And you understand that I am not..." I could tell that she was searching for a word which would enable her not to use the one that came to her lips. She gave up "... a virgin."

I took both her hands and held them in mine. "From all that you have told us," I said, "You have never given yourself in love. You have never been taken with love. Your soul is as immaculate as any virgin. And I would that you would give yourself to me. As my wife."

Her eyes still shone with unfallen tears, and then one slipped over her pale lashes and onto her cheek. I released one of her hands and brushed the drop away with my thumb. She opened her mouth to speak, but I stopped it, gently, with my lips. We did not move, but sat, our lips touching, while eternity spun around us. She was the first to pull, very slightly, away. When she spoke, I could feel her breath on my face.

"Wulf, I… I am not sure."

"Lucet!"

"Wait, listen. I am sure of you, yes. And I am sure that I could love you. That I will love you. That I *do* love you. My love for you is inside me, like a child growing there, in a place that I thought no longer existed. That I thought had been taken from me long ago. You are right to say that much of my childhood was taken from me, too… and for that reason I would ask that I live a little of that childhood now, before I become wife and, with God's blessing, mother. Just a little more time to get to know who I am. The thrall Lucet, Lucet the companion-woman, or the Lady Lucet de Rouen. Will you wait for me to grow up?"

"Yes, Lucet, I will wait for you." Of course I would. "I will wait…" I fear I was about to launch into some flowery declaration of unending patience. This time, she stopped my lips with her fingers.

"You do not have to wait for everything," she said. "I am certainly old enough to be kissed!"

I know not how long it was before the evening bell rang to summon us to the High Table.

))))))(((((

Elfrith had ensured that there was a fine board for this first night of our stay. The food and wine were superb and on the lower tables, the ale appeared to be just as well received. A Great Chair had been placed at the centre of the top table for the King, but he graciously insisted that our hostess should be seated in it, which, with a pretty acquiescence, she agreed to do. On her right sat Edward, to her left, her son. Aetna sat beside him, with Meryasek to her own left. The "Lady" Lucet, had the honour of sitting beside the King, whilst, to my delight I was at her right hand. Meryasek then had the pleasure of the house priest's company, whilst my own other neighbour was none other than Master Slean. He had certainly not embarrassed himself – his attire was entirely fitting for the occasion which, I must admit, somewhat surprised me. I did not recall him ever appearing so at Wintancaestre although, perhaps, I mused, he had always been something of the popinjay, but had never been invited to the High Table to demonstrate it. Mayhap that was somewhat the reason for this popularity with the lasses in the town. I made some slight remark as to his finery as he took his seat.

"Her Majesty does not permit ragamuffins at her board!" he replied sharply, as though he was quite aware of the expected dress code. I raised an eyebrow, but before I could speak again, the King rose to his feet.

"My esteemed and beloved stepmother, Queen Elfrith and her son, my brother, the Aetheling Ethelred, friends. I give you the *was heil*. I rejoice to be at Corf once again. Formality is set aside. We are family!"

"*Drynke heil!*" cried Ethelred, his young voice rising just a fraction in anticipation of everyone else. He looked anxiously at his mother in case he had overstepped, but for once she seemed sanguine. She even smiled.

"Yes, indeed," she said. "Family! *Was heil!*"

There was a resounding second *Drynke heil* in reply and the meal began in earnest. The conversation ebbed and flowed pleasantly and I observed that Ethelred was making great effort to be adult. He chatted animatedly with my sister, but also remained quiet when Meryasek spoke, listening to his companion and tutor. There was a great affection there. For his part, Meryasek was clearly delighted to be seated alongside Aetna. As I had reflected upon our visit last year, he must be leading something of a lonely life. Elfrith and Edward appeared to be getting along famously. She smiled and acquiesced at all his comments and laughed at his jokes. Only the brooding presence of Morwen at her shoulder reminded me that this was the way in which she often behaved in the early days of her marriage to Edgar... because from time to time, as then, when Edward turned away and spoke to Lucet, or one of the servers, she and the dark crow would catch each other's eye and something indefinable would pass between them.

After some time, when the evening was beginning to grow late, Edward rose the topic of the hunt.

"Step-mother, as we rode through the woodlands it seemed as though you had done still more to improve them. You have worked wonders since our first visit. I hope sending my man Slean to you in advance of our arrival was not too impertinent, but I am keen to hear a huntsman's opinion on the improvements. Master Slean has been in for the kill at almost every hunt this past twelvemonth at Wintancaestre. So, what say you, man?" He looked along the table to where Slean sat. "Shall my brother and I have a fine time of it?"

Slean leaned forward, the better that he might see the King. "Sire, the rides and clearings are well kept and the quarry much increased from that which you told me you saw yourself but last year. I have ridden well through the estate – I am honoured to say that Her Majesty has been gracious enough to accompany me on occasion – and I am certain that you will not be disappointed."

"Oho! Riding with a queen, eh? You will have much to drink upon when you return to Wintancaestre, will you not, Master Slean?" Edward laughed. Slean inclined his head as if in appreciation of the royal jest, but I thought he somewhat bridled at the comment. His eyes slipped toward Elfrith, who sat erect and apparently unconcerned by the mild innuendo. Edward had drunk quite deep and was in a mischievous mood. "Come, we have too few ladies among us to remain in the same seats all evening. Wulf, allow Master Meryasek and my brother the pleasure of the Lady Lucet's company – Lucet, swap places with the Lady Aetna – and, Wulf, you take my place beside Her Majesty, while I discuss more of the chase with Master Slean."

With good humour, we all exchanged places and I found myself seated between my sister and Elfrith. Aetna and I exchanged a brief look and then I attempted to make conversation with Her Majesty. But her attention, which had never focussed upon me, had entirely evaporated.

"Excuse me a moment, sire," she said over my head and in the direction of the King. "There is a matter which demands my attention." Edward waved a hand in her direction.

"Of course, Step-mother."

Elfrith left the table, her dark shadow in attendance.

I was sorry to have lost Lucet's immediate company, but was pleased to see that she seemed quite at ease. Young Ethelred remembered her from previous encounters, and whether or not he recalled her previous lower social status, or wondered at her current elevation, he was obviously delighted to renew the acquaintance. His still unbroken, boyish voice was raised in merriment. "Lady Lucet!" he laughed at some jest. To my left Aetna was enquiring of the King whether she might join the hunt – it had been decided that they would ride on the morrow – for, although ladies often took part, it was at the discretion of the highest-ranking participant.

"Of course, of course, we shall make a great day of it! Wulf, you too! And Master Meryasek, come, let us tear you away from your books for the day. And what say you, Lady Lucet, are you for the hunt, too?"

The King's enthusiasm was infectious and from all sides came affirmation. "That's settled then," he said. "And now, I fear, I am for my pillow! It has been a long day and a hard ride. Let us all retire, the better to be fresh on the morn. We will set out early. Master Slean, pray tell the Master of Hounds and the Horse-master of our plans. We shall be abroad as soon as our fasts are broken!"

)))))))((((((

The following was the first of several happy, apparently carefree days we spent together. Elfrith eschewed participation in the hunt, but was content that Ethelred should take part, and although Meryasek was not at his most comfortable on horseback, he acquitted himself passably – even staying mounted during some rough riding when a lesser horseman might well have taken a tumble. He was determined to stay close to Ethelred. Aetna and Lucet revelled in the chase and the King was relaxed and happy. On the evening after the first hunt, tired and fulfilled, we trotted home toward the Gate, the huntsmen bearing a couple of small deer, and Ethelred proudly carrying his own kill – a fine hare, coursed by his hound and then despatched by an arrow from his bow. He was delighted with it and Edward had praised his marksmanship. Now, the Aetheling jogged along beside his tutor, explaining, for the umpteenth time how this feat had been achieved. The good-humoured Meryasek listened with apparently rapt attention.

The King spurred his horse up toward Aetna and Lucet, and I followed. "Friends," he said, guiding his horse carefully. The trackway was wide, but there was only just room enough for all of us to ride abreast, "I am decided upon a plan of action."

"Sire?" Aetna was the first to speak, and the rest of us intimated our curiosity also.

"As you know, I wanted to make this trip before Easter, in order that I should be back in Wintancaestre before the Holy days of our Lord's resurrection. But I am also persuaded now, that upon that most auspicious of days I shall make public my marriage. I shall announce that I am a man wed, and that my wife is to be crowned Queen, and my two daughters recognised. I have waited long enough. My stepmother has been naught but gracious this twelvemonth – see how she has welcomed us, I feel certain that she has accepted my rightful place as King – and I would that Ethelred should meet his nieces! I shall suggest that they accompany us back to Court when we return in preparation for the celebration. What say you? Shall it not be a merry time?"

We were all taken something aback by the suddenness of this declaration, but Edward's words did not come as a real surprise, for we had all felt that he would not be willing to remain apart from Alfreth and his children much longer. He was beginning often to make mention of them – less than cautiously – and it would be better that an announcement be made officially than a rumour-mill spring up unregulated.

I spoke up. "Well, sire, if that is your decision, then of course, it must be so. But may I still advise caution..."

"Yes, yes, Wulf, I know! Caution. Why, sometimes you sound like an old nursemaid! Of course. But it is only right that Elfrith and Ethelred should be told before the rest of the kingdom, surely you can see that?"

"Well..."

"It is settled then. I shall tell Her Majesty, quietly, this evening. Then she will have time to think upon the matter before we return to

Wintancaestre." He reigned in his mount and fell back to ride with his brother. We could hear their light-hearted chatter as we trotted on ahead.

"Well, the time has come," said Aetna.

"Indeed," I replied.

"Perhaps the Queen's ambitions have tempered in the last year," said Lucet. "She does seem more amiable than on previous visits. Sometimes I think she recognises me but forebears to mention anything. And what about her allowing Master Slean to the High Table... the Queen Elfrith of the past would never have permitted that, surely?"

Aetna snorted – it really was not one of her more pleasant habits! "I was passing by the kitchens on the way to the chapel last eve and heard the serving girls gossiping – though they should mind themselves, for tongues have been snipped out for less: they say that the High Table is not the only place that Master Slean has been allowed to visit! The Queen's bedchamber is an odd place to discuss the merits of woodland clearance!"

"Aetna!"

"Lady!"

Lucet and I looked behind us, but Edward was deep in discussion of the hunt with Ethelred and Meryasek. The first day's chase had passed, and with it some of our peace of mind, but it seemed that Elfrith took Edward's news in her stride when, later, it was imparted. Late that night the King and Wulf scratched upon my chamber door and said that I could rest easy, for Her Majesty was quite content, she had said, with her lot. She would be delighted to accompany us back to Wintancaestre, but in the meantime, she hoped we would, as we had planned, enjoy a week's hunting as her honoured guests. She cautioned that she thought it better not to tell Ethelred just yet. Let him enjoy Edward's undivided attention for just one more visit before he felt obliged to share his affection with the little princesses, she suggested.

Master Slean had, indeed, taken his commission from Edward most seriously. It seemed he had acquainted himself with all the rides and tracks through the forest, knew the deer runs and the boars' favourite haunts and, beginning with that first hunt on the day after our arrival had steadily increased the complexity and demands of each outing until, a week later, all but the King and myself, Master Slean and the huntsmen and slippers (who had no say in the matter) declared that they had had their fill of the chase. All but Ethelred, that is.

During the postnoon of the seventeenth day of March, Ethelred had bounded into the *solarium*, which had become our regular place of meeting and relaxation during days when the hunt was not taking place. It was not a favourite of the Queen, so we mostly had it to ourselves, as on that day. Aetna and Lucet were about their embroidery and Meryasek had been reciting a long poem from memory. Aetna had insisted that we share the news of the King's marriage with Meryasek – she thought highly of him after his previous loyalty to the King and was certain of his discretion.

Ethelred was longing to impart some news, but his affection for his tutor was such that he did not wish to interrupt. He was, though, hopping from one foot to the other in his excitement. Meryasek came to the end of his recitation, to our applause, and Ethelred could contain himself no longer.

"Brother, Sire, I just heard Master Slean tell Mama that tomorrow's hunt would be the one to end them all! We are to pursue the old black boar, the big one that we glimpsed only once a few days ago when chasing the deer – do you remember? He is as big as a horse and as mean as... the Chief Ealdorman!"

"Brother!" laughed Edward. "That is no way to speak of Ealdorman Alfhere, though now you do...!" We could, none of us, contain our amusement. "What would your mother say?"

That was obviously a consequence Ethelred was anxious to avoid. "Oh, you will not tell her, will you? I only meant..."

"Tush, Ethelred, of course not. You are among friends," said the King. "But the old boar... are you certain? Master Slean knows that there will only be a few in tomorrow's party. That animal will be a difficult kill. And I am sorry, Brother, but you will not be coming, not if that is to be our prey! Your Mama would never allow it."

"Oh, but, Sire... I would not get in the way. I would..."

"No Ethelred, it cannot be, this will be a hard chase, even for me and Wulf – and Master Slean. But, I tell you what! I will bring you the boar's tail. How about that? And you can have the tanner make it into a bookmark so that when you are at your studies this year you can think of me and look forward to all our hunting next spring."

Ethelred looked crestfallen and little impressed by the promise.

"That will be a fine thing," said Meryasek. "You should thank His Majesty."

Ethelred pouted slightly, but he was in too fine a mood to be ill-tempered for long. "Thank you, Sire," he said and then, with the beginnings of a mischievous grin, "Brother, I heard something else that Mama said."

"Your Highness, have you been climbing about inside the walls again?" said Aetna, looking up from her needlework and catching Lucet's eye. "You should be careful..."

"Oh, Lady, I am, and how else am I to know what is going on, for once you all return to Court it will once again be just Master Meryasek and me and no-one telling us anything."

"And what is this other thing you have heard?" asked Lucet, lightly.

"Mama was speaking to Black Morwen – that's what the kitchen thralls call her. She was saying that we were soon all to be travelling to Wintancaestre – for a coronation!"

"Well, now, young man," said Edward, "little mice have big ears, do they not? Your mama is right. But we were going to save it as a surprise for you!"

"So who is the King we will see crowned?" asked Ethelred, his excitement mounting. "For you are our King, so it must be someone from far away, and why is he to be crowned here?"

"No, no, Brother, you heard your mother wrongly: it is a queen to be crowned, it is…"

"I did NOT hear wrongly, sire! A king, she said, a new king!" Ethelred was beginning to grow frustrated with the turn of the conversation – he was like his brother in that he did not appreciate being gainsaid. "I heard Mama…" But at that moment his nurse-maid scratched upon the *solarium* door and came to take him away.

"Your Highness, your mother the Queen desires to see you."

Meryasek rose to his feet to accompany Ethelred. "Take your ease, Master Meryasek," said the nurse, "Her Majesty asked me to bring only the Aetheling." With only the barest good grace Ethelred allowed himself to be led away.

At the door he turned back to us, and favoured us with a rueful smile. "Brother, I am sorry, I did not mean to argue with you… I am sure you must be right. I would much rather stay here with you than…" but he was hustled away.

We looked at each other in silence for a moment, each wrapped in their own thoughts. Meryasek spoke first.

"If he was listening through the wall it is difficult to hear clearly," he said. "Perhaps he was mistaken."

"Even so…" said Aetna. "I do not like it. What is she planning now?"

"Aetna," the King was chuckling. "Come, you see conspiracy behind Elfrith's every word. I am sure that there is none. My brother was mistaken. He as good as admitted it. His head is full of Kings and crowns and battles, just as mine was at his age. He thought he heard the word King – he wanted to hear it – and so he heard it. They spoke but of Alfreth's coronation, I am sure. Her Majesty was simply planning her wardrobe with her companion-woman, nothing more, nothing less."

"I hope you are right. But take care, sire, do not let her blind you with her false affections as she did your father."

"And do not you overstep your place, Lady," replied Edward sharply, his face darkening. These men of Wessex: their tempers could change in a flash from sunny to stormy. "Queen Elfrith has accepted me as King, knows of my marriage and has sworn to honour it. I will hear no more on the matter." He looked at each of us in turn, though we avoided catching his eye. Then he turned and stalked out of the chamber. Again, we sat in silence. The ladies continued with their sewing. Then Aetna stabbed the needle into the fabric and left it quivering there as she threw the piece to one side.

"In the name of Heaven," she said, "when will that woman allow us some peace of mind?"

)))))))(((((((

The next day dawned fair and bright. Edward was abroad early and did not wake me as he left our chamber, only rousing me when he returned, smelling of sweet new hay and, faintly, of horses. He had been to see that his mount was well prepared for the chase.

He shook my shoulder. "Up, up, Lord Lie-a-bed," he shouted in my ear. Any ill temper of the night before seemed to have disappeared with the dawn. "It is a fine day for our last outing. Come, let us break our fasts and be away!"

We descended into the Great Hall, to find Aetna and Lucet already at the board, with Ethelred explaining animatedly his plans to allow his young bitch to have puppies with one of the huntsman's dogs. "... and they shall be the best hounds that you did ever see! I shall start my own pack with them, shall I not Master Meryasek!"

"Indeed, my Prince, you shall, but you will need to take advice other than mine, for I fear that such matters fall outside my mien. Perhaps you should ask Master Slean."

"Hmph!" Ethelred did not seem over-enamoured of that suggestion. His smile broadened as he saw his brother approach. "Perhaps next year we may take some of my own dogs on the chase, Sire? I was just telling..." and he prattled on merrily.

Aetna and Lucet rose to their feet as the King reached the table. "Good day to you, ladies."

"Your Majesty," said Aetna, "I fear I angered you last eve. I am sorry!"

"Hush, Lady, it was nothing. You are but too wary on my behalf, how can I fault you for that? Put it out of your mind. Can I truly not tempt you and the fair Lucet to ride with us this day?"

Aetna was relieved that Edward's temper was so restored. She glanced at Lucet. "Sire, I cannot speak for others, but for myself, I fear that my lust for the chase is fully sated this trip. I would for a quiet day with my silks! Lucet, do not let me stop you, though, if the forest calls!"

"Sire," said Lucet, "I fear that I, too, have reached the limits of my ability... Master the Black Boar must be yours and yours alone!"

"He shall be mine and Wulf's, then!" cried Edward. "Are you fully refreshed, man?" he said to me. We had eaten bread, cheese and cold venison, washed down well with small ale, and I did, indeed, feel ready for the day. All seemed fair.

"I am, sire! Come, ladies, will you not see us mount and wave us off?" Ethelred was sitting with his red bitch beside him on the bench, feeding her titbits, a little crestfallen now that he recalled that he was not to be taking part in the day's main activity. "Prince Ethelred, bring Trixet along so that she might see her spouse-to-be lead the pack. She is a fine-looking dog – her pups will be great coursers one and all!" The Aetheling beamed at me. "And do not forget that His Majesty will be bringing you the boar's tail!"

As we rose from the board, Morwen materialised at the King's shoulder in her customary, unnerving manner. How did she do it? One moment the woman was nowhere to be seen, and the next... but no matter. "Your Majesty," she said, "My Mistress, the Queen, sends her greetings for a good morning and bids me give you her best wishes for the hunt. She is somewhat occupied at present and hopes you will forgive her not seeing you depart for the day in person."

"Of course, Morwen," Edward replied. It was a gracious gesture to use the serving woman's given name. "Thank her Majesty and bid her, too, a good morning. I will see her this eve."

"Indeed, sire." Morwen dropped a curtsey and retreated.

We were a light-hearted party as we left the Great Hall and crossed the courtyard to the stable block. The lads had brought out our horses – Master Slean was already mounted, his beast pawing the ground in anticipation of the off. His horse was bridled and reined in fine red leather. I commented upon it.

"A gift from Her Majesty, one of a pair," he replied. "For my advice upon improving the forest rides still further," he added.

The huntsmen and some of our men-at-arms were also mounted and reining back their horses as the hounds milled around their hooves, deftly avoiding their irritable stamping. They, too, were anxious to be away. A long legged red and tan hound was giving tongue. "That's him," Ethelred whispered to me, "That's Maxwell, the head huntsman's best hound. Shall he not be a fine mate for my Trixet?"

"Indeed, he shall, my Prince," I said, admiringly, as one of the stable thralls handed me the reins of my horse. Aetna came up beside me and put her hand on my arm. "Wulf," she whispered urgently, as I was about to mount. "Wulf! Be careful. Remember the... just... take care!"

"What?" I said, slightly impatiently. "Why?" And then suddenly I remembered. "Oh, Aetna," I said, more good-naturedly, "Surely you are not still fearful at Thella's warning of all those years ago? How many hunts have I – have we – been on since then with no ill befalling?"

"Remember Uncle Ethelwold!"

"That was so long past! But do not worry, I will take care, I promise. I do not take your fears lightly, you know that, sister." She smiled, but there was still doubt hovering behind her eyes. Lucet came up beside her and they linked arms. "Enjoy your stitching, ladies," I called from the saddle.

"… and we shall compare notes upon our days' activities this eve!" cried Edward. He lightly spurred his horse and cantered out of the courtyard, the rest of us in his train.

At first, we took one of the wide rides we had taken before, the woods on either side carpeted with early bluebells, just opening, their flowers flushed with purple. The hammering of woodpeckers could be heard, even above the muffled pounding of our horses' hooves, together with the sleepy call of pigeons echoing from the trees above. A startled doe jumped across our path, with a fawn at her heels. The hounds made to follow, but the whippers brought them in… mother and baby lived to run and jump another day. I was pleased. I would have been sad to see such beauty brought down on so fine a day. We penetrated further into the woods, the track becoming narrower and less familiar, the trees closing above our heads, their pale young leaves massing together until only glimpses of the spring sky could be seen through them. Dappled yellow-green and grey shadows played about us. I could hear the huntsmen and our men-at-arms chatting amicably behind me, the hounds alternately running up to my horse's heel and then falling back to their whippers, snuffling and giving an occasional bay when a scent was discovered and then left behind as we followed the way which, I noticed, was already marked out. Strips of rag were knotted upon twigs spaced out along the ride. I was happy to ride alone – my thoughts were turned once again to Lucet – and the morning wore on pleasantly enough as we passed deeper and deeper into the forest.

Master Slean rode ahead with the King, and I could see him gesticulating – indicating the direction in which we were to proceed – away from our present ride and into an area of the forest we had not yet visited. Edward reined back his horse and turned in the saddle, beckoning me to ride up and join them.

"Apparently the old boar favours a lair to the west of here," he said. "He is known to be a bolter – and once he runs, he will find a hiding place, for he knows every inch of his territory like the bristles upon his snout. Master Slean suggests we send the body of the hunt around toward his rear, cutting off his retreat, so that we may approach him more effectively. Then if he flees, the hounds will be on his heels all the quicker. We will ride on to the next fork in the track and then part company with the pack. Wulf, you will stay with me."

"Very well, sire, but shall we not keep some few of the men with us?"

"Master Slean tells me that the fewer we are, the better chance we shall have of surprising the old fellow. He has survived this many years by having ears that can hear a cat approach."

I felt a pang of dis-ease, but shook it off. It was perfectly logical advice from a man who had made a study of these woodlands on the King's order, for just this purpose. After only a short while we came to the place where the track split, and sent the main party off to the right, Master Slean instructing them to go straight ahead past two turnings, and then begin to work their way around to the left, by taking the next fork, and continuing in like manner. Slean then took the lead in our little triumvirate, the King behind him, myself in the rear and we trotted on some distance along the left-hand path, the trail becoming increasingly hard to follow. Eventually, we stopped.

"Sire, I believe the boar's lair to be a little way ahead. Rest you here for a short while, and I shall go ahead on foot to espy him out. If you ready your spear, should he make a break this way you will be ready for him. Keep watching in the direction I go… it may take me a short time…" He was already setting off.

"Master Slean," called the King in a loud whisper. "You are defenceless, if the boar should scent you and turn…"

"Don't worry, sire." Slean turned back for a moment, and I fancied that I saw what almost looked like regret in his eyes. "I have all I need."

Still keeping his voice to a whisper, Edward said "Well, I suppose we must wait then … but time for a pull on that skin of wine I brought with me, eh?" He winked.

"I thank you, sire, but I shall keep to my small ale!" I said, pulling out my own drinking skin. We both uncorked our vessels and drank. "I know not who filled this," I said, looking at mine, "But this ale is far from small. I fear it is the full brew!" I had taken a long, deep swig before I realised what I was drinking. At all costs, I thought, I must keep a clear head. There was something…

"Pah!" said Edward, pulling again at his wineskin. "Time to brace up for the fight." Since the men-at-arms had left us, the King had been carrying his own spear, supported upright by a leather grip to one side of his saddle, and cradled in the crook of his right arm. Now he pulled it up, out of the cup in which it sat, and balanced it in his right hand, feeling its weight and finding the textured grooves which ran around its middle and allowed it to be held without slipping. Time passed. The King hefted the spear into his left hand, for it was becoming heavy. As he stretched the muscles in his right fingers, wincing slightly as their cramp was released, the spear slipped and with a dull thud hit the forest floor. He swore and immediately dived from his saddle to retrieve the weapon – to be unarmed in the vicinity of a boar was sheer folly – and upon the instant a whir, as of a huge dragonfly, buzzed through the air, accompanied by a blur of shining metal. Then there was a dagger quivering inches above his head, embedded in the tree trunk at his side.

"What the…?"

"Sire, get down, down upon the ground, quickly!" I cried, sliding from my horse and drawing my sword. It was impossible to say exactly where the knife had come from, the breeze was playing with the leaves and branches of all the trees and bushes all around us – movement was everywhere. But behind us, in the opposite direction to that in which we had been looking, we heard the thud of hooves. I ran toward the receding sound. Just a few yards from the track there was the cut off end of a tether, still tied to a sapling.

I ran back to the King. "Edward!" Fear for his life displaced the need for title. "Are you unharmed?"

"Yes, by God, but had the dagger flown a moment earlier, or had I dropped my spear an instant later, I would have been taken through the throat. Could you see who it was? He'll hang by all that's holy – or worse, much worse!"

"I could see nothing, he was gone too quickly, but see this…" I held out the piece of tether. It was fine leather, tanned and dyed red.

"There was only one… traitor? Are you sure? Murdering bastard!" He was shaking. He reached for the wineskin and took another long pull. "Find Slean… we return to the Gate! Now!"

"Edward, I cannot leave you alone, mount up and we will find Master Slean together. I believe the threat is passed for now."

We both remounted and trotted our horses further along the trackway, with no heed for silence. Discovering the boar was now far from our minds. He could run where he would, we wanted to find Slean and be away from that place. After a short distance, my wits somewhat returning, I reined back and put my hand on the King's arm, to stop him, too.

"Sire, who could have known that we would be here? Nobody was following us, of that I am sure, we were so silent. There was no-one who knew our destination – except Slean himself."

"But his horse is still here!" said Edward, turning in the saddle. Slean's horse, untethered and unwilling to stand alone in the forest had followed us.

"He could have had another – tethered off the track, hidden in the trees. We would not have noticed it as we rode by." Suddenly, too, I remembered the red tack… "He could have left us, gone along this path until he was out of our sight and worked his way back through the wood until he was behind us. Remember he made great play that we should keep our eyes firmly on the path ahead. He could creep into a place where he had you in view and..."

"We would have heard him!"

"Sire, he is a skilled hunter – that is why you sent him here! It is his talent to approach his quarry neither seen nor heard. And, may the Saints curse him, you were his quarry!"

"And he had sent the huntsmen and others off to chase wild geese..."

"Come, your Majesty, you must get back to safety. Having failed, he may try again, or God forbid, there may be others in this plot. We must get back to Corf. To your other men-at-arms, for we cannot stumble about these woods searching for the rest of the hunt – they are likely lost, as I fear we may be." It had occurred to me that I was by no means certain of the route back to the main track. Slean's markers had ceased some way before we reached this point.

We turned the horses, pushed back past Slean's loose mount, and began picking our way back along the narrow pathway. It seemed even more remote than it had upon the outward ride, and I was increasingly fearful that other murderous assassins might be lying in wait, but it seemed not, as eventually we found ourselves upon the slightly wider track and then, thankfully, saw the markers which had indicated the inward route. Still cautious, we increased our speed, anxious now to regain proper shelter and be away from the forest. We reached the fork in the track where the main body of the hunt had pressed onward to make its way behind the boar – had the animal ever really had its hideaway in this vicinity, or was that just a ruse to get the King to such an isolated, lonely spot?

"Perhaps we should try to find the men-at-arms," said Edward. "Surely they cannot be too far away." We held our breath and listened, but there was not a sound among the trees other than the usual woodland noises – birds, the rustling of the leaves, the light scamper of small creatures.

"Sire, I fear Slean will have set them upon some path that took them well away from us," I said. "Perhaps he even sent them toward the boar's real lair, knowing that the dogs would become aroused and noisy and lead them off still further."

"I cannot fathom such treachery," said the King. "Was I not ever generous to Master Slean... why, he was in train for honours, had he but been loyal. Why must those we trust..." but he said no more and I led the way back toward the Hall, now cantering my horse and increasing in speed as we began to near the Corf Gate. Trees began to thin out and the track widened still further, until we were able to ride abreast. We were now galloping at speed and at last I felt that we were approaching safety. Wherever Slean had gone, he was surely not fool enough to try anything this close to the Hall. We were almost out of the shadow of the trees when, suddenly, my horse stumbled. The earth here was rough and pitted from the passing of many hooves, and a jagged stone shifted beneath us, throwing him off his stride, and buckling his foreleg beneath him. He fell heavily, and I only just managed to roll off his back at the last moment, avoiding being trapped beneath him. Slean's horse, still following, took a leap and sailed over us. I felt a sharp crack on the side of my head as one of its hooves clipped my skull. It careered off toward the Hall. Edward reined in and turned back toward me.

"Wulf, Wulf, are you hurt? I am coming!"

I was badly winded and my horse was thrashing dangerously close beside me, but I managed to call out to him. "Edward, no! Go! Get to safety! I am not hurt, I will follow on the moment. Get within the palisade, for the love of God. I will be there soon!" He hesitated. In that instant I loved him as my King and my friend. Even in his own peril, he thought to help me. "Go!" I repeated, waving him onward.

"I will send help," he cried as he rode away.

Slowly, so slowly it seemed, my breath began to flow freely once again. My shoulder felt on fire where I had landed hard upon a fallen tree trunk, but I could move my arm, so I believed there was no break. My leg felt badly jarred, and there was a trickle of blood from the corner of my mouth, where I had bitten my tongue, I thought. The pain in my shoulder was such that I hardly noticed the sharp, but oddly fluctuating sensation on the side of my head. My sight seemed a little blurred, but it appeared I had survived the fall with no worse injury. I was relieved to see that my horse was beginning to calm, too. He allowed me to feel his foreleg, and whinnied in pain as I examined the tendons, but he struggled to his feet and was able to walk, barely putting any weight on the injured limb. With luck, I thought – and surely we deserved some – he, too, would survive. We hobbled out of the shadows and into the evening sunlight slanting across the open ground which separated the forest from the approach to the Hall. There was no sign of the King. Pray God he had reached safety. At any moment now, there would be a party out of the gates, come to my aid, likely with Aetna on her own horse, ready to remonstrate with me for ignoring Thella's foretelling – once again.

My horse and I made painfully slow progress up the incline toward the Hall. The barrows loomed menacingly to my left. Where was everyone? Admittedly, news of the attack on the King would be foremost in everyone's mind, but surely... The throbbing in my shoulder increased with every step and my horse was beginning to fail when we finally reached the gate in the palisade. Head down, I was concentrating on putting one foot before the other and watching the ground for possible pitfalls, when I saw it. Blood.

A splash of blood, no, there was more than that, a trail. Deep grooves in the soft earth and places where the grass had been gouged out as if by… what? And everywhere, blood.

I stood dumbfounded – dazed by my fall and foolish, in my incomprehension, swaying slightly, as a body of mounted men swept past me, following the trail. What had happened? I looked through the open gates. Aetna and Lucet were running toward me. As they reached me, my legs gave out beneath me and I slipped into unconsciousness.

)))))))(((((((

When I awoke, I had no idea how much time had elapsed. My last memories were vivid; I recalled everything until the moment I passed out, but then the blackness had been absolute, and now… I was in my – our – chamber, on my palliasse with Aetna beside me, sitting, holding my hand.

"Wulf? Oh, Wulf, thanks be to the Saints. But you have a hard head, I have said so before. My own has been throbbing this last day since we carried you in. And my shoulder." She smiled and smoothed her cool hand over my forehead.

I tried to sit up a little. "Edward! The King! Where is he?"

Aetna pushed me back upon my pillow, straightening the bere, which I could see was spotted with blood – mine. Oh, by God, what was that other blood I had seen?

"Wulf, lie quiet. I will tell you all… yes, yes, now… but you must stay still, just for a while at the least."

The door opened and Lucet came in. Lucet! She stood beside my sister, and they clasped hands. "How long has he…?"

"Only this moment, my dear," said Aetna. And then to me, "Lucet has been at your side from the instant you were found. We both have. This place is not safe."

Once again, I tried to rise and again was pushed back, but this time I managed to sit up a little straighter. Lucet had brought a bowl of warm pottage – perhaps to share with Aetna – but now she offered it to me. My hands were shaking slightly, but I managed to hold it, and the wooden spoon.

"Eat," Lucet said. "We must away from this benighted Hall as soon as we can."

"Then tell me…"

They exchanged glances, and then Aetna took a deep breath. "Brother, it is the worst news and I cannot lessen it, though I would with all my heart that I might. The King is dead. Edward is… he is dead."

Somehow, I had known this was what I would hear. Known but did not want to believe. My voice was flat. "How?"

552

I will not tell the tale in the words of my sister and my beloved. It was broken by too many tears, too many fearful asides, too many outbursts of accusation and anger. But I will tell it.

After we had left the Great Hall that morning, the day passed in its usual manner. As they had promised themselves, Aetna and Lucet repaired to the *solarium* with their embroidery and had enjoyed several pleasant hours. They had shared their midday repast with Prince Ethelred and Master Meryasek in the Great Hall, and then taken a walk outside the palisade, Ethelred playing with his wooden sword and Meryasek entertaining them with riddles and poetry. Toward late postnoon they returned to the Hall. They had not seen Elfrith all day, but that was not unusual, she often kept to her own withdrawing chambers.

They were beginning to expect our return, and Ethelred was on tenterhooks to hear of the hunt, when a solitary rider galloped through the gates, just opened in anticipation of our arrival. He had a long, dark, nondescript cloak with a hood pulled low over his face which made it impossible to see who it was and such was the speed of his horse's dash and its precipitate halt directly in front of the great doors that the guards were taken quite unawares. However, they received no rebuke, as the doors opened and none other than Black Morwen herself ushered the apparent stranger straight into the Great Hall and thence to the Queen's withdrawing chamber.

Whether Elfrith was aware of how loudly she shouted, or whether she simply cared not, as her son, his tutor and the ladies entered the Hall, her words could clearly be heard.

"You fool! How much simpler could it have been?"

There was the low murmur of a male voice in response and then Elfrith's again.

"Well, you will have to! I have not come this far along the path to..." And then her tone lowered. Aetna thought she caught the words "How much time do he have?"

Again, a murmur of response, and some more words from Elfrith that could not be fully heard. Morwen hurried out of the chamber and into the Great Hall, where the ladies were divesting themselves of their outer cloaks. She stopped, a look of surprise on her face at seeing the party, and then, realising that Ethelred was with them said "Aetheling, your mother the Queen desires your presence."

"But I am awaiting the King and the hunt," he replied. "They will be back any moment and..."

"Do you disobey your mother? Come along at once!" She gripped him with vice-like fingers around his wrist and almost dragged him into the withdrawing chamber.

"It seems his Highness is excused his postnoon lessons this day," said Meryasek.

"Shall we to the *solarium* once more to await this eve?" said Lucet. "I confess that my own delight at the sight of a butchered pig – be he ever so black – is not such that I wish to wait for it here!" There was laughter and they made their way through the length of the Hall to the chambers against its western wall.

They heard nothing of the King's arrival. It was only later, when Meryasek told Aetna and Lucet what Ethelred had imparted to him, between the boy's tears and stifled gasps of pain, that the full story became clear. A story which today cannot be spoken aloud.

Morwen had almost forced Ethelred into the withdrawing chamber, such was Elfrith's urgent demand. Once there, he found Master Slean in her presence, clearly in a state of terror, only slightly lessened by the Queen's now more reassuring tone.

"There is no time to lose, then," Elfrith was saying. "Slean, go you to the great doors and wait." Then turning to Ethelred, "My son, this day will seal your destiny, for aught or else, and I am determined that by the time the sun sets you will be King. Come with me."

Ethelred did not understand his mother's words. How could be King? He was old enough now to understand that his brother was the rightful monarch, but he was still a slight child, and between Morwen's physical strength and Elfrith's authority he assumed his usual compliant demeaner. They hustled him out of the withdrawing chamber into the Great Hall and toward the doors, where Slean had concealed himself from anyone approaching through the courtyard. Morwen went to the kitchens and returned with a large silver chalice containing red wine.

Elfrith took the cup and passed it to Ethelred. "Take this, my son. Your brother will return at any moment and will need refreshment. We shall greet him upon the steps and you will offer him to drink." She gripped his shoulder tightly and they stood, silent, as minutes passed.

"Mama," began Ethelred, "the cup is heavy... I shall not be able to reach..."

"Then your brother will have to lean down, will he not?" said the Queen.

"But..."

"Be quiet. Do as you are told!"

Moments later, the guards at the gate stood to attention. The thud of approaching hooves could be heard from without and Edward's horse galloped into the courtyard. The King was shouting something. Ethelred could not catch the words, but knew that there was an urgency to them: something was wrong. And where was Wulf? His mother's grip upon his shoulder tightened still further and she rushed him forward, through the great door and down the steps. He sensed movement behind them as Slean shifted his position, better to see what was happening.

Everything took place so quickly. Edward was shouting, Elfrith telling him to be calm, to speak more slowly... would he not take a drink, look, Ethelred had the cup ready... he was frightening the child... Ethelred offered the cup, but his reach was far short of his brother's hand. The King appeared to take a deep breath, steadying himself to explain the urgency and leaned down low to take the chalice from the boy. And at that instant Slean appeared on the steps, his movements so fluid, the knife in his hand like quicksilver, wicked and deadly. Two strikes, one to the King's right arm, as he bent toward the cup and a second in the middle of his back.

Edward cried out, in pain, shock and disbelief. He jerked away, losing his hold upon his horse's rein's, and his seat in the saddle. He fell backward, one foot becoming loose from its stirrup, the other twisting and becoming tightly enmeshed in its own. The horse, already distressed, bolted, first in the direction of the chapel and then, seeing the gates still open, back the way it had come, out into the grassy area beyond the palisade, dragging its hapless captive in its wake. There was blood now, blood on the ground from the attack, blood where the King was trailed brutally on the hard earth, and blood where the horse's hooves, with no ill intent, but with catastrophic effect smashed into his skull, splintering bone.

The guards, at first, had run across the courtyard toward the great doors, but they now doubled back toward the gate, although hopelessly outpaced by the bolting horse. Some of the men-at-arms, who had been taking their ease, made toward the stable and mounted their own horses – bareback in their haste – and fell in to follow the mad chase. But Ethelred saw no more. His mind was in a state of unimaginable horror. The chalice had crashed to the ground, spilling its contents all over him, and for a moment he thought that he, too, was covered in blood. Then his mother and Morwen hustled him inside, back, back through the Great Hall and into the withdrawing chamber. He was in tears. Hysteria was fast rising in his throat.

"Edward! Edward! Brother...! Mother, what? What, where is Slean? He did it, he killed the King. My brother is dead... or mayhap not, what think you, Mama could he still be...? Oh, but the blood! Mama!"

Elfrith slapped him hard across his face. "Shut up! You are King. Yes, that wicked man has killed your brother, but now YOU are King. Act like it. We will... we will send to arrest Master Slean. Morwen, see to it, send out the men to find him... see, Ethelred, he will be found, as you command. But now, now..."

"But you must find Edward, Mama... it matters not, now, to find Slean, find Edward! He may yet live!"

"I think not, son."

"But, Mother!"

"Ethelred, compose yourself. You will have the entire household in this room in moments, and you are not fit to... very well, we will send to find poor Edward, remember you said not to search for Slean, and you are King. Morwen, stay where you are, the King commands it. Ethelred, you held the cup while Slean struck, some may say you knew... so keep your counsel, my son. I am here to help you. To protect you. No matter what the others may..."

"But, Mother, what are you saying? I knew nothing. I... you told me to offer the cup. What? Mama, I cannot think, please!" The boy was becoming frenzied.

Elfrith could contain her temper no longer. "You ungrateful little... grow up! See what we have done. We have made you King and this is how you behave." The evening was already approaching and candles burned in tall holders on a nearby table. Elfrith seized one and brought it down with all her strength upon her son's arm as he reached for her seeking comfort. And again, smashing it into his ribs. A third blow, again, and Ethelred felt something crack in his chest.

"Morwen, take him to his nurse... or his tutor... I care not, get him out of my sight. There are things to be taken care of!"

All this Ethelred sobbed to Meryasek and he, appalled and revolted, reported the same to Aetna, as she sat beside my unconscious body, not knowing when or whether I would wake. But such knowledge was dangerous. Aetna and Lucet decided not to admit to it: they had been in the *solarium* throughout, seeing and hearing nothing. All they knew was that Master Slean had lost his wits and attacked the King. And now? Now, he was gone. Ethelred had commanded that all efforts be concentrated upon finding Edward.

A few hours before I awoke, that sad task was completed. Some ceorls had been seen hurrying toward the village, agitated and in a state of alarm. They were questioned by the men-at-arms searching for the King. The well at the crossroads, they said, was emitting a bright light, like sunlight through a coloured window, and they had heard a strange ringing sound, like the tinkling of golden bells. The well was searched, and there, there was the King's poor broken body. His horse was found wandering nearby. It was inexplicable. It was terrible. It was finished.

POST SCRIPTUM

THE AT ABBEY AT SCEPTESBERIE
20th February, The Year of Our Lord 981

AETNA

Is it wrong to be so light-hearted, so happy, on such a solemn day? Surely not. Can joy in the hearts of true friends ever be less than a blessing? I feel certain that Edward would say it could never be. He, above all, knew what it was to love.

It is almost two years since the terrible day when the King's horse, led by one of his men-at-arms, carried his body through the gates at Corf and back within those cursed walls. I was almost in despair. Wulf had still not awakened from the little-death he was suffering after the injuries he sustained before the horrific events of the rest of that night unfurled. Lucet and I were in fear of our lives – and his – for we knew the secret of how Edward had died: that it was not the mad act of a deranged man, but the outcome of a shameful plot, a plot which had failed in its first attempt, but succeeded only too well at its second. The so-called lunatic, Slean, had never been caught – had never again been seen. Had he taken payment for his awful deed and escaped, or been bloodily despatched himself to cover the tracks of more important conspirators? That we did not know, nor ever would. Thankfully, the fact that we held such knowledge as we did was not known by the Queen. As soon as Wulf felt able to move, we left that place. My brother and I and Lucet, the three of us, took those men-at-arms who wished to return to Wintancaestre and fled. Well, it felt like flight... and in truth I wished that we had been able to bring Ethelred and Meryasek with us, but their wyrd lay elsewhere.

It was clear who would be crowned King and successor to Edward: there would be no candidate other than Ethelred. Before his brother's body was cold in the ground at Warham, laid to rest in a hasty and less than honourable service contrived by Elfrith, she had sent riders out to members of the Witan, convening a Witangemot. Ethelred's coronation, at Kingestun, took place exactly two weeks after his brother's death. Dunstan presided, what else could he do? We did not attend, nor did many Ealdormen, citing the short notice. By the time those beside the Temes were bending the knee to the newly anointed King Ethelred, Wulf and I were back at Radendunam, for there was no place for us at Elfrith's Court.

And it was *her* Court, mistake me not. Hers and Chief Ealdorman Alfhere's, for they were Regents in all but name. Poor Ethelred.

Oh, but it was good to see Eastseaxe again! I did not realise how much I had missed it. The softly undulating landscape, the big open skies of the East, the grey blue sea. Of course, Lucet came with us. Wulf announced to anyone who cared to listen that he was determined that she should be his wife and found no opposition, either from our aunt and uncle or, after a very short while, from Lucet herself. But first, she insisted, she wanted to spread her wings, just a little. And, I confess, after a short while I felt the wanderlust again, too. How fortunate then, that in the summer of 979 Wulfstan and Ethelmaer arrived at Radendunam. They stayed until the early autumn and then began preparations for their return to the road – our father continuing his storytelling, and Ethelmaer his itinerant evangelism. Oh, how I wanted to go with them, to get to know my father better and to be with...

For many a long night Lucet and I sat listening to the murmur of the brook and discussing whether we should – whether we could – take time out of the lives we might be expected to live and be part of their world. Lucet had a knack for many things, that much was clear: her history had prepared her well for such an adventure, but me? Well, I said at last, I was my mother's daughter and what she could do, so could I. But all of that is a story for another day.

This day we are all reunited. Wulf and Lucet, Aunt Aelflaed and Uncle Brithnoth, our aunt the Dowager Queen Aethelflaed. Ethelwine is here with his brothers, and even Oswig and Leoflada with some few of their children! And me and Ethelmaer.

Dear Edward is here, too. He is in a finely-wrought sarcophagus, draped with embroidered cloths and is brought into this great abbey church of Sceptesberie where the nuns will tend his mortal remains for as long as songs are sung. He is laid to rest, now, on the North side of the High Altar. There are chants of praise in the air and it is sweet with incense. It is said that those who came to honour him in his poor, low grave at Warham arrived sick and leprous and left hale and clean. His remains have performed miracles. The poor and wealthy alike began to say that the dishonour he received in death was a shame which would bring ill fortune upon us all. He is being called a martyr. Much against her wishes, Elfrith had to agree to this translation of his body – paid for by the Chief Ealdorman – and now we are all here to pay our respects to his corporeal remains and his eternal soul. Edward, you would have loved this.

His body was taken up at Warham and escorted by a hundred priests and men-at-arms throughout the twenty-five-mile journey to Sceptesberie. It took seven days, the procession stopping overnight every few miles to allow the crowds which gathered at every village and crossroads to see his coffin and pray for miracles – many of which were granted. This morning they arrived in Shaftesbury, followed by a huge pilgrimage of the faithful and now, at last, he is at rest. I have just overheard gossip that when Elfrith tried to join the cortege, riding her high-stepping, gorgeously attired horse, the beast refused to step forward into the procession. It would not budge. She had to dismount and try with another horse, but it, too, refused to carry her. She either had to forego attending the interment and risk the wrath of the people or walk – Elfrith! Walk! – behind Edward's coffin. That I should ever see the day!

We are seated at the front of the abbey church, with the royal party – at King Ethelred's insistence. He has some little authority over such mundane matters, at the least. He is now almost twelve – how many years will it be before he can shuffle off the unwelcome dominance of others? The Queen Mother sits in full state beside the young King. The faithful Meryasek is afforded a place just behind him. Our seats had been reserved and as we entered through the West door, we passed through throngs of ceorls, serving people, farmers, shop-keepers, bakers. All here to honour Edward one last time. Taverners, too. As we passed there was a low voice which caught my attention.

"Lady Aetna!"

I turned. There was Alfreth, slim, lovely Alfreth with two little girls clinging to her skirts – and a baby boy in her arms. And with his arm around her waist, and an expression of adoration in his eyes when he looked at her, was Garreth.

"Alfreth!" I knew not what to say. We had corresponded, briefly, but then she had written no more, after saying that it was too dangerous. If our letters had been intercepted her life and that of her children would be at risk. Princesses grow up to have children of their own – and any boys would be pretenders to Ethelred's throne. Alfreth's marriage to Edward must never be revealed.

"Lady, I believe you know my husband – Master Garreth. We run the best tavern in Wessex. This is our boy – we have called him Edward." But I was being swept away by the procession. I blew her a kiss.

"I will visit!" I called as Ethelmaer gently pulled me through the throng and back to his side.

Oh, yes, back to his side. But that is a story for another day, too.

FINIS

The story of THE NEEDLE AND THE SWORD will continue in the next book of the series.

AUTHOR'S NOTES

PEOPLE, PLACES AND PHRASES

"The past is a foreign country; they do things differently there" wrote L. P. Hartley in the prologue to his masterpiece *The Go-Between*. Indeed, they do, but in the millennium-plus which separates the tenth and the twenty-first centuries human nature has changed little. Most actions are still predicated by the same emotions: love, lust, ambition, sympathy, guilt and so on. It is a long list. What makes the past seem a foreign country is the way in which its events are recorded and our attempts to make sense of them in a manner contemporary to our own experiences.

In writing this book, which had the first stirrings of life some thirty years ago, I have tried to transport myself and the reader back into that foreign country which is late Anglo-Saxon England. Whilst of necessity the story is written in the language of modern English, I have avoided using words, phrases and concepts which simply would not have existed or occurred to the people of those earlier times. Where they do not have a literal modern English translation, I have used the Anglo-Saxon. Similarly, modern place names have been replaced by the names used in the tenth century or thereabouts. I have, however, simplified the spellings somewhat and avoided using diphthongs and characters which no longer exist in our own alphabet. This is the case, too, with personal names.

The seminal events in the story are real and documented. Well, they are documented! Some are undoubtedly real, such as coronations and other national celebrations. Plagues and natural disasters, astronomical phenomena and threats of war and civil unrest are similarly noted in a number of places, most notably the *Anglo-Saxon Chronicle*. With a similarly straight pen are variously recorded "facts" such as that a crucifix spoke with the voice of God, a building collapsed leaving, among the death and destruction, only one man completely unscathed – thus affording proof positive of intervention of the miraculous – and that the corpses of kings can emit bright light and the sounds of tinkling bells. Such were the facts in that foreign time and place.

PEOPLE

The royal persons in this book are, as closely as possible, given all the traits and attributes, physical appearance and actions that they were accorded during their lifetimes and during the immediate aftermaths of their deaths. I have tried to avoid later interpretations in order than I might more effectively create my own. Crowned Royals, both male and female, are indicated by **bold type** cast of characters on pages 3 – 5. Characters of my own invention and historical veracity interact with them, as far as logically permitted, within the parameters of known "facts".

PLACES

Late Anglo-Saxon place names sound, to us, both strange and yet oddly familiar, as though of long-ago holiday destinations, once visited and now largely lost amid the hiatus of everyday modern life. Often the inflection and vowel sounds remain the same, sometimes it is the first few letters that remain unchanged over the centuries and in many locations a pidgin incorporation of Latin tells us that the place was once important to the Legions, and was later equally strategic to those who came after. *"Caestre"*, derived from Latin denotes "castle", telling us immediately that the place once had military significance.   In using these wonderful, evocative names throughout – with as little alteration as possible – I believe that the character of the Saxon nation resonates more clearly down the centuries.   Villages, towns, cities and generalised areas, rivers and woodlands are given below. The concepts of national identity, both Saxon and foreign are discussed in the Glossary of words and phrases, though it needs little historical or archaeological experience to recognise "Englaland" as "England".

Locations – Anglo Saxon into Modern English

Avreberie	Avebury
Baltunesberge	Baltonsborough
Bathe	Bath
Bedeford	Bedford
Bryttania	The island comprising present day England, Wales and Scotland
Bedricsworth	(literally "the estate of Bedric", later Bury St. Edmunds)
Brycgstowe	Bristol
Cantuaria	Canterbury
Caresia	Kersey
Caune	Calne
Caestre	Chester
Celmereford	Chelmsford
Cent	Kent
Chepeham	Chippenham
Coche-felda	Cockfield

Colencaestre	Colchester
Corf	Corfe
Coteham	Cotteham
Cyrnecaestre	Cirencester
Derhest	Deerhust
Diton	Ditton
Duibhlinn	Dublin
Dulligham	Dullingham
Dumnonia	Devon
Eastseaxe	Essex
Einulusberie	Eynesbury (later St. Neots)
Elig	The Isle of Ely
Eligburg	Ely (the town)
Englaland	England
Eoforwic	York
Escancaestre	Exeter
Escanmor	Exmoor
Ethendon	Site of the Battle of Ethendon, exact location uncertain
Evesham	Evesham
Enylesberie	Eynsbury
Fordeham	Fordham
Froweholt	Ladywood, exact location uncertain
Glestingaberg	Glastonbury
Glewcaestre	Gloucester
Grantabrycgscir	Cambridgeshire
Grantebrige	Cambridge
Huntedunburg	Huntingdon
Huntedunburgscir	Huntingdonshire
Icenilde Way	Icknield Way
Iraland	Ireland
Ivelcaestre (I'lcaestre)	Ivelchester (I'lchester)
Kernow	Cornwall
Kingestun	Kingston (upon Thames)
Lincylene	Lincoln
Londinium (Latin)	London, barely occupied and retaining its Latin name
Londonia	Informal name for Londinium
Merleberge Downs	Marlborough Downs
Monig	The Isle of Anglesey
Persore	Pershore
Petrideburg	Peterborough
Petroc-stowe	Padstow

Polesteda	Polstead
Pryckewillowewayter	River Lark
Purbecig	Isle of Purbeck
Radendunam	Rettendon
Rammesig	Ramsey (town and island)
Reche	Reach
River Alor	River Alre
River Deva	River Dee
River Escan	River Exe
River Marden,	flowing through Caune
River Saverna	River Sever
River Stur	River Stour
River Tamaer	River Tamar
River Temes	River Thames
Rycebroc	Rushbrook
Saham	Soham
Sawtrede	Sawtry
Sceptesberie	Shaftsbury
Sceo	Village near Bathe, exact location uncertain
Sceptesberie	Shaftesbury
Scotti (Latin)	"Scotland", as we understand it today, did not exist.This refers to a loose alliance of Northern petty kingdoms, also referred to as "Caledonia"
Silcaestre	Silcaestre
Spaldevice	Spaldwick
Stecworthe	Stetchworth
Stoche	Stoke Eleigh
Sumersaete	Somerset
Suthbyrig	Sudbury
Tamweorthig	Tamworth
Tavestoch	Tavistock
Thornig	Thorney (Island)
Uphude	Upwood
Wakenig	Wakering
Waldringa-felda	Waldringfield
Walha	Wales
Warham	Wareham
Wenberie	Wanborough
Westmonaster	Westminster
Wintancaestre	Winchester
Wirecaestre	Worcester
Wivelingham	Willingham

PHRASES AND WORDS

Words, expressions and concepts in the text and spoken by the characters, which need no translation to convey their everyday use, do not appear in this glossary.   However, those which simply cannot be conveyed in modern English, or which would lose impact if removed from their original tongue are *italicized*. Those which require some explanation, even if given without the benefit of italics, are also included.

GLOSSARY

Baecbord
Port side of a ship

Beadlorbrocc
Badger

Beor
Cider

Bottler
A position which came to prominence in the late 10th century. Most great households, including the Royal Court, had a bottler who was in charge of the day to day running of the practical aspects of the kitchen and, with increasing emphasis, the cellars. The term was corrupted to "Butler" in later centuries.

Breotenwealda
King of the British people

Bridd-braegen
Literally: "Bird-brain"

Byrth-faeder
"Birth father"

Cataya
Any or all of the territories now encompassed by China. The extreme East.

Companion-man/women
Officially appointed companion (of the same sex) to a nobleman or
woman, King or Queen

Cunte
"Lady-parts", generally used as a term of insult.

Drynke heil
Literally "Drink hale", "hale" meaning healthy. The traditional reply to
"Was heil".

Ealdorman
Nobleman appointed by the King. Ealdormanries of particular shires (e.g.
East Anglia, Essex, Mercia) were not hereditary, but often passed between
family members. Ealdormen could also be appointed to lesser areas of
land.

Elf-shot
Basically, ill. It was believed that many maladies were the result of
malicious entities attacking the infirm, most often with invisible arrows.

Espier
Spy

Faeder ures   Literally "Our Father". The Lord's Prayer spoken in the
common tongue.

Fafnir
Dragon who defended the Hoard of the Rhine.   Fafnir featured
prominently in early Scandinavian story telling.

Full-punt
One pint (roughly equivalent to a modern Imperial pint).

Fyrd
Local militia.   The responsibility for raising the Fyrd lay with the
ealdorman of each Shire or other nominated area.

Germania (Latin)
The area roughly corresponding to modern Germany and/or the German
peoples.

Girl-childe
Little girl

Great Hall
The Great Hall was the main gathering space in any Hall (see Hall), usually accessed directly from the courtyard. Used for all communal activities, including eating, meetings, entertainments and often sleeping.

Haelf-scilling
Half shilling

Hall
The concept of a "castle" was not one which the Anglo Saxons enjoyed. Rather, the Hall was generally the largest building at a homestead, village or town. The term "castle" (*caestre*) was more often reserved for the remains of Roman buildings – possibly remodelled and put to contemporary use.

Hel
The Underworld, not to be confused with the modern concept of "hell". Residence in the Underworld did not connotate wrong doing or punishment in the same manner as in later centuries.

High Table
Corresponding to the modern concept of the "top table" at formal events, the High Table was set apart from the lower trestles and reserved for those of the highest status at any gathering.

Lufestre
Sweetheart

Lustling
Man obsessed with sex

Mallow water
Common mallow was used as a soap to wash face, body and delicate fabrics. Rubbed in warm water it produced a pleasingly scented foam.

Medicus (Latin)
Someone skilled in medicine, often, though not exclusively, a monk. The concept of a "doctor" did not exist as we understand it. A *medicus* was the respectable face of doctoring, in some ways less and in some ways more skilled than the local wise-woman or hedge witch.

Morgen hours

The Anglo-Saxon day was divided into eight periods, with three hours to each period, totalling twenty-four. Each period was given a name. The Morgan hours roughly equate to between 6.00 a.m. and 9.00 a.m. today. By the 10th century this was considered a somewhat archaic method of time-keeping. The bells tolled regularly to tell the hours of the monastic offices, which served for the common people, and time keeper candles were fairly accurate, if expensive, serving the same purpose for those better off. The working day was considered to be from around (in modern terms) 6.00 a.m. to 6.00 p.m. or from sunrise to sunset in the winter. Consequently, if a man worked from the end of the Morgen hours (9.00 a.m.) until the end of the working day (6.00 p.m.) and was prepared to be paid for only half a day, he would be considered something of a fool – or desperate.

Morgengifu

Literally "morning gift". A gift given to a bride on the morning after the wedding night, originally as a compensation for the loss of her virginity. *Morgengifu* was the absolute property of the woman, and could not be taken from her even if the marriage failed.

Mother-daughter
Sister

Musbane

Literally "the bane of mice". Pet name for a cat.

Mus-brod

Literally "mouse-bread". Bread laced with rat poison.

"Music from the West"

Ill fortune. Opinions vary as to the origin of this phrase. Some say it was because the common folk stood at the west end of the church and their singing was less than expert. Another theory holds that as the east was generally considered to be "holy" any inexplicable sounds from the west must portend something bad. The expression survives in the phrase to "face the music", i.e., square up to a threat or punishment.

Pantomimus (Latin)

Foolish and comedic performance.

Pars minuta prima (Latin)
Literally "At any moment"

Ran
A Celtic sea god

Reeve
A reeve was appointed by the King (or other official, depending on the level of his responsibility) to oversee the practical running of a village, town, city or shire. The term Sherriff is a derivation of "Shire Reeve" the highest of the positions and a term which was just in its infancy in the tenth century.

Saccellus (Latin)
A small bag to carry specifics necessary to a person's profession, often medical. The origin of the term "satchel", it might be made of leather or fabric.

Saussiche
Sausage

Serabaite
A vagrant or beggar, not necessarily, but often, purporting to be a wandering, itinerant monk or priest. It was considered a word of extreme insult, as it also carried connotations of sexual misconduct and even child abuse or bestiality.

Sigimund and Sigilind
Twins in the Saga of the Rheingold. Best known today as characters in the *"Ring Cycle"* by Wagner.

Sirop
Syrup, probably sweetened with honey.

Sister-son
Nephew

Sixfot
Literally: "six feet". A man over six feet tall, sometimes used metaphorically to suggest a hero.

Skop
Story-teller and musician, usually travelling from Hall to Hall.

Steorbord
Starboard side of a ship.

Synod of Whitby
Influential conclave of Christian Church in England which took place in the year 664, at which the tenets of the Celtic Church were largely superseded by those of the Church of Rome. It marked the beginning of the decline and ultimate near extinction of the Celtic tradition, which allowed priests to marry and was far more tolerant of the "Old Gods" than its rival.

Tertium
One third of the Fyrd – rostered onto duty every three months when needed.

Tesoro (Old Italian)
Treasure

Tibbert
"The King of Cats" according to early French folk tales. He was companion and friend to Reynard the Fox. The name was variously styled: Tybert, Tybald and most famously, some centuries later in Shakespeare's *Romeo and Juliet* as Tybalt, 'Prince of Cats'. 'Tibs' I still a popular name for pet cats.

Vill
Village or small town.

Walhacynn
The Welsh people.

Was heil
Literally: "Be hale" (healthy). The traditional toast which has survived in the expression "Good health!" when a drink is taken. Also, the root of "wassail".

Weosuling
Weasel

Weregild
Weregild is a strange concept to modern thinking. It is not fine, compensation nor ransom, yet incorporates something of all three. On a

personal level, weregild could be paid to a widow or dependants by a man's murderer. Other punishment might never be extracted. The term is also applied to the huge sums of money paid to dissuade an aggressor in war, or to secure the safety of a town under siege.

Wyrd
Most easily described as "fate".

AND LASTLY...

The days of the week with their names, in the opinion of some Anglo Saxon churchmen, bearing too close an affinity to those of the old gods, and the days of the months (accorded similar mistrust, given that some of them were even named after foreign – Roman – deities) were often deemed of less importance than the Saints' days with which they coincided. There was a feast-day with its attendant Mass for almost every day of the year. In many ways it still might be easier to agree to meet someone in the fore-noon of the Feast of Saint Cunibert of Cologne than to specify "next Thursday fortnight": the good Cunibert's day occurred only once a year.

"Christmas", the literal meaning of which, recent polls suggest, is unknown to a huge proportion of the population was – and still is – The Christ's Mass. Whether Edgar's second Queen, Elfrith, brought a tree into the Great Hall at Winchester upon that holy day is open to debate, but the tradition is certainly many hundreds of years older than the once popular belief that Prince Albert, in the 19th century, was the first to bring it to these shores.

Perhaps Anglo-Saxon England is a foreign country, but it is one in which we might find ourselves more at home than we had anticipated. The axiom of Saint Ambrose (7th December) might prove good advice: "*When in Rome...*"

Welcome to Englaland.

ACKNOWLEDGEMENTS

My primary thanks have to go those anonymous writers who compiled the collection of texts which have come to be known as *"The Anglo-Saxon Chronicles"*. Without them and other, largely unacknowledged diarists, chartists and testators the world of Anglo-Saxon Englaland would be almost entirely unknown to us. It is thanks to innumerable historians and scholars of this period of history that the expression "Dark Ages" is now rarely used. A light has been shone upon that era which has allowed my fiction at least a foundation of reality.

To patient friends who have endured my long-standing passion for retelling the stories of the tenth century and infuriating them with Anglo-Saxon riddles, you have my love and appreciation. To all the devotees of my embroidery who have encouraged me to write this, my first novel, after some twelve forays into non-fiction, I also owe a debt of thanks.

I hope my Latin teacher, Mr Rex Wingfield, now long passed, who, no doubt, came to regret offering to help me translate "Anglo-Saxon Latin" into modern English, would have approved of what I did with his assistance – assistance given some thirty years ago.

Janice, thank you for reading my first drafts – and for being my friend and "still crazy after all these years". Steve, just thank you!

CPSIA information can be obtained
at www.ICGtesting.com
Printed in the USA
LVHW020910210920
666634LV00002B/219